THE
HEAVENLY TWINS

BY

MADAME SARAH GRAND

AUTHOR OF " IDEALA," ETC. ETC.

" They call us the Heavenly Twins."
" What, signs of the Zodiac?" said the Tenor.
" No ; signs of the times," said the Boy.

NEW YORK
THE CASSELL PUBLISHING CO.
31 EAST 17TH ST. (UNION SQUARE)

THE MERSHON COMPANY PRESS.
RAHWAY, N. J.

MADAME SARAH GRAND.

The time is racked with birth-pangs ; every hour
Brings forth some gasping truth, and truth new-born
Looks a misshapen and untimely growth,
The terror of the household and its shame,
A monster coiling in its nurse's lap
That some would strangle, some would starve ;
But still it breathes, and passed from hand to hand,
And suckled at a hundred half-clad breasts
Comes slowly to its stature and its form,
Calms the rough ridges of its dragon scales,
Changes to shining locks its snaky hair,
And moves transfigured into Angel guise,
Welcomed by all that cursed its hour of birth,
And folded in the same encircling arms
That cast it like a serpent from their hold !
—Oliver Wendell Holmes.

PROEM.

Mendelssohn's " Elijah."

He, watch-ing o-ver Is - ra - el, slumbers not, nor sleeps.

FROM the high Cathedral tower the solemn assurance floated forth to be a warning, or a promise, according to the mental state of those whose ears it filled ; and the mind, familiar with the phrase, continued it involuntarily, carrying the running accompaniment, as well as the words and the melody, on to the end. After the last reverberation of the last stroke of every hour had died away, and just when expectation had been succeeded by the sense of silence, they rang it out by day and night—the bells—and the four winds of heaven by day and night spread it abroad over the great wicked city, and over the fair flat country, by many a tiny township and peaceful farmstead and scattered hamlet, on, on, it was said, to the sea—to the sea, which was twenty miles away !

But there were many who doubted this ; though good men and true, who knew the music well, declared they had heard it, every note distinct, on summer evenings when they sat alone on the beach and the waves were still ; and it sounded then, they said, like the voice of a tenor who sings to himself softly in murmurous monotones. And some thought this must be true, because those who said it knew the music well, but others maintained that it could not be true just for that very reason ; while others again, although they confessed that they knew nothing of the distance sound may travel under special circumstances, ventured, nevertheless, to assert that the chime the people heard on those occasions was ringing in their own hearts ; and, indeed, it would have been strange if those in whose mother's ears it had rung before they were born, who knew it for one of their first sensations, and felt it to be, like a blood relation, a part of themselves, though having a separate existence, had not carried the memory of it with them wherever they went, ready to respond at any moment, like sensitive chords vibrating to a touch.

But everything in the world that is worth a thought becomes food for controversy sooner or later, and the chime was no exception to the rule. Differences of opinion regarding it had always been numerous and extreme, and it was amusing to listen to the wordy warfare which was continually being waged upon the subject.

There were people living immediately beneath it who wished it far enough, they said, but they used to boast about it nevertheless when they went to other places—just as they did about their troublesome children, whom they declared, in like manner, that they expected to be the death of them when they and their worrying ways were within range of criticism. It was a flagrant instance of the narrowness of small humanity which judges people and things, not on their own merits, but with regard to their effect upon itself ; a circumstance being praised to-day because importance is to be derived from *its* importance, and blamed to-morrow because a bilious attack makes thought on any subject irritating.

Other people liked the idea of the chime, but were not content with its arrangement ; if it had been set in another way, you know, it would have be so different, they asserted, with as much emphasis as if there were wisdom in the words. And some said it would have been more effective if it had not rung so regularly, and some maintained that it owed its power to that same regularity which suggested something permanent in this weary world of change. Among the minor details of the discussion there was one point in particular which exercised the more active minds, but did not seem likely ever to be settled. It was as to whether the expression given to the announcement by the bells did not vary at different hours of the day and night, or at different seasons of the year at all events ; and opinion differed as widely upon this point as we are told they did on one occasion in some other place with regard to the question whether a fish weighed heavier when it was dead than when it was alive—a question that would certainly never have been settled either, had it not happened, after a long time and much discussion, that someone accidentally weighed a fish, when it was found there was no difference.

The question of expression, however, could not be decided in that way, expression being imponderable; and it was pretty generally acknowledged that the truth could not be ascertained and must therefore remain a matter of opinion. But that did not stop the talk. Once, indeed, someone declared positively that the state of a man's feelings at the moment would influence his perceptions, and make the chimes sound glad when he was glad, and mournful when he was melancholy; but nobody liked the solution.

Let them wrangle as they might, however, the citizens were proud of their chime, and for a really good reason. It meant something! It was not a mere jingle of bells, as most chimes are, but a phrase with a distinct idea in it which they understood as we understand a foreign language when we can read it without translating it. It might have puzzled them to put the phrase into other words, but they had it off pat enough as it stood, and they held it sacred, which is why they quarrelled about it, it being usual for men to quarrel about what they hold sacred, as if the thing could only be maintained by hot insistence—the things they hold sacred, that is—although they cannot be sure of them, like the forms of a religion which admit of controversy, as distinguished from the God they desire to worship about whom they have no doubt, and therefore never dispute.

In this latter respect, however, the case of the people of Morningquest was just the reverse of that which obtains in most other places, for in consequence of the hourly insistence of the chime, their most impressive monitor. they talked much more of Him whom they should worship than of various ways to worship him; and the most persistent of all the questions which occupied their attention arose out of the involuntary but continuous effort of one generation after another to define with scientific accuracy and to everybody's satisfaction his exact nature and attributes; in consequence of which efforts there had come to be several most distinct but quite contradictory ideas upon the subject. There were some simple-minded folk to whom the chime typified a God essentially masculine, and like a man, hugely exaggerated, but somewhat amorphous, because they could not see exactly in what the exaggeration consisted except in the size of him. They pictured him sitting alone on a throne of ivory and gold inlaid with precious stones; and recited the catalogue of those mentioned in the Book of the Revelation by preference as imparting

a fine scriptural flavor to the idea. And he sat upon the throne
day and night, looking down upon the earth, and never did
anything else nor felt it monotonous. Buddha himself, in
Nirvana, could not have attained to a greater perfection of
contemplation than that with which they credited this curious
divinity, who served solely for a finish to their mental range
as the sky was to their visual ; a useful point at which to aim
their rudimentary faculty of reverence.

But others, again, of a different order of intelligence, had
passed beyond this stage and saw in him more

> of a creature
> Moving about in worlds not realized ;

very like Jove, but unmarried. He was both beneficent and
jealous, and had to be propitiated by regular attendance at
church ; but further than that he was not exacting ; and therefore they ventured to take his name in vain when they were
angry, and also to call upon him for help, with many apologies,
when there was nobody else to whom they could apply ; although, so long as the current of their lives ran smoothly on,
they seldom troubled their heads about him at all.

There were deeper natures than those, however, who were
not content with this small advance, and these last had by
degrees, as suited their convenience but without perceiving
it, gradually discovered in him every attribute, good, bad, or
indifferent, which they found in themselves, thus ascribing to
him a nature of a highly complex and most extraordinarily
inconsistent kind, less that of a God than of a demon. To
them he was still a great shape like a man, but a shape to be
loved as well as feared : a God of peace who patronized war ;
a gentle lamb who looked on at carnage complacently ; a just
God who condemned the innocent to suffer ; an omnipotent
God who was powerless to make his law supreme ; and they
reserved to themselves the right of constantly adding to or
slightly altering this picture ; but having completed it so far,
they were thoroughly well satisfied with it, and, incongruous
as it was, they managed to make it the most popular of all the
presentments, partly because, being so flexible, it could be
adjusted to every state of mind ; but also because there was
money in it. Numbers of people lived by it, and made name
and fame besides ; and these kept it going by damaging anybody who ventured to question its beauty. For there is no
faith that a man upholds so forcibly as the one by which he
earns his livelihood, whether it be faith in the fetish he has

helped to make, or in a particular kind of leather that sells quickest because it wears out so fast.

In these latter days, however, it began to appear as if the supremacy of the great masculine idea was at last being seriously threatened, for even in Morningquest a new voice of extraordinary sweetness had already been heard, not *his*, the voice of man ; but *theirs*, the collective voice of humanity, which declared that " He, watching," was the all-pervading good, the great moral law, the spirit of pure love, Elohim, mistranslated in the book of Genesis as " He " only, but signifying the union to which all nature testifies, the male and female principles which together created the universe, the infinite father and mother, without whom, in perfect accord and exact equality, the best government of nations has always been crippled and abortive.

Those who heard this final voice were they who loved the chime most truly, and reverenced it ; but they did not speak about it much : only, when the message sounded, they listened with that full-hearted pleasure which is the best praise and thanks. Mendelssohn must have felt it when the melody first occurred to him, and the words had wedded themselves to the music in his soul !

He, watch-ing o-ver Is-ra-el, slumbers not, nor sleeps.

And the chime certainly had power to move the hearts of many ; but it would be hard to say when it had most power, or upon whom. Doubtless, the majority of those who had ears to hear in the big old fashioned city heard not, use having dulled their faculties ; or if, perchance, the music reached them it conveyed no idea to their minds, and passed unheeded. It was but an accustomed measure, one more added to the myriad other sounds that make up the buzz of life, and help, like each separate note of a chord, to complete the varied murmur which is the voice of " a whole city full."

But of course there were times when it was specially apt to strike home—in the early morning, for instance, when the mind was fresh and hope was strong enough to interpret the assurance into a promise of joy ; and again at noon, when fatigue was growing and the mind perceived a sympathetic melancholy in the tones which was altogether restful; but it was at midnight it had most power. It seemed to rise then to the last pitch of enthusiasm, sounding triumphant, like the special effort that finishes a strain, as if to speed the departing interval of time ; but when it rang again, after the first hour of the new day, its voice had dropped, as it were, to that tone of indifference which expresses the accustomed doing of some monotonous duty which has become too much of a habit to excite either pleasure or pain. To the tired watcher then, for whom the notes were mere tones conveying no idea, the soft melancholy cadence, dulled by distance, was like the half-stifled echo of her own last stifled sigh.

It is likely, however, that the chime failed less of its effect outside the city than it did within ; but there again it depended upon the hearer. When the mellow tones floated above the heath where the gipsies camped, only one, perchance, might listen, lifting her bright eyes with pleasure and longing in them, dumbly, as a child might, yet showing for a moment some glimmering promise of a soul. But to many in the village close at hand the chime brought comfort. It seemed to assure the sick, counting the slow hours, that they were not forsaken, and helped them to bear their pain with patience ; it seemed to utter to the wayworn a word which told them their trouble was not in vain ; it seemed to invite all those who waited and were anxious to trust their care to Him and seek repose. It was all this, and much more, to many people : and yet, when it spread in another direction over the fields, it meant nothing to the yawning ploughman, either musical or poetical, had no significance whatever for him if it were not of the time of day, gathered, however, with the help of sundry other sensations of which hunger and fatigue were chief. It probably conveyed as much, and neither more nor less, to the team he drove.

But perhaps of all the affairs of life with which the chime had mingled, the most remarkable, could they be collected and recorded, would be the occasions on which the hearing of the message had marked a turning point in the career of some one person, as happened, once on a summer afternoon, when it was heard by a Lancashire collier—a young lad with an unkempt mop of golden hair, delicate features, and limbs which were too refined for his calling, who was coming up the River Morne on a barge.

The river winds for a time through a fertile undulating bit of country, and nothing of the city can be seen until you are almost in it, except the castle of the Duke of Morningquest, high perched on a hill on the farther side, and the spire of the cathedral, which might not attract your attention, however, if it were not pointed out to you above the trees. When the chime floated over this sparsely peopled tract, filling the air with music, but coming from no one could tell whence, there was something mysterious in the sound of it to an imaginative listener in so apparently remote a place ; and once, twice, as the long hours passed, the young collier heard it ring, and wondered. He had nothing to do but listen, and watch the man on the bank who led the horse that was towing the barge; or address a rare remark to his solitary companion—an old sailor, dressed in a sou'-wester, blue jersey, and the invariable drab trowsers, tar-besprent, and long boots, of his calling, who steered automatically, facing the meadows in beautiful abstraction. He would have faced an Atlantic gale, however, with that same look.

When the chime rang out for the third time, the young collier spoke :

" It's the varse of a song, maybe ? " he suggested.

" Aye, lad," was the laconic rejoinder.

The barge moved on—passed a little farmhouse close to the water's edge ; passed some lazy cattle standing in a field flicking off flies with their tails ; passed a patient fisherman, who had not caught a thing that day, and scarcely expected to, but still fished on. The sun sparkled down on the water ; the weary man and horse plodded along the bank ; far away, a sweet bird sang ; and the collier spoke again.

" Dost tha' know the varse ? " he said.

The old man had been brought up in those parts ; he knew it well ; and slowly repeated it to the lad, who listened without a sign, sitting with his dreamy eyes fixed on the water :

" He, watching over Israel, slumbers not, nor sleeps."

There was another long silence, and then the lad spoke once more, with apathetic gravity, asking: " Who's *He ?* "

The old man kept his eyes fixed on a distant reach of the river, and moved no muscle of his face.

" I guess it's Christ," he said at last.

" Ah niver 'eerd tell on 'im," the collier answered slowly.

" Hast 'niver 'eerd tell on Christ ? " the old man asked in measured machine-like tones. " I thowt ivery one know'd on 'im. Why, what religion are you ? "

" Well, me feyther's a Liberal—leastways 'im as brought me up," was the passionless rejoinder, slowly spoken ; " but ah doan't know no one o' the name o' Christ, an', what's more, ah's sure 'e doan't work down our way,"—with which he sauntered forward with his hands in his trowser pockets, and sat in the bow ; and the old man steered on as before.

How like a mind is to a river ! both may be pure and transparent and lovable, and strong to support and admirable ; each may mirror the beauties of earth and sky, and still have a wonderful beauty of its own to delight us ; both are always moving onward, bound irresistibly to be absorbed in a great ocean mystery, to be swept away irreclaimably, without hope of return, but leaving memories of themselves in good or evil wrought by them ; and both are pure at the outset, but can be contaminated, when they in turn contaminate ; and, being perverted in their use, become accursed, and curse again with all the more effect because the province of each was to bless.

The collier lad in the bow of the barge felt something of the fascination of the river that day. He saw it sparkle in the sunshine, he heard it ripple along its banks, he felt the slow and dreamy motion of the boat it bore ; and his mind was filled with unaccustomed thought, and a strange yearning which he did not understand. There was something singularly attractive about the lad, although his clothes were tattered, his golden hair and delicate skin were begrimed, his great bright eyes had no intelligent expression in them, and there was that discontented undisciplined look about his mouth which is common to uneducated men. He had no human knowledge, but he had capacity, and he had music, the divine gift, in his soul, and the voice of an angel to utter it.

What passed through his dim consciousness in the interval which followed his last remark, no one will ever know ; but the chime had once more sounded ; and, suddenly, as he sat there, he took up the strain, and sang it—and the labourers in the fields, and the loiterers by the river, and the ladies in their gardens, even the very cattle in the meadows, looked up and listened, wondering, while he varied the simple melody, as singers can, finding new meaning in the message, and filling the summer silence with perfect raptures of ecstatic sound.

It was a voice to gladden the hearts of men, and one who heard it knew this, and followed the barge, and took the lad and had him taught, so that in after days the world was ready to fall at his feet and worship the gift.

And so time passed. Change followed change, but the chime was immutable. And always, whatever came, it rang out calmly over the beautiful old city of Morningquest, and entered into it, and was part of the life of it, mixing itself impartially with the good and evil ; with all the sin and suffering, the pitiful pettiness, the indifference, the cruelty, and every form of misery-begetting vice, as much as with the purity above reproach, the charity, the self-sacrifice, the unswerving truth, the patient endurance, and courage not to be daunted, which are in every city—mixing itself with these as the light and air of heaven do, and with effects doubtless as unexpected and as fine ; and ready also to be a help to the helpless, a guide to the rash and straying, a comfort to the comfortless, a reproach to the reckless, and a warning to the wicked. Perhaps an ambitious stranger, passing through the city, would hear the chime, and pause to listen, and in the pause a flash of recollection would show him the weary way he had gone, the disappointments which were the inevitable accompaniments of even his most brilliant successes in the years of toil that had been his since he made the world his idol and swerved from the Higher Life ; and then he would ask himself the good of it all, and finding that there was no good, he would go his way, cherishing the new impression, and asking of all things,

" Is it too late now ? "

And perhaps at the same moment a lady rolling past in her carriage would say, " How sweet ! " or the beauty of the bells might win some other thoughtless tribute from her, if she heard the chime at all ; but probably she never heard it, because the accustomed tones were as familiar as the striking of the hour—the striking of an hour that bore no special significance for her, and therefore set no chord vibrating in her soul. The thoughts of her mind deafened her heart to it as completely as the thunder of a waggon had at the same time deafened the waggoner's ears while the bells uttered their message above him. And so it was with the doctor, over-worked and anxious, hurrying on his rounds ; the grasping lawyer, absorbed in calculation, and all the other money-grubbers ; the indolent woman, the pleasure-seeker, and the hard-pressed toiler for daily bread : if they heard they heeded not because their hour had not yet come. At least this is what some thought, who believed that for every one a special hour would come, when they would be called, and then left to decide, as it were, between life and death-in-life ; if they accepted life, the next message would be fraught with strength and help and blessing ; but if they rejected it, the bells would utter their condemnation, and leave them to their fate.

CONTENTS.

BOOK I.

CHILDHOODS AND GIRLHOODS.

The spring is the pleasantest of the seasons ; and the young of most animals, though far from being completely fashioned, afford a more agreeable sensation than the full grown ; because the imagination is entertained with the promise of something more, and does not acquiesce in the present object of the sense.—*Burke on the Sublime.*

I am inclined to agree with Francis Galton in believing that education and environment produce only a small effect on the mind of anyone, and that most of our qualities are innate.—*Darwin.*

THE HEAVENLY TWINS.

CHAPTER I.

AT nineteen Evadne looked out of narrow eyes at an untried world inquiringly. She wanted to know. She found herself forced to put prejudice aside in order to see beneath it, deep down into the sacred heart of things, where the truth is, and the bewildering clash of human precept with human practice ceases to vex. And this not of design, but of necessity. It was a need of her nature to know. When she came across something she did not understand, a word, a phrase, or an allusion to a phase of life, the thing became a haunting demon only to be exorcised by positive knowledge on the subject. Ages of education, ages of hereditary preparation had probably gone to the making of such a mind, and rendered its action inevitable. For generations knowledge is acquired, or, rather, instilled by force in families, but, once in a way, there comes a child who demands instruction as a right ; and in her own family Evadne appears to have been that child. Not that she often asked for information. Her faculty was sufficient to enable her to acquire it without troubling herself or anybody else, a word being enough on some subjects to make whole regions of thought intelligible to her. It was as if she only required to be reminded of things she had learnt before. Her mother said she was her most satisfactory child. She had been easy of education in the schoolroom. She had listened to instruction with interest and intelligence, and had apparently accepted every article of faith in God and man which had been offered for her guidance through life with unquestioning confidence ; at least she had never been heard to object to any time-honoured axiom. And she did, in fact, accept them all, but only provisionally. She wanted to know. Silent, sociable, sober, and sincere, she had walked over the course of her early education and gone on far beyond it with such ease that those in authority over her never suspected the extent to which she had outstripped them.

It was her father who struck the keynote to which the tune of her early intellectual life was set. She was about twelve years old at the time, and they were sitting out on the lawn at Fraylingay one day after dinner, as was their wont in the summer—he, on this occasion, under the influence of a good cigar, mellow in mind and moral in sentiment, but inclining to be didactic for the moment because the coffee was late; she in a receptive mood, ready to gather silently, and store with care, in her capacious memory any precept that might fall from his lips, to be taken out and tried as opportunity offered.

"Where is your mother?" he asked.

"I don't know, father," Evadne answered. "I think she is in the drawing room."

"Never say you *think*, my dear, about matters of fact," he said. "When it is possible to *know* it is your business to find out, and if you cannot find out you must say you don't know. It is moral cowardice, injurious to yourself, not to own your ignorance; and you may also be misleading, or unintentionally deceiving, someone else."

"How might the moral cowardice of not owning my ignorance be injurious to myself, father?" she asked.

"Why, don't you see," he answered, "you would suffer in two ways? If the habit of inaccuracy became confirmed, your own character would deteriorate; and by leading people to suppose that you are as wise as themselves, you lose opportunities of obtaining useful information. They won't tell you things they think you know already."

Evadne bent her brows upon this lesson and reflected; and doubtless it was the origin of the verbal accuracy for which she afterward became notable. Patient investigation had always been a pleasure, but from that time forward it became a principle also. She understood from what her father had said that to know the facts of life exactly is a positive duty; which, in a limited sense, was what he had intended to teach her; but the extent to which she carried the precept would have surprised him.

Her mind was prone to experiment with every item of information it gathered, in order to test its practical value; if she could turn it to account she treasured it; if not, she rejected it, from whatever source it came. But she was not herself aware of any reservation in her manner of accepting instruction. The trick was innate, and in no way interfered with her faith in her friends, which was profound. She might have justified it, however, upon her father's authority, for she once heard him say to one of her brothers : "Find out for your-self, and form your own opinions," a lesson which she had laid to heart also. Not that her father would have approved of her putting it into practice. He was one of those men who believe emphatically that a woman should hold no opinion which is not of masculine origin, and the maxims he had for his boys differed materially in many respects from those which he gave to his girls. But these precepts of his were, after all, only matches to Evadne which fired whole trains of reflection, and lighted her to conclusions quite other than those at which he had arrived himself. In this way, however, he became her principal instructor. She had attached herself to him from the time that she could toddle, and had acquired from his con-versation a proper appreciation of masculine precision of thought. If his own statements were not always accurate it was from no want of respect for the value of facts ; for he was great on the subject, and often insisted that a lesson or principle of action is contained in the commonest fact ; but he snubbed Evadne promptly all the same on one occasion when she mentioned a fact of life, and drew a principle of action therefrom for herself. "Only confusion comes of women thinking for themselves on social subjects." he said. "You must let me decide all such matters for you, or you must refer them to your husband when you come under his control."

Evadne did not pay much attention to this, however, because she remembered another remark of his with which she could not make it agree. The remark was that women never had thought for themselves, and that therefore it was evident that they could not think, and that they should not try. Now, as it is obvious that confusion cannot come of a thing that has never been done, the inaccuracy in one or other of these state-ments was glaring enough to put both out of the argument. But what Evadne did note was the use of the word control.

As she grew up she became her father's constant companion in his walks, and, flattered by her close attention, he fell into the way of talking a good deal to her. He enjoyed the fine flavour of his own phrase-making, and so did she, but in such a silent way that nothing ever led him to suspect it was having any but the most desirable effect upon her mind. She never attempted to argue, and only spoke in order to ask a question on some point which was not clear to her, or to make some

small comment when he seemed to expect her to do so. He
often contradicted himself, and the fact never escaped her
attention, but she loved him with a beautiful confidence, and
her respect remained unshaken.

When she had to set herself right between his discrepancies
she did not dwell on the latter as faults in him, but only thought
of how wise he was when he warned her to be accurate, and
felt grateful. And in this way she formed her mind upon his
sayings ; and as a direct result of the long, informal, generally
peripatetic lectures to which she listened without prejudice, and
upon which she brought unsuspected powers of discrimination
to bear, he had unconsciously made her a more logical, reason-
ing, reasonable being than he believed it possible for a woman
to be. Poor papa ! All that he really knew of his most
interesting daughter was that she was growing up a good child,
physically strong and active, morally well educated, with a
fortunately equable temper ; and that she owed a great deal
to him. What, precisely, was never defined. But when the
thought of his kindness recurred to him it always suffused him
with happiness.   ·

He was a portly man, with a place in the country, and a
house in town; not rich for his position, but well off; a magistrate, and much respected ; well educated in the ideas of the
ancients, with whom his own ideas on many subjects stopped
short, and hardly to be called intellectual ; a moderate Churchman, a bigoted Conservative, narrow and strongly prejudiced
rather than highly principled. He was quite ignorant of the
moral progress of the world at the present time, and ready to
resent even the upward tendency of evolution when it presented itself to him in the form of any change, including, of
course, changes for the better, and more especially so if such
change threatened to bring about an improvement in the position of women, or increase the weight of their influence for
good in the world. The mere mention of the subject made
him rabid, and he grew apoplectic whenever he reflected upon
the monstrous pretensions of the sex at the present time. But
the thing that roused his scorn and indignation most was when
a woman ventured to enter any protest against the established
order of iniquity. He allowed that a certain number of women
must of necessity be abandoned, and raised no objection to
that ; but what he did consider intolerable was that any one
woman should make a stand against the degradation of her
own sex. He thought that immoral.

He was well enough to live with, however, this obstinate English country gentleman, although without sympathetic insight, and liable to become a petty domestic tyrant at any moment. " Sound " was what he would have called himself. And he was a man to be envied upon the whole, for his family loved him, and his friends knew no ill of him.

CHAPTER II.

EVADNE, like the Vicar of Wakefield, was by nature a lover of happy human faces, and she could be playful herself on occasion; but she had little if any of the saving sense of humor.

Her habit was to take everything *au grand serieux*, and to consider it. When other people were laughing she would be gravely observant, as if she were solving a problem ; and she would sooner have thought of trying to discover what combination of molecules resulted in a joke, with a view to benefiting her species by teaching them how to produce jokes at will, than of trying to be witty herself. She had, too, a quite irritating trick of remaining, to all outward seeming, stolidly unmoved by events which were causing an otherwise general commotion ; but in cases of danger or emergency she was essentially swift to act—as on one occasion, for instance, when the Hamilton House twins were at Fraylingay.

The twins had arrived somewhat late in the married lives of their parents, and had been welcomed as angel visitants, under which fond delusion they were christened respectively Angelica and Theodore. Before they were well out of their nurse's arms, however, society, with discernment, had changed Theodore's name to Diavolo, but " Angelica " was sanctioned, the irony being obvious.

The twins were alike in appearance, but not nearly so much so as twins usually are. It would have been quite easy to distinguish them apart, even if one had not been dark and the other fair, and for this mercy everybody connected with them had reason to be thankful, for as soon as they reached the age of active indiscretion they would certainly have got themselves mixed if they could. Angelica was the dark one, and she was also the elder, taller, stronger, and wickeder of the two, the organizer and commander of every expedition. Before they were five years old everybody about the place was upon the alert, both in self-defence and also to see that the twins did not kill themselves. Bars of iron had to be put on the upstairs windows to prevent them making ladders of the traveller's joy and wisteria, modes of egress which they very much preferred to commonplace doors ; and Mr. Hamilton-Wells had been reluctantly obliged to have the moat, which was deep and full of fish, and had been the glory of Hamilton House for generations, drained for fear of accidents. Argument was unavailing with the twins as a means of repression, but they were always prepared to argue out any question of privilege with their father and mother cheerfully. Punishment, too, had an effect quite other than that intended. They were interested at the moment, but they would slap each other's hands and put each other in the corner for fun five minutes after they had received similar chastisement in solemn earnest

They would have lived out of doors altogether by choice, and they managed to make their escape in all weathers. If the vigilant watch that was kept upon them were relaxed for a moment, they disappeared as if by magic, and would probably only be recovered at the farthest limit of their father's property, or in the kitchen of some neighbouring country gentleman, where they were sure to be popular. They were always busy about something, and when every usual occupation failed, they fought each other. After a battle they counted scars and scratches for the honour of having most, and if there were not bruises enough to satisfy one of them, the other was always obligingly ready to fight again until there were.

Mr. Hamilton-Wells had great faith in the discipline of the Church service for them, and was anxious that they should be early accustomed to go there. They behaved pretty well while the solemnity was strange enough to awe them, and one Sunday when Lady Adeline—their mother—could not accompany him, Mr. Hamilton-Wells ventured to go alone with them. He took the precaution to place them on either side of him so as to separate them and interpose a solid body between them and any signals they might make to each other ; but in the quietest part of the service, when everybody was kneeling, some movement of Diavolo's attracted his attention for a moment from Angelica, and when he looked again the latter had disappeared. She had discovered that it was possible to creep from pew to pew beneath the seats, and had started to explore the church. On her way, however, she observed a pair of stout legs belonging to a respectable elderly woman who was too deep in her devotion to be aware of the intruder, and, being somewhat astonished by their size, she proceeded to test their quality with a pin, the consequence being an appalling shriek from the woman, which started a shrill treble cry from herself. The service was suspended, and Mr. Hamilton-Wells, the most precise of men, hastened down the aisle, and fished his daughter out, an awful spectacle of dust, from under the seat, incontinently.

When Mr. and Lady Adeline Hamilton-Wells went from home for any length of time they were obliged to take their children with them, as servants who knew the latter would rather leave than be left in charge of them, and this was how it happened that Evadne made their acquaintance at an early age.

It was during their first visit to Fraylingay, while they were still quite tiny, and she was hardly in her teens, that the event referred to in illustration of one of Evadne's characteristics occurred.

The twins had arrived late in the afternoon, and were taken into the dining room, where the table was already decorated for dinner. It evidently attracted a good deal of their attention, but they said nothing. At dessert, however, to which Evadne had come down with the elder children, the dining room door was seen to open with portentous slowness, and there appeared in the aperture two little figures in long nightgowns, their forefingers in their mouths, their inquisitive noses tilted in the air, and their bright eyes round with astonishment. It was like the middle of the night to them, and they had expected to find the room empty.

" Oh, you naughty children ! " Lady Adeline exclaimed.

" The *darlings !* " cried Mrs. Frayling, Evadne's mother. "*Do* let them come in," and she picked up Angelica, and held her on her knee, one of the other ladies at the opposite end of the long table taking Diavolo up at the same time. But the moment the children found themselves on a level with the table they made a dart for the centre piece simultaneously on their hands and knees, regardless of the smash of dessert plates, decanters, wineglasses, and fruit dishes, which they upset by the way.

" It *is !* " shrieked Angelica, thumping the flat mirror which was part of the table decorations triumphantly.

" It is *what ?* " cried Lady Adeline, endeavoring to reach the child.

" It's looking-glass, mamma.   Diavolo said it was water."

There was much amusement at the words, and at the quaint spectacle of the two little creatures sitting amid the wreckage in the middle of the table not a bit abashed by the novelty of their conspicuous position.   Only Evadne, who was standing behind her mother's chair, remained grave.   She seemed to be considering the situation severely, and, acting on her own responsibility, she picked Diavolo up in the midst of the general hilarity, and carried him out of the room with her hand pressed tight on his thigh.   The child had come down armed with an open penknife, with which to defend Angelica should they encounter any ogres or giants on the stairs, and in scrambling up the table he had managed to strike himself in the thigh with it, and had severed the femoral artery ; but, with the curious shame which makes some children dislike to own that they are hurt, he had contrived to conceal the accident for a moment with his nightgown under cover of the flowers, and it was only Evadne's observant eye and presence of mind that had saved his life.   No one in the house could make a tourniquet, and she sat with the child on her knee while a doctor was being fetched, keeping him quiet as by a miracle, and stopping the hemorrhage with the pressure of her thumb, not even his parents daring to relieve her, since Diavolo had never been known to be still so long in his life with anybody else. She held him till the operation of tying the artery was safely accomplished, by which time Mr. Diavolo was sufficiently exhausted to be good and go to sleep ; and then she quietly fainted.   But she was about again in time to catch him when he woke, and keep him quiet, and so by unwearied watching she prevented accidents until all danger was over.

Diavolo afterward heard his parents praise her in unmeasured terms to *her* parents one day in her absence.   She happened to return while they were still in the room, and, being doubtless wide awake to the advantages of such a connection, he took the opportunity of promising solemnly, in the presence of such respectable witnesses, to marry her as soon as he was able.

She had added the word " tourniquet " to her vocabulary during this time, and having looked it up in the dictionary, she requested the doctor to be so good as to teach her to make one.   While doing so the doctor became interested in his silent, intelligent pupil, and it ended in his teaching her all that a young lady could learn of bandaging, of antidotes to poisons, of what to do in case of many possible accidents, and also of nursing, theoretically.

But this was not a solitary instance of the quiet power of the girl which already compelled even elderly gentlemen much overworked and self-absorbed, to sacrifice themselves in her service.

CHAPTER III.

IT is a notable thing that in almost every instance it was her father's influence which forced Evadne to draw conclusions in regard to life quite unlike any of his own, and very distasteful to him. He was the most conservative of men, and yet he was continually setting her mind off at a tangent in search of premises upon which to found ultra-liberal conclusions.

His primitive theories about women and "all that they are good for," for one thing, which differed so materially from the facts as she observed them every day, formed a constant mental stimulus to which her busy brain was greatly indebted. "Women should confine their attention to housekeeping," he remarked once when the talk about the higher education of women first began to irritate elderly gentlemen. "It is all they are fit for."

"Is it ?" said Evadne.

"Yes. And they don't know arithmetic enough to do that properly."

"Don't they ? why ?" she asked.

"Because they have no brains," he answered.

"But some women have been clever," she ventured seriously.

"Yes, of course ; exceptional women. But you can't argue from exceptional women."

"Then ordinary women have no brains, and cannot learn arithmetic ?" she concluded.

"Precisely," he answered irritably. Such signs of intelligence always did irritate him, somehow.

Evadne found food for reflection in these remarks. She had done a certain amount of arithmetic herself in the schoolroom, and had never found it difficult, but then she had not gone far enough, perhaps. And she went at once to get a Colenso or a Barnard Smith to see. She found them more fascinating when she attacked them of her own free will and with all her intelligence than she had done when necessity, in

the shape of her governess, forced her to pay them some
attention, and she went through them both in a few weeks at
odd times, and then asked her father's advice about a book
on advanced mathematics.

" Advanced mathematics ! " he exclaimed.   " Can you keep
accounts ? "

" I don't know," she answered doubtfully.

" Then what is this   nonsense   about   advanced   mathematics ? "

" Oh, I have finished Barnard Smith, and I thought I should
like to go on," she explained.

" Now, isn't that like your sex ? " he observed, smiling at his
own superiority.   " You   pick   things   up   with   a   parrot-like
sharpness, but haven't intelligence enough to make any practical application of them.   A woman closely resembles a parrot
in her mental processes, and in the use she makes of fine
phrases which she does not understand to produce an effect of
cleverness—such as 'advanced mathematics ! ' "

Evadne bent her brow, and let him ruminate a little in
infinite self-content, then asked abruptly : " Can men keep
accounts who have never seen accounts kept ? "

" No, of course not," he answered, seeing in this a new
instance of feminine imbecility, and laughing.

" Ah," she observed, then added thoughtfully as she moved
away : " I should like to see how accounts are kept."

She never had any more conversation with her father upon
this subject, but from that time forward mathematics, which
had before been only an incident in the way of lessons, became
an interest in life, and a solid part of her education.   But,
although she found she could do arithmetic without any great
difficulty, it never occurred to her either that her father could
be wrong or that there might be in herself the making of an
exceptional woman.   The habit of love and respect kept her
attention from any point which would have led to a judgment
upon her father, and she was too unconscious of herself as a
separate unit to make personal application of anything as yet.
Her mind at this time, like the hold of a ship with a general
cargo, was merely being stored with the raw materials which
were to be distributed over her whole life, and turned by degrees
to many purposes, useful, beautiful—not impossibly detestable.

But that remark of her father's about " all that women are
fit for," which he kept well watered from time to time with
other conventional expressions of a contemptuous kind, was

undoubtedly the seed of much more than a knowledge of the higher mathematics. It was that which set her mind off on a long and patient inquiry into the condition and capacity of women, and made her, in the end of the nineteenth century, essentially herself. But she did not begin her inquiry of set purpose ; she was not even conscious of the particular attention she paid to the subject. She had no foregone conclusion to arrive at, no wish to find evidence in favour of the woman which would prove the man wrong. Only, coming across so many sneers at the incapacity of women, she fell insensibly into the habit of asking why. The question to begin with was always : " Why are women such inferior beings ?" But, by degrees, as her reading extended, it changed its form, and then she asked herself doubtfully : " Are women such inferior beings ?" a position which carried her in front of her father at once by a hundred years, and led her rapidly on to the final conclusion that women had originally no congenital defect of inferiority, and that, although they have still much way to make up, it now rests with themselves to be inferior or not, as they choose.

She had an industrious habit of writing what she thought about the works she studied, and there is an interesting record still in existence of her course of reading between the ages of twelve and nineteen. It consists of one thick volume, on the title page of which she had written roundly, but without a flourish, " Commonplace Book," and the date. The first entries are made in a careful, unformed, childish hand, and with diffidence evidently ; but they became rapidly decided both in caligraphy and tone as she advanced. The handwriting is small and cramped, but the latter probably with a view to economy of space, and it is always clear and neat. There are few erasures or mistakes of grammar or spelling, even from the first, and little tautology ; but she makes no attempt at literary style or elegance of expression. Still, all that she says is impressive, and probably on that account. She chooses the words best calculated to express her meaning clearly and concisely, and undoubtedly her meaning is always either a settled conviction or an honest endeavour to arrive at one. It is the honesty, in fact, that is so impressive. She never thinks of trying to shine in the composition of words ; there was no idea of budding authorship in her mind ; she had no more consciousness of purpose in her writing than she had in her singing, when she sang about the place. The one was as involuntary as the other, and the outcome of similar sensations. It pleased her to write, and it pleased her to sing, and she did both when the impulse came upon her. She must, however, have had considerable natural facility of expression. Writing seems always to have been her best mode of communication. She was shy from the first in conversation, but bold to a fault with her pen. Some of the criticisms she wrote in her " Commonplace Book " are quite exhaustive ; most of them are temperate, although she does give way occasionally to bursts of fiery indignation at things which outrage her sense of justice ; but the general characteristic is a marked originality, not only in her point of view, but also in the use she makes of quite unpromising materials. In fact, the most notable part of the record is the proof it contains that all the arguments upon which she formed her opinions were found in the enemy's works alone. She had drawn her own conclusions ; but after having done so, as it happened, she had the satisfaction of finding confirmation strong in John Stuart Mill on " The Subjection of Women," which she came across by accident—an accident, by the way, for which Lady Adeline Hamilton-Wells was responsible. She brought the book to Fraylingay, and forgot it when she went home, and Evadne, happening to find it throwing about, took charge of it, read it with avidity, and found for herself a world of thought in which she could breathe freely.

" The Vicar of Wakefield " was one of her early favourites. She read it several times, and makes mention of it twice in her "Commonplace Book." Her first notice of it is a childish little synopsis, very quaint in its unconscious irony ; but interesting, principally from the fact that she was struck even then by the point upon which she afterward became so strong.

" The vicar," she says, " was a good man, and very fond of his wife and family, and they were very fond of him, but his wife was queer, and could only read a little. *And he never taught her to improve herself, although* he had books and was learned.* He had two daughters, who were spiteful and did not like other girls to be pretty. They had bad taste, too, and wanted to go to church overdressed, and thought it finer to ride a plough-horse than walk. It does not say that they ever read anything, either. If they had they would have known

---

* This is the point alluded to.

better. There is a very nasty man in the book called Squire Thornhill, and a nice one called Sir William Thornhill, who was his uncle. Sir William marries Sophia, and Squire Thornhill marries Olivia, although he does not intend to. Olivia was a horrid deceitful girl, and it served her right to get such a husband. They have a brother called Moses, who used to talk philosophy with his father at dinner, and once sold a cow for a gross of green spectacles. A gross is twelve dozen. Of course they were all annoyed, but the vicar himself was cheated by the same man when he went to sell the horse. He seemed to think a great deal of knowing Latin and Greek, but it was not much use to him then. It was funny that he should be conceited about what he knew himself, and not want his wife to know anything. He said to her once : ' I never dispute your abilities to make a goose pie, and I beg you'll leave argument to me ' ; which she might have thought rude, but perhaps she was not a lady, as ladies do not make goose pies. I forgot, though, they had lost all their money. They had great troubles, and the vicar was put in prison. He was very ill, but preached to the prisoners, and everybody loved him. I like ' The Vicar of Wakefield ' very much, and if I cannot find another book as nice I shall read it again. ' Turn, Gentle Hermit ' is silly. I suppose *Punch* took Edwin and Angelina out of it to laugh at them."

Quite three years must have elapsed before she again mentions " The Vicar of Wakefield," and in the meantime she had been reading a fair variety of books, but for the most part under schoolroom supervision, carefully selected for her. Some, however, she had chosen for herself—during the holidays when discipline was relaxed ; but it was a fault which she had to confess, and she does so always, honestly. Lewes' " Life of Goethe " was one of these. She wrote a glowing description of it, at the end of which she says :

" I found the book on a sofa in the drawing room, and began it without thinking, and read and read until I had nearly finished it, quite forgetting to ask leave. But of course I went at once to tell father as soon as I thought of it. Mother was there too, and inclined to scold, but father frowned, and said : ' Let her alone. It will do her no harm ; she won't understand it.' I asked if I might finish it, and he said, ' Oh, yes,' impatiently. I think he wanted to get rid of me, and I am sorry I interrupted him at an inconvenient time. Mother often does not agree with father, but she always gives in.

Very often she is right, however, and he is wrong. Last week she did not want us to go out one day because she was sure it would rain, but he did not think so, and said we had better go It did rain—poured—and we got wet through and have had colds ever since, but when we came in mother scolded me for saying, 'You see, you were right.' She said I should be saying 'I told you so!' next, in a nasty jeering way as the boys do, which really means rejoicing because somebody else is wrong, and is not generous. I hope I shall never come to that; but I know if I am ever sure of a thing being right which somebody else thinks is wrong, it won't matter what it is or who it is, I shall not give in. I don't see how I could."

Her pen seldom ran away with her into personal matters like these, in the early part of the book; but from the first she was apt to be beguiled occasionally by the pleasure of perceiving a powerful stimulant under the influence of which everything is lost sight of but the point perceived. She had never to fight a daily and exhausting battle for her private opinions as talkative people have, simply because she rarely if ever expressed an opinion; but her father stood ready always, a post of resistance to innovation, upon which she could sharpen the claws of her conclusion silently whenever they required it.

When next she mentions "The Vicar of Wakefield," she says expressly :

" I do not remember what I wrote about it the first time I read it, and I will not look to see until I have written what I think now, because I should like to know if I still agree with myself as I was then."

And it is interesting to note how very much she does agree with herself as she " was then"; the feeling, in fact, is the same, but it has passed from her heart to her head, and been resolved by the process into positive opinion, held with conscious knowledge, and delivered with greatly improved power of expression.

" ' The Vicar of Wakefield ' makes me think a good deal," she continues, " but there is no order in my thoughts. There is, however, one thing in the book that strikes me first and foremost and above all others, which is that the men were educated and the women were ignorant. It is not to be supposed that the women preferred to be ignorant, and therefore I presume they were not allowed the educational advantages upon which the men prided themselves. The men must accordingly have withheld these advantages by main force, yet they do not scorn to sneer at the consequences of their injustice. There is a sneer implied in the vicar's remark about his own wife : 'She could read any English book without much spelling.' That her ignorance was not the consequence of incapacity is proved by the evidence which follows of her intelligence in other matters. Had Mrs. Primrose been educated she might have continued less lovable than the vicar, but she would probably have been wiser. The vicar must always have been conscious of her defects, but had never apparently thought of a remedy, nor does he dream of preventing a repetition of the same defects in his daughters by providing them with a better education. He takes their unteachableness for granted, remarking complacently that an hour of recreation 'was taken up in innocent mirth between my wife and daughters, and in philosophical arguments between my son and me,' as if 'innocent mirth' were as much as he could reasonably expect from such inferior beings as a wife and daughters must necessarily be. The average school girl of to-day is a child of light on the subject of her own sex compared with the gentle vicar, and incapable, even before her education is half over, of the envy and meanness which the latter thinks it kindest to take a humourous view of, and of the disingenuousness at which he also smiles as the inevitable outcome of feminine inferiority— at least *I* never met a girl in my position who would not have admired Miss Wilmot's beauty, nor do I know one who would not answer her father frankly, however embarrassing the question might be, if he asked her opinion of a possible lover."

The next entry in the book is on the subject of "Mrs. Caudle's Curtain Lectures," and, like most of the others, it merits attention from the unexpected view she takes of the position. It does not strike her as being humourous, but pathetic. She feels the misery of it, and she had already begun to hold that human misery is either a thing to be remedied or a sacred subject to be dwelt on in silence ; and she considers Mrs. Caudle entirely with a view to finding a cure for her case.

"The Caudles were petty tradespeople," she says, "respectable in their own position, but hardly lovable according to our ideas. Mr. Caudle, with meek persistency, goes out to amuse himself alone when his day's work is done. Mrs. Caudle's day's work never is done. She has the wearing charge of a large family, and the anxiety of making both ends

meet on a **paltry** income, which entails much self-denial and
sordid parsimony, but is conscientiously done, if not cheerfully, nevertheless.   It is Mr. Caudle, however, who grum-
bles, making no allowance for extra pressure of work on
washing days, when she is too busy to hash the cold mutton.
The rule of her life is weariness and worry from morning till
night, and for relaxation in the evening she must sit down and
mend the children's clothes ; and even when that is done she
goes to bed with the certainty of being roused from her hard-
earned rest by a husband who brings a sickening odour of bad
tobacco and spirits home with him, and naturally her temper
suffers.   She knows nothing of love and sympathy ; she has
no pleasurable interest in life.   Fatigue and worry are succeeded by profound disheartenment.   One can imagine that
while she was young, the worn garments she was wont to
mend during those long lonely evenings were often wet with
tears.   The dulness must have been deadly, and dulness
added to fatigue time after time ended at last not in tears, but
in peevish irritation, ebullitions of spleen, and ineffectual resistance   The woman was thoroughly embittered, and the man
had to pay the penalty.   Whatever pleasure there might have
been in their joint lives he had secured for himself, leaving
her to stagnate for want of a little variety to keep her feelings
flowing wholesomely ; and she did stagnate dutifully, but she
was to blame for it.   Had she gone out and amused herself
with other wives similarly situated, and had tobacco and beer,
if she liked them, every evening, it would have been better for
herself and her husband."

There must have been some system in Evadne's reading,
for " The Naggletons" came immediately after " Mrs. Caudle," and are dismissed curtly enough :

"Vulgar, ill-bred, lower class people," she calls them.
" Objectionable to contemplate from every point of view.
But a book which should enlighten the class whom it describes
on the subject of their own bad manners.   *We* don't nag."

She owed her acquaintance with the next two books she
mentions to the indirect instigation of her father, and she
must have read them when she was about eighteen, and
emancipated from schoolroom supervision, but not yet fairly
entered upon the next chapter of her existence ; for they are
among the last she notices before she came out.

The date is fixed by an entry which appears on a subse-
quent page with the note :   " I was presented at court to-day

by my mother." After this entry life becomes more interesting than literature, evidently, for the book ceases to be a
record of reading and thought with an occasional note on
people and circumstances, and becomes just the opposite, viz.,
a diary of events interspersed with sketches of character and
only a rare allusion to literature. But, judging by the number and variety and the careful record kept of the works she
read, the six months or so immediately preceding her presentation must have been a time of the greatest intellectual
activity, her father's influence being, as usual, often apparent
as primary instigator. Once, when they were having coffee
out on the lawn after dinner, he began a discussion in her
hearing about books with another gentleman who was staying
in the house, and in the course of it he happened to praise
"Roderick Random" and "Tom Jones" eloquently. He
said they were superior in their own line to anything which
the present day has produced. "They are true to life in
every particular," he maintained, "and not only to the life of
those times, but of all time. In fact, you feel as you read
that it is not fiction, but human nature itself that you are
studying; and there is an education in moral philosophy on
every page."

Evadne was much impressed, and being anxious to know
what an education in moral philosophy might be, she got
"Roderick Random" and "Tom Jones" out of the library
when she went in that evening, and took them to her own
room to study. They were the two books already referred to
as being among the last she read just before she came out.
They did not please her, but she waded through them from
beginning to end conscientiously, nevertheless, and then she
made her remarks.

Of "Roderick Random" she wrote :

"The hero is a kind of king-can-do-no-wrong young man ;
if a thing were not right in itself he acted as if the pleasure
of doing it sanctified it to his use sufficiently. After a career
of vice, in which he revels without any sense of personal degradation, he marries an amiable girl named Narcissa, and
everyone seems to expect that such a union of vice and virtue
would be productive of the happiest consequences. In point
of fact he should have married Miss Williams, for whom he
was in every respect a suitable mate. If anything, Miss Williams was the better of the two, for Roderick sinned in weak
wantonness, while she only did so of necessity. They repent

together, but she is married to an unsavoury manservant named Strap as a reward ; while Roderick considers himself entitled to the peerless Narcissa. Miss Williams, moreover, becomes Narcissa's confidential friend, and the whole disgraceful arrangement is made possible by Narcissa herself, who calmly accepts these two precious associates at their own valuation, and admits them to the closest intimacy without any knowledge of their true characters and early lives. The fine flavour of real life in the book seems to me to be of the putrid kind which some palates relish, perhaps ; but it cannot be wholesome, and it may be poisonous. The moral is : Be as vicious as you please, but prate of virtue."

"Tom Jones" she dismissed with greater contempt, if possible :

"Another young man," she wrote, "steeped in vice, although acquainted with virtue. He also marries a spotless heroine. Such men marrying are a danger to the community at large. The two books taken together show well the self-interest and injustice of men, the fatal ignorance and slavish apathy of women ; and it may be good to know these things, but it is not agreeable."

The ventilation of free discussion would doubtless have been an advantage to Evadne at this impressionable period, when she was still, as it were, more an intellectual than a human being, travelling upon her head rather than upon her heart—so to speak—and one cannot help speculating about the probable modification it would have wrought in some of her opinions. Unfortunately, however, her family was one of those in which the *clôture* is rigorously applied when any attempt is made to introduce ideas which are not already old and accustomed. It was as if her people were satisfied that by enforcing silence they could prevent thought.

CHAPTER IV.

IT is interesting to trace the steps by which Evadne advanced : one item of knowledge accidentally acquired compelling her to seek another, as in the case of some disease mentioned in a story-book, the nature of which she could not comprehend without studying the construction of the organ it affected. But haphazard seems to have determined her pursuits much more than design as a rule. Some people in after life, who liked her views, said they saw the guiding hand of Providence directing her course from the first ; but those who opposed her said it was the devil ; and others again, in idleness or charity, or the calm neutrality of indifference, set it all down to the Inevitable, a fashionable first cause at this time, which is both comprehensive, convenient, and inoffensive, since it may mean anything, and so suits itself to everybody's prejudices.

But she certainly made her first acquaintance with anatomy and physiology without design of her own. Her mother sent her up to a lumber room one day to hunt through an old box of books for a story she wanted her to read to the children, and the box happened to contain some medical works, which Evadne peeped into during her search. A plate first attracted her attention, and then she read a little to see what the plate meant, and then she read a little more because the subject fascinated her, and the lucid language of a great scientific man, certain of his facts, satisfied her, and carried her on insensibly. She continued standing until one leg tired, then she rested on the other ; then she sat on the hard edge of the box, and finally she subsided on to the floor, in the dust, where she was found hours later, still reading.

"My dear child, where *have* you been?" her mother exclaimed irritably, when at last she appeared. "I sent you to get a book to read to the children."

"There it is, mother—'The Gold Thread,'" Evadne answered. "But I cannot read to the children until after their tea. They were at their lessons this morning, and we are all going out this afternoon." She had neither forgotten the children nor the time they wanted their book, which was eminently characteristic. She never did forget other people's interests, however much she might be absorbed by the pleasure of her own pursuits.

"And I found three other books, mother, that I should like to have ; may I ?" she continued. "They are all about our bones and brains, and the circulation of the blood, and digestion. It says in one of them that muriatic acid, the chemical agent by which the stomach dissolves the food, is probably obtained from muriate of soda, which is common salt contained in the blood. Isn't that interesting ? And it says that pleasure—not excitement, you know—is the result of the action of living organs, and it goes on to explain it. Shall I read it to you ?"

"My dear child, what nonsense have you got hold of now?"
Mrs. Frayling exclaimed, laughing.

"It is all here, mother," Evadne remonstrated, tapping her
books. "Do look at them."

Mrs. Frayling turned over a few pages with dainty
fingers : "Tracing from without inward, the various cover-
ings of the brain are," she read in one. "The superior ex-
tremity consists of the shoulder, the arm, the forearm, and the
hand," she saw in another. "Dr. Harley also confirms the
opinion of M. Chaveau that the sugar is not destroyed in any
appreciable quantity during its passage through the tissues,"
she learned from the third "Oh, how nasty!" she ejaculated,
alluding to the dust on the cover. "And what a state you
are in yourself ! You seem to have a perfect mania for grub-
bing up old books. What do you want with them ? You
cannot possibly understand them. Why, *I* can't ! It is all
vanity, you know. Here, take them away."

"But, mother, I want to keep them. They can't do me any
harm if I don't understand them."

"You really *are* tiresome, Evadne," her mother rejoined.
"It is quite bad taste to be so persistent."

"I am sorry, mother ; I apologize. But I can read them, I
suppose, as you don't see anything objectionable in them."

"Don't *you* see, dear child, that I am trying to write a letter ?
How do you suppose I can do so while you stand chattering
there at my elbow ! You won't understand the books, but
you are too obstinate for anything, and you had better take
them and try. I don't expect to hear anything more about
them," she added complacently, as she resumed her letter.
Nor did she, but she felt the effect of them strongly in after
years.

When Evadne went out for a ride with three of her sisters
that afternoon her mind was full to overflowing of her morning studies, and she would liked to have shared such interesting
information with them, but they discouraged her.

"Isn't it curious," she began, "our skulls are not all in one
piece when we're born——"

"I call it simply *nasty*," said Julia. She was the one who
screamed at a mouse.

"You'll be a bore if you don't mind," cried Evelyn, who
monopolized the conversation, as a rule.

Barbara politely requested her to "Shurrup !" a word of
the boys which she permitted herself to borrow in the exuber-

ance of her spirits and the sanctity of private life whenever Evadne threatened, as on the present occasion, to be "*too* kind."

Evadne turned back then and left them, not because they vexed her, but because she wanted to have her head to the wind and her thick brown hair blown back out of her eyes, and full leisure to reflect upon her last acquisition as she cantered home happily.

CHAPTER V.

EVADNE was never a great reader in the sense of being omnivorous in her choice of books, but she became a very good one. She always had a solid book in hand, and some standard work of fiction also ; but she read both with the utmost deliberation, and with intellect clear and senses unaffected by anything. After studying anatomy and physiology, she took up pathology as a matter of course, and naturally went on from thence to prophylactics and therapeutics, but was quite unharmed, because she made no personal application of her knowledge as the coarser mind masculine of the ordinary medical student is apt to do. She read of all the diseases to which the heart is subject, and thought of them familiarly as " cardiac affections," without fancying she had one of them ; and she obtained an extraordinary knowledge of the digestive processes and their ailments without realizing that her own might ever be affected. She possessed, in fact, a mind of exceptional purity as well as of exceptional strength, one to be enlightened by knowledge, not corrupted ; but had it been otherwise she must certainly have suffered in consequence of the effect of the curiously foolish limitations imposed upon her by those who had charge of her conventional education. Subjects were surrounded by mystery which should have been explained. An impossible ignorance was the object aimed at, and so long as no word was spoken on either side it was supposed to be attained. The risk of making mysteries for an active intellect to feed upon was never even considered, nor did anyone perceive the folly of withholding positive knowledge, which, when properly conveyed, is the true source of healthy-mindedness, from a child whose intelligent perception was already sufficiently keen to require it. Principles were dealt out to her, for one thing, with a generous want of definition which must have made them fatal to all progress had she been able to take them intact. Her mother's favourite and most inclusive dictum alone, that "everything is for the best, and all things work together for good," should have forced her to a matter of fact acceptance of wickedness as a thing inevitable which it would be waste of time to oppose, since it was bound to resolve itself into something satisfactory in the end, like the objectionable refuse which can be converted by ingenious processes into an excellent substitute for butter. But she was saved from the stultification of such a position by finding it impossible to reconcile it practically with the constant opposition which she found herself at the same time enjoined to oppose to so many things. If everything is for the best, it appeared to her, clearly we cannot logically oppose ourselves to anything, and there must accordingly be two trinities in ethics, good, better, best, and bad, worse, worst, which it is impossible to condense into one comprehensive axiom.

But most noticeably prominent, to her credit, through all this period are the same desirable characteristics, viz., that provisional acceptance already noticed of what she was taught by those whom she delighted to honor and obey, and the large-minded absence of prejudice which enabled her to differ from them, when she saw good cause, without antagonism. " Drop the subject when you do not agree : there is no need to be bitter because you know you are right," was the maxim she used in ordinary social intercourse ; but she was at the same time forming principles to be acted upon in opposition to everybody when occasion called for action. Another noticeable point, too, was the way in which her mind returned from every excursion into no matter what abstruse region of research, to the position of women, her original point of departure. "Withholding education from women was the original sin of man," she concludes.

Mind as creator appealed to her less than mind as recorder, reasoner, and ruler ; and for one gem of poetry or other beauty of purely literary value which she quotes, there are fifty records of principles of action. The acquisition of knowledge was her favourite pastime, her principal pleasure in life, and there were no doubts of her own ability to disturb her so long as there was no self-consciousness. Unfortunately, however, for her tranquillity, the self-consciousness had to come. She approached the verge of womanhood. She was made to do up her hair. She was encouraged to think of being presented, coming out, and having a home of her own eventually. Her liberty of action was sensibly curtailed, but all supervision in the matter of her mental pursuits was withdrawn. She had received the accustomed education for a girl in her position, which her parents held, without knowing it themselves, perhaps, to consist for the most part in being taught to know better than to read anything which they would have considered objectionable. But the end of the supervision, which should have been a joy to her, brought the first sudden sense of immensity, and was chilling. She perceived that the world is large and strong, and that she was small and weak ; that knowledge is infinite, capacity indifferent, life short—and then came the inevitable moment. She does not, say what caused the first overwhelming sense of self in her own case ; but the change it wrought is evident, and the disheartening doubts with which it was accompanied are expressed. She picks her

> Flower in the crannied wall,

and realizes her own limitations :

> . . . but if I could understand
> What you are, root and all, and all in all,
> I should know what God and man is.

And from this time forward there is less literature and more life in the "Commonplace Book."

CHAPTER VI.

MR. and Lady Adeline Hamilton-Wells, with the inevitable twins, came constantly to Fraylingay while Evadne was in the schoolroom, and generally during the holidays, that she might be at liberty to look after the twins, whose moral obliquities she was supposed to be able to control better than anybody else. They once told their mother that they liked Evadne, "because she was so good" ; and Lady Adeline had a delicious moment of hope. If the twins had begun to appreciate goodness they would be better themselves directly, she was thinking, when Diavolo exclaimed : "We can shock her easier than anybody," and hope died prematurely. They had been a source of interest, and also of some concern to Evadne from the first. She took a grave view of their vagaries, and entertained doubts on the subject of their salvation should an "all-wise Providence" catch them peering into a sewer, resolve itself into a poisonous gas, and cut them off suddenly —a fate which had actually overtaken a small brother of her own who was not a good little boy either—a fact which was the cause of much painful reflection to Evadne. She understood all about the drain and the poisonous gas, but she could not fit in the "all-wise Providence acting only for the best," which was introduced as primary agent in the sad affair by "their dear Mr. Campbell," as her mother called him, in "a most touching and strengthening" discourse he delivered from the pulpit on the subject. If Binny were naughty—and Binny *was* naughty beyond all hope of redemption, according to the books ; there could be no doubt about that, for he not only committed one, but each and every sin sufficient in itself for condemnation, all in one day, too, when he could, and twice over if there were time. He disobeyed orders. He fought cads. He stole apples. He told lies—in fact, he preferred to tell lies ; truth had no charm for him. And all these things he was in the habit of doing regularly to the best of his ability when he was "cut off"; and how such an end could be all for the best, if the wicked must perish, and it is not good to perish, was the puzzle. There was something she could not grasp of a contradictory nature in it all that tormented her. The doctrine of Purgatory might have been a help, but she had not heard of it.

She told the twins the story of Binny's sad end once in the orthodox way, as a warning, but the warning was the only part of it which failed to impress them. "And do you know," she said solemnly, "there were some green apples found in his pockets after he was dead, actually !"

"What a pity !" Diavolo exclaimed. If they had been found in his stomach it would have been so much more satisfactory. "How did he get the apples ? Off the tree or out of the storeroom ?"

" I don't know," said Evadne.

"They wouldn't have green apples in the storeroom," Angelica thought.

"Oh, yes, they might," Diavolo considered. " Those big cooking fellows, you know—they're green enough."

" But they're not nice," said Angelica.

" No, but you don't think of that till you've got them," was the outcome of Diavolo's experience. " Is your storeroom on the ground floor ?" he asked Evadne.

" No," she answered.

"Is there a creeper outside the window?" he pursued.

"No, creepers won't grow because a big lime tree over-hangs it."

The children exchanged glances.

"I shouldn't have made that room a storeroom," said Angelica. "Lime trees bring flies. There's something flies like on the leaves."

"But any tree will bring flies if you smear the leaves with sweet stuff," said Diavolo. "You remember that copper-beech outside papa's dressing room window, Angelica?"

"Yes," she said thoughtfully. "He had to turn out of his dressing room this summer; he couldn't stand them."

"But was Binny often caught, Evadne?" Diavolo asked.

"Often," she said.

"And punished?"

"*Always.*"

"But I suppose he had generally eaten the apples?" Angelica suggested anxiously.

"It's better to eat them at once," sighed Diavolo. "Did you say he did everything he was told not to do?"

"Yes."

"I expect when he was told not to do a thing he could not think of anything else until he *had* done it," said Angelica.

"And now he's in heaven," Diavolo speculated, looking up through the window with big bright eyes pathetically.

The twins thought a good deal about heaven in their own way. Lady Adeline did not like them to be talked to on the subject. They were indefatigable explorers, and it was pop-ularly supposed that only the difficulty of being present at an inquest on their own bodies, which they would have thoroughly enjoyed, had kept them so far from trying to obtain a glimpse of the next world. They discovered the storeroom at Fraylingay half an hour after they had discussed the improv-ing details of Binny's exciting career, and had found it quite easy of access by means of the available lime tree. They both suffered a good deal that night, and they thought of Binny. "But there's nothing in *our* pockets, that's one comfort," Diavolo exclaimed suddenly, to the astonishment of his mother, who was sitting up with him. Angelica heaved a sigh of satis-faction.

Evadne's patience with the twins was wonderful. She always took charge of them cheerfully on wet days and in other times of trouble, and managed them with infinite tact.

"How do you do it, my dear?" Lady Adeline asked. "Do you talk to them and tell them stories?"

"No," said Evadne, "I don't talk much; I—just don't lose sight of them—or interfere—if I can possibly help it."

The twins had no reverence for anything or anybody. One day they were in Evadne's little sitting room which overlooked the courtyard. It was an antechamber to her bedroom, and peculiarly her own by right of primogeniture. Nobody ever thought of going there without her special permission—except, of course, the twins; but even they assumed hypocritical airs of innocent apology for accidental intrusion when they wanted to make things pleasant for themselves.

On this particular occasion Evadne was sitting beside her little work-table busy with her needle, and the twins were standing together looking out of the window.

"There's papa," said Diavolo.

"He's going for a ride," said Angelica.

"Doesn't he mount queerly?" Diavolo observed. "He'd be safer in a bath chair."

"Not if we were wheeling him," Angelica suggested, with a chuckle.

"What shall we do?" yawned Diavolo. "Shall we fight?"

"Yes; let's," said Angelica.

"You must do no such thing," Evadne interfered.

"Not fight! Why?" Angelica demanded.

"We *must* fight, you know," Diavolo asserted.

"I don't see that," said Evadne. "Why should you fight?"

"It's good for the circulation of the blood," said Angelica. "Warms a body, you know."

"And there's the property, too!" said Diavolo. "We've got to fight for that."

Evadne did not understand, so Angelica kindly explained: "You see, I'm the eldest, but Diavolo's a boy, so he gets the property because of the entail, and we neither of us think it fair; so we fight for it, and whichever wins is to have it. I won the last battle, so it's mine just now; but Diavolo may win it back if we fight again before papa dies. That's why he wants to fight now, I expect."

"Yes," Diavolo candidly confessed. "But we generally fight when we see papa go out for a ride."

"Because you are afraid he will catch you and punish you, as you deserve, if he's at home, I suppose, you bad children."

"Not at all," said Angelica. "It's because he looks so unsafe on a horse ; you never know what'll happen."

"It's a kind of a last chance," said Diavolo, "and that makes it exciting."

"But wouldn't you be very sorry if your father died ? " Evadne asked.

The twins looked at each other doubtfully.

"Should we ? " Diavolo said to Angelica.

"I wonder ? " said Angelica.

One wet day they chose to paint in Evadne's room because they could not go out. She found pictures, and got everything ready for them good-naturedly, and then they sat themselves down at a little table opposite each other ; but the weather affected their spirits, and made them both fractious. They wanted the same picture to begin with, and only settled the question by demolishing it in their attempts to snatch it from each other. Then there was only one left between them, but happily they remembered that artists sometimes work at the same picture, and it further occurred to them that it would be an original method—or "funny," as they phrased it—for one of them to work at it wrong side up. So Angelica daubed the sky blue on her side of the table, and Diavolo flung green on the fields from his. They had large genial mouths at that time, indefinite noses, threatening to turn up a little, and bright dark eyes, quick glancing, but with no particular expression in them—no symptom either of love or hate, nothing but living interest. It was pretty to see Diavolo's fair head touching Angelica's dark one across the little table ; but when it came too close Angelica would dunt it sharply out of the way with her own, which was apparently the harder of the two, and Diavolo would put up his hand and rub the spot absently. He was too thoroughly accustomed to such sisterly attentions to be altogether conscious of them.

The weather darkened down.

"I wish I could see," he grumbled.

"Get out of your own light," said Angelica.

"How can I get out of my own light when there isn't any light to get out of ? "

Angelica put her paint brush in her mouth, and looked up at the window thoughtfully.

"Let's make it into a song," she said.

"Let's," said Diavolo, intent upon making blue and yellow into green.

> " No light have we, and that we do resent,
>   And. learning this, the weather will relent,
>   Repent ! Relent ! Ah-men,"

Angelica sang. Diavolo paused with his brush halfway to his mouth, and nodded intelligently.

" Now ! " said Angelica, and they repeated the parody together, Angelica making a perfect second to Diavolo's exquisite treble.

Evadne looked up from her work surprised. Her own voice was contralto, but it would have taken her a week to learn to sing a second to the notes, and she had never dreamt of making one.

" I didn't know you could sing," she said.

" Oh, yes, we can sing," Angelica answered cheerfully. " We've a decided talent for music."

" Angelica can make a song in a moment," said Diavolo. " Let me paint your nose green, Evadne."

" You can paint mine if you like," said Angelica.

" No, I shan't. I shall paint my own."

" No, you paint mine and I'll paint yours," Angelica suggested.

" Well, both together, then," Diavolo answered.

" Honest Injin," Angelica agreed, and they set to work.

Evadne sat with her embroidery in her lap and watched them. Their faces would have to be washed in any case, and they might as well be washed for an acre as for an inch of paint. She never nagged with, " Don't do this," and " Don't do that " about everything, if their offences could be summed up, and wiped out in some such way all at once.

" We'll sing you an anthem some day," Angelica presently promised.

" Why not now ? " said Evadne.

" The spirit does not move us," Diavolo answered.

" But you may forget," said Evadne.

" We never forget our promises," Angelica protested as proudly as was possible with a green nose.

Nor did they, curiously enough. They made a point of keeping their word, but in their own way, and this one was kept in due course. The time they chose was when a certain Grand Duke was staying in the house. They had quite captivated him, and he expressed a wish to hear them sing.

" Shall we ? " said Diavolo.

" We will," said Angelica. " Not because he's a prince, but

because we promised Evadne an anthem, and we might as well do it now," she added with true British independence.

The prince chuckled.

"What shall it be?" said Diavolo, settling himself at the piano. He always played the accompaniments.

"*Papa*, I think," said Angelica.

"What is '*Papa*'?" Lady Adeline asked anxiously.

"Very nice, or you wouldn't have married him," answered Angelica. "Go on, Diavolo. If you sing flat, I'll slap you."

"If you're impertinent, miss, I'll put you out," Diavolo retorted.

"Go on," said Evadne sharply, fearing a fight.

But to everybody's intense relief the prince laughed, and then the twins' distinguished manners appeared in a new and agreeable light.

"*Papa—Papa—Papa*,"—they sang—"*Papa says—that we —that we—that we are little devils! and so we are—we are— we are and ever shall be—world without end.*"

"*I am a chip*," Diavolo trilled exquisitely; "*I am a chip.*"

"*Thou art a chip—Thou art a chip*," Angelica responded.

"*We are both chips*," they concluded harmoniously—"*chips of the old—old block! And as it was in the beginning, is now, and ever shall be, world without end. Amen!*"

"You sang that last phrase flat, you—*pulp!*" cried Angelica.

"I can't both sing and play," Diavolo protested.

"You'll say you can't eat and breathe next," she retorted, giving his hair a tug.

"What did you do that for?" he demanded.

"Just to waken you up," she answered.

"Are they always like this?" the prince asked, much edified.

"This is nothing," groaned Mr. Hamilton-Wells.

"Nothing if it is not genius," the prince suggested grace-fully.

"The ineffectual genius of the nineteenth century, I fancy, which betrays itself by strange incongruities and contrasts of a violent kind, but is otherwise unproductive," Mrs. Orton Beg whispered to Mr. Frayling incautiously.

Lady Adeline looked up: "I could not help hearing," she said.

"Oh, Adeline, I am sorry!" Mrs. Orton Beg exclaimed.

"*I* thank you," said Lady Adeline, sighing. "Courtly phrases are pleasant plums, even to latter-day palates which are losing all taste for such dainties ; but they are not nourishing.   I would rather know my children to be merely naughty, and spend my time in trying to make them good, than falsely flatter myself that there is anything great in them, and indulge them on that plea, until I had thoroughly confirmed them in faults which I ought to have been rigorously repressing."

"You're right there," said Mr. Frayling ; "but all the same, you'll be able to make a good deal of that boy or I'm much mistaken   And as for Angelica, why, when she is at the head of an establishment of her own, she will require all her smart-ness.   But teach her housekeeping, Lady Adeline ; that is the thing for *her*."

Evadne was sitting near her father, not taking part in the conversation, but attending to it ; and Lady Adeline happen-ing to look at her at this moment, saw something which gave her " pause to ponder."   Evadne's face recalled somewhat the type of old Egypt, Egypt with an intellect added.   Her eyes were long and apparently narrow, but not so in reality—a trick she had of holding them half shut habitually gave a false im pression of their size, and veiled the penetration of their glance also, which was exceptionally keen.   In moments of emotion, however, she would open them to the full unexpectedly, and then the effect was startling and peculiar ; and it was one of these transient flashes which surprised Lady Adeline when Mr. Frayling made that last remark.   It was a mere gleam, but it revealed Evadne to Lady Adeline as a flash of lightning might have revealed a familiar landscape on a dark night.   She saw what she expected to see but all transformed, and she saw some-thing beyond, which she did not expect, and could neither comprehend nor forget. So far she had only thought of Evadne as a nice, quiet little thing with nothing particular in her; from that evening, however, she suspended her opinion, suspecting something, but waiting to know more.   Evadne was then in her eighteenth year, but not yet out.

CHAPTER VII.

MRS. ORTON BEG was a sister of Mrs Frayling's and an oracle to Evadne.   Mrs. Frayling was fair, plump, sweet, yielding, commonplace, prolific.   Mrs. Orton Beg was a barren widow, slender, sincere, silent, firm, and tender. Mrs. Frayling, for lack of insight, was unsympathetic, Mrs. Orton Beg was just the opposite ; and she and Evadne understood each other, and were silent together in the most companionable way in the world.

When Evadne went to her own room on the evening made memorable by the twins' famous anthem, she was haunted by that word "ineffectual," which Mrs. Orton Beg had used. "Ineffectual genius"—there was something familiar as well as high sounding in the epithet ; it recalled an idea with which she was already acquainted ; what was it ? She opened her " Commonplace Book," and sat with her pen in her hand, cogitating comfortably. She had no need to weary her fresh young brain with an irritating pursuit of what she wanted ; she had only to wait, and it would recur to her. And presently it came. Her countenance brightened. She bent over the book and wrote a few lines, read them when she had blotted them, and was satisfied.

" I have it," she wrote. " Shelley=genius of the nineteenth century—' Beautiful and ineffectual angel, beating in the void his luminous wings in vain.'—*Matthew Arnold.*"

When she had done this she took up a book, went to the fire, settled herself in an easy-chair and began to read. The book was " Ruth," by Mrs. Gaskell, and she was just finishing it. When she had done so she went back to the table, and copied out the following paragraph :

" The daily life into which people are born, and into which they are absorbed before they are aware, forms chains which only one in a hundred has moral strength enough to despise, and to break when the right time comes—when an inward necessity for independent action arises, which is superior to all outward conventionalities."

She stopped here, and pushed the volume away from her. It was the only passage in it which she cared to remember.

She had lost the confidence of the child by this time, and become humbly doubtful of her own opinion ; and instead of summing up " Ruth " boldly, as she would have done the year before, she paused now a moment to reflect before she wrote with diffidence &

" The principal impression this book has made upon me is that Mrs. Gaskell must have been a very lovable woman.*

---

* George Eliot thought so too, years before Evadne was born, and expressed the thought in a letter in which she also prophesied that " Ruth " would not live through a generation. The impression the book made upon Evadne is another proof of prescience in the great writer.

The story seems to me long drawn out, and of small significance. It is full of food for the heart, but the head goes empty away, and both should be satisfied by a work of fiction, I think. But perhaps it is my own mood that is at fault. At another time I might have found gems in it which now in my dulness I have failed to perceive."

Somebody knocked at the door as she blotted the words.

"Come in, auntie," she said, as if in answer to an accustomed signal ; and Mrs. Orton Beg entered in a long, loose, voluminously draped white wrapper.

Evadne drew an easy-chair to the fire for her.

"Sit down, auntie," she said, "and be cosey. You are late to-night. I was afraid you were not coming."

Mrs. Orton Beg was in the habit of coming to Evadne's room every evening when she was at Fraylingay, to chat, or sit silently sociable over the fire with her before saying good-night.

"Do I ever fail you ? " she asked, smiling.

"No. But I have been afraid of the fatal fascination of that great fat foreign prince. He singled you out for special attention, and I have been jealous."

"Well, you need not have been, for he singled me out in order to talk about you. He thinks you are a nice child. You interest him."

"Defend me ! " said Evadne. "But you mistake me, dear aunt. It was not of him I was jealous, but of you. The fat prince is nothing to me, and you are a very great deal."

Mrs. Orton Beg's face brightened at the words, but she continued to look into the fire silently for some seconds after Evadne had spoken, and made no other visible sign of having heard them.

"I don't think I ought to encourage you to sit up so late," she said presently. "Lady Adeline has just been asking me who it is that burns the midnight oil up here so regularly."

"Lady Adeline must be up very late herself to see it," said Evadne. "I suppose those precious twins disturb her. I wish she would let me take entire charge of them when she is here. It would be a relief, I should think ! "

"It would be an imposition," said Mrs. Orton Beg. "But you are a brave girl, Evadne. *I* would not venture."

"Oh, they delight me," Evadne answered. "And I know them well enough now to forestall them."

"When I told Lady Adeline that these were your rooms,"

her aunt pursued, " she said something about a lily maid high in her chamber up a tower to the east guarding the sacred shield of Lancelot."

" Singularly inappropriate," said Evadne. " For my tower is south. and west, thank Heaven."

" And there isn't a symptom of Lancelot," her aunt concluded.

" Young ladies don't guard sacred shields nowadays," said Evadne.

" No," answered her aunt, glancing over her shoulder at the open book on the table. " They have substituted the sacred 'Commonplace Book'—full of thought, I fancy."

" You speak regretfully, auntie; but isn't it better to think and be happy, than to die of atrophy for a sentiment ? "

" I don't think it better to extinguish all sentiment. Life without sentiment would be so bald."

" But life with that kind of sentiment doesn't last, it seems, and nobody is benefited by it. It is extreme misery to the girl herself, and she dies young, leaving a legacy of lifelong regret and bitterness to her friends. I should think it small comfort to become the subject for a poem or a picture at such a price. And surely, auntie, sentiments which are silly or dangerous would be better extinguished ? "

Mrs. Orton Beg smiled at the fire enigmatically.

" But the poem or the picture may become a lasting benefit to mankind," she suggested presently.

" Humph ! " said Evadne.

" You doubt it ? "

" Well, you see, auntie, there are two ways of looking at it. When you first come across the poem or the picture which perpetuates the sentiment that slew the girl, and beautifies it, you feel a glow all over, and fancy you would like to imitate her, and think that you would deserve great credit for it if you did. But when you come to consider, there is nothing very noble, after all, in a hopeless passion for an elderly man of the world who is past being benefited by it, even if he could reciprocate it. Elaine should have married a man of her own age, and made him happy. She would have done some good in her time so, and been saved from setting us a bad example. I think it a sin to make unwholesome sentiments attractive."

" Then Lancelot does not charm you ? "

" No," said Evadne thoughtfully. " I should have preferred the king."

"Ah, yes. Because he was the nobler, the more ideal man?"

"No, not exactly," Evadne answered. "But because he was the more wholesome."

"My dear child, are you speaking literally?"

"Yes, auntie."

"Good Heavens!" Mrs. Orton Beg ejaculated softly. "The times *have* changed."

"Yes, we know more now," Evadne answered tranquilly.

"You are fulfilling the promise of your youth, Evadne," her aunt remarked after a thoughtful pause. "I remember reading a fairy tale of Jean Ingelow's aloud to you children in the nursery long ago. I forget the name of it, but it was the one into which 'One morning, oh, so early,' comes; and you started a controversy as to whether, speaking of the dove, when the lark said 'Give us glory,' she should have made answer, 'Give us peace' or 'peas.' The latter, you maintained, as being the more natural, and the most sensible."

"I must have been a horrid little prig in those days," said Evadne, smiling. "But, auntie, there can be no peace without plenty. And I think I would rather be a sensible realist than a foolish idealist. You mean that you think me too much of a utilitarian, do you not?"

"You are in danger, I think."

"Utilitarianism is Bentham's *greatest happiness principle,* is it not?" Evadne asked.

"Yes—greatest human happiness," her aunt replied.

"Well, I don't know how that can be dangerous in principle. But, of course, I know nothing of such questions practically. Only I do seem to perceive that you must rest on a solid basis of real advantages before you can reach up to ideal perfection with any chance of success."

"You seem to be very wide awake to-night, Evadne," Mrs. Orton Beg rejoined. "This is he first I have heard of your peculiar views."

"Oh, I am a kind of owl, I think, auntie," Evadne answered apologetically. "You see, I never had anything to do in the schoolroom that I could not manage when I was half asleep, and so I formed a habit of dozing over my lessons by day, and waking up when I came to bed at night. Having a room of my own always has been a great advantage. I have been secure all along of a quiet time at night for reading and thought —and that is real life, auntie, isn't it? I don't care to talk much, as a rule, do you ? I like to listen and watch people. But I always wake up at this time of the night, and I feel as if I could be quite garrulous now when everybody else is going to sleep. But, auntie, don't use such an ominous expression as 'peculiar views' about anything I say, *please ;* 'views' are always in ill odour, and peculiarities, even peculiar perfections, would isolate one, and that I *do* dread. It would be awful to be out of sympathy with one's fellow-creatures, and have them look suspiciously at one ; and it would be no comfort to me to know that want of sympathy is the proof of a narrow nature, and that suspicion is the inevitable outcome of ignorance and stupidity. I don't want to despise my fellow-creatures. I would rather share their ignorance and conceit and be sociable than find myself isolated even by a very real superiority. The one would be pleasant enough, I should think ; the other pain beyond all bearing of it."

Mrs. Orton Beg's heart contracted with a momentary fear for her niece, but she dismissed it promptly.

" The room to yourself has been a doubtful advantage, I fancy," she said. " It has made you theoretical. But you will lose all that by and by. And in the meantime, you must remember that in such matters we have small choice. We are born with superior or inferior faculties, and must make use of them, such as they are, to become inferior cooks or countesses or superior ditto, as the case may be. But there are always plenty of one's own kind, whichever it is, to consort with. Birds of a feather, you know. You need not be afraid of being isolated."

" You are thinking of ordinary faculties, auntie. I was think-ing of extraordinary. But even with ordinary ones we are hampered. Birds of a feather would flock together if they could, of course, but then they can't always ; and suppose, being superior, you find yourself forced to associate with infe-rior cooks of your kind, what then ? "

" Be their queen."

" Which, unless you were a queen of hearts, would really amount to being an object of envy and dislike, and that brings us back to the point from which we started."

" Evadne, you talk like a book ; go to bed !" Mrs. Orton Beg exclaimed, laughing.

" It is you who have made me talk, then," Evadne rejoined promptly, " and I feel inclined to ask now, with all proper respect, what has come to you ? It must be the prince ! "

"Yes, it must be the prince!" Mrs. Orton Beg responded, raising her slender white hand to smother a yawn. "And it must be good-night, too—or rather, good-morning! Just look at the clock. It is nearly three."

CHAPTER VIII.

THE next morning all the guests left Fraylingay, and the family there settled into their accustomed grooves. Evadne and her father walked and rode, conversing together as usual, he enjoying the roll and rumble and fine flavour of his own phrase-making amazingly, and she also impressed by the roll and rumble. But when it was all over, and he had marched off in triumph, she would collect the mutilated remains of the argument and examine them at her leisure, and in nine cases out of ten it proved to be quartz that he had crushed and con- temned, overlooking the gold it contained, but releasing it for her to find and add exultingly to her own collection. In this way, therefore, she continued to obtain her wealth of ore from him, and both were satisfied—he because he was sure that, thanks to him, she was " a thoroughly sensible girl with no non- sense of new-fangled notions about her " ; and she because, being his daughter, she had not altogether escaped the form of mental myopia from which he suffered, and was in the habit of seeing only what she hoped and wished to see in those she loved. Man, the unjust and iniquitous, was to her always the outside, vague, theoretical man of the world, never the dear undoubted papa at home.

Evadne was the eldest of six girls, and their mother had a comfortable as-it-was-in-the-beginning-is-now-and-ever-shall-be feeling about them all ; but she prided herself most upon Evadne as answering in every particular to the conventional idea of what a young lady should be.

"The dear child," she wrote to Lady Adeline, "is *all* and *more* than we dared to hope to have her become. I can assure you she has never caused me a moment's anxiety in her life, except, of course, such anxiety for her health and happi- ness as every mother must feel. I have had her educated with the utmost care, and her father has, I may say, *devoted* himself to the task of influencing her in the right direction in matters of opinion, and has ably seconded all my endeavours in other respects. She speaks French and German *well*, and knows a little Italian ; in fact, I may say that she has a special aptitude for languages. She does not draw, but is a fair musician, and is still having lessons, being most anxious to improve herself; and she sings very sweetly. But, best of all, as I am sure you will agree with me, I notice in her a deeply religious disposition. She is *really* devout, and beautifully reverential in her manner both in church and to us, her parents, and, indeed, to all who are older and wiser than herself. She is very clever too, they tell me ; but of course I am no judge of that. I do know, however, that she is perfectly innocent, and I am indeed thankful to think that at eighteen she knows nothing of the world and its wickedness, and is therefore eminently qualified to make somebody an excellent wife ; and all I am afraid of is that the destined somebody will come for her all too soon, for I cannot bear to think of parting with her. She is not *quite* like other girls in *some* things, I am afraid—mere trifles, however—as, for instance, about her presentation. I know *I* was in quite a flutter of excitement for days before *I* was presented, and was quite bewildered with agitation at the time; but Evadne displayed no emotion whatever. I never knew *anyone* so equable as she is ; in fact, *nothing* seems to ruffle her wonderful calm ; it is almost provoking sometimes ! On the way home she would not have made a remark, I think, if I had not spoken to her. 'Don't you think it was a very pretty sight ?' I said at last. 'Yes,' she answered doubtfully ; and then she added with genuine feeling : ' *Mais il y a des longuers !* Oh, mother, the hours we have spent hanging about draughty corridors, half dressed and shivering with cold ; and the crowding and crushing, and unlovely faces, all looking so miserable and showing the discomfort and fatigue they were enduring so plainly ! I call it positive suffering, and I never want to see another Drawing Room. My soul desires nothing now but decent clothing and hot tea.' And that is all she has ever said about the Drawing Room in my hearing. But wasn't it a very curious view for a girl to take ? Of course the arrangements are detestable, and one does suffer a great deal from cold and fatigue, and for want of refreshments ; but still *I* never thought of those things when *I* was a girl ; did you ? I never thought of anything, in fact, but whether I was looking my best or not. Don't let me make you imagine, however, that Evadne was whining and querulous. She never is, you know ; and I should call her tone sorrowful if it were not so absurd for a girl to be saddened by the sight of other people in distress—well, not quite in distress—that is an exaggeration—but at all events not quite comfortably situated—on what was really one of the greatest occasions of her own life. I am half inclined to fear that she may not be quite so strong as we have always thought her, and that she was depressed by the long fasting and fatigue, which would account for a momentary morbidness.

"But excuse my garrulity. I always have so much to say to *you !* I will spare you any more for the present, however ; only *do* tell me all about yourself and your own lovely children. And how is Mr. Hamilton-Wells ? Remember that you are to come to us, twins and all, on your way home as usual this year. We are anxiously expecting you, and I hope your next letter will fix the day.

"Ever, dear Adeline, your loving friend,
"ELIZABETH FRAYLING.

"P. S.—We return to Fraylingay to-morrow, so please write to me there."

· The following is Lady Adeline's reply to Mrs. Frayling's letter :

"HAMILTON HOUSE, MORNINGQUEST, 30th July.
"MY DEAR ELIZABETH :

" I am afraid you will have been wondering what has become of us, but I know you will acquit me of all blame for the long delay in answering your letter when I tell you that I have only just received it ! We had left Paris before it arrived for (what is always to me) a tiresome tour about the continent, and it has been following us from pillar to post, finally reaching me here at home, where we have been settled a fortnight. I had not forgotten your kind invitation, but I am afraid I must give up all idea of going to you this year. We hurried back because Mr. Hamilton-Wells became homesick suddenly while we were abroad, and I don't think it will be possible to get him to move again for some time. But won't you come to us ? Do, dear, and bring your just-come-out, and, I am sure, most charming, Evadne for our autumn gayeties. If Mr. Frayling would come too we should be delighted, but I know he has a poor opinion of *our* coverts, and I despair of being able to tempt him from his own shooting ; and therefore I ask *you* first and foremost, in the hope that you will be able to come whether he **does or** not.

"I have been thinking much of all you have told me about Evadne. She had already struck me as being a most interesting

child and full of promise, and I do hope that now she is out of
the schoolroom I shall see more of her. I know you will trust
her to me—although I do think that in parts of her education
you have been acting by the half light of a past time, and following a method now out of date. I cannot agree, for instance,
that it is either right or wise to keep a girl in ignorance of the
laws of her own being, and of the state of the community in
which she will have to pass her existence. While she is at an
age to be influenced in the right way she should be fully in-
structed, by those she loves, and not left to obtain her knowledge of the world haphazard from anyone with whom accident
may bring her acquainted—people, perhaps, whose point of
view may not only differ materially from her parents', but be
extremely offensive to them. The first impression in these matters, you know, is all important, and my experience is that what
you call 'beautiful innocence,' and what I consider *dangerous
ignorance*, is not a safe state in which to begin the battle of life.
In the matter of marriage especially an ignorant girl may be
fatally deceived, and indeed I know cases in which the man
who was liked well enough as a companion was found to be
objectionable in an unendurable degree as soon as he became
a husband.

"You will think I am tainted with new notions, and I do
hope I am in so far as these notions are juster and better than
the old ones. For, surely, the elder ages did not discover all
that is wisdom ; and certainly there is still room for 'nobler
modes of life' and 'sweeter manners, purer laws.' If this were
not allowed moral progress must come to a standstill. So I
say, 'instruct ! instruct !' The knowledge must come sooner
or later ; let it come wholesomely. A girl must find out for
herself if she is not taught, and she may, in these plain-spoken
times, obtain a wholly erroneous theory of life and morality
from a newspaper report which she reads without intention in
an idle moment while enjoying her afternoon tea. We are in
a state of transition, we women, and the air is so full of ideas
that it would be strange if an active mind did not catch some
of them ; and I find myself that stray theories swallowed whole
without due consideration are of uncertain application, difficult
in the working, if not impracticable, and apt to disagree.
Theories should be absorbed in detail as dinner is if they are to
become an addition to our strength, and not an indigestible
item of inconvenience, seriously affecting our mental temper.

"But you ask me about my twins. In health they continue

splendid, in spirits they are tremendous, but their tricks are simply terrible. We never know what mischief they will devise next, and Angelica is much the worst of the two. If we had taken them to Fraylingay it would have been in fear and trembling ; but we should have been obliged to take them had we gone ourselves, for they somehow found out that you had asked them, and they insisted upon going, and threatened to burn down Hamilton House in our absence if we did not take them, a feat which we doubt not they would have accomplished had they had a mind to. Indeed, I cannot tell you what these children are ! Imagine their last device to extort concessions from their father. You know how nervous he is ; well, if he will not do all that they require of him they blow him up literally and actually ! They put little trains of gunpowder about in unexpected places, with lucifer matches that go off when they are trodden upon, and you can imagine the consequence ! I told him what it would be when he would spoil them so, but it was no use, and now they rule him instead of him them, so that he has to enter into solemn compacts with them about not infringing what they call their rights ; and, only fancy, he is so fond to foolishness as to be less annoyed by their naughtiness than pleased because, when they promise not to do anything again ' honest Injun,' as they phrase it, they keep their word. Dr. Galbraith calls them in derision ' The Heavenly Twins.'

" But have I told you about Dr. Galbraith ? He is the new master of Fountain Towers, and a charming as well as remarkable man, quite young, being in fact only nine-and-twenty, but already distinguished as a medical man. He became a professional man of necessity, having no expectation at that time of ever inheriting property, but now that he is comparatively speaking a rich man he continues to practice for the love of science, and also from philanthropic motives. He is a fine looking young man physically, with a strong face of most attractive plainness, only redeemed from positive ugliness, in fact, by good gray eyes, white teeth, and an expression which makes you trust him at once. After the first five minutes' conversation with him I have heard people say that they not only could but would positively have enjoyed telling him all the things that ever they did, so great is the confidence he inspires. He, and Sir Daniel Galbraith's adopted son—Sir Daniel is Dr. Galbraith's uncle— were my brother Dawne's great friends at Oxford, where the three of them were known as Shadrach, Meshach, and Abednego, because they passed unscathed through the burning fiery furnace of temptation to which young men of position at the universities are exposed. Dr. Galbraith is somewhat abrupt in manner, and quick of temper, but most good-naturedly long-suffering with my terrible children nevertheless. Of course they impose upon his good nature. And they are always being punished ; but that they do not mind. In fact, I heard Angelica say once : 'It is all in the day's work,' when she had a long imposition to do for something outrageous ; and Diavolo called to her over the stairs only yesterday, 'Wait for me a minute in the hall till I've been thrashed for letting the horses and dogs loose, and then we'll go and snare pheasants in the far plantation !' They explained to me once that being found out and punished added the same zest to their pleasures that cayenne pepper does to their diet ; a little too much of it stings, but just the right quantity relieves the insipidity and adds to the interest ; and then there is the element of uncertainty, which has a charm of its own : they never know whether they will 'catch it hot' or not ! When they *are* found out they always confess everything with a frankness which is quite provoking, because they so evidently enjoy the recital of their own misdeeds ; and they defend themselves by quoting various anecdotes of the naughty doings of children which have been written for our amusement. And it is in vain that I explain to them that parents who are hurt and made anxious by their children's disobedience cannot see anything to laugh at in their pranks—at least not for a very long time afterward. They pondered this for some time, and then arrived at the conclusion that when they were grown up and no longer a nuisance to me, I should be a 'very jolly old lady,' because I should have such a lot of funny stories all my own to tell people.

"But I shall weary you with this inexhaustible subject. You must forgive me if I do, for I am terribly anxious about my young Turks. If they are equal to such enormities in the green leaf, I am always asking myself, what will they do in the dry ? I own that my sense of humour is tickled sometimes, but never enough to make me forget the sense of danger, present and to come, which all this keeps forever alive. Come and comfort me, and tell me how you have made your own children so charming.

"Ever lovingly yours,
"ADELINE HAMILTON-WELLS."

Mrs. Frayling wrote a full account of Evadne's presentation at court to her sister, Mrs. Orton Beg—who was wandering about Norway by herself at the time—and concluded her description of the dear child's gown, very charming appearance, and dignified self-possession with some remarks about her character to the same effect as those which she had addressed to Lady Adeline. It was natural, perhaps, that the last conversation Mrs. Orton Beg had had with Evadne at Fraylingay, which was in fact the first articulate outcome of Evadne's self-training, coming as it did at the end of a day of pleasurable interest and excitement, should have made no immediate impression upon her tired faculties; but she recollected it now and smiled as she read her sister's letter. "If that is all you know of your daughter, my dear Elizabeth," was her mental comment, "I fancy there will be surprises at Fraylingay!" But in reply she merely observed that she was glad Evadne was so satisfactory. She was too wise a woman to waste words on her sister Elizabeth, who, in consequence of having had them in abundance to squander all her life long, had lost all sense of their value, and would have failed to appreciate the force which they collect in the careful keeping of such silent folk as Mrs Orton Beg.

Mrs. Frayling was not able to accept Lady Adeline's invitatain that year.

CHAPTER IX.

THIS was the period when Evadne looked out of narrow eyes at an untried world inquiringly, and was warmed to the heart by what she saw of it. Theoretically, people are cruel and unjust, but practically, to an attractive young lady of good social position and just out, their manners are most agreeable; and when Evadne returned to Fraylingay after her first season in town, she thought less and sang more.

> " A little bird in the air,
> Is singing of Thyri the fair,
> 　The sister of Svend the Dane ;
> And the song of the garrulous bird
> In the streets of the town is heard,
> 　And repeated again and again,"

she carolled about the house, while the dust collected upon her books. She took up one old favourite after another when she first returned, but her attention wandered from her best beloved, and all that were solid came somehow to be set aside and replaced, the nourishing fact by inflated fiction, reason and logic by rhyme and rhythm, and sense by sentimentality, so far had her strong, simple, earnest mind deteriorated in the unwholesome atmosphere of London drawing rooms. It was only a phase, of course, and she could have been set right at once had there been anybody there to prescribe a strengthening tonic ; but failing that, she tried sweet stimulants that soothed and excited, but did not nourish : tales that caused chords of pleasurable emotion to vibrate while they fanned the higher faculties into inaction—vampire things inducing that fatal repose which enables them to drain the soul of its life blood and compass its destruction. But Evadne escaped without permanent injury, for, fortunately for herself, among much that was far too sweet to be wholesome she discovered Oliver Wendell Holmes' " The Breakfast Table Series," " Elsie Venner," and " The Guardian Angel" and was insensibly fixed in her rightful place and sustained by them.

The sun streaming into her room one morning at this time awoke her early and tempted her up and out. There was a sandy space beyond the grounds, a long level of her father's land extending to the eastern cliffs, and considered barren by him, but rich with a certain beauty of its own, the beauty of open spaces which rest and relieve the mind ; and of immensity in the shining sea-line beyond the cliffs, and the arching vault of the sky overhead dipping down to encircle the earth ; and of colour for all moods, from the vividest green of grass and yellow of gorse to the amethyst ling, and the browns with which the waning year tipped every bush and bramble—things which, when properly appreciated, make life worth living. It was in this direction that Evadne walked, taking it without design but drawn insensibly as by a magnet to the sea.

She had thought herself early up, but the whole wild world of the heath was before her, and she began to feel belated as she went. There was a suspicion of frost in the air which made it deliciously fresh and exhilarating. The early morning mists still hung about, but the sun was brightly busy dispelling them. The rabbits were tripping hither and thither, too intent on their own business to pay much heed to Evadne. A bird sprang up from her feet, and soared out of sight, and she paused a moment with upturned face, dilated eyes, and lips apart, to watch him. But a glimpse of the gorse recalled her, and she picked some yellow blooms with delicate finger tips, and carried them in her bare hand savouring the scent, and at the same time looking and listening with an involuntary straining to enjoy the perception of each separate delicate delight at once, till presently the enthusiasm of nature called forth some further faculty, and she found herself sensible of every tint and tone, sight and sound, distinguishing, deciphering, but yet perceiving all together as the trained ear of a musician does the parts played by every instrument in an orchestra, and takes cognizance of the whole effect as well.

At the end of the waste there was a little church overlooking the sea. She saw that the door was open as she approached it, and she paused to look in. The early weekday service was in progress. A few quiet figures sat apart in the pews. The light was subdued. Something was being read aloud by a voice of caressing quality and musical. She did not attend to the words, but the tone satisfied. It seemed to her that the peace of God invited, and she slipped into the nearest pew. She found a Bible on the seat beside her, and opening it haphazard her eyes fell upon the words :

" They that go down to the sea in ships, that do business in great waters ; these see the works of the Lord, and his wonders in the deep."

The lap of the little waves on the beach below was distinctly audible, the bird calls, and their twitterings, intermittent, incessant, persistent, came close and departed ; and the fragrance of the blossoms, crushed in her hand, rose to remind her they were there.

" They that go down to the sea in ships."

It was a passage to be felt at the moment with the sea itself so near, and as she paused to ponder it her mind attuned itself involuntarily to the habit of holy thought associated with the place, while the scents and sounds of nature streamed in upon her, forming now a soft undercurrent, now a delicious accompaniment which filled the interval between what she knew of this world and all that she dreamt of the next. The cycle of sensation was complete, and in a moment her whole being blossomed into gladness. Her intellectual activity was suspended—her senses awoke. It was the morning of life with her, and she sank upon her knees, and lifted up her heart to express the joy of it in one ecstatic note : "O blessed Lord!"

Lord of the happy earth ! Lord of the sun and our senses,

He who comes to us first in Love's name, and bids us rejoice and be glad ; not he who would have us mourn.

CHAPTER X.

AFTER the experiences of that early morning's walk Evadne did not go to bed so late ; she got up early and went to church. The agreeable working of her intellectual faculties during the early part of her absorbing self-education had kept her senses in abeyance ; but when the discipline of all regular routine was relaxed, they were set free to get the upper hand if they would, and now they had begun to have their way—a delicate, dreamy way, of a surety, but it was a sensuous way nevertheless, and not at all a spiritual way, as her mother maintained it to be, because of the church-going. Sometimes sense, sometimes intellect, is the first to awake in us—supposing we are dowered with an intellect ; but pain, which is the perfecting of our nature, must precede the soul's awakening, and for Evadne at that age, with her limited personal knowledge of life and scant experience of every form of human emotion which involves suffering, such an awakening was impossible. The first feeling of a girl as happily situated, healthy-minded, and physically strong as she was is bound to be pleasurable ; and had she been a young man at this time she would not improbably have sought to heighten and vary her sensations by adding greater quantities of alcohol to her daily diet ; she would have grown coarse of skin by eating more than she could assimilate ; she would have smelt strongly enough of tobacco, as a rule, to try the endurance of a barmaid ; she would have been anxious about the fit of coats, fastidious as to the choice of ties, quite impossible in the matter of trousers, and prone to regard her own image in the glass caressingly. She would have considered that every petticoat held a divinity, or every woman had her price according to the direction in which nature had limited her powers of perception with a view to the final making of her into a sentimental or a vicious fool. When she should have been hard at work she would have stayed in bed in the morning flattering her imagination with visions of the peerless beauties who would all adore her, and the proud place she would conquer in the world ; and she would have gone girl-stalking in earnest—*probably*—had she been a young man. But being as she was, she got up early

and went to church. It was the one way she had of expressing the silent joy of her being, and of intensifying it. She
practised an extreme ritual at this time, and found in it the
most complete form of expression for her mood possible.
And in those early morning walks when she brushed the dew-
bespangled cobwebs from the gorse, and startled the twitter-
ing birds from their morning meal—in the caressing of
healthy odours, the uplifting of all sweet natural sounds, the
soothing of the great sea-voice, the sense of infinity in the
level landscape, of beauty in form and colour, of rest and peace
in the grateful shadow of the little church on the cliff, but,
above all, in the release from mental tension, and the ease of
feeling after the strain of thought, she found the highest form
of pleasure she had tasted, the most rarefied, the most intense.
The St. Valentine's Day of her development was approaching,
and her heart had begun already to practise the notes of the
song-significant into which she would burst when it came.

It is a nice question that, as to where the sensuous ends,
and the spiritual begins. The dovetail is so exact just at the
junction that it is impossible to determine, and it is there that
" spirit and flesh grow one with delight " on occasion ; but the
test of the spiritual lies in its continuity. Pleasures of the
senses pall upon repetition, but pleasures of the soul continue
and increase. A delicate dish soon wearies the palate, but
the power to appreciate a poem or a picture grows greater
the more we study them—illustrations as trite, by the way,
as those of the average divine in his weekly sermon, but calculated to comfort to the same extent in that they possess the
charm of familiarity which satisfies self-love by proving that
we know quite as much of some subjects as those who profess to teach them. Still, a happy condition of the senses
may easily be mistaken for a great outpouring of spiritual
enthusiasm, and many an inspiring soul unconsciously stimu-
lates them in ways less pardonable perhaps than the legitimate
joy of a good dinner to a hungry man, or the more subtle
pleasure which a refined woman experiences while sharing
the communion of well-dressed saints on a cushioned seat,
listening to exquisite music in a fashionable church. Sensations of gladness send some people to church whom grief of
any kind would drive from thence effectually. It is a matter
of temperament. There are those who are by nature grateful for every good gift, who even bow their heads and suffer
meekly if they perceive that they will have their reward, but

are ready to rebel with rage against any form of ineffectual pain. This was likely to be Evadne's case. Yet her mother had been right about her having a deeply religious disposition.

The vicar in charge of the church on the cliff—he of the musical voice, Mr. Borthwick by name—became aware at once of Evadne's regular attendance. He was a young man, very earnest, very devout, worn thin with hard work, but happy in that he had it to do, and with that serene expression of countenance which comes of the habit of conscientious endeavour. As a matter of course, with such men at the present time, he sought solace in ritual. His whole nature thrilled to the roll of the organ, to the notes of a grateful anthem, to the sight and scent of his beautiful flowers on the altar, and to the harmony of colour and conventional design on the walls of his little church. He spent his life and his substance upon it, doing what he could to beautify it himself, in the name of the Lord, and finding in the act of worship a refinement of pleasure difficult of attainment, but possible and precious. And while all that sufficed for him, he honestly entertained the idea of celibacy as a condition necessary for the perfect purification of his own soul, and desirable as giving him a place apart which would help to maintain and strengthen his influence with his people. A layman may remain a bachelor without attracting attention, but a priest who abjures matrimony insists that he makes a sacrifice, and deserves credit for the same. He says that the laws of nature are the laws of God, yet arranges his own life in direct opposition to the greatest of them. He can give no unanswerable reason for maintaining that the legitimate exercise of one set of natural functions is less holy than the exercise of the others, but that is what he believes, and curiously inconsistent as the conclusion is, the Rev. Henry Borthwick had adopted this view emphatically at the outset of his clerical career, and had announced his intention of adhering to it for the rest of his life. But, just as the snow under the cool and quiet stars at dusk might feel full force in itself to vow to the rising moon that it will not melt, and find nevertheless of necessity when the sun appears that it cannot keep its vow, so did the idea of celibacy pass from the mind of the Rev. Henry Borthwick when Evadne began to attend his morning services. Insensibly his first view of the subject vanished altogether, and was immediately replaced, first by an uplifting vision of the advantages of having a wife's help in the parish, then by a glimpse of the tender pleasure of a wife's

presence in the house ; and—extraordinary as it may seem, this
final thought occurred to him while the Psalms were being sung
in church one morning, so uncertain is the direction of man's
mind at any time—he even had a vision of the joy of a wife's
kiss when the sweet red lips that gave it were curved like those
of the girl before him.   He felt a great outpouring of spiritual
grace during that service ; his powers of devotion were intensified.   But the moment it was over he hurried to the vestry,
tore off his surplice and threw it on the floor, met Evadne as
she left the church, and lingered long on the cliffs with her in
earnest conversation

She was late for breakfast that morning, and her mother
asked her what had detained her.

" Mr. Borthwick was talking to me about the sacraments of
the Church, mother," she answered, her calm true eyes meeting her mother's without confusion ; " and about the necessity
for, and the advantage of, frequent communions."

" And what do you think about it, dear ? "

" I think I should like it."

Her mother said no more.   Young Borthwick was a cadet
of good family with expectations in the way of money, influence enough to procure him a deanery at least, and with a
reputation for ability which, with his other advantages,
gave him as fair a prospect as anybody she knew of a bish-
opric eventually—just the thing for Evadne, she reflected, so
she did not interfere.

This was really a happy time for Evadne.   The young priest
frequently met her after the early service, and she liked his
devotion.   She liked his clean-featured, close-shaven face too,
and his musical voice.   He was her perfection of a priest, and
when he did not meet her she missed him.   She did not care
for him so much when he called at the house, however.   She
associated him somehow with her morning moods, with religious discourses, and the Church service ; but when he ventured
beyond these limits, they lost touch, and so she held him down
to them rigorously   He tried to resist.   He even conceived
a distaste for ecclesiastical subjects, and endeavoured to float
her attention from these on little boats of fancy phrases made
out of the first freshness of new days, the beauty of the sun
on the sea, the jade-green of grass on the cliffs, the pleasure
he took in the songs of birds, and other more mundane matters ; but he lost her sympathetic interest when he did so,
receiving her polite attention instead, which was cold in com-

parison, and therefore did not satisfy him, so he determined to try and come to a perfect understanding, and during one of their morning walks, he startled her by making her a solemn and abrupt offer of marriage.

She considered the proposition in silence for some time. Then she looked at him as if she had never seen him before. Then she said, not knowing she was cruel, and only desiring to be frank : " I have never thought of you as a man, you know—only as a priest ; and in that character I think you perfect. I respect and reverence you. I even love you, but——"

" But what ? " he asked eagerly, his delicate face flushing, his whole being held in suspense.

" But I could not marry a priest. It would seem to be a sort of sacrilege."

She was very pale when she went in that morning, and her mother noticed it, and questioned her.

" Mr. Borthwick asked me to marry him, mother," she answered straight to the point, as was her wont. " He surprised me."

" I am not surprised, dear," her mother rejoined, smiling.

" Did you suppose he would, mother ?'

" Yes. I was sure of it."

" Oh, I wish you had warned me ! "

" Then you haven't accepted him, Evadne ?"

" No. I have always understood that it is not right for a priest to marry, and the idea of marrying one repels me. He has lowered himself in my estimation by thinking of such a thing. I could not think of him as I do of other men. I cannot dissociate him from his office. I expect him somehow to be always about his reading-desk and pulpit."

Mrs. Frayling's face had fallen, but she only said : " I wish you could have felt otherwise, dear."

Evadne went up to her room, and stood leaning against the frame of the open window, looking out over the level landscape. The poor priest had shown deep feeling, and it was the first she had seen of such suffering. It pained her terribly.

She got up early next morning, and went out as usual ; but the scent of the gorse was obtrusive, the bird-voices had lost their charm, the far-off sound of the sea had a new and melancholy note in it, and the little church on the cliff looked lonely against the sky. She could not go there again to be reminded of what she would fain have forgotten. No ; that phase was over. The revulsion of feeling was complete, and to banish all recollection of it she tried with a will to revive the suspended animation of her interest in her books.

CHAPTER XI.

"ALL excitements run to love in women of a certain—let us not say age, but youth," says the professor. " An electrical current passing through a coil of wire makes a magnet of a bar of iron lying within it, but not touching it. So a woman is turned into a love-magnet by a tingling current of life running round her. I should like to see one of them balanced on a pivot properly adjusted, and watch if she did not turn so as to point north and south, as she would if the love-currents are like those of the earth, our mother."

This passage indicates exactly the point at which Evadne had now arrived, and where she was pausing.

The attempt to return to her books had been far from successful. Her eye would traverse page after page without transferring a single record to her brain, and she would sit with one open in her lap by the hour together, not absorbed in thought, but lost in feeling. She was both glad and sad at the same time, glad in her youth and strength, and sad in the sense of something wanting ; what was it ?

> If she had—Well ! She longed, and knew not wherefore.
> Had the world nothing she might live to care for ?
> No second self to say her evening prayer for ?

The poor little bird loved the old nest, but she had unconsciously outgrown it, and was perplexed to find no ease or comfort in it any more.

She certainly entertained the idea of marriage at this time. She had acquired a sort of notion from her friends that it was good to marry, and her own inclinations seconded the suggestion. She meant to marry when she should find the right man, but the difficulty of choice disturbed her. She had still much of the spirit which made her at twelve see nothing but nonsense in the "Turn, Gentle Hermit of the Dale" drivel, and she was quite prepared to decide with her mind. She never took her heart into consideration, or the possibility of being overcome by a feeling which is stronger than reason.

She made her future husband a subject of prayer, however. She prayed that he might be an upright man, that he might come to her soon; she even asked for some sign by which she should know him. This was during the morning service in church one Sunday—not the little one on the cliff, which was only a chapel-of-ease; but the parish church to which the whole family went regularly. Her thoughts had wandered away, from the lesson that was being read, to this subject of private devotion, and as she formulated the desire for a sign, for some certainty by which she might know the man whom the dear Lord intended to be her husband, she looked up, and from the other side of the aisle she met a glance that abashed her. She looked away, but her eyes were drawn back inevitably, and this time the glance of those other eyes enlightened her. Her heart bounded—her face flushed. This was the sign, she was sure of it. She had felt nothing like it before, and although she never raised her eyes again, she thrilled through the rest of the service to the consciousness that there, not many yards away, her future husband sat and sighed for her.

After the service, the subject of her thoughts claimed her father's acquaintance, and was introduced by him to her as Major Colquhoun. He looked about thirty-eight, and was a big blond man, with a heavy moustache, and a delicate skin that flushed easily. His hair was thin on the forehead · in a few more years he would be bald there.

Mr. Frayling asked him to lunch, and Evadne sat beside him. She scarcely spoke a word the whole time, or looked at him; but she knew that he looked at her; and she glowed and was glad. The little church on the cliff seemed a long way off, and out in the cold now. She was sorry for Mr. Borthwick. She had full faith in the sign. Was not the fact that Major Colquhoun, whom she had never even heard of in her life before, was sitting beside her at that moment, confirmation strong, if any were wanting? But she asked no more.

After lunch her father carried his guest off to smoke, and she went up to her own room to be alone, and sat in the sun by the open window, with her head resting on the back of her chair, looking up at the sky; and sighed, and smiled, and clasped her hands to her breast, and revelled in sensations.

Major Colquhoun had been staying with a neighbouring county gentleman, but she found when she met him again at afternoon tea that her father had persuaded him to come to Fraylingay for some shooting. He was to go back that night, and return to them the following Tuesday. Evadne heard of the arrangement in silence, and unsurprised. Had he gone and *not* returned, she would have wondered ; but this sudden admission of a stranger to the family circle, although unusual, was not unprecedented at Fraylingay, where, after it was certain that you knew the right people, pleasant manners were the only passport necessary to secure a footing of easy intimacy ; and, besides, it was inevitable—that the sign might be fulfilled. So Evadne folded her hands as it were, and calmly awaited the course of events, not doubting for a moment that she knew exactly what that course was to be.

She did not actually *see* much of Major Colquhoun in the days that followed, although, when he was not out shooting, he was always beside her ; but such timid glances as she stole satisfied her. And she heard her mother say what a fine-looking man he was, and her father emphatically pronounced him to be " a very good fellow." He was Irish by his mother's side, Scotch by his father's, but much more Irish than Scotch by predilection, and it was his mother tongue he spoke, exaggerating the accent slightly to heighten the effect of a tender speech or a good story. With the latter he kept Mr. Frayling well entertained, and Evadne he plied with the former on every possible occasion.

His visit was to have been for a few days only, but it extended itself to some weeks, at the end of which time Evadne had accepted him, the engagement had been announced in the proper papers, Mrs. Frayling was radiant, congratulations poured in, and everybody concerned was in a state of pleasurable excitement from morning till night.

Mrs. Frayling was an affectionate woman, and it was touching to see her writing fluent letters of announcement to her many friends, the smiles on her lips broken by ominous quiverings now and then, and a handkerchief held crumpled in her left hand, and growing gradually damper, as she proceeded, with the happy tears that threatened her neat epistle with blots and blisters.

" It has been the prettiest idyl to us onlookers," she wrote to Lady Adeline. " Love at first sight with both of them, and their first glimpse of each other was in church, which we all take to be the happiest omen that God's blessing is upon them, and will sanctify their union. Evadne says little, but there is such a delicate tinge of colour in her cheeks always, and such a happy light in her eyes, that I cannot help looking at her. George is senior major, and will command the regiment in a very short time, and his means are quite ample enough for them to begin upon. There is twenty years difference in their ages, which sounds too much theoretically, but practically, when you see them together, you never think of it. He is very handsome, every inch a soldier, and an Irishman, with all an Irishman's brightness and wit, and altogether the most taking manners. I tell Evadne I am quite in love with him myself! He is a thoroughly good Churchman too, which is a great blessing—never misses a service, and it is a beautiful sight to see him kneeling beside Evadne as rapt and intent as she is. He was rather wild as a young man, I am sorry to say, but he has been quite frank about all that to Mr. Frayling, and there is nothing now that we can object to. In fact, we think he is exactly suited to Evadne, and we are thoroughly satisfied in every way. You can imagine that I find it hard to part with her, but I always knew that it would be the case as soon as she came out, and so was prepared in a way; still, that will not lessen the wrench when it comes. But of course I must not consider my own feelings when the dear child's happiness is in question, and I think that long engagements are a mistake; and as there is really no reason why they should wait, they are to be married at the end of next month, which gives us only six weeks to get the trousseau. We are going to town at once to see about it, and I think that probably the ceremony will take place there too. It would be such a business at Fraylingay, with all the tenants and everything, and altogether one has to consider expense. But do write at once and promise me that we may expect you, and Mr. Hamilton-Wells, and the *dear* twins, wherever it is. In fact, I believe Evadne is writing to Theodore at this moment to ask him to be her page, and Angelica will, of course, be a bridesmaid."

During the first days of her absorbing passion Evadne's devotion to God was intensified. "Sing to the Lord a new song" was forever upon her lips.

When the question of her engagement came to be mooted she had had a long talk with her father, following upon a still longer talk which he had with Major Colquhoun.

"And you are satisfied with my choice, father?" she said. "You consider George in every respect a suitable husband for me?"

" In all respects, my dear," he answered heartily.   " He is
a very fine, manly fellow."

" There was nothing in his past life to which I should
object ?" she ventured timidly.

" Oh, nothing, nothing," he assured her.   " He has been
perfectly straightforward about himself, and I am satisfied
that he will make you an excellent husband."

It was all the assurance she required, and after she had
received it she gave herself up to her happiness without a
doubt, and unreservedly.

The time flew.   Major Colquhoun's leave expired, and he
was obliged to return to his regiment at Shorncliffe ; but they
wrote to each other every day, and this constant communion
was a new source of delight to Evadne.   Just before they
left Fraylingay she went to see her aunt, Mrs. Orton Beg.
The latter had sprained her ankle severely, and would therefore not be able to go to Evadne's wedding.   She lived in
Morningquest, and had a little house in the Close there.
Morningquest was only twenty miles from Fraylingay, but
the trains were tiresomely slow, and did not run in connection,
so that it took as long to get there as it did to go to London,
and people might live their lives in Fraylingay, and know
nothing of Morningquest.

Mrs. Orton Beg's husband was buried in the old cathedral
city, and she lived there to be near his grave.   She could
never tear herself away from it for long together.   The light
of her life had gone out when he died, and was buried with
him ; but the light of her love, fed upon the blessed hope of
immortality, burnt brighter every day.

Her existence in the quiet Close was a very peaceful, dreamy
one, soothed by the chime, uplifted by the sight of the beautiful old cathedral, and regulated by its service.

Evadne found her lying on a couch beside an open window
in the drawing room, which was a long, low room, running the
full width of the house, and with a window at either end, one
looking up the Close to the north, the other to the south, into
a high-walled, old-fashioned flower garden ; and this was the
one near which Mrs. Orton Beg was lying.

" I think I should turn to the cathedral, Aunt Olive,"
Evadne said.

" I do," her aunt answered ; " but not at this time of day.
I travel round with the sun."

" It would fill my mind with beautiful thoughts to live

here," Evadne said, looking up at the lonely spire reverently.

"I have no doubt that your mind is always full of beautiful thoughts," her aunt rejoined, smiling. "But I know what you mean. There are thoughts carved on those dumb gray stones which can only come to us from such a source of inspiration. The sincerity of the old workmen, their love and their reverence, were wrought into all they produced, and if only we hold our own minds in the right attitude, we receive something of their grace. Do you remember that passage of Longfellow's?—

> "Ah! from what agonies of heart and brain,
>   What exultations trampling on despair,
> What tenderness, what tears, what hate of wrong,
>   What passionate outcry of a soul in pain,
> Uprose this poem of the earth and air,
>   This mediæval miracle, . . . !

Sitting here alone, sometimes I seem to feel it all—all the capacity for loving sacrifice and all the energy of human passion which wrought itself into that beautiful offering of its devotion, and made it acceptable. But, tell me, Evadne—are you very happy?"

"I am *too* happy, I think, auntie. But I can't talk about it. I must keep the consciousness of it close in my own heart, and guard it jealously, lest I dissipate any atom of it by attempting to describe it."

"Do you think, then, that love is such a delicate thing that the slightest exposure will destroy it?"

"I don't know what I think. But the feeling is so fresh now, auntie, I am afraid to run the risk of uttering a word, or hearing one, that might tarnish it."

She strolled out into the garden during the afternoon, and sat on a high-backed chair in the shade of the old brick wall, with eyes half closed and a smile hovering about her lips. The wall was curtained with canaryensis, virginia creeper rich in autumn tints, ivy, and giant nasturtiums. Great sunflowers grew up against it, and a row of single dahlias of every possible hue crowded up close to the sunflowers. They made a background to the girl's slender figure.

She sat there a long time, happily absorbed, and Mrs. Orton Beg's memory, as she watched her, slipped back inevitably to her own love days, till tears came of the inward

supplication that Evadne's future might never know the terrible blight which had fallen upon her own life.

Evadne walked through the village on her way back to
Fraylingay. A young woman with her baby in her arms was
standing at the door of her cottage looking out as she passed,
and she stopped to, speak to her. The child held out his little
arms, and kicked and crowed to be taken, and when his
mother had intrusted him to Evadne, he clasped her tight
round the neck, and nibbled her cheek with his warm, moist
mouth, sending a delicious thrill through every fibre of her
body, a first foretaste of maternity.

She hurried on to hide her emotion.

But all the way home there was a singing at her heart, a
certainty of joys undreamt of hitherto, the tenderest, sweetest,
most womanly joys—her own house, her own husband, her
own children—perhaps ; it all lay in that, her *own !*

CHAPTER XII.

THE next few weeks were decked with the richness of
autumn tints, the glory of autumn skies ; but Evadne was
unaware of either. She had no consciousness of distinct days
and nights, and indeed they were pretty well mingled after she
went to town, for she often danced till daylight and slept till
dusk. And it was all a golden haze, this time, with impressions of endless shops ; of silks, satins, and lovely laces ; of
costly trinkets ; of little notes flying between London and
Shorncliffe ; and of everybody so happy that it was impossible
to help sitting down and having a good cry occasionally.

The whirl in which she lived during this period was entered
upon without thought, her own inclinations agreeing at the
time to every usage sanctioned by custom ; but in after years
she said that those days of dissipation and excitement appeared
to her to be a curious preparation for the solemn duties she
was about to enter upon.

Evadne felt the time fly, and she felt also that the days were
never ending. It was six weeks at first ; and then all at once,
as it seemed, there was only one week ; and then it was "to-
morrow ! " All that last day there was a terrible racket in
the house, and she was hardly left alone a single moment, and
was therefore thankful when finally, late at night, she managed
to escape to her own room—not that she was left long in peace

even then, however, for two of her bridesmaids were staying in the house, and they and her sisters stormed her chamber in their dressing-gowns, and had a pillow fight to begin with, and then sat down and cackled for an hour, speculating as to whether they should like to be married or not. They decided that they should, because of the presents, you know, and the position, and the delight of having such a lot of new gowns, and being your own mistress, with your own house and servants; they thought of everything, in fact, but the inevitable husband, the possession of whom certainly constituted no part of the advantages which they expected to secure by marriage. Evadne sat silent, and smiled at their chatter with the air of one who has solved the problem and knows. But she was glad to be rid of them, and when they had gone, she got her sacred "Commonplace Book," and glanced through it dreamily. Then, rousing herself a little, she went to her writing table, and sat down and wrote: "This is the close of the happiest girlhood that girl ever had. I cannot recall a single thing that I would have had otherwise."

When she had locked the book away, with some other possessions in a box that was to be sent to await her arrival at her new home, she took up a photograph of her lover and gazed at it rapturously for a moment, then pressed it to her lips and breast, and placed it where her eyes might light on it as soon as she awoke.

She was aroused by a kiss on her lips and a warm tear on her cheek next morning. "Wake, darling," her mother said. "This is your wedding day."

"Oh, mother," she cried, flinging her arms round her neck; "how good of you to come yourself! I *am* so happy!"

Mr. Hamilton-Wells, Lady Adeline, and the Heavenly Twins had been at the Fraylings' since breakfast, and nothing had happened.

Lady Adeline, having seen the children safely and beautifully dressed for the ceremony, Angelica as a bridesmaid, Diavolo as page, left them sitting, with a picture-book between them, like model twins.

"Really," she said to Mr. Hamilton-Wells, "I think the occasion is too interesting for them to have anything else in their heads."

But the moment she left them alone those same heads went up, and set themselves in a listening attitude.

"*Now*, Diavolo : *quick!*" said Angelica, as soon as the sound of her mother's departing footsteps had died away.

Diavolo dashed the picture-book to the opposite side of the room, sprang up, and followed Angelica swiftly but stealthily to the very top of the house.

When the wedding party assembled in the drawing room the twins were nowhere to be found. Mr. Hamilton-Wells went peering through his eyeglass into every corner, removed the glass and looked without it, then dusted it, and looked once more to make sure, while Lady Adeline grew rigid with nervous anxiety.

The search had to be abandoned, however ; but when the party went down to the carriages, it was discovered, to everybody's great relief, that the children had already modestly taken their seats in one of them with their backs to the horses. Each was carefully covered with an elegant wrap, and sitting bolt upright, the picture of primness. The wraps were superfluous, and Mr. Hamilton-Wells was about to remonstrate, but Lady Adeline exclaimed : " For Heaven's sake, *don't* interfere ! It is such a *trifle*. If you irritate them, goodness knows *what* will happen."

But, manlike, he could not let things be.

" Where have you been, you naughty children ? ' he demanded in his precisest way. " You have really given a great deal of trouble."

"Well, papa," Angelica retorted hotly, at the top of her voice through the carriage window for the edification of the crowd, " you said we were to be good children, and not get into everybody's way, and here we have been sitting an hour as good as possible, and quite out of the way, and you aren't satisfied ! It's quite unreasonable ; isn't it, Diavolo? Papa can't get on, I believe, *without* finding fault with us. It's just a bad habit he's got, and when we give him no excuse he invents one."

Mr. Hamilton-Wells beat a hasty retreat, and the party arrived at the church without mishap, but when the procession was formed there was a momentary delay. They were waiting for the bride's page, who descended with the youngest bridesmaid from the last carriage, and the two came into the church demurely, hand in hand. " What darlings ! " " Aren't they pretty ? " " What a sweet little boy, with his lovely dark curls ! " was heard from all sides ; but there was also an audible titter. Lady Adeline turned pale, Mrs. Frayling's fan dropped.

Evadne lost her countenance. The twins had changed clothes.

There was nothing to be done then, however; so Angelica obtained the coveted pleasure of acting as page to Evadne, and Diavolo escaped the trouble of having to hold up her train, and managed besides to have some fun with a small but amorous boy who was to have been Angelica's pair, and who, knowing nothing of the fraud which had been perpetrated, insisted on kissing the fair Diavolo, to that young gentleman's lasting delight.

It was a misty morning, with only fitful glimpses of sunshine.

Mrs. Frayling was not a bit superstitious (nobody is), but she had been watching the omens (most people do), and she would have been better satisfied had the day been bright; but still she felt no shadow of a foreboding until the twins appeared. Then, however, there arose in her heart a horrified exclamation : " It is unnatural ! It will bring bad luck."

There was no fun for the Heavenly Twins apart, so they decided to sit together at the wedding breakfast, and nobody dared to separate them, lest worse should come of it.

Diavolo bet he would drink as much champagne as Major Colquhoun, and having secured a seat opposite to an uncorked bottle, he proceeded conscientiously to do his best to win the wager. Toward the end of breakfast, however, he lost count, and then he lost his head, and showed signs of falling off his chair.

" You must go to sleep under the table now," said Angelica. " It's the proper thing to do when you're drunk. *I'm* going to. But I'm not far enough gone yet. My legs are queer, but my head is steady. Get under, will you ? I'll be down directly." And she cautiously but rapidly dislodged him, and landed him at her feet, everybody's attention being occupied at the moment by the gentleman who was gracefully returning thanks for the ladies. When the speech was over Lady Adeline remembered the twins with a start, and at once missed Diavolo.

" Where is he ? " she asked anxiously.

" He is just doing something for me, mamma," Angelica answered.

He was acting at that moment as her footstool under the table. She did not join him there as she had promised, however, because when the wine made her begin to feel giddy she

took no more.   She said afterward she saw no fun in feeling
nasty, and she thought a person must be a fool to think there
was, and Diavolo, who was suffering badly at the moment
from headache and nausea, the effect of his potations, agreed.
That was on the evening of the eventful day at their own
town house, their father and mother having hurried them off
there as soon after Diavolo was discovered in a helpless condition as they could conveniently make their escape.   The
twins had been promptly put to bed in their respective rooms,
and told to stay there, but, of course, it did not in the least
follow that they would obey, and locking them up had not
been found to answer.   Angelica did remain quiet, however,
an hour or so, resting after all the excitement of the morning ;
but she got up eventually, put on her dressing gown, and
went to Diavolo ; and it was then they discussed the drink
question.   Discussion, however, was never enough for the
twins ; they always wanted to *do* something : so now they went
down to the library together, erected an altar of valuable
books, and arrayed themselves in white sheets, which they tore
from the parental couch for the purpose, considerably disar-
ranging the same ; and the sheets they covered with crimson
curtains, taken down at imminent risk of injuring themselves
from one of the dining room windows, with the help of a
ladder, abstracted from the area by way of the front door,
although they *were* in their dressing-gowns, the time chosen
for this revel being when their parents were in the drawing
room after dinner, and all the servants were having their
supper and safe out of the way.   The ladder was used to go
down to the coal cellar, and never, of course, replaced, the consequence being that the next person who went for coal fell in
in the dark, and broke her leg, an accident which cost Mr.
Hamilton-Wells from first to last a considerable sum, he being
a generous man, and unwilling to let anyone suffer in pocket
in his service ; he thought the risks to life and limb were
sufficient without that.

Having completed these solemn preparations the twins
swore a ghastly oath on the altar never to touch drink again,
and might they be found out in everything they did on earth
if they broke it, and never see heaven when they died !

The wedding breakfast went off merrily enough, and when
the bride and bridesmaids left the table, and the dining room
door was safely shut, there was much girlish laughter in the
hall, and an undignified scamper up the stairs, also a tussle as

to who should take the first pin from the bride's veil and be married next, and much amusement when Mrs. Frayling's elderly maid unconsciously appropriated it herself in the way of business.

Evadne hugged her, exclaiming : " You dear old Jenny ! You *shall* be married next, and I'll be your bridesmaid ! "

" Oh, no you won't ! " cried one of the girls. " You'll never be a bridesmaid again."

Then suddenly there was silence. " Never again " is chilling in effect ; it is such a very long time.

As Evadne was leaving the room in her travelling dress she noticed some letters lying on her dressing table, which she had forgotten, and turned back to get them. They had come by the morning's post, but she had not opened any of them, and now she began to put them into her pocket one by one to read at her leisure, glancing at the superscriptions as she did so. One was from Aunt Olive : dear Aunt Olive, how kind of her ! Two were letters of congratulation from friends of the family. A fourth was from the old housekeeper at Fraylingay ; she kissed that. The fifth was in a strange and peculiar hand which she did not recognize, and she opened it first to see who her correspondent might be. The letter was from the North, and had been addressed to Fraylingay, and she should have received it some days before. As she drew it from its envelope she glanced at the signature and at the last few words, which were uppermost, and seemed surprised. She knew the writer by name and reputation very well, although they had never met, and, feeling sure that the communication must be something of importance, she unfolded the letter, and read it at once deliberately from beginning to end.

When she appeared among the guests again she was pale, her lips were set, and she held her head high. Her mother said the dear child was quite overwrought, but she saw only what she expected to see through her own tear-bedimmed eyes, and other people were differently impressed. They thought Evadne was cold and preoccupied when it came to the parting, and did not seem to feel leaving her friends at all. She went out dry-eyed after kissing her mother, took her seat in the carriage, bowed polite but unsmiling acknowledgments to her friends, and drove off with Major Colquhoun with as little show of emotion, and much the same air as if she had merely been going somewhere on business, and expected to return directly.

"Thank goodness, all that is over!" Major Colquhoun exclaimed. She looked at him coolly and critically.

He was sitting with his hat in his hand, and she noticed that his hair was thin on his forehead, and there was nothing of youth in his eyes.

"I expect you are tired," he further observed.

"No, I am not tired, thank you," Evadne answered.

Then she set her lips once more, leant back, and looked out of the carriage window at the street all sloppy with mud, and the poor people seeming so miserable in the rain which had been falling steadily for the last hour.

"Poor weary creatures!" she thought. "We have so much, and they so little!" But she did not speak again till the carriage pulled up at the station, when she leant forward with anxious eyes, and said something confusedly about the crowd.

Major Colquhoun thought she was afraid of being stared at. He took out his watch.

"You will only have to cross the platform to the carriage," he said, "and the train ought to be up by this time. But if you don't mind being left alone a moment, I'll just go myself and see if it is, and where they are going to put us, and then I can take you there straight, and you won't feel the crowd at all."

He was not gone many minutes, but when he returned the carriage was empty.

"Where is Mrs. Colquhoun?" he said.

"She followed you, sir," the coachman answered, touching his hat.

"Confound——" He pulled himself up. "She'll be back in a moment, I suppose," he muttered.

"Dover express! Take your seats!" bawled a porter. "Are you for the Dover express?"

"Yes," said Major Colquhoun.

"Engaged carriage, sir?"

"Yes—oh, by the way, perhaps she's gone to the carriage," and he started to see, the porter following him. "Did you notice a young lady in a gray dress pass this way?" he asked the man as they went.

"With a pink feather in 'er 'at, sir?"

"Yes."

"Not pass up this way, sir," the man rejoined. "She got into a 'ansom over there, and drove off—if it was the same young lady." Major Colquhoun stopped short. The compartment reserved for them was empty also.

"Dover express! Dover express!" the guard shouted as he came along banging the carriage doors to.

"For Dover, sir?" he said in his ordinary voice to Major Colquhoun.

"No. It seems not," that gentleman answered deliberately.

The guard went on: "Dover express! Dover express! All right, Bill!" This was to someone in front as he popped into his own van, and shut the door.

Then the whistle shrieked derisively, the crank turned, and the next moment the train slid out serpent-like into the mist. Major Colquhoun had watched it off like any ordinary spectator, and when it had gone he looked at the porter, and the porter looked at him.

"Was your luggage in the train, sir?" the man asked him.

"Yes, but only booked to Dover," Major Colquhoun answered carelessly, taking out a cigarette case and choosing a cigarette with exaggerated precision. When he had lighted it he tipped the porter, and strolled back to the entrance, on the chance of finding the carriage still there, but it had gone, and he called a hansom, paused a moment with his foot on the step, then finally directed the man to drive to the Fraylings'.

"Swell's bin sold some'ow," commented the porter. "And if I was a swell I wouldn't take on neither."

CHAPTER XIII.

THE Fraylings had decided to postpone all further festivities till the bride and bridegroom's return, so that the wedding guests had gone, and the house looked as drearily commonplace as any other in the street when the hansom pulled up a little short of the door for Major Colquhoun to alight.

The servant who answered his ring made no pretense of concealing his astonishment when he saw who it was, but Major Colquhoun's manner effectually checked any expression of it. He was not the kind of a man whom a servant would ever have dared to express any sympathy with, however obviously things might have gone wrong. But there was nothing in Major Colquhoun's appearance at that moment to show that anything had gone wrong, except his return when he should have been off on his wedding journey. There was probably a certain amount of assumption in his apparent indifference. He had always cultivated an inscrutable bearing, as being " the thing " in his set, so that it was easy for him now to appear to be cooler and more collected than he was. His attitude, however, was largely due to a want of proper healthy feeling, for he was a vice-worn man, with small capacity left for any great emotion.

He walked into the hall and hung up his hat.

" Is Mr. Frayling alone ? " he said.

" Yes, sir—with Mrs. Frayling—and the family—upstairs in the drawing room," the man stammered.

" Ask him to see me down here, please. Say a gentleman." He stepped to a mirror as he spoke and carefully twisted the ends of his blond moustache.

" Very good, sir," said the servant.

Major Colquhoun walked into the library in the same deliberate way, and turned up the gas. Mr. Frayling came hurrying down, fat and fussy, and puffing a little, but cheerfully rubicund upon the success of the day's proceedings, and apprehending nothing untoward. When he saw his son-in-law he opened his eyes, stopped short, turned pale, and gasped.

" Is Evadne here ? " Major Colquhoun asked quietly.

" Here ? No ! What should she be doing here ? What has happened ? " Mr. Frayling exclaimed aghast.

" That is just what I don't rightly know myself if she is not here," Major Colquhoun replied, the quiet demeanour he had assumed contrasting favourably with his father-in-law's fuss and fume.

" Why have you left her ? What are you doing here ? Explain," Mr. Frayling demanded almost angrily.

Major Colquhoun related the little he knew, and Mr. Frayling plumped down into a chair to listen, and bounced up again, when all was said, to speak.

" Let me send for her mother," he began, showing at once where, in an emergency, he felt that his strength lay. " No, though, I'd better go myself and prepare her," he added on second thought. " We mustn't make a fuss—with all the servants about too. They would talk." And then he fussed off himself, with agitation evident in every step.

Something like a smile disturbed Major Colquhoun's calm countenance for a moment, and then he stood, twisting the

ends of his fair moustache slowly with his left hand, and
gazing into the fire, which shone reflected in his steely blue
eyes, making them glitter like pale sapphires, coldly, while he
waited.

Mr. Frayling returned with his wife almost immediately.
The latter had had her handkerchief in her hand all day, but
she put it in her pocket now.

Major Colquhoun had to repeat his story.

" Did you look for her in the waiting rooms?" Mrs. Frayling asked.

" No."

" She may be there waiting for you at this very moment."

It was a practical suggestion.

" But the porter said he saw her get into a hansom," Major
Colquhoun objected.

" He said he saw a young lady in gray get into a hansom, I
understood you to say," Mrs. Frayling corrected him. " A
young lady in gray is not necessarily Evadne. There might
be a dozen young ladies in gray in such a crowd."

" There might, yes," Mr. Frayling agreed.

" And the proof that it was not Evadne is that she is not
here," her mother proceeded. " If she had been seen getting
into a hansom it could only have been to come here."

" A hansom might break down on the way," said Major
Colquhoun, entertaining the idea for a moment.

" That is not impossible," Mr. Frayling decided.

" But why should she come here?" Major Colquhoun
slowly pursued, looking hard at his parents-in-law. " Had she
any objection to marrying me? Was she overpersuaded
into it?"

" Oh, *no!*" Mrs. Frayling exclaimed emphatically. " How
can you suppose such a thing? We should never have *dreamed*
of influencing the dear child in such a matter. If there were
ever a case of love at first sight it was one. Why, her first
words on awaking this morning, were: ' Oh, mother! I *am* so
happy!' and that doesn't sound like being overpersuaded!"

" Then what, in God's name, is the explanation of all this?"
Major Colquhoun exclaimed, showing some natural emotion
for the first time.

" That is it," said Mr. Frayling energetically. " There
must be some explanation."

" Heaven grant that the dear child has not been entrapped
in some way and carried off, and robbed, and murdered, or

something *dreadful*," Mrs. Frayling cried, giving way to the strain all at once, and wringing her hands.

Then they looked at each other, and the period of speculation was followed by a momentary interregnum of silence, which would in due course be succeeded by a desire to act, to do something, if nothing happened in the meantime. Something did happen, however. The door bell rang violently. They looked up and listened. The hall door was opened. Footsteps approached, paused outside the library, and then the butler entered, and handed Mr. Frayling a telegram on a silver salver.

" Is there any answer, sir ?" he asked.

Mr. Frayling opened it with trembling hands and read it. " No ; no answer," he said.

The butler looked at them all as if they interested him, and withdrew.

" Well," cried Mrs. Frayling, her patience exhausted. " Is it from her ?"

" Yes," Mr. Frayling replied. " It was handed in at the General Post Office at——"

" The General Post Office ! " Major Colquhoun ejaculated. " What on earth took her there ?"

" The hansom, you know," said Mrs. Frayling. " Oh, dear "—to her husband—" *do* read it."

" Well, I'm going to, if you'll let me," he answered irritably, but delaying, nevertheless, to mutter something irrelevant about women's tongues. Then he read : " ' Don't be anxious about me. Have received information about Major C.'s character and past life which does not satisfy me at all, and am going now to make further inquiries. Will write.' "

" Information about my character and past life ! " exclaimed Major Colquhoun. " Why, what is wrong with my character ? What have I done ?"

" Oh, the child is mad ! she must be mad !" Mrs. Frayling ejaculated.

Mr. Frayling fumed up and down the room in evident perturbation. He had not a single phrase ready for such an occasion, nor the power to form one, and was consequently compelled to employ quite simple language.

" You had better make inquiries at the post office," he said to Major Colquhoun, " and try and trace her. You must follow her and bring her back at once, if possible."

" Not I, indeed." was Major Colquhoun's most unexpected

rejoinder; " I shall not give myself any trouble on her account ; she may go."

" Oh, for Heaven's sake, don't say that, George !" Mrs. Frayling exclaimed. " You *do* love her, and she loves *you ;* I *know* she does. Some *dreadful* mischief-making person has come between you. But wait, *do* wait, until you know more. It will all come right in the end. I am *sure* it will."

Major Colquhoun compressed his lips and looked sullenly into the fire.

CHAPTER XIV.

ON the third day after Evadne's wedding, in the afternoon, Mrs. Orton Beg was sitting alone in her long, low drawing room by the window which looked out into the high-walled garden. She had found it difficult to occupy herself with books and work that day. Her sprained ankle had been troublesome during the night, and she had risen late, and when her maid had helped her to dress, and she had limped downstairs on her crutches, and settled herself in her long chair, she found herself disinclined for any further exertion, and just sat, reclining upon pale pink satin cushions, her slender hands folded upon her lap, her large, dark luminous eyes and delicate, refined features all set in a wistful sadness.

There was a singular likeness between herself and Evadne in some things, a vague, haunting family likeness which continually obtruded itself but could not be defined. It had been more distinct when Evadne was a child, and would doubtless have grown greater had she lived with her aunt, but the very different mental attitude which she gradually acquired had melted the resemblance, as it were, so that at nineteen, although her slender figure, and air, and carriage continually recalled Mrs. Orton Beg, who was then in her thirty-fifth year, the expression of her face was so different that they were really less alike than they had been when Evadne was four years younger. Evadne's disposition, it must be remembered, was essentially swift to act. She would, as a human being, have her periods of strong feeling, but that was merely a physical condition in no way affecting her character ; and the only healthy minded happy state for her was the one in which thought instantly translated itself into action.

With Mrs. Orton Beg it was different. Her spiritual nature predominated, her habits of mind were dreamy. She lived for

the life to come entirely, and held herself in constant communion with another world. She felt it near her, she said. She
believed that its inhabitants visit the earth, and take cognizance of all we do and suffer ; and she cherished the certainty
of one day assuming a wondrous form, and entering upon a
new life, as vivid and varied and as real as this, but far more
perfect. Her friends were chiefly of her own way of thinking ;
but her faith was so profound, and the charm of her conversation so entrancing, that the hardest headed materialists were
apt to feel strange delicious thrills in her presence, forebodings
of possibilities beyond the test of reason and knowledge ; and
they would return time after time to dispute her conclusions
and argue themselves out of the impression she had produced,
but only to relapse into their former state of blissful sensation
so soon as they once more found themselves within range of
her influence. Opinions are germs in the moral atmosphere
which fasten themselves upon us if we are predisposed to entertain them ; but some states of feeling are a perfume which
every sentient being must perceive with emotions that vary
from extreme repugnance to positive pleasure through diverse
intermediate strata of lively interest or mere passive perception ; and the feeling which emanated from Mrs. Orton Beg
is one that is especially contagious. For, in the first place,
the beauty of goodness appeals pleasurably to the most
depraved ; to be elevated above themselves for a moment is a
rare delight to them ; and, in the second, there is a deeply
implanted leaning in the heart of man toward the something
beyond everything, the impalpable, impossible, imperceptible,
which he cannot know and will not credit, but is nevertheless
compelled to feel in some of his moods, or in certain presences,
and having once felt, finds himself fascinated by it, and so
returns to the subject for the sake of the sensation. In that
long, low drawing room of Mrs. Orton Beg's, with the window
at either end, in view of the gray old cathedral towering above
the gnarled elms of the Lower Close, itself the scene of every
form of human endeavour, every expression of human passion,
in surroundings so heavy with memories of the past, and listening to the quiet tone of conviction in which Mrs. Orton Beg
spoke, with the double charm of extreme polish and simplicity
combined—in that same room even the worldliest had found
themselves rise into the ecstasy of the higher life, spiritually
freed for the moment, and with the desire to go forth and do
great deeds of love.

Mrs. Orton Beg had sat idle an hour looking out of the window, her mind in the mood for music, but bare of thought.

A gale was blowing without. The old elms in the Close were tossing their stiff, bare arms about, the ground was strewed with branches and leaves from the limes, and a watery wintry sun made the misery of the muddy ground apparent, and accentuated the blight of the flowers and torn untidiness of the creepers, and all the items which make autumn gardens so desolate. The equinoctial gales had set in early that year. They began on Evadne's wedding day with a fearful storm which raged all over the country, and burst with especial violence upon Morningquest, and the wind continued high, and showed no sign of abating. It was depressing weather, and Mrs. Orton Beg sighed more than once unconsciously.

But presently the cathedral clock began to strike, and she raised her head to listen. One, two, three, four, the round notes fell ; then there was a pause ; and then the chime rolled out over the storm-stained city :

He, watch-ing o-ver Is-ra-el, slumbers not, nor sleeps.

Mechanically Mrs. Orton Beg repeated the phrase with each note as it floated forth, filling the silent spaces ; and then she awoke with a start to thought once more, and knew that she had been a long, long time alone.

She was going to ring, but at that moment a servant entered and announced : " Mrs. and Miss Beale."

They were the wife and daughter of the Bishop of Morningquest, the one a very pleasant, attractive elderly lady, the other a girl of seventeen, like her mother, but with more character in her face.

" Ah, how glad I am to see you ! " Mrs. Orton Beg exclaimed, trying to rise, " and what a delicious breath of fresh air you have brought in with you ! "

" My dear Olive, don't move," Mrs. Beale rejoined, preventing her. " We have been nearly blown away walking this short distance. Just look at Edith's hair."

" I feel quite tempest tossed," said Edith, getting up and going to a glass before which she removed her hat, and let down her hair, which was the colour of burnished brass, and fell to her knees in one straight heavy coil without a wave.

" You remind me of some Saxon Edith I have seen in a picture," said Mrs. Orton Beg, looking at her admiringly.

" But, dear child," her mother deprecated, " should you make a dressing room of the drawing room ? "

"I know Mrs. Orton Beg will pardon me," said Edith, rolling her hair up deftly and neatly as she spoke, with the air of a privileged person quite at home.

Mrs. Orton Beg smiled at her affectionately ; but before she could speak the door opened once more, and the servant announced : " Lord Dawne."

And there entered a grave, distinguished looking man between thirty and forty years of age, apparently, with black hair, and deep blue eyes at once penetrating and winning in expression.

Mrs. Orton Beg greeted him with pleasure, Mrs. Beale with pleasure also, but with more ceremony, Edith quite simply and naturally, and then he sat down. He was in riding dress, with his whip and hat in his hand.

" This is an unexpected pleasure. I did not know you were at Morne," said Mrs. Orton Beg. " Is Claudia with you ? "

" No, I have only come for a few days," Lord Dawne replied. " I came to see Adeline specially, but they don't return from town till to-morrow. They have all been assisting at the marriage of a niece of yours, I hear, and the Heavenly Twins have been prolonging the festivities on their own account. Adeline wrote to me in despair, and I have come to see if I can be of any use. My sister," he added, turning to Mrs. Beale with his bright, almost boyish smile, which was like his nephew Diavolo's, and made them both irresistible—" my sister flatters herself that I have some influence with the children, and as it is quite certain that nobody else has, I am careful not to dispel the illusion. It is a comfort to her. But the twins will not allow me to deceive myself upon that head. They put me in my place every time I see them. The last time we had a serious talk together I noticed that Diavolo was thinking deeply, and hoped for a moment that it was about what I was saying ; but that, apparently, had not interested him at all, for I had the curiosity to ask, just to see if I had, perchance, made any impression, and discovered that he had had something else in his mind the whole time. ‘I was just wondering,’ he answered, ‘if you care much about being Duke of Morningquest.’ ‘No, not very much,’ I assured him ; ‘why ?’ ‘Well, I was pretty certain you didn't,’ he replied ; ‘and, you see, *I* do ; so I was just thinking couldn't you remain as you are when grandpapa dies, and let me walk into the title? Then I'd give Angelica the Hamilton House property, and it would be very jolly for all of us.' 'But, look here,' Angelica broke in, in her energetic way, 'if you're going to be a duke I won't be left plain Miss Hamilton-Wells.' 'You couldn't be "plain" Miss anything,' Diavolo gallantly assured her, bowing in the most courtly way. But Angelica said, with more force than refinement, that that was all rot, and then Diavolo lost his temper and pulled her hair, and she got hold of his and dragged him out of the room by his—my presence of course counted for nothing. And the next I saw of them they were on their ponies in a secluded grassy glade of the forest, tilting at each other with long poles for the dukedom. Angelica says she means to beat Demosthenes hollow—I use her own phraseology to give character to the quotation; that delivering orations with a natural inclination to stammering was nothing to get over compared to the disabilities which being a girl imposes upon her; but she means to get over them all by hook, which she explains as being the proper development of her muscles and physique generally, and by crook, which she defines as circumventing the slave drivers of her sex, a task which she seems to think can easily be accomplished by finessing."

"And what was the last thing?" Mrs. Orton Beg inquired, smiling indulgently.

"Oh, that was very simple," Lord Dawne rejoined. "Diavolo, dressed in velvet, was caught and taken up by a policeman for recklessly driving a hansom in Oxford Street, Angelica being inside the same disguised in something of her mother's."

"I wonder it was Angelica who went inside!" Mrs. Orton Beg exclaimed.

"Well, that was what her mother said," Lord Dawne replied; "and both her parents seem to think the matter was not nearly so bad as it might have been in consequence. Mr. Hamilton-Wells had to pay a fine for the furious driving, and use all his influence with the Press to keep the thing out of the papers."

"But where did the children get the hansom?" Mrs. Beale begged to be informed.

"I regret to say that they hailed it through the dining room window, and plied the driver with raw brandy until his venal nature gave in to their earnestly persuasive eloquence and the contents of their purses, and he consented to let Diavola 'just try what it was like to sit up on that high box,'

Angelica having previously got inside, and, of course, the moment the young scamp had the reins in his hands he drove off full tilt."

"Oh, dear, *poor* Lady Adeline!" Mrs. Beale exclaimed.

Lord Dawne smiled again, and changed the subject. "Did you feel the storm much here?" he asked. "My trees have suffered a great deal, I am sorry to say."

"Ah, that reminds me." Mrs. Beale began. "A very strange and solemn thing happened on the day of the storm; have you heard of it, Olive?"

"No," Mrs. Orton Beg answered with interest. "What was it?"

"Well, you know the dean's brother has a large family of daughters," Mrs. Beale replied, "and they had a very charming governess, Miss Winstanley, a lady by birth, and an accomplished person, and extremely *spirituelle*. Well, on the morning of the storm she was sitting at work with one of her pupils in the schoolroom, when another came in from the garden, and uttered an exclamation of surprise when she saw Miss Winstanley. 'How did you get in, and take your things off so quickly?' she said. 'I have not been out,' Miss Winstanley answered. "Why, I saw you—I ran past you over by the duck pond!' 'Dear child, you must be mistaken. I haven't been out to-day,' the governess answered, smiling. Well, that child got out her work and sat down, but she had hardly done so when another came in, and also exclaimed: 'Oh, Miss Winstanley! How *did* you get here? I saw you standing looking out of the window at the bottom of the picture gallery as I ran past this minute.' 'I must have a double,' said Miss Winstanley lightly. 'But it *was* you,' the child insisted; 'I saw you quite well, flowers and all.' The governess was wearing some scarlet geranium. 'You know what they say if people are seen like that where they have never been in the body?' she said jokingly. 'They say it is a sign that that person is going to die.' In the afternoon," Mrs. Beale continued, lowering her voice and glancing round involuntarily— and in the momentary pause the rush of the gale without sounded obtrusively—"in the afternoon of that same day she went out alone for a walk, and did not return, and they became alarmed at last, and sent some men to search for her when the storm was at its height, and they found her lying across a stile. She had been killed by the branch of a tree falling on her."

"How do you explain that?" Mrs. Orton Beg said softly to Lord Dawne.

" I should not attempt to explain it," he answered, rising.

" Must you go?"

" Yes, I am sorry to say. Claudia and Ideala charged me with many messages for you."

" They are together as usual, and well, I trust?"

" Yes," he answered, " and most anxious to hear a better account of your foot."

"Ah, I hope to be able to walk soon," she said, holding out her hand to him.

" What a charming man he is," Mrs. Beale remarked when he had gone. " There is no hope of his marrying, I suppose," she added, trying not to look at her daughter.

" Oh, no!" Mrs. Orton Beg exclaimed in an almost horrified tone.

Lord Dawne's friends made no secret of his grand and chivalrous devotion to the distinguished woman known to them all as Ideala. Every one of them was aware, although he had never let fall a word on the subject, that he had remained single on her account—every one but Ideala herself. She never suspected it, or thought of love at all in connection with Lord Dawne—and, besides, she was married.

When her friends had gone that day Mrs. Orton Beg sat long in the gathering dusk, watching the newly lighted fire burn up, and thinking. She was thinking of Evadne chiefly, wondering why she had had no news of her, why her sister Elizabeth did not write, and tell her all about the wedding; and she was just on the verge of anxiety—in that state when various possibilities of trouble that might have occurred to account for delays begin to present themselves to the mind, when all at once, without hearing anything; she became conscious of a presence near her, and looking up she was startled to see Evadne herself.

" My dear child!" she gasped, " what has happened? Why are you here?"

"Nothing has happened, auntie; don't be alarmed," Evadne answered. " I am here because I have been a fool."

She spoke quietly but with concentrated bitterness, then sat down and began to take off her gloves with that exaggerated show of composure which is a sign in some people of suppressed emotion.

Her face was pale, but her eyes were bright, and the pupils were dilated.

"I have come to claim your hospitality, auntie," she pursued, "to ask you for shelter from the world for a few days, *because* I have been a fool.   May I stay?"

"Surely, dear child," Mrs. Orton Beg replied, and then she waited, mastering the nervous tremor into which the shock of Evadne's sudden appearance had thrown her with admirable self-control.   And here again the family likeness between aunt and niece was curiously apparent.   Both masked their agitation because both by temperament were shy, and ashamed to show strong feeling.

Evadne looked into the fire for a little, trying to collect herself.   "I knew what was right," she began at last in a low voice, "I knew we should take nothing for granted, we should never be content merely to feel and suppose and hope for the best in matters about which we should know exactly.   And yet I took no trouble to ascertain.   I fell in love, and liked the sensation, and gave myself up to it unreservedly.   Certainly, I was a fool—there is no other word for it."

"But are you married, Evadne?" Mrs. Orton Beg asked in a voice rendered unnatural by the rapid beating of her heart.

"Let me tell you, auntie, all about it," Evadne answered hoarsely.   She drew her chair a little closer to the fire, and spread her hands out to the blaze.   There was no other light in the room by this time.   The wind without howled dismally still, but at intervals, as if with an effort.   During one of its noisiest bursts the cathedral clock began to strike, and hushed it, as it were, suddenly.   It seemed to be listening, to be waiting, and Evadne waited and listened too, raising her head. There was a perceptible, momentary pause, then came the chime, full, round, mournful, melodious, yet glad too, in the strength of its solemn assurance, filling the desolate regions of sorrow and silence with something of hope whereon the weary mind might repose :

He, watch-ing o-ver   Is-ra-el,   slumbers not, nor sleeps.

When the last reverberation of the last note had melted out of hearing, Evadne sighed ; then she straightened herself, as if collecting her energy, and began to speak.

"Yes, I am married," she said, "but when I went to change my dress after the ceremony I found this letter   It was intended, you see, to reach me some days before it did, but unfortunately it was addressed to Fraylingay, and time was lost in forwarding it." She handed it to her aunt, who raised her eyebrows when she saw the writing, as if she recognized it, hastily drew the letter from its envelope, and held it so that the blaze fell upon it while she read. Evadne knelt on the hearthrug, and stirred the fire, making it burn up brightly.

Mrs. Orton Beg returned the letter to the envelope when she had read it. "What did you do?" she said.

"I read it before I went downstairs, and at first I could not think what to do, so we drove off together, but on the way to the station it suddenly flashed upon me that the proper thing to do would be to go at once and hear all that there was to tell, and fortunately Major Colquhoun gave me an opportunity of getting away without any dispute. He went to see about something, leaving me in the carriage, and I just got out, walked round the station, took a hansom, and drove off to the General Post Office to telegraph to my people."

"But why didn't you go home?"

"For several reasons," Evadne answered, "the best being that I never thought of going home. I wanted to be alone and think. I fancied that at home they either could not or would not tell me anything of Major Colquhoun's past life, and I was determined to know the truth exactly. And I can't tell you how many sayings of my father's recurred to me all at once with a new significance, and made me fear that there was some difference between his point of view and mine on the subject of a suitable husband. He told me himself that Major Colquhoun had been quite frank about his past career, and then, when I came to think, it appeared to me clearly that it was the frankness which had satisfied my father; the career itself was nothing. You heard how pleased they were about my engagement?"

"Yes," Mrs. Orton Beg answered slowly, "and I confess I was a little surprised when I heard from your mother that your *fiancé* had been 'wild' in his youth, for I remembered some remarks you made last year about the kind of man you would object to marry, and it seemed to me from the description that Major Colquhoun was very much that kind of man."

"Then why didn't you warn me?" Evadne exclaimed.

"I don't know whether I quite thought it was a subject for warning," Mrs. Orton Beg answered, "and at any rate, girls *do* talk in that way sometimes, not really meaning it. I thought it was mere *youngness* on your part, and theory ; and I don't know now whether I quite approve of your having been told—of this new departure," she added, indicating the letter.

"*I* do," said Evadne decidedly. " I would stop the imposition, approved of custom, connived at by parents, made possible by the state of ignorance in which we are carefully kept—the imposition upon a girl's innocence and inexperience of a disreputable man for a husband."

Mrs. Orton Beg was startled by this bold assertion, which was so unprecedented in her experience that for a moment she could not utter a word ; and when she did speak she avoided a direct reply, because she thought any discussion on the subject of marriage, except from the sentimental point of view, was indelicate.

" But tell me your position exactly," she begged—" what you did next : why you are here ! "

" I went by the night mail North," Evadne answered, " and saw them. They were very kind. They told me everything. I can't repeat the details ; they disgust me."

" No, pray don't ! " Mrs. Orton Beg exclaimed hastily. She had no mind for anything unsavoury.

" They had been abroad, you know," Evadne pursued ; " Otherwise I should have heard from them as soon as the engagement was announced. They hoped to be in time, however. They had no idea the marriage would take place so soon."

Mrs. Orton Beg reflected for a little, and then she asked in evident trepidation, for she had more than a suspicion of what the reply would be : " And what are you going to do ? "

" Decline to live with him," Evadne answered.

This was what Mrs. Orton Beg had begun to suspect, but there is often an element of surprise in the confirmation of our shrewdest suspicions, and now she sat upright, leant forward, and looked at her niece aghast. "*What ?* " she demanded.

" I shall decline to live with him," Evadne repeated with emphasis.

Mrs. Orton Beg slowly resumed her reclining position, acting as one does who has heard the worst, and realizes that there is nothing to be done but to recover from the shock.

" I thought you loved him," she ventured, after a prolonged pause.

" Yes, so did I," Evadne answered, frowning—" but I was mistaken. It was a mere affair of the senses, to be put off by the first circumstance calculated to cause a revulsion of feeling by lowering him in my estimation—a thing so slight that, after reading the letter, as we drove to the station—even so soon ! I could see him as he is. I noticed at once—but it was for the first time—I noticed that, although his face is handsome, the expression of it is not noble at all." She shuddered as at the sight of something repulsive. " You see," she explained, "my taste is cultivated to so fine an extent, I require something extremely well-flavoured for the dish which is to be the *pièce de resistance* of my life-feast. My appetite is delicate, it requires to be tempted, and a husband of that kind, a moral leper "—she broke off with a gesture, spreading her hands, palms outward, as if she would fain put some horrid idea far from her. " Besides, marrying a man like that, allowing him an assured position in society, is countenancing vice, and "— she glanced round apprehensively, then added in a fearful whisper—" *helping to spread it.*"

Mrs. Orton Beg knew in her head that reason and right were on Evadne's side, but she felt in her heart the full force of the custom and prejudice that would be against her, and shrank appalled by the thought of what the cruel struggle to come must be if Evadne persisted in her determination. In view of this, she sat up in her chair once more energetically, prepared to do her best to dissuade her ; but then again she relapsed, giving in to a doubt of her own capacity to advise in such an emergency, accompanied by a sudden and involuntary feeling of respect for Evadne's principles, however peculiar and unprecedented they might be, and for the strength of character which had enabled her so far to act upon them. " You must obey your own conscience, Evadne," was what she found herself saying at last. " I will help you to do that. I would rather not influence you. You may be right. I cannot be sure—and yet—I don't agree with you. For I know if I could have my husband back with me, I would welcome him, even if he were—a leper." Evadne compressed her lips in steady disapproval. " I should think only of his future. I should forgive the past."

" That is the mistake you good women all make," said Evadne. " You set a detestably bad example. So long as women like you will forgive anything, men will do anything. You have it in your power to set up a high standard of excellence for men to reach in order to have the privilege of associating with you. There is this quality in men, that they will have the best of everything ; and if the best wives are only to be obtained by being worthy of them, they will strive to become so. As it is, however, why should they? Instead of punishing them for their depravity, you encourage them in it by overlooking it ; and besides," she added, "you must know that there is no past in the matter of vice. The consequences become hereditary, and continue from generation to generation."

Again Mrs. Orton Beg felt herself checked.

"Where did you hear all this, Evadne!" she asked.

"I never heard it. I read—and I thought," she answered. "But I am only now beginning to understand," she added. "I suppose moral axioms are always the outcome of pained reflection. Knowledge cries to us in vain as a rule before experience has taken the sharp edge off our egotism—by experience, I mean the addition of some personal feeling to our knowledge."

"I don't understand you in the least, Evadne," Mrs. Orton Beg replied.

"Your husband was a good man," Evadne answered indirectly. "You have never thought about what a woman ought to do who has married a bad one—in an emergency like mine, that is. You think I should act as women have been always advised to act in such cases, that I should sacrifice myself to save that one man's soul. I take a different view of it. I see that the world is not a bit the better for centuries of self-sacrifice on the woman's part and therefore I think it is time we tried a more effectual plan. And I propose now to sacrifice the man instead of the woman."

Mrs. Orton Beg was silent.

"Have you nothing to say to me, auntie?" Evadne asked at last, caressingly.

"I do not like to hear you talk so. Evadne. Every word you say seems to banish something—something from this room —something from my life to which I cling. I think it is my faith in love—and loving. You may be right, but yet—the consequences! the struggle, if we must resist! It is best to submit. It is better not to know."

"It is easier to submit—yes ; it is disagreeable to know," Evadne translated.

There was another pause, then Mrs. Orton Beg broke out : "Don't make me think about it. Surely I have suffered enough? Disagreeable to know! It is torture. If I ever let myself dwell on the horrible depravity that goes on unchecked, the depravity which you say we women license by ignoring it when we should face and unmask it, I should go out of my mind. I do know—we all know; how can we live and not know? But we don't think about it—we can't—we daren't. See! I try always to keep my own mind in one attitude, to keep it filled for ever with holy and beautiful thoughts. When I am alone, I listen for the chime, and when I have repeated it to myself slowly—

He, watching over Israel, slumbers not nor sleeps—

my heart swells. I leave all that is inexplicable to Him, and thank him for the love and the hope with which he feeds my heart and keeps it from hardening. I thank him too," she went on hoarsely, "for the terrible moments when I feel my loss afresh, those early morning moments, when the bright sunshine and the beauty of all things only make my own barren life look all the more bare in its loneliness; when my soul struggles to free itself from the shackles of the flesh that it may spread its wings to meet that other soul which made earth heaven for me here, and will, I know, make all eternity ecstatic as a dream for me hereafter. It is good to suffer, yes; but surely I suffer enough? My husband—if I cry to him, he will not hear me; if I go down on my knees beside his grave, and dig my arms in deep, deep, I shall not reach him. I cannot raise him up again to caress him, or move the cruel weight of earth from off his breast. The voice that was always kind will gladden me no more; the arms that were so willing to protect—the world—just think how big it is! and if I traverse it every yard, I shall not find him. He is not anywhere in all this huge expanse. Ah, God! the agony of yearning, the ache, the ache; why must I live?"

"Auntie!" Evadne cried. "I am selfish." She knelt down beside her and held her hand. "I have made you think of your own irreparable loss, compared with which I know my trouble is so small. Forgive me."

Mrs. Orton Beg put her arms round the girl's neck and kissed her: "Forgive *me*," she said. "I am so weak, Evadne, and you—ah! you are strong."

CHAPTER XV.

THE Fraylings had sent their children and the majority of their servants back to Fraylingay the day after the wedding, but had decided to stay in London themselves with Major Colquhoun until Evadne wrote to relieve their anxiety, which was extreme, and gave them some information about her movements and intentions.

Mr. Frayling spent most of the interval in prancing up and down. He recollected all his past grievances, real and imaginary, and recounted them, and also speculated about those that were to come, and mentioned the number of things he was always doing for everybody, the position he had to keep up and consider for the sake of his family, the scandal there would be if this story got about ; and described in one breath both his determination to hush it up, and his conviction that it would be utterly impossible to do so. Whenever the postman knocked he went to the door to look for a letter, and coming back empty-handed each time, he invariably remarked that it was disgraceful, simply disgraceful, and he had never heard of such a thing in all his life. There was blame and severity in his attitude toward poor Mrs. Frayling ; he seemed to insinuate that she might and should have done something to prevent all this ; while there was a mixture of sympathy, deprecation, and apology in his manner to his son-in-law, combined with a certain air of absolving himself from all responsibility in the matter.

Major Colquhoun's own attitude was wholly enigmatical. He smoked cigars, read novels, and said nothing except in answer to such remarks as were specially addressed to him, and then he confined himself to the shortest and simplest form of rejoinder possible.

" The dear fellow's patience is exemplary," Mrs. Frayling remarked to her husband as they went to bed one night. " He conceals his own feelings *quite*, and never utters a complaint."

" Humph !" grunted Mr. Frayling, who scented some reproach in this remark ; " if the dear fellow does not suffer from impatience, and has no feelings to conceal, it is not much marvel if he utters no complaint. I believe he doesn't care a rap, and is only thinking of how to get out of the whole business."

" Oh, my dear, how *dreadful !* " Mrs. Frayling exclaimed.

" I am sure you are quite mistaken. You don't understand him at all."

Mr. Frayling shrugged his shoulders and snorted. He despised feminine conclusions too much to reply to them, but not nearly enough to be wholly unmoved by them.

Mrs. Frayling spent the three days in sitting still, embroidering silk flowers on a satin ground, and watering them well with her tears. But on the morning of the fourth day, by the first post, letters arrived which put an end to their suspense. One was from Mrs. Orton Beg and the other from Evadne herself. Mrs. Frayling read them aloud at the breakfast table, and the three sat for an hour in solemn conclave, considering them.

Mrs. Orton Beg had had time to recover herself and reflect before she wrote, and the consequence was some modification of her first impression.

" My Dear Elizabeth :

"Evadne is here ; she arrived this afternoon. On her wedding day she received a letter from a lady, whose name I am not allowed to mention here, but written under the impression that Evadne was being kept in ignorance of Major Colquhoun's past life, and offering to give her any information that had been withheld so that she might not be blindly entrapped into marrying him under the delusion that he was a worthy man. The letter arrived too late, but Evadne went off nevertheless on the spur of the moment to make further inquiries, the result of which is great indignation on her part for having been allowed to marry a man of such antecedents, and a determination not to live with him. She wishes to stay here with me for the present, and I am very glad to have her. I give her an asylum, but I shall not speak a word to influence her decision in any way if I can help it. It is a matter of conscience with her, and I perceive that her moral consciousness and mine are not quite the same ; but in the present state of my ignorance, I feel that it would be presumption on my part to set my own up as superior, and therefore I think it better not to interfere in any way.

" You need not be in the least anxious about Evadne. She is quite well, has an excellent appetite, and is not at all inclined to pose as a martyr. I confess I should have thought myself she would have suffered more in the first days of her disillusion, for she certainly was very much in love with Major Colquhoun;

but her principles are older than her acquaintance with him, and ingrained principle is a force superior to passion, it seems —which is as it should be.

"I am sorry for you all, and for you especially, dear, in this dilemma, for I know how you will feel it ; and I am the more sorry because I cannot say a single word which would relieve the state of perplexity you must be in, or be in any way a comfort to you.

"Your loving sister,
"Olive Orton Beg."

Evadne's letter ran thus :

"The Close, Morningquest, 4th October.

"My Dear Father and Mother :

"Aunt Olive has kindly written to tell you exactly why I am here, so that my letter need only be a supplement to hers. For whatever trouble and anxiety I may have caused you, forgive me. The thought of it will be a pang to me as long as I live.

"Since I left you I have been fully informed of circumstances in Major Colquhoun's past career which make it impossible for me to live with him as his wife. I find that I consented to marry him under a grave misapprehension of his true character—that he is not at all a proper person for a young girl to associate with, and that in point of fact his mode of life has very much resembled that of one of those old-fashioned heroes, Roderick Random or Tom Jones, specimens of humanity whom I hold in peculiar and especial detestation.

"I consider I should be wanting in all right feeling if I held myself bound to him by vows which I took in my ignorance of his history. But I am afraid there will be some difficulty about the legal business. Kindly find out for me what will be the best arrangement to make for our separation, and tell me also if I ought to write to Major Colquhoun myself. I should like it better if my father would relieve me of this dreadful necessity.

"Until we have arranged matters, I should prefer to stay here with Aunt Olive. I am very well, and happier too, than I should have expected to be after the shock of such a disappointment, though perhaps less so than I ought in gratitude to be, considering the merciful deliverance I have had from what would have been the shipwreck of my life.

"Your affectionate daughter,
"Evadne."

"Good Heavens! good Heavens!" Mr. Frayling ejaculated several times.

Major Colquhoun had curled his moustache during the reading of the letter, with the peculiar set expression of countenance he was in the habit of assuming to mask his emotions.

"What language! what ideas!" Mr. Frayling proceeded. "I have been much deceived in that unhappy child," and he shook his head at his wife severely, as if it were her fault.

Major Colquhoun muttered something about having been taken in himself.

After the reading of the letter, Mrs. Frayling's comely plump face looked drawn and haggard. She could not utter a word at first, and had even exhausted her stock of tears. All at once, however, she recovered her voice, and gave sudden utterance to a determination.

"I must go to that child!" she exclaimed. "I must—I must go at once."

"You shall do no such thing," her husband thundered. He had no reason in the world for opposing the motherly impulse; but it relieves the male of certain species to roar when he is irritated, and the relief is all the greater when he finds some sentient creature to roar at, that will shrink from the noise, and be awed by it.

Mrs. Frayling looked up at him pathetically, then riveted her eyes upon the tablecloth, and rocked herself to and fro, but answered never a word.

Major Colquhoun, with the surface sympathy of sensual men, who resent anything that produces a feeling of discomfort in themselves, felt sorry for her, and relieved the tension by asking what was to be said in reply to Evadne's letter.

This led to a discussion of the subject, which was summarily ended by Mr. Frayling, who deputed to his wife the task of answering the letter, without allowing her any choice in the matter. It was never his way to do anything disagreeable if he could insist upon her doing it for him.

But Mrs. Frayling was nothing loth upon this occasion.

"Well," she began humbly, "I undertake the task since you wish it, but I should have thought a word from you would have gone further than anything I can say. However,"—she ventured to lift a hopeful head,—"I have certainly always been able to manage Evadne,"—she turned to Major Colquhoun,—"I can assure you, George, that child has never given me a moment's anxiety in her life ; and,"—she added in a broken voice,—" I never, never thought that she would live to quote books to her parents."

Mr. Frayling found in his own inclinations a reason for everything. He was very tired of being shut up in London, and he therefore decided that they should go back to Fraylingay at once, and suggested that Major Colquhoun should follow them in a few days if Evadne had not in the meantime come to her senses. Major Colquhoun agreed to this. He would have hidden himself anywhere, done anything to keep his world in ignorance of what had befallen him. Even a man's independence is injured by excesses. As the tissues waste, the esteem of men is fawned for instead of being honestly earned, criticism is deprecated, importance is attached to the babbling of blockheads, and even to the opinion of fools. What should have been self-respect in Major Colquhoun had degenerated into a devouring vanity, which rendered him thin-skinned to the slightest aspersion. He had married Evadne in order to win the credit of having secured an exceptionally young and attractive wife, and now all he thought of was " what fellows would say " if they knew of the slight she had put upon him. To conceal this was the one object of his life at present, the thought that forever absorbed him.

Mr. Frayling felt that it would be a relief to get away from his son-in-law : " If the fellow would only speak ! " he exclaimed when he was alone with his wife. " What the deuce he's always thinking about I can't imagine."

" He is in great grief," Mrs. Frayling maintained.

As soon as she was settled at Fraylingay she wrote to Evadne :

" MY POOR MISGUIDED CHILD :

" Your whole action since your marriage and your extraordinary resolution have occasioned your dear father, your poor husband, and myself the very greatest anxiety and pain. We have grave fears for your sanity. I have never in my life heard of a young lady acting in such a way. Your poor husband has been very sweet and good all through this dreadful trial. He very much fears the ridicule which of course would attach to him if his brother officers hear what has happened ; but so far, I am thankful to say, no inkling of the true state of the case has leaked out. The servants talk, of course, but they *know* nothing. What they suspect, however, is, I believe, that you have gone out of your mind, and I even ventured to suggest something of the kind to Jenny, who, after all these years, is naturally concerned at the sight of my deep distress. I assure you I have taken nothing since your letter arrived but a little tea. So do, dear child, end this distressing state of things by returning to your right state of mind *at once*. You are a legally married woman, and you must obey the law of the land ; but of course your husband would rather not invoke the law and make a public scandal if he can help it. He does not wish to force your inclinations in any way, and he therefore generously gives you more time to consider. In fact he says : ' She must come back of her own free will.' * And he is as ready, I am sure, as your father and myself are, to forgive you freely for all the trouble and anxiety you have caused him, and is waiting to welcome you to his heart and home with open arms.

"And, Evadne, remember : a woman has it in her power to change even a reprobate into a worthy man—and I know from the way George talks that he is far from being a reprobate now. And just think what a work that is ! The angels in heaven rejoice over the sinner that repents, and you have before you a sphere of action which it should gladden your heart to contemplate. I don't deny that there *were* things in George's past life which it is very sad to think of, but women have always much to bear. It is our *cross*, and you must take up yours patiently and be sure that you will have your reward. *Whom the Lord loveth he chasteneth.* I wish now that I had talked to you on the subject before you were married, and prepared you to meet some forms of wickedness in a proper spirit ; you would not then have been at the mercy of the wicked woman who has caused all this mischief. She is some clever designing adventuress, I suppose, and she must have told you dreadful things which you should never have heard of at your age, and I suspect that jealousy is at the bottom of it all. She may herself have been cast off in her wickedness for my own sweet innocent child's sake. When I think of all the happiness she has destroyed, of these dark days following such bright prospects, I could see her *whipped*, Evadne, I could indeed. Everything had arranged itself so beautifully. He

---

* What he did say exactly was : "She wen.. of her own accord, and she must come back of her own accord, or not at all. Just as she likes. *I* shall not trouble about her."

is an excellent match. The Irish property, which he *must*
have, is one of the best in the country, and as there is only one
fragile child between him and the Scotch estates, you might
almost venture to calculate upon becoming mistress of them
also. And then, he certainly is a handsome and attractive
man of most charming manners, so what more do you want ?
He is a good Churchman too. You know how regularly he
accompanied you to every service. And, *really* if you will just
think for a *moment*, I am sure you will see yourself that you
have made a terrible mistake, and repent while it is called to-
day. But we do not blame you entirely, dear. You have surprised and distressed us, but we all freely forgive you, and if
you will come back at once, you need fear *no* reproaches, for
not another word will *ever* be said on the subject.—I am, dear
child,

" Ever your loving mother,

" Elizabeth Frayling."

" P. S.—Your father is so horrified at your conduct that he
declares he will neither write to you nor speak to you until
you return to your duty."

Evadne took a day and a half to consider her mother's
letter, and then she wrote the following reply :

"The Close, Morningquest, 9th October.

" My Dear Mother :

"I answer your postscript first, because I am cut to the
quick by my father's attitude   I was sure that, large-minded
and just as I have always thought him, he would allow that a
woman is entitled to her own point of view in a matter which,
to begin with, concerns her own happiness more than anybody else's, and that if she accepts a fallen angel for a husband,
knowing him to be such, she shows a poor appreciation of her
own worth. I am quite ready to rejoice over any sinner that
repents if I may rejoice as the angels themselves do, that is to
say, at a safe distance. I would not be a stumbling block in
the way of any man's reformation. I only maintain that I am
not the right person to undertake such a task, and that if
women are to do it at all, they should be mothers or other experienced persons, and not young wives.

"I am pained that you should make such a cruel insinuation
against the character and motives of the lady whom I have to

bless for my escape from a detestable position. But even if she had been the kind of character you describe, do I understand you to mean that it would have been a triumph for me to have obtained the reversion of her equally culpable associate? that I ought, in fact, to have gratefully accepted a secondhand sort of man! You would not counsel a son of yours to marry a society woman of the same character as Major Colquhoun, and neither more nor less degraded, for the purpose of reforming her, would you, mother? I know you would not. And as a woman's soul is every bit as precious as a man's, one sees what cant this talk of reformation is. It seems to me that such cases as Major Colquhoun's are for the clergy, who have both experience and authority, and not for young wives to tackle. And, at any rate, although reforming reprobates may be a very noble calling, I do not, at nineteen, feel that I have any vocation for it ; and I would respectfully suggest that you, mother, with your experience, your known piety, and your sweet disposition, would be a much more suitable person to reform Major Colquhoun than I should be. His past life seems to inspire you with no horror ; the knowledge of it makes *me* shrink from him. My husband must be a Christ-like man. I have very strong convictions, you see, on the subject of the sanctity and responsibilities of marriage. There are certain conditions which I hold to be essential on both sides. I hold also that human beings are sacred and capable of deep desecration, and that marriage, their closest bond, is sacred too, the holiest relationship in life, and one which should only be entered upon with the greatest care, and in the most reverent spirit. I see no reason why marriage should be a lottery. But evidently Major Colquhoun's views upon the subject differ widely from mine, and it seems to me utterly impossible that we should ever be able to accommodate ourselves to each other's principles. Had I known soon enough that he did not answer to my requirements, I should have dismissed him at once, and thought no more about him, and all this misery would never have occurred ; but having been kept in ignorance, I consider that I was inveigled into consenting, that the vow I made was taken under a grave misapprehension, that therefore there is nothing either holy or binding in it, and that every law of morality absolves me from fulfilling my share of the contract. This, of course, is merely considering marriage from the higher and most moral point of view ; but even when I think of it in the lower and more ordinary way, I find the same conclusion forces itself upon me. For there certainly is no romance in marrying a man old already in every emotion, between whom and me the recollection of some other woman would be forever intruding. My whole soul sickens at the possibility, and I think that it must have been women old in emotion themselves who first tolerated the staleness of such lovers.

"I feel that my letter is very inadequate, mother. The thought that I am forced to pain and oppose you distracts me. But I have tried conscientiously to show you exactly what my conviction and principles are, and I do think I have a right to beg that you will at least be tolerant, however much you may disagree with me.

"Your affectionate daughter,

"EVADNE."

Mrs. Frayling's reply to this letter arrived by return of post, red hot. Evadne, glancing at the envelope, frowned to find herself addressed as " Mrs. Colquhoun." The name had not struck her on her mother's first communication, which was also the first occasion upon which she had been so addressed, and it had not occurred to her until now that she would have to be " Mrs. Colquhoun " from thenceforth, whether she liked it or not. She felt it to be unjust, distinctly ; a gross infringement of the liberty of the subject, and she opened her mother's letter with rage and rebellion at her heart, and found the contents anything but soothing to such a state of mind. It ran as follows ·

" YOU MOST UNNATURAL CHILD :
" We shall all be disgraced if this story gets out. So far, the world knows nothing, and there is time for you to save yourself. I warn you that your father's anger is extreme. He says he shall be obliged to put you in a lunatic asylum if you do not give in at once, and consent to live with your husband. And there is the law, too, which your husband can invoke. And think of your five sisters. Will anybody marry them after such a business with you ? Their prospects will be simply ruined by your heartless selfishness. No girl in my young days would have acted so outrageously. It is not decent. It is positively immodest. I repeat that your father is the proper person to judge for you. You know nothing of the world. and even if you did, you are not old enough to

think for yourself. You do not imagine yourself to be a sort
of seer, I hope, better informed by intuition than your parents
are by wisdom and knowledge, for that would be a certain
sign of insanity. Your father thinks your opposition is mere
conceit, and certainly no good can come of it. All right
minded women have submitted and suffered patiently, and
have had their reward. Think of the mother of St. Augus-
tin! Her husband returned to her penitent after years of
depravity. ' Every wise woman buildeth her house ; but the
foolish pluck it down,' and that is what you are doing. ' A
continual dropping on a rainy day and a contentious woman are
alike.' For Heaven's sake, my child, do not become a contentious woman. See also Prov. viii. If only you had read
your Bible regularly every day, prayed humbly for a contrite
heart, and *obeyed your parents*, as you have always been taught
to do, we should never have had all this dreadful trouble with
you; but you show yourself wanting in respect in every way
and in all right and proper feeling, and really I don't know
what to do. I don't indeed. Oh, do remember that forgiveness is still offered to you, and repent while it is called to-day.
I assure you that your poor husband is even more ready than
your father and myself to forgive and forget.

" I pray for you continually, Evadne, I do indeed. If you
have any natural feeling at all, write and relieve my anxiety at
once.

" Your affectionate mother,

" ELIZABETH FRAYLING."

Evadne read this letter in the drawing room, and stood for
a little leaning against the window frame looking up at the
Close, at the old trees dishevelled by the recent gale, and at
the weather-beaten wall of the south transept of the cathedral,
from which the beautiful spire sprang upward ; but she rendered no account to herself of these marvels of nature and art.

Something in her attitude as she stood there, with one hand
resting flat upon the window frame high above her head and
the other hanging down beside her loosely holding her
mother's letter, attracted Mrs. Orton Beg's attention, and
made her wonder what thought her niece was so intent upon.
Not one of the thoughts of youth, which are " long, long
thoughts," apparently, for the expression of her countenance
was not far away, and neither was it sad nor angry, but only
intent. Presently, she turned from the window, languidly

strolled to the writing table, re-read her letter, and began to write without moving a muscle of her face. As she proceeded, however, she compressed her lips and bent her brows portentously, and Mrs. Orton Beg was sure that she heard no note of the mellow chime which sounded once while she was so engaged, and seemed to her aunt to plead with her solemnly to cast her care on the great Power watching, and continue passively in the old worn grooves, as Mrs. Orton Beg herself had done.

Evadne began abruptly :

"THE CLOSE, MORNINGQUEST, 13th October.
" DEAR MOTHER :

" You say that no girl in your young days would have behaved so outrageously as I am doing. I wish you had said ' so decidedly,' instead of ' outrageously,' for I am sure that any resistance to the old iniquitous state of things is a quite hopeful sign of coming change for the better. We are a long way from the days when it was considered right and becoming for women in our position to sit in their ' parlours,' do Berlin woolwork, and say nothing. We should call that conniving now. But, happily, women are no longer content to be part of the livestock about the place ; they have acquired the right of reason and judgment in matters concerning themselves in particular, and the welfare of the world at large. Public opinion now is composed of what *we* think, to a very great extent. You remind me of what other women have done, and how patiently they have submitted. I have found the same thing said over and over again in the course of my reading, but I have not yet found any particular mention made of the great good which would naturally have come of all the submission which has been going on for so many centuries, if submission on our part is truly an effectual means of checking sin. On the contrary. St. Monica doubtless made things pleasanter for her own husband by rewarding him with forgiveness, a happy home, and good nursing, when he returned to her exhausted by vice, but at the same time she set a most pernicious example. So long as men believe that women will forgive anything they will do anything. Do you see what I mean ? The mistake from the beginning has been that women have practised self-sacrifice, when they should have been teaching men self-control. You say that I do not know the world, but my father does, and that, therefore, I must let him judge for me. He probably does know the world, but he quite evidently does not know me. Our point of view, you see, is necessarily very different. I have no doubt that Major Colquhoun is agreeable in the temporary good fellowship of the smoking room, and he is agreeable in the drawing room also, but society and his own interests require him to be so; it is a trick of manner, merely, which may conceal the most objectionable mind. Character is what we have most to consider in the choosing of a partner for life, and how are we to consider it except by actions, such as a man's misdeeds, which are specially the outcome of his own individuality, and are calculated in their consequences to do more injury to his family than could be compensated for by the most charming manners in the world.

" Of course I deprecate my father's anger, but I must again repeat I do not consider that I deserve it.

" The lunatic asylum is a nonsensical threat, and the law I am inclined to invoke myself for the purpose of ventilating the question. Do I understand that Major Colquhoun presumes to send *me* messages of forgiveness? What has *he* to forgive, may I ask? Surely *I* am the person who has been imposed upon. Do not, I beg, allow him to repeat such an impertinence.

But, mother, why do you persistently ignore my reason for refusing to live with Major Colquhoun? Summed up it comes to this really, and I give it now vulgarly, baldly, boldly, and once for all. *Major Colquhoun is not good enough, and I won't have him.* That is plain, I am sure, and I must beg you to accept it as my final decision. The tone of our correspondence is becoming undignified on both sides, and the correspondence itself must end here. I shall not write another word on the subject, and I only wish you had not compelled me to write so much. Forgive me, mother, do, for being myself—I don't know how else to put it; but I know that none of the others could do as I have done, and yet I cannot help it. I cannot act otherwise and preserve my honesty and self-respect. It is conscience, and not caprice, that I am obeying; I wish I could make you realize that. But, at all events, don't write me any more hard words, mother. They burn into my memory and obliterate the loving thoughts I have of you. It is terrible to be met with bitterness and reproach, where hitherto one has known nothing but kindness and indulgence, so, I do entreat you, mother, once more to forgive me for being myself, and above everything, to say nothing which will destroy my affection for you.

"Believe me, I always have been, and hope always to be,
                    "Your most loving child,
                                        "Evadne."

The last lines were crowded into the smallest possible space, and there had hardly been room enough for her name at the end. She glanced at the clock as she folded the letter, and finding that there was only just time to catch the post she rang for a servant and told her to take it at once. Then she took her old stand in the window, and watched the girl hurrying up the Close, holding the white letter carelessly, and waving it to and fro on a level with her shoulder as she went.

"I wish I had had time to re-write it," Evadne thought; "shall I call her back? No. Anything will be better for mother than another day's suspense. But I think I might have expressed myself better. I don't know, though." She turned from the window, and met her aunt's kind eyes fixed upon her.

"You are flushed, Evadne," the latter said. "Were you writing home?"

"Yes, auntie," Evadne answered wearily.

"You are looking more worried than I have seen you yet."

"I *am* worried, auntie, and I lost my temper. I could not help it, and I am dissatisfied. I know I have said too much, and I have said the same thing over and over again, and gone round and round the subject, too, and altogether I am disheartened."

"I cannot imagine you saying too much about anything, Evadne," Mrs. Orton Beg commented, smiling.

"When I am speaking, you mean. But that is different. I am always afraid to speak, but I dare write anything. The subject is closed now, however. I shall write no more." She advanced listlessly, and leaned against the mantelpiece close beside the couch on which her aunt was lying.

"Have you ever felt compelled to say something which all the time you hate to say, and afterward hate yourself for having said? That is what I always seem to be doing now." She looked up at the cathedral as she spoke. "How I envy you your power to say exactly what you mean," she added.

"Who told you I always say exactly what I mean?" her aunt asked, smiling.

" Well, exactly what you ought to say, then," Evadne answered, responding to the smile.

Mrs. Orton Beg sighed and resumed her knitting. She was making some sort of wrap out of soft white wool, and Evadne noticed the glint of her rings as she worked, and also the delicacy of her slender white hands as she held them up in the somewhat tiring attitude which her position on the couch necessitated.

" How patient you are, auntie," Evadne said, and then she bent down and kissed her forehead and cheeks.

" It is easy to be patient when one's greatest trial is only the waiting for a happy certainty," Mrs. Orton Beg answered. " But you will be patient too, Evadne, sooner or later. You are at the passionate age now, but the patient one will come all in good time."

" You have always a word of comfort," Evadne said.

" There is one word more I would say, although I do not wish to influence you," Mrs. Orton Beg began hesitatingly.

" You mean *submit*," Evadne answered, and shook her head. " No, that word is of no use to me. Mine is *rebel*. It seems to me that those who dare to rebel in every age are they who make life possible for those whom temperament compels to submit. It is the rebels who extend the boundary of right little by little, narrowing the confines of wrong, and crowding it out of existence."

She stood for a moment looking down on the ground with bent brows, thinking deeply, and then she slowly sauntered from the room, and presently passed the south window with her hat in her hand, took one turn round the garden, and then subsided into the high-backed chair, on which she had sat and fed her fancy with dreams of love a few weeks before her marriage. The day was one of those balmy mild ones which come occasionally in mid-October. The sheltered garden had suffered little in the recent gale. From where Mrs. Orton Beg reclined there was no visible change in the background of single dahlias, sunflowers, and the old brick wall curtained with creepers, nor was there any great difference apparent in the girl herself. The delicate shell-pink of passion had faded to milky white, her eyes were heavy, and her attitude somewhat fatigued, but that was all ; a dance the night before would have left her so exactly, and Mrs. Orton Beg, watching her, wondered at the small effect of " blighted affection " as she saw it in Evadne, compared with the terrible consequences

which popular superstition attributes to "a disappointment."
Evadne had certainly suffered, but more because her parents,
in whom she had always had perfect confidence, and whom
she had known and loved as long as she could remember anything, had failed her, than because she had been obliged to
cast a man out of her life who had merely lighted it for a few
months with a flame which she recognized now as lurid at
the best, and uncertain, and which she would never have
desired to keep burning continually with that feverish glare to
the extinguishing of every other interesting object. She would
have been happiest when passion ended and love began, as it
does in happy marriages.

And she was herself comparing the two states of mind as she
sat there. She was conscious of a blank now, dull and dispir-
iting enough, but no more likely to endure than the absorbing
passion it succeeded. She knew it for an interregnum, and
was thinking of the books she would send for when she had
mastered herself sufficiently to be interested in books again. It
was as if her mind had been out of health, but was convalescent
now and recovering its strength ; and she was as well aware
of the fact as if she had been suffering from some physical ail-
ment which had interrupted her ordinary pursuits, and was making plans for the time when she should be able to resume them.

While so engaged, however, she fell asleep, as convalescents
do, and Mrs. Orton Beg smiled at the consummation. It was
not romantic, but it was eminently healthy.

At the same time, she heard the hall door opened from
without as by one who had a right to enter familiarly, and a
man's step in the hall.

"Come in," she said, in answer to a firm tap at the door,
and smiled, looking over her shoulder as it opened.

It was Dr. Galbraith on his way back through Morningquest
to his own place, Fountain Towers.

"I am so glad to see you," said Mrs. Orton Beg as he took
her hand.

"I am on my way back from the Castle," he rejoined, sitting down beside her ; "and I have just come in for a moment
to see how the ankle progresses."

"Quicker now, I am thankful to say," she answered. "I
can get about the house comfortably if I rest in between times.
But is there anything wrong at the Castle ?"

"The same old thing," said Dr. Galbraith, with a twinkle in
his bright gray eyes. "The Duke has been seeing visions—

determination of blood to the head ; and Lady Fulda has been dreaming dreams—fatigue and fasting. Food and rest for her—she will be undisturbed by dreams to-night ; and a severe course of dieting for him."

Mrs. Orton Beg smiled. "Really life is becoming too prosaic," she said, "since you dreadfully clever people began to discover a reason for everything. Lady Fulda's beauty and goodness would have been enough to convince any man at one time that she is a saint indeed, and privileged to heal the sick and converse with angels ; but you are untouched by either."

"On the contrary," he answered, "I never see her or think of her without acknowledging to myself that she is one of the loveliest and most angelic women in the world. And she has the true magnetic touch of a nurse too. There is healing in it. I have seen it again and again. But that is a natural process. Many quite wicked doctors are endowed in the same way, and even more strongly than she is. There can be no doubt about that——" He broke off with a little gesture and smiled genially.

"But anything *beyond!*" Mrs. Orton Beg supplemented ; "anything supernatural, in fact, you ridicule."

"One cannot ridicule *anything* with which Lady Fulda's name is associated," he answered. "But tell me," he exclaimed, catching sight of Evadne placidly sleeping in the high-backed chair, with her hat in her hand held up so as to conceal the lower part of her face ; "Are visions about? *Is* that one that I see there before me? If I were Faust, I should love such a Marguerite. I wish she would let her hat drop. I want to see the lower part of her face. The upper part satisfies me. It is fine. The balance of brow and frontal development are perfect."

Mrs. Orton Beg coloured with a momentary annoyance. She had forgotten that Evadne was there, but Dr. Galbraith had entered so abruptly that there would have been no time to warn her away in any case.

"No vision," she began—"or if a vision, one of the nineteenth century sort, tangible, and of satisfying continuance. She is a niece of mine, and I warn you in case you have a momentary desire to forsake your books and become young in mind again for her sake that she is a very long way after Marguerite, whom I think she would consider to have been a very weak and foolish person. I can imagine her saying about Faust : 'Fancy sacrificing one's self for the transient pleasure

of a moonlight meeting or two with a man, and a few jewels
however unique, when one can *live !* ' in italics and with a note
of admiration. ' Why, I can put my elbow here on the arm of
my chair and my head on my hand, and in a moment I perceive delights past, present, and to come, of equal intensity,
more certain quality, and longer continuance than passion. I
perceive the gradual growth of knowledge through all the
ages, the clouds of ignorance and superstition slowly parting,
breaking up, and rolling away, to let the light of science
shine—science being truth. And there is all art, and all
natural beauty from the beginning—everything that lasts and
is life. Why, even to think on such subjects warms my whole
being with a glow of enthusiasm which is in itself a more
exquisite pleasure than passion, and not alloyed like the latter
with uncertainty, that terrible ache. I might take my walk in
the garden with my own particular Faust like any other girl,
and as I take my glass of champagne at dinner, for its pleasurably stimulating quality, but I hope I should do both in
moderation. And as to making Faust my all, or even giving
him so large a share of my attention as to limit my capacity
for other forms of enjoyment, absurd ! We are long past the
time when there was only one incident of interest in a woman's
life, and that was its love affair ! There was no sense of proportion in those days !' "

"Is that how you interpret her?" he said. "One who holds
herself well in hand, bent upon enjoying every moment of her
life and all the variety of it, perceiving that it is stupid to narrow it down to the indulgence of one particular set of emotions, and determined not to swamp every faculty by constant
cultivation of the animal instincts to which all ages have created altars ! Best for herself, I suppose, but hardly possible
at present. The capacity, you know, is only coming. Women
have been cramped into a small space so long that they cannot
expand all at once when they *are* let out ; there must be a great
deal of stretching and growing, and when they are not on their
guard, they will often find themselves falling into the old
attitude, as newborn babes are apt to resume the ante-natal
position. She will have the perception, the inclination ; but
the power—unless she is exceptional, the power will only be
for her daughter's daughter."

"Then she must suffer and do no good?"

"She must suffer, yes ; but I don't know about the rest
She may be a seventh wave, you know ! "

" What is a seventh wave ? "

" It is a superstition of the fisher-folks. They say that when the tide is coming in it pauses always, and remains stationary between every seventh wave, waiting for the next, and unable to rise any higher till it comes to carry it on ; and it has always seemed to me that the tide of human progress is raised at intervals to higher levels at a bound in some such way. The seventh waves of humanity are men and women who, by the impulse of some one action which comes naturally to them but is new to the race, gather strength to come up to the last halting place of the tide, and to carry it on with them ever so far beyond." He stopped abruptly, and brushed his hand over his forehead. " Now that I have said that," he added, " it seems as old as the cathedral there, and as familiar, yet the moment before I spoke it appeared to have only just occurred to me. If it is an ill-digested reminiscence and you come across the original in some book, I am afraid you will lose your faith in me forever ; but I pray you of your charity make due allowance. I must go."

"Oh, no, not yet a moment !" Mrs. Orton Beg exclaimed. " I want to ask you : How are Lady Adeline and the twins ? "

" I haven't seen Lady Adeline for a month," he answered, rising to go as he spoke. " But Dawne tells me that the twins are as awful as ever. It is a question of education now, and it seems that the twins have their own ideas on the subject, and are teaching their parents. But take care of your girlie out there," he added, his strong face softening as he took a last look at her. " Her body is not so robust as her brain, I should say, and it is late in the year to be sitting out of doors."

" Tell me, Dr. Galbraith," Mrs. Orton Beg began, detaining him, " you are a Scotchman, you should have the second sight ; tell me the fate of my girlie out there. I am anxious about her."

" She will marry," he answered in his deliberate way, humouring her, " but not have many children, and her husband's name should be George."

" Oh, most oracular ! a very oracle ! a Delphic oracle, only to be interpreted by the event ! "

" Just so ! " he answered from the door, and then he was gone.

" Evadne, come in ! " Mrs. Orton Beg called. " It is getting damp." Evadne roused herself and entered at once by the window.

"I have been hearing voices through my dim dreaming consciousness," she said. "Have you had a visitor?"

"Only the doctor," her aunt replied. "By the way, Evadne," she added, "what is Major Colquhoun's Christian name?"

"George," Evadne answered, surprised. "Why, auntie?"

"Nothing; I wanted to know."

CHAPTER XVI.

WHEN breakfast was over at Fraylingay next morning, and the young people had left the table, Mrs. Frayling helped herself to another cup of coffee, and solemnly opened Evadne's last letter. The coffee was cold, for the poor lady had been waiting, not daring to take the last cup herself, because she knew that the moment she did so her husband would want more. The emptying of the urn was the signal which usually called up his appetite for another cup. He might refuse several times, and even leave the table amiably, so long as there was any left; but the knowledge or suspicion that there was none, set up a sense of injury, unmistakably expressed in his countenance, and not to be satisfied by having more made immediately, although he invariably ordered it just to mark his displeasure. He would get up and ring for it emphatically, and would even sit with it before him for some time after it came, but would finally go out without touching it, and be, as poor Mrs. Frayling mentally expressed it: "Oh, dear! quite upset for the rest of the day."

On this occasion, however, the pleasure of a wholly new grievance left no space in his fickle mind for the old-worn item of irritation, and he never even noticed that the coffee was done. "Dear George" sat beside Mrs. Frayling. She kept him there in order to be able to bestow a stray pat on his hand, or make him some other sign of that maternal tenderness of which she considered the poor dear fellow stood so much in need.

Mr. Frayling sat at the end of the table reading a local paper with one eye, as it were, and watching his wife for her news with the other. A severely critical expression sat singularly ill upon his broad face, which was like a baked apple, puffy, and wrinkled, and red, and there was about him a queerly pursed-up air of settled opposition to everything which did duty for both the real and spurious object of his attention.

Mrs. Frayling read the letter through to herself, and then she put it down on the table and raised her handkerchief to her eyes with a heavy sigh.

"Well, what does she say now," Mr. Frayling exclaimed, throwing down the local paper and giving way to his impatience openly.

"Dear George" was perfectly cool.

"She says," Mrs. Frayling enjoined between two sniffs, "that Major Colquhoun isn't good enough, and she wont have him."

"Well, I. understand that, at all events, better than anything else she has said," Major Colquhoun observed, almost as if a weight had been removed from his mind. "And I am quite inclined to come to terms with her, for I don't care much myself for a young lady who gets into hysterics about things that other women think nothing of."

"Oh, *don't* say think *nothing* of, George," Mrs. Frayling deprecated. "We lament and deplore, but we forgive and endure."

"It comes to the same thing," said Major Colquhoun.

A big dog which sat beside him, with its head on his knee, thumped his tail upon the ground here and whined sympa-thetically; and he laid one hand caressingly upon his head, while he twirled his big blond moustache with the other. He was fond of children and animals, and all creatures that fawned upon him and were not able to argue if they disagreed with him, or resent it if he kicked them, actually or metaphor-ically speaking; not that he was much given to that kind of thing. He was agreeable naturally as all pleasure-loving peo-ple are; only when he did lose his temper that was the way he showed it. He would cut a woman to the quick with a word, and knock a man down; but both ebullitions were momentary as a rule. It was really too much trouble to cherish anger.

And just then he was thinking quite as much about his moustache as about his wife. It had once been the pride of his life, but had come to be the cause of some misgivings; for "heavy moustaches" had gone out of fashion in polite society.

Mr. Frayling followed up the last remark. "This is very hard on you, Colquhoun, very hard," he declared, pushing his plate away from him; "and I may say that it is very hard on me too. But it just shows you what would come of the Higher

Education of Women ! Why, they'd raise some absurd standard of excellence, and want to import angels from Eden if
we didn't come up to it."

Major Colquhoun looked depressed.

"Yes," Mrs. Frayling protested, shaking her head. "She
says her husband must be a Christlike man. She says men
have agreed to accept Christ as an example of what a man
should be, and asserts that therefore they must feel in themselves that they *could* live up to his standard if they chose."

"There now !" Mr. Frayling exclaimed triumphantly.
"That is just what I said. A Christlike man, indeed ! What
absurdity will women want next ? I don't know what to
advise, Colquhoun. I really don't."

"Can't you *order* her ?" Mrs. Frayling suggested.

"Order her ! How can *I* order her ? She belongs to
Major Colquhoun now," he retorted irritably, but with a fine
conservative regard for the rights of property.

"And this is the way she keeps her vow of obedience,"
Major Colquhoun muttered.

"Oh, but you see—the poor misguided child considers that
she made the vow under a misapprehension," Mrs. Frayling
explained, her maternal instinct acting on the defensive when
her offspring's integrity was attacked, and making the position
clear to her. "Don't you think, dear,"—to her husband—
"that if you asked the bishop, he would talk to her."

"The bishop !" Mr. Frayling ejaculated with infinite scorn
"*I* know what women are when they go off like this. Once
they set up opinions of their own, there's *no* talking to them.
Why, haven't they gone to the stake for their opinions ? She
wouldn't obey the whole bench of bishops in her present frame
of mind ; and, if they condescended to talk to her, they
would only confirm her belief in her own powers. She would
glory to find herself opposing what she calls her opinions to
theirs."

"Oh, the child is mad !" Mrs. Frayling wailed. "I've said
it all along. She's quite mad."

"Is there any insanity in the family ?" Major Colquhoun
asked, looking up suspiciously.

"None, none whatever," Mr. Frayling hastened to assure
him. "There has never been a case. In fact, the women
on both sides have always been celebrated for good sense
and exceptional abilities—*for* women, of course ; and several
of the men have distinguished themselves, as you know."

"That does not alter *my* opinion in the least!" Mrs Frayling put in. "Evadne must be mad."

"She's worse, I think," Major Colquhoun exclaimed in a tone of deep disgust. "She's worse than mad. She's clever. You can do something with a mad woman; you can lock her up; but a clever woman's the devil. And I'd never have thought it of her," he added regretfully. "Such a nice quiet little thing as she seemed, with hardly a word to say for herself. You wouldn't have imagined that she knew what 'views' are, let alone having any of her own. But that is just the way with women. There's no being up to them."

"That is true," said Mr. Frayling.

"Well, I don't know where she got them," Mrs. Frayling protested, "for I am sure *I* haven't any. But she seems to know so much about—*everything!*" she declared, glancing at the letter. "At *her* age I knew *nothing!*"

"I can vouch for that!" her husband exclaimed. He was one of those men who oppose the education of women might and main, and then jeer at them for knowing nothing. He was very particular about the human race when it was likely to suffer by an injurious indulgence on the part of women, but when it was a question of extra port wine for himself, he never considered the tortures of gout he might be entailing upon his own hapless descendants. However, there was an excuse for him on this occasion, for it is not every day that an irritated man has an opportunity of railing at his wife's incapacity and the inconvenient intelligence of his daughter both in one breath. "But how has Evadne obtained all this mischievous information? I cannot think how she could have obtained it!" he ejaculated, knitting his brows at his wife in a suspicious way, as he always did when this importunate thought recurred to him. In such ordinary everyday matters as the management of his estate, and his other duties as a county gentleman, and also in solid comprehension of the political situation of the period, he was by no means wanting; but his mind simply circled round and round this business of Evadne's like a helpless swimmer in a whirlpool, able to keep afloat, but with nothing to take hold of. The risk of sending the mind of an elderly gentleman of settled prejudices spinning "down the ringing grooves of change" at such a rate is considerable.

During the day he wandered up to the rooms which had been Evadne's. They were kept very much as she was

accustomed to have them, but there was that something of
bareness about them, and a kind of spick-and-spanness conveying a sense of emptiness and desertion which strikes cold
to the heart when it comes of the absence of someone dear.
And Mr. Frayling felt the discomfort of it. The afternoon
sunlight slanted across the little sitting room, falling on the
backs of a row of well worn books, and showing the scars of
use and abuse on them. Without deliberate intention, Mr.
Frayling followed the ray, and read the bald titles by its un-
compromising clearness—histology, pathology, anatomy, physiology, prophylactics, therapeutics, botany, natural history,
ancient and outspoken history, not to mention the modern
writers and the various philosophies. Mr. Frayling took out
a work on sociology, opened it, read a few passages which
Evadne had marked, and solemnly ejaculated, " Good Heavens ! " several times. He could not have been more horrified
had the books been " Mademoiselle de Maupin," " Nana," " La
Terre," " Madame Bovary," and " Sapho " ; yet, had women
been taught to read the former and reflect upon them, our
sacred humanity might have been saved sooner from the depth
of degradation depicted in the latter.

The discovery of these books was an adding of alkali to
the acid of Mr. Frayling's disposition at the moment, and he
went down to look for his wife while he was still effervescing.
How did Evadne get them ? he wanted to know. Mrs. Frayling could not conceive. She had forgotten all about Evadne's
discovery of the box of books in the attic, and the sort of
general consent she had given when Evadne worried her for
permission to read them.

" She must be a most deceitful girl. I shall go and talk to
her myself," Mr. Frayling concluded.

And doubtless, if only he had had a pair of wings to spread,
he would presently have appeared sailing over the cathedral
into the Close at Morningquest, a portly bird, in a frock coat,
tall hat, and a very bad temper.

But, poor gentleman ! he really was an object for compassion. All his ideas of propriety and the natural social order
of the universe were being outraged, and by his favourite
daughter too, the one whom everybody thought so like him.
And in truth, she was like him, especially in the matter of
sticking to her own opinion ; just the very thing he had no
patience with, for he detested obstinate people. He said so
himself. He did not go, however. Having preparations to

make and a train to wait for, gave him time to reflect, and, perceiving that the interview must inevitably be of a most disagreeable nature, he decided to send his wife next day to reason with her daughter.

Mrs. Frayling came upon Evadne unawares, and the shock it gave the girl to see her mother all miserably agitated and worn with worry, was a more powerful point in favour of the success of the latter's mission than any argument would have been.

The poor lady was handsomely dressed, and of a large presence calculated to inspire awe in inferiors unaccustomed to it. She was a well-preserved woman, with even teeth, thick brown hair, scarcely tinged with gray, and a beautiful soft transparent pink and white complexion, and Evadne had always seen her in a state of placid content, never really interrupted except by such surface squalls as were caused by having to scold the children, or the shedding of a few sunshiny tears ; and had thought her lovely. But when she entered now, and had given her daughter the corner of her cheek to kiss for form's sake, she sat down with quivering lips and watery eyes all red with crying, and a broken-up aspect generally which cut the girl to the quick.

"Oh, mother !" Evadne cried, kneeling down on the floor beside her, and putting her arms about her. "It grieves me deeply to see you so distressed."

But Mrs. Frayling held herself stiffly, refusing to be embraced, and presenting a surface for the operation as unyielding as the figurehead of a ship.

"If you are sincere," she said severely, "you will give up this nonsense at once."

Evadne's arms dropped, and she rose to her feet, and stood, with fingers interlaced in front of her, looking down at her mother for a moment, and then up at the cathedral. Her talent for silence came in naturally here.

"You don't say anything, because you know there is nothing to be said for you," Mrs. Frayling began. "You've broken my heart, Evadne, indeed you have. And after everything had gone off so well too. What a tragedy ! How could you forget ? And on the very day itself ! Your wedding day, just think ! Why, we keep ours every year. And all your beautiful presents, and such a trousseau ! I am sure no girl was ever more kindly considered by father, mother, friends— everybody ! "

She was obliged to stop short for a moment. Ideas, by

which she was not much troubled as a rule, had suddenly crowded in so thick upon her when she began to speak, that she became bewildered, and in an honest attempt to make the most of them all, only succeeded in laying hold of an end of each, to the great let and hindrance of all coherency as she herself felt when she pulled up.

" Yes, you may well look up at the cathedral," she began again, unreasonably provoked by Evadne's attitude. " But what good does it do you ? I should have supposed that the hallowed associations of this place would have restored you to a better frame of mind."

" I do feel the force of association strongly," Evadne answered ; " and that is why I shrink from Major Colquhoun. People have their associations as well as places, and those that cling about him are anything but hallowed."

Mrs. Frayling assumed an aspect of the deepest depression : " I never heard a girl talk so in my life," she said. " It is positively indelicate. It really is. But *we* have done all we could. Now, honestly, have you anything to complain of ?"

" Nothing, mother, nothing," Evadne exclaimed. " Oh, I wish I could make you understand ! "

" Understand ! What is there to understand ? It is easy enough to understand that you have behaved outrageously. And written letters you ought to be ashamed of. Quoting Scripture too, for your own purposes. I cannot think that you are in your right mind, Evadne, I really cannot. No girl ever acted so before. If only you would read your Bible properly, and say your prayers, you would see for yourself and repent. Besides, what is to become of you ? We can't have you at home again, you know. How we are any of us to appear in the neighbourhood if the story gets about—and of course it must get about if you persist—I cannot think. And every-body said, too, how sweet you looked on your wedding day, Evadne ; but I said, when those children changed clothes, it was unnatural, and would bring bad luck ; and there was a terrible gale blowing too, and it rained. Everything went so well up to the very day itself ; but, since then, for no reason at all but your own wicked obstinacy, all has gone wrong. You ought to have been coming back from your honeymoon soon now, and here you are in hiding—yes, literally *in hiding like a criminal*, ashamed to be seen. It must be a terrible trial for my poor sister, Olive, and a great imposition on her good nature, having you here. You consider no one. And I might have been a grandmother in time too, although I don't so much mind about that, for I don't think it is any blessing to a military man to have a family. They have to move about so much. But, however, all that it seems is over. And your poor sisters—five of them—are curious to know what George is doing all this time at Fraylingay, and asking questions. You cannot have imagined *my* difficulties, or you never would have been so selfish and unnatural. I had to box Barbara's ears the other day, I had indeed, and who will marry them now, I should like to know? If only you had turned Roman Catholic and gone into a convent, or died, or never been born— oh, dear! oh, dear!"

Evadne looked down at her mother again. She was very white, but she did not utter a word.

"Why don't you speak?" Mrs. Frayling exclaimed. "Why do you stand there like a stone or statue, deaf to all my arguments?"

Evadne sighed: "Mother, I will do anything you suggest except the one thing. I will not live with Major Colquhoun as his wife," she said.

"I thought so!" Mrs. Frayling exclaimed. "You will do everything but what you ought to do. It is just what your father says. Once you over-educate a girl, you can do nothing with her, she gives herself such airs; and you have managed to over-educate yourself somehow, although *how* remains a mystery. But one thing I am determined upon. Your poor sisters shall never have a book I don't know off by heart myself. I shall lock them all up. Not that it is much use, for no one will marry them now. No man will ever come to the house again to be robbed of his character, as Major Colquhoun has been by you. I am sure no one ever knew anything bad about him—at least *I* never did, whatever your father may have done—until you went and ferreted all those dreadful stories out. You are shameless, Evadne, you really are. And what good have you done by it all, I should like to know? When you might have done so much, too."

Mrs. Frayling paused here, and Evadne looked up at the cathedral again, feeling for her pitifully. This new view of her mother was another terrible disillusion, and the more the poor lady exposed herself, the greater Evadne felt was the claim she had upon her filial tenderness.

"Why don't you say something?" Mrs. Frayling recommenced.

" Mother, what *can* I say?"

" If you knew what a time I have had with your father and your husband, you would pity me. I can assure you George has been so sullen there was no doing anything with him, and the trouble I have had, and the excuses I have made for you, I am quite worn out. He said if you were that kind of girl you might go, and I've had to go down on my knees to him almost to make him forgive you. And now I will go down on my knees to you "—she exclaimed, acting on a veritable inspiration, and suiting the action to the word—" to beg you for the sake of your sisters, and for the love of God, not to disgrace us all!"

"Oh, mother—no! Don't do that. Get up—do get up! This is too dreadful!" Evadne cried, almost hysterically.

"Here I shall kneel until you give in," Mrs. Frayling sobbed, clasping her hands in the attitude of prayer to her daughter, and conscious of the strength of her position.

Evadne tried in vain to raise her. Her bonnet had slipped to one side, her dress had been caught up by the heels of her boots, and the soles were showing behind ; her mantle was disarranged , she was a figure for a farce ; but Evadne saw only her own mother, shaken with sobs, on her knees before her.

" Mother—mother," she cried, sinking into a chair, and covering her face with her hands to hide the dreadful spectacle : " Tell me what I am to do ! Suggest something ! "

"If you would even consent," Mrs. Frayling began, gathering herself up slowly, and standing over her daughter ; " if you would even consent to live in the same house with him until you get used to him and forget all this nonsense, I am sure he would agree   For he is *dreadfully* afraid of scandal, Evadne. I never knew a man more so. In fact, he shows nothing but right and proper feeling, and you will love him as much as ever again when you know him better, and get over all these exaggerated ideas. *Do* consent to this, dear child, for my sake. You shall have your own way in everything else. And I will arrange it all for you, and get his written promise to allow you to live in his house quite independently, like brother and sister, as long as you like, and there will be no awkwardness for you whatever. Do, my child, do consent to this," and the poor old lady knelt once more, and put her arms about her daughter, and wept aloud.

Evadne broke down. The sight of the dear face so distorted, the poor lips quivering, the kind eyes all swollen and blurred with tears was too much for her, and she flung her arms round her mother's neck and cried : " I consent, mother, for your sake—to keep up appearances ; but only that, mother, you promise me. You will arrange all that ? "

" I promise you, my dear, I promise," Mrs. Frayling rejoined, rising with alacrity, her countenance clearing on the instant, her heart swelling with the joy and pride of a great victory. She knew she had done what the whole bench of bishops could not have done—nor that most remarkable man, her husband, either, for the matter of that, and she enjoyed her triumph.

As she had anticipated, Major Colquhoun made no difficulty about the arrangement.

" I should not care a rap for an unwilling wife," he said. " Let her go *her* way, and I'll go mine. All I want now is to keep up appearances. It would be a deuced nasty thing for me if the story got about. Fellows would think there was more in it than there is."

" But she will come round," said Mrs. Frayling. " If only you are nice to her, and I am sure you will be, she is sure to come round."

" Oh, of course she will," Mr. Frayling decided.

And Major Colquhoun smiled complacently. He often asserted that there was no knowing women ; but he took credit to himself for a superior knowledge of the sex all the same.

CHAPTER XVII.

BEFORE writing the promise which Evadne required, Major Colquhoun begged to be allowed to have an interview with her, and to this also she consented at her mother's earnest solicitation, although the idea of it went very much against the grain. She perceived, however, that the first meeting must be awkward in any case, and she was one of those energetic people who, when there is a disagreeable thing to be done, do it, and get it over at once. So she strengthened her mind by adding a touch of severity to her costume, and sat herself down in the drawing room with a book on her lap when the morning came, well nerved for the interview. Her heart began to beat unpleasantly when he rang, and she heard him in the hall, doubtless inquiring for her. At the sound of his voice she arose from her seat involuntarily, and stood,

literally awaiting in fear and trembling the dreadful moment
of meeting.

" What a horrible sensation ! " she ejaculated mentally.

"Colonel Colquhoun," the servant announced.

He entered with an air of displeasure he could not conceal,
and bowed to her from a distance stiffly ; but, although she
looked hard at him, she could not see him, so great was her
trepidation. It was she, however, who was the first to speak.

"I—I'm nervous," she gasped, clasping her hands and holding them out to him piteously.

Colonel Colquhoun relaxed. It flattered his vanity to perceive that this curiously well-informed and exceedingly strong-
minded young lady became as weakly emotional as any
ordinary school girl the moment she found herself face to
face with him. " There is nothing to be afraid of," he blandly
assured her.

"Will you—sit down," Evadne managed to mumble, dropping into her own chair again from sheer inability to stand
any longer.

Colonel Colquhoun took a seat at an exaggerated distance
from her. His idea was to impress her with a sense of his
extreme delicacy, but the act had a contrary effect upon her.
His manners had been perfect so far as she had hitherto seen
them, but thus to emphasize an already sufficiently awkward
position was not good taste, and she registered the fact against
him.

After they were seated, there was a painful pause. Evadne
knit her brows and cast about in her mind for something to
say. Suddenly the fact that the maid had announced him as
"Colonel" Colquhoun recurred to her.

"Have you been promoted?" she asked very naturally.

" Yes," he answered.

"I congratulate you," she faltered.

Again he bowed stiffly.

But Evadne was recovering herself. She could look at him
now, and it surprised her to find that he was not in appearance
the monster she had been picturing him—no more a monster,
indeed, than he had seemed before she knew of his past.
Until now, however, except for that one glimpse in the carriage, she had always seen him through such a haze of feeling
as to make the seeing practically null and void, so far as any
perception of his true character might be gathered from his
appearance, and useless for anything really but ordinary pur-

poses of identification. Now, however, that the misty veil of passion was withdrawn from her eyes, the man whom she had thought noble she saw to be merely big ; the face which had seemed to beam with intellect certainly remained fine-featured still, but it was like the work of a talented artist when it lacks the perfectly perceptible, indefinable finishing touch of genius that would have raised it above criticism, and drawn you back to it again, but, wanting which, after the first glance of admiration, interest fails, and you pass on only convinced of a certain cleverness, a thing that soon satiates without satisfying. Evadne had seen soul in her lover's eyes, but now they struck her as hard, shallow, glittering, and obtrusively blue ; and she noticed that his forehead, although high, shelved back abruptly to the crown of his head, which dipped down again sheer to the back of his neck, a very precipice without a single boss upon which to rest a hope of some saving grace in the way of eminent social qualities. "Thank Heaven, I see you as you are in time !" thought Evadne.

Colonel Colquhoun was the next to speak.

"I shall be able to give you rather a better position now," he said.

"Yes," she replied, but she did not at all appreciate the advantage, because she had never known what it was to be in an inferior position.

"May I speak to you with reference to our future relations ?" he continued.

She bowed a kind of cold assent, then looked at him expectantly, her eyes opening wide, and her heart thumping horribly in the very natural perturbation which again seized upon her as they approached the subject ; yet, in spite of her quite perceptible agitation, there was both dignity and determination in her attitude, and Colonel Colquhoun, meeting the unflinching glance direct, became suddenly aware of the fact that the timid little love-sick girl with half-shut, sleepy eyes he had had such a fancy for, and this young lady, modestly shrinking in every inch of her sensitive frame, but undaunted in spirit, nevertheless, were two very different people. There had been misapprehension of character on both sides, it seemed, but he liked pluck, and, by Jove ! the girl was handsomer than he had imagined. Views or no views, he would lay siege to her senses in earnest ; there would be some satisfaction in such a conquest.

"Is there no hope for me, Evadne ?" he pleaded.

"None—none," she burst out impetuously, becoming desperate in her embarrassment. "But 1 cannot discuss the subject. I beg you will let it drop."

Her one idea was to get rid of this big blond man, who gazed at her with an expression in his eyes from which, now that her own passion was dead, she shrunk in revolt.

Again Colonel Colquhoun bowed stiffly. "As you please," he said. "My only wish is to please you." He paused for a reply, but as Evadne had nothing more to say, he was obliged to recommence : "The regiment," he said, "is going to Malta at once, and I must go with it. And what I would venture to suggest is, that you should follow when you feel inclined, by P. and O. Fellows will understand that I don't care to have you come out on a troopship. And I should like to get your rooms fitted up for you, too, before you arrive. I am anxious to do all in my power to meet your wishes. I will make every arrangement with that end in view ; and if you can suggest anything yourself that does not occur to me I shall be glad. You had better bring an English maid out with you, or a German. Frenchwomen are flighty." He got up as he said this, and added : "You'll like Malta, 1 think. It is a bright little place, and very jolly in the season."

Evadne rose too. "Thank you," she said. "You are showing me more consideration than I have any right to expect, and I am sure to be satisfied with any arrangement you may think it right to make."

"I will telegraph to you when my arrangements for your reception are complete," he concluded. "And I think that is all."

"I can think of nothing else," she answered.

"Good-bye, then," he said.

"Good-bye," she rejoined, "and I wish you a pleasant voyage and all possible success with your regiment."

"Thank you," he answered, putting his heels together, and making her a profound bow as he spoke.

So they parted, and he went his way through the old Cathedral Close with that set expression of countenance which he had worn when he first became aware of her flight. But, curiously enough, although he had no atom of lover-like feeling left for her, and the amount of thought she had displayed in her letters had shocked his most cherished prejudices on the subject of her sex, she had gained in his estimation. He liked her pluck. He felt she could be nothing but a credit to him.

She remained for a few seconds as he had left her, listening to his footsteps in the hall and the shutting of the door ; and then from where she stood she saw him pass, and watched him out of sight—a fine figure of a man, certainly ; and she sighed. She had been touched by his consideration, and thought it a pity that such a kindly disposition should be unsupported by the solid qualities which alone could command her lasting respect and affection.

She walked to the window, and stood there drumming idly on the glass, thinking over the conclusion they had come to, for some time after Colonel Colquhoun had disappeared. She felt it to be a lame one, and she was far from satisfied. But what, under the circumstances, would have been a better arrangement? The persistent question contained in itself its own answer. Only the prospect was blank—blank. The excitement of the contest was over now ; the reaction had set in. She ventured to look forward ; and, seeing for the first time what was before her, the long, dark, dreary level of a hopelessly uncongenial existence, reaching from here to eternity, as it seemed from her present point of view, her over-wrought nerves gave way ; and, when Mrs. Orton Beg came to her a moment later, she threw herself into her arms and sobbed hysterically : "Oh, auntie ! I have suffered horribly ! I wish I were dead !"

CHAPTER XVIII.

THE first news that Evadne received on arriving in Malta was contained in a letter from her mother. It announced that her father had determined to cut her off from all communication with her family until she came to her senses.

She had remained quiety with Mrs. Orton Beg until it was time to leave England. She did not want to go to Fraylingay. She shrank from occupying her old rooms in her new state of mind, and she would not have thought of proposing such a thing herself ; but she did half expect to be asked. This not liking to return home, not recognizing it as home any longer, or herself as having any right to go there uninvited, marked the change in her position, and made her realize it with a pang. Her mother came and went, but she brought no message from her father nor ever mentioned him. Something in ourselves warns us at once of any change of feeling in a friend, and Evadne asked no questions, and sent no messages either. But this attitude did not satisfy her father at all. He thought it her duty clearly to throw herself at his feet and beg for mercy and forgiveness ; and he waited for her to make some sign of contrition until his patience could hold out no longer, and then he asked his wife : " Has Evadne—eh—what is her attitude at present ? "

"She is perfectly cheerful and happy," Mrs. Frayling replied.

"She expresses no remorse for her most unjustifiable conduct ? "

"She thinks she only did what is right," Mrs. Frayling reminded him.

"Then she is quite indifferent to my opinion ? " he began, swelling visibly and getting red in the face. "Has she asked what I think ? Does she ever mention me ? "

"No, never," Mrs. Frayling declared apprehensively.

"A most unnatural child," he exclaimed in his pompous way ; "a most unnatural child."

It was after this that he became obstinately determined to cut Evadne off from all communication with her friends until she should become reconciled to Colonel Colquhoun as a husband. Mr. Frayling was not an astute man. He was simply incapable of sitting down and working out a deliberate scheme of punishment which should have the effect of bringing Evadne's unruly spirit into what he considered proper subjection. In this matter he acted, not upon any system which he could have reduced to writing, but rather as the lower animals do when they build nests, or burrow in the ground, or repeat, generation after generation, other arrangements of a like nature with a precision which the cumulative practice of the race makes perfect in each individual. He possessed a certain faculty, transmitted from father to son, that gives the stupidest man a power in his dealings with women which the brightest intelligence would not acquire without it ; and he used to obtain his end with the decision of instinct, which is always neater and more effectual than reason and artifice in such matters. He denied hotly, for instance, that Evadne had any natural affection, and yet it was upon that woman's weakness of hers that he set to work at once, proving himself to be possessed of a perfect, if unconscious, knowledge of her most vulnerable point ; and he displayed much ingenuity in his manner of making it a means of torture He let no hint of the cruel edict be breathed before she went abroad ; she might have altered her arrangements had she known of it before, and remained with Mrs. Orton Beg—and there was something of foresight too, in timing her mother's tear-stained letter of farewell, good advice, pious exhortation, and plaintive reproach to meet her on her arrival, to greet her on the threshold of her new life, and make her realize the terrible gulf which she was setting between herself and those who were dearest to her, by her obstinacy.

The object was to make her suffer, and she did suffer ; but her father's cruelty did not alter the facts of the case, or appeal to her reason as an argument worthy to influence her decision.

Mrs. Orton Beg ventured to express her opinion to Mr. Frayling on the subject seriously. She often said more to him in her quiet way than most people would have dared to.

"I think you are making a mistake," she said.

"What!" he exclaimed, ready to bluster ; "Would you have me countenance such conduct? Why, it is perfectly revolutionary. If other women follow her example, not one man in ten will be able to get a wife when he wants to marry."

"It is very terrible," she answered in her even way, "to hear that so large a majority will be condemned to celibacy ; but I have no doubt you have good grounds for making the assertion. That is not the point, however. What I was thinking of was the risk you run of bringing more serious trouble on yourself by cutting Evadne adrift from every influence of her happy childhood, and casting her lot among strangers, and into a world of intrigue alone."

"She will come to her senses when she finds herself so situated, perhaps," he retorted testily ; "and if she does not, it will just show that she is incorrigible."

Evadne answered this last letter of her mother's with dignity.

"Of course I regret my father's decision [she wrote], and I consider it neither right nor wise. But I shall take the liberty of writing to you regularly every mail nevertheless. I know my letters will be a pleasure to you although you cannot answer them. But where is the reason and right, mother, in this decision of my father's? We both know, you and I, that it is merely the outcome of irritation caused by a difference of opinion, and no more binding in reason upon you than upon me."

When Mrs. Frayling received this letter, she wrote a hurried note to Evadne, saying that she did think her husband unreasonable, and also that he had no right to separate her from any of her children, and that therefore she should write to Evadne as often as she liked, but without letting him know it. She thought his injustice quite justified such tactics ; but Evadne answered, " No ! "

" There has been too much of that kind of cowardice among women already [she wrote]. Whatever we do we should do openly and fearlessly. We are not the property of our husbands ; they do not buy us. We are perfectly free agents to write to whomsoever we please, and so long as we order our lives in all honour and decency, they have no more right to interfere with us than we with them. Tell him once for all that you see no reason in his request, and write openly. What can he do ? Storm, I suppose. But storming is no proof of his right to interfere between you and me. Once on a time the ignorant were taught to believe that the Lord spoke in the thunder, and they could be influenced through their terror and respect to do anything while an opportune storm was raging ; and when women were weak and ignorant men used their wrath in much the same way to convince them of error. To us, educated as we are, however, an outburst of rage is about as effectual an argument as a clap of thunder would be. Both are startling I grant, but what do they prove ? I have seen my father in a rage. His face swells and gets very red, he prances up and down the room, he shouts at the top of his voice, and presents altogether a very disagreeable spectacle which one never quite forgets. But he cannot go like that forever, mother. So tell him gently you have been thinking about his proposition, and are sorry that you find you must differ from him, but you consider that it is clearly your duty to correspond with me. Then sit still, and say nothing, and let him storm till he is tired ; and when he goes out and bangs the door, finish your letter, and put it in a conspicuous position on the hall table to be posted. He will scarcely tear it up, but if he does, write another, send it to the post yourself, and tell him you have done so, and shall continue to do so. Be open before everything, and stand upon your dignity. Things have come to a pretty pass, indeed, when an honourable woman only dares to write to her own daughter surreptitiously, **as if she were doing something she should be ashamed of.**"

Poor Mrs. Frayling was not equal to such opposition. She would rather have faced a thunderstorm than her husband in his wrath, so she concealed Evadne's letter from him, and wrote to her again surreptitiously in order to reproach her for seeming to insinuate that she, her mother, would stoop to do anything underhand. Evadne sighed when she received this letter, and thought of letting the matter drop. Why should she dislike to see her father in the position unreasonable husbands and fathers usually occupy, that of being ostensibly obeyed while in reality they are carefully kept in the dark as to what is going on about them? And why should she object to allow her mother to act as so many other worthy but weak women daily do in self-defence and for the love of peace and quietness? There seemed to be no great good to be gained by persisting, and she might perhaps have ended by acquiescing under protest if her mother had not added by way of post-script : "I doubt very much if I shall be allowed to receive your letters. Your father will probably send any he may capture straight back to you ; and, at any rate, he will insist upon seeing them, so do not, my dear child, allude to having heard from me. I earnestly entreat you to remember this."

But the request only made Evadne's blood boil again. She did not belong to the old corrupt state of things herself, and she would not submit to anything savouring of deceit. If her mother were too weak to assert her own independence she felt herself forced to do it for her, so she wrote to her father sharply :

"My mother tells me that you intend to stop all communication between her and myself. I consider that you have no right to do anything of the kind, and unless I hear from her regularly in answer to my letters, I shall be reluctantly compelled to send a detailed statement of my case to every paper in the kingdom in order to find out from my fellow country-women what their opinion of your action in the matter is, and also what they would advise us to do. You know my mother's affection for you. You have never had any reason to complain of want of devotion on her part, and when you make your disagreement with me a whip to scourge her with, you are guilty of an unjustifiable act of oppression."

This letter arrived at Fraylingay late one afternoon, and was handed to Mr. Frayling on his return from a pleasant

country ride. He read it standing in the hall, and lost his
equanimity at once.

"Where is Mrs. Frayling?" he asked a servant who happened to be passing, speaking in a way which caused the man
to remark afterward that "Mrs. Frayling was going to catch
it about somethin'; and 'e seemed to think I'd made away
with 'er."

Mrs. Frayling was in the drawing room, writing one of her
pleasant chatty letters to a friend in India, with a cheerful
expression on her comely countenance, and all recollections of
her domestic difficulties banished for the moment.

When Mr. Frayling entered in his riding dress, with his
whip in his hand and his hat on his head (he was one of those
men who are most punctilious with strange ladies, but do not
feel it necessary to behave like gentlemen in the presence of
their own wives, making it appear as if the latter had lost cast
and forfeited all claim to their respect by marrying them) Mrs.
Frayling looked round from her writing and smiled.

"Have you had a nice ride, dear?" she said.

"Read that!" he exclaimed, slapping Evadne's letter with
his whip, and then throwing it down on the table before her
rudely: "Read that, and tell me what you think of your
daughter now!" Mrs. Frayling's fair face clouded on the
instant, and her affectionate heart, which had been so happily
expanded the moment before by the kind thoughts about her
absent friend that came crowding as she wrote to her, contracted now with a painful spasm of nervous apprehension.

She read the letter through, and then put it down on the
table beside her without a word. She did not look at her
husband, but at some miniatures which hung on the wall
before her. They were portraits of her own people, father,
mother, grandmother, a great aunt and uncle, and other near
relations, together with a brother and sister much older than
herself, and both dead, and forgotten as a rule : but at that
moment all that she had ever known of them, details of merry
games together, and childish naughtinesses which got them into
trouble at the time but made them appear to have been only
amusingly mischievous now, recurred to her in one great flash
of memory, which showed her also some lost illusions of her
early girlhood about a husband's love and tenderness, his constant friendship, the careful, patient teaching of the more
powerful mind which was to strengthen her mind and enlarge
it too, and the constant companionship which would banish

for ever the indefinite gnawing sense of loneliness from which
all healthy, young, unmated creatures suffer. She had actually expected at one time to be more to her husband than
the mere docile female of his own kind which was all he
wanted his wife to be. She had had aspirations which had
caused her to yearn for help to develop something beyond the
animal side of her, proving the possession in embryo of faculties other than those which had survived Mr. Frayling's rule ;
but her nature was plastic ; one of those which requires the
strong and delicate hand of a master to mould it into distinct
and lovely form. Motherhood, as it had appeared to her in
the delicate dreams of those young days, had promised to be a
beautiful and blessed privilege, but then the children of her
happy imaginings had been less her own than those of the
shadowy perfection who was to have been her husband. She
had little sense of humour, but yet she could have smiled
when, in this moment of absolute insight, see saw the ideal
compared with the real husband, this great fat country gentleman. The folly of having expected even motherhood with
such a father for her children to be anything but unsatisfactory
and disappointing at the best, dawned upon her for an instant
with disheartening effect. But, fortunately, the outlook was
so hopeless there seemed nothing more to sigh for, and so she
sat for once, looking up at the miniatures without washing out
with tears the little mental strength she had left.

Mr. Frayling waited impatiently for her to make some
remark when she had read Evadne's letter. Almost anything
she could have said must have given him some further food
for provocation, and there is nothing more gratifying to an
angry man than fresh fuel for his wrath. However, silence
sometimes fans the flame as effectually as words, and it did so
on this occasion, for, having waited till he could contain himself no longer, he burst out so suddenly that Mrs. Frayling
raised her large soft white hand to the heavy braids which it
was then the fashion to pile high on the head and have hanging down in two rows to the nape of the neck behind, as if
she expected them to be disarranged by the concussion.

"May I ask if you approve of that letter ?" he demanded.

But she only set her lips.

Mr. Frayling took a turn about the room with his hands
behind his back, holding his riding whip upright, and flicking
himself between the shoulders with it as he went.

"Let her write to the papers !" he exclaimed, addressing the

pictures on the walls as if he were sure of their sympathy.
" Let her write to the papers. I don't care what she does.
I cast her off forever. This comes of the higher education
of women ; a promising specimen ! Woman's rights, indeed !
Woman's shamelessness and want of common decency
once she is let loose from proper control. She'll make the
matter public, will she ? A girl of nineteen ! and take the
opinion of her fellow countrywomen on the subject, egad !
because I won't let her mother write to her : and my not doing
so is an unjustifiable act of oppression, is it ? What do you
consider it yourself ? " he demanded of his wife, striding up to
her, and standing over her in a way which, with a flourish of
the whip, was unpleasantly suggestive of an impulse to visit
her daughter's offence upon her shoulders actually as well as
figuratively.

Mrs. Frayling did not shrink, but her comely pink and
white face, usually so lineless in its healthy matronly plump-
ness, suddenly took on a look of age and hardness, the one
moment of horrid repulsion marking it more deeply than years
of those household cares which write themselves on the mind
without contracting the heart had done.

" Do you consider, ' he repeated, " that I have been guilty
of an unmanly act of oppression ? "

" I think you have been very unkind, ' she answered, meaning the same thing   " Her conduct was bad enough to begin
with, but now it will be ten times worse. She will write to the
papers, if she says she will. Evadne is as brave—- ! You
can't understand her courage. She will do anything she
thinks right. And now there will be a public scandal after
all we have done to prevent it, and you will never be able to
show your face again anywhere, for there isn't a mother in the
country from her Majesty downward, who will not take my
part and say you have no right to separate me from my
daughter."

" I know what the end of it will be." he roared. " I know
what happens when women leave the beaten track. They go
to the bad altogether. That's what will happen, you'll see.
She'll write a volume next to prove that she has a right to be
an immoral woman if she chooses. She'll be a common hussey
yet, I promise you."

" *Sir !* " said Mrs. Frayling, stung into dignity for a moment,
and rising to her feet in order to confront him boldly while
she spoke. " Sir, I have been a good and loyal wife to you,

as my daughter says, and it seems she was right too, when she declared that you are capable of making your disapproval of her opinions a whip to scourge me with ; but I warn you, if you do not instantly retract that cowardly insult, I shall walk straight out of your house, and make the matter public myself."

Mr. Frayling stared at her. "I—I beg your pardon, Elizabeth," he faltered in sheer astonishment. "What with you and your daughter, I am provoked past endurance. I don't know what I am saying."

"No amount of provocation justifies such an attack upon your daughter's reputation," Mrs. Frayling rejoined, following up her advantage. "If she had been that kind of girl she would not have objected to Colonel Colquhoun ; and at any rate she has every right to as much of your charity as you give him."

"Women are different," Mr. Frayling ventured feebly.

"Are they?" said Mrs. Frayling, some of Evadne's wisdom occurring to her with the old worn axiom upon which for untold ages the masculine excuse for self-indulgence at the expense of the woman has rested. "I believe Evadne is right after all. I shall get out her letters, and read them again. And what is more, I shall write to her just as often as I please."

Mr. Frayling stared again in his amazement, and then he walked out of the room without uttering another word. He had not foreseen the possibility of such spirited conduct on the part of his wife ; but since she had ventured to revolt, the question of a public scandal was disposed of, and that being a consummation devoutly to be wished, he said no more, salving his lust of power with the reflection that, by deciding the question for herself, she had removed all responsibility from his shoulders, and proved herself to be a contumacious woman and blameworthy. So long as there is no risk of publicity the domestic tyrannies of respectable elderly gentlemen of irascible disposition may be carried to any length, but once there is a threat of scandal they coil up.

By that one act of overt rebellion, Mrs. Frayling secured some comfort in her life for a few months at least, and taught her husband a little lesson which she ought to have endeavoured to inculcate long before. It was too late then, however, to do him any permanent good ; the habit of the slave-driver was formed. When a woman sacrifices her individuality and the right of private judgment at the outset of her married life, and limits herself to " What thou biddest, unargued I obey," taking it for granted that " God is thy law," without making any inquiries, and accepting the assertion that " To know no more is woman's happiest knowledge, and her praise," as confidently as if the wisdom of it had been proved beyond a doubt, and its truth had never been known to fail in a single instance, she withdraws from her poor husband all the help of her keener spiritual perceptions, which she should have used with authority to hold his grosser nature in check, and leaves him to drift about on his own conceit, prejudices, and inclinations, until he is past praying for.

There was a temporary lull at Fraylingay after that last battle, during which Mrs. Frayling wrote to her daughter freely and frequently. She described the fight she had had for her rights, and concluded : " Now the whole difficulty has blown over, and I have no more opposition to contend against"—to which Evadne had replied in a few words judiciously, adding:

> " Before the curing of a strong disease,
> Even in the instant of repair and health,
> The fit is strongest ; evils that take leave,
> On their departure most of all show evil."

CHAPTER XIX.

IT came to be pretty generally known that all had not gone well with the Colquhouns immediately after their marriage. Something of the story had of necessity leaked out through the servants ; but, as the Fraylings had the precaution, common to their class, to keep their private troubles to themselves, nobody knew precisely what the difficulty had been, and their intimate friends, whom delicacy debarred from making inquiries, least of all. Lady Adeline just mentioned the matter to Mrs. Orton Beg, and asked, Is it a difficulty that may be discussed ? "

" No, better not, I think," the latter answered, and of course the subject dropped.

But poor Lady Adeline was too much occupied with domestic anxieties of her own at that time to feel more than a passing gleam of sympathetic interest in other people's. As Lord Dawne had hinted to Mrs. Orton Beg, it was now a question of how best to educate the twins. Their parents had made what they considered suitable arrangements for their instruction ; but the children, unfortunately, were not satisfied with these. They had had a governess in common while they were still quite small ; but Mr. Hamilton-Wells had old-fashioned ideas about the superior education of boys, and consequently, when the children had outgrown their nursery governess, he decided that Angelica should have another, more advanced ; and had at the same time engaged a tutor for Diavolo, sending him to school being out of the question because of the fear of further trouble from the artery he had severed. When this arrangement became known, the children were seen to put their heads together.

" Do we like having different teachers ? " Diavolo inquired tentatively.

" No, we don't," said Angelica.

Lady Adeline had tried to prepare the governess, but the latter brought no experience of anything like Angelica to help her to understand that young lady, and so the warning went for nothing. " A little affection goes a long way with a child," she said to Lady Adeline, " and I always endeavour to make my pupils understand that I care for them, and do not wish to make their lessons a task, but a pleasure to them."

" It is a good system, I should think," Lady Adeline observed, speaking dubiously, however.

" Can you do long division, my dear," the governess asked Angelica when they sat down to lessons for the first time.

" No, Miss Apsley," Angelica answered sweetly.

" Then I will show you how. But you must attend, you know,"—this last was said with playful authority.

So Angelica attended.

" How did you get on this morning ? " Lady Adeline asked Miss Apsley anxiously afterward.

" Oh, perfectly " the latter answered. " The dear child was all interest and endeavour."

Lady Adeline said no more ; but such docility was unnatural, and she did not like the look of it at all.

Next day Angelica, with an innocent air, gave Miss Apsley a long division sum which she had completed during the night. It was done by an immense number of figures, and covered four sheets of foolscap gummed together. Miss Apsley worked at it for an hour to verify it, and, finding it quite correct, she decided that Angelica knew long division enough, and must go on to something else. Her first impression was that she had secured a singularly apt pupil, and she was much surprised, when she began to teach Angelica the next rule in arithmetic, to find that she could *not* make the dear child see it. Angelica listened, and tried, with every appearance of honest intention, getting red and hot with the effort ; and she would not put the slate down ; she would go on trying till her head ached, she was so eager to learn ; but work as she might, she could do nothing but long division. Miss Apsley said she had never known anything so singular. Lady Adeline sighed.

For about a week, the twins " lay low."

The tutor had found it absolutely impossible to teach Diavolo anything. The boy was perfectly docile. He would sit with his bright eyes riveted on his master's face, listening with might and main apparently ; but at the end of every explanation the tutor found the same thing. Diavolo never had the faintest idea of what he had been talking about.

At the end of a week, however, the children changed their tactics. When lessons ought to have begun one morning Diavolo went to Miss Apsley, and sat himself down beside her in Angelica's place, with a smiling countenance and without a word of explanation ; while Angelica presented herself to the tutor with all Diavolo's books under her arm.

" Please, sir," she said, " there must have been some mistake. Diavolo and I find that we were mixed somehow wrong, and I got his mind and he got mine. I can do his lessons quite easily, but I can't do my own ; and he can do mine, but he can't do these "—holding up the books. "It's like this, you see. I can't learn from a lady, and he can't learn from a man. So I'm going to be your pupil, and he's going to be Miss Apsley's. You don't understand twins, I expect. It's always awkward about them ; there's so often something wrong. With us, you know, the fact of the matter is that *I* am Diavolo and *he* is me."

The tutor and governess appealed to Mr. Hamilton-Wells, and Mr. Hamilton-Wells sent for the twins and lectured them, Lady Adeline sitting by, seriously perplexed. The children stood to attention together, and listened respectfully ; and then went back to their lessons with undeviating cheerfulness ; but Diavolo did Angelica's, and Angelica did his diligently, and none other would they do.

But this state of things could not continue, and in order to end it, Mr. Hamilton-Wells had recourse to a weak expedient which he had more than once successfully employed unknown to Lady Adeline.   He sent for the twins, and consulted their wishes privately.

" What do you want? " he asked.

" Well, sir," Diavolo answered, " we don't think it's fair for Angelica only to have a beastly governess to teach her when she knows as much as I do, and is a precious sight sharper."

" I taught you all you know, Diavolo, didn't I ? " Angelica broke in.

" Yes," said Diavolo, with a wise nod.

" And it is beastly unfair," she continued, " to put me off with a squeaking governess and long division, when I ought to be doing mathematics and Latin and Greek."

" My dear child, what use would mathematics and Latin and Greek be to you ? " Mr. Hamilton-Wells protested.

" Just as much use as they will to Diavolo," she answered decidedly.   " He doesn't know half as much about the good of education as I do.   Just ask him."   She whisked round on her brother as she spoke, and demanded :   " Tell papa, Diavolo, what *is* the use of being educated ? "

" I am sure I don't know," Diavolo answered impressively.

" My dear boy, mathematics are an education in themselves." Mr. Hamilton-Wells began didactically, moving his long white hands in a way that always suggested lace ruffles.   " They will teach you to reason."

" Then they'll teach me to reason too," said Angelica, setting herself down on the arm of a chair as if she had made up her mind, and intended to let them know it.   All her movements were quick, all Diavolo's deliberate.   " Men are always jeering at women in books for not being able to reason, and I'm going to learn, if there's any help in mathematics," she continued.   " I found something the other day—where is it now ? "   She was down on her knees in a moment, emptying the contents of her pocket on to the floor, and sifting them. There were two pocket-handkerchiefs of fine texture, and exceedingly dirty, as if they had been there for months (the one she used she carried in the bosom of her dress or up her sleeve), a ball of string, a catapult and some swan shot, a silver pen, a pencil holder, part of an old song book, a pocket book, some tin tacks, a knife with several blades and scissors, etc.; also a silver fruit knife, two coloured pencils, indiarubber, and a scrap of dirty paper wrapped round a piece of almond toffee. This was apparently what she wanted, for she took it off the toffee, threw the latter into the grate—whither Diavolo's eyes followed it regretfully—and spread the paper out on her lap, whence it was seen to be covered with cabalistic-looking figures.

"Here you are," she said. "I copied it out of a book the other day, and put it round the toffee because I knew I should be wanting that, and then I should see it every time I took it out of my pocket, and not forget it."

"But why did you throw the toffee away?" said Diavolo.

"Shut up, and listen," Angelica rejoined from the floor politely; and then she began to read: 'Histories make men wise; poets witty; mathematics subtle; natural philosophy, deep, moral, grave; logic and rhetoric, able to contend.' Now that's what I want, papa. I want to know all that, and have a good time; and I expect I shall have to contend to get it!"

"You'll soon learn how," said Diavolo encouragingly.

Mr. Hamilton-Wells had always enjoyed his children's precocity, and, provided they amused him, they could make him do anything. So after the conference he announced that he had been questioning Angelica, and had found that she really was too far advanced for a governess, and he had therefore decided that she should share Diavolo's lessons with the tutor. The governess accordingly disappeared from Hamilton House, the first tutor found that he had no vocation for teaching, and left also, and another was procured with great difficulty, and at considerable expense, for the fame of the Heavenly Twins was wide-spread, and their parents were determined besides not to let any candidate engage himself under the pleasing delusion that the task of teaching them would be something of a sinecure.

The tutor they finally secured turned out to be a very good fellow, fortunately; a gentleman, and with a keen sense of humour which the twins appreciated, so that they took to him at once, and treated him pretty well on the whole; but lessons were usually a lively time. Angelica, who continued to be the taller, stronger, and wickeder of the two, soon proved herself the cleverer also. Like Evadne, she was consumed by the rage to know, and insisted upon dragging Diavolo on with her. It was interesting to see them sitting side by side, the dark head touching the fair one as they bent together intently over some problem. When Diavolo was not quick enough, Angelica would rouse him up in the old way by knocking her head, which was still the harder of the two, against his.

"Angelica, did I see you strike your brother?" Mr. Ellis

sternly demanded, the first time he witnessed this performance.

" I don't know whether you saw me or not, sir, but I certainly did strike him," Angelica answered irritably.

" Why ? "

" To wake him up."

" You see, sir," Diavolo proceeded to explain in his imperturbable drawl ; " Angelica discovered that I was born with a
hee-red-it-air-ee predisposition to be a muff. We mostly are
on father's side of the family——"

" And if he isn't one, it's because I slapped the tendency
out of him as soon as I perceived it," Angelica interrupted.
" Get on, Diavolo, I've no patience with you when you're so
slow. You know you don't want to learn this, and that's why
you're snailing."

It was rather a trick of Diavolo's " to snail " over his lessons,
for in that as in many other things he was very unlike the good
little boy who loved his book, besides evincing many other
traits of character equally unpopular at the present time.
Diavolo would not work unless Angelica made him, and the
worst collision with the tutor was upon this subject.

" Wake up, Theodore, will you ! " Mr. Ellis said, during the
first week of their studies.

" Not until you call me Diavolo," was the bland response.

Mr. Ellis resisted for some time, but Diavolo was firm and
would do nothing, and Lady Adeline cautioned the tutor to
give in if he saw an opportunity of doing so with dignity.

" But the young scamp will be jeeringly triumphant if I do,"
Mr. Ellis objected.

" Oh, no," Lady Adeline answered. " Diavolo prides himself upon being a gentleman, and he says a gentleman never
jeers or makes himself unpleasant. His ideas on the latter
point, by the way, are peculiarly his own, and you will probably differ from him as to what is or is not unpleasant."

Mr. Ellis made a point of calling the boy " Diavolo " in a
casual way, as if he had forgotten the dispute, as early as possible after this, and found that Lady Adeline was right. Diavolo showed not the slightest sign of having heard, but he got
out his books at once, and did his lessons as if he liked them.

Mr. Hamilton-Wells had a habit of always saying a little
more than was necessary on some subjects. He was either a
born *naturalist* or had never conquered the problem of what
not to say, and he was so incautious as to come into the school-

room one morning while lessons were going on, and warn Mr.
Ellis to be most careful about what he gave the twins to read
in Latin, because some of the classic delicacies which boys are
expected to swallow without injury to themselves are much too
highly seasoned for a young lady : " You must make judicious
excerpts," he said.

Slap came the dictionary down upon the table, and Angelica
was deep in the " ex's " in a moment.   Excerpt, she found,
was to pick or take out.   She passed the dictionary to Diavolo,
who studied the definition ; but neither of them made a
remark.   From that day forth, however, they spent every
spare moment they had in poring over Latin text-books, until
they mastered the language, simply for the purpose of finding
out what it was that Angelica ought not to know.

There were, as has already been stated, some lively scenes at
lessons.

" Talk less and do more," Mr. Ellis rashly recommended in
the early days of their acquaintance, and after that, when they
disagreed, they claimed that they had his anthority to settle
the difference by tearing each other's hair or scratching each
other across the table ; and when he interfered, sometimes
they scratched him too.   Mr. Hamilton-Wells raised his salary
eventually.

The children invariably had a discussion about everything
as soon as it was over.   They called it " talking it out " ; and
after they had sinned and suffered punishment, their great
delight was to come and coax the tutor " to talk it out."   They
would then criticize their own conduct and his, impartially,
point out what they might have done, and what he might have
done, and what ought to have been done on both sides.

These discussions usually took place at the schoolroom tea,
a meal which both tutor and children as a rule thoroughly
enjoyed.   Mr. Ellis was not bound to have tea with the twins,
but they had politely invited him on the day of his arrival,
explaining that their parents were out, and it would give them
great pleasure to entertain him.

Tea being ready, they took him to the schoolroom, where
he found a square table, just large enough for four, daintily
decorated with flowers, and very nice china.

" We have to buy our own china, because we break so
much," Angelica said, seeing that the tutor noticed it.   " That
was the kind of thing papa got for us "—indicating a hugely
thick white cup and saucer, which stood on the mantelpiece

on a stand of royal blue plush, and covered with a glass shade.

"We broke the others, but we had that one mounted as a warning to him. Papa has no taste at all."

The tutor's face was a study. It was the first of these remarks he had heard.

The children decided that it would balance the table better if he poured out the tea, and he good-naturedly acquiesced, and sat down with Angelica on his right, and Diavalo on his left. The fourth seat opposite was unoccupied, but there was a cover laid, and he asked who was expected.

"Oh, that is for the Peace Angel," said Diavolo casually.

"Prevents difficulties at tea, you know," Angelica supplemented. "*We* don't mind difficulties, but we thought you might object, so we asked his holiness"—indicating the empty chair—"to preserve order."

Mr. Ellis did not at first appreciate the boon which was conferred on him by the presence of the Peace Angel, but he soon learnt to.

"I am on my honour and thick bread and butter to-day," said Diavolo, looking longingly at the plentiful supply and variety of cakes on the table.

"What does that mean exactly?" Mr. Ellis asked, pausing with the teapot raised to pour.

"Why, you see, he was naughty this morning," Angelica explained. "And as mamma was going out, she put him on his honour, as a punishment, not to eat cake."

"I've a good mind not to eat anything," said Diavolo, considering the plate of thick bread and butter beside him discontentedly.

"Then you'll be cutting off your nose to vex your face," said Angelica.

Diavolo caught up a piece of bread and butter to throw at her ; but she held up her hand, crying : "I appeal to the Peace Angel !"

"I forgot," said Diavolo, transferring the bread to his plate.

The children studied the tutor during tea.

He was a man of thirty, somewhat careworn about the eyes, but with an excessively kind and pleasant face, clean shaven ; and thick, reddy-brown hair. He was above the middle height, a little stooped at the shoulders, but of average strength.

"I like the look of you," said Angelica frankly.

" Thank you," he answered, smiling.

" And I vote for a permanent arrangement," she said, look-ing at Diavolo.

He was just then hidden behind a huge slice of bread, biting it, but he nodded intelligently.

The permanent arrangement referred to was to have the tutor to tea, and he agreed, wisely stipulating, however. that the presence of the Peace Angel should also be permanent. He even tried to persuade the twins to invite him to lessons ; but that they firmly declined.

" You'll like being our tutor, I think," Diavolo observed during this first tea.

" He will if we like him," said Angelica significantly.

" Are we going to ? " Diavolo asked.

" Yes, I think so," she answered, taking another good look at Mr. Ellis. " I like the look of that red in his hair."

" Now, isn't that a woman's reason ? " Diavolo exclaimed, appealing to Mr. Ellis.

" Yes, it is," said Angelica, preparing to defend it by shuf-fling a note-book out of her pocket, and ruffling the leaves over : " Listen to this "—and she read—" ' A tinge of red in the hair denotes strength and energy of character and good staying power.' We don't want a muff for a tutor, do we ? There are born muffs enough in the family without importing them.   And a woman's reason is always a good one, as men might see if they'd only stop chattering and listen to it."

" It mayn't be well expressed, but it will bear examination," Mr. Ellis suggested.

" Do you like being a tutor ? " Diavolo.

" It depends on whom I have to teach."

" If you're a good fellow, you'll have a nice time here—on the whole—I hope, sir," Angelica observed.   " But why are you a tutor ? "

" To earn my living," Mr. Ellis answered, smiling again.

The children remembered this, and when they were having tea under the shadow of the supposititious Peace Angel's wing, after the first occasion on which, when the tutor tried to separate them during a fight at lessons, they had turned simul-taneously and attacked him, they made it the text of some recommendations.   He expressed a strong objection to having manual labour imposed upon him as well as his other work ; but they maintained that if only he had called the affray " a **struggle for daily bread** " or " **a fight for a livelihood**," he would quite have enjoyed it ; and they further suggested that such diversion must be much more interesting than being a mere commonplace tutor who only taught lessons. They could not understand why a fight was not as much fun for him as for them, and thought him unreasonable when they found he was not to be persuaded to countenance that way of varying the monotony. Not that there was ever much monotony in the neighbourhood of the Heavenly Twins ; they managed to introduce variety into everything, and their quickness of action, when both were roused, was phenomenal. One day while at work they saw a sparrow pick up a piece of bread, take it to the roof-tree of an angle of the house visible from the schoolroom window, drop it, and chase it as it fell ; and the twins had made a bet as to which would beat, bird or bread, quarrelled because they could not agree as to which had bet on bird and which on bread, and boxed each other's ears almost before the race was over.

Mr. Ellis, although continually upon his guard, was not by any means always a match for them. Over and over again he found that his caution had been fanned to sleep by flattering attentions, while traps were being laid for him with the most innocent air in the world, as on one occasion when Diavolo betrayed him into a dissertation on the consistency of the Scriptures, and Angelica asked him to kindly show her how to reconcile Prov. viii. 2 : " For wisdom is better than rubies; and all the things that may be desired are not be compared to it," with Eccles. i. 18 : " For in much wisdom is much grief ; and he that increaseth knowledge increaseth sorrow."

His way with them was admirable, however, and he completely won their hearts. The thing that they respected him for most was the fact that he took in *Punch* on his own account, and could show you a lot of things in it that you could never have discovered yourself, as Angelica said, and read bits in a way that made them seem ever so much funnier than when *you* read them ; and could tell you who drew the pictures the moment he looked at them—so that " *Punch* Day " came to be looked forward to by the children as one of the pleasantest events of the week. Lessons were suspended the moment the paper arrived, if they had been good ; but when they were naughty Mr. Ellis put the paper in his pocket, and that was the greatest punishment he could inflict upon them— the only one that ever made them sulk. They would be good for hours in advance to earn the right of having *Punch* shown to them the moment it came. And it was certainly by means of his intelligent interpretation of it that their tutor managed to cultivate their tastes in many ways, and give them true ideas of art, and the importance of art, at the outset, and also of ethics. He was as careful of Angelica's physical as of her mental education, being himself strongly imbued by the then new idea that a woman should have the full use of her limbs, lungs, heart, and every other organ and muscle, so that life might be a pleasure to her and not a continual exertion. He had a strong objection to the artificial waist, and impressed the beauty of Tenniel's classical purity of figure upon the children by teaching them to appreciate the contrast it presents to the bulging vulgarities made manifest by Keene; and showed them also that while Du Maurier depicted with admirable artistic interpretation the refined surroundings and attenuated forms of women as they are, Linley Sambourne, that master of lovely line, pointed the moral by drawing women as they should be. There was nothing conventional about the Heavenly Twins, and it was therefore easy to make a good impression upon them in this direction, and the tutor soon had a practical proof of his success which must have been eminently satisfactory if a trifle embarrassing.

The children were out on the lawn in front of the house one afternoon when a lady arrived to call upon their mother. They were struck by her appearance as she descended from her carriage, and followed her into the drawing room to have a good look at her. She was one of those heroic women who have the constancy to squeeze their figures in beyond the V shape, which is the commonest deformity, to that of the hourglass which bulges out more above and below the line of compression.

There were a good many other people in the room, whom the Heavenly Twins saluted politely ; and then they sat down opposite to the object of their interest and gazed at her.

" Why are you tied so tight in the middle ? " Angelica asked at last in a voice that silenced everybody else in the room. " Doesn't it hurt? I mean to have a *good* figure when I grow up, like the Venus de Medici, you know. I can show you a picture of her, if you like. She hasn't a stitch on her."

" She looks awfully nice, though," said Diavolo, "and Angelica thinks she'd be able to eat more with that kind of figure."

" Yes," Angelica candidly confessed, looking at her victim

compassionately. " I shouldn't think, now, that you can eat both pudding and meat, can you ? "

" Not to mention dessert ! " Diavolo ejaculated with genuine concern.

" Mr. Ellis, will you get those children out of the room, somehow," Lady Adeline whispered to the tutor, who had come in for tea.

" Is it true, do you think," Mr. Ellis began loudly, addressing Mr. Hamilton-Wells across the room—" Is it true that Dr. Galbraith is going to try some horrible experiments in vivisection this afternoon ? "

" What is vivisection ? " asked Angelica, diverted.

" Cutting up live animals to find out what makes them go," said the tutor.

In three minutes there wasn't a vestige of the Heavenly Twins about the place.

CHAPTER XX.

THE twins had a code of ethics which differed in some respects from that ordinarily accepted in their state of life. They honoured their mother—they couldn't help it, as they said themselves, apologetically ; but their father they looked upon as fair game for their amusement.

" What was that unearthly noise I heard this morning ? " Mr. Ellis asked one day.

" Oh, did we wake you, sir ? " Diavolo exclaimed. " We didn't mean to. We were only yowling papa out of bed with our fiddles. He's idle sometimes, and won't get up, and it's so bad for him, you know."

" I wish you could see him scooting down the corridor after us," Angelica observed. " And do you know, he speaks just the same at that time of day in his dressing gown, as he does in the evening in dress clothes. You'd die if you heard him."

Another habit of the twins was to read any letters they might find lying about.

" It is dishonourable to read other people's letters," Mr. Ellis admonished them severely when he became aware of this peculiarity.

" It isn't for us," Angelica answered defiantly. " You might as well say its dishonourable to squint. We've always done it, and everybody knows we do it. We warn them not to leave their letters lying about, don't we, Diavolo?"

" That is because it is greater fun to hunt for them," Diavolo interpreted precisely. When Angelica gave a reason he usually cleared it of all obscurity in this way.

" And how are we to know what goes on in the family if we don't read the letters?" Angelica demanded.

" What necessity is there for you to know?"

" Every necessity!" she retorted. " Not be interested in one s own family affairs? Why, we should we wanting in intelligence, and we're not that, you know! And we should be wanting in affection, too, and every right feeling; and I hope we are not that either. Mr. Ellis, *quite*. But you needn't be afraid about your own letters. We shan't touch them."

" No," drawled Diavolo. " Of course that would be a very different thing."

" I am glad you draw the line somewhere," Mr. Ellis observed sarcastically. He was far from satisfied, however, but he noticed eventually that the dust collected on letters of his own if he left them lying about, and he soon discovered that when his intelligent pupils gave their word they kept it uncompromisingly. It was one of their virtues, and the other was loyalty to each other. Their devotion to their mother hardly counted for a virtue, because they never carried it far enough to make any sacrifice for her sake. But they would have sacrificed their very lives for each other, and would have fought for the right to die until there was very little left of either of them to execute; of such peculiar quality were their affections.

They had gone straight to Fountain Towers by the shortest cut across the fields that afternoon when Mr. Ellis suggested vivisection as a possible occupation for Dr. Galbraith. They never doubted but that they should discover him hard at work, in some underground cellar most likely, to which they would be guided by the cries of his victims, and would be able to conquer his reluctance to allow them to assist at his experiments, by threats of exposure; and they were considerably chagrined when, having carefully concealed themselves in a thick shrubbery, in order to reconnoitre the house, they came upon him in the garden, innocently occupied in the idle pursuit of pruning rose trees.

He was somewhat startled himself when he suddenly saw

their hot red faces, set like two moons in a clump of greenery, peeping out at him with animated eyes.

" Hollo ! " he said. " Are you hungry ? " The faces disappeared behind the bushes.

" Are we, Angelica ? " Diavolo whispered anxiously.

" Of course we are," she retorted.

" I thought we were too angry—disgusted—disappointed—*something*," he murmured apologetically, but evidently much relieved.

Dr. Galbraith went on with his pruning, and presently the twins appeared walking down the proper approach to the garden hand in hand demurely.

After they had saluted their host politely, they stood and stared at him.

" Well ? " he said at last.

" I suppose we are too late ? " said Angelica.

" For what ? " he asked, without pausing in his occupation.

" For the viv-viv-vivinesectionining."

" Vivinesectionining ! What on earth—Oh ! " Light broke in upon him. " Who told you I was ? "

" Mr. Ellis," said Angelica.

" No, he didn't tell us you were exactly," Diavolo explained with conscientious accuracy. " He asked papa if it was true that you were going to this afternoon ? "

" And what were *you* doing ? " Dr. Galbraith asked astutely.

" We were in the drawing room," Angelica answered, " trying to find out from a lady why she tied herself up so tight in the middle."

" And so you came off here to see ? "

" Yes," said Diavolo. " We wanted to catch you at it."

" You little brute, misbegotten by the——" Dr. Galbraith began, but Diavolo interrupted him.

" *Sir !* " he exclaimed, drawing himself up with an expression of as much indignation as could be got into his small patrician features. " If you do not instantly withdraw that calumny, I shall have to fight you on my mother's behalf, and I shall consider it my duty to inform her of the insinuation which is the cause of offence." ·

" I apologize," said Dr. Galbraith, taking off his hat and bowing low. " I assure you the expression was used as a mere *façon de parler.*"

" I accept your explanation, sir," said Diavolo, returning the salute. " But I caution you to be careful for the future. What is a *façon de parler*, Angelica?" he whispered as he put his hat on.

"Oh, just a way of saying it," she answered. "I wish you wouldn't talk so much. Men are always cackling by the hour all about nothing. If people come to see me when *I* have a house of my own, I shall not forget the rites of hospitality."

The doctor put up his pruning knife. There was a twinkle in his gray eyes.

"If you will do me the favour to come this way," he said, "my slaves will prepare a small collation on the instant."

"Oh, yes," said Diavolo. "Arabian Nights, you know! You must have fresh fruits and dried fruits, choice wines, cakes, sweets, and nuts.

"It shall be done as my lord commands," said the doctor.

That same evening, when he took the children home, Dr. Galbraith found Lady Adeline alone. She was a plain woman, but well-bred in appearance; and tender thoughts had carved a sweet expression on her face.

Next to her brother Dawne, Dawne's most intimate friend, Dr. Galbraith, was the man in the world upon whom she placed the greatest reliance.

"I have brought back the children," he said.

"Ah, then they *have* been with you!" she answered in a tone of relief. "We hoped they were."

"Oh, yes," he said smiling. "They showed me exactly what the difficulty here had been, and I have been endeavouring to win back their esteem, for they made it appear plainly that they despised me when they found me peacefully pruning rose trees instead of dismembering live rabbits, as Mr. Ellis had apparently led them to expect."

"They told you, then?"

"Oh, exactly, I am sure—about the lady tied too tight in the middle, and everything."

"They are terrible, George, those children," Lady Adeline declared. "My whole life is one ache of anxiety on their account. I am always in doubt as to whether their unnatural acuteness portends vice or is promising; and whether we are doing all that ought to be done for them."

"I am sure they are in very good hands now," he answered cheerfully. "Mr. Ellis is an exceedingly good fellow; they like him too, and I don't think anybody could manage them better."

"No," said Lady Adeline : "but that only means that no one can manage them at all. They are everywhere. They know everything. They have already mastered every fact in natural history that can be learnt upon the estate ; and they will do almost anything, and are so unscrupulous that I fear sometimes they are going to take after some criminal ancestor there may have been in the family, although I never heard of one, and go to the bad altogether. Now, what is to be done with such children ? I hardly dare allow myself to hope that they have good qualities enough to save them, and yet—and yet they are lovable," she added, looking at him wistfully.

"Most lovable, and I am sure you need not disturb yourself seriously," he answered with confidence. "The children have vivid imaginations and incomparable courage ; and their love of mischief comes from exuberance of spirits only, I am sure. When Angelica's womanly instincts develop, and she has seen something of the serious side of life—been made to *feel* it, I mean—she will become a very different person, or I am much mistaken. Her character promises to be as fine, when it is formed, as it will certainly be unusual. And as for Diavolo— well, I have seen no sign of any positive vice in either of them."

"You comfort me," said Lady Adeline. "How did you entertain them ?"

"Oh, we had great fun !" he replied, laughing. "We had an impromptu Arabian Night's entertainment with all the men and women about the place disguised as slaves ; and they all entered into the spirit of the thing heartily. I assure you, I never enjoyed anything more in my life. But I must go. I am on my way to town to-night to read a paper to-morrow morning upon a most interesting case of retarded brain development, which I have been studying for the last year. If I am right in my conclusions, we are upon the high road to some extraordinary and most valuable discoveries."

"Now, that is a singular man," Lady Adeline remarked to Mr. Ellis afterward. She had been telling the tutor about the success of his stratagem. "He spent valuable hours to-day playing with my children, and he says he never enjoyed anything so much in his life, and I quite believe him ; and to-morrow he will probably astonish the scientific world with a discovery of the last importance."

"I call him a human being, perfectly possessed of all his faculties," Mr. Ellis answered.

The twins worked well by fits and starts ; but when they did not chose to be diligent, they considerately gave their tutor a holiday. The last threat of a thrashing for Diavolo happened to be on the first of these occasions.

"It looks a good morning for fishing," he remarked casually to Angelica, just after they had settled down to lessons.

"Yes, it does," she answered.

There was a momentary pause, and then away went their books, and they were off out of the window.

But Mr. Ellis succeeded in capturing them, and, laying hold of an arm of each, he dragged them before the paternal tribunal in the library. He was not intimate with the peculiar relations of the household to each other at that particular time, and he thought Mr. Hamilton-Wells would prefer to order the punishment himself for so serious an offence. Angelica shook her hair over her face, and made sufficient feint of resistance to tumble her frock on the way, while Diavolo pretended to be terror-stricken ; but this was only to please Mr. Ellis with the delusion that fear of their father gave him a moral hold over them, for the moment Mr. Hamilton-Wells frowned upon them they straightened themselves and beamed about blandly.

Mr. Hamilton-Wells ordered Diavolo to be thrashed, and Diavolo dashed off for the cane and handed it to his tutor politely, saying at the same time : "Do be quick, Mr. Ellis, I want to get out."

"You wouldn't dare to thrash him if he were big enough to thrash you back," Angelica shrieked, waltzing round like a tornado; "and it isn't fair to thrash him and not me, for I am much worse than he is. You know I am, papa ! and I shall *hate* you if Diavolo is thrashed, and teach him how to make your life a burden to you for a month, I *shall* "—stamping her foot.

It always made her blood boil if there were any question of corporal punishment for Diavolo. She could have endured it herself without a murmur, but she had a feminine objection to knowing that it was being inflicted, especially as she was not allowed to be present.

"Don't be an idiot, Angelica," Diavolo drawled. "I would rather be thrashed, and have done with it. It does fellows good to be thrashed; makes them manly, they say in the books. And it hurts a jolly sight less than being scratched by *you*, if that is any comfort."

"Oh, you *are* mean!" Angelica exclaimed. "Wait till we get outside!"

"I think, sir," Mr. Ellis ventured to suggest in answer to an appealing glance from Mr. Hamilton-Wells, and looking dubiously at the cane—"I think, since Diavolo doesn't care a rap about being flogged, I had better devise a form of punishment for which he will care."

"Then come along, Diavolo," Angelica exclaimed, making a dash for the door. "They won't want us while they're devising."

Mr. Ellis would have followed them, but Mr. Hamilton-Wells gently restrained him. "It is no use, Mr. Ellis," he said, sighing deeply. "I would recommend you to keep up a show of disapproval for form's sake, but I beg that you will not give yourself any unnecessary trouble. They are quite incorrigible."

"I hope not," the tutor answered.

"Well, I leave them to you, make what you can of them!" their father rejoined. "I wash my hands of the responsibility while you are here."

The Heavenly Twins got their day's sport on that occasion, and returned with a basket full of trout for tea, fishy themselves, and tired, but bland and conciliatory. They dressed for the evening carefully, and without coercion, which was always a sign of repentance; and then they went down to the schoolroom, where they found Mr. Ellis standing with his back to the fireplace, reading a newspaper. He looked at them each in turn as they entered, and they looked at him, but he made no remark.

"I wish you would give us a good scolding at once, and have done with it," Angelica observed.

He made no sign of having heard, however, but quietly turned the paper over, chose a fresh item of information, and began to read it. Angelica sat down in her place at table, leant back with her short frock up to her knees and her long legs tucked under her chair, and reflected. Diavolo did the same, yawning aggressively.

"I'd sell my birthright for a mess of pottage with pleasure this minute," he exclaimed.

"What was pottage, Mr. Ellis?" Angelica asked insinuatingly.

"You don't suppose the recipe has been handed down in the Ellis family, do you?" said Diavolo.

Angelica looked round for a missile to hurl at him, but there being nothing handy, she tried the effect of a withering glance, to which he responded by making a face at her. A storm was evidently brewing, but fortunately just at that moment the tea arrived, and caused a diversion which prevented further demonstrations. Happily for those in charge of the twins, their outbursts of feeling were all squalls which subsided as suddenly as those of the innocent babe which howls everybody in the house out of bed for his bottle, and is beyond all comfort till he gets it, when his anger instantly goes out, and only a few gurgling "Oh's" of intense satisfaction mark the point from which the racket proceeded.

For a week Mr. Ellis maintained an attitude of dignified reserve with the twins, and their sociable souls were much exercised to devise a means to break down the barrier of coldness which they found between themselves and their tutor. They tried everything they could think of to beguile him back to the old friendly footing, and it was only after all other means had failed that they thought at last of apologising for their unruly conduct. It was the first time that they had ever done such a thing in their lives spontaneously, and they were so proud of it that they went and told everybody they knew

Mr. Ellis, having graciously accepted the apology, found himself expected to discuss the whole subject at tea that evening.

"Of course, we were quite in the wrong," said Angelica, taking advantage of the Peace Angel's presence to sum up comprehensively ; "but you must acknowledge that we were not altogether to blame, for you really have not been making our lessons sufficiently interesting to rivet our attention lately."

"That is true," said the diligent Diavolo. "My attention has not been riveted for weeks."

After the twins had made their memorable apology, they were so impressed by the importance of the event that they determined to celebrate it in some special way. They wanted to do something really worthy of the occasion.

"We'll do some good to somebody, shall we ?" said Angelica.

"Not unless there's some fun in it," said Diavolo.

"Well, who proposed to do anything without fun in it ?" Angelica wanted to know. "You've no sense at all, Diavolo. When people get up fancy fairs and charity balls, do they pretend to be doing it for fun? No! They say, ' Oh, my dear, I *am* so busy, I hardly know what to do first; but what keeps me up is the object! the good object!' And then they're enjoying it as hard as they can all the time. And that's what we'll do. We'll give the school children a treat."

The twins were allowed an hour to riot about the place after their early dinner, and then a bell was rung to summon them in to lessons, but on that particular day Mr. Ellis waited in vain for them. Angelica had concealed her riding habit in a loft, and as soon as they got out they ran to the stables, which were just then deserted, the men being at their dinner; and Angelica changed her dress while Diavolo got out their ponies and saddled them, and having carefully stolen through a thick plantation on to the high road, they scampered off to Morningquest as hard as their lively little steeds could carry them.

They were well known in Morningquest, and many an admiring as well as inquiring glance followed them as they cantered close together side by side through the quaint old streets. The people were wondering what on earth they were up to.

" Everybody looks so pleased to see us," said Diavolo, smiling genially; " I think we ought to come oftener."

" We will," said Angelica.

They pulled up at the principal confectioner's in the place, and bought as many pounds of sweets as they could carry, desiring the proprietor in a lordly way to send the bill to Hamilton House at his earliest convenience; and then they rode off to the largest day school in the city, stationed themselves on either side of a narrow gateway through which both girls and boys had to pass to get in, and pelted the children with sweets as they returned from their midday dinners; and as they had chosen sugar almonds, birds' eggs, and other varieties of a hard and heavy nature, which, although interesting in the mouth of a child, are inconvenient when received in its eyes, and cause irritation, which is apt to be resented, when pelted at the back of its head, the scene in a few minutes was extremely animated. This was what the Heavenly Twins called giving the school children a treat, and they told Mr. Ellis afterward that they enjoyed doing good very much.

"What shall we do now ?" said Diavolo as they walked their ponies aimlessly down the street when that episode was over.

" Let's call on grandpapa and the bishop," Angelica sug‎gested.

" The bishop first, then," said Diavolo. " They've such good cakes at the palace."

" Well, that's just why we should do grandpapa first," said Angelica. " Don't you see ? We can have cake at Morne ; and we shall be able to eat the ones at the palace too, if they're better."

" Yes," said Diavolo, with grave precision. " I notice my‎self, that, however much I have had, I can always eat a little more of something better."

" That's what they mean by tempting the appetite," observed Angelica sagely.

When the children arrived at the castle, it occurred to them that it would be a very good idea to ride right in and go up‎stairs on their ponies ; but they only succeeded in mounting the broad steps and entering the hall, where they were captured by the footmen and respectfully persuaded to alight. They announced that they had come to call on the Duke of Morning‎quest, and were conducted to his presence with pomp and ceremony enough to have embarrassed any other equally dusty dishevelled mortals, but the twins were not troubled with self-consciousness, and entered with perfect confidence. The duke was delighted. If there was one thing which could give him more pleasure than another in his old age, it was the wicked ways of the Heavenly Twins, and especially of the promising Angelica, who very much resembled him both in appearance, decision of character, and sharpness of temper. She promised, however, to be on a much larger scale, for the duke was diminutive. He looked like one who stands in a picture at the end of a long line of ancestors, considerably reduced by the perspective, and it was as if in his person an attempt had been made to breed the race down to the vanish‎ing point. His high-arched feet were admired as models of size and shape, and so also were his slender delicate hands ; but neither were agreeable to an educated eye and an intelli‎gence indifferent to the dignity of dukes, but nice in the matter of proportion.

The children found their grandfather in the oriel room, so called because of the great oriel window, which was a small room in itself, although it looked, as you approached the castle, no bigger than a swallow's nest on the face of the solid masonry, being the only excrescence visible above the trees from that point of view. The castle stood on a hill which descended precipitously from under the oriel, so that the latter almost overhung the valley in which the city lay below, and commanded a magnificent view of the flat country beyond, thridded by a shining winding ribbon of river. The hill was wooded on that side to the top, and the castle crowned it, rising above the trees in irregular outline against the sky imposingly. The old duke sat in the oriel often, looking down at the wonderful prospect, but thinking less of his own vast possessions than of the great cathedral of Morningquest, which he coveted for Holy Church. He had become a convert to Roman Catholicism in his old age, and his bigotry and credulity were as great now as his laxity and scepticism had been before his conversion.

He was sitting alone with his confessor and private chaplain, Father Ricardo, a man of middle age, middle height, attenuated form, round head with coarse black hair, piercing dark eyes, aquiline nose somewhat thick, and the loose mouth characteristic of devout Roman Catholics, High Church people, and others who are continually being wound up to worship an unseen Deity by means of sensuous enjoyment; the uncertain lines into which the lips fall in repose indicating fairly the habitual extent of their emotional indulgences. His manners were suave and deferential, his motives sincerely disinterested in the interests of the Church, his method of gaining his ends unhampered by any sense of the need of extreme verbal accuracy. He was reading to the duke when the children were announced, and rose and bowed low to them as they entered, with a smile of respectful and affectionate interest.

Diavolo raised his dusty cap to his chest and returned the bow with punctilious gravity. Angelica tossed him a nod as she passed up the room in a business-like way to where her grandfather was sitting facing the window. The old duke looked round as the children approached and his face relaxed; he did not absolutely smile, but his eyes twinkled.

Angelica plumped down on the arm of his chair, put her arm round his neck, and deposited a superficial kiss somewhere in the region of his ear, while Diavolo wrung his hand more ceremoniously, but with much energy. Both children seemed sure of their welcome, and comported themselves with their usual unaffected ease of manner. The old duke controlled his mouth, but there was something in the expression of his countenance which meant that he would have chuckled if his old sense of humour had not been checked by the presence of the priest, which held him somehow to his new professions of faith, and the severe dignity of demeanour that best befits the piety of a professional saint.

He was wearing a little black velvet skull cap, and Angelica, still sitting on the arm of his chair, took it off as soon as she had saluted him, looked into it, and clapped it on to the back of his head again, somewhat awry.

" I am glad you have your black velvet coat on to-day," she said, embracing the back of his chair with an arm, and kicking her long legs about in her fidgety way. " It goes well with your hair, and I like the feel of it."

" Have you a holiday to-day ? " the duke demanded with an affectation of sternness.

" Yes," said Angelica absently, taking up one of his delicate hands and transferring a costly ring from his slender white forefinger to her own dirty brown one.

" No," the more exact Diavolo contradicted ; " we gave Mr. Ellis a holiday."

" To tell you the truth, grandpapa, I had forgotten all about lessons," said Angelica candidly. " I fancy Mr. Ellis is fizzing by this time, don't you, Diavolo ? "

" What are you doing here if you haven't a holiday ? " their grandfather asked.

" Visiting you, sir," Diavolo answered in his peculiar drawl, which always left you uncertain as to whether he intended an impertinence or not. He was lying at full length on the floor facing his grandfather, with the back of his head resting on the low window sill, and the old gentleman was looking at him admiringly. He was not at all sure of the import of Diavolo's last reply, but had the tact not to pursue the subject.

The priest had remained standing, with his hands folded upon the book he had been reading, and a set smile upon his thin intellectual face, behind which it was easy to see that the busy thoughts came crowding.

Angelica turned on him suddenly, flinging herself from the arm of her grandfather's chair on to a low seat which stood with its back to the window, in order to do so.

" I say, Papa Ricardo, I want to ask you," she began. " What do you think of that Baronne de Chantal, whom you call Sainte, when her son threw himself across the threshold of their home to prevent her leaving the house, and she stepped across his body to go and be *religieuse ?* "

"It was the heroic act of a holy woman," the priest replied.

"But I thought Home was the woman's sphere?" said Angelica.

"Yes," the priest rejoined, "unless God calls them to religion."

"But did God give her all those children?" Angelica pursued.

"Yes, indeed," said Father Ricardo. "Children are the gift of God."

"Well, so I thought I had heard," Angelica remarked, with a genial air of being much interested. "But it seems such bad management to give a lady a lot of children, and then take her away so that she can't look after them."

The poor old duke had been dull all day. His mind, under the influence of his father confessor, had been running on the horrors of hell, and such subjects, together with the necessity of accomplishing certain good works and setting aside large sums of money in order to excuse himself from such condemnation as the priest had ventured to hint courteously that even a great duke might entail upon himself by the quite excusable errors of his youth; but since the Heavenly Twins arrived the old gentleman had begun to see things again from a point of view more natural to one of his family, and his countenance cleared in a way which denoted that his spirits were rising. Father Ricardo was accustomed to say that the dear children's high spirits were apt to be too much for his Grace; but this was a mistake, due doubtless to his extreme humility, which would not allow him to mention himself, for whom there was no doubt the dear children *were* apt to be too much.

The old duke, upon that last remark of Angelica's, twinkled a glance at his Father Confessor which had an effect on the latter that made itself apparent in the severity of his reply: "The ways of the Lord are inscrutable," he said, "and it is presumptuous for mortals, however great their station, to attempt to fathom them."

"I have heard that before too, often," said Diavolo, with a wise nod of commendation.

"So have I," said Angelica; and then both children beamed at the priest cordially, and the long-suppressed chuckle escaped from the duke.

Father Ricardo retired into himself.

"Grandpapa," Diavolo resumed—the Heavenly Twins never

allowed the conversation to flag—"Grandpapa, do you believe there ever was a little boy who never, never, told a lie?"

"I hope, sir, you do not mean me to infer that you are mendacious?" the old gentleman sternly rejoined.

"Mendacious?" Diavolo repeated; "that's do I tell lies, isn't it? Well, you see, sir, it's like this. If I'd been up to something, and you asked me if I'd done it, I'd say 'Yes' like a shot; but if Angelica had been up to something, and I knew all about it, and you asked me if she'd done it, I'd say 'No' flatly."

"Do I understand, sir, that you would tell me a lie 'flatly'?"

"Yes," said Diavolo decidedly, "if you were mean enough to expect me to sneak on Angelica."

"Father Ricardo," the latter began energetically, "when you tell a lie do you look straight at a person or just past the side of their heads?"

"*I* always look straight at a person myself," said Diavolo, gravely considering the priest; "I can't help it."

"It's the best way," said Angelica with the assurance of one who has tried both. "I suppose, grandpapa," she pursued, "when people get old they have nothing to tell lies about. They just sit and listen to them;" and again she looked hard at Father Ricardo, whose face had gradually become suffused with an angry red.

"I should think, Father Ricardo," said Diavolo, observing this, "if you were a layman, you would be feeling now as if you could throttle us?"

But before the poor priest could utter the reproof which trembled on his lips, the door opened and the duke's unmarried daughter and youngest child, the beautiful Lady Fulda, entered, and changed the moral atmosphere in a moment.

Both children rose to receive her tender kisses affectionately.

Their passionate appreciation of all things beautiful betrayed itself in the way they gazed at her; and hers was the only presence that ever subdued them for a moment.

"I like her in white and gold," Angelica remarked to Diavolo when she had looked her longest.

"So do I," Diavolo rejoined with a nod of satisfaction.

"My dear children!" Lady Fulda exclaimed. "You must not discuss my appearance in that way. You speak of me as if I were not here."

"You never seem to be here, somehow," said Diavolo,

struggling with a big thought he could not express. " I always feel when you come in as if you were miles and miles away from us. Now, mamma is always close to us, and papa gets quite in the way ; but you seem to be "—he raised both hands high above his head, with the palms spread outward, and then let his arms sink to his sides slowly. The gesture expressed an immeasurable distance above and beyond him.

"Yes," said Angelica, " I feel that too. But sometimes, when there's music and flowers and no light to speak of—in church, you know—and you feel as if angels might be about, or even the Lord himself, I rise up beside you somehow, and come quite close."

Lady Fulda's eyes deepened with feeling as Angelica spoke, and drawing the child to her side, she smoothed her hair, and gazed down into her face earnestly, as if she would penetrate the veil of flesh that baffled her when she tried to see clearly the soul of which Angelica occasionally gave her some such glimpse.

The old duke glanced round at the clock, and instantly the attentive priest stepped to the window and opened it wide. Then the duke raised his hand as if to enjoin silence, and presently the music of the bells of the city clocks, striking the hour in various tones, and all at different moments, causing a continuous murmurous sea of sound, arose from below. When the last vibration ceased there was a quite perceptible pause. The duke took off his little round black velvet cap, and leant forward, listening intently ; Lady Fulda bent her head and her lips moved ; the priest folded his hands and looked straight before him with the unconscious eyes of one absorbed in thought or prayer who sees not ; the twins, assuming a sanctimonious expression, bowed their hypocritical heads and watched what was going on out of the corners of their eyes. There was a moment's interval, and then came the chime, mellowed by distance, but clear and resonant :

He. watch-ing o - ver Is - ra - el, slumbers not, nor sleeps.

It was the habit of the old duke to listen for it hour by hour, and while it rang, he, and those of his household who shared his faith, offered a fervent prayer for the restoration of Holy Church.

Lady Fulda insisted on sending the children home under proper escort. They strongly objected. They said they were not going straight home ; they had to call on the Bishop of Morningquest.

" Why are you going to call on the Bishop of Morningquest ?" their aunt asked.

" We wish to see him," Angelica answered stiffly.

" On the subject of rotten potatoes," Diavolo supplemented Lady Fulda stared.

" Sainte Chantal, you know," said the ready Angelica. The reason was new to her, but the twins usually understood each other like a flash. " They put a rotten potato on her plate one day at dinner, and she ate it."

" She was so hungry ?" suggested Lady Fulda, trying hard to remember the story.

" No, so humble," Angelica answered ; " at least so they say in the book ; but we don't think it could have been humility ; it must have been horrid bad taste ; but we're going to ask the bishop. He's so temperate, you know. We tried to discuss the matter with Father Ricardo, but he shut us up promptly."

" My dear child ! " Lady Fulda exclaimed, " what an expression ! "

" I assure you it is the right one, Aunt Fulda," Angelica maintained. " He got quite red in the face."

" Yes," said Diavolo, gazing at Father Ricardo thoughtfully. " He looked hot enough to set fire to us if he'd touched us."

" I should think he would have been invaluable in the Inquisition," said Angelica, to whom that last remark of Diavolo's had opened up a boundless field of speculation and retrospect. " Wouldn't you like to hear a heretic go off pop on a pile?" she inquired, turning to Father Ricardo.

The duke and Lady Fulda glanced at him involuntarily, and very good-naturedly tried to smile. This, however, did not necessitate such an effort as the mere cold reading of the twins' remark might make it appear, for they both had a certain charm of manner, expressive of an utter absence of any intention to offend, which no kindly disposed person could resist ; and Father Ricardo was essentially kindly disposed.

The twins were taking their leave by this time. Angelica proceeded to deposit one of her erratic kisses somewhere on the old duke's head, with an emphasis which caused him to wince perceptibly. Then she went up to Father Ricardo, and shook hands with him.

"I hope the next time we come you will be able to tell us some nice bogey stories about death and the judgment, and hell, and that kind of thing," she said politely. "They interest us very much. You remember, you told us some before?"

"It must be very jolly for grandpapa to have you here always, ready to make his blood run cold whenever he feels dull," Diavolo observed, looking up at the priest admiringly. "You do it so well, you know, just as if you believed it all."

"We tried it once with some children we had to spend the day with us at Hamilton House," Angelica said. "We took them into a dark room—the long room, you know, Aunt Fulda ; and Diavolo rubbed a match on the wall at the far end, and I explained that that was a glimmer of hell-fire at a great distance off ; and then we told them if they didn't keep quite still the old devil himself would come creeping up behind without any noise, and jump on their backs."

"And the little beggars howled," Diavolo added, as if that consequence still filled him with astonishment.

"My dear children, I am afraid you tell dreadful stories," Lady Fulda exclaimed in a horrified tone.

"Yes," said Angelica, with her grave little nod ; "and we're improving ; but we cannot come up to Father Ricardo yet in that line."

"Not by a long chalk," said Diavolo.

"But, my *dear* child," Lady Fulda solemnly asserted, "Father Ricardo tells you *nothing* but what is *absolutely* true."

"How do you know?" Angelica asked.

"Oh—oh!" Lady Fulda stammered, and then looked at the priest appealingly.

"When you are older, and able to understand these things," Father Ricardo began with gentle earnestness, "perhaps you will allow me——"

"But how do you *know* it's true yourself?" Angelica demanded.

> "Did you ever *see* the devil,
> With his little spade and shovel,
> Digging praties in the garden
> With his tail cocked up?"—

Diavolo chanted, accompanying the words with a little dance, in which Angelica, holding up her habit, joined incontinently.

Lady Fulda remained grave, but the old duke and Father Ricardo himself were moved to mirth, and there was no more talk of Revealed Religion, the Power of the Popedom, and the glory of the Church on earth, at Morne that day.

Lady Fulda had been firm about sending the children home under escort, and they found a steady old groom waiting ready to mount a spirited horse when they went down to the courtyard to get on their ponies. They had discovered a box of croquet mallets on their way downstairs, and borrowed one each.

As they descended the steep hill leading from the castle, at a walk, they began to discuss recent events, as their habit was.

"What did you do when the chime went, and you hung your head?" said Angelica.

"I hoped there'd be hot cakes for tea ; but I didn't mean it for a prayer," Diavolo answered, as if the matter admitted of a doubt.

"I'm glad we decided to go secondly to the palace ; I didn't think much of grandpapa's tea," Angelica observed. "It was all china, and no cakes—to speak of ; no crisp ones, you know."

"Well, you see his teeth are bad," said Diavolo indulgently.

"He has enough of them, then!" Angelica answered.

"Yes, but they aren't much good, they're so loose, you know ; every now and again you can see them waggle," said Diavolo.

"I'd like to see him bite a fig!" said Angelica, chuckling.

"They'd stick, I suppose," said Diavolo meditatively. "I expect there will be great improvements in those matters by the time we want to be patched."

The groom, who had been riding at a respectful distance behind, suddenly perceived that he had lost sight of the children altogether. The descent was steep just there, and winding ; and, knowing with whom he had to deal, the man urged his horse on, straining his eyes at every turn to catch a glimpse of the twins, but vainly, till he reached the bottom of the hill, when they bounced out on him suddenly from among the trees on either side of the road, whooping and flourishing their mallets wildly. The horse, which was very fresh, gave one great bound and bolted, and the Heavenly Twins, shrieking with delight, hunted him hard into Morningquest.

When they arrived at the palace, Angelica asked with the utmost confidence if the bishop were at home ; and, being

Informed by an obsequious footman that he was, the twins marched into the hall, and were ushered into the presence of Mrs. Beale and her daughter Edith.

"Tell his lordship we are here," Angelica said to the servant authoritatively, before she performed her salutations. When these were over, the twins sat down opposite to Edith and inspected her.

"We've just been seeing Aunt Fulda," Diavolo remarked.

Angelica caught the connection : "Your hair is about the same colour as hers, but your face is smoother," she observed. "It looks like porcelain. Hers has little stipples, you know, about the nose, when you go close. They seem to come as you get older."

"Uncle Dawne calls you Saxon Edith," said Diavolo. "Don't you wonder he doesn't want to marry you ? *I* do. When I'm old enough I'm going to propose to you ; do you think you will have me ? "

"Have you ! I should think not, indeed !" Angelica exclaimed with a jealous flash. At that time the notion of sharing her brother's affection with anybody always enraged her.

Diavolo was irritated by her scornful manner.

"I am a little afraid," he began, addressing Mrs. Beale in his deliberate way : "I am a little afraid Angelica will stand in the way of my making a good match. No respectable wife would have her about."

Quick as thought, Angelica had him by the hair, and the two were tumbling over each other on the floor.

Mrs. Beale and Edith sprang forward to separate them, but that was impossible until the twins had banged each other to their heart's content, when they got up, with their feelings thoroughly relieved, and resumed their seats and the conversation as if nothing had happened. The skirmish, however, had been severe although short. Diavolo had a deep scratch over his right eyebrow which began to bleed profusely. Angelica was the first to notice it, and tearing out a handkerchief which was up her sleeve, she rolled it into a bandage roughly, whirled over to Diavolo, and tied it round his head, covering his right eye, and leaving a great knot and two long ends sticking up like rabbit's ears amongst his fair hair, and a pointed flap hanging down on the opposite side.

"I must cut my nails," she remarked, giving a finishing touch to this labour of love, which made Diavolo rock on his chair, but he accepted her attentions as a matter of course, merely drawling : " Angelica is *so* energetical ! " as he recovered his balance.

Just at this moment the bishop bustled in. He had been engaged upon some important diocesan duties when the twins were announced ; but, thinking they must have come with an urgent message, he suspended the work of the diocese, and hurried up to see what was the matter.

The twins rose to receive him with their usual unaffected affability. He was a short stout man with a pleasant face, and a cordial well-bred manner ; a little apt to be fussy on occasion, and destitute of any sense of humour in other people, although given to making his own little jokes. He was a bishop of the old-fashioned kind, owing his position to family influence rather than to any special attainment or qualification ; but he was a good man, and popular, and the See of Morningquest would have had much to regret if the back door by which he got into the Church had been shut before he passed through it.

" I am afraid there has been an accident," he said with concern when he saw Diavolo's head tied up in a handkerchief.

" Oh, no, thank you, sir," that young gentleman assured him. " It is only a scratch."

" *I* did it," said the candid Angelica ; " and it looked unpleasant, so I tied it up."

" Oh," the bishop ejaculated, glancing inquiringly at his wife and daughter. " You wanted to see me ? "

" Yes," said Diavolo, preparing to suit his conversation to the bishop's taste. " There are a great many things we want to discuss with you ; what were they, Angelica ? I am sure I have forgotten them all."

" Let me see," said Angelica—Sainte Chantal and the rotten potato had quite gone out of her mind. " It was just to have a little interesting conversation, you know."

" We're getting on very well with our lessons," Diavolo gravely assured him, anticipating the inevitable question.

" We've just come from Morne." said Angelica.

" Indeed," the bishop answered. " How is your grandfather ? "

" Rather flat to-day," said Angelica. " He didn't say anything of interest ; didn't even lecture us."

" No ; but he looked pleasant," said Diavolo.

" I like him to lecture," Angelica insisted. " I like him to talk about the Church, how it is going to encompass the earth, the sea, and all that in them is ; and that kind of thing, you know—boom, boom ! He makes you feel as if every word he uttered ought to be printed in capital letters ; and it seems as if your eyes opened wider and wider, and your skin got tight."

Diavolo nodded his head to one side in intelligent acquiescence.

Not being troubled with self-consciousness, he wore the handkerchief with which his head was decorated with the grave dignity of his best behaviour.

"I sometimes think, sir," he began, addressing the bishop exactly in his father's precise way, "that there is something remarkable about my grandfather. He is a kind of a prophet, I imagine, to whom the Lord doesn't speak."

Edith walked to the window, Mrs. Beale got out her handkerchief hastily ; the bishop's countenance relaxed.

"I suppose you wouldn't like us to be converted ?" Angelica asked.

"We call it *perverted*, dear child," said Mrs. Beale.

"Well, they call it *converted* just as positively up at the castle," Angelica rejoined, not argumentatively, merely stating the fact.

"I wonder what the angels call it," said Diavolo, looking up in their direction out of a window opposite, and then glancing at the bishop as if he thought he ought to know.

"I don't suppose they care a button what we call it," Angelica decided off-hand, out of her own inner consciousness. "But you would not like us to be either ' con ' or ' per,' would you ?" she asked the bishop.

"I am afraid I must not discuss so serious a question with you to-day," he answered. "I am very busy, and I must go back to my work."

"I thought you looked unsettled," Angelica observed. "I know what it is when you've got to come to the drawing room, and want to be somewhere else. They won't excuse us at home as a rule, but we'll excuse you, if you like."

"Eh—thank you," the old gentleman answered, glancing with a smile at his wife.

"But I should think some tea would do you good," Diavolo suggested.

"Have you not had any tea ?" Edith asked, stretching her hand out toward the bell.

" Well, yes," he answered. " We've had a little "—the tone implied, " but not nearly enough."

" We always like your cakes, you know," said Angelica; "and ours at Hamilton House are generally nice ; but at Morne they're sometimes sodden."

The bishop withdrew at this point, and the children devoted the rest of their attention to the cakes.

" Now we've got to go and settle with Mr. Ellis," Diavolo remarked to Angelica, yawning, as they walked their ponies out of the palace grounds.

" Well, at any rate, we've done the celebration thoroughly,' she answered, "and enjoyed it.   He won't be able to help that now.   Oh—by the way ! here's grandpapa's ring.   I forgot it."

" It doesn't matter," said Diavolo.   " He knows you'll take care of it."

Almost at the same moment the old duke at Morne missed the ring, and remarked : " Ah, I remember, Angelica has it. She put it on her finger when she was sitting beside me this afternoon."

" Shall I go at once to Hamilton House, and bring it back with me ? " Father Ricardo asked, somewhat officiously.

" No, sir, thank you," said the duke with dignity.   " My grand-daughter will return the ring when it suits her convenience."

Next day Angelica begged her father to take the ring back for her with a note of apology explaining that she had forgotten it, and expressing her regret.

CHAPTER XXI.

PART of the old gray palace at Morningquest had been a monastery.   The walls were thick, the windows gothic, the bedrooms small, the reception rooms huge, as if built for the accommodation of a whole community at a time ; and with unexpected alcoves and angles and deep embrasures, all very picturesque, and also extremely inconvenient ; but Edith Beale, who had been born in the palace and grown up there, under the protection of the great cathedral, as it were, and the influence of its wonderful chime, was never conscious of the inconvenience, and would not, at any rate, have exchanged it for the comfort and luxury of the best appointed modern house.

The Bishop of Morningquest and Mrs. Beale had three sons,

but Edith was their only daughter, their white child, their pearl ; and certainly she was a lovely specimen of a well-bred English girl.

On the day following that upon which the Heavenly Twins had celebrated the important occasion of their first spontaneous " Kow-tow," as they called it, in the early morning Edith, being still asleep, turned toward the east window of her room, the blind of which was up, and fell into a dream. The sun, as he rose, smiled in upon her. She had flung her left hand up above her head with the pink palm outward, and the fingers half bent ; the right lay on the sheet beside her, palm downward, spread out, and all relaxed. Her whole attitude expressed the most complete abandonment of deep and restful sleep.

The night had been warm, and the heavier draperies had slipped from her bed on the farther side, leaving only the sheet.

Her warm bright hair, partly loosened from the one thick braid into which it had been plaited, fell from off the pillow to the floor on her right, and the sun, looking in, lit it up and made it sparkle. She left that window with the blind undrawn so that he might arouse her every morning ; and now, as the first pale ray gleamed over her face, her eyelids quivered, and half opened, but she was still busy with her dream and did not wake. She lived in an atmosphere of dreams and of mystic old associations. Events of the days gone by were often more distinctly pictured in her mind than incidents of yesterday. Mrs. Orton Beg, her mother, and all the gentle mannered, pure-minded women among whom she had grown up, thought less of this world, even as they knew it, than of the next as they imagined it to be ; and they received and treasured with perfect faith every legend, hint, and shadow of a communication which they believed to have come to them from thence. They neglected the good they might have done here in order to enjoy their bright and tranquil dreams of the hereafter. Their spiritual food was faith and hope. They kept their tempers even and unruffled by never allowing themselves to think or know, so far as it is possible with average intelligence not to do either in this world, anything that is evil of anybody. They prided themselves on only believing all that is good of their fellow-creatures ; this was their idea of Christian charity. Thus they always believed the best about everybody, not on evidence, but upon principle ; and then they acted as if their attitude had made their acquaintances all they desired them to be. They seemed to think that by ignoring the existence of sin, by refusing to obtain any knowledge of it, they somehow helped to check it ; and they could not have conceived that their attitude made it safe to sin, so that, when they refused to know and to resist, they were actually countenancing evil and encouraging it. The kind of Christian charity from which they suffered was a vice in itself. To keep their own minds pure was the great object of their lives, which really meant to save themselves from the horror and pain of knowing.

Edith, by descent, by teaching, by association, and in virtue of the complete ignorance in which she had been kept, was essentially one of that set. It is impossible for any adult creature to be more spiritually minded than she was. She lived in a state of exquisite feeling. The whole training of her mind had been so directed as to make her existence one long beatific vision, and she was unconsciously prepared to resent in her gentle way, and to banish at once, if possible, any disturbing thought that might break in upon it.

In her dream that morning ·he smiled at first, and then she fairly laughed. She had met the Heavenly Twins, and they were telling her something—what was it ? The most amusing thing she had ever heard them say ; she knew it by the way it had made her laugh—why couldn't she repeat it? She was trying to tell her mother, and while in the act, she became suddenly aware of a strange place, and Diavolo kneeling at her feet, clasping her left hand, and kissing it. She felt the touch of his lips distinctly ; they were soft and warm. He was beseeching her to marry him, she understood, and she was going to laugh at him for being a ridiculous boy, but it was the steadfast, dark blue eyes of Lord Dawne that met hers, and she was looking up at him, and not down at the fair-haired Diavolo kneeling before her. She caught the gloss on Lord Dawne's black hair, the curve of his slight moustache, and the gleam of his white teeth. He was grave, but his lips were parted, and he carried a little child in his arms, and the expression of his face was like the dear Lord's in a picture of the Good Shepherd which she had in her room. He held the little child out to her. She took it from him, smiling, raised its little velvet cheek to hers, and then drew back to look at it, but was horrified because it was not beautiful at all as it had been the moment before, but deformed, and its poor little body was covered with sores. The sight sickened her, and

she tried to cover it with her own clothes. She tore at the
skirt of her gown. She struggled to take off a cloak she wore.
She stripped herself in the endeavour and cried aloud in her
shame, but she could not help herself, and Dawne could not
help her, and in the agony of the attempt she awoke, and
sprang up, clutching at the bedclothes, but was not able to
find them at first, because they had fallen on the floor; and
she fancied herself still in her horrible dream. Big drops of
perspiration stood on her forehead, her eyes were dazzled by
the sun, and she was all confused. She jumped out of bed
and stood a moment, trying to collect herself; and the first
thing she saw distinctly was the picture of the Saviour on the
wall. A *Prie-dieu* stood beneath it, and she went and knelt
there, her beautiful yellow hair streaming behind her, her eyes
fixed on the wonderful, sad, sweet face.

"Dear Lord," she prayed passionately, "keep me from all
knowledge of unholy things,"—by which she meant sights and
circumstances that were unlovely, and horrified.

She knelt for some minutes longer, with all articulate
thought suspended; but by degrees there came to her that
glow in the chest, that expansion of it which is the accompaniment of the exalted sentiment known to us as adoration, or
love; love purged of all earthly admixture of doubt and fear,
which is the most delicious sensation human nature is capable
of experiencing. And presently she arose, free from the painful impression made by the revolting details of her dream, put
her hands under her hair at the back of her neck, and then
raised them up above her head and her hair with them, stretching herself and yawning slightly. Then she brought her hair all
around to the right in a mass, and let it hang down to her knees,
and looked at it dreamily; and then began to twist it slowly,
preparatory to coiling it round her head. She went to the
dressing-table for hairpins to fasten it, holding up her long
nightdress above her white feet with one hand that she might
not trip, and, standing before the mirror, blushed at the beauty
of her own reflection. When she had put her hair out of the
way, she glanced at her bed somewhat longingly, then at her
watch. It was very early, and the morning was chilly, so she
put on her white flannel dressing gown, got a book, returned to
her bed, and propped herself up in a comfortable position for
reading; and so she spent the time happily until her maid came
to call her. Her book that morning was " The Life of Frances
Ridley Havergal," and she found it absorbingly interesting.

CHAPTER XXII.

THE ladies of an artist's family usually arrange and decorate their rooms in a way which recalls the manner called artistic, more especially when the artist is a figure or subject, as distinguished from a landscape painter, for the latter lives too much in the free fresh air to cultivate draperies, even if he does not absolutely detest them as being stuffy ; and in the same way the bedroom of the only daughter of the Bishop of Morningquest would have made you think of matters ecclesiastical.   The room itself, with its thick walls, high stone mantelpiece, small gothic windows, and plain ridged vault, was so in fact ; and a sense of suitability as well as the natural inclination of the occupant had led her to choose the furniture and decoration as severely in keeping as possible.   The pictures consisted of photographs or engravings of sacred subjects, all of Roman Catholic origin.   There was a " Virgin and Child," by Botticelli, and another by Perugini ; " Our Lady of the Cat," by Baroccio ; the exquisite " Vision of St. Helena," by Paolo Veronese ; Correggio's " Ecce Homo " ; and others less well-known ; with a ghastly Crucifixion too painful to be endured, especially by a young girl, had not custom dulled all genuine perception of the horror of it.   The whole effect, however, was a delicious impression of freshness and serenity, which inspired something of the same respect for Edith's sanctum that one felt for Edith herself, as was evident on one occasion, when, the ladies of his family being absent, the Bishop of Morningquest had taken Mr. Kilroy of Ilverthorpe, a gentleman who had lately settled in that neighbourhood, over the palace.   When they came to Edith's room, he had opened the door absently, and then, remembering whose it was, he said : " My daughter's room," and they had both looked in without entering, and both becoming aware at the same moment that they had their hats on, removed them involuntarily.

Edith's dress too, was characteristic.   All the ornamentation was out of sight, the lining of her gowns being often more costly than the materials of which they were made.   In the same way, her simple unaffected manners were the plain garment which concealed the fine quality and cultivation of her mind. She might have done great good in the world had she known of the evil ; she would have fought for the right in defiance of every prejudice, as women do. But she had never been allowed to see the enemy. She had been fitted by education to move in the society of saints and angels only, and so rendered as unsuited as she was unprepared to cope with the world she would have to meet in that state of life to which, as she herself would have phrased it, it had pleased God to call her.

When she left her room that morning she went to her mother's sitting room, which was on the same floor.

Edith and her mother usually breakfasted here together. Sometimes the bishop joined them and chatted over an extra cup of tea; but he was an early riser, and had generally breakfasted with his chaplain and private secretary, and done an hour's work or so before his wife appeared. For Mrs. Beale was delicate at that time, and obliged to forego the early breakfast with her husband which had hitherto been the habit and pleasure of her whole married life.

The bishop did not come up to the sitting room that morning, however, and when Edith and her mother had breakfasted they read the Psalms for the day together, and a chapter of the Bible, verse by verse. Then Edith wrote some notes for her mother, who was busy making a cushion for a bazaar; after which she went into the garden and gathered flowers in one of the conservatories, which she brought in to paint on a screen she was making, also for the bazaar.

Mother and daughter worked together without any conversation to speak of until lunch: they were too busy to talk. After lunch they drove out into the country and paid a call. On the way back Edith noticed a beggar, a young, slender, very delicate-looking girl, lying across the footpath with her feet toward the road. A tiny baby lay on her lap. Her head and shoulders were pillowed upon the high bank which flanked the path, her face was raised as if her last look had been up at the sky above her, her hands had slipped helplessly on to the ground on either side of her, releasing the child, which had rolled over on to its face and so continued inertly.

Edith caught only a passing glimpse of the group, and she made no remark until they had driven on some distance; but then she asked : " Did you notice that poor girl, mother ? "

"No," Mrs. Beale answered. " Where was she ? "

" Lying on the ground. She had a baby on her lap. I think she was ill."

They were in an open carriage, and Mrs. Beale looked round over the back of it. It was a straight road, but she could only see something lying on the footpath, which looked like a bundle at that distance.

"Are you sure it was a girl?" she said.

"Yes, quite, mother," Edith answered.

"Stop the carriage, then," said Mrs. Beale; "and we will turn back and see what we can do."

They found the girl in the same attitude. Edith was about to alight, but her mother stopped her.

"Let Edwards" (the footman, who was an old servant), "see what is the matter," she said.

Edith instantly sat down again, and the footman went and stood by the girl, looking down at her curiously. Then he stooped, took off his glove, and put the points of the four fingers of his right hand on her chest, like an amateur doctor afraid of soiling his hands, a perfunctory way of ascertaining if she still breathed.

"I know who it is, ma'am," he said, returning to the carriage. "She's French, and was a dressmaker in Morning-quest. There were two of them, sisters, doing a very good business, but they got to know some of the gentry——"

Mrs. Beale stopped him. She would not have heard the story for the world.

"She's not dead, is she?" Edith asked in a horrified tone.

The man looked at the girl again from where he stood; "No, miss," he answered, "I think not. She's dead beat after a long tramp. The soles are wore off her shoes. Or likely she's fainted. It's a pity of her," he added for the relief of his own feelings, looking at her again compassionately.

"Oh, mother! can't we do something?" Edith exclaimed.

"But what *can* we do?" Mrs. Beale responded helplessly, looking at Edwards for a suggestion.

"We're not very far from the workus," he said, looking down the road they had just retraversed. "We might call there as we pass, and leave a message for them to send and take her in."

"Let us go at once," said Mrs. Beale in a tone of relief.

Edith, whose face was pale, looked pityingly once more at the girl and her little child as they drove off. It had not occurred to either of the two ladies, gentle, tender, and good as they were, to take the poor dusty disgraced tramp into their carriage, and restore her to "life and use and name and fame" as they might have done.

The incident, however, had naturally made a painful impression upon them both ; and when they returned to the palace they ordered tea in the drawing room immediately, feeling that they must have something, and went there with their things still on to wait for it. Neither of them could get the tramp and her baby out of their heads, but they had not mentioned her since they came in, until Mrs. Beale broke a long silence by exclaiming : "We will drive that way again to-morrow, and find out how they are."

Edith needed no explanation as to whom she was alluding. "They would take her in at once, of course, mother ? They could not put it off ? " she said.

" Oh, no ! not when we asked them," her mother answered.

The tea was brought at this moment, and immediately afterward the footman announced from the door; "Sir Mosley Menteith," and a tall, fair-haired man about thirty, with a small, fine, light-coloured moustache, the ends of which were waxed and turned up toward the corners of his eyes, entered and shook hands with Mrs. Beale, looking into her face intently as he did so, as if he particularly wanted to see what she was like ; then he turned to Edith, shook hands, and looked at her intently also, and taking a seat near her he continued to scrutinize her in a way that brought the blood to her cheeks, and caused her to drop her eyes every time she looked at him. But they were old acquaintances, and she was not displeased.

He was a good-looking young man, although he had a face which some people called empty because of the singular immobility of every feature except his eyes ; but whether the set expression was worn as a mask, or whether he really had nothing in him, was a question which could only be decided on intimate acquaintance ; for although some effect of personality continually suggested the presence in him of thoughts and feelings disguised or concealed by an affectation of impassivity, nothing he did or said at an ordinary interview ever either quite confirmed or destroyed the impression.

" I thought you had gone abroad with your regiment," said Mrs. Beale, who had received him cordially.

" No, not yet," he answered, looking away from Edith for a minute in order to scrutinize her mother.

He always seemed to be inspecting the person he addressed, and never spoke of anyone without describing their charms or blemishes categorically. "Fact is, I've just come to say good-

bye.   I've been abroad on leave for two months.   Took mine
at the beginning of the season."

He looked intently at Edith again when he had said this.

"Mrs. Orton Beg," the servant announced.

Mrs. Orton Beg's ankle was strong enough now for her to
walk from her little house in the Close to the palace, but she
had to use a stick.   She was bleached by being so much
indoors, and looked very fragile in the costly simplicity of her
black draperies as she entered.

Mrs. Beale and Edith received her affectionately, and Sir
Mosley rose and transferred his scrutinizing gaze to her while
they were so occupied.   He inspected her dark glossy hair;
eyes, nose, mouth, and figure, down to her feet; then looked
into her eyes again, and bowed on being presented by Mrs.
Beale.

"Sir Mosley is in the Colquhoun Highlanders," the latter
explained to Mrs. Orton Beg.   "He is just going out to Malta
to join them."

Mrs. Orton Beg looked up at him with interest from the low
chair into which she had subsided: "Then you know my
niece, I suppose," she said—"Mrs. Colquhoun?"

"I have not yet the pleasure," he answered, smiling so
that he showed his teeth.   They were somewhat discoloured
by tobacco, but the smile was a pleasant one, to which people
instantly responded.   He went to the tea table when he had
spoken, and stood there waiting to hand Mrs. Orton Beg a cup
of tea which Mrs. Beale was pouring out for her.   "But I have
seen Mrs. Colquhoun," he added.   "I was at the wedding—
she looked remarkably well."   He fixed his eyes on vacancy
here, and turned his attention inward in order to contemplate
a vision of Evadne in her wedding dress.   His first question
about a strange woman was always; "Is she good-looking?"
and his first thought when one whom he knew happened to be
mentioned was always as to whether she was attractive in
appearance or not.   He was one of several of Colonel Colquhoun's brother officers who had graced the wedding.   There
was not much variety amongst them.   They were all excessively
clean and neat in appearance, their manners in society were
unexceptionable, the morals of most of them not worth describing because there was so little of them; and their comments
to each other on the occasion neither original nor refined;
generations of them had made the same remarks under similar
circumstances.

The bishop came in during the little diversion caused by handing tea and cake to Mrs. Orton Beg.

" Ah, how do you do?" he said, shaking hands with the latter. " How is the foot? Better? That's right. Oh! is that you, Mosley? I beg your pardon, my dear boy "—here they shook hands—" I did not see you at first. Very glad you've come, I'm sure. How is your mother? Not with your regiment, eh?" He peered at Sir Mosley through a pair of very thick glasses he wore, and seemed to read an answer to each question as he put it, written on the latter's face.

" Will you have some tea, dear?" said Mrs. Beale.

" Eh, what did you say, my dear? Tea? Yes, if you please. That is what I came for."

He turned to the tea table as he spoke, and stood over it rubbing his hands, and beaming about him blandly.

Sir Mosley Menteith had been a good deal at the palace as a youngster. He and Edith still called each other by their Christian names. The bishop had seen him grow up from a boy, and knew all about him—so he would have said—although he had not seen much of him and had heard absolutely nothing for several years.

" So you are not with your regiment?" he repeated interrogatively.

" I am just on my way to join it now," the young man answered, looking up at the bishop from the chair near Edith on which he was again sitting, and giving the corners of his little light moustache a twirl on either side when he had spoken. All his features, except his eyes, preserved an imperturbable gravity; his lips moved, but without altering the expression of his face. His eyes, however, inspected the bishop intelligently; and always, when he spoke to him, they rested on some one point, his vest, his gaiters, his apron, the top of his bald head, the end of his nose.

" Dr. Galbraith," the footman announced; and the doctor entered in his easy, unaffected, but somewhat awkward way. He had his hat in his hand, and there was a shade of weariness or depression on his strong pale face; but his deep gray kindly eyes—the redeeming feature—were as sympathetically penetrating as usual.

He shook hands with them all, except Sir Mosley, at whom he just glanced sufficiently long to perceive that he was a stranger.

Mrs. Beale named them to each other, and they both bowed

slightly, looking at the ground, and then they exchanged glances.

"Not much like a medico if you are one," thought Menteith.

"Not difficult to take your measure," thought the doctor; after which he turned at once to the tea table, like one at home, and stood there waiting for a cup. His manner was quite unassuming, but he was one of those men of marked individuality who change the social atmosphere of a room when they enter it. People became aware of the presence of strength almost before they saw him or heard him speak. And he possessed that peculiar charm, common to Lord Dawne and others of their set, which came of giving the whole of their attention to the person with whom they were conversing for the moment. His eyes never wandered, and if his interest flagged he did not allow the fact to become apparent, so that he drew from everybody the best that was in them, and people not ordinarily brilliant were often surprised, on reflection, at the amount of information they had been displaying, and the number of ideas which had come crowding into their usually vacant minds while he talked with them.

He turned his attention to Mrs. Beale now. "I was afraid I should be late for tea," he said. "I had to turn back—about something. I was delayed."

"We were late ourselves this afternoon," said Mrs. Beale.

Curiously enough the same cause had delayed them both, for Dr. Galbraith, coming into Morningquest by the road Mrs. Beale had chosen for her drive that day, had noticed the insensible girl and her baby lying on the footpath, and had got down, lifted them into his carriage, and driven back some miles with them in order to leave them at the house of one of his tenants, a respectable widow whom he had trained as a nurse, and to whose kind care he now confided them with strict orders for their comfort, and the wherewithal to carry the orders out.

Dr. Galbraith took his tea now and sat down. He had come for a special purpose, and hastened to broach the subject at once.

"Have you decided where to go this winter?" he asked Mrs. Beale. "You will be having another attack of bronchitis, and then you will not be able to travel. It is not safe to put it off too long."

His orders were that she should winter abroad that year,

and Edith was to accompany her; but they were both reluctant to go because of the bishop, whose duties obliged him to remain behind alone. Mrs. Beale glanced at him now affectionately. He was leaning back in a low chair, paunch protuberant, and little legs crossed; and he answered the look with a smile which was meant to be encouraging, but was only disturbed. He was a perfect coward, this ruler of a great diocese, in matters which were of moment to the health and well-being of his own family; he hated to have to decide for them.

"Why not come to Malta?" Sir Mosley suggested.

"That would be nice for Evadne," Mrs. Orton Beg exclaimed, her mind taking in at a glance all the advantage for the latter of having a companion of her own age, and without quirks, like Edith, and the womanly restraining influence of a friend like dear old Mrs. Beale.

"What kind of a place is Malta?" the bishop asked generally, tapping the edge of his saucer with his teaspoon; then, addressing Dr. Galbraith in particular, he added : "Would it be suitable?"

"Just the thing," the latter answered. "Picturesque, good society, and delightful climate at this time of the year. Accessible, too; you can go directly by P. and O., and the little sea voyage would be good for Mrs. Beale."

"It would be nice to have Evadne there," said Edith, considering the proposition favourably. "I have hardly seen her at all since we were both in the nursery."

"She was such a quiet child," said Mrs. Beale. "Unnaturally so; but they used to say she was clever."

"She is," said Mrs. Orton Beg, "decidedly so, and original —or, rather, *advanced.* I believe that is the proper word now."

"Oh, dear!" said Mrs. Beale. "Is that nice?"

"Well," Mrs. Orton Beg answered, smiling, "I cannot say. It is not a matter of law, you know, but of opinion. Evadne is nice, however; so much I will venture to declare!"

"She used to be very good to the little Hamilton-Wellses," Mrs. Beale gave out as a point in her favour.

"Oh—*did* you hear about the Heavenly Twins yesterday?" Edith exclaimed, addressing Dr. Galbraith : "They came to call on papa, and he couldn't make out what they wanted. He did look so puzzled! and they sat down and endeavoured to draw him into a theological discussion, after having had a fight on the floor—the children, I mean, not papa, of course!"

" They always endeavour to adapt themselves to the people with whom they happen to be," said Dr. Galbraith. " When they call upon me they come primed with medical matters, and discuss the present condition of surgical practice, and the future prospects of advance in that direction. And I rather suspect that my own books and papers are the sources from which they derive their information. I lock up my library and consulting rooms now as a rule when I go out, but sometimes I forget to shut the windows."

" They are very singular little people," said the bishop, with his benign smile ; " very singular ! "

" They are very *naughty* little people, I think ! " said Mrs. Beale.

Dr. Galbraith laughed as at some ludicrous reminiscence.

" But will you come to Malta ? " said Sir Mosley. " Because if you will, and would allow me, I could see about making arrangements for your accommodation."

" You are very kind," said the bishop.

" But when should we be obliged to go ? " Mrs. Beale asked, meaning, " How long may we stay at home ? "

" You must go as soon as possible," Dr. Galbraith decided inexorably.

And so the matter was settled after some little discussion of details, during which Lady Adeline Hamilton-Wells and Mrs. Frayling came in. The latter was in Morningquest for the day doing some shopping. She had lunched with her sister, Mrs. Orton Beg, and had come to have tea with Mrs. Beale ; and she and Lady Adeline had encountered each other at the door.

Mrs. Frayling looked very well. She was a wonderfully preserved woman, and being of an elastic temperament, a day away from home always sufficed to smooth out the wrinkles which her husband's peculiar method of loving and cherishing her tended to confirm. And she was especially buoyant just then, for it was immediately after the Battle of the Letters, and Mr. Frayling was so meek in his manner, and she felt altogether so free and independent, that she had actually ventured to come into Morningquest that day without first humbly asking his permission. She had just informed him of her intention, and walked out before he could recover himself sufficiently to oppose it.

Dr. Galbraith had taken his leave when they entered the room, and only waited a moment afterward to exchange a word with Lady Adeline. When he had gone, Sir Mosley asked the latter, who had known him since he was a boy, but did not love him, " Is that ugly man a medical doctor ? "

" Yes," she answered in her gentle but downright way, " he *is* a medical man, but not an ' ugly ' man at all."

" Is Mosley calling Dr. Galbraith ugly ? " Mrs. Beale exclaimed, " Now, *I* think he has the *nicest* face ! "

" A most good-looking kind of ugliness," said Mrs. Orton Beg.

Menteith perceived that any attempt to disparage Dr. Galbraith in that set was a mistake, and retired from the position cleverly. " There is a kind of ugliness which is attractive in a man," he said with his infectious smile.

Edith responded, and then they drew apart from the rest, and began to talk to each other exclusively.

There was a bright tinge of colour in her transparent cheeks, her eyes sparkled, and a pleased perpetual smile hovered about her lips. The entrance of Sir Mosley Menteith had changed the unemotional feminine atmosphere. He was an eligible, and his near neighbourhood caused the girl's heart to swell with a sensation like enthusiasm. She felt as if she could be eloquent, but no suitable subject presented itself, and so she said little. She was very glad, however, and she looked so ; and naturally she thought no more for the moment of the poor little French girl—who was just then awaking to a sense of pain, mental and physical, to horror of the past, and fear for the future, and the heavy sense of an existence marred, not by reason of her own weakness so much as by the possession of one of the most beautiful qualities in human nature—the power to love and trust.

" Is the old swing still on the elm ? " said Sir Mosley.

" Yes," Edith answered. " Not exactly the same rope, you know ; but we keep a swing there always."

" Who uses it now ? "

" Children who come to see us," she said. " And sometimes I sit in it myself ! " she added laughing.

" I should very much like to see it again," he said.

" Come and see it then," she answered, rising as she spoke. " Mosley wants to see the old swing," she said to her mother as they left the room together.

" What a nice looking young man," Mrs. Frayling observed.

"His head is too small," Lady Adeline said. "Has he anything in him?"

"Oh—yes. Well, good average abilities, I should say," Mrs. Beale rejoined. "Too much ability, you know, is rather dangerous. Men with many ideas so often get into mischief."

"That is true," said Mrs. Frayling; "and it is worse with women. When *they* have ideas, as my husband was saying only this morning, they become quite outrageous—*new* ideas, of course I mean, you know."

"He seems to admire Edith very much," Mrs. Orton Beg observed.

Mrs. Beale smiled complacently.

Edith sat long in her room that night on the seat of the window that faced the east. She had taken off her evening dress and put on her white flannel wrapper. The soft material draped itself to her figure, and fell in heavy folds to her feet. Her beautiful hair, which was arranged for the night in one great plait with the ends loose, hung down to the ground beside her.

The moon was high in the heavens, but not visible from where she sat. Its light, however, flooded the open spaces of the garden beneath her, and cast great shadows of the trees across the lawn. The sombre afternoon had cleared to a frosty night, and the deep indigo sky was sparsely sprinkled with brilliant stars.

Edith looked out. She saw the stars, and the earth with its heavy shadows, and the wavering outlines of the trees and shrubs, and felt a kinship with them.

She was very happy, but she did not think. She did not want to think. When any obtrusive thought presented itself she instantly strove to banish it, and at first she succeeded. She wanted to recall the pleasurable sensations of the day, and to prolong them.

The last sixteen hours seemed longer in the retrospect than any other measure of time with which she had been acquainted. She felt as if the terrible dream from which she had awakened that morning in affright had happened in some other state of being which ended abruptly while she was pacing the shady walks of the old palace garden with Mosley Menteith in the afternoon, and was now only to be vaguely recalled. Some great change in herself had taken place since then; she would not define it; she imagined she could not; but she knew what it was all the same, and rejoiced.

They were going to Malta.

The feeling resolved itself into that clear idea inevitably ; and after a little pause it was followed by the question : "Well, and what then ? "

But either her mind refused to receive the reply, or else in the Book of Fate the answer was still unwritten, for none came to her consciousness.

Turning at last from the window, she found the eyes of the Good Shepherd in the picture fixed upon her, the beautiful benign eyes she loved so well ; and looking up at him responsively, she waited a moment for her heart to expand anew, and then set herself to meditate upon his life. It was a religious exercise she had taught herself, not knowing that the Roman Catholics practise it as a duty always. She thought of him first as the dear Lord who died for her, and her heart awoke trembling with joy and fear at the realization of the glorious deed. His tenderness came upon her, and she bowed her head to receive it. Her ears were straining as it were to hear the sweetness of his voice. She sank on her knees before his image to be the nearer to him while she dwelt on the mystery of his divine patience, and felt herself filled with the serene intensity of his holy love. She recalled the faultless grace and beauty of his person, and revelled in the thought of it, till suddenly a deep and sensuous glow of delight in him flooded her being, and her very soul was faint for him. She called him by name caressingly : "Dear Lord !" She confessed her passionate attachment to him. She implored him to look upon her lovingly. She offered him the devotion of her life. And then she sank into a perfect stupor of ecstatic contemplation. This was the way she worshipped, dwelling on the charms of his person and character with the same senses that her delicate maiden mind still shrank from devoting to an earthly lover ; calling him what she would have had her husband be : "Master ! "—the woman's ideal of perfect bliss : " A strong support !" " A sure refuge ! "—praying him to strengthen her, to make her wise, to keep her pure ; to help, to guide, to comfort her ! and finding in each repetition of familiar phrases the luxurious gladness of a great enthusiasm.

But these emotional excesses were not to be indulged in with impunity. When Edith arose from her knees, she had already begun to suffer the punishment of a chilling reaction. The love-light faded from her face. The glow of ecstatic passion was extinguished in her heart. The festal robes of enraptured feeling feh from her consciousness and were replaced by the rags of unwelcome recollections. She thought of the poor delicate little French girl lying by the wayside exhausted, and longed to know if she were at that moment sheltering in the workhouse, and rested and restored. She wondered what it was like to be in the workhouse—alone— without a single friend to speak kindly to her; but the bare thought of such a position made her shudder. If only she could have befriended that poor creature and her little child? The sweet maternal instinct of her own being set up a yearning which softened her heart the more tenderly toward the mother because of the child. She did so wish that she could have done something for both of them, and then she recollected her horrible dream, and began involuntarily to piece the vision of the morning to the incident of the afternoon in order to find some faint foreshadowing for her guidance of the one event in the other. Next day, she persuaded her mother to send to the workhouse directly after breakfast to ask if the girl had been taken in, and how she was. Edwards, the old footman, could have told his mistress the girl's whole history, and she knew him also to be an honest man, of simple speech, not given to exaggerate; but she scented something "unpleasant" in the whole affair, and she would have looked coldly for the rest of her life on anyone as being a suspicious character, who had ventured to suggest that she should make herself acquainted with the details of such a case. She considered that any inquiries of that kind would have been improper to the last degree.

She sent Edwards to the workhouse, however, to know if the girl had been found; and when he brought back word that she had not, although the most careful search for her had been made in the neighbourhood, Mrs. Beale concluded that she had recovered sufficiently to continue her weary tramp, and very gladly dismissed the whole matter from her mind.

END OF BOOK I.

BOOK II.

A MALTESE MISCELLANY.

Death itself to the reflecting mind is less serious than marriage. The elder plant is cut down that the younger may have room to flourish ; a few tears drop into the loosened soil, and buds and blossoms spring over it Death is not a blow, is not even a pulsation ; it is a pause But marriage unrolls the awful lot of numberless generations. Health, genius, honour are the words inscribed on some ; on others are disease, fatuity, and infamy. —*Walter Savage Landor.*

The great leading idea is quite new to me, viz., that during late ages the mind will have been modified more than the body ; yet I had not got as far as to see with you, that the struggle between the races of man depended entirely on intellectual and *moral* qualities.—*Darwin · Letter to A. R. Wallace.*

CHAPTER I.

MEANWHILE the Colquhouns at Malta had been steadily making each other's acquaintance.

Colonel Colquhoun had met Evadne on board the steamer on her arrival, and had found her enchanted by her first glimpse of the place, and too girlishly glad in the excitement of change, the bustle and movement and novelty, to give a thought to anything else. The healthy young of the human race have a large capacity for enjoyment, and they have also the happy knack of banishing all thought which threatens to be an interruption to pleasurable sensation. When a thing was once settled it was Evadne's disposition to have done with it, and since she had come to satisfactory terms with Colonel Colquhoun and recovered from the immediate effects of the painful contest, the matter had not troubled her. She had perfect confidence in his word of honour as a gentleman, and was prepared to find it no more awkward to live in his house and have him for an occasional companion, than it would to be a guest of good position in any other establishment.

His own attitude was that of a kind of pleased curiosity. He considered their bargain a thing to be carried out to the letter so long as she held him to it, like a debt of honour, not legally binding but morally, and he was prepared, with gentlemanly tack, to keep faith without further discussion of the subject. The arrangement did not trouble him at all. It was original, and therefore somewhat piquant, and so was Evadne.

They met therefore without more than a momentary embarrassment, and his first glimpse of her fresh young face, flushed with excitement, and full of intelligent interest and of unaffected pleasure in everything, was an unexpected revelation of yet another facet of her manifold nature, and a bright one too. What a pity she had "views"! But there was always a hope the determination to live up to them was merely an infantile disease of which society would soon cure her. Society has views too. It believes all it hears in the churches without feeling at all bound to practise any inconvenient precept implied in the faith.

Colonel Colquhoun had gone out on a government **steam** launch to meet the mail as soon as she was signalled, and finding Evadne on deck had remained there with her watching the wonderful panorama of the place gradually unfolding itself.   He showed her the various points of interest as they came along, and she smiled silent acknowledgments of the courtesy.

The sun was just dispelling the diaphanous mists of early morning, making them hang luminous a moment and then disperse, like tinted gauze that flutters slowly upward in a breeze and vanishes.   Great white clouds, foam-like and crisp, piled themselves up fantastically and floated off also, leaving the deep blue vault to mirror itself in the answering azure of the sea ; the eternal calm above, awful in its intensity of stillness ; the ceaseless movement below, a type of life, throbbing, murmurous, changeful, more interesting than awe-inspiring, more to be wondered at than revered.

Colonel Colquhoun pointed out the lighthouses of St. Elmo, patron saint of sailors, on the right, and Ricasoli on the left. Then they were met by a rainbow fleet of dghaisas, gorgeous in colour, and propelled by oarsmen who stood to their work, and were also brightly clad—both boats and boatmen, clothed by the sun, as it were, having blossomed into colour unconsciously as the flowers do in genial atmospheres.   The boats, carrying fruits, flowers, tobacco, cheap jewellery, and coarse clothing for sailors, each cargo adding something of picturesqueness to the scene, formed a gay flotilla about the steamer and accompanied her, she towering majestically above them, and appearing to attract them and hold them to her sides as a great cork in the water does a handful of chopped straw.   The boatman held up their wares, chattering and gesticulating, their sun-embrowned faces all animation and changeful as children's.   One moment they would be smiling up and speaking in wheedling tones to the passengers, and the next they would be frowning round at each other, and resenting some offence with torrents of abuse.   So the mail glided into the Grand Harbour, Evadne wondering at the fortifications, and straining her eyes to make out somewhat of the symbols, alternate eye and ear, carved on the old watch tower of St. Angelo ; noticing, too, the sharp outline of everything in the pellucid atmosphere, and feeling herself suddenly aglow with warmth and colour, a part of the marvellous beauty and brightness, and uplifted in spirit out of the everyday world above all thought and care into regions of the purest pleasure.

"What a lovely place !" she exclaimed. "It looks like a great irregular enchanted palace !"

"It's very jolly," said Colonel Colquhoun, smiling upon the scene complacently, and looking as important as if he were himself responsible for the whole arrangement, but was too magnanimous to mention the fact. "I thought you'd like it. But wait till you see it by moonlight! We'll come off and dine with one of the naval fellows some night. I'm sure you'll be delighted. It's just like a photograph."

Evadne found that Colonel Colquhoun had secured a good house for her, and had bestowed much care upon the arrangement of it. It was the kind of occupation in which he delighted, and he did it well. He showed Evadne over the house himself as soon as she arrived, and what struck her as most delightful were the flowers and foliage plants which decorated every available corner, and nearly all growing; oranges and oleanders in great tubs, and palms and ferns in oriental china stands and in Majolica vases.

"One only sees it so for a ball at home," she said ; "or some other special occasion."

He looked at her keenly a moment. Her face was serenely content.

"Well, this is a kind of a special occasion with me," he said rather gloomily.

He went on as he spoke, Evadne following him from room to room, pleased with everything, and looking it; which is a much more convincing token of appreciation than the best chosen words.

But when they came to the rooms which were to be hers, she was quite overcome. For Colonel Colquhoun had chosen two opening into each other, as nearly as possible like those she had occupied at Fraylingay, and had filled them with all the beloved possessions, books, pictures, and ornaments, which she had left behind her.

"How good you are ! How very good you are !" she exclaimed impulsively. "I hope we shall be friends."

"Oh, we shall be friends," he answered with affected carelessness, but really well pleased. "I thought you would settle better if you had your own pet things to begin with. I had a great fight with your father about the books. He said you'd got all your nonsense out of them, but I suggested that it might be a case of a little learning being a dangerous thing, so I captured all the old ones, and I've got a lot more for you; see, here's Zola and Daudet complete, and George Sand, You'll like them better, I fancy, when you get into them than Herbert Spencer and Francis Galton. But I've got you some more of their books as well—all that you hadn't got."

"You are really *too* good," said Evadne.

Getting her the books was like putting butter on the paws of a strange cat to make it settle. She sat down beside them and began to take off her gloves at once. Colonel Colquhoun smiled beneath his blond moustache, then, pleading regimental duty, left her to her treasures, assuring himself as he went that he really did know women, exceptional or otherwise.

He had arranged the books himself, placing Zola and Daudet in prominent positions, and anticipating much entertainment from the observation of their effect upon her. He expected that she would end by making love to him; in which case he promised himself the pleasure of paying her off by acting for a time after the manner proposed by the Barber's Fifth Brother.

When they met again, Evadne had read her mother's letter, and she at once took him into her confidence about it.

"What would you do if you were me?" she asked.

"I should write to the papers," he answered gravely, as if he meant it.

He did not at all understand the strong, simple, earnest nature, incapable of flippancy, with which he had to deal, nor appreciate the danger of playing with it; and he never dreamt that she would seriously consider the suggestion.

"I cannot understand why my father should continue to feel vexed about this arrangement of ours," she said seriously. "We do not interfere with his domestic affairs, why should he meddle with ours? It is not at all his business; do you think it is?" This taking it for granted that the arrangement was as satisfactory to him as it was to her, and appealing to him in good faith against himself and his own interests as it were, touched Colonel Colquhoun's sense of the ludicrous pleasurably. It was always the unexpected apparently that was likely to happen with Evadne, and he appreciated the charm of the unexpected, and began to believe he should find more entertainment at home than he had thought possible even at the outset of his matrimonial venture, when all appeared most promising. He got on very well with her father, but, nevertheless, when it had at last dawned upon him that she was taking his suggestion about writing to the papers seriously, it jumped with his peculiar sense of humour—which had never developed beyond the stage into which it had blossomed in his subaltern days—to egg her on "to draw" the testy old gentleman by threats of publicity. It was his masculine mind, therefore, that was really responsible for her "unnatural" action in that matter. In bygone days when there was any mischief afoot the principle used to be, *chercher la femme*, and when she was found the investigation stopped there ; but modern methods of inquiry are unsatisfied with this imperfect search, and insist upon looking behind the woman, when lo, invariably, there appears a skulking creature of the opposite sex who is not ashamed to be concealed by the petticoats gen-erously spread out to screen him. While the world approves man struts and crows, taking all the credit ; but, when there is blame about, he whines, street-arab fashion : "It wasn't me. *Cherchez la femme.*"

CHAPTER II.

MRS. BEALE and Edith arrived in Malta almost immedi-ately after Evadne herself, and it so happened that the latter, when she went with Colonel Colquhoun to call upon them, met for the first time in their drawing room most of the people to whom she was to become really attached during her sojourn in Malta. There were Mrs. Sillenger, wife of the colonel of one of the other regiments stationed on the island; Mrs. Malcomson, also the wife of a military man ; the Rev. Basil St. John, a man of good family, pronounced refinement, and ultra-ritualistic practices; and Mr. Austin B. Price, a distinguished American diplomatist and man of letters, to whom she became specially attached. Mrs. Beale and Edith also were from that time forward two of her dearest and most valued friends. She looked very charming on the occasion of that first visit.

Mrs. Beale received her with quite effusive kindliness. She had promised Mrs. Orton Beg to be a mother to her, and had been building a little aerial castle wherein she saw herself installed as principal adviser, comforter, confidential friend, and invaluable help generally under certain circumstances of peculiar trial and happy interest to which young wives are subject.

Evadne and Edith looked at each other with a kind of pleased surprise.

"How tall you have grown!" said Evadne.

"And how young you are to be married!" Edith rejoined.
"I was so glad when Mrs. Orton Beg told us you were here.
That was one of the reasons which decided us to come, I think."

"I hope we shall see a good deal of each other," said
Evadne.

"That would be delightful," Edith answered. Then suddenly she blushed. She had recognized someone who had
just entered the room, and Evadne, narrowing her eyes to see
who it was, recognized him as Sir Mosley Menteith, a captain
in the Colquhoun Highlanders, whose acquaintance she had
made the day before, when he called upon her for the first
time. He shook hands with Mrs. Beale and stood talking to
her, looking down at her intently, until someone else claimed
her attention. Then he turned away, rested the back of his
left hand, in which he was holding his hat, on his haunch,
fixed an eyeglass in his eye, and looked round with an expression of great gravity, twirling first one end and then the
other of his little light moustache slowly as he did so. He
was extremely spic-and-span in appearance, and wore light-
coloured kid gloves. The room was pretty full by that time,
and he seemed to have some little difficulty in finding the person whom he sought, but at last he made out Edith and
Evadne sitting together, and going over to them, greeted them
both, and then took a vacant chair beside them. He began by
inspecting first one and then the other carefully in turn, as if
he were comparing them point by point, uttering little remarks
the while of so thin and weak a nature that Evadne had to
make quite an effort to grasp them. She had thawed under
the influence of Edith's warm frank cordiality, but now she
froze again suddenly, and began to have disagreeable thoughts.
She noticed something repellent about the expression of Sir
Mosley's mouth. She acknowleged that his nose was good,
but his eyes were small, peery, and too close together, and his
head shelved backward like an ape's. She could not have
kept up a conversation with him had she wished to, but she
preferred to withdraw herself and let him monopolize Edith.

"I like you best in blue," Sir Mosley was saying. "Will
you wear blue at our dance?"

"Oh, no!" Edith rejoined archly, smiling up at him with
lips and eyes. "I have worn nothing but blue lately. I shall
soon be known as the blue girl! I must have a change. Gray
and pink are evidently *your* colours, Evadne!"

Evadne looked down at her draperies as a polite intimation
that she had heard. But just then her attention was diverted
by the conversation of two ladies and a gentleman, who were
sitting together in a window on her right. The gentleman
was Mr. St. John, the ritualistic divine, whose clean-shaven
face, with its firm, well-disciplined mouth, finely formed nose
with sensitive nostrils, and deep-set kindly dark eyes, attracted
her at once. He was very fragile in appearance, and had a
troublesome cough.

"Ah, Mrs. Malcomson!" he was saying, " I should be very
sorry to see the old exquisite ideal of womanhood disturbed
by these new notions. What can be more admirable, more elevating to contemplate, more powerful as an example, than her
beautiful submission to the hardships of her lot?"

" Or less effectual—seeing that no good, but rather the contrary has come of it all!" Mrs. Malcomson answered. "That
is the poetry of the pulpit ; and the logic too, I may add," she
said, leaning back in her chair luxuriously. "For what could
be less effectual for good than the influence has been of those
women, poor wingless creatures of the ' Sphere,' whose ideal
of duty rises no higher than silent abject submission to all the
worst vices we know to be inseparable from the unchecked
habitual possession of despotic authority? What do you say,
Mrs. Sillenger?"

The other lady smiled agreement. She was older than Mrs.
Malcomson, and otherwise presented a contrast to the latter,
being taller, slighter, with a prettier, sweeter, and altogether
more womanly face, as some people said. A stranger might
have thought that she had less character too, but that was not
the case. She suffered neither from weakness nor want of
decision ; but her manner was more diffident, and she said
less.

Mrs. Malcomson belonged to a somewhat different order of
being. She had a strong and handsome face with regular
features ; a proud mouth, slightly sarcastic in expression ;
and dark gray eyes given to glow with fiery enthusiasm. Her
hair was dark brown, but showed those shades of red in certain lights which betoken an energetic temperament, and good
staying power. It was crisp, and broke into little natural
curls on her forehead and neck, or wherever it could escape
from bondage ; but she had not much of it, and it was usually
rather picturesque than tidy. Mrs. Sillenger's, on the contrary,
was straight and luxuriant, and always neat. It had been light

golden-brown in her youth, but was somewhat faded. Mrs. Malcomson spoke as well as she looked, the resonant tones of her rich contralto voice pleasing the ear more than her opinions startled the understanding. She owed half her success in life to the careful management of her voice. By simple modulations of it she could always differ from an opponent without giving personal offence, and she seldom provoked bitter opposition because nothing she said ever sounded aggressive. If she had not been a good woman she would have been a dangerous one, since she could please eye and ear at will, a knack which obtains more concessions from the average man than the best chosen arguments.

"It seems to me that your 'poetry of the pulpit' is very mischievous," she pursued. "You have pleased our senses with it for ages. You have flattered us into in action by it, and used it as a means to stimulate our vanity and indolence by extolling a helpless condition under the pompous title of 'beautiful patient submission.' You have administered soothing sedatives of 'spiritual consolation,' as you call it, under the baleful influence of which we have existed with all our highest faculties dulled and drugged. You have curtailed our grand power to resist evil by narrowing us down to what you call the 'Woman's Sphere,' wherein you insist that we shall be unconditional slaves of man, doing always and only such things as shall suit his pleasure and convenience.

"Ah, but when you remember that the law which man delivers to woman he receives direct from God, you must confess that that alters the whole aspect of the argument," Mr. St. John deprecated.

"I confess that it would alter it if it were true," Mrs. Malcomson replied. "But it is not true. Man does not deliver the law of God to us, but the law of his own inclinations. And by assuming to himself the right, among other things, of undisputed authority over us, he has held the best half of the conscience of the race in abeyance until now, and so checked the general progress; he has confirmed himself in his own worst vices, arrogance, egotism, injustice, and greed, and has developed the worst in us also, among which I class that tendency to sycophantic adulation, which is an effort of nature to secure the necessaries of life for ourselves."

"But women generally do not think that any change for the better is necessary in their position. They are satisfied," Mr. St. John observed, smiling.

"Women generally are fools," Mrs. Malcomson ruefully confessed. "And the 'women generally' to whom you allude as being satisfied are the women well off in this world's goods themselves, who don't think for others. The first symptom of deep thought in a woman is dissatisfaction."

"I wonder men like yourself, Mr. St. John," Mrs. Sillenger began in her quiet diffident way, "continue so prejudiced on this subject. How you could help on the moral progress of the world, if only you would forget the sweet soporific 'poetry of the pulpit,' as Mrs. Malcomson calls it, and learn to think of us women, not as angels or beasts of burden—the two extremes between which you wander—but as human beings——"

"Oh!" he protested, interrupting her, "I hope I have not made you imagine that I do not recognize certain grave injustices to which women are at present subject. Those I as earnestly hope to see remedied as you do. But what I do think objectionable is the way in which women are putting themselves forward——"

"You are right there," said Mrs. Sillenger. "I think myself that men might be allowed to continue to monopolize the right of impudent self-assertion."

"But do not lend yourself to the silencing system any longer, Mr. St. John," Mrs. Malcomson implored. "The silent acquiescence of women in an iniquitous state of things is merely an indication of the sensual apathy to which your ruinous 'poetry of the pulpit' has reduced the greater number of us."

"I quite agree with you!" Evadne exclaimed; then stopped, colouring crimson. She had forgotten in her interest that she was a stranger to these people; and only remembered it when they all looked at her—rather blankly, as she imagined. "I beg your pardon," she said, addressing Mrs. Malcomson. "I could not help overhearing the discussion, and I am deeply interested. I am—Mrs. Colquhoun," she broke off, covered with confusion.

"Oh, I am very glad to make your acquaintance," Mrs. Malcomson said warmly. "I called on you to-day on my way here, but you were out."

"And so did I," said Mrs. Sillenger.

"And I hope to have the pleasure very soon," Mr. St. John added, bowing.

Mrs. Beale joined the group just then.

"You have been talking so merrily in this corner," she said, sitting down on a high chair as she spoke, "I have been wondering what it was all about!"

"*Woman's Rights!*" Mrs. Malcomson uttered in deeply tragic tones.

"Woman's Rights! Oh, dear me, how dreadful!" Mrs. Beale exclaimed comfortably. "I won't hear a word on the subject."

"Not on the subject of cooking?" said Mrs. Malcomson.

"What has cooking to do with it?" Mrs. Beale asked.

"Why, everything!" Mrs. Malcomson answered, smiling. "If only Mr. St. John and a few other very good men would stand up in their pulpits boldly and assure those who dread innovation that their food will be the better cooked, and the 'Sphere' itself will roll along all the more smoothly for the changes we find necessary; there would be an end of their opposition. I would not promise women cooks, for I really think myself that the men are superior, they put so much more feeling into it. And I can never understand why they do not quarrel with us for the possession of that department. I am sure we are quite ready to resign it! and really, when one comes to think of it, it is obvious that the kitchen is much more the man's sphere than the woman's, for it is there that his heart is!"

"You beguile me, my dear," Mrs. Beale said, smiling; "but I will not listen to your wicked railleries." She looked at Mrs. Sillenger. "I came to ask you if you would be so kind as to play us something," she said.

Mrs. Sillinger was a perfect musician; and as Evadne listened, her heart expanded. When the music ceased, she looked up and about her blankly like one who is bewildered by the sudden discovery of an unexpected loss; and with that expression still upon her face she met the bright, penetrating, kindly eye of a small thin elderly gentleman with refined features, a wrinkled forehead, and thick gray hair, who was looking at her so fixedly from the other side of the room that at first her own glance fell; but the next moment she felt an irresistible impulse to look at him again. The attraction was mutual. He got up at once from the low ottoman on which he was sitting, and came across to her; and she welcomed his approach with a smile.

"Excuse the liberty of an old man who has not been introduced," he said. "You are Mrs. Colquhoun, I know, and my name is Price. I am an American, and I came to Europe on official business for my country first of all ; but I am now travelling for my own pleasure."

"I am very glad to make your acquaintance," Evadne answered.

Before they could say another word to each other, however, there was a general move of guests departing, and Colonel Colquhoun came to carry her off. She held out her hand to Mr. Price. " We shall meet again ? " she said.

"With your permission, I will call," he answered.

CHAPTER III.

MR. ST. JOHN and Mr. Price were staying at the same hotel, and they walked back to it together. They had only just made each other's acquaintance, and were feeling the attraction which there is in a common object pursued by the most dissimilar means. They were both humanitarians, Mr. Price by choice and of set purpose, Mr. St. John of necessity—seeing that he was a good man, but unconsciously, the consequence being much confusion of mind on the subject, and a wide difference between his words and his deeds. He preached, for instance, the degrading doctrine that we ought to be miserable in this world, that all our wonderful powers of enjoyment were only given to us to be suppressed; and further blasphemed our sacred humanity by maintaining that we are born in sin, and sinners we must remain, fight as we will to release ourselves from that bondage; but yet his whole life was spent in trying to make his fellow-creatures better. and the world itself a pleasanter place to live in. The means which he employed, however, was the old anodyne : " Believe the best "—that is to say, " Cultivate agreeable feelings." Mr. Price's motto, on the other hand, was : " Know the worst." The foe must be known, must be recognized, must be met and fought in the open if he is to be subdued at all.

This was the difference which drew the two together; each felt the deepest interest in the point where the other diverged, and yearned to convert him to his own way of thought. Mr. Price would have had the clergyman know the world; Mr. St. John would have taught Mr. Price to ignore it, " to look up ! " as he called it, or, in other words, to sit and sigh for heaven while the heathen raged, and the wicked went their way here undisturbed—although he had not realized up to the present that that was practically what his system amounted to. He belonged by birth to the caste which is vowed to the policy of ignoring, and was as sensitive as a woman about delicate matters. Nationally, Mr. Price was the Englishman's son, and had advanced a generation. Men are what women choose to make them. Mr. St. John's mother was the best kind of woman of the old order, Mr. Price was the product of the new; and the two were typical representatives of the chivalry of the past, high-minded, ill-informed, unforeseeing—and the chivalry of the present, which reaches on always into futurity with the long arm of knowledge, not deceiving itself with romantic misrepresentations of things by the way, but fully recognizing what is wrong from the outset, and making direct for the root of the evil instead of contenting itself by lopping a branch here and there.

"I think you said you were going to winter here?" Mr. Price remarked, as they stepped into the street.

"Yes—if the place suits me," Mr. St. John answered; "and so far,—that is to say for the last month,—it has done so very well. Are you a resident?"

"Well, no, not exactly," the old gentleman answered; "but I have been in the habit of coming here for years."

"It is an interesting place," said Mr. St. John, "teeming with historical associations."

"Yes, it is an interesting place," Mr. Price agreed, making a little pause before he added—"full of food for reflection. Life at large is represented at Malta during the winter season, and in a little place like this humanity is under the microscope as it were, which makes it a happy hunting ground for those who have to know the world."

"Ah!" Mr. St. John ejaculated deliberately. "I should think there are some very nice people here."

"Yes—and some very nasty ones," Mr. Price rejoined. "But, of course, one must know both."

"Oh, I differ from you there!" Mr. St. John answered, smiling. "Walk not in sinners' way, you know!"

"On the contrary, I should say," Mr. Price rejoined, smiling responsively, and twitching his nose as if a gnat had tickled it; "but I allow you have got to have a good excuse when you do."

Mr. St. John smiled again slightly, but said nothing.

"There were elephants once in Malta, I am told," he began after a little pause, changing the subject adroitly "but they dwindled down from the size which makes them so useful by way of comparison, till they were no bigger than Shetland ponies, before they finally became extinct."

"And there is a set in society on the island now," Mr. Price pursued, "formed of representatives of old English houses that once brought men of notable size and virile into the world, but are now only equal to the production of curious survivals, tending surely to extinction like the elephant, and by an analogous process."

"Here we are," said Mr. St. John, as they arrived at their place of abode. "Will you come to my room and smoke a cigarette with me?"

"Thank you, I don't smoke, but I'll go to your room, and see *you* smoke one, with pleasure," Mr. Price responded.

When they got to Mr. St. John's room, the latter took off his clerical coat and waistcoat, and put on a coloured smoking jacket, which had the curious effect of transforming him from an ascetic looking High Churchman into what, from his refined, intellectual, clean-shaven face, and rather long straight hair, most people would have mistaken for an actor suffering from overwork.

Having provided Mr. Price with a comfortable seat in the window, which was open, he lighted a cigarette, drew up another easy-chair, and stretched himself out in it luxuriously. He was easily fatigued at that time, and the rest and quiet were grateful after the talk and crowd at Mrs. Beale's. There was a little wooden balcony outside his window, full of flowers and foliage plants; and from where he sat he saw the people passing on the opposite side of the street below, and could also obtain a glimpse of the Mediterranean, appearing between the yellow houses at the end of the street, intensely blue, and sparkling in the rays of the afternoon sun. It was altogether a soothing scene; and had he been alone he would have sunk into that state of intellectual apathy which is so often miscalled contemplative. The homely duties of hospitality, however, compelled him to exert himself for the entertainment of his guest. Several of the people they had just met at Mrs. Beale's went past together, laughing and talking, and *à propos* of this he remarked, "It's a bright little world."

"Yes, on the smoothly smiling surface of society, I allow it's bright," Mr. Price rejoined. "The surface, however, is but a small part of it."

Mr. St. John took a whiff of his cigarette.

" Do you see that man?" Mr. Price pursued, indicating a man below the middle height, with broad shoulders, a black beard and moustache streaked with brown, a ruddy complexion, and obtrusively blue eyes, who was passing at the moment.

"Captain Belliot, of H. M. S. *Abomination*," Mr. St. John answered, using the ship's nickname, and holding out his cigarette between his finger and thumb as he spoke, his fluent patrician English losing in significance what it gained in melody compared with the slow dry *staccato* intonation of the American.

"Yes, sir," Mr. Price rejoined. "Now, he is one of the survivals I just now mentioned—a typical specimen."

" I rather like the man," Mr. St. John answered. "He isn't a friend of mine, but he's pleasant enough to meet."

"Just so," Mr. Price rejoined. " The manners of the kind are agreeable—on the surface. One must give the devil his due. But on closer acquaintance you won't find that their general characteristics are exactly pleasant. Their minds are hopelessly tainted with exhalations from the literary sewer which streams from France throughout the world, and their habits are not nicer than their books.

" Ah, well," said Mr. St. John, whose sensitive lip had curled in dislike of the subject, " it is never too late to mend. I believe, too, that the evil is exaggerated. But at all events they repent and marry, and become respectable men eventually."

" Well, yes, sir, they marry as a rule," Mr. Price rejoined ; " and that's the worst of it."

Mr. St. John held his cigarette poised in the air on the way to his mouth, and looked at him interrogatively.

" Will what you call repentance restore a rotten constitution ?" Mr. Price responded. " Will it prevent a drunkard's children from being weakly vicious ? or the daughters of a licentious man from being foredoomed to destruction by an inherited appetite for the vices which you seem to flatter yourself end in effect when they are repented of ? You do not take into consideration the fact that the once vicious man becomes the father of vicious children and the grandfather of criminals. You persuade women to marry these men. The arrangement is perfect. Man's safety, and man's pleasure ; if there is any sin in it, *damn the woman.* She's weak ; she can't retaliate."

Mr. St. John's cigarette went out. He had begun to think.

"These are horrors!" he ejaculated. "But I know, thank Heaven, that the right feeling of the community is against the perpetration of them."

"That's so," said the American. "Unfortunately, it is not with the right feeling of the community, but with the wrong feeling of individuals, that women have to deal."

"Heaven forbid that women should ever know anything about it!"

"I say so too," said Mr. Price. "At present, however, Heaven permits them by the thousand to make painful personal acquaintance with the subject. And I assure you, sir, that the indignation which has long been simmering in whispers over tea tables in the seclusion of scented boudoirs, amongst those same delicate dames whom you have it in your mind to keep in ignorance of the source of most of their sufferings, mental and physical, is fast approaching the boiling point of rebellion."

"Do you know this for a fact?"

"I do. And the time is at hand, I think, for a thorough ventilation of the subject. It is the question of all others which must either be ignored until society is disintegrated by the licence that attitude allows, or considered openly and seriously. That is why I mentioned it. I see in you every inclination to help and defend the suffering sex, and every quality except the habit of handling facts. The subject's repulsive enough, I allow. Right-minded people shrink in disgust even from what is their obvious duty in the matter, and shirk it upon various pretexts, visiting their own pain—like *Betsey Trotwood*, when she boxed the ears of the doctor's boy—upon the most boxable person they can reach, and that is generally the one who has forced their attention to it."

There was a pause after this, then the clergyman observed: "One knows that there are sores which must be exposed to view if they are to be prescribed for at all or treated with any chance of success."

"Yes, yes, that is just it," Mr. Price exclaimed. "You will perceive, if you reflect for a moment, that there must have been a good deal that was disagreeable in the cleansing of the Augean stables to which people in the neighbourhood would certainly and very naturally object at the time; but it has since been pretty generally conceded that the undertaking was a very good sanitary measure nevertheless; and had Hercules

lived in our day, and survived the shower of stones with which
he was sure to have been encouraged during his conduct of
the business, we should doubtless have given him a dinner, or
in the other case, an epitaph at least. But there is work for
the strong man still. The Augean stable of our modern civilization must be cleansed, and it is a more difficult task than the
other was, and one to put him on his mettle and win him great
renown because it is held to be impossible."

He rose as he spoke, and looked at Mr. St. John with concern, as the latter struggled with a bad fit of coughing.

" I am afraid I have talked too much for your strength," he
added.

" Oh, no," Mr. St. John answered as soon as he could speak.
"On the contrary, I assure you. You have taken me out of
myself, and that is always good. Must you go ? "

" I must, thank you. Don't rise."

But Mr. St. John had risen, and was surprised to find himself towering over the little gentleman as they shook hands—
a feeling which recurred to him always afterward when they
met, there being about Mr. Price the something that makes the
impression of size and strength and courage which is usually
only associated with physical force.

CHAPTER IV.

NEXT day there was an afternoon dance on board Captain
Belliot's ship, H. M. S. *Abomination*—facetiously so-called
for no particular reason ; and Evadne was there with Colonel
Colquhoun. She was dressed in white, heavily trimmed with
gold, and, being a bride, was an object of special attention
and interest. It was the first entertainment of the kind she
had appeared at since her arrival, and, not having a scrap of
morbid sentiment about her, she was prepared to enjoy it
thoroughly, but in her own way, of course, which, as she was
new to the place and the people, would naturally be a very
quiet observant way.

Captain Belliot received her when she came on board, and
they shook hands.

She was taller than he was, and looking down at him while
in the act, noticed the streaks of brown in his black beard,
his brick-red skin, tight as a gooseberry's, and his obtrusively
blue eyes.

"Queen's weather!" he remarked.

"Yes," she answered, looking out at the sparkling water.

"It's a pretty place," he continued,

"Yes," she agreed, glancing toward the shore, but seeing only with the mind's eye. Her pupils dilated, however, as she recalled the way she had come, the narrow picturesque steep streets, almost all stone-steps, well worn; with high irregular houses on either side, yellow, with green wooden verandas jutting out; the wharf on which they had waited a moment for the man-of-war's boat to take them off, and the Maltese ruffians with their brown faces and brightly coloured clothing, lying idly about in the sun, or chattering together at the top of their voices in little groups. They had seemed to look at her, too, with friendly eyes. And she saw the sapphire sea which parted in dazzling white foam from the prow of the boat as they came along, saw the steady sweep of the oars rising and falling rhythmically, the flash of the blades in the sunshine, the well-disciplined faces of the men who looked at her shyly, but with the same look which she took to be friendly; and their smart uniforms. She would liked to have shaken hands with them all. And there was more still in her mind when Captain Belliot asked her if she thought the place "pretty," yet all she found for answer was the one word, "Yes"; and he, being no physiognomist, rashly concluded that was all she had in her.

"Do you dance?" he proceeded, making one more effort to induce her to entertain him.

"Not in the afternoon," she said.

Sir Mosley Menteith tried next.

"You come from Morningquest, do you not?" he asked, looking into her eyes.

"My people live near Morningquest," she answered.

"Ah, then I suppose you know everybody there," he observed, looking hard at her brooch.

She reflected a moment, then answered deliberately: "Not by any means, I should think. It is a large neighbourhood."

He twisted each side of his little light moustache, and changed the subject, inspecting her figure as he did so.

"Do you ride?" he asked.

"Yes," she said.

There was a pause, during which she noticed a suspicion of powder on his face, and he felt dissatisfied because she didn't seem to be going to entertain him.

The band struck up a waltz.

" Do you dance ?" he said, looking down from her face to her feet.

" Not in the afternoon," she answered.

The dance had begun, and a pair came whirling down toward them.

Evadne moved back to be out of the way, and Menteith, looking round for a partner, saw Mrs. Guthrie Brimston opposite smiling at him.

He went over to her.

" Well, what do you make of the bride ?" she asked.

" Her conversation is not exactly animated," he answered, looking into Mrs. Guthrie Brimston's face intently.

She was a round, flat-faced, high-hipped, high-shouldered woman, short in the body, and tight-laced ; and she had a trick of wagging her skirts and perking at a man when talking to him.

She did so now, nodding and smiling in a way that made her speech piquant with the suggestion that she thought or knew a great deal more than she meant to say.

" You have made her acquaintance, I suppose ?" Menteith added.

" Oh, yes," she answered. " Her husband is an old friend of ours, you know, so Bobbie thought we ought to call at once."

The tone in which she spoke suggested that she and " Bobbie " merely meant to tolerate Mrs. Colquhoun for her husband's sake. " Bobbie " was Major Guthrie Brimston, a very useful little man to his wife by way of reference. When she wanted to say a smart thing which might or might not be considered objectionable, according to the taste of the person she addressed—and she very often did—she always presented it as a quotation from him. " Bobbie thinks," she added now, " that if there were an Order of the Silent Sewing Machine, Mrs. Colquhoun would be sure to be a distinguished member of it."

A Royal personage whom Evadne had met at home recognized her at this moment, and shook hands with her with somewhat effusive cordiality, making a remark to which she responded quietly.

" She seems to be a pretty self-possessed young woman, too," Menteith observed. " Her composure is perfect."

" Ah !" Mrs. Guthrie Brimston ejaculated ; " those stupid

people have no nerves ! Now, *I* should shake all over in such a position ! "

The band played the next few bars hard and fast, the dancers whirled like teetotums, then stopped with the final crash of the instruments, and separated, scattering the groups of onlookers, who re-arranged themselves into new combinations immediately. Mrs. Guthrie Brimston leaned against the bulwarks. Colonel Beston, of the Artillery, and Colonel Colquhoun joined her, also her Bobbie, and Menteith remained. The conversation was animated. Evadne, having moved, could now hear every word of it, and thought it extremely stupid. It was all what "he said" and "she said"; what they ought to have said, and what they really meant. Mrs. Guthrie Brimston made some cutting remarks. She talked to all the men at once, and they appeared to appreciate her sallies ; but their own replies were vapid. She seemed to be the only one of the party with any wit. Mrs. Beston joined her. She was a little dark woman with a patient anxious face, and eyes that wandered incessantly till she discovered her husband with Mrs. Guthrie Brimston. Evadne surprised the glance—entreating, reproachful, loving, helpless—what was it ? The look of a woman who finds it a relief to know the worst. Evadne's heart began to contract ; the girlish gladness went out of her eyes.

Mrs. Beale and Edith arrived and joined her, and Menteith came and attached himself to them at once.

" You *have* put on the blue frock," he said softly to Edith, looking down at her with animal eyes and a flush partly of gratified vanity on his face.

Edith smiled and blushed. She could not reason about him. Her wits had forsaken her.

"That's a case, I think," said Mrs. Guthrie Brimston. Several more men had joined her by this time, and they all looked across at Edith and Menteith. Half the men on the island took their opinions, especially of the women, from Mrs. Guthrie Brimston. She was forever lowering her own sex in their estimation, and they, with sheep-like docility, bowed to her dictates, and never dreamt of judging for themselves.

Mr. Price persuaded Mr. St. John to come and look on at the dance. They were leaning now against the bulwarks beside Mrs. Guthrie Brimston, who tried to absorb them into her circle, but found them heavy. Mr. Price despised her, and Mr. St. John was occupied with his own thoughts. He

had passed the night in painful reflection, and when he arose
in the morning he was more than half convinced that Mr.
Price had not exaggerated ; but now, with the smiling surface
of society under observation, and his senses both soothed and
exhilarated by the animated scene and the lively music, he
could not believe it.   He had thought for the moment that
the old American minister was a strong and disinterested
philanthropist, but now he saw in him only the victim of a
diseased imagination.   The habit of seeing society through a
haze of feeling as it should be was older than the American's
entreaties that he should learn to know it as it is, and he
deliberately chose to be unconvinced.

"The person is casting covetous eyes at the bishop's pretty
ewe lamb," Colonel Beston observed to Mrs. Guthrie Brimston
sotto voce.

A kind of bower had been made of the stern sheets by
screening them off from the main deck with an awning, and
from out of this a lady, a young widow, stepped just at this
moment, followed by a young man.   They had been out of
sight together, innocently occupied leaning over, watching the
fish darting about down in the depths of the transparent
water.   The moment they appeared, however, the men about
Mrs. Guthrie Brimston exchanged glances of unmistakable
significance, and the young widow, perceiving this, flushed
crimson with indignation.

"Guilty conscience!" Major Guthrie Brimston remarked
upon this, with a chuckle.

Mr. St. John had witnessed the incident and overheard the
remark, and the import of both forced itself upon his attention.
Mr. Price's words recurred to him : "You are right," he
remarked.   "They are gross of nature, these people.   The
animal in them predominates—at present.   But the spiritual,
the immortal part, is there too.   It must be.   It has not been
cultivated, and therefore it is undeveloped.   We should direct
our whole energies to the cultivation of it.   It is a serious
subject for thought and prayer."

Mr. Price twitched his nose, and studied the physiognomies
about him : "I doubt myself if the spiritual nature has been as
generally diffused as you seem to imagine," he remarked in his
crisp, dry way.   "But if the germ of it is anywhere it is in the
women.   Help them out of their difficulties, and you will help
the world at large.   Now, there is one "—indicating Evadne,
who was sitting in the same place still, quietly observant.

"I was looking at her," Mr. St. John broke in. "She seems to me to be one of those sensitive creatures, affected by sun and wind and rain, and all atmospheric influences, to their joy or sorrow, who will suffer a martyrdom in secret with beautiful womanly endurance."

"And be very much to blame for it!" Mr. Price interrupted. "That is your idea of her character? Now mine is different. I should say that she is a being so nicely balanced, so human, that either senses or intellect might be tipped up by the fraction of an ounce. Which is right, surely; since the senses are instrumental in sustaining nature, while the intellect helps it to perfection. And as to her beautiful womanly endurance"— he shrugged his shoulders, and turned the palms of his hands upward—"I don't know, of course; but I am no judge of character if she does not prove to be one of the new women, who are just appearing among us, with a higher ideal of duty than any which men have constructed for women. I expect she will be ready to resent as an insult every attempt to impose unnecessary suffering either upon herself or her sex at large."

"Well, I hope she will not become a contentious woman," Mr. St. John said. "The way in which women are putting themselves forward just now on any subject which happens to attract their attention is quite deplorable, I think; and pushing themselves into the professions, too, and entering into rivalry with men generally; you must confess that all that is unwomanly."

"It seems to me to depend entirely upon how it is done," Mr. Price answered judicially. "And I deny the rivalry. All that women ask is to be allowed to earn their bread honestly; but there is no doubt that the majority of men would rather see them on the streets." The old gentleman stopped, and compressed his lips into a sort of smile. "I can see," he said, "that you are dissenting from every word I say; but I am not disheartened. I feel sure that the scales will fall from your eyes some day, and then you will look back, and see clearly for yourself the way in which all moral progress has been checked for ages by the criminal repression of women."

"Repression of women!" exclaimed Captain Belliot, who caught the words just as the band stopped—"Good Lord! I beg your pardon, St. John—but it's a subject I feel very strongly upon. It's impossible to tell what the devil women will be at next. Why, I went into a hotel in Devonport for a brandy and soda just before I sailed, and I happened to remark to a fellow that was with me that something was 'a damned nuisance '; and the barmaid leant over the counter : ' A shilling, sir,' she said, with the coolest cheek in the world. 'What for ?' I demanded. ' A fine, sir, for swearing,' she answered, with the most perfect assurance. ' Now, look here, young woman,' I said, ' you just shut up, for I'm not going to stand any of your damned nonsense.' ' Two shillings, sir,' she said, in just the same tone. I wanted to argue the question, but she wouldn't say a word more. She just sent for the pro-prietor, and he said it was his wife's orders. She wouldn't have any female in her service insulted by bad language, and that fellow, the proprietor, actually supported his wife. What do you think of that for petticoat government? He made me pay up too, by Jove ! I was obliged to do it to save a row. Now, what do you think of that for a sign of the times ? "

Mr. Price twitched his nose, and looked at Mr. St. John.

" Some signs of the times are hopeful, certainly," the latter said enigmatically.

" What ! talking seriously in these our hours of ease ?" Mrs. Guthrie Brimston broke in. " What is it all about ? "

" I was just about to remark that I like a woman to *be* a woman," Captain Belliot rejoined, ogling the lady, and with the general air of being sure that she at least could have no higher ambition than to attain to his ideal. " These bold creatures who put themselves forward, as so many of them do nowadays, are highly antipathetic to me ; and if you saw them ! the most awful old harridans—with voices !—' Shriek-ing sisterhood ' doesn't half come up to it ! "

Mrs. Malcomson passed at that moment.

" Should you call *her* an old harridan ? " Mr. St. John asked, smiling involuntarily.

" No," the naval man was obliged to confess ; " she's deuced handsome ; but she presumes on her good looks, and doesn't trouble herself to be agreeable. I took her in to dinner the other night, and could hardly get a word out of her—not that she can't talk, mind you ; she just wouldn't—to pique my inter-est, you know. You may take your oath that was it. There's no being up to women. But she'll find herself stranded, if she doesn't take care. *I* shan't bother myself to pay her any more attention ; and I'm a bad prophet if the other men in the place go out of their way to be civil to her much longer either. Besides," he said to Mr. Price, lowering his voice, but not enough to prevent Mr. St. John hearing—" her husband's jealous ! " He turned up his eyes—" Game's not worth—you know ! "

Again Mr. Price looked at Mr. St. John. The band struck up ; another waltz began ; scarcely anything else had been danced.

" Oh, this eternal one, two, three ! " Mr. Price ejaculated ; " how it wearies the mind ! Society has sacrificed its most varied, wholesome, and graceful recreation—dancing—to this monotonous one, two, three ! "

He passed on, leaving Mr. St. John to his reflections.

Captain Belliot bent before Mrs. Guthrie Brimston ; " Our dance, I think," he said, offering her his arm.

She took it, perking and preening herself, and began to say something about Mrs. Malcomson in agreement with his last remark : " You are quite right about her," Mr. St. John over-heard. " She is always jeering at men. She abuses you whole-sale. I've heard her often."

Captain Belliot's face darkened ; but he put his arm round his partner, and they glided off together slowly.

When next they passed Mr. St. John, their faces wore a simi-lar expression of drowsy sensuous delight, which gave them for the moment a curious likeness to each other. They looked incapable of speech or thought, or anything but the slow measure of their interwoven paces, and inarticulate emotion.

The scene made a painful impression on Mr. St. John, and he began to feel as much out place as he looked.

' We churchmen are a failure," he thought. " We have done no good, and are barely tolerated. Poetry of the pulpit—spiritual anodyne—what is it ? Something I cannot grasp ; but something wrong somewhere. Is Mrs. Malcomson right ? Is Mr. Price ? Where are they ? "

He looked about, but the dancers with parted lips and drowsy dreamy eyes, intoxicated with music and motion, floated past him in endless, regular succession, hemming him in, so that he could not move till the music stopped.

CHAPTER V.

MRS. MALCOMSON had made her way over to where Evadne and Mrs. Beale were sitting. Both welcomed her cordially, and Evadne, in particular, brightened visibly when she saw her approach. She was wearied by these vapid

men, who had all said the same thing, and looked at her with
the same expression one after the other the whole afternoon.
Mrs. Sillenger and Mr. Price were also of the party, and Mrs.
Malcomson, in a merry mood, was holding forth brightly when
Mr. St. John joined them.

" Oh, yes, we have our reward, we Englishwomen," she was
saying   "We religiously obey our men.   We do nothing of
which they disapprove.   We are the meekest sheep in the
world.   We scorn your independent, out-spoken American
women, Mr. Price ; we think them bold and unwomanly, and
do all we can to be as unlike them as possible.   And what
happens?   Do our men adore us?   Well, they continue to
say so.   But it is the Americans they marry.

Mr. Price twitched his nose and smiled.

"But, tell me, Mr. Price," Mrs. Malcomson rattled on :
" The fate of nations has hung upon your opinion, and your
decisions are matter of history ; so kindly condescend, of your
goodness and of your wisdom, to tell us if you think that '*true*
womanliness' is endangered by our occupations, or the cut
of our clothes—I have it !" she broke off, clasping her hands.
" Make us a speech !   *Do ! !*"

" Oh, yes, *do !*" the rest exclaimed simultaneously.

Mr. Price's mobile countenance twitched all over.   He
looked from one to the other, then, entering good-humouredly
into the jest, he struck an attitude : " If true womanliness has
been endangered by occupation or the fashion of a frock in
the past, it will not be so much longer, or the signs of the
times are most misleading," he began, with the ease of an
orator.   " The old ideals are changing, and we regret them—
not for their value, for they were often mischievous enough ;
but as a sign of change, to which, in itself, mankind has an
ineradicable objection—yet these changes must take place if
we are ever to progress.   For myself," he continued—" I
should be very sorry to say that anything which honourable
women of the day consider a reform, and propose to adopt, is
' unwomanly ' or ' unsexing,' until it has been thoroughly tried,
and proved to be so.   It sounds mere idiotcy, the thing is so
obvious, when one reduces it to words, but yet neither men
nor women themselves—for the most part—seem to recognize
the fact that womanliness is a matter of sex, not of circumstances, occupation, or clothing ; and each sex has instincts
and proclivities which are peculiar to it, and do not differ to
any remarkable extent even in the most diverse characters ;

from which we may be sure that those instincts are safe whatever happens. And as to the value of cherished 'ideals of womankind'—well, we have only to look back at many of the old ones, which had to be abandoned, and have been held up to the laughter and contempt of succeeding ages—although doubtless they were dear enough to the heart of man in their own day—to appreciate the worth of such. That little incident of Jane Austin, hiding away the precious manuscript she was engaged upon, under her plain sewing, when visitors arrived, ashamed to be caught at the 'unwomanly' occupation of writing romances, and shrinking with positive pain from the remarks which such poor foolish people as those she feared would have made about her—that little incident alone, which I remarked very early in life, has saved me from braying with the rest of the world upon this subject. If those brave women, sure of themselves and of their message, who have written in the face of all opposition, had not dared to do so, how much the poorer and meaner and worse we should all, men and women alike, have been to-day for want of the nourishment of strength and goodness with which they have kept us provided. And you will find it so in these questions of our day. Women are bringing a storm about their ears, but they are prepared for that, and it will not deter them ; for they have an infallible prescience in these matters which men have not, and they know what they are doing and why, and could make their motives plain to us if it were not for our own stupid prejudices and density. Ah ! these are critical times, but I believe what a fellow-countryman of mine has already written—I believe that the women will save us. I do not fear the fate of the older peoples. I am sure that we shall not fall into nothingness from the present height of our civilization, by reason of our sensuality and vice, as all the great nations have done heretofore. The women will rebel. The women will not allow it. But "—he added with his benign smile, dropping into a lighter tone, as if he felt that he had been more serious than the occasion warranted, and addressing Mrs. Malcomson specially—"but you must not despise your personal appearance. Beauty is a great power, and it may be used for good as well as for evil. Beauty is beneficent as well as malign. Angels are always allowed to be beautiful, and our highest ideal of manhood is associated with physical as well as moral perfection. Yes ! Be sure that beauty is a legitimate means of grace ; and I will venture to suggest that you who have it should use it as such." Here he was interrupted by applause. " True beauty, I mean, of course," he added, descending from the rostrum, as it were, and speaking colloquially—" not the fashionable travesty of it."

" Well, that is a piece of servility I have never been so degraded as to practise," Mrs. Malcomson exclaimed.

" Ah, my dear, it does not do to be singular," Mrs. Beale mildly remonstrated.

A dance concluded just at this moment, and Edith joined the group, followed by Sir Mosley Menteith

The ladies looked at her as she approached with affectionate interest and admiration.

" I am always conscious of their presence," she was saying.

" Whose presence, dear?" her mother asked.

" The presence of those who love us, mother, in the other life," she said, looking out into space with great serious eyes, as if she saw something grand and beautiful, and also love-inspiring. The words and her presence changed the whole mental attitude of the group. The intellectual element subsided, the spiritual, which trenches on sensation and is warm, began to glow in their breasts. Edith was the actor now, and Mrs. Malcomson became a mere spectator. Mr. St. John was the first to appreciate the change. Edith's presence, more than her words, was enough in itself to relax the tension of pained reflection which had possessed him the whole afternoon. It was as if a draught of the sacred anodyne to which he had been so long accustomed were being held out to him, and he had drained it eagerly, to excite feeling, and to drown thought.

" Mosley does not think they are so near us as I know them to be," Edith pursued ; " but I tell him, if only he would allow himself, he would perceive their presence just as I do. He says this scene is so worldly it would frighten them ; but I answer that they cannot be frightened ; they are incorruptible, so that there is nothing for them to fear for themselves —but they may fear for us, and when they do, we know that it is then that they are nearest to us. They come to guard us."

Menteith's glance wandered over her person as she spoke, and returned again to meet her eyes. He quite enjoyed a thrill of superstitious awe ; it was an excellent *sauce piquante* to what he called his " sentiments "—by which he meant the state of his senses at the moment. He recognized in Edith no higher quality than that of innocence, which is so appetizing.

But a gentle thrill, as of an electric shock, had passed through them all, silencing them. Mrs. Beale, with a sigh, released herself from the uneasy impression Mrs. Malcomson's words had made upon her, and felt the peace of mind, which she managed to preserve by refusing to know of anything that might disturb it and rouse her soul from its apathetic calm to the harassing point of action, restored. Mrs. Sillenger gave herself up for the moment also. Her fine nature, although highly tempered and exceedingly sensitive, was too broad to allow her to delude herself by imagining that it is right to countenance evil by ignoring it. She shrank from knowledge, but still she had the courage to possess herself of it ; and, fortunately, her very sensitiveness enabled her to turn with ease from the consideration of terrible facts to the enjoyment of a fine idea.

Mrs. Malcomson and Mr. Austin Price looked at each other involuntarily. The new element was not congenial to either of them. But Mr. St. John was satisfied. His heart had expanded to the full : "Mr. Price is wrong, Mrs. Malcomson is wrong," was the new measure to which he set his thoughts. " They exaggerated the evil ; they have never perceived in what the good consists. And what do they do with all their wondrous clever talk ? They withdraw our attention from the contemplation of holy things only to pain and excite us ; for sin must continue, and suffering must continue, and we can do no more than we have done. Example—a good example ! We have only each to set one, and say nothing. Talk, talk, talk ; I will listen no more to such tattle ! It is mere pride of intellect, which is put to shame by the first gentle innocent girl who comes, strong in purity and faith, and simply bids us all look up ! Did not our heart burn within us? Was not the worst among us and the most worldly moved to repent ? " He looked across at Menteith, but suddenly the exaltation ceased, and his soul shot with a pang to another extreme. " He is not worthy of her—he is not worthy of her—no ! no ! Heaven help me to save her from such a fate ! " His mind had been nourished upon inconsistencies, and he was as unconscious of any now as he was when he preached—as he had been taught—that God orders all things for the best, and at the same time prayed him to avert some special catastrophe.

Menteith was bending over Edith.

" I want to lunch with you to-morrow," he said. " Do let me. I love to hear you talk. Just to be near you makes a better man of me. But you can make anything you like of me ; you know you can. May I come ? "

Edith glanced up at him and smiled, and the young man, taking this for acquiescence, bowed and withdrew in triumph, making way for Colonel Colquhoun.

Evadne looked up at the latter and smiled too. " Shall we go ? " she said.

" I came to see if you were ready," he answered, and then she rose, took leave of the friends about her, crossed the deck to where Captain Belliot, her host, was standing, shook hands with him, and left the ship. Many eyes had followed her with curiosity and interest ; and many tongues made remarks about her when she was gone, expressing positive opinions with the confident conceit of mediocrity, although she had not at that time made any sign of what manner of person she really was. She had only been a week amongst them, and her mind had been in a state of passive receptivity the whole time, subject to the impressions which might be made upon it, but not itself producing any. It was her appearance that they presumed to judge her by. But her intellect had been both nourished and stimulated that afternoon, and when she went to her room at night she hunted up a manuscript book suitable for the purpose, and resumed her old habit of noting everything of interest which she had seen and heard. There were blank pages still in the old " Commonplace Book," and she had it with her, but she never dreamt of making another note in it. She had written her last there once for all the night before her wedding, expecting to enter upon a new phase of existence ; and she had indeed entered upon a new phase, although not at all in the way she had expected ; and now she felt that only a new volume would be appropriate to contain the record of it.

She ended her notes that night with a maxim which probably contained all the wisdom she had been able to extract from her late experiences :—" Just do a thing, and don't talk about it," she wrote, expressing herself colloquially. " This is the great secret of success in all enterprises. Talk means discussion, discussion means irritation, irritation means opposition ; and opposition means hindrance always, whether you are right or wrong."

CHAPTER VI.

EVADNE settled down into her new position at once. She took charge of the household and managed it well. Colonel Colquhoun was scrupulous in matters of etiquette, and Evadne's love of order and exactitude made her punctilious too, so that there was one subject which they agreed upon perfectly, and it very soon came to be said of them that they always did the right thing. They appeared together everywhere, at the Palace receptions, the opera, entertainments on naval vessels, dinners and dances, polo and picnics, and at church. If there was one thing that Colquhoun was more particular about than another it was, in the language of his own profession, church parade. Watching Evadne to detect the first symptom of new tactics on her part, became one of the interests of his life. It wouldn't have been good form to take another man into his confidence for betting purposes, seeing that the lady was "Mrs. Colquhoun"; but a wager laid upon the chances of change in her "views" was the only zest lacking to the pleasure he took in the study of this new specimen of her sex. He used to dance a good deal himself, and danced well too, but after Evadne joined him he gave it up to a great extent, and might often have been seen leaning against a pillar in a ball room gravely observing her. It was a kind of curiosity he suffered from, a sort of rage to make her out. He was very attentive to her at that period, treating her always with the deference due to a young lady, and for that reason she accepted his attentions gratefully, because they were delicately paid and he was really kind, but also as a matter of course. They had begun well together from the very first day, and she was soon satisfied that her position at Malta was the happiest possible. The beautiful place, the bright clear atmosphere, the lively society, all suited her. She had none of the trials peculiar to married life to injure her health and break her spirit, none of the restrictions imposed upon a girl to limit her pleasures, and she enjoyed her independence thoroughly. But of course there were drawbacks, and the thing of all others she disliked most was being toadied. There was one pair of inveterate toadies in the garrison, Major and Mrs. Guthrie Brimston. They belonged to a species well-known in the service, and tolerated on the principle of *Damne-toi, pourvu que tu nous amuse.* Major Guthrie

Brimston claimed to be one of the Morningquest family, and he had a portrait of the duke, as the head of the house, in his dressing room. It was balanced on the right by *Ecce Homo*, and on the left by the *Sistine Madonna*, but it was popularly supposed that he worshipped the duke. The pair acted the rôle of devoted husband and wife successfully, being in fact sincere in their habit of playing into each other's hands for their own selfish purposes ; and people who wished for an excuse to tolerate them because they were amusing, might say of them quite truly : "Well, whatever their faults, they are certainly devoted to each other." But it was a partnership of self-interest, enhanced by a little sentimentality, and they understood it themselves, for Mrs. Guthrie Brimston confessed in a moment of expansion that she knew "Bobbie" would marry again directly if she died, and certainly she would do the same if she lost him ; why shouldn't she ?"

Mrs. Guthrie Brimston was a nasty-minded woman, of extremely coarse conversation, and, without compromising herself, she was a fecund source of corruption in others. No younger woman of undecided character could come under her influence without being tainted in mind if not in manners. She delighted in objectionable stories, and her husband fed her fancy from the clubs liberally. Her stock-in-trade consisted for the most part of these stories, which she would retail to her lady friends at afternoon teas. She told them remarkably well too, and knew exactly how to suit them to palates which were only just beginning to acquire a taste for such fare, and were still fastidious. Wherever she came there was laughter among the ladies, of the high hysteric bacchante kind, not true mirth, but a loud laxity, into which they were beguiled for the moment, and which was the cause of self-distrust, disgust, and regret, upon reflection, to the better kind. If the question of motive is to be taken into account in considering the words and deeds of people, it may be confidently asserted that the Guthrie Brimstons never said a good-natured thing nor did a kind one. "I say, Minnie, if I give that sergeant of mine a goose at Christmas, I think I'll get more work out of the fellow next year," Major Brimston said to his wife at breakfast one morning.

"Yes, do," his wife answered sympathetically. "And I say, Bobbie, I'm going to work Captain Askew a bedspread. He's an awfully useful little man."

One form of pleasantry the Guthrie Brimstons greatly

affected was nicknaming. They nicknamed everybody, always opprobriously, often happily in the way of hitting off a salient peculiarity; but they were not in the least aware that they were themselves the best nicknamed people in the service. And they would not have liked it had they known it, for they were both exceedingly touchy. They held no feelings of another sacred, but their own supreme. Mrs. Guthrie Brimston was known as "The Brimston Woman."

Her conversation bristled with vain repetitions. She was always "a worm" when asked after her health, and everything that pleased her was "pucka." She knew no language but her own, and that she spoke indifferently, her command of it being limited for the most part to slang expressions, which are the scum of language; and a few stock phrases of polite quality for special occasions. But she used the latter awkwardly, as workmen wear their Sunday clothes.

Of the Guthrie Brimston morals it is safe to say that they would neither of them have broken either the sixth, seventh, or eighth commandments; but they bore false witness freely— not in open assertion, however, for that could be easily refuted, and fair fight was not at all in their line. But when false witness could be meanly conveyed by implication and innuendo, it formed the staple of their conversation.

"Those Guthrie Brimstons should be public prosecutors," Evadne said to Colonel Colquhoun at breakfast one morning, commenting upon some story of theirs which he had just retailed to her. "I notice when anyone's character is brought forward to be judged by society they are always Counsel for the Prosecution."

These were the people whom Colonel Colquhoun first introduced to Evadne. They amused him, and therefore he encouraged them to come to the house. Mrs. Guthrie Brimston suited him exactly. To use their own choice language, he would have given her away at any time, and she him; but that did not prevent them enjoying each other's society thoroughly.

True to her determination to make things pleasant for Colonel Colquhoun if possible, and seeing that he found these people congenial, Evadne did her best to cultivate their acquaintance for his sake. Never successfully, however. A mere tolerance was as far as she got; but even that was intermittent; and the undercurrent of criticism which streamed through her mind in their presence could never be checked.

But she was slow to read character. Her impulse was always to believe in people, and to like them; and she had to acquire a knowledge of their faults painfully, bit by bit. But Colonel Colquhoun helped her here. He was an inveterate gossip, very much in the manner of Mrs. Guthrie Brimston herself, only that he was more refined when he talked to Evadne; and at breakfast, their one *tête-à-tête* meal in the day, it was his habit to tell her such club stories as were sufficiently decent, and what "he said" and what "she said" of each other, upon which he would strike an average to arrive at the probable truth.

"Do you happen to know what is at the bottom of the feud between Mrs. Guthrie Brimston and Mrs. Malcomson?" he asked her one morning at breakfast.

"Mrs. Guthrie Brimston's defects of character obviously," said Evadne sententiously.

"Then you prefer Mrs. Malcomson?" he suggested. "Now, *I* can't get on with her a bit. She always appears to me so cold and censorious."

"Does she?" said Evadne thoughtfully. "But she is not really so at all. She is judicial though, and sincere, which gives one a sense of security in her presence."

"But she is deadly dull," said Colonel Colquhoun.

"Oh, no!" Evadne exclaimed, smiling. "You mistake her entirely. She made me laugh immoderately only yesterday."

"I should like to see you laugh immoderately," said Colonel Colquhoun.

Major Guthrie Brimston surprised Evadne more, perhaps, than his wife did. She began by overlooking the little man somehow without the least intending it, and as he seemed to himself to fill the horizon when in society and block out all view of anybody else, he could only believe that she did it on purpose.

He was by way of being an amateur actor, a low comedy man; but he was not sincere enough to personate any character, or be anything either on the stage or off it but his own small inartistic self; and no amount of bawling could make him an actor, though he bawled himself hoarse as a rule, mistaking sound for the science of expression. Still, it was the fashion to consider him funny. People called him "Grigsby" and "Kickleberry Brown," and laughed when he twiddled his thumbs. He was forever buffooning, and if he sat on a high stool with his toes just touching the floor, his head on one side, a sad expression of countenance, and the tips of his fingers touching, he was supposed to be doing something amusing, and the effort would be rewarded with laughter, in which, however, Evadne could not join. These performances outraged her sense of the dignity of poor human nature, which it is easy enough to discount, but very difficult to maintain ; and made her sorry for him.

His hands were another offence to her. They were fat and podgy, with short pointed fingers, indicative of animalism and ill-nature, the opposite of all that is refined and beautiful— truly of necessity an offence to her.

It was at first that she had overlooked him, but after a time, when she began to know him better, the little, fat, funny man magnetized her attention. She could not help gravely considering him wherever she met him, and wondering about him —wondering about them both in fact. She wondered, for one thing, why they were so fond of eating and drinking, her own taste in those matters being of the simplest description.

" I never deny myself anything," said Mrs. Guthrie Brimston. And she looked like it.

Evadne wondered also at their meanness, when she saw them saving money by borrowing the carriages of people whom she had heard them class as " Nothing but shopkeepers, you know. We shouldn't speak to them anywhere else." And whom they ridiculed habitually for the mispronunciation of words, and for accents unmistakably provincial.

What could Evadne have in common with these flippant people—scum themselves, forever on the surface, incapable even of seeing beneath, their every idea and motive a falsification of something divine in life or thought ? They did not even speak the same language. To their insidious slang she opposed a smooth current of perfect English, which seemed to reflect upon the inferior quality of their own expressions and led to mutual embarrassment. Evadne meant every word she uttered, and was careful to choose the one which should best express her meaning. Mrs. Guthrie Brimston's meanings, on the other hand, told best when half concealed. Another difficulty was, too, that Evadne's clear, decided speech had the effect of exposing innuendo and insincerity, and making both " bad form," which, socially speaking, is a much more terrible stigma to bear than an accusation of dishonesty, however well authenticated. And even their very manner of

expressing legitimate mirth was not the same, for Mrs. Guthrie Brimston laughed aloud, while Evadne's laugh was sound-
less.

Evadne suffered when she found herself being toadied by
these people. She said nothing, however. They were Colonel Colquhoun's friends, and she felt herself forced to be civil
to them so long as he chose to bring them to the house. And
they were besides an evil out of which good came to her
quickly. For as soon as she understood their manners and
their modes of thought, she felt her heart fill with earnest
self-congratulation : "If these are the kind of people whom
Colonel Colquhoun prefers," was her mental ejaculation,
" what an escape I have had ! Thank Heaven, he is nothing
to me."

CHAPTER VII.

SOCIETY in Malta during the sunny winter is very much
like the society of a London season, only that it is more
representative because there are fewer specimens of each class,
and those who do go out are like delegates charged with a
concentrated extract of the peculiarities and prejudices of
their own set. When Evadne arrived, at the beginning of
the winter, the rest of the party had already assembled.
There were naval people, military, commercial, landed gentry,
clerical, royalty, and beer. The principal representative of
this latter interest was a lady whom Mrs. Guthrie Brimston
called the Queen of Beersheba because of her splendid habili-
ments, and this is a fair specimen of Mrs. Guthrie Brimston's
wit.

Evadne was received in silence, as it were, for abroad the
question is not generally " Who are you ?" as at home, but
" What are you like ?" or " How much can you do for us ?"
and people were waiting till she showed her colours. She
never did show any decided colours of the usual kind, however. She was not " a beauty beyond doubt "—some people
did not admire her in the least. She was not " the same "
or " nice " to everybody, for she had strong objections to
certain people, and showed that she had ; and she was not
" by way of entertaining " at all, although she did " as much
of that kind of thing " as other ladies of her station. But yet,
with all these negatives, she made a distinct impression on the
place as soon as she appeared. It sounds paradoxical, but

she was celebrated at once for her silence and for what she had said. The weight of her occasional utterances told. And if it were fair to call Mrs. Guthrie Brimston counsel for the prosecution, Evadne might have been set up as counsel for the defence; for it so happened that when she did speak in those early days it was usually in defence of something or somebody—people, principles, absent friends, *or* enemies ; anything unfairly attacked. Generally, when she said anything cutting, it was so clearly incisive you hardly knew for a moment where you were injured. She did it like the executioner of that Eastern potentate who decapitated a criminal with such skill and with so sharp an instrument that the latter did not know when he was executed and went on talking, his head remaining *in situ* until he sneezed. There was one old gentleman, Lord Groome, whom she had disposed of several times in that way without, however, being able to get rid of him quite, because his stupidity was a hardy perennial which came up again all the fresher and stronger for having been lopped. He was a degenerated, ridiculous-looking old object, a man with the most touching confidence in his tailor, which the latter invariably betrayed by never making him a garment that fitted him. He had begun by admiring Evadne, and had endeavoured to pay his senile court to her with fulsome flatteries in the manner approved of his kind—but he ended by being afraid of her.

His first collision with Evadne was on the subject of "those low Radicals," against whom he had been launching out in unmeasured terms. "Why low, because Radical ?" she asked. "I should have thought, among so many, that some must be honest men, and nothing honest can be low."

"I tell you, my dear lady," he replied, his temper tried by her words, but controlled by her appearance, "I tell you the Radicals are a low lot, the whole of them."

"Ah ! Then I suppose you know them all," she said, looking at him thoughtfully.

The want of intelligence in the community at large was made painfully apparent by the stories of her peculiar opinions which were freely circulated and seldom suspected. The Queen of Beersheba declared that Evadne approved of the frightful cruelties which the people inflicted on the nobles during the Reign of Terror, that she had heard her say so herself.

What Evadne did say was : "The revolutionary excesses

were inevitable. They came at the swing of the pendulum which the nobles themselves had set in motion; and if you consider the sufferings that had been inflicted on the people, and their long endurance of them, you will be more surprised to think that they kept their reason so long than that they should have lost it at last. 'Pour la populace ce n'est jamais par envie d'attaquer qu'elle se soulève, mais par impatience de souffrir.'"

But the French Revolution is an abstract subject of impersonal interest compared with the Irish question at the present time; and the commotion which was caused by the misrepresentation of Evadne's remarks about the Reign of Terror was insignificant compared with what followed when her feeling for Ireland had been misinterpreted. She gave out the text which called forth the second series of imbecilities during a dinner party at her own house one night, her old friend, Lord Groome, supplying her with a peg upon which to hang her conclusions, by making an intemperate attack upon the Irish.

CHAPTER VIII.

CAPTAIN BELLIOT was not one of the guests at that dinner party of Evadne's, but he happened to call on Mrs. Guthrie Brimston next day, and finding her alone, had tea with her *tête-à-tête*; and of course she entertained him with her own version of what had occurred the night before.

"The dinner itself was very good," she said. "All their dinners are, you know. But Mrs. Colquhoun was"—she raised her hands, and nodded her head—"well, just *too* awful!" she concluded.

"Indeed!" he observed, leaning back in his chair, crossing his legs, and settling himself for a treat generally. "You surprise me, because she has never struck me as being the kind of person who would set the Thames on fire in any way."

Mrs. Guthrie Brimston smiled enigmatically: "Do you admire her very much?" she asked with the utmost suavity.

"Well," he answered warily, "she is rather peculiar in appearance, don't you know."

Mrs. Guthrie Brimston drew her own conclusions, not from the words, but from the wariness, and proceeded: "It is not in appearance only that that she is peculiar, then. She astonished us all last night, I can assure you."

" How ? " he asked, to fill up an artistic pause.

" By the things she said ! " Mrs. Guthrie Brimston answered, with an affectation of reserve.

"Now you do surprise me !" Captain Belliot declared. " Because I cannot imagine her saying anything but ' How do you do ? ' and ' Good-bye,' ' Yes ' and ' No,' ' Indeed ! ' ' Please,' ' Thank you,' and ' Do you think so ? ' On my honour, those words are all I have ever heard her utter, and I have met her as often as anybody on the island. Now, *I* like a woman with something in her," he concluded, ogling Mrs. Guthrie Brim-ston.

" Well, then, she must have been hibernating, or something, when she first came out, for she has begun to talk now with a vengeance," Mrs. Guthrie Brimston answered smartly.

" But what has she been saying ? " he asked, with great curiosity.

" I simply cannot tell you ! " she answered pointedly.

" So bad as that ? " he said, raising his eyebrows.

" Yes. Things that *no* woman should have said," she sub-joined with emphasis.

There was, of course, only one conclusion to be drawn from this, and it would have been drawn at the club later in the day inevitably, even if other ladies had not also declared that Mrs. Colquhoun had said such dreadful things that they really could not repeat them. It is true that some of the men of the party mentioned the matter in a different way, and one, when asked what it was exactly that Mrs. Colquhoun had said, even answered casually : " Oh, some rot about the Irish ques-tion ! " But the explanation made no impression, and was immediately forgotten. Captain Belliot himself was so excited by the news that he hurried away from Mrs. Guthrie Brimston as soon as he could possibly excuse himself without giving offence, and went at once to call upon Evadne in order to inspect her from this unexpected point of view.

He found her talking tranquilly to Mr. St. John, Edith, and Mrs. Beale ; and although he sat for half an hour, she never said a word of the slightest significance. That, however, proved nothing either one way or the other, and he left her with his confidence in Mrs. Guthrie Brimston's insinuations quite unshaken, his theory being that the women whose minds are in reality the most corrupt are as a rule very carefully guarded in their conversation, although, of course, they always betray themselves sooner or later by some such slip as that with which he credited Evadne—an idea which he proceeded to expand at the club with great effect.

Evadne's reputation was in danger after that, and she risked it still further by acting in defiance of the public opinion of the island generally, in order to do what she conceived to be an act of justice.

Mrs. Guthrie Brimston went to her one morning, brimming over with news.

"My husband has just received a letter from a friend of his in India, Major Lopside, telling him to warn us all not to call on Mrs. Clarence, who has just joined your regiment," she burst out. "I thought I ought to let you know at once. She met her husband in India, Major Lopside says, and it was a runaway match. But that is not all. For he says he knows for a fact that they travelled together for three hundred miles down country, sleeping at all the dak bungalows by the way, before they *were* married!"

"Waiting until they came to some place where they could be married, I suppose?" Evadne suggested.

Mrs. Guthrie Brimston laughed. "Taking a sort of trial trip, I should say!" she ventured. "But it was very good of Major Lopside to let us know. I should certainly have called if he hadn't."

"You make me feel sick——" Evadne began.

"I knew I should!" Mrs. Guthrie Brimston interposed triumphantly.

"Sick at heart," Evadne pursued, "to think of an Englishman being capable of writing a letter for the express purpose of ruining a woman's reputation."

Mrs. Brimston changed countenance. "*We* think it was awfully kind of Major Lopside to let us know," she repeated, perking.

"Well, *I* think," said Evadne, her slow utterance giving double weight to each word—"*I* think he must be an exceedingly low person himself, and one probably whom Mrs. Clarence has had to snub. He could only have been actuated by animus when he wrote that letter. One may be quite sure that a man is never disinterested when he does a low thing."

"It was a private letter written for our *private* information," Mrs. Guthrie Brimston asserted. She was ruffled considerably by this time.

"No, not written for your private information," Evadne rejoined, "or if it were, you are making a strange use of it. I have no doubt, however, that it was designed for the very purpose to which you are putting it—the purpose of spoiling the Clarences' chance of happiness in a new place. And it is precisely to the ' private ' character of the document that I take exception. If this Major Lopside has any accusation to bring against Captain Clarence, he should have done it publicly, and not in this underhand manner. He should have written to Colonel Colquhoun."

"Nonsense," said Mrs. Guthrie Brimston, her native rudeness getting the better of her habitual caution at this provocation. "Major Lopside would not be fool enough to report a man to his own chief. Why, he might get the worst of it himself if there were an inquiry."

"Exactly," Evadne answered. " He thinks it safer to stab in the dark. Will you kindly excuse me? I am very busy this morning, writing my letters for the mail. But many thanks for letting me know about this malicious story."

There was nothing for it but to retire after this, which Mrs. Guthrie Brimston did, discomfited, and with an uneasy feeling, which had been growing upon her lately, that Evadne was not quite the nonentity for which she had mistaken her.

Colonel Colquhoun had lunched at mess that day, and Evadne did not see him until quite late, when she met him on the Barraca with the Guthrie Brimstons.

It was the hour when the Barraca is thronged, and Evadne had gone with a purpose, expecting to find him there.

He left the Guthrie Brimstons and joined her as soon as she appeared.

"I have been home to look for you," he said, "but I found that you had gone out without an escort, no one knew where."

" I have been making calls," Evadne answered—"and making Mrs. Clarence's acquaintance also. Oh, there she is, leaning against that arch with her husband. Have you met her yet? Let me introduce you. She is charmingly pretty, but very timid."

Colonel Colquhoun's brow contracted.

"I thought Mrs. Guthrie Brimston had warned you——"

"*Warned* me?" Evadne quietly interposed. "Mrs. Guthrie Brimston brought me a scandalous story which had the effect of making me call on Mrs. Clarence at once. I suppose you have seen this precious Major Lopside's letter?"

"Yes," he answered. "And I am sorry you called without consulting me. You really ought to have consulted me. It will make it doubly awkward for you, having called. **But** we'll rush the fellow. I'll make him send in his papers at once."

"Why is it awkward for me—what is awkward for me?" Evadne asked.

"Why, having a lady in the regiment you can't know, to begin with, and having to cut her after calling upon her," he answered. "If you would only condescend to consult me occasionally I could save you from this kind of thing."

"But why may I not countenance Mrs. Clarence?"

"You cannot countenance a woman there is a story about," he responded decidedly.

"But where is the proof of the story?" she asked,

Colonel Colquhoun reflected : "A man wouldn't write a letter of that kind without some grounds for it," he said.

"We must find out what the exact grounds were," said Evadne.

"Well, you see none of the other ladies are speaking to her," Colonel Colquhoun observed, with the air of one whose argument is unanswerable.

"They are sheep," said Evadne, "but they can be led aright as well as astray, I suppose. We'll see, at all events. But don't let me keep you from your friends. I want to speak to Mrs. Malcomson."

There was a quiet sense of power about Evadne when she chose to act which checked opposition at the outset, and put an end to argument. Colonel Colquhoun looked disheartened, but like a gentleman he acted at once on the hint to go. He did not rejoin the Guthrie Brimstons, however, but sat alone under one of the arches of the Barraca, turning his back on the entrancing view of the Grand Harbour, a jewel of beauty, set in silence.

Colonel Colquhoun was watching. He saw Mrs. Clarence turn from the strange Christian women who eyed her coldly, and lean over the parapet ; he saw the influence of the scene upon her mind in the sweet and tranquil expression which gradually replaced the half-pained, half-puzzled look her face had been wearing. He saw her husband standing beside her, but with his back to the parapet, looking at the people gloomily and with resentment, but also half-puzzled, perceiving that his wife was being slighted, and wondering why.

Colonel Colquhoun saw Mrs. Guthrie Brimston also, going from one group to another with the peculiar ducking-forward gait of a high-hipped, high-shouldered woman, followed by her little fat "Bobbie," smiling herself, and met with smiles which were followed by noisy laughter; and he noticed, too, that invariably the eyes of those she addressed turned upon Mrs. Clarence, and their faces grew hard and unfriendly; and not one person to whom she spoke looked the happier or the better for the attention when she left them. Colonel Colquhoun, with a set countenance, slowly curled his blond moustache. Only his eyes moved, following Mrs. Guthrie Brimston for a while, and then returning to Evadne. She was speaking to Mrs. Malcomson, and the latter looked, as she listened, at Mrs. Guthrie Brimston. Then Evadne took her arm, and the two sauntered over to Mrs. Beale—an important person, who always adopted the last charitable opinion she heard expressed positively, and acted upon it.

It was Mrs. Malcomson who spoke to her, and the effect of what she said was instantaneous, for the old lady bridled visibly, and then set out, accompanied by Edith, with the obvious intention of heading the relief party herself that very minute. She stationed herself beside Mrs. Clarence, and stood, patting the poor girl's hand with motherly tenderness; smiling at her, and saying conventional nothings in a most cordial manner.

Colonel Colquhoun had watched these proceedings, understanding them perfectly, but remaining impassive as at first. And Mrs. Guthrie Brimston had also seen signs of the re-action the moment it set in, and shown her astonishment. She was not accustomed to be checked in full career when it pleased her to be down upon another woman, and she didn't quite know what to do. She looked first at Colonel Colquhoun, inviting him to rejoin her, but he ignored the glance; and she therefore found herself obliged either to give him up or to go to him. She decided to go to him, and set out, attended by her own "Bobbie." By the time she had reached him, however, the last act of the little play had begun. Evadne was standing apart with Captain Clarence, looking up at him and speaking—with her usual unimpassioned calm, to judge by the expression of her face, but Mrs. Guthrie Brimston had begun to realize that when Evadne did speak it was to some purpose, and she watched now and awaited the event in evident trepidation.

"She's not telling him! She never would dare to!" slipped from her unawares.

"They are coming this way," Colonel Colquhoun observed significantly.

" I shall go ! " cried Mrs. Guthrie Brimston.   " Come, Bob-bie ! "

It was too late, however ; they were surrounded.

" Be good enough to remain a moment," Captain Clarence exclaimed authoritatively. Then turning to Colonel Colqu-houn, he said ; " I understand that these people have in their possession a letter containing a foul slander against my wife and myself, and that they have been using it to injure us in the estimation of everybody here. If it be possible, sir, I should like to have an official inquiry instituted into the cir-cumstances of my marriage at once."

" Very well, Captain Clarence," Colonel Colquhoun answered ceremoniously.

" I'll apologise," Major Guthrie Brimston gasped.

But Captain Clarence turned on his heel, and walked back to his wife as if he had not heard.

How the inquiry was conducted was not made public. But when it was *said* that the Clarences had been cleared, and *seen* that the Guthrie Brimstons had not suffered, society declared it to have been a case of six of one and half-a-dozen of the other, which left matters exactly where they were before. Those who chose to believe in the calumny continued to do so, and *vice versa*, the only difference being that Evadne's generous action in the matter brought blame upon herself from one set, and also—what was worse—brought her into a kind of vogue with another which would have caused her to rage had she understood it. For the story that she had " said things which no woman could repeat," added to the fact that she was seen everywhere with a lady whose reputation had been attacked, made men of a certain class feel a sudden in-terest in her. " Birds of a feather," they maintained ; then spoke of her slightingly in public places, and sent her bouquets innumerable.

Her next decided action, however, put an effectual stop to this nuisance.

CHAPTER IX.

COLONEL COLQUHOUN came to Evadne one day, and asked her if she would not go out.

She put down her work, rose at once, smiling, and declared that she should be delighted.

There had been a big regimental guest night the day before, and Colonel Colquhoun had dined at mess, and was consequently irritable. Acquiescence is as provoking as opposition to a man in that mood, and he chose to take offence at Evadne's evident anxiety to please him.

"She makes quite a business of being agreeable to me," he reflected while he was waiting for her to put her hat on. "She requires me to be on my good behaviour as if I were a school-boy out for a half-holiday, and thinks it her duty to entertain me by way of reward, I suppose."

And thereupon he set himself determinedly against being entertained, and accordingly, when Evadne rejoined him and made some cheerful remark, he responded to it with a sullen grunt which did small credit to his manners either as a man or a gentleman, and naturally checked the endeavour for the moment so far as she was concerned.

As he did not seem inclined to converse, she showed her respect for his mood by being silent herself. But this was too much for him. He stood it as long as he could, and then he burst out ; "Do you never talk ?"

"I don't know !" she said, surprised. "Do you like talkative women ?"

"I like a woman to have something to say for herself."

While Evadne was trying in her slow way to see precisely what he meant by this little outbreak, they met one of the officers of the regiment escorting a very showy young woman, and as everybody in Malta knows everybody else in society, and this was a stranger, Evadne asked—more, however, to oblige Colonel Colquhoun by making a remark than because she felt the slightest curiosity on the subject ; "Who is that with Mr. Finchley ? A new arrival, I suppose ?"

"Oh, only a girl he brought out from England with him," Colonel Colquhoun answered coarsely, staring hard at the girl as he spoke, and forgetting himself for once in his extreme irritability. "He ought not to bring her here, though," he added carelessly.

Mr. Finchley had passed them, hanging his head, and pretending not to see them. Evadne flushed crimson.

"Do you mean that he brought out a girl he is not married to, and is living with her here ?" she asked.

"That is the position exactly," Colonel Colquhoun rejoined, "and I'll see him in the orderly room to-morrow and interview him on the subject. He has no business to parade her publicly where the other fellows' wives may meet her ; and I'll not have it."

Evadne said no more. But there was a ball that evening, and during an interval between the dances, when she was standing beside Colonel Colquhoun and several ladies in a prominent position and much observed, for it was just at the time when she was at the height of her unenviable vogue—Mr. Finchley came up and asked her to dance.

She had drawn herself up proudly as he approached, and having looked at him deliberately, she turned her back upon him.

There was no mistaking her intention, Colonel Colquhoun's hand paused on its way to twirl his blond moustache, and there was a perceptible sensation in the room.

Captain Belliot shook his head with the air of a man who has been deceived in an honest endeavour to make the best of a bad lot, and is disheartened.

"She took me in completely," he said. "I should never have guessed she was that kind of woman. What is society coming to?"

"She must be deuced nasty-minded herself, you know, or she wouldn't have known Finchley had a woman out with him," said Major Livingston, whom Mrs. Guthrie Brimston called "Lady Betty" because of his nice precise little ways with ladies.

"Oh, trust a prude!" said Captain Brown. "They spy out all the beastliness that's going."

Colonel Colquhoun did not take this last proof of Evadne's peculiar views at all well. He was becoming even more sensitive as he grew older to what fellows say or think, and he was therefore considerably annoyed by her conduct, so much so, indeed, that he actually spoke to her upon the subject himself.

"People will say that I have married Mrs. Grundy," he grumbled.

"1 suppose so," she answered tranquilly. "You see I do not feel at all about these things as you do. I wish you *could* feel as I do, but seeing that you cannot, it is fortunate, is it not, that we are not really married?"

"It sounds as if you were congratulating yourself upon the fact of our position," he said.

"But don't *you* congratulate yourself?" she answered in surprise. "Surely you have had as narrow an escape as I had? you would have been miserable too?"

He made no answer. It is perhaps easier to resign an inferior husband than a superior wife.

But he let the subject drop then for the moment; only for
the moment, however, for later in the day he had a conversation with Mrs. Guthrie Brimston.

That little business about the Clarences had not interrupted
the intimacy between Colonel Colquhoun and the Guthrie
Brimstons. How could it? Mrs. Guthrie Brimston was as
amusing as ever, and Colonel Colquhoun remained in command of a crack regiment, and was a handsome man, well
set-up and soldier like into the bargain. It was Evadne who
had caused all the annoyance, and consequently there was
really no excuse for a rupture—especially as Evadne met the
Guthrie Brimstons herself with as much complacency as ever.
Colonel Colquhoun had gone to Mrs. Guthrie Brimston's that
afternoon for the purpose of discussing the advisability of getting some experienced woman of the world to speak to Evadne
with a view to putting a stop to her nonsense, and the consultation ended with an offer from Mrs. Guthrie Brimston to
undertake the task herself. Her interference, however, produced not the slightest effect on Evadne.

CHAPTER X.

THOSE who can contemplate certain phases of life and still
believe that there is a Divine Providence ordering all
things for the best, will see its action in the combination of
circumstances which placed Evadne in the midst of a community where she must meet the spirit of evil face to face
continually, and, since acquiescence was impossible, forced her
to develop her own strength by steady and determined resistance. But her position was more than difficult : it was desperate. There was scarcely one, even amongst the most indulgent of her friends, who did not misunderstand her and
blame her at times. She kept the pendulum of public opinion
swaying vehemently during the whole of her first season in
Malta. Major Livingston shook his head about her from the
first.

"I can't get on with her," he said, as if the fact were not
at all to her credit. He was a survival himself, one of the old-
fashioned kind of military men who were all formed on the
same plan ; they got their uniform, their politics, their vices,

and their code of honour cut and dried, upon entering the service, and occasionally left the latter with their agents to be taken care of for them while they served.

Evadne gave offence to representatives of the next generation also. Seeing that she was young and attractive, it was clearly her duty to think only of meriting their attention, and when she was discovered time after time during a ball hanging quite affectionately on the arm of Mr. Austin B. Price, "a dried up old American," and pacing the balcony to and fro with him in the moonlight by the hour together when there were plenty of young fellows who wanted to dance with her ; and when, worse still, it was observed that she was serenely happy on these occasions, listening to Mr. Austin B. Price with a smile on her lips, or even and actually talking herself, why, they declared she wasn't womanly—she couldn't be !

Mr. St. John was one of the friends who very much deprecated Evadne's attitude at this time. He did not speak to her himself, being diffident and delicate, but he went to Mr. Price, who was, he knew, quite in her confidence.

" You have influence with her, *do* restrain her ; " he said. " No good is done by making herself the subject of common gossip."

" My dear fellow," Mr. Price replied, " she is quite irresponsible. Certain powers of perception have developed in her to a point beyond that which has been reached by the people about her, and she is forced to act up to what she perceives to be right. They blame her because they cannot see so far in advance of themselves, and she has small patience with them for not at once recognizing the use and propriety of what comes so easily and naturally to her. So far, it is easy enough to understand her, surely ? But further than that it is impossible to go, because she is as yet an incomplete creature in a state of progression. With fair play, she should continue on, but, on the other hand, her development may be entirely arrested. It is curious that priesthoods, while preaching perfection, invariably do their best to stop progress. You will never believe that any change is for the better until it is accomplished, and there is no denying it, and so you hinder forever when you should be the first to help and encourage ; and you are bringing yourselves into disrepute by it. Just try and realize the difference between the position and powers of judgment of women now and that which obtained among them at the beginning of the century ! And think, too, of the hard battles they have had to fight for every inch of the way they have made, and of the desperate resolution with which they have stood their ground, always advancing, never receding, and with supernumeraries ready, whenever one falls out exhausted, to step in and take her place, however dangerous it may be. Oh, I tell you, man, women are grand !—grand ! "

"But I don't see how we have imposed upon women," Mr. St. John objected.

"I can show you in a minute," Mr. Price rejoined, twitching his face. " It was the submission business, you know, to begin with. Not so many years ago we men had only to insist that a thing was either right or necessary, and women believed it, and meekly acquiesced in it. We told them they were fools to us, and they believed it ; and we told them they were angels of light and purity and goodness whose mission it was to marry and reform us, and above all pity and sympathize with us when we defiled ourselves, because we couldn't help it, and they believed it. We told them they didn't really care for moral probity in man, and they believed it. We told them they had no brains, that they were illogical, unreasoning, and incapable of thought in the true sense of the word, and, by Jove ! they took all that for granted, such was their beautiful confidence in us, and never even *tried* to think—until one day, when, quite by accident, I feel sure, one of them found herself arriving at logical conclusions involuntarily. Her brain was a rich soil, although untilled, which began to teem of its own accord ; and that, my dear fellow, was the beginning of the end of the old state of things. But I believe myself that all this unrest and rebellion against the old established abuses amongst women is simply an effort of nature to improve the race. The men of the present day will have a bad time if they resist the onward impulse ; but, in any case, the men of the future will have good reason to arise and call their mothers blessed. Good-day to you. Don't interfere with Evadne, and don't think. Just watch—and—and pray if you like ! " The old gentleman smiled and twitched his face when he had spoken, and they shook hands and parted in complete disagreement, as was usually the case.

CHAPTER XI.

WHEN any difference of opinion arose between Evadne and Colonel Colquhoun they discussed it tranquilly as a rule, and with much forbearance upon either side, and having done so, the subject was allowed to drop. They each generally remained of the same opinion still, but neither would interfere with the other afterward. Had he had anything in him ; could he have made her feel him to be superior in any way, she must have grown to love him with passion once more ; but as it was, he remained only an erring fellow-creature in her estimation, for whom she grew gradually to feel both pity and affection, it is true ; but toward whom her attitude generally speaking was that of most polite indifference.

She had her moments of rage, however. There were whole days when her patient tolerance of the position gave way, and one wild longing to be free pursued her ; but she made no sign on such occasions, only sat

> With lips severely placid, felt the knot
> Climb in her throat, and with her foot unseen,
> Crushed the wild passion out against the floor,
> Beneath the banquet, where the meats become
> As wormwood—

and uttered not a word. Yet there was nothing in Colonel Colquhoun's manner, nothing in his treatment of her, in the least objectionable ; what she suffered from was simply contact with an inferior moral body, and the intellectual starvation inevitable in constant association with a mind too shallow to contain any sort of mental sustenance for the sharing.

The pleasing fact that he and Evadne were getting on very well together dawned on him quite suddenly one day ; but it was she who perceived that the absence of friction was entirely due to the restriction which polite society imposes upon the manners of a gentleman and lady in ordinary everyday intercourse when their bond is not the bond of man and wife.

" I should say we are very good friends, Evadne, shouldn't you ? " he remarked, in a cheerful tone.

" Yes," she responded cordially.

They were both in evening dress when this occurred—she sitting beside a table with one bare arm resting upon it, toying with the tassel of her fan ; he standing with his back to the fireplace, looking down upon her. It was after dinner, and they were lingering over their coffee until it should be time to stroll in for an hour or so to the opera.

" By-the-way," he said after a pause, " have you read any of those books I got for you—any of the French ones ? "

Her face set somewhat, but she looked up at him, and answered without hesitation : " Yes. I have read the ' Nana,' La Terre,' ' Madame Bovary,' and ' Sapho.' "

She stopped there, and he then waited in vain for her to express an opinion.

" Well," he said at last, " what has struck you most in them ? "

" The suffering, George," she exclaimed—" *the awful, needless suffering !* "

It was a veritable cry of anguish, and as she spoke, she threw her arms forward upon the table beside which she was sitting, laid her face down on them, and burst into passsionate sobs.

Colonel Colquhoun bit his lip. He had not meant to hurt the girl—in that way, at all events. He took a step toward her, hesitated, not knowing quite what to do ; and finally left the room.

When next Evadne went to her bookshelves she discovered a great gap. The whole of those dangerous works of fiction had disappeared.

CHAPTER XII.

COLONEL COLQUHOUN had gradually fallen into the habit of riding out or walking alone with Mrs. Guthrie Brimston continually, and of course people began to make much of the intimacy, and to talk of the way he neglected his poor young wife ; but the only part of the arrangement which was not agreeable to the latter was having to entertain Major Guthrie Brimston sometimes during his lady's absence, and the lady herself when she stayed to tea. For there was really no harm in the flirtation, as Evadne was acute enough to perceive. Mrs. Guthrie Brimston was one of those women who pride themselves upon having a train of admirers, and are not above robbing other women of the companionship of their husbands in order to swell their own following ; while many men rather affect the society of these ladies because " They are not a bit stiff, you know," and allow a certain laxity of language which

is particularly piquant to the masculine mind when the complacent lady is no relation and is really " all right herself, you
know."

Mrs. Guthrie Brimston was " really quite right, you know."
She and her husband understood each other perfectly, while
Evadne, on her part, was content to know that Colonel Colquhoun was so innocently occupied. For she was beginning
to think of him as a kind of big child, of weak moral purpose, for whose good behaviour she would be held responsible,
and it was a relief when Mrs. Guthrie Brimston took him off
her hands.

No healthy-minded human being likes to dwell on the misery
which another is suffering or has suffered, and it is, therefore, a
comfort to know that upon the whole, at this period of her life,
Evadne was not at all unhappy. She had her friends, her pleasures, and her occupations ; the latter being multifarious. The
climate of Malta, at that time of the year, suited her to perfection, and the picturesque place, with its romantic history and
strange traditions, was in itself an unfailing source of interest
and delight to her.

Dear old Mrs. Beale had kept her heart from hardening into
bitterness just by loving her, and giving her a good motherly
hug now and then. When Evadne was inclined to rail she
would say : " Pity the wicked people, my dear, pity them.
Pity does more good in the world than blame, however well
deserved. You may soften a sinner by pitying him, but never
by hard words ; and once you melt into the mood of pity yourself, you will be able to endure things which would otherwise
drive you mad."

Mrs. Malcomson helped her too. During that first burst of
unpopularity which she brought upon herself by daring to act
upon her own perception of right and wrong in defiance of the
old established injustices of society, when even the most kindly
disposed hung back suspiciously, not knowing what dangerous sort of a new creature she might eventually prove herself
to be—at the earliest mutter of that storm, Mrs. Malcomson
came forward boldly to support Evadne ; and so also did Mrs.
Sillinger.

Mr. St. John was another of Evadne's particular friends.
He had injured his health by excessive devotion to his duties,
and been sent to Malta in the hope that the warm bright climate might strengthen his chest, which was his weak point,
and restore him ; but it was not really the right place for him,

and he had continued delicate throughout the winter, and required little attentions which Evadne was happily able to pay him ; and in this way their early acquaintance had rapidly ripened into intimacy. He was a clever man in his own profession, of exceptional piety, but narrow, which did not, however, prevent him from being congenial to one side of Evadne's nature. She had never doubted her religion. It was a thing apart from all her knowledge and opinions, something to be *felt*, essentially, not *known* as anything but a pleasurable and elevating sensation, or considered except in the way of referring all that is noble in thought and action to the divine nature of its origin and influence ; and she preserved her deep reverence for the priesthood intact, and found both comfort and spiritual sustenance in their ministrations. She still leaned to ritual, and Mr. St. John was a ritualist, so that they had much in common ; and while she was able to pay him many attentions and show him great kindness, for the want of which, as a bachelor and an invalid in a foreign place, he must have suffered in his feeble state of health, he had it in his power to take her out of herself. She said she was always the better for a talk with him ; and certainly the delicate dishes and wines and care generally which she lavished upon him had as much to do as the climate with the benefit he derived from his sojourn in Malta. They remained firm friends always ; and many years afterward, when he had become one of the most distinguished bishops on the bench, he was able, from the knowledge and appreciation of her character which he had gained in these early days, to do her signal service, and save her from much stupid misrepresentation.

And last, among her friends, although one of the greatest, was Mr. Austin B. Price. Evadne owed this kind, large-hearted, chivalrous gentleman much gratitude, and repaid him with much affection. He was really the first to discover that there was anything remarkable about her ; and it was to him she also owed a considerable further development of her originally feeble sense of humour.

Mr. Price's first impression that she was an uncommon character had been confirmed by one of those rapid phrases of hers which contained in a few words the embodiment of feelings familiar to a multitude of people who have no power to express them. She delivered it the third time they met, which happened to be at another of those afternoon dances, held on board the flag ship on that occasion. Colonel Colquhoun liked her to show herself although she did not dance in the afternoon, so she was there, sitting out, and Mr. Price was courteously endeavouring to entertain her.

"It surprises me," he said, "as an American, to find so little inclination in your free and enlightened country to do away with your—politically speaking—useless and extremely expensive Royal House."

"Well, you see," said Evadne, "we are deeply attached to our Royal House, and we can well afford to keep it up."

It was this glimpse of the heart of the proud and patriotic little aristocrat, true daughter of a nation great enough to disdain small economies, and not accustomed to do without any luxury to which it is attached, that appealed to Mr. Price, pleasing the pride of race with which we contemplate any evidence of strength in our fellow-creatures, whether it be strength of purpose or strength of passion, more than it shocked his utilitarian prejudices.

When it was evident that Evadne had brought a good deal that was disagreeable upon herself by her action in the matter of the Clarences, old Mrs. Beale came to her one day in all kindliness to tell her the private opinion of the friends who had stood by her loyally in public.

"I am sure you did it with the best motive, my dear, and it was bravely done," the old lady said, patting her hand; "but be advised by those who know the world, and have had more experience than you have had. Don't interfere again. Interference does no good; and people will say such things if you do! They will make you pay for your disinterestedness."

"But it seems to me that the question is not *Shall I have to pay?* but *Am I not bound to pay?*" Evadne rejoined. "Neglecting to do what is, to me, obviously the right thing, and making no endeavour but such as is sure to be applauded—working in the hope of a reward, in fact, seems to me to be a terribly old-fashioned idea, miserable remnant of the bribery and corruption of the Dark Ages, when the people were kept in such dense ignorance that they could be treated like children, and told if they were good they should have this for a prize, but if they were bad they should be punished."

"You are quite right, I am sure, my dear," rejoined Mrs. Beale; "but all the same. I don't think I should interfere again, if I were you."

"It seems that I have not done the Clarences any good," Evadne murmured one day to Mr. Price.

"Well, that was hardly to be expected," he answered—at which she raised her eyebrows interrogatively. "Calumnies which attach themselves to a name in a moment take a life-time to remove, because such a large majority of people prefer to think the worst of each other. The Clarences will have to live down their own little difficulty. And what you have to consider now is, not how little benefit they have derived from your brave defence of them, but how many other people you may have saved from similar attacks. I fancy it will be some time before people will venture to spread scandals of the kind here in Malta again. You have taught them a lesson ; you may be sure of that ; so don't be disheartened and lose sight of the final result in consideration of immediate conse-quences. The hard part of teaching is that the teacher him-self seldom sees anything of the good he has done."

It was very evident at this time that Evadne's view of life was becoming much too serious for her own good ; and, per-ceiving this, Mr. Price let fall some words one day in the course of conversation which she afterward treasured in her heart to great advantage. "It is our duty to be happy," he said. "Every human being is entitled to a certain amount of pleasure in life. But, in order to be happy, you must think of the world as a mischievous big child ; let your attitude be one of amused contempt so long as you detect no vice in the mischief ; once you do, however, if you have the gift of lan-guage, use it, lash out unmercifully ! And don't desist because the creature howls at you. The louder it howls the more you may congratulate yourself that you have touched it on the right spot, which is sure to be tender."

But he did not limit his kindly attentions to the giving of good advice ; in fact, he very seldom gave advice at all ; what he chiefly did was to devise distractions for her which should take her out of herself ; and one of these was a children's party which he induced her to give at Christmas.

The party was to take place on Christmas Eve, and the whole of the day before and far into the night the Colquhoun house was thronged with actors rehearsing charades and *tableaux,* and officers painting and preparing decorations, and putting them up. All were in the highest spirits ; the talk and laughter were incessant ; the work was being done with a will, and none of them looked as if they had ever had a sor-

rowful thought in their lives—least of all Evadne, whose
gaiety seemed the most spontaneous of all.

Late at night she had come to the hall with nails for the
decorators, and was handing them up as they were wanted by
those on the ladders.   The men were in their shirt sleeves, the
most becoming dress that a gentleman ever appears in ; and
during a pause she happened to notice Colonel Colquhoun,
who had stepped back to judge the effect of some drapery he
was putting up.   Mr. Price was a little behind him, and two
of the younger men, the three making an excellent foil to
Colonel Colquhoun.   Evadne was struck by the contrast.
The outside aspect of the man still pleased her.   There was
no doubt that he was a fine specimen of his species, a splendid
animal to look at ; what a pity he should have had a regrettable
past, the kind of past, too, which can never be over and done
with !   A returned convict is always a returned convict, and a
vicious man reformed is not repaired by the process.   The
stigma is in his blood.

Evadne sighed.   She was too highly tempered, well-balanced
a creature to be the victim of any one passion, and least of all
of that transient state of feeling miscalled " Love."   Physical
attraction, moral repulsion : that was what she was suffering
from ; and now involuntarily she sighed—a sigh of rage for
what might have been ; and just at that moment, Colonel Colquhoun, happening to look at her, found her eyes fixed on
him with a strange expression.   Was there going to be a
chance for him after all ?

He did not understand Evadne.   He had no conception of
the human possibility of anything so perfect as her self-control ;
and when she showed no feeling, he took it for granted that it
was because she had none.   But during the games next day
he obtained a glimpse of her heart which surprised him.   She
had paid a forfeit, and, in order to redeem it, she was requested
to state her favourite names, gentlemen's and ladies'.

" Barbara, Evelyn, Julia, Elizabeth, Pauline, Mary, Bertram,
and Evrard," she answered instantly.   " I do not know if I
think them the most beautiful names, but they are the ones
that I love the best, and have always in my mind."

Colonel Colquhoun's countenance set upon this.   They were
the names of her brothers and sisters, whom she never mentioned to him by any chance, and whom he had not imagined
that she ever thought of ; yet it seemed that they were always
in her mind !   He had so little conception of the depth and

tenderness of her nature, or of her fidelity, that had he been
required to put his feelings on the subject into words before
this revelation, he would, without a moment's hesitation, have
declared her to be cold, and wanting in natural affection, a
girl with "views," and no heart. But after this, a few questions and a very little observation served to convince him that
she not only cared for her friends, especially her brothers and
sisters, but fretted for their companionship continually in
secret, and felt the separation all the more because her father's
harsh prohibition was still in force, and none of them were
allowed to write to her, her mother excepted, whose letters,
however, came but rarely now, and were always unsatisfactory.
The truth was that the poor lady had relapsed into slavery,
and been nagged into an outward show of acquiescence in her
husband's original mandate which forbade her to correspond
with her recalcitrant daughter ; and, in her attempts to conceal
her relapse from the latter, and at the same time to keep Mr.
Frayling quiet under the conviction that her submission was
genuine, the style of her letters suffered considerably, and
their numbers tended always to diminish. But the thing that
touched Colonel Colquhoun was the care which Evadne had
taken to conceal her trouble from him, the fact that she had
not allowed a single complaint to escape her, or made a sign
that might have worried him by implying a reproach. He
had his moments of good feeling, however, and his kindly
impulses too, being, as already asserted, anything but a
monster ; and under the influence of one of them, he sat down
and wrote a sharp remonstrance to Mr. Frayling, which, however, only drew from that gentleman an expression of his
sincere admiration for his son-in-law's generous disposition,
and of his regret that a daughter of his should behave so badly
to one who could show himself so nobly forgiving, with a
reiteration of his determination, however, not to countenance
her until she should "come to her senses"—so that no actual
good was done, although doubtless Colonel Colquhoun himself was the better for acting on the impulse.

It was about this time that he became aware of the fact that
Evadne had gradually formed a party of her own, and was
making his house a centre of attraction to all the best people
in the place. He knew that such support was an evidence of
her strength, and would only confirm her in her "views,"
especially when even those who had opposed her most bitterly
at first were caught intriguing to get into the Colquhoun

house clique; but naturally he was gratified by a position which reflected credit upon himself; his respect for Evadne increased, and consequently they became, if possible, better friends than ever.

CHAPTER XIII

ON the day following her children's party, Evadne went to see Edith. She always went there when she felt brain-fagged and world-weary, and came away refreshed. Edith's ignorance of life amazed and perplexed her. She thought it foolish, and she thought it unsafe for a mature young woman to know no more of the world than a child does, but still she shrank from sharing the pain of her own knowledge with her, and had never had the heart to say a word that might disturb her beautiful serenity. She showed some selfishness in that. She could be a child in mind again with Edith, and only with Edith, and it was really for her own pleasure that she avoided all serious discussion with the latter, although she firmly persuaded herself that it was entirely out of deference to Mrs. Beale's wishes and prejudices.

She owed a great deal, as has already been said, to Mrs. Beale. When her attitude began to attract attention and provoked criticism, the old lady declined emphatically to hear a word against her from anybody, and so supported her in public; while in private the influence of her sweet old-fashioned womanliness was restraining in the way that Mrs. Orton Beg had foreseen; it was a check upon Evadne, and prevented her from going too far and fast at a time. Argument would not have hindered her; but when Mrs. Beale was present, she often suppressed a fire-brand of a phrase, because it would have wounded her.

As she went out that afternoon she met old Lord Groome on the doorstep, just coming to call on her, and hesitated a moment between asking him in or allowing him to accompany her as far as Mrs. Beale's, but decided on the latter because she would get rid of him so much the sooner. Her attitude toward him, however, was kindly and tolerant as a rule, and she was even amused by his curious conceit. He was always ready to express what he called an opinion on any subject, but more especially when it bore reference to legislation and the government of peoples generally, for he was comfortably confident that he had inherited the brain power necessary for a legislator as well as a seat in the House of Lords and the position of one—a pardonable error, surely, since it is so very common. Socially he lived in a comfortable conception of the fitness of things that were agreeable to him, morally he did not exist at all, religiously he supported the Established Church, and politically he believed in every antiquated error still extant, in which respect most of his friends resembled him.

"Ah, and so you are going to see Miss Beale? That's right," he observed patronisingly. "I like to see one young lady with her work in her hand tripping in to sit and chat with another, and while away the long hours till the gentlemen return. One can imagine all their little jests and confidences. Young ladyhood is charming to contemplate."

The implication that a young lady has no great interest in life but in "the return of the gentlemen," and that, while awaiting them, her pursuits must of necessity be petty and trivial, both amused and provoked Evadne, and she answered with a dry enigmatical, "Yes-s-s."

A few steps further on, they overtook that soft-voiced person of "singular views," Mrs. Malcomson, from whom Lord Groome would have fled had he seen her in time, for they detested each other cordially, and she never spared him. She was strolling along alone with her eyes cast down, humming a little tune to herself, and thinking. There was a tinge of colour in her cheeks, for the air was fresh for Malta; her eyes were bright, her hair as usual had broken from bondage into little brown curls, all crisp and shining, on her forehead and neck, and her lips were parted as if they only waited for an excuse to break into a smile. A healthier, pleasanter, happier, handsomer young woman Lord Groome could not have wished to encounter, and consequently his disapproval of those "absurd new-fangled notions of hers" which were "an effectual bar, sir," as he said himself, "the kind of thing that destroys a woman's charm, and makes it impossible to get on with her," mounted to his forehead in a frown of perplexity.

"What are you so busy about?" Evadne asked her.

"My profession," she answered laconically.

"And what is that?" Lord Groome inquired, with that ponderous affectation of playfulness which he believed to be acceptable to women.

"The Higher Education of Man," she rejoined, then darted down a side street, laughing.

"I am afraid you are too intimate with that lady," Lord

Groome observed severely. "You must not allow yourself to be bitten by her revolutionary ideas. She is a dangerous person."

" Not ' revo '—but evolutionary," Evadne answered, smiling. "Yes. Mrs. Malcomson has taught me a great deal. She is a very remarkable person. The world will hear more of her, I am sure, and be all the better for her passage through it. But here we are. Thank you for accompanying me. What a hot afternoon! Good-bye!"

She shook hands with him, then opened the door and walked in, leaving him outside.

He felt the dismissal somewhat summary, but shrugged his shoulders philosophically and walked on, reflecting, *à propos* of Mrs. Malcomson : " That's just the way with women ! When they begin to have ideas they spread them everywhere, and all the other women in the neighbourhood catch them, and are spoiled by them."

Evadne's spirits had risen in the open air, but the moment she found herself alone a reaction set in.

The hall was dark and cool, and she stopped there, thinking—Oh, the dissatisfaction of it all !

There were no servants about, and the house seemed curiously still. She heard the ripple of running water from an unseen fountain somewhere, and the intermittent murmur of voices in a room close by, but there is a silence that broods above such sounds, and this it was that Evadne felt.

Close to where she stood was a divan with some tall foliage plants behind it, and she sat down there, and, leaning forward with her arms resting on her knees, began listlessly to trace out the pattern of the pavement with the point of her parasol. She had no notion why she was lingering there alone, when she had come out for the sole purpose of not being alone; but the will to do anything else had suddenly forsaken her. Her mind, however, had become curiously active all at once, in a jerky, disconnected sort of way.

" Lord Groome—thank Heaven for having got rid of him so easily ! I was afraid it would be more difficult. Poor foolish old man ! Yes. It is ridiculous that the destinies of nations should hang on the size of one man's liver. Where did I hear that now ? It seems as old—old—as the iniquity itself. Subjects get into the air—I heard someone say that too, by-the-way—here—soon after I came out. Who was it ? Oh—the dance on the *Abomination.* Mrs. Malcomson and Mr.

Price. *He* said subjects were diseases which got into the air; *she* said they were more like perfumes. Now, *I* should not have compared them with either——"

The door of the room where the voices had been murmuring intermittently opened at that moment, and Edith came out, followed by Menteith.

It was a vision which Evadne never forgot.

Edith was dressed in ivory white, and wore a brooch of turquoise and diamonds at her throat, a buckle of the same at her waist, and a very handsome ring, also of turquoise and diamonds, on the third finger of her left hand. Evadne took the ornaments in at a glance. She had seen all that Edith had hitherto possessed, and these were new; but she did not for a moment attach any significance to the fact. It was Edith's radiant face that riveted her attention. A bright flush flickered on her delicate cheek, deepening or fading at every breath; her large eyes floated in light; even the bright strands of her yellow hair shone with unusual lustre; her step was so buoyant she scarcely seemed to touch the ground at all; she was all shy smiles; and as she came, with her slender white right hand she played with the new ring she wore on her left, fingering it nervously. But anyone more ecstatically happy than she seemed it is impossible to imagine. Menteith could not take his eyes off her. He seemed to gloat over every item of her appearance.

"Oh, here is Evadne!" she exclaimed in a voice of welcome, running up to the latter and kissing her with peculiar tenderness. Then she turned and looked up at Menteith, then back again at Evadne, wanting to say something, but not liking to.

With a start of surprise, Evadne awoke to the significance of all this, and she knew, too, what was expected of her; but she could not say, "I congratulate you!" try as she would. "I will wait for you in the drawing room," was all she was able to gasp, and she hastened off in that direction as she spoke.

"How can you care so much for that cold, unsympathetic woman?" Menteith exclaimed.

"She is not cold and unsympathetic," Edith rejoined emphatically. "I am afraid there is something wrong. I must go and see what it is. O Mosley! I feel all chilled! It is a bad omen!"

"This is a bad damp hall," he answered, laughing at her, "you are too sensitive to changes of temperature."

It seemed so really, for her colour had faded, and she had not recovered it when she appeared in the drawing room.

Evadne was standing in the middle of the room alone, waiting for her.

" Edith ! You are not going to marry that dreadful man ? " she exclaimed.

Edith stopped short, astonished.

" *Dreadful man !* " she gasped. " You must be mad, Evadne ! "

Mrs. Beale came into the room just as Edith uttered these words, and overheard them. She had been on the point of happy smiles and tears, expecting kind congratulations, but at the tone of Edith's voice almost more than at what she had said, and at the sight of the two girls standing a little apart looking into each other's faces in alarm and horror, her own countenance changed, and an expression of blank inquiry succeeded the smiles, and dried the tears.

" Oh, Mrs. Beale ! " Evadne entreated ; " you are not going to let Edith marry that dreadful man ! "

" Mother ! she will keep saying that ! " Edith exclaimed.

" My dear child, what *do* you mean ? " Mrs. Beale said gently to Evadne, taking her hand.

" I mean that he is bad—thoroughly bad," said Evadne.

" Why ! Now tell me, what do you know about him ? " the old lady asked, leading Evadne to a sofa, and making her sit down beside her upon it. Her manner was always excessively soothing, and the first heat of Evadne's indignation began to subside as she came under the influence of it.

" I don't know anything about him," she answered confusedly ; " but I don't like the way he looks at me ! "

" Oh, come, now ! that is childish ! " Mrs. Beale said, smiling.

" No, it is not ! I am sure it is not ! " Evadne rejoined, knitting her brows in a fruitless endeavour to grasp some idea that evaded her, some item of information that had slipped from her mind. " I feel—I have a consciousness which informs me of things my intellect cannot grasp. And I *do* know ! " she exclaimed, her mental vision clearing as she proceeded. " I have heard Colonel Colquhoun drop hints."

" And you would condemn him upon hints ? " Edith interjected contemptuously.

" I know that if Colonel Colquhoun hints that there is something objectionable about a man it must be something very objectionable indeed," Evadne answered, cooling suddenly.

Edith turned crimson.

" Evadne—*dear*," Mrs. Beale remonstrated, patting her hand emphatically to restrain her. " Edith has accepted him because she loves him, and that is enough."

" If it were love it would be," Evadne answered. " But it is not love she feels. Prove to her that this man is not a fit companion for her, and she will droop for a while, and then recover. The same thing would happen if you separated them for years without breaking off the engagement. Love which lasts is a condition of the mature mind ; it is a fine compound of inclination and knowledge, controlled by reason, which makes the object of it, not a thing of haphazard, but a matter of choice. Mrs. Beale," she reiterated, "you will not let Edith marry that dreadful man ! "

" My dear child," Mrs. Beale replied, speaking with angelic mildness, " your mind is quite perverted on this subject, and how it comes to be so I cannot imagine, for your mother is one of the sweetest, truest, most long suffering *womanly* women I ever knew. And so is Lady Adeline Hamilton-Wells—and Mrs. Orton Beg. You have been brought up among womanly women, none of whom ever even *thought* such things as you do not hesitate to utter, I am sure."

" I once heard a discussion between Lady Adeline and Aunt Olive," Evadne rejoined. " It was about a lady who had a very bad husband, and had patiently endured a great deal. ' It is beautiful—pathetic—pitiful to see a woman making the best of a bad bargain in that way,' Aunt Olive said. ' It may be all that,' Lady Adeline answered ; ' *but is it right?* If this generation would object to bad bargains, the next would have fewer to make the best of.' "

" Ah, that is so like dear Adeline ! " Mrs. Beale observed. " But what a memory you have, my dear, to be able to give the exact words ! "

Evadne's countenance fell. She was disheartened, but still she persisted.

" It is you good women," she said, clasping Mrs. Beale's hand in both of hers, and holding it to her breast : " It is you good women who make marriage a lottery for us. You, for instance. Because you drew a prize yourself, you see no reason why every other woman should not be equally fortunate."

" I think, when people make *quite* sure beforehand that they love each other, they are safe—even when the man has *not* been all that he ought to have been. Love is a great purifier, and love for a good woman has saved many a man," Mrs. Beale declared with the fervour of full conviction.

" That is presuming that a man ' who has not been all that he ought to have been " is still able to love," said Evadne, " which is not the case. We are all endowed with the power to begin with ; but love is a delicate essence, as volatile as it is delicious ; and when a man's moral fibre is loosened, his share of love escapes. But this is not the point," she broke off, dropping Mrs. Beale's hand, and gathering herself together. " The trouble now is that you are going to let Edith throw herself away on a man you know nothing about——"

" Ah, my dear, *there* you are mistaken," Mrs. Beale interrupted, comfortably triumphant. " They have known each other all their lives. They used to play together as children ; and when I wrote to ask her father's consent to the engagement, he replied that the one thing which could reconcile him to parting with Edith was her choice of a man who had grown up under our own eyes. I can assure you that we know his faults quite as well as his good qualities."

" I thought you would like to have me in the regiment, Evadne," Edith ventured with timid reproach.

" I would not like to have you anywhere as that man's wife," Evadne answered.

" Well, if he is," said Edith, with a flash of enthusiasm, " if he is *bad*, I will make him good ; if he is lost, I will save him ! "

" Spoken like a true woman, dearest ! " her mother said, rising to kiss her, and then standing back to look up at her with yearning love and admiration.

Evadne rose also with a heavy sigh. " I know how you feel," she said to Edith drearily. " You glow and are glad from morning till night. You have a great yearning here," she clasped her hands to her breast. " You find a new delight in music, a new beauty in flowers ; unaccountable joy in the warmth and brightness of the sun, and rapture not to be contained in the quiet moonlight. You despise yourself, and think your lover worthy of adoration. The consciousness of him never leaves you even in your sleep. He is your last thought at night, your first in the morning. Even when he is away from you, you do not feel separated from him as you do from other people, for a sense of his presence remains with you, and you flatter yourself that your spirits mingle when your bodies are apart. You think, too, that the source of all this ecstasy is holy because it is pleasurable; you imagine it will last forever!"

Edith stared at her. That Evadne should know the entrance-ment of love herself so exactly, and not reverence it as holy, amazed her.

"And you call it love," Evadne added, as if she had read her thought; "but it is not love. The threshold of love and hate adjoin, and it—this feeling—stands midway between them, an introduction to either. It is always a question, as marriages are now made, whether, when passion has had time to cool, husband and wife will love or detest each other. But what is the use of talking?" she exclaimed. "You will not heed me. It is too late now." She turned and walked toward the door; but Edith caught her by the arm and stopped her.

"Evadne! Do not go like this!" she entreated, with a sob in her voice. "Wish me well at least!"

"I *do* wish you well," said Evadne. "With what other motive could I have said so much? But I ask again, what is the use? Your parents are content to let you marry a man of whose private life they have no knowledge whatever——"

Mrs. Beale interrupted her: "This is not quite the case," she confessed. "We *do* know that there have been errors; but all that is over now, and it would be wicked of us not to believe the best, and hope for the best. A young man in his position has great temptations——"

"And if he succumbs, he is pardoned because of his position!"

"Oh, come, now, Evadne!" Mrs. Beale remonstrated. "You cannot think that such a consideration affects our decision. His position and property are very nice in themselves, and indeed all that we care about in that way for Edith, but we were not thinking about either when we gave our consent. It is the dear fellow himself that we want——"

"I can make him all that he ought to be! I know I can!" Edith exclaimed fervently, clasping her hands, and looking up, with bright eyes full of confidence and passion.

Evadne said not another word, but kissed them both, and left the house.

"Mother! how strange Evadne is!" Edith ejaculated.

Mrs. Beale shook her head several times. "I heard that she

had some trouble at the outset of her own married life," she said. " I don't know what it was ; but doubtless it accounts for her manner to-day. Don't think about it, however. She will recover her right-mindedness as she grows older. A little shock upsets a girl's judgment very often ; but she is so clever and conscientious, she will certainly get over it. But you are quite agitated yourself, dear. Come ! think no more about what she said ! Her own marriage quite disproves all her arguments, for Colonel Colquhoun was notoriously just the kind of man she would have us believe Mosley is, and see what she has done for him, and how well they get on together ! Think no more about it, dear child, but come out with me The air will tranquillize us both."

On her way home, Evadne overtook Mr. St. John He was walking slowly with his chin on his chest, looking down, and his whole demeanour was expressive of deep dejection.

He looked up with a start when Evadne overtook him, and their eyes met.

" You have heard ? " she said.

He made an affirmative gesture.

" I never—never dreamt of such a thing," she went on. " I thought—I hoped—pardon me, but I hoped it would be you. She liked you so much. I know she did."

" But not enough, for she refused me," he answered gently. " But doubtless it is all for the best. *His* ways are not our ways, you know, and we suffer because we are too proud to resign ourselves to manifestations of His wisdom, which are beyond our comprehension. When you came up, I was feeling as if I could never say ' Thy will be done ' with my whole heart, fervently, in this matter, but since you spoke to me, I think I can "

Evadne took his arm, and the gentle pressure of her hand upon it expressed her heartfelt sympathy-eloquently.

" If it had been anyone else, I thought at first—but, doubt-less, doubtless, it is all for the best ! " he added ; and then he raised his head, and changed the subject bravely.

But Evadne did not hear what he was saying, for suddenly she found herself on the cliffs at home, and it was a scented summer morning ; the air was balmy, the sun was shining, the little waves rippled up over the sand, the birds were singing, and the dew-drops hung on the yellow gorse ; but that joy in her own being which lent a charm to these was wanting, and the songs seemed tuneless, the scent oppressive, the sea all sameness, the land a waste, and the sun itself a glaring garish baldness of light, that accentuated her own disconsolation, the length of a life that is not worth living, and the size of a world which contains no corner of comfort in all its pitiless expanse. And it was the same story too. She was witnessing the same mystery of love rejected—the same worthiness for the same unworthiness ; the same fine discipline of resignation, which made the pain of it endurable ; listening to the same old pulpit platitudes even, which have such force of soothing when reverently expressed. She and Edith were very different types of girlhood, and it seemed a strange coincidence that their opportunities should have been identical nevertheless ; but not singular that their action should have been the same, because the force of nature which controlled them is a matter of constitution more than of character, and subject only to a training which neither of them had received, and without which, instead of ruling, they are ruled erratically.

Evadne had quite forgotten by this time all her first fine feelings on the subject of a celibate priesthood. She now held that the laws of nature are the laws of God, and marriage is a law of nature which there is no evidence that God has ever rescinded.

Evadne had not heard what Mr. St. John was saying, and she did not care to hear ; she knew that it was not relevant to anything which either of them had in their minds ; but still held his arm, and looked up at him sympathetically when he paused for a reply, and at that moment Colonel Colquhoun, accompanied by Sir Mosley Menteith, turned out of a side street just behind them, and followed on in the same direction. When Menteith saw the two walking so familiarly arm in arm, he glanced at Colonel Colquhoun out of the corners of his eyes to see how he took it. But Colonel Colquhoun's face remained serenely impassive.

"Easy !" he said. "We won't overtake them till we arrive at the house. I expect he is seeing her home, and as Mrs. Colquhoun is only at her best *tête-à-tête*, it would be a shame to deprive him of the small recompense he will get for his trouble." He twisted his moustache and continued to look at the pair thoughtfully when he had spoken, and Menteith glanced at him again to see if he might not perchance be concealing some secret annoyance under an affectation of easy indifference, but there was not a trace of anything of the kind apparent.

" There is no doubt that women *do* cling to the clergy," was the outcome of Colonel Colquhoun's reflections—" I mean metaphorically speaking, of course," he hastened to add with a laugh, perceiving the double construction that might be put on the remark in view of the situation. " Now, there is only one fellow on the island that Evadne cares for as much as she does for her friend there. I think she likes the other better though."

" You mean yourself, of course," said Menteith.

" No, I don't mean myself, of course," Colonel Colquhoun answered. " Putting myself out of the question. It is Price, I mean."

" That dried-up old chap ? " Menteith exclaimed. " Well, he's pretty safe, I should say ! And I should never be jealous of a parson myself. Women always treat them *de haut en bas.*"

" I believe, sir, that Mrs. Colquhoun is perfectly ' safe ' with anyone whom she may choose for a friend." Colonel Colquhoun said with an emphasis which made Menteith apologize immediately.

Colonel Colquhoun asked Evadne that evening what she thought of the projected marriage.

" I think it detestable," she answered.

" Well, I think it a pity myself," he said. " She's such a nice looking girl too."

Evadne turned to him with a flash of hope. " Can't you do something ? " she exclaimed. " Can't you prevent it ? "

" Absolutely impossible," he answered. " And I beg as a favour to myself that you won't try."

" I have done my best already," she said.

" Then you have made your friends enemies for life," he declared. " A girl like that won't give up a man she loves even for such considerations as have made you indifferent to my happiness—and welfare."

Evadne perceived the contradiction involved in commending Edith for doing what he considered it a pity that she *should* do ; but she recognized her own impotence also, and was silent. It was the system, the horrid system that was to blame, and neither he, nor she, nor any of them.

Colonel Colquhoun ruminated for a little.

" It is rather curious," he finally observed, " that you should both have shied at the parsons, seeing how very particular you are."

"Who told you we had both—refused a clergyman?" Evadne asked.

"Everybody in Malta knows that St. John proposed to Miss Beale," he answered, "and your father told me about the offer you had. He remarked at the time that girls will only have manly men, and that therefore we soldiers get the pick of them.

Evadne was silent. She was thinking of something her father had once remarked in her presence on the same sub-ject: "I have observed," he had said, in his pompous way, "that the clergy carry off all the nicest girls. You will see some of the finest, who have money of their own too, marry quite commonplace parsons. But the reason is obvious. It is their faith in the superior moral probity of Churchmen which weighs with them."

The Beales went home the following week to prepare for the wedding, which was to take place immediately. They both wrote to Evadne kindly before they left, and she replied in the same tone, but she could not persuade herself to see them again, nor did they wish it.

END OF BOOK II.

BOOK III.

DEVELOPMENT AND ARREST OF DEVELOPMENT.

Fury. Blood thou canst see, and fire ; and canst hear groans;—
Worse things, unheard, unseen, remain behind.

Prometheus : Worse?

Fury :   In each human heart terror survives
The ravin it has gorged.   The loftiest fear
All that they would disdain to think were true :
Hypocrisy and Custom make their minds
The fanes of many a worship now outworn.
They dare not devise good for man's estate,
And yet they know not that they do not dare.
The good want power but to weep barren tears :
The powerful goodness want,—worse need for them :
The wise want love : and those who love want wisdom :
And all best things are thus confused to ill.
Many are strong and rich and would be just,
But live among their suffering fellow-men
As if none felt : they know not what they do.
                  —Prometheus Unbound

CHAPTER I.

EDITH was married in the cathedral at Morningquest, and of course the twins were present at the wedding. From what social gathering were they ever excluded if they chose to be present? Mrs. Beale had not thought of asking them at all, but Angelica intimated, in her royal way, that she wished to be a bridesmaid, and Diavolo must be a page, and Lady Adeline begged Mrs. Beale for Heaven's sake to arrange it so, lest worse should come of it.

But the twins did not enjoy the occasion at all, for the truth was that they were not as they had been. Angelica was rapidly outstripping Diavolo, as was inevitable at that age. He was still a boy, but she was verging on womanhood, and already had thoughts which did not appeal to him, and moods which he could not comprehend, the consequence being continual quarrels between them,—those quarrels in which people are hottest and bitterest, not because of their hate, but because of their love for each other. There is such agony in misunderstanding and blame when all has hitherto been comprehension, approval, and sympathy. The shadow of approaching maturity, which would separate them inevitably for the next few years, already touched Angelica perceptibly; and, although to the onlookers they seemed to treat each other as usual, both children felt that there was something wrong, and their discomfort was all the greater because neither of them could account for the change. Angelica had been for some time in her most hoydenish, least human stage, during which she had given up hugging Diavolo, and taken to butting him in the stomach instead. But she was growing beyond that now, and was in fact just on the borderland, hovering between two states: in the one of which she was a child, all nonsense and mischievous tricks; and in the other a girl with tender impulses and yearning senses seeking some satisfaction.

She and Diavolo had promised themselves some fun at Edith's wedding, but when the morning came Angelica was moody and irritable, and Diavolo watched her and waited in vain for a suggestion. When they were in the cathedral, during the ceremony, she had a strange feeling that there was something in it all that specially concerned her, and she looked at Edith and listened to the service intently, in an involuntary effort to obtain some clue to her own sensations.

Diavolo, who was all sympathy when there was anything really wrong with her, became alarmed.

"Does your stomach ache?" he whispered. (They were kneeling side by side.)

"No!" she answered shortly.

"Oh, then, I suppose there is something *morally* wrong," he observed, in a satisfied tone, as if he knew from experience that that was a small thing compared with the other complaint.

They sat together at the wedding breakfast, but Angelica continued silently observant.

Diavolo had brought a big boiled shrimp in his pocket.

It was black and of great age, and he managed to fasten it adroitly on the shoulder of the lady who sat next him, so that its long antennæ tickled her neck, and provoked her attention to it.

Glancing down sideways, and catching a glimpse of black eyes and many legs, she thought it was some horrid creature with a sting, and jumped up, shrieking wildly, to everybody's consternation.

Angelica declared it was a stupid trick.

"Well, you put me up to it yourself," Diavolo grumbled.

"Did I?" she snapped. "Then I was wrong."

Somebody began to make a speech, which was all in praise of the lovely bride; and Diavolo, listening to it, and remembering that he had wished to marry her himself, became intensely sentimental. He recovered his shrimp, and laying it out on the cloth before him gazed at it in a melancholy way.

"All the nice girls marry," he complained, thinking of Evadne.

"Well, what's that to you?" Angelica demanded, with a jealous flash.

"Only that I suppose you also will marry and leave me some day," he readily responded. Diavolo was nothing if not courtly.

But Angelica knew him, and resented this attempt to impose upon her.

"I despise you!" she exclaimed; and then she turned to Mr. Kilroy of Ilverthorp, who was her neighbour on the right, and made great friends with him to spite Diavolo ; but the latter was engrossed in his breakfast by that time, and took no notice.

When they got back to Hamilton House, Mr. Ellis asked her how she had enjoyed the wedding.

" It made me feel *sick*," she said ; and then she got a book, and flinging herself down on a window seat, with her long legs straggling out behind her and her face to the light, made a pretence of reading.

Diavolo hovered about her with a dismal face, trying to devise some method of taking her out of herself.

" My ear does bother me," he said at last, sitting down beside her with his back to the window, and his *legs* stretched straight out before him close together. " I feel as if I could tear it off."

" No, don't ; you might want it again ! " Angelica retorted, and then, the observation striking her as ludicrous, she looked up at him and grinned, and so broke the ice.

Mr. Ellis was the first to notice signs of the impending change in Angelica. Although she was over fifteen, she had no coquettish or womanly ways, insisted on wearing her dresses up to her knees, expressed the strongest objection to being grown-up and considered a young lady, and had never been known to look at herself in the glass ; but she began to be less teasing and more sympathetic, and sometimes now, if the tutor were tired or worried, she noticed it, and pulled Diavolo up for being a nuisance.

The day after the wedding, in the afternoon, Dr. Galbraith walked over from Fountain Towers to Hamilton House, through the fields, and encountered Lord Dawne in the porch. It was lovely summer weather.

" I am looking for the children," Lord Dawne said. " I have come over from Morne with a message for them from their grandfather. Do you happen to have seen them anywhere ? "

" Yes, I have," Dr. Galbraith answered drily, but with a twinkle in his eyes. " I discovered them just now in a field of mine—a hayfield—not that they were making any pretence of hiding themselves, however," he hastened to add, " for they were each sitting on the top of a separate haycock, carrying on an animated discussion in tones as elevated as their position, so that I heard them long before I saw them. They will end the discussion by demolishing my haycocks, I suppose," he concluded resignedly.

"What was it all about?" Lord Dawne asked.

"Well, I believe they started with the vexed question of primogeniture," Dr. Galbraith replied; "but when I came up with them they were quarrelling because they could not agree as to whether they were more their father's or their mother's children. Angelica maintained the latter, for reasons which she gave at the top of her voice with admirable accuracy. When I appeared they both appealed to me to confirm their opinions, but I fled. I am not so advanced as the Heavenly Twins."

Lord Dawne looked grave: "What will become of the child, Angelica?" he said.

"Oh, you needn't be anxious about her," Dr. Galbraith replied, looking full at him with sympathy and affection in his kind gray eyes. "She has no vice in her whatever, and not a trace of hysteria. Her talk is mere exuberance of intellect."

"I don't know," her uncle answered. "*Qui peut tout dire arrive à tout faire*, you know."

"I find that falsified continually in my profession," Dr. Galbraith rejoined. "It depends entirely as a rule upon how the thing is said, and why. If it be a matter of inclination only, controlled by fear of the law or public opinion which is expressed, the aphorism would hold, probably; but language which is the outcome of moods or phases that are transient makes no permanent mark upon the character."

Lord Dawne took Dr. Galbraith to the drawing room, where they found Lady Adeline with Mr. Hamilton-Wells and the tutor. Mr. Ellis had been a great comfort to Lady Adeline ever since he came to the house. She felt, she said, that she should always owe him a deep debt of gratitude for his patient care of her terrible children.

"You are just in time for tea, George," she said to Dr. Galbraith. "Dawne, you had better wait here for the children. They won't be late this afternoon, I am sure, because Mr. Kilroy of Ilverthorpe is here, and Angelica likes him to talk to."

"Ah, now you do surprise me," said Dr. Galbraith, "for I should have thought that Mr. Kilroy was the last person in the world to interest Angelica."

"And so he is," Mr. Hamilton-Wells observed in his precisest way, "and she does not profess to find him interesting. But what she says is that she must talk, and he does for a target to talk at."

Lady Adeline looked anxiously at the door while her husband was speaking. She was in terror lest Mr. Kilroy should come in and hear him, for Mr. Hamilton-Wells had a habit of threshing his subject out, even when it was obviously unfortunate, and would not allow himself to be interrupted by anybody.

He made his favourite gesture with his hands when he had spoken, which consisted in spreading his long white fingers out as if he wore lace ruffles which were in the way, and was shaking them back a little. He had a long cadaverous face, clean shaven; straight hair of suspicious brownness, parted in the middle and plastered down on either side of his head; and a general air of being one of his own Puritan ancestors who should have appeared in black velvet and lace; and his punctilious manners strengthened this impression. The one trinket he displayed was a ring, which he wore on the forefinger of his right hand, a handsome intaglio carved out of crimson coral. It seemed to be the only part of his natural costume which had survived, and came into play continually.

Mr. Kilroy entered the room in time to hear the concluding remark, but naturally did not take it to himself, and Lord Dawne, seeing his sister's trepidation, came to the rescue by diverting the subject into another channel.

They were all sitting round an open window, and just at that moment the twins themselves appeared in sight, straggling up the drive in a deep discourse, with their arms round each other's necks, and Angelica's dark head resting against Diavolo's fair one.

"Harmony reigns among the heavenly bodies, apparently," said Dr. Galbraith.

"The powers of darkness plotting evil, more likely," said their uncle Dawne.

"Naughty children! What have they done with their hats?" Lady Adeline exclaimed.

"Discovered some ingenious method of doing damage to my hay with them, most probably," Dr. Galbraith observed.

They all leant forward, watching the children.

"Angelica is growing up," said Lord Dawne.

"She has always been the taller, stronger, and wickeder of the two, and will remain so, I expect," said Dr. Galbraith.

"But how old is she now exactly?" Mr. Kilroy wished to know.

"Nearly sixteen," Lady Adeline answered. "But a very

young sixteen in some ways, I am thankful to say. And I
believe we have you to thank, Mr. Ellis, for keeping her so."

The tutor's strong but careworn face flushed sensitively;
but he only answered with a deprecating gesture.

"Then how old is Diavolo?" Mr. Kilroy pursued absently.

"About the same age," Mr. Hamilton-Wells replied, without moving a muscle of his face.

Lady Adeline looked puzzled: "Of course they are the
same age," she said, as if the point could be disputed.

Mr. Kilroy woke up: "Oh, of course, of course!" he
exclaimed with some embarrassment.

The twins had gone round the house by this time, and
presently Diavolo appeared in the drawing room alone. His
thick fair hair stood out round his head like a rumpled mop:
his face and hands were not immaculate, and his clothes were
creased; but he entered the room with the same courtly yet
diffident air and high-bred ease which distinguished his uncle
Dawne, whom he imitated as well as resembled in most
things.

He took his seat beside him now, and remarked that it was
a nice day, and——

But before he could finish the affable phrase, the door
burst open from without, and Angelica entered.

"Hollo! Are you all here?" she said. "How are you,
Uncle Dawne?"

"I wish you would not be so impetuous," Diavolo remonstrated gently. "You quite startle one."

"You *are* a coon!" said Angelica.

"My dear child——" Lady Angeline began.

"Well, mamma, no matter *what I* do, Diavolo grumps at
me," Angelica snapped.

"What expressions you use!" sighed Lady Adeline.

Angelica plumped down on the arm of her uncle's chair,
and hugged him round the head with one hand. She smelt
overpoweringly strong of hay and hot weather, but he patiently
endured the caress, which was over in a moment as it happened, for Angelica caught sight of her cat lurking under a
sofa opposite, and bending down double, whistled to it. Then
she turned her attention to a huge slice of bread, butter, and
jam she held in her hand. Diavolo's soul appeared in his face
and shone out of his eyes when she bit it.

"Have some?" said Angelica, going over to him, and edg-
ing him half off his chair so as to make room for herself

beside him.   She held the bread and butter to his mouth as
she spoke, and they finished it together, bite and bite about.

"Now I am ready for tea," said Angelica when they had
done.

"So am I," said Diavolo, with a sigh of satisfaction.

"Let us have afternoon tea with you here to-day, Mr.
Ellis," Angelica coaxed.   "It's so much more sociable.   And
I want to talk to Mr. Kilroy."

She jumped up in her impetuous way, plumped down again
on a low stool in front of that gentleman, clasped her hands
round her knees, and looked up in his face as she spoke.

"That's a nice place you've got at——" she was beginning,
but Mr. Ellis interrupted her by throwing up his head and
ejaculating "Grammar!"

"*Bother!*" Angelica exclaimed testily.   "Now you've put
me all out.   Oh!—I was going to say *you have* a nice place at
Ilverthorpe.   We were over there the other day and inspected
it."

"Very happy—glad, I am sure, you did not stand upon
ceremony," Mr. Kilroy answered.

But this politeness seemed altogether superfluous to Angelica, and she did not therefore acknowledge it in any way.

"I suppose you will go into Parliament now," she pursued.

Mr. Kilroy looked surprised.   The idea had occurred to
him lately, but he was not aware of having mentioned it to
anyone.

"I hope you will at all events," she continued, "and let me
write your speeches for you.   That is what Diavolo is going
to do.   You see I shall want a mouthpiece until I get in
myself, and I don't mind having two if you are clever at learning by heart.   You've a pleasant voice and good address to
begin with, and that is all in your favour.   Oh, you needn't
exchange glances with papa," she broke off.   "He doesn't
know how I mean to order my life in the least."

"But you will allow him some voice in the ordering of it—
at least until you marry, I suppose," Mr. Kilroy observed.

"That depends," Angelica answered decidedly.   "You see,
a child comes into the world for purposes of its own, and not
in order to carry out any preconceived ideas its father may
have of what it is good for.   And as to marrying—well, that
requires consideration."

"Now, I call that a very proper spirit in which to approach
the subject," Mr. Kilroy declared.   "You have every right to

expect to make the best match possible, and the choice for a young lady in your position will be restricted."

"Not at all," said Angelica bluntly "Is thy servant a slave of a princess that she should marry a rickety king? I have quite other views for myself. In fact, I think the wisest plan for me would be to buy a nice clean little boy, and bring him up to suit my own ideas. I needn't marry him, you know, if he doesn't turn out well." She slipped from the footstool on to the floor as she spoke, and began to make friendly overtures to the cat.

" I always thought you had designs on Dr. Galbraith !" said Diavolo, meaning to provoke her.

" Did you ?" she answered. " Then you must have thought me of a suicidal tendency. Why, he would pound me up in a mortar if I disagreed with him. You have heard him slam a door ? "

"He *is* irascible," Diavolo answered, quite as if Dr. Galbraith were not present listening to him. "He called me a little brute on one occasion."

"Which reminds me," said Dr. Galbraith. "What have you done to my decoy? The birds have forsaken it."

"We never did anything to your decoy," rejoined Angelica in a positive tone. "You just went down there yourself one day and exploded some long words at the ducks, and, naturally, they scooted."

"Well, I warn you," said Dr. Galbraith, frowning with decision—"I warn you that I am going to have keys made for everything about the place that will lock up ; and, all the same, I shall only allow you to come under escort of the chief constable, and I shall keep a posse of detectives concealed about the grounds to watch for you carefully."

The twins exploded with delight.

"Didn't I promise you I'd draw him this afternoon?" Diavolo exclaimed.

" You did," Angelica responded, with tears in her eyes.

Lord Dawne got up.

"Won't you stay for tea?" Lady Adeline exclaimed. "It is just coming."

" I don't care for any, thank you," he answered. "And I really ought not to have stayed so long. I only came to ask if you would let the children come. Both my father and Fulda have set their hearts upon having them."

"Are we to go to Morne?" cried Angelica.

"For a visit—to stay?" said Diavolo.

"If you behave yourselves," their mother answered.

"Oh, in that case!" said Diavolo, shrugging his shoulders as at an impossibility.

"It would never do for us to be good there," said Angelica. "Grandpapa would be so dreadfully disappointed if we were."

"Quite so," said Diavolo.

And then they scampered out together into the hall, and kicked each other in the exuberance of their spirits, but without ill-will.

CHAPTER II.

AS soon as the Heavenly Twins were safely settled at Morne, Mr. Hamilton-Wells played them a huge trick. He made Lady Adeline pack up and set off with him for a voyage round the world without them. When their parents were well on the way, and the news was broken to the children, the people at Morne expected storm and trouble ; but the Heavenly Twins saw the joke at once, and chuckled immoderately.

"I wonder how long it took him to think it out?" said Diavolo.

"It must have been a brilliant impromptu," Angelica supposed—"because, you know, our coming here was all arranged in a moment. If you remember, we came because they looked so sure that we shouldn't. I expect as soon as we had gone, it was such a relief, that papa said : 'Adeline, my dear, we must prolong this period of peace.' And he's just about hit on the only way to do so."

"I should like to have seen him, though, popping in and out of the train whenever it stopped. He must have been in a perfect fever until they were safe on board and out at sea, fearing we might have heard that they were off, and found some means of following them."

"We might do so still," said Angelica thoughtfully.

"No. Too much bother," said Diavolo. "And, besides, there is good deal going on here, you know," he added significantly. "But, I say," he demanded, becoming parent-sick suddenly, "do you understand how they could go off like that without saying good-bye to us? I call it beastly unnatural."

"Oh, give them their due!" said Angelica. "They did say good-bye to us. Don't you remember how particularly affectionate they were the last time they came? And all the good advice they gave us? 'Do attend to Mr. Ellis'; 'Don't worry your grandfather,' and that sort of thing. They must have relieved their own feelings thoroughly."

"Well, then, they didn't consider ours much," Diavolo grumbled; "and they might have allowed us, poor grass-orphans, the comfort of bidding them farewell."

"We'll write them a letter," said Angelica.

Diavolo grinned.

And this was how it happened that the Heavenly Twins, who had only gone to Morne for a month, remained a year there, and one of the most important years of their lives, as was afterward evident. It was during this time that they managed to identify themselves completely with their grandfather in the estimation of the people of Morningquest. Charming manners were a family trait, and the Heavenly Twins had always been popular in the city on their own account; their spontaneity and extreme affability having usually been held to balance their monkey tricks. Hamilton House, however, was ten miles distant from Morningquest, and they had hitherto been thought of as Hamilton-Wells; but after that year at the Castle, they became identified with the old stock, the alien Hamilton-Wells being dropped out of sight altogether.

The duke himself had always been popular. He had, like his ancestors, lived much in his castle on the hill overlooking the city, and had dominated the latter by his personality as well as by his place, so that the people, predisposed by the pressure of hereditary habit to recognize the pre-eminence of one of his family, and being no longer subject to the authority of their duke as in the old days when he was a ruler who must be obeyed, looked up to him involuntarily as an example to be followed.

Which was how it came to pass that, for the last half century, there had been two influences at work in Morningquest: that of the chime, full fraught with spiritual suggestion; and that of the duke, which was just the opposite. They were the influences of good and evil, and, needless to say, the effect of the latter was much the more certain of the two.

A great change, however, came over the duke toward the end of his life. In his youth he had filled the place with riot and debauchery; in middle age he had concealed his doings under respectable cloaks of excuse, such as the County Club and business ; but now he was old and superstitious, and sought to sway the people in another direction altogether. For when his youngest daughter, the beautiful Lady Fulda, became a Roman Catholic, she wrought upon him by her earnestness so as to make him fear the flames, and drove him in that way to seek solace and salvation in the Church as well; and when he had done so himself, he rather expected, and quite intended, that everybody else should do likewise. But the people of Morningquest who had adopted his vices did not fear the flames themselves, and would have nothing to do with his piety. They were like the children in " Punch," who, when threatened with the policeman at the corner, exclaimed in derision : " Why, that's father ! " And, besides, the times were changing rapidly, and the influence which remained to the aristocracy was already only dominant so long as it went the way of popular feeling and was human ; directly it retro-graded to past privileges, ideas, superstitions, and tastes, the people laughed at it. They knew that the threatened rule of the priest was a far-fetched anachronism which they need not fear for themselves in the aggregate, and they therefore gave themselves up with interest to the observation of such evi-dences of its effect on the individual as the duke should betray to them from time to time. Their theory was that, having grown too old for worldly dissipation, he had entered the Church in search of new forms of excitement, and to vary the monotony generally, as so many elderly coquettes do when they can no longer attract attention in any other way. This, the people maintained, was the nature of such religious consolation as he enjoyed ; and upon that supposition certain lapses of his were accounted for uncharitably.

But, in truth, the duke was perfectly sincere. He had turned so late in life, however, that he was apt, by force of habit, to get muddled. His difficulty was to disconnect the past from the present, the two having a tendency to mix themselves up in his mind. The great interest of his old age was the build-ing of a Roman Catholic Cathedral in Morningquest, but occasionally—and always at the most inconvenient times—he would forget it was a cathedral, and imagine it was an opera house he was supporting ; and when he went to distribute the prizes in the schools, he would compliment the pretty girls on their good looks, instead of lecturing them on the sin of vanity ; and promise that they should sing in the chorus, or dance in the ballet if their legs were good, when he should have been discoursing about the dangers of the vain world, and pointing the moral of happy humble obscurity. On these occasions, Lady Fulda, who was always beside him, suffered a good deal. She would pull him up in a whisper which he sometimes made her repeat, until everyone in the place had heard it but himself, and then, at last, when he did understand, he would hasten to correct himself. But, of course, it was the mistake and not the correction which made the most lasting impression.

Lady Fulda was not at all clever. In the schoolroom she was always far behind her sisters, Lady Adeline and Lady Claudia, and before his conversion, her father used to say that she had the appearance of a Juno, and the cow-like capacity one would naturally expect from the portraits of that matron now extant. But this was not fair to her intelligence, for she had a certain range which included sympathetic insight, and the knack of saying the right thing both for her own purpose and for the occasion.

She had a full exterior of uncrumpled, lineless, delicately tinted flesh ; a voice that made " Good-morning " impressive when she said it ; a sincerity which paused upon every expression of opinion to weigh its worth. She would hardly say ; " It is a fine day," without first glancing at the weather, just to be sure that it had not changed since she decided to make the remark. And she had a great loving heart. If she did not sigh for husband and children, it was because she was never in the presence of any creature for many minutes without feeling a flood of tenderness for them suffuse her whole being, so that her affections were always satisfied. Because of her grand presence people expected great things of her, and none of them ever went disappointed away. She filled their hearts, and nobody ever complains of the head when the heart is full. Love was the secret both of her beauty and her power.

The twins arrived late one day at Morne, and immediately afterward the whole castle was pervaded by their presence, and signs of them appeared in the most unlikely places. A mysterious packet, rolled up in a sheet of the *Times*, considerably soiled. and known as " Angelica's work," which nobody had ever seen opened, was found in the oriel room on the seat of the chair sacred to the duke himself ; and a cricket cap of Diavolo's was discovered on one of the tall candles which stood on the altar in the private chapel of the castle, as if it had been used as an extinguisher. A peculiar intentness was also observed in the expression of the children's countenances which was thought to betoken mischief, because always hither-to it had been noticed that when the gravity of their de-meanour was most exemplary, the wickedness of the design upon which they were engaged was sure to be extreme. But all the old symptoms were misleading at this time, for the twins settled down at once, with lively intelligent interest, to the innocent occupation of studying the ways of the household, their own conduct being distinguished for the most part by a masterly inactivity. For the truth was they were thinking. They had lately taken to reading the books and papers and magazines of the day, which they found in the library at Hamilton House ; and at Morne they followed the same occupation, and thus had an opportunity of seeing the ques-tions which interested them treated from different points of view. At home all had been Liberal, Protestant, and progres-sive ; but at Morne the tendency of everything was Roman Catholic, Conservative, and retrograde ; and they were doing their best, as their conversations with different people at this time showed, to discover the why and wherefore, and right and wrong of the difference. Angelica was naturally the first to draw definite conclusions for herself, and having made up her own mind she began to instruct Diavolo. She was teaching him to respect women, for one thing ; when he didn't respect them she beat him ; and this made him thoughtful.

"You wouldn't strike me if you didn't know that I can't strike you back, because you're a girl," he remonstrated.

"And you wouldn't say that if you didn't know that the cruellest thing you can do to a woman is to hurt her feelings," she retorted.

" Oh, feelings ! " exclaimed Diavolo. " You've got castanets that clack where you should have feelings."

Angelica raised her hand, and then dropped it by her side again, and looked at him.

" What do you mean by this nonsense ? " she demanded. "We always *have* fought everything out ever since we were born."

" Yes," he said regretfully, " and you used to be as hard as nails. When I got a good hit at you it made my knuckles tingle. But now you're getting all boggy everywhere. Just look at your arms ! "

Angelica ripped her tight sleeve open to the shoulder with one of her sudden jerks, and looked at her arm.

"Now, see mine," said Diavolo, taking off his coat, and turning his shirt sleeve up in his more deliberate way.

Angelica held out her arm beside his to compare them. Hers was round and white and firm, with every little blue vein visible beneath the fine transparent skin ; his was all hard muscle and bone, burnt brown with the sun, and coarse of texture compared with hers.

"You see, now !" he said.

Angelica slowly drew down the tattered remains of her sleeve, and then she looked at Diavolo thoughtfully, and from him to a full-length reflection of herself in a long mirror on the wall.

"We're growing up !" she said, in a surprised sort of tone.

" *You* are," he said. "*I* seem to be just about as young as ever I was."

"All the more reason that I should teach you, then," said Angelica. " Education matures the mind, and the principal instrument of education for your sex has always been a stick. Women are open to reason from their cradles, but men have to be whopped. They are thrashed at school, that being, as they have always maintained themselves, the best way to deal with them. ' He that spareth the rod hateth his son : but he that loveth him chasteneth him betimes.' And ' Withhold not correction from the child : for if thou beatest him with the rod, he shall not die.' It is only the boys, you see, that have their minds enlarged in that way, because, if you tell a girl a thing, she understands it at once. And when men grow up and things go wrong, they still think they ought to thrash each other. That is also their primitive way of settling the disputes of nations ; they just hack each other down in hundreds, sacrificing the lives which are precious to the women they should be loving, for the sake of ideas that are always changing. You certainly *are* the stupid part of humanity !" she concluded. " And how you ever discovered the way to manage each other, I can't imagine. But it was the right one. ' A whip for the horse, a bridle for the ass, and a rod for the fool's back.' "—and so saying, she flounced out of the room, without, however, administering the parting slap of another kind which he expected.

But the episode made a lasting impression on Diavolo, as was apparent in much that he said, and particularly in some remarks which he made during a conversation he had with his grandfather toward the end of the year.

A capital understanding had always existed between Diavolo

and his grandfather, a fact which caused Lady Adeline's heart
to sink every time she observed it, but had an opposite effect
on the duke himself—a quite exhilarating effect, indeed, which
was the cause of certain of those lapses which Lady Fulda had
so often to deplore—as when, for instance, he aided and abetted
Diavolo in some of his worst tricks, and then had to sit sheepishly by, saying nothing, when the boy was found out and
corrected. Lady Fulda was puzzled by the intelligent glances
that passed between the two at such times, but Diavolo was
perfectly loyal, and never once got his grandfather into
trouble.

One of the dreams of the old duke's life was to make a good
Catholic of Diavolo, and to that end his conversation was
often directed—intermittently it is true, because Diavolo was
skilled in the art of beguiling him into other subjects when it
suited himself.

The duke was turning his attention at this time, under Lady
Fulda's direction, to the spiritual welfare of that class of
women which in former times he had been accustomed to
countenance in quite another way. Lady Fulda had established a refuge for these in Morningquest, and her father was
deeply interested in the success of the undertaking. The
Heavenly Twins were also much interested. At first they
could not make out why their Aunt Fulda so often breakfasted
in her outdoor dress, and whether she had just come in or was
just going out.

If there were no visitors staying at the castle, the party at
breakfast was small, there being only the old duke, Father
Ricardo, Mr. Ellis, and the Heavenly Twins, as a rule. When
Lady Fulda did appear the meal was usually half over.

The duke sat at the end of the long table, with the twins on
either side of him, but he was generally limp and querulous in
the morning, and more kindly disposed toward Father Ricardo
than to his own flesh and blood, as Angelica pointed out on
one occasion.

When Lady Fulda came in she always went up to her father
and kissed him. He did not rise to receive the salute, but he
invariably held her hand some seconds, and asked : " Any
news ? " anxiously ; to which she always answered " Yes " or
" No " ; and then he would say : " You must tell me afterward. Go to your seat now. Take plenty of rest and refreshment Both are necessary ; both are necessary ! "

The Heavenly Twins were inclined to regard this scene with

the scorn and contempt of ignorance at first ; but when Lord
Dawne came to the castle for a few days, with their widowed
aunt Lady Claudia and Ideala, and all these paid the same
reverent attention to Lady Fulda's report as the duke and
Father Ricardo did, they reserved judgment until they should
know more about the matter.

They asked Mr. Ellis for an explanation, but he told them
bluntly to mind their own business, and further puzzled them
by a remark which they chanced to hear him make about
Lady Fulda to Dr. Galbraith.   They did not overhear what Dr.
Galbraith had said to lead up to it, but Mr. Ellis answered:
"Grasp her character ?   She is not a character at all !   She's
a beautiful abstraction.   Now Ideala is human."

Although the twins were Protestants by education—and also
by nature, one may say—it had pleased them to go regularly
to certain services in the chapel from the day of their arrival
at the castle.

"We enjoy them very much," Angelica said, to the great
delight of her aunt and grandfather.

"I am sure the atmosphere of devotion in which we live
will have its effect upon the children," the latter said several
times.

And so it had.   It was never the low mass, however, at
which they appeared, but the more sensuous, sumptuous functions, when there was music, of which they both were exceedingly fond, both of them being excellent musicians.

Soon after her arrival at the castle Angelica bought a big
drum.   She said she couldn't express her feelings on any
other instrument on Sunday, her spiritual fervour was so excessive.   Her behaviour in chapel, however, was for the most
part exemplary.   Her aunt noticed that she often knelt all
through the service with a book before her, thoroughly absorbed.
Lady Fulda was anxious to know what the book was, and on
one occasion, when Angelica remained on her knees after the
congregation had dispersed, with her handkerchief pressed to
her face, apparently deeply moved, her aunt stole up behind
her softly, and peeped over her shoulder, expecting to see a
holy "Imitation," or something of that kind ; but, to her
horror, she found that the book was Burnand's "Happy
Thoughts," and that Angelica's gurglings were not tears of
repentance, but suppressed explosions of hearty laughter.

This happened during what proved to be rather a trying
time for Lady Fulda.   It was while Lord Dawne, Lady Claudia,

and Ideala were at the castle, and the old duke was, as Lady Fulda delicately phrased it to her sister Claudia in private, " inclined to be tiresome." It was at this time that he had several relapses. One of these happened in chapel during benediction.

The choir had been singing *O Salutaris, Hostia!* at the conclusion of which everybody was startled by a senile cheer from the stalls. The duke had dozed off into a dream of the opera, and had awakened suddenly, under the impression that a wooden image of the Blessed Virgin opposite had just completed a lovely solo, and was unexpectedly following it up by an audacious *pas seul.*

"Aren't our ancestors like us?" Diavolo whispered to Angelica enthusiastically. But Angelica dampened his ardent admiration of the *coup* by refusing to believe that the diminutive duke had "done it on purpose."

CHAPTER III.

THE next day Diavolo happened to stroll into the oriel room about tea-time, and finding his grandfather sitting there alone, looking down upon Morningquest from his accustomed seat in the great deep window, which was open, he carefully chose a soft cushion, placing it on the low sill so that he could rest his back against it, and stretching himself out on the floor, looked up at the old gentleman sociably.

" You're growing a big fellow, sir," the latter observed.

" But not growing so fast as Angelica is," said Diavolo.

" Ah, women mature earlier," said the duke. " But their minds never get far beyond the first point at which they arrive."

" I suppose you mean when they marry at seventeen, or their education is otherwise stopped short for them, just when a man is beginning his properly?" Diavolo languidly suggested.

The duke frowned down at him. " Where is your sister?" he asked.

" That I can't tell you," Diavolo answered.

" Don't you know?" the duke said sharply.

" Yes," was the cool rejoinder; " but I don't happen to have my sister's permission to say."

The old man's face relaxed into a smile: " That's right

my boy, that's right," he said. " Loyalty is a grand virtue. Be loyal to the ladies "—he shook his head in search of an improving aphorism, but only succeeded in extracting a familiar saw. " Kiss, but never tell," he said, " it's vulgarly put, my boy, but there's a whole code in it, and a damned chivalrous code, too. I tell you, men were gentlemen when they stuck to it."

There was a sound of stealthy footsteps in the room at this moment, and the old duke glanced over his shoulder apprehensively, while Diavolo bent to one side to peer round the chair his grandfather was sitting in, which was between him and the door.

" It's one of the dogs," he said carelessly. " Father Ricardo is out, I think."

The duke looked relieved.

" Well," Diavolo resumed, reflectively, " I should have thought myself that it was playing it pretty low down to sneak on a woman. But, I say, sir," he asked innocently, " how would you define a lady-killer ? "

" Lady-killer," said the little old gentleman, taking hold of his collar to perk himself up out of his clothes, as it were, on the strength of his past reputation : " A lady-killer is a—eh—a fellow whom ladies—eh—admire."

" Do you mean real ladies, or only pretty women ? " said Diavolo.

" Both, my boy, both," the duke answered complacently. He was beginning to enjoy himself.

" You were one once, were you not, sir ? " said Diavolo. " I suppose you had a deuced good time ? "

" Ah ! " the duke ejaculated, with a sigh of retrospective satisfaction. Then, suddenly remembering his new rôle, he pulled himself up, and added severely. " But keep clear of women, my boy, keep clear of women. Women are the very devil, sir."

" But supposing they run after *you ?* " said Diavolo. " Nowadays, you know, a fellow gets so hunted down—they say."

" Oh—ah—then. In that case, you see." said the duke, relapsing, " the principle has always been to take the goods the gods may send you, and be thankful."

There was a pause after this, during which the duke again recollected himself.

" We were talking about women," he sternly recommenced,

"and I was warning you that their wiles are snares of the evil one, who finds them ever ready to carry out his worst behests. Women are bad."

" Are they, now ? " said Diavolo. " Well, I should have thought, taking them all round, you know, that they're a precious sight better than *we* are."

" It was a woman, my boy," the duke said solemnly, " who compassed the fall of man."

" Well," Diavolo rejoined, with a calmly judicial air, " I've thought a good deal about that story myself, and it doesn't seem to me to prove that women are weak, but rather the contrary. For you see, the woman could tempt the man easily enough ; but it took the very old devil himself to tempt the woman."

" Humph ! " said the duke, looking hard at his grandson.

" And, at any rate," Diavolo pursued, " it happened a good while ago, that business, and it's just as likely as not that it was Adam whom the devil first put up to a thing or two, and Eve got it out of him—for I grant you that women are curious—and then they both came a cropper together, and it was a case of six of one and half a dozen of the other. It mostly is, I should think, in a business of that kind."

" Well, yes," said the duke. " In my own experience, I always found that we were just about one as bad as the other "—and he chuckled.

" Then, we may conclude that there is a doubt about that Garden of Eden story whichever way you look at it, and it's too old for an argument at any rate," said Diavolo. " But there is no doubt about the redemption. It was a woman who managed that little affair. And, altogether, it seems to me, in spite of the disadvantage of being classed by law with children, lunatics, beggars, and irresponsible people generally, that, in the matter of who have done most good in the world, women come out a long chalk ahead of us."

" Why the devil don't you speak English, sir ! " the duke burst out testily.

Diavolo started. " Good gracious, grandpapa ! " he began with his customary deliberation, " how sudden you are ! You quite made me jump. Is it the slang you don't like ? "

" Yes sir, it *is* the slang I don't like."

" Then you've only got to say so," said Diavolo in a tone of mild remonstrance. " You really quite upset me when you're so sudden. Angelica will tell you I never could stand being startled. She's tried all kinds of things to cure me. You can't frighten me, you know. It's just the jump I object to."

" Oh, you object, do you ?" said the duke, bending his brows upon him. " Then I apologise."

" Oh, no ! pray don't mention it, sir," said Diavolo. " I didn't mean you to go so far as that, you know. And it's over in a minute."

Angelica burst into the room at this point, followed by two or three dogs, and immediately took up her favourite position on the arm of her grandfather's chair.

" I want some tea," she said.

" It's coming," said Diavolo.

" You say that because you don't want the trouble of getting up to ring," Angelica retorted.

Diavolo looked at her provokingly, and she was about to say something tart, when a footman opened the door wide, and two others entered carrying the tea-things, and at the same time the rest of the party began to assemble.

Lady Fulda was the first to arrive with her widowed sister, Lady Claudia. They presented a great contrast, the one being so perfectly lovely, the other so decidedly plain. Lady Claudia was a tall gaunt woman, hard in manner, with no pretension to any accomplishments ; but wise, and of a faithful, affectionate disposition, which deeply endeared her to her friends.

Lord Dawne came in next, with Dr. Galbraith and Mr. Kilroy of Ilverthorpe, and these were followed by Father Ricardo and Mr. Ellis, after whom came Ideala herself, alone.

This was before she made her name, but already people spoke of her ; and theoretically men were supposed not to like her " because of her ideas, don't you know," which were strongly opposed in some circles, especially by those who either did not know or could not understand them. There is no doubt that mankind have a rooted objection to be judged when the judge is a woman. If they cannot in common honesty deny the wisdom of her decisions they attack her for venturing to decide at all.

" Now," said Angelica, skipping over to a couch beside which Mr. Kilroy was sitting, " *now*, we shall have a little interesting conversation ! "

" I hope you will kindly allow us to have a little interesting tea first," said Diavolo, who had risen politely when the other ladies entered the room, a formality which he omitted in Angelica's case because he insisted that she wasn't a lady.

When the tea was handed round, and the servants had withdrawn, he lounged over to the couch where she was, in his
deliberate way, sat down beside her, and put his tea cup on the
floor ; and then they put their arms round each other, slanted
their heads together, and sat expectant. This had been a
favourite position of theirs from the time they could sit up at
all, and when there was a good deal of gossip going on about
them it had always been a treat to see them sitting so, with
blank countenances and ears open, collecting capital doubtless
for new outrages on public decency.

"What do you want to talk about, Angelica ? " Ideala asked,
smiling.

"Oh, a lot of things," Angelica exclaimed, straightening
herself energetically, and giving Diavolo's head a knock with
her own to make him move it out of the way. "I've been
reading, you know, and I want you to explain. I want to know
how people can be so silly."

"In what way ? " Ideala asked.

"Well, I'm thinking of Aunt Fulda," said the candid
Angelica. "You know, she very much wants to make a
Roman Catholic of me, and she gave me some books to read,
and of course I read them. They were all about the Church
being the true church and all that sort of thing. And then I
got a lot of books about other churches, and each said that *it*
was the true church just as positively, and Aunt Fulda told
me that anyone who would read about *her* church *must* be
convinced that it is the true church, but the difficulty is to get
people to read; so when I found these other books I took
them to her to show her all about the other true churches, and
I told her she ought to read them, because if there were truth
in any of them, we could none of us possibly be saved unless
we belonged to *all* the different churches. But do you know,
she wouldn't look at a book ! She said she wasn't allowed to !
Now ! what do you think of that? and after telling me what
a mistake it was not to read ! "

Lady Fulda and her father were talking together in the
window, and did not therefore overhear these remarks, but
Father Ricardo was listening, and Ideala flashed a mischievous
glance at him as Angelica spoke.

"Then," the latter continued before anyone could answer
her, "Aunt Fulda is just as good as she possibly *can* be, and
Father Ricardo says it is because she has submitted to *his*
Holy Church ; and Mrs. Orton Beg and mamma are also as

good as they possibly can be, and the Bishop of Morning-quest says that Mrs. Orton Beg is a holy woman because she is a humble follower of Christ, but he rather shakes his head about mamma. Uncle Dawne, however, and Dr. Galbraith both maintain that mamma is admirable, because she doesn't trouble her head about churches and creeds any longer. She used to do so once, but now she thinks only of what is *morally* right or wrong, and leaves the ecclesiastical muddle for the divines to get out of as best they can. Mamma used to dread bringing us to Morne when we were younger; we were always so outrageous here; and we told her it was Aunt Fulda who made us so, because she is too good, and the balance of nature has to be preserved. But, now, I am sure Aunt Claudia is quite as good as she is, and so are you, and mamma, and Mrs. Orton Beg."

Ideala smiled at her. "And so you are puzzled ?" she said. "Well, now, I will explain. Your aunts and mother, and Mrs. Orton Beg, are all of those people born good, who would have been saints in any calendar, Buddhist, Christian, or Jewish. They come occasionally—these good people—to cause confusion on the subject of original sin, and overthrow the pride of professors who maintain that their own code of religious ethics must be the right one because it produces the best specimens of humanity. There was a Chinese lady living at Shanghai a few years ago, a devout Buddhist, who, in her habits of life, her character, her prayers, her penances, and her sweetness of disposition, exactly resembled your Aunt Fulda, the only difference between them being the names of the ideal of goodness upon whom they called for help. Their virtues were identical, and the moral outcome of their lives was the same."

"I see what you mean ! " Angelica burst out. "And you wouldn't say either 'convert' or 'pervert' yourself, would you ?"

"Well, no," Ideala acknowledged, "I always adopt a little pleonasm myself to avoid Christian controversy, and say 'when So-and-so became' a Roman or Anglican Catholic, a Protestant, Positivist, or whatever else it might be; and I let them say 'convert' or 'pervert,' whichever they like, to me, because I know that it really cannot matter, so long as they are agreeable—not that anybody ever expects them to be, poor little people ! although they know quite well that they should never let their angry passions rise. They have no sense of humour at all! But just fancy, how silly it must seem to the angels when Miss Protestant throws down a book she is reading and shrieks, '*Convert*, indeed!' while Miss Catholic at the same moment groans, '*Pervert*,' indignantly! Must be 'something rotten in the state of Denmark,' surely, or one or other of them would have proved their point by this time. Or do you suppose," she added, looking at Lord Dawne, "that the opposition is mercifully preordained by nature to generate the right amount of heat by friction to keep things going so that we do not come to a standstill on the way to human perfection? It is very wonderful any way," she added—"to the looker on; wonderfully funny!"

"I did not know that Lady Adeline had definitely left the Church of England," Mr. Kilroy observed, "and I am surprised to hear it."

"Are you?" said Ideala. "Now, we were not. Adeline has always been of a deeply religious disposition; but it was not bound to be, and it was never likely to be, the religion of any church which would secure her lasting reverence."

"I wonder what the religion of the future will be?" Mr. Kilroy remarked.

"It will consist in the deepest reverence for moral worth, the tenderest pity for the frailties of human nature, the most profound faith in its ultimate perfectibility," Ideala answered. "The religion of the future must be a thing about which there can be no doubt, and consequently no dispute. It will be for the peace and perfecting of man, not for the exercise of his power to outwit an antagonist in an argument; and there are only the great moral truths, perceived since the beginning of thought, but hard to hold as principles of action because the higher faculties to which they appeal are of slower growth than the lower ones which they should control, and the delights they offer are of a nature too delicate to be appreciated by uncultured palates; but it is in these, the infinite truths, known to Buddha, reflected by Plato, preached by Christ, undoubted, undisputed even by the spirit of evil, that religion must consist, and is steadily growing to consist, while the questionable man-made gauds of sensuous service are gradually being set aside. The religion of the future will neither be a political institution, nor a means of livelihood, but an expression of the highest moral attribute, human or divine—disinterested love."

She sat for some time, looking down at the floor, and lost in thought when she had said this; and then, rousing herself, she turned to Father Ricardo. "I had a fit of Roman Catholicism once myself," she said to him, pleasantly. "I enjoyed it very much while it lasted. But you do a great deal of harm, you clergy! In the first place you begin by setting up Christ as an ideal of perfect manhood, and then you proceed to demolish him as a possible example, by maintaining that he was not a man, but a God, and therefore a being whom it is beyond the power of man to imitate! Oh, you terrible, terrible clergy! You preach the parable of the buried talents, and side by side with that you have always insisted that women should put theirs away; and you have soothed their sensitive consciences with the dreadful cant of obedience—not obedience to the moral law, but obedience to the will of man; for what moral law could be affected by the higher education of women?"

"The Anglican Church is rather countenancing the higher education of women, is it not?" said Mr. Kilroy.

"You don't put it properly," Ideala answered. "Women, after a hard battle, secured for themselves their own higher education, and now that it is being found to answer, the churches are coming in to claim the credit. Dear, how rapidly reforms are carried out when we take them in hand ourselves!" she exclaimed. "All the spiritual power is ours, and while we refuse to know, it must be wasted for want of direction."

"But that is what you reject," said Father Ricardo. "The Church is ever ready to direct her children."

"For her own advantage, and very badly," Ideala answered. "Does her direction ever benefit the human race generally, or anybody but herself in particular? Every great reform has been forced on the Church from outside. Just consider the state of degradation, and the dense ignorance of the people of every country upon which the curse of Catholicism rests! 'Wherever churches and monasteries abound the people are backward' it is written. Just lately, there has been a little revival of Catholicism, a flash in the pan, here in England, due to Cardinal Newman and Cardinal Manning, who introduced some good old Protestant virtues into your teaching; but that cannot last. You carry the instrument of your own destruction along with you in the degrading exercises with which you seek to debase our beautiful, wonderful, perfectible human nature."

"But the Church has done all that is possible for the people," Father Ricardo began lamely. "The Church has always taught, for one thing, that the labourer is worthy of his hire."

"But the Church never used its influence to make the hire worthy of the labourer; instead of that, it has always sought to grind the last penny out of the people, and then it pauperized them with alms," said Ideala.

"Why have the priests done so little good, Uncle Dawne?" Diavolo asked.

"Because they are no better than other people," was the answer, "and when they get money they use it just as everybody else does, to strengthen their own position, and make a display with."

"Ah, the terrible mistake it has been, this making a paid profession of the doing of good!" Ideala exclaimed.

Angelica, who had put her arm round Diavolo again, and was sitting with her head against his, listening gravely, now looked at Ideala: "I want to know where the true spirit of God is," she said.

"I can tell you," Ideala answered fearlessly. "It is in us *women.* *We* have preserved it, and handed it down from one generation to another of our own sex unsullied; and very soon we shall be called upon to prove the possession of it, for already"—she turned to Father Ricardo here, and specially addressed him, speaking always in gentle tones, without emphasis—"already I—that is to say Woman—am a power in the land, while you—that is to say Priest—retain ever less and less even of the semblance of power.

"Pardon me, dear lady," the priest replied; "but it shocks me to hear you assume such an arrogant tone."

"I don't think the tone was in the least arrogant," Angelica put in briskly; "and, at any rate, it's your own tone exactly, for I've heard you say as much and more, speaking of the priesthood."

"Not exactly," Diavolo corrected her. "Father Ricardo always says: 'Heaven, for some great inscrutable purpose, has mercifully vouchsafed this wondrous power to us, poor '—or humble or unworthy; the first adjective of that kind he can catch—'priests.' I like the short way of putting it myself."

"But why do you always try to make out that it is our duty to be *miserable* sinners?" Angelica asked.

"If we taught ourselves to be happy in this world, we should grow to love it too much, and then we should not strive to win the next."

"And that would impoverish the Church?" Diavolo suggested.

" But why not let *us* be happy, and you raise money in some other way ?" Angelica wanted to know. " Miracles—now I should try some miracles ; a miracle must be much better than a bazaar to raise the funds."

" Oh, but you forget the nunneries Father Ricardo was telling us about the other day," Diavolo said ; " the austere orders where they only live a few years, you know."

" I had forgotten for the moment, but I read up the subject at the time, and found out that when the nuns die all their money remains in the Church ; is that what you mean ?" said the practical Angelica.

" Yes," said Diavolo. " You see, it would hardly cost ten shillings a week to keep a nun, and of course," he said to Father Ricardo, " the more fasting you counsel the less outlay there would be ; so I don't wonder you promise them more goodies in the next world, the more austerities they practise in this."

" It must really work like a provision of nature for the enrichment of Holy Church—so many nuns worked off on the prayer and fasting mill per annum, so many unencumbered fortunes added to the establishment," Angelica observed.

" *Jerusalem !*" said Diavolo. " How easy it is to gull the public !"

The Heavenly Twins had been speaking in a confidential tone, as if they were behind the scenes with Father Ricardo, and now they watched him, seeming to wait for him to wink—at least, that was how Dr. Galbraith afterward interpreted the look. Nothing of this kind coming to pass, however, they both got up, and both together strolled out of the room, yawning undisguisedly.

" That child, Angelica, will be one of us," Ideala whispered to Lord Dawne.

" Yes," he answered gravely ; " They will both be of us eventually ; only we must make no move, but wait in patience ' Until the day break, and the shadows flee away.' "

CHAPTER IV.

THERE was much high talk of doing good and living for others at Morne in these days, to which the twins listened attentively. It is evident from the thoughts they expressed at this time that the minds of both were in a state of fermentation, and that the more active pursuits in which they still indulged occasionally were the mere outcome of habit. When the conversation was interesting, they would sit beside Father Ricardo (whom they insisted on classing with themselves as an inferior being) and watch the speakers by the hour together, and Father Ricardo too, gauging his moral temperature, and noting every sigh of pity or shiver of disapprobation that shook his sensitive frame.

"Where does it hurt you, *dear?*" Diavolo asked him once. "I know you are a bad, bad man, because you say so yourself——"

"I never said so!" Father Ricardo exclaimed with a puzzled air.

"Well, you said you were a miserable sinner, not worthy, *et cetera*, and it comes to the same thing," Diavolo rejoined; "and I don't wonder you are disheartened when you see how impossible it is for you to be as disinterestedly good as Uncle Dawne and Dr. Galbraith. I feel so myself sometimes."

"Oh, I hope I am disinterested," Father Ricardo protested.

"I can't make it out if you are," said Diavolo, shaking his head. "You don't seem to love goodness for its own sake, but for the reward here and hereafter. The whole system you preach is one of reward and punishment."

Father Ricardo had an innocent hobby. He was fond of old china, and had made a beautiful collection, with the help of such friends as Lord Dawne, Dr. Galbraith, and Lady Adeline Hamilton-Wells, who never failed to bring him back any good specimen they might find in the course of their travels.

One day at this time, after the talk had been running, as usual, upon self-sacrifice and living for others, he invited the whole party to inspect his collection; and they all went, with the exception of the Heavenly Twins, who were not to be found at the moment. When the others reached the room in which Father Ricardo kept his treasures, however, they were surprised to find the cabinets comparatively speaking bare, and with great gaps on the shelves as if someone had been weeding them indiscriminately. The good Father looked very blank at first; but the windows were wide open, and before he could think what had happened, a noise on the lawn below attracted everybody's attention, and on looking out to see what was the matter, they beheld the Heavenly Twins apparently intent upon organizing a revel. They were very busy at the moment, and had been for some hours evidently, for they had collected an organ man with a monkey ; a wandering musician with a harp ; a man with a hammer who had been engaged in breaking stones ; a Punch and Judy party, consisting of a man, woman, and boy, with their Toby-dog ; five christy minstrels in their war paint ; a respectable looking mechanic with his wife and three children who were tramping from one place to another in search of work ; and a blind beggar ; and all these were seated in more or less awkward and constrained attitudes on easy-chairs, covered with satin, velvet, or brocade, about the lawn, with little tables before them on which was spread all the cooked food, apparently, that the castle contained. When their admiring relatives first caught sight of the twins, Angelica—who had coiled up her hair, and wore a long black dress, borrowed from her Aunt Fulda's wardrobe ; a white apron with a bib, and a white cap like a nurse's, the property of one of the lady's maids—was pouring tea out of a silver urn, and Diavolo, in his shirt sleeves, with a serviette under his arm like a waiter in a restaurant, was standing beside her with a salver in his hand, waiting to carry it to the mechanic's lady.

"What on earth are you children doing ? " Lord Dawne exclaimed.

"Feeding the hungry, sir," Diavolo drawled cheerfully.

"Well," groaned the poor priest, "you needn't have taken all my best china for that purpose."

"We did that, sir," Diavolo replied with dignity, " in order that you, all unworthy as you are, might have the pleasure of participating in this good work. But, there ! " he said to Angelica, " I told you he wouldn't appreciate it ! "

To the credit of the Heavenly Twins and their guests, it must be recorded that no harm happened either to the china or the plate.

The next day was a Saint's day, and the children announced at breakfast that they intended to keep it. They said they were going to compose a religion for themselves out of all the most agreeable practices enjoined by other religions, and they proposed to begin by making that day a holiday.

Mr. Ellis would have remonstrated at the waste of time, and Father Ricardo at the absence of proper intention, but the way the twins had put the proposition happened to amuse the duke, and therefore they gained their point. But, having gained it, they did not know very well what to do with themselves. Angelica wouldn't make plans. She was thinking of the long dress she had worn the day before, and feeling a vague desire to have her own lengthened ; and she wanted also to take that mysterious packet known as her " work " to her Aunt Fulda's sitting room, where the ladies usually spent the morning, so as to be with them, but she knew that Diavolo would scorn her if she did ; and the outcome of all this vagueness of intention was a fit of excessive irritability. She wanted sympathy, but without being aware of the fact herself, and the way she set about obtaining it was by being excessively disagreeable to everybody. There was a rose in a glass beside her plate, and she took it out, and began to twiddle it between her fingers and thumb impatiently, till she managed to prick herself with the thorns, and then she complained of the pain.

" Oh, that sort of thing doesn't hurt much," Diavolo declared.

" It *does* hurt," she maintained aggressively ; " and pain is pain, whether the seat of it be your head, heart, or hindquarters."

"*Angelica !* " Lady Fulda exclaimed with tragic emphasis. " Someone must really talk to you *seriously !* you are positively *vulgar !* "

" Thank Heaven ! " Angelica ejaculated fervently. " I knew I was going to be something ! "

She got up as she spoke, and walked out of the room with her head in the air, affecting a proud consciousness of having had greatness suddenly thrust upon her.

Lady Fulda looked helplessly, first at Father Ricardo, then at Mr. Ellis.

" Can't you do something ? " she said to the latter.

Mr. Ellis replied by an almost imperceptible shrug of his shoulders. " We know better than to interfere when she's in one of her bad-language tantrums," Diavolo explained.

When his grandfather left the table, he followed him uninvited on a tour of inspection around the castle and grounds, and, finally, retiring with him to the library, whither the old duke usually went to rest, read, or meditate sometime during the morning, he coiled himself up in an armchair, took a small book out of his pocket, and began to study it dilligently.

His grandfather glanced at him affectionately and with interest from time to time. He was lonely in his old age, and liked to have the boy about. He had nobody left to him now who could touch his heart or take him out of himself as Diavolo did, for nobody else attached themselves to him in the same way, or showed such an unaffected preference for having him all to themselves.

"What are you reading, sir?" he asked him at last.

"'Euripides,' sir," Diavolo answered, glancing over the top of his book for a moment as he spoke. "I'm just where Hippolytus exclaims: 'O Jove! wherefore indeed didst thou place in the light of the sun that specious evil to men—woman?'"

"Are you reading 'Euripides' with a 'Key'?" his grandfather asked sternly.

"No, I am reading a key to 'Euripides,'" Diavolo answered.

"Don't you know your Greek, sir?" his grandfather demanded.

"I'm just looking to see, sir," Diavolo rejoined, returning to his book.

When he had finished the page, he looked up at his grandfather, who was sitting with his hands folded upon a large volume he held open on his knee, meditating, apparently.

"Beastly bad tone about women in the Classics," Diavolo remarked; "don't you think so, sir?"

"Ah, my boy, you don't know women yet!" the old duke responded.

"Then I've not made the most of my opportunities," Diavolo said with a grin, "for we meet with a fine variety in the houses about here! But what I object to in these classical chaps," he resumed, "is the way they sneaked and snivelled about women's faults, as if they had none of their own! and then their mean trick of going back upon the women, and reproaching them with their misfortunes."

"What do you mean by that?" his grandfather asked.

"Well, sir, I suppose you would call old age a misfortune to a pretty woman?" Diavolo answered. "And just look at the language in which that fellow Horace taunts Lydia and Lyce when they grow old, and after the sickening way he fawned upon them when they were young, too! And here again," he said, holding up his book, "is that fellow Hippolytus. Just because one woman has shocked him, he says '. . . Never shall I be satisfied in my hatred against women. . . For in some way or other they are always bad.' And a little further back, too"—he scuffed the leaves over—"he says that woman is a great evil *because* men squander away the wealth of their houses upon them. If the men were such

superior beings, why don't they show it somehow? Horace
was as spiteful himself as any old woman ; we should have
called him a cad nowadays. And all this abuse "—he shook
his 'Euripides '—" is beastly bad form whichever way you look
at it." He ruffled his thick tow-hair as he spoke, and yawned
in conclusion.

"Then you are coming out as a champion of women?"
said the duke.

"Oh, by Jove, no!" Diavolo exclaimed, straightening himself. "I haven't the conceit to suppose they would accept
such a champion, and besides, I think it's the other way on now ;
we shall want champions soon. You see, in the old days,
women were so ignorant and subdued, they couldn't retaliate
or fight for themselves in any way ; they never thought of such
a thing. But, now, if you hit a woman, she'll give you one
back promptly," he asseverated, rubbing a bump on his head
suspiciously. "She'll put you in *Punch*, or revile you in the
Dailies ; Magazine you ; write you down an ass in a novel ;
blackguard you in choice language from a public platform ; or
paint a picture of you which will make you wish you had never
been born. Ridicule!" he ejaculated, lowering his voice.
"They ridicule you. That's the worst of it. Now, there's
Ideala, she can make a fellow ridiculous without a word.
When old Lord Groome came back from Malta the other day,
he called, and began to jeer at Mrs. Churston's feet for being
big and ugly. Ideala let him finish ; and then she just looked
down at his own feet, and you could see in a minute that he
wished himself an Eastern potentate with petticoats to hide
them under ; for they were ugly enough to be indecent."

The duke stretched out one of his own miniature models of
feet upon this, and glanced at it complacently.

"Where do you get all these ideas?" he asked. "At your
age I never had any ; and if I had, I should have been ashamed
to own it. You'll be a prig, sir, if you don't mind."

"*I* don't mind," Diavolo rejoined. "I've heard you say
that ladies dearly love a prig, and therefore I rather think of
cultivating that tone."

"You should have been sent to a public school," his grandfather said. "It would have made a man of you."

"Oh, time will do that just as well," Diavolo answered
encouragingly.

At that moment the door opened, and Lady Fulda entered.

"Papa, may I speak to you now?" she asked, and Diavolo

got up politely and lounged off to look for Angelica. He did
not succeed in finding her, however, because she had driven
into Morningquest to do some shopping with her Aunt Claudia
and Ideala. She hated shopping as a rule, and could seldom
be persuaded to do any; but that morning, after breakfast,
she had gone to Lady Fulda's room, where the three ladies
were sitting, and after fidgeting them to death by wandering
up and down, doing nothing, with a scowl on her face, and
an ugly look of discontent in her fine dark eyes, she had burst
out suddenly : "Aunt Fulda ! I want some long dresses."
Lady Fulda looked up at her in blank amazement ; but Lady
Claudia, who was all energy, rolled up her work on the instant,
rang the bell, ordered the carriage, and answered : " Come,
then, and get what you like."

And ten minutes afterward they had started.

Several unsuccessful attempts had been made to persuade
Angelica to wear long dresses, and Lady Claudia felt that
now, when she proposed it herself, it would never do to check
the impulse ; and accordingly, in less than a week from that
day, Angelica, the tom-boy, was to all appearance no more,
and Miss Hamilton-Wells astonished the neighbourhood.

She came down to the drawing room quite shyly in her first
long dinner dress, with her dark hair coiled neatly high on
her head. She had met Mr. Kilroy on the stairs, and he had
looked at her in a strange, startled way, but he said nothing ;
and neither did anybody else when she entered the room.
Her grandfather, however, opened his eyes wide when he saw
her, and smiled as if he were gratified. Lord Dawne gave
her a second glance, and seemed a little sad ; and Ideala went
up to her and kissed her, and then looked into her face for a
moment very gravely, making her feel as if she were on the
eve of something momentous. But Diavolo would not look
at her a second time. One glimpse had been enough for him,
and during the whole of dinner he never raised his eyes.

His uncle Dawne saw what was wrong with the boy, and
glanced at him from time to time sympathetically. He meant
to talk to him when the ladies had left the table, but Diavolo
escaped unobserved before he could carry out his intention.

Mr. Ellis, however, had seen him go, and followed him.
He found him in the schoolroom, crying as if his heart would
break, his slender frame all shaken with great convulsive sobs,
and the old books and playthings which had suddenly assumed
for him the bitterly pathetic interest that attaches to once

loved things when they are carelessly cast aside and forgotten, scattered about him. Mr. Ellis sat down beside, him, and touched his hand, and tried to comfort him, but the tutor was sad at heart himself.

Before very long, however, Angelica burst in upon them, with her hair down, and in the shortest and oldest dress she possessed. Her passionate love for her brother had always been the great hopeful and redeeming point of her character, and if she did show it principally by banging his head, she never meant to hurt him. Almost any other sister would have owed him a grudge for not admiring her in her first fine gown, and so spoiling her pleasure ; but Angelica saw that he was thinking that the old days were over, and there had come a change now which would divide them, and she thought only of the pain he was suffering on that account. So, when she found that he was not going to join the ladies in the drawing room, she rushed upstairs to her own room, which her maid was arranging for the night, and relieved her feelings by tearing off her dinner dress, rolling it in a whisp, and throwing it at the woman. Her petticoats followed it, and then she kicked off her white satin shoes, one of which lit on the mantelpiece, the other on the dressing table ; and, tearing out her hairpins, flung them about the floor in all directions.

" My old brown gown, Elizabeth," she demanded, stamping.

" What's the matter, Miss——"

But Angelica had snatched the gown from the wardrobe, put it on, and was halfway downstairs, buttoning it as she went, before the maid could finish the sentence.

When she entered the schoolroom, she threw herself on her knees beside Diavolo, and hugged him tight, as if she been going to lose him altogether, or he had just escaped from a great danger.

" I won't wear long dresses if you don't like them," she protested.

" Well, you can't go about like that," he grumbled, recovering himself the moment he felt her close to him again, and struck by a sense of impropriety in her short skirt after the grown-up appearance she had presented in the long one. " You look like a beggar."

" Well, if I *do* wear a long one," she declared, " it shall only be a disguise. I promise you I'll be just as bad as ever in it," and she drew a handkerchief out of her pocket, which had been left there for months and was frowsy, and wiped her own eyes and Diavolo's abruptly. "Your feelings are quite boggy, Diavolo," she said, giving a dry sob herself as she spoke. "You can't touch them at all without coming to water. You cry when you laugh."

Mr. Ellis had stolen softly out of the room as soon as he could do so unobserved, and now the twins were sitting together in their favourite position on the same chair, with their arms around each other, and Angelica's dark head slanted so as to lean against Diavolo's fair one.

He had rewarded her last remark with a melancholy grin ; but the clouds had broken, and it now only required time for them to roll away.

"You'll get a moustache in time," Angelica proceeded, in her most matter-of-fact tone. "I can see signs of it now in some lights, only it's so fair it doesn't show much."

"I'll shave it to make it darker," he suggested.

"No, you mustn't do that," she answered, "because that'll make it coarse, and I want you to have one like Uncle Dawne's. But when it comes it will make you look as much grown up as my long dresses do me, and then we'll study some art and practise it together, and not be separated all our lives."

"We will," said Diavolo.

"But I think we ought to begin at once," Angelica added thoughtfully. "Just give me time to consider. And come out into the grounds for a frolic. I feel smothered in here ; and there's a moon ! "

CHAPTER V.

EDITH BEALE had now been married for more than a year to Sir Mosley Menteith, and the whole of their life together had been to her a painful period of gradual disillusion—and all the more painful because she was totally unprepared even for the possibility of any troubles of the kind which had beset her. Parental opinion and prejudice, ignorance, education, and custom had combined to deceive her with regard to the transient nature of her own feeling for her lover ; and it was also inevitable that she should lend herself enthusiastically to the deception ; for who would not believe, if they could, that a state so ecstatic is enduring ? Even people who do know better are apt to persuade themselves that an exception will be made in their favour, and this being so, it naturally follows that a girl like Edith, all faith and fondness, is foredoomed by every circumstance of her life and virtue of her nature, to make the fatal mistake. But, as Evadne told her, passion stands midway between love and hate, and is an introduction to either ; and there is no doubt that, if Menteith had been the kind of repentant erring sinner she imagined him, her first wild desire would have cooled down into the lasting joy of tranquil love. Menteith, however, was not at all that kind of man, and, consequently, from the first the marriage had been a miserable example of the result of uniting the spiritual or better part of human nature with the essentially animal or most degraded side of it. In that position there was just one hope of happiness left for Edith, and that was in her children. If such a woman so situated can be happy anywhere it will be in her nursery. But Edith's child, which arrived pretty promptly, only proved to be another whip to scourge her. Although of an unmistakable type, he was apparently healthy when he was born, but had rapidly degenerated, and Edith herself was a wreck.

They had been out to Malta for a short time, but had come home, Menteith being invalided, and were now at a bracing sea-side place, trying what the air would do for them all.

It was Edith's habit to send the child out with his nurse directly after breakfast, and having done so as usual one morning, she remained alone with her husband in the breakfast room, which looked out upon the sands. She had her hands idly folded on her lap, and was watching Menteith as she might have watched a stranger about whom she was curious. He sat at some distance from her reading a paper, and there was no perceptible change in him ; but she had changed very much for the worse. Why was she not recovering her strength ? Why had it pleased Heaven to afflict her ? That was what she was thinking, but at the same time she blamed herself for repining, and, in order to banish the thought, she rose, and, going over to her husband, laid her hand gently on his shoulder, courting a caress. He had been lavish enough of caresses at first, but all that was over now, and he finished the paragraph he was reading before he noticed Edith at all. Then he glanced at her, but his eyes were cold and critical.

" You certainly are not looking well," he observed, evidently meaning not attractive, as if he were injured by the fact. He got up when he had spoken, so that in the act of rising he dislodged her hand from his shoulder. Then he yawned and lounged over to the window, which was wide open, the weather being warm ; and stood there with his legs apart, and his hands in his pockets, looking out.

One little loving caress or kindly word would have changed the whole direction of Edith's thoughts ; but, wanting that, she stood where he had left her for some moments, lost in pained reflection ; and then she followed him listlessly, seated herself in a low easy-chair, and looked out also.

There were crowds of people on the sands, and her dull eyes wandered from group to group, then up to the sky, and down again to the sea and shore. The sun shone radiantly ; sparkles of light from the rippling wavelets responded to his ardent caress. The sea-sweet air fanned her face. But neither light, nor air, nor sound availed to move her pleasurably.

" Is this to be my life ? " she thought.

The tide was coming in over the sands. Some children with their shoes and stockings off were playing close to the water's edge. They had made a castle, and were standing on the top of it, all crowded together, waiting for a big wave to come and surround them ; and when at last it came, it carried half their fortress away with it, and they all hopped off into the water, and splashed up through it helter-skelter, with shouts of laughter, to the dry land.

" I should have enjoyed that once," thought Edith.

A party of grown-up people cantered past upon donkeys, driven by boys with big sticks. The women were clinging to the pommels of their saddles, and shrieking as they bumped along, while the men shouted, and beat and kicked the donkeys with all their might.

" Horrid, common, cruel people ! " thought Edith. " How dreadful it would be to have to know them ! "

A girl came riding past alone on a hired horse. She wore a rusty black skirt over her petticoats. It was gathered in by a drawing string at the waist, and made her look ludicrously bunchy. Her stirrup was too short ; and she clung desperately with both hands to whip and reins and saddle, only venturing to guide her horse now and then in a timid, half apologetic sort of way, as if she were afraid he would resent it. She must have felt far from comfortable, but probably the dream of her life had been to ride, and now that she *was* riding she admired herself extremely.

Edith involuntarily drew a mental picture of the contrast she herself presented on horseback. " But that girl is well and happy," she objected, to her own disadvantage.

She became aware at this moment of another girl who was passing on foot. She was one of those good-looking girls of the middle class who throng to fashionable watering-places in the season—young women with senses rampant, and minds undisciplined, impelled by natural instinct to find a mate, and practising every little art of dress and manner which they imagine will help them to that end by making them attractive. Their object is always evident in their eyes, which rove from man to man pathetically, pleadingly, anxiously, mischievously, according to their temperaments, but always with the same inquiry : " Will it be you ? "

This girl had made herself by tight-lacing into a notable specimen of the peg-top figure, bulgy at the bust and shoulders, and tapering off at the waist. She had also squeezed her feet into boots that were much too small for them, and fluffed her hair out till her head seemed preposterously large —by which means she had achieved the appearance known to her set as "stylish."

When Edith first saw her she was walking along very quickly with a dissatisfied look on her face ; but as she approached the window she glanced up, and, seeing Menteith, her countenance cleared ; and she slackened her speed, seeming suddenly to become uncertain of the direction she wished to take. First, she half stopped, and appeared to be thinking ; then she hastily put her hand in her pocket, and looked back the way she had come, as if she had lost something ; then shrugged her shoulders to signify that it didn't much matter, and with a far-away look in her eyes walked slowly into the sea ; this was in order that she might spring nimbly out again with a fine pretence of confusion at her affected fit of absent-mindedness.

Menteith watched these manœuvres attentively, patiently awaiting the inevitable moment when she would look at him again. So far, she had pretended to ignore him, but he understood her tactics, and as he observed them, he twisted first one end and then the other of his little light moustache, with a self-complacency not to be concealed. He had been feeling bored all the morning, but now his interest in life revived. He had only the one interest in life, and when the girl on the beach had done all she could to excite it, she glanced at him again, and saw by the look with which he responded that she had succeeded. Then she sat down on the sand, placing her-self so that she could meet his eyes every time she looked up, and taking a letter out of her pocket she began to read it, varying the expression of her countenance the while, to show that she derived great pleasure from the perusal. This was to pique Menteith into supposing that he had a rival

The girl had not troubled herself about Edith's presence, but the latter had also been watching her wiles—dully enough, however, until all at once a thought occurred to her, a hateful thought.

It was the emotional rather than the intellectual side of her nature which had been developed by early associations. She had been accustomed to feel more than to think, and now, when all food for elevating emotions had been withdrawn from her daily life, others, mostly of a distressing kind, took posses-sion of her mind. She had gone through all the phases of acute misery to which a girl so trained and with such a hus-band is liable. She had been weakened into dependence by excess of sympathy, and now was being demoralised for want of any. Menteith had hung upon her words at first, had been responsive to her every glance ; but latterly he had become indifferent to both ; and she knew it, without, however, com-prehending the why and wherefore of the change, or of the growing sense of something wanting which was fast becoming her own normal condition. She was still fighting hard to pre-serve the spiritual fervour which had been the predominant characteristic of her girlhood ; but, at this period of their inter-course, she knew better than to attempt to re-arouse in him that semblance of spirituality which had deluded her in their early passion-period. But she had from the first cultivated a passive attitude toward him, and that even when the natural instinct of her womanhood impelled her to war with him. In any case, however, instinct is not safeguard enough for creat-ures living under purely artificial conditions ; they must have knowledge ; and Edith had been robbed of all means of self-defence by the teaching which insisted that her only duty as a wife consisted in silent submission to her husband's will. Her intellectual life, such as it was, had stopped short from the time of her intimate association with Menteith ; and her spiritual nature had been starved in close contact with him ; only her senses had been nourished, and these were now being rendered morbidly active by disease. The shadow of an awful form of insanity already darkened her days. The mental torture was extreme ; but she fought for her reason with the fearful malady valiantly ; and all the time presented outwardly only the same dull apathy, giving no sign and speaking no word which could betray the fury of the rage within.

This last thought took her unawares as usual, and followed an accustomed course. She had entertained it for a moment, turning it over in her mind with interest before she realized its nature. When she did so, however, her soul sickened. " What am I coming to ? " she mentally ejaculated, recovering herself with an effort ; which resulted also in a sudden resolution.

" I want to go home," she said. Her voice was very husky.

Menteith, startled from the absorbing occupation of ogling the girl on the beach, looked at her sharply. Had she noticed what he was up to, and was she jealous by any chance, as these confounded unreasonable women are apt to be ? No, he concluded, after carefully scrutinizing her face and attitude ; there was not a trace of that kind of thing, and she evidently only meant what she had said. " And, by Jove ! " he thought, " it's an excellent idea, for she's looking anything but nice at present. Marriage is certainly a lottery ! A fellow chooses a girl for her health and beauty, and gives her everything she can want in the world, and in less than a year she's a wreck ? " The injury done to himself, implied in this last reflection, caused a certain amount of irritation, which betrayed itself in the politely " nagging " tone of his reply :

" What precisely do you mean by ' home ' ? " he asked.

" I mean Morningquest," she answered.

" Ah ! " he ejaculated. " That was what I inferred."

" I hope I have not said anything to annoy you ? " she exclaimed.

" Oh, dear, no ! " he assured her. " I know your sex too well to be annoyed by any of its caprices. But still," he added, " a wife does not usually make her ' home ' with her parents."

" But we have no settled home," she remonstrated.

" Do you mean that for a reproach, because my want of means at present obliges me to keep my houses shut up ? " he asked.

" No," she answered with a gleam of spirit, " and you know I do not."

There was a pause after this. It pleased him to make her

ask for his permission to go to her mother, in so many words. He perceived that she found it difficult to do so, and there was satisfaction in the respect and fear which he thought were betokened by her hesitation. The sense of power and possession flattered his self-esteem and enlivened him.

"Do you object?" she ventured at last.

"To what, dear?" he asked, without interrupting an exchange of amorous glances which was just then going on between himself and the girl on the beach.

"To my going home?"

"Oh, no!" he exclaimed, smiling. "Only to that way of putting it. By the way," he added pleasantly, taking up a pair of opera glasses that were lying on a table beside him, and adjusting the sight, "shall I accompany you?"

Edith had taken it for granted that he would, as they had never yet been separated since their marriage ; and the question, striking as it did another note of change, surprised and hurt her. But as it was evident that he would not have asked it had he wished to go, she answered quietly : 'Oh, no! Why should you trouble yourself?"

"It would be no trouble, I assure you," he answered, confirming her first impression that he did not wish to go.

"Oh, no!" she repeated. "I could not think of taking you away from here—if the air is doing you good."

"Ah, well," he answered, catching at the excuse, "I suppose I ought to forego the pleasure, for I am just beginning at last to feel some benefit from the change, and I should probably lose the little good it has done me if I go away now. Morningquest is relaxing. However, I shall join you as soon as I can, you know!" This was said with a plausible affectation of being impelled by a sense of duty to act contrary to his inclination, which did not, however, impose upon Edith ; and the thought that the wish to be with her now was not imperative *although* she was ill became another haunting torment during the short remaining time they were together ; but, happily for herself, she never perceived that he did not care to accompany her principally *because* she was ill.

She left that afternoon with her servants and child, and he saw to the preparations for their departure with cheerful alacrity. She was depressed, and he told her she must keep up her spirits for—everybody's—sake! and set her a good example by keeping his own up manfully. He saw her off at the station, and stood smiling and bowing, with his hat in his hand, until she was out of sight ; and then he turned on his heel and went with a jaunty air to look for the girl on the beach.

Up to the last moment, Edith would have been thankful for any excuse to change her mind and stay ; but when she found herself alone, and the journey had fairly begun, she experienced a sudden sense of relief.

She had not realized the fact : but latterly her husband's presence had oppressed her.

CHAPTER VI.

THE Beales had not seen their daughter and grandson for some months, and the appearance of both was a shock to them. They said not a word to each other at first, but neither of them could help looking at Edith furtively from time to time on the evening of her arrival. When the bishop came up to the drawing room after dinner and had settled himself in his accustomed easy-chair, Edith had crept to his side, and, slipping her hand through his arm, sat leaning her head against his shoulder, and staring straight before her, neither speaking nor listening except when directly addressed. Her father, between whom and herself there had always been a great deal of sympathy, was inexpressively touched by this silent appeal to his love ; and letting the paper lie on his lap, he sat silent also, and serious, feeling, without in any way knowing, that all was not well.

Mrs. Beale was also depressed, although she assured herself again and again that such deep devotion between father and daughter was an elevating and beautiful sight, which it was a privilege to witness ; and tried to persuade herself that they were all extremely happy in the tranquil joy of this peaceful evening spent alone together, with the world shut out.

" That child is not right," the Bishop said, when Edith had gone to bed. " Have you noticed her face ? I don't like the look of it at all ; not at all."

" Isn't that rather unkind, dear ? " Mrs. Beale replied. " I always recovered in time."

" You never were as ill as the poor child evidently is," he answered ; and retired to his library, much disturbed.

But Mrs. Beale determined not to worry herself, and managed to dismiss the subject from her mind until next day, when she was sitting alone with her daughter in the morning room up stairs. They were both working, but the conversation flagged, and Mrs. Beale, from wondering why Edith was so uncommunicative, found herself involuntarily repeating the bishop's observation : " That child is not right," and the question : "What is the matter with your face, dearest?" slipped from her unawares.

" I don't know, mother," Edith answered shortly.

She had never before in her life spoken to her mother in that tone, and the latter was surprised and hurt for a moment ; but then persuaded herself that some irritability was only natural if the child were out of health. and at once made proper allowances.

Edith got up when she had spoken, and left the room.

She was occupying one of the state departments of the palace then, but on the way to it she had to pass the room which had been hers as a girl. The door was open, and she went in. Nothing was changed there ; but the moment she entered she felt that there was a direful difference in herself. The sad, benignant Christ, with tender, sympathetic eyes, looked down upon her from the picture on the wall ; but she returned the glance indifferently at first, and then, remembering the rapture with which she had been wont to kneel at his feet, she looked again. The recollection of the once dear delight tantalized her now, however, because it did not renew it ; and, turning from the picture impatiently, she went to the window, and there sank on to the seat from whence she had looked out at the moonlight and the shadows on the night of the day on which it had been arranged that she should winter with her mother at Malta. And here again she endeavoured to recall the glow of sensation which had thrilled her then ; but only the lifeless ashes of that fire remained, and they were burnt out past all hope of rekindling them. Even the remembrance of what her feelings had been eluded her, and she could think of nothing but after experiences—experiences of her married life, and those precisely which it was not wise to recall. They were not exactly thoughts, however, that occupied her, but emotions, to which, looking out on the sunlit garden with rounded eyes and pupils dilated to the uttermost, she had unconsciously lent herself for some time, as on other occasions, before she realized what she was doing. Suddenly, however, she came to her senses, and fled in affright to the morning room, where she threw herself down on her knees beside her mother impetuously, and buried her face in her lap.

"Take care, dear child!" Mrs. Beale exclaimed. "You will hurt yourself."

"Mother! Mother!" Edith cried. "I have such terrible, terrible thoughts! I cannot control them. I cannot keep them away. The torment of my mind is awful. I could kill myself."

Mrs. Beale turned pale. "Pray, dearest!" she ejaculated.

"I do, I do, mother," Edith wailed; "but they mingle with my prayers. God is a demon, isn't he?"

Mrs. Beale threw her arms round her daughter, and almost shook her in her consternation. "Edith, darling, do you know what you are saying?" she demanded.

Edith looked into her face in a bewildered way. "No, mother, what was it?" she answered.

Then all outward sign of Mrs. Beale's agitation subsided. Some shocks stun, and some strengthen and steady us. The piteous appeal in Edith's eyes, the puzzle and the pain of her face as she made an effort to recall her words and understand them, had the latter effect upon her mother.

"I am afraid you are very weak, dear child," the poor lady bravely responded. "Weakness makes people unhealthy-minded. You must see the doctor, and have a tonic."

"The doctor again!" Edith groaned. "It has been nothing but the doctor and 'tonics' ever since I have been married."

"What does he say is the matter exactly?" Mrs. Beale asked.

"All his endeavour seems to be not to say what is the matter exactly," Edith replied.

Mrs. Beale reflected, caressing her daughter the while, and under the soothing influence of her loving touch, Edith's countenance began to relax.

"When is Mosley coming?" her mother said at last.

Edith's face contracted again, and she rose to her feet. "I don't know, mother," she answered coldly.

The chime rang out at this moment, and she frowned as she listened to it.

"I wish those bells could be stopped!" she exclaimed. "They deafen me."

Mrs. Beale had also risen from her chair, smiling mechanically, but with pain and perplexity at her heart. "I am sure it is the journey," she said. "It has quite upset you. Your nerves are all jarred. You must really lie down for a little—see, dearest, here on the couch ; and keep quite quiet." She arranged the cushions.

"Come, dear," she urged, "like a good child, and I will cover you up."

Edith had been accustomed to this kind of gentle compulsion all her life, and as she yielded to it now she began to feel more like herself. "I knew I should be better with you, mother," she said sighing ; and then she reached up her arm, and drew her mother's face down to hers. "Kiss me, mother, and tell me you forgive me for being impatient."

"Dear child, you are not impatient," her mother answered, adding to herself, as she returned to her seat ; "I hope it is only impatience ! "

Edith had turned her face to the wall, and soon appeared to be asleep. Then her mother went down to the library The bishop rose from his writing table when she entered. It was a habit of his to be polite to his wife.

"I think you were right last night about Edith," she said. "She is not as she should be. Write to Dr. Galbraith. Ask him to come here to-morrow. Ask him to dine and stay the night, as if it were only an ordinary visit—not to alarm her, you know. But tell him why we want him to come. I am nervous about her.

Mrs. Beale's face quivered, and she burst into tears as she spoke.

"Oh, my dear ! I am sure there is no need to agitate yourself," the bishop exclaimed. "Now do—now don't, really ! See ! I will write at once."

He sat down, and began, "My dear George," and then looked up at his wife to see if she were not already relieved.

Mrs. Beale could not speak, but she stroked his head once or twice in acknowledgment of his great kindness. Then more tears came because he *was* so very kind ; and finally she was obliged to go to her own room to recover herself.

As the day wore on, however, she became reassured. Edith seemed much refreshed by her sleep, and, in the afternoon when the three ladies came from the castle to call upon her, bringing Angelica with them, she quite roused up.

"What, Angelica a grown up young lady in a long dress!"
she exclaimed. "But where is Diavolo?"

"We had a slight difference of opinion this morning,"
Angelica answered stiffly.

"Dear me! that is a new thing!" Mrs. Beale commented.

"No, it is not," Angelica contradicted, bridling visibly.
"Only, when we were younger we used to—settle our differences—at once, and have done with them. But now that I am
in long dresses Diavolo won't do that, so we have to sulk like
married people."

"But, my dear child, I don't see why you should quarrel at
all," Mrs. Beale remonstrated.

"You would if you were with us, I expect," Angelica
answered, and then she turned her attention to Edith, but not
by a sign did she betray the slightest consciousness of the
latter's disfigurement—unless making herself unusually agreeable was a symptom of commiseration; and in this she succeeded so thoroughly that when the others rose to go Edith
did not feel inclined to part with her.

"Won't you stay with me here a few days?" she entreated.

Angelica reflected. "It would do him good, I should think,"
she said at last.

"I should think it would!" Edith agreed, laughing.

"Did I speak?" said Angelica.

"Yes," Edith answered. "You informed me that you are
going to stay here in order to punish Diavolo by depriving him
of your society for a time."

"I am sure I did not say all that!" Angelica exclaimed.

"Well, not exactly, perhaps," Edith confessed; "but you
led me to infer it."

"Well, I will stay," Angelica decided. "Aunt Fulda, I'm
going to stay here for a few days with Edith," she answered.

"Very well, dear," her aunt meekly rejoined. "Are you
going to stay now?"

"Yes. Tell Elizabeth to bring me some wearing apparel."

As they drove back to Morne, Lady Claudia scolded Lady
Fulda for so weakly allowing Angelica to have her own way in
everything.

"I thought you would agree with me that the sweet womanly
influence at the palace would do her good," Lady Fulda
answered, in an injured tone.

"'Sweet womanly' *nonsense!*" said Lady Claude. "She
will twist them all round her little finger, and turn the whole

place upside down before she leaves, or I am much mistaken."

"Well, dear, if you would only make Angelica do what *you*
wish while you are here to influence her I should be thankful," Lady Fulda rejoined with gentle dignity.

Lady Claudia said no more.

Things went merrily at the palace for the rest of the day.
Mrs. Orton Beg called, and Mr. Kilroy of Ilverthorpe, between
whom and Angelica there was always an excellent understanding; and she entertained him now with observations and
anecdotes which so amused Edith that, as Mrs. Beale said to
the bishop afterward : "The dear, naughty child quite took
her out of herself."

Angelica had never been in the same house with a baby
before, and she was all interest.   Whatever defects of character the new women may eventually acquire, lack of maternal
affection will not be one of them.

"Have you seen the baby?" she asked Elizabeth, when the
latter was brushing her hair for dinner.   He had not been
visible during the afternoon, but Angelica had thought of him
incessantly.

"Yes, Miss," Elizabeth answered.

"Is he a pretty baby?" Angelica wanted to know.

Elizabeth pursed up her lips with an air of reserve.

"You don't think so?" Angelica said—she had seen the
maid's face in the mirror before her.   "What is he like?"

"He's exactly like the bishop, Miss."

Angelica broke into a broad smile at herself in the glass.
"What! a little old man baby!" she exclaimed.

"Yes, Miss—with a cold in his head," the maid said
seriously.

When she was dressed, Angelica went to make his acquaintance.   On the way she discovered her particular friend, the
bishop, going furtively in the same direction, and slipped her
hand through his arm.

"We'll go together," she said confidentially, taking it for
granted that his errand was the same as her own.

The nurse was undressing the child when they entered, and
Edith sat watching her.   She was already dressed for the
evening, and looked worse in an elaborate toilet than she had
done in her morning dress.   A stranger would have found it
hard to believe that only the year before she had been radiantly
healthy and beautiful.   The puzzled, pathetic expression was

again in her eyes as she watched the child. She had no smile for him, and uttered no baby words to him—nor had he a smile for her. He was old, old already, and exhausted with suffering, and as his gaze wandered from one to the other it was easy to believe that he was asking each dumbly why had he ever been born?

"Is *that* Edith's baby?" Angelica exclaimed in her astonishment and horror under her breath, slipping her hand from the bishop's arm.

She had seen enough in one momentary glance, and she fled from the room. The bishop followed her. Mrs. Beale was there when they entered, standing behind her daughter's chair, but she did not look at her husband, nor he at her. For the first time in their married life, poor souls, they were afraid to meet each other's eyes.

CHAPTER VII.

NEXT day, in the afternoon, Mrs. Beale being otherwise engaged, Edith proposed that she and Angelica should go for a drive together. Edith was feeling better, and Angelica had recovered her equanimity. She suggested that they should drive toward Fountain Towers. Edith had not been on that road since her marriage, and when they passed the place where she and her mother had seen the young French girl lying insensible on the pathway with her baby beside her she was reminded of the incident, and described it to Angelica, adding : "I have so often longed to know what became of her."

"I can tell you," said Angelica. "I know her quite well by sight. She is living with Nurse Griffiths, in Honeysuckle Cottage, on Dr. Galbraith's estate. Nurse Griffiths told us he brought her there one day in his carriage very ill, and she has been there ever since. He always gets angry and snaps at you if he's bothered about anybody who's ill or unfortunate, and Diavolo and I met him that day coming away from the cottage, and he spoke to us so shortly we were sure there was something bad the matter, so we went to see what it was, and Nurse Griffiths said she was French. I've not been there since, but I expect it's the same girl. Shall we stop and see? We pass the end of the lane where the cottage is."

Edith agreed eagerly. She said it would be a relief to her mind to know that the girl was well cared for and happy.

"Oh, everybody is well cared for and happy on Dr. Galbraith's estate," said Angelica. "His tenants worship him. And they would rather be abused by him than complimented by anybody else."

The cottage, covered with the honeysuckle from which it took its name, stood in a large old-fashioned garden, at the edge of a fir plantation, which sheltered it from the northeast wind at the back, and filled the air about it with balsamic fragrance.

Edith and Angelica left the carriage at the end of the lane and walked up.

"What a lovely spot!" Edith exclaimed. "On a still bright day like this it makes one realize what the Saints meant by 'holy calm.' I think I should like to live in such a place, and never hear another echo from the outside world."

"I suppose you would just like to add dear Mosley to the establishment," Angelica suggested.

Edith's heart contracted. She had not thought of her husband, and now when she did it was with a pang, because she could not include him in her idea of Eden.

The French girl was standing at the door of the cottage with a child in her arms.

"Is Nurse Griffiths in?" Angelica asked.

Edith looked at the child. It should have been running about by that time, but it was small and rickety, with bones that bent beneath its weight, slight as it was. Edith had looked at it first with some interest, but its unhealthy appearance repelled her. She managed, however, to speak to the girl about it kindly.

"What is your baby's name?" she asked.

"Mosley Menteith," was the answer.

For a moment it seemed to Edith as if all the world were blotted out, and then again the hum of bees, the chirrup of birds, the fall of a fir-cone, the call of the cock-pheasant in the wood sounded obtrusively, making the girl's voice as she continued speaking appear far off and indistinct.

"I called him after his father, then, didn't I?" she was saying to the baby in good English, but with a French accent. "And he's to grow up, and be a big strong fellow and beat his father, isn't he, for he's a bad, bad man!"

Nurse Griffiths hearing voices in the porch came out.

"Hush, Louise," she said to the girl. "You've no call to talk in that way now. You must excuse her," she added to the ladies. "She's had a bad bringing up."

"I can't—believe you," Edith faltered. "Tell me— exactly."

"Well, it was in this way," the girl rejoined, speaking in the prosaic tone in which her countrywomen are accustomed to discuss matters that inspire ours with too much disgust to be mentioned. "Menteith came after me, and my sister wanted money, so she made me believe that he couldn't marry me because there was a law, to prevent it. She said he loved me, and if I loved him well enough, it would be a noble thing to disregard the law. and he gave her seventy-five pounds for that. I found her letter to Menteith about it, and I've got it here," tapping the bosom of her gown. "He took me abroad when he wanted to get rid of me, and left me in Paris with five pounds in my pocket ; but it was enough to bring me back. I was sick when I landed at Dover, and they sent me to the workhouse ; and when I got well again I told them I had friends in Morningquest, and they gave me a little help to get there ; but I had to tramp most of the way, and I was weak— I couldn't have got as far as I did if I hadn't wanted to kill them both."

"Now, hush !" said Nurse Griffiths. "The Lord saved you from such a sin."

"The Lord !" said the girl derisively. "If the Lord had been inclined to help me, he wouldn't have waited till I came to murder. It wasn't the Lord saved *me*."

"She will say that, and I can't cure her," Nurse Griffiths declared. "But I'm afraid you're feeling the heat, ma'am, and you are not very strong," she added, addressing Edith, who was clinging to the porch for support, looking strangely haggard. "Won't you come in and sit down a bit?"

"No, thank you, it is nothing," Edith answered steadily, recovering herself.

"Will you come and sit down with me on that seat ?" she said to Louise, indicating a rustic bench under an old pear tree at the end of the garden. "I want to talk to you."

Nurse Griffiths and Angelica remained in the porch.

"Who is that lady, Miss ?" the nurse asked when Edith was out of hearing.

"Lady Menteith," Angelica answered.

The woman threw up her hands. "O Lord ! have mercy upon her—and upon us ! What a cruel, cruel shame ! She's showing her the letter. Eh ! it's enough to kill her. You generally know all the mischief that's going, Miss ! Why did you bring her here ?"

"I wish I had known this, then," said Angelica, whose heart

was thumping painfully. "If any harm comes of it, I shall always think it was my fault."

"Well, there's no call to do that if you didn't know," the woman answered. "I see she was a great lady myself, but I never thought it was *her*. Eh! but it's the dirty men makes the misery."

On the way back, Edith stopped the carriage at the telegraph office, and despatched a message to her husband to come to her, "Come at once."

They only arrived in time to dress hurriedly for dinner, and when they went down to the drawing room they found Dr. Galbraith there with the bishop and Mrs. Beale.

"Where have you two been the whole afternoon?" the latter asked.

"We had tea in the library at Fountain Towers," Angelica answered easily, "and obtained some useful knowledge from your books."

Dr. Galbraith looked hard at her: "I wonder what devilment you've been up to now?" he thought.

But Angelica's manner was as unconcerned as possible. Edith's was not, however. Her face was flushed, her eyes unnaturally glittering, and she became excited about trifles, and talked loudly at table; and in the drawing room after dinner she could not keep still. Mrs. Beale asked Angelica to play, and Angelica tried something soothing at first, but Edith complained impatiently that those things always made her melancholy. Then Angelica played some bars of patriotic music, stirring in the extreme, but Edith stopped her again.

"That wearies my brain," she said, and began to pace about the room, up and down, up and down. Her mother watched her anxiously. Angelica closed the piano. Dr. Galbraith and the bishop came in from the dining room, and then Edith declared that driving in the open air had made her so sleepy she must go to bed.

Angelica noticed that Dr. Galbraith scrutinized her face sharply as he shook hands with her.

"God bless you, my dear child," the bishop said when she kissed him, and his lips moved afterward for some seconds as if he were in prayer. Her mother followed her out of the room; and then silence settled on the three who were left. The bishop was obviously uneasy. Dr. Galbraith's good-looking plainness was softened by a serious expression which added much to the attractiveness of his strong kind face.

Angelica shivered, and was about to break the spell of silence boldly in her energetic way, when suddenly, and apparently overhead, a heavy bell tolled once.

It was only the cathedral clock striking the hour, but it sounded portentously through the solemn stillness of the night, and with quickened attention they all looked up and listened.

Slowly the big bell boomed forth ten strokes. Then came a pause; and then the chime rolled through the room, a deafening volume of sound, in long reverberations, from amidst which the constant message disentangled itself as it were, but distinctly, although to each listener with a different effect:

He, watch-ing o-ver Is-ra-el, slumbers not, nor sleeps.

It awoke Dr. Galbraith from a train of painful reflections; it reassured the bishop; and it made Angelica fret for Diavolo remorsefully.

CHAPTER VIII.

ANGELICA must have fallen asleep the moment she got into bed that night, and just as instantly she began to dream. She had never hitherto felt a throb of passion. She had given the best love of her life to her brother, and had made no personal application of anything she had heard, or seen, or read of lovers, so that the possibility of ever having one of her own had never cost her a serious thought. But the excitement of that day and the occupations had so wrought upon her imagination that when she slept she dreamt, and in her dream she saw a semblance, the semblance of a man, a changing semblance, the features of which she could not discern, although she tried with frenzied effort, because she knew that when she saw him fully face to face he would be hers. They were not in this world, nor in the next. They were not even in the universe. They were simply each the centre of a great light which formed a sphere about them, and separated them from one another; and heaven and hell, and earth and sky, and night and day, and life and death were all added to the glory of those spheres of light. And she knew *how;* but there is no word of human speech to express it. She lay on light, she stood on light, she sat on light, she swam in light; and wallowed, and walked, and ran, and leaped, and soared, rolling along in her own sphere until the monotony made her giddy; and all her endeavour was to reach her lover, not for himself so much as because she knew that if their two lights could be added in equal parts to each other and mingled into one, their combined effulgence would make a pathway to heaven. But try as she would she could not attain her object, and finally she became so exhausted by the struggle that she was obliged to desist. The moment she did so, however, the other sphere turned of its own accord, and rolled up to her. "Dear me!" said Angelica. "How easily things are done when the right time comes!" The semblance now took shape, and kissed her. "How nice!" thought Angelica, returning the kiss. "This is love. Love is life. I am his. He is mine. Most of all, he is *mine!*" "No, we can't allow that!" said a chorus of men from the earth. "You' re beginning to know too much. You'll want to be paid for your labour next just as well as we are, and that is *unwomanly!*" But Angelica only laughed and kissed her lover. "Talk does no good," she said; "this is the one thing the great man-boy-booby understands at present!" So she kissed him again, and every time she kissed him, he changed. He was Samson, Abraham, Lot, Antony, Cæsar, Pan, Achilles, Hercules, Jove; he was Lancelot and Arthur, Percival, Galahad and Gawaine. He was Henry VIII., Richelieu, Robespierre, Luther, and several Popes. He was David the Psalmist, beloved of the man-god of the Hebrews. He was golden-haired Absalom, and St. Paul in his unregenerate days. But he never was Solomon. She saw hundreds of women dividing Solomon among them, and cherishing the little bits in the Woman's Sphere of their day, and they offered her a portion, but she refused to take it. She said she would have the whole of him or none at all, and they were horribly shocked. They said: "Fie! you are no true woman! A woman is satisfied with very little, and silently submits." But Angelica answered: "Rubbish! What do you know of womanhood and truth? you talk like a bishop!" And the clergy were dreadfully offended at this. They said she was all wrong. They said it mildly. They shouted it rudely. They whispered it persuasively, and then they blustered. "We are right, and you are wrong!" they maintained. "Well, I have only your word for that," said Angelica, which provoked them again. "We speak in the name of the Lord!" they answered.

"Oh, anybody could do that," said Angelica, "but it wouldn't prove that they have the Lord's permission to use his name." Then they reminded her that the true spirit of God had been bestowed upon them for transmission, and she answered : "Yes, but it was taken from you again for your sins, and confided to us; and wherever a virtuous woman is, there is the spirit of God, and the will of God, and there only !" Then they drew off a little and consulted, and when they spoke again they had lowered their tone considerably. "But you will allow, I suppose, that we have done some good in the world ?" they said collectively. "Oh, yes," she answered, "you have done your duty here and there to the best of your ability, but your ability was considerably impaired by vice. However, you have brought the world up out of the dark ages of physical force at our instigation, and helped to prepare it for us; now step down gracefully, take your pensions and perquisites, and hold your tongues. Men are the muscle, the hard working material of the nation; women are the soul and spirit, the directing intelligence." They were about to reply, but before they could do so, a stentorian voice proclaimed :

"Home is the Woman's Sphere !"

"Who are you ?" said Angelica coolly. "I am the Pope of Rome," he answered, strutting up to her with dignity. "And what do *you* know about the Woman's Sphere ?" she said laughing. "I am informed of God !" he declared. But she answered that she had much later information, and slammed the doors of the Sphere in his face. Then she peeped through the keyhole, and saw that the pope was in consultation with the Archbishops of Canterbury and York, and two popular cardinals. They were very quiet at first, but presently they began to quarrel. "Don't make such a noise," she shrieked through the keyhole : "go away and be good, will you ? We're very busy in here, and you disturb us. We're revising the moral laws." The shock of this intelligence electrified them, and while they stared at each other helplessly, not knowing what to do, she armed herself with the vulgar vernacular, which was the best weapon, she understood, to level at cant. "Lord," she said to herself, "how Diavolo would enjoy this ! I wish he was here !" She found the work of the Sphere very heavy, and she tried to remember the name of some saint, but for the life of her she couldn't think of any, so she called upon Ouida and Rhoda Broughton. Then she peeped through the keyhole again, and finding that the pope was listening, she squirted water into his ear. The other Ecclesiastical Commissioners remained in the background, looking anxious. "We're attending to man the iniquitous now," she called to them kindly to relieve their minds. "He's been too much for you, it seems, but we'll soon settle him." "You're a nasty-minded woman," said the pope. "Always abusive, old candles and vestments," Angelica retorted. "Candles and vestments—*in excess*," said the Archbishop of York hurriedly. "Where?" And he went off to see about them. "To the pure all things are pure," a powerful voice proclaimed at that moment. "Ah, that is St. Paul!" said Angelica, surprised and delighted, and then she shook hands with him. "The sacred duties of wife and mother," one of the cardinals began to pipe—— "There you are meddling again," Angelica interrupted him rudely; "will you go away, and let us mind our own business?" "This is all your fault," the pope said to the Archbishop of Canterbury. The archbishop defended himself courteously, but another quarrel seemed inevitable nevertheless. Before it could come off, however, it suddenly appeared that if it were anything it was UNWOMANLY! About that they were quite in accord; and having made the discovery they went their several ways, shaking their several heads impressively. "Now I shall have time to consider the state of the Sphere," said Angelica. "Just wait till I can come and teach you your duty," she called to the women there. "I am not Esther, most decidedly! But I am Judith. I am Jael. I am Vashti. I am Godiva. I am all the heroic women of all the ages rolled into one, not for the shedding of blood, but for the saving of suffering." They did not understand her a bit, however, they were so dazed, and they all looked askance at her. "I see," she said; "I shall have to save you in spite of yourselves." But when she had looked a little longer, and seen men, women, and children crowding like loathsome maggots together, she was disheartened. "All this filth will breed a pestilence," she said, "and I shouldn't be surprised if that pestilence were ME!" But just at that moment the light went out, someone uttered a cry, and Angelica awoke. The room was flooded with moon-light. "I am awake now," she said to herself, "and that was a real cry. It was 'murder!' I think"—and she rose intrepidly to rush to the rescue. She was going off at once, just as she was, in her nightdress; but the house was so still at the moment that she thought she might be mistaken. She was determined to go and see for herself, however, in order to make sure ; and having pinned up her hair, she put on her shoes and stockings and a dressing gown, and opened the door, her heart beating wildly all the time. It was a sickening sensation. But as she listened she became aware of voices speaking naturally, and people moving to and fro, which somewhat reassured her. She left the room, however, and ran down the corridor.

At the farther end a bright shaft of light streamed across it from a half-open door, and she heard Edith speaking wildly.

" My poor child ! my poor child," Mrs. Beale answered with tears in her voice. " Do try and calm yourself. Won't you tell us this story that is troubling you now ? You will feel better if you tell us."

" No, no," Edith answered quickly. " I will not tell you until he comes, any of you. But *when* he comes ! " There was a pause, then she asked feebly : " Doctor, what is the matter with my head ? " But before he could answer, she broke out into a stream of horrid imprecations.

Angelica put her hands to her ears, and flew back past her own room to the top of the stairs. There she encountered the bishop. He was trembling. He was at a loss. Nothing he had ever studied either in theology or metaphysics had in the slightest degree prepared him for the state of things in society which he was now being forced to consider.

" My dear child ! " he exclaimed, " What are you doing here ? "

" Oh, I'm frightened ! I'm frightened ! " Angelica cried, thumping him hard on the chest with both fists. " Let us go away and hide ourselves ! " She seized his hand impetuously, and dragged him downstairs after her sideways, a mode of descent which was more rapid than either safe or graceful for a little fat bishop in evening dress.

" Come, come, come to the library with me, and talk about God and good angels, and that kind of thing," she cried.

" But this is the middle of the night," the bishop objected.

" Well, and is there any time like the present ? " Angelica exclaimed. " Come at once—come and say nice soothing things from the psalms."

As she spoke, she dragged him across the hall and into the library from whence he had just issued, and then slammed the door. The bishop reproved her for this, and wanted her to go to bed, but she refused. " Go to bed, and lie awake in the dark with horrid words about, how can you expect it ? " she demanded. "I shall not go to bed unless you come and sit beside me all night long."

Poor Angelica! impetuous, imperious, but in that she was her father's daughter, not saved by her wonderful intelligence from being fantastical. There must inevitably have been an element of broad farce in the veriest tragedy into which she might have been brought at that time, an element which was rendered all the more conspicuous by her own inability to perceive at the moment that she was behaving ridiculously, and making others ridiculous. But the bishop himself was not conscious of any absurdity or loss of dignity. It was only the inconvenience that he felt just then. For he was fresh from a painful interview with Dr. Galbraith, and every nerve was jarring in response to the horror that had come upon him. His heart was wrung, and his conscience did not acquit him. He did recognize now, however, that Angelica was in no fit state of mind to be left alone, and sitting down beside a little table on which stood his constant companion and friend for many years, a large quarto copy of the Bible, he folded his hands upon it, seeming to pray, while he waited patiently until she should have calmed herself.

Her indignation had driven her to seek a more popular form of relief than the bishop had chosen. As she paced up and down the room in evident agitation, every now and then stopping short to wring her hands when terrible thoughts came crowding, she became in her own mind exceedingly abusive.

She revised and enlarged her reply to that cardinal who had piped to her earlier in the night about the sacred duties of wife and mother. "What do *you* know about 'the Sacred Duties of Wife and Mother'?" she jeered, increasing her pace as her passion waxed. "Wait until you're a wife and mother yourself, and then perhaps you'll be able to give an opinion; and, meanwhile, attend to your own 'Sacred Duties.' You *will* come poking your nose into the Sphere where it's not wanted"—she shook her fist at him—"with your theories." She exclaimed: "You meddling priest! What you're afraid of is that there won't be slaves enough in the world to make money for you; or poor enough to bear witness to your Christian charity! You needn't be afraid, though. So long as we have *you* there'll be poverty in plenty!" Here she became conscious of the attitude of her companion. The bishop blotted out the cardinal. His wrinkled hands, meekly folded; his white head bowed; his benign face expressive of

intense mental suffering heroically borne, impressed her.
"Resignation? No, not resignation exactly," her thoughts ran
on. "To be resigned is to acquiesce. Resistance? Yes. To
resist—but not to resist with rage. Be firm, but be gentle."
She sat down at last in an easy-chair and leaned back, looking
up at the ceiling. In a few minutes she was fast asleep. When
she awoke the room was empty, but outside she heard receding footsteps, and springing up with characteristic impetuosity
she followed after "to see for herself."

The shutters were still closed in the library, and the lamps
were burning; but it was broad daylight in the hall, and a
heavy squall of rain was beating against the windows with
mournful effect. Angelica saw a manservant standing beside
some baggage as she passed, and wondered who had arrived.

At the foot of the stairs she overtook Dr. Galbraith, and
caught his arm.

"Is Edith better?" she exclaimed.

Dr. Galbraith looked down at her, clasped both her hands in
one of his as they rested on his arm, and led her upstairs.
Before they reached the top, his firm, cool touch had steadied
her nerves, and calmed her.

"This is your room, I think," he said, stopping when they
reached it.

Angelica took the hint, and went in, but she did not shut
the door. "You might have told me, you pig, and then perhaps I should have been satisfied," she reflected, standing just
inside her room, holding her head very high, and straining her
ears to listen. She heard Dr. Galbraith go to the end of the
corridor, and then, as the sound of his footsteps ceased, she
knew that he must have gone into Edith's room. The house
was oppressively still. "I suppose I am to be tortured with
suspense because I am young," she thought, and then she
followed Dr. Galbraith.

The shutters were still closed in Edith's room, and the gas
was burning. Nobody had thought of letting the daylight in.
The door was open, and a screen was drawn across it, but
Angelica could see past the screen. She saw Edith first. She
was lying on her bed, still dressed, and sensible now, but
exhausted. Her yellow hair, all in disorder, fell over the
pillow to one side, and on the same side her mother sat facing
her, rocking herself to and fro, and holding Edith's hand,
which she patted from time to time in a helpless, piteous sort
of way.

Edith was lying on her back, with her face turned toward Angelica. There were deep lines of suffering marked upon it, and her eyes glittered feverishly, but otherwise she was gray and ghastly, and old. It was the horrible look of age that impressed Angelica. There were three gentlemen present, the bishop, Dr. Galbraith, and Sir Mosley Menteith.

Edith was looking at her father. "That is why I sent for you all," she was saying feebly—"to tell you, you who represent the arrangement of society which has made it possible for me and my child to be sacrificed in this way. I have nothing more to say to any of you—except "—she sat up in bed suddenly, and addressed her husband in scathing tones—" except to you. And what I want to say to you is—Go! go! Father! turn him out of the house. Don't let me ever see that dreadful man again!"

She fell back on her pillow, white and still, and shut her eyes.

"My darling, you will kill yourself!" her mother exclaimed.

Dr. Galbraith stepped to the side of the bed hurriedly, and bent over her. The bishop stood at the foot, holding on to the rail with both hands, his whole face quivering with suppressed emotion. Menteith gave them a vindictive glance, and then stole quietly away. Angelica had made her escape, and was standing at the head of the stairs, wringing her hands. She was trembling with rage and excitement. "I am Jael—I am Judith—No! I am Cassandra," she was saying to herself. "I must speak!"

"I wish to God I hadn't answered that telegram so promptly —coming to be made an exhibition of by a sick woman in her tantrums," Menteith reflected as he walked down the corridor. "I'm surprised at Edith. But it is so like a woman; you never can count upon them." Here he caught sight of Angelica, and quite started with interest. "That's a deuced fine girl," he thought, and followed her to the library instinctively.

A servant had just opened the shutters. Angelica went to one of the windows and, throwing it up to the top, inhaled a deep breath of the fresh morning air. The rain had stopped. The servant put out the lamps and withdrew, after standing aside for a moment respectfully to allow Sir Mosley Menteith to enter. The latter glanced round the room, but Angelica was hidden by the curtain in the deep embrasure of the window. Menteith bit his nails and stood still for some time. Then the bishop came, followed by Dr. Galbraith, and walked straight up to him. It was a bad moment for Sir Mosley Menteith. He tried to inspect his father-in-law coolly, but his hand was somewhat tremulous as he raised it to twist the ends of his little light moustache.

"My daughter wishes you to leave the house," the bishop said sternly ; "and—eh—I may say that I—that *we*—eh—her father and mother, also wish you to go—eh—now, at once."

Angelica sprang from her hiding place. "And take that," she cried, "for a present, you father of a speckled toad !" And seizing the heavy quarto Bible from the table, she flung it with all her might full in his face. It happened to hit him on the bridge of his nose, which it broke.

CHAPTER IX.

LATER in the day Lord Dawne, who had ridden in, saw Dr. Galbraith's carriage waiting before Mrs. Orton Beg's little house in the Close. He reined in his horse, which was fidgety, and at the same moment Dr. Galbraith came out.

"Nothing wrong here, I hope ?" Lord Dawne inquired.

"No," was the curt response, "it is that poor child at the palace. I have been up with her all night."

"What is the matter now ?" Lord Dawne inquired.

"Now—it is her brain," the doctor answered ; then stepped into his carriage and was driven away.

Lord Dawne dismounted and met Mrs. Orton Beg, who was coming out with her bonnet on.

"No hope, I suppose !" he said in a tone of deep commiseration.

"Oh, it is worse than death !" she answered. "I am going there now. Dr. Galbraith says I shall be of use."

The bishop and Angelica spent some time in the library together that morning. The bishop had sent for Angelica to talk to her, and she had come to talk to the bishop ; and, being quicker of speech than he, she had taken the initiative.

"Did you ever feel like a horse with a bearing rein, champing his bit ?" she began the moment she burst into the room.

"No, I never did," said the bishop severely.

"Ah ! then I can never make you understand how I feel now !" she said, throwing herself on to a chair opposite to him, sideways, so that she could clasp the back. "You look very unsympathetic," she remarked.

" It seems to me," the bishop began with increased severity, " that you have no respect for anybody."

" No, I have not," she answered decidedly—" at least not for bishops and doctors who let Menteith miscreants loose in society to marry whom they please."

The bishop winced.

" I am sorry to have to reprove you seriously," he recommenced, shaking his head. " But I feel that I should not be doing my duty if I neglected to point out to you the extremely reprehensible nature of your conduct, first in causing grievous distress of mind to Edith, in consequence of which partly she is now lying dangerously ill upstairs——"

Angelica stopped him by suddenly assuming a dignified position on her chair. She looked hard at him, and as she did so great tears came into her eyes, and ran down her cheeks. " If I have done Edith any injury," she exclaimed, " I shall never forgive myself."

" Well, well," said the bishop kindly——

" But do you think I was so much to blame?" Angelica demanded, interrupting him. " I only did what you and Mrs. Beale and everybody else did—took it for granted that she had married a decent man. But go on," said Angelica, throwing herself back in her chair, and folding her arms. " What else have I done ?"

" You have grievously injured a fellow-creature."

" Oh, ' fellow ' if you like, and ' creature ' too," said Angelica; " but the injury I did him was a piece of luck for which I expect to be congratulated."

" You took the sacred word of God," the bishop began——

" Because of the weight of it," Angelica interrupted again, " figuratively, too, it was most appropriate. I call it poetical justice, whichever way you look at it, and "—she burst into a sudden squall of rage—" if you nag me any more I'll throw Bibles about until there isn't a whole one in the house ! "

The bishop looked at her steadily. " I shall say no more," he observed very gently ; " but I beg of you to reflect." Then he opened the quarto Bible and began to read to himself. Angelica remained sitting opposite to him, looking moodily at the floor ; but now and then they stole furtive glances at each other, and every time the bishop looked at Angelica he shook his head.

" Things have gone wrong in the Sphere," slipped from Angelica at last.

"'The Sphere'?" said the bishop looking up. "What Sphere?"

"*The Woman's Sphere!*" Angelica answered solemnly, and then she told him her dream. It took her exactly an hour to relate it with such comments and elucidations as she deemed necessary, and the bishop heard her out. When she finished he was somewhat exhausted; but he said that he thought it a very remarkable dream.

"If you had been able to manage the Sphere, you see," Angelica concluded, "and to regulate the extent of it, you would have been able to make it a proper place for us to live in by this time."

"My dear child, you are talking nonsense!" the bishop exclaimed.

"Well, it may sound so to you at present," Angelica answered temperately; "but there is a small idea in my mind which won't be nonsense when it grows up." She was silent for a little after that, and then she ejaculated: "I shouldn't be surprised if that pestilence were Me!"

"Eh?" said the bishop.

"Did I speak?" said Angelica.

"Yes."

"Ah, then, that is because I am tired out. I shall go to bed. Don't, for the life of you, let anybody disturb me."

She got up and left the room, yawning desperately; and very soon afterward her aunts came to take her back to Morne; but the bishop obeyed her last injunction implicitly, and they were obliged to return without her.

The news that Edith had returned to the palace, bringing her little son for the first time, was soon known in the neighbourhood. The arrival of the boy was one of those events of life, originally destined to be a great joy, which soften the heart and make it tender. And very soon carriages came rolling up with ladies leaning forward in them all in a flutter of sympathy and interest, eager to offer their congratulations to the young mother, and to be introduced to the child. And meanwhile Mrs. Beale sat beside her daughter's bed, patting her slender white hand from time to time as it lay upon the coverlet, with that little gesture which had struck Angelica as being so piteous. Edith had not spoken for hours; but suddenly she exclaimed: "Evadne was right!"

Mrs. Beale rocked herself to and fro, and the tears gathered in her eyes and slowly trickled down her cheeks. "Edith, darling," she said at last with a great effort, "do you blame me?"

"Oh, no, mother! oh, no!" Edith cried, pressing her hand, and looking at her with a last flash of loving recognition. "The same thing may happen now to any mother—to any daughter—and *will* happen so long as we refuse to know and resist." A spasm of pain contracted her face. She pressed her mother's hand again gently, and closed her eyes.

Presently she laughed. "I am quite, quite mad!" she said. "Do you know what I have been doing? I've been murdering him! I've been creeping, creeping, with bare feet, to surprise him in his sleep; and I had a tiny knife—very sharp—and I felt for the artery"—she touched her neck—"and then stabbed quickly! and he awoke, and knew he must die—and cowered! and it was all a pleasure to me. Oh, yes! I am quite, quite mad!"

She did not notice the coming and going of people now, or anything that was done in her room that day. Only once when she heard a servant outside the door whisper: "For her ladyship," she asked what it was, and a silver salver was brought to her covered with visiting cards. She looked at one or two. "Kind messages," she said, "great names! and I am a great lady too, I suppose! I made a splendid match. And now I have a lovely little boy—the one thing wanting to complete my happiness. What numbers of girls must envy me! Ah! they don't know! But tell them—tell them that I'm quite, quite mad!"

Mrs. Beale was at last persuaded to go and rest, and Mrs. Orton Beg replaced her.

"I am glad you have come," said Edith. "I want to show you my lovely little son. Naturally I want to show him to everyone!" and she laughed.

Late in the evening, when the room was lighted up, Edith noticed her father and mother and Dr. Galbraith. Angelica was there too, but in the background.

"Oh-h!" Edith exclaimed with a sudden shriek, starting up in bed—"I want to kill—I want to kill *him*. I want to kill that monstrous child!"

Dr. Galbraith was in time to prevent her springing out of bed.

"I know I am mad," she moaned in a broken voice. "I am quite, quite mad! I never hurt a creature in my life—never thought an evil thought of anyone; why must I suffer so?

Father, my head." Again she started up. "Can't you—can't you save me?" she shrieked. "Father, my head! my head!"

Angelica stole away to her own room, put on her things, and walked back to Morne alone.

CHAPTER X.

ANGELICA had been baptized into the world of anguish. She had assisted at horrid mysteries of life and death, and the experience was likely to be warping.

She had fled from the palace, first, because she could not bear the place any longer, and secondly, because she felt imperatively that she must see Diavolo. He had been in bed and asleep for some time when she went to his room that night, and awoke him by flashing a light in his face. He was startled at first, but when he saw who it was, he remembered their last quarrel and the base way she had deserted him by going to stay at the palace, and he thought it due to his wounded heart to snap at her.

"What *do* you mean by disturbing me so late at night?" he drawled plaintively; "bringing in such a beastly lot of fresh air with you too. You make me shiver."

"Don't be a fool, Diavolo," Angelica answered. "You know you're delighted to see me. How nice you look with your hair all tousled! I wish my hair was fair like yours. Oh! I have such a lot to tell you."

"Get on then," he said, lying back on his broad white pillows resignedly; "or go away, and keep your confidences till to-morrow. If you would be so good as to kindly consult my inclinations, that is what I should ask," he added politely.

Angelica curled herself up on the end of his bed, and leant against the foot-rail. The room was large and lofty, and the only light in it was that of the candle which she still held in her hand. She had a walking jacket on over an evening dress, and a hat, but this she took off and threw on the floor.

"I've run away," she said. "I walked home all alone."

"What, up all that long dark hill!" he exclaimed, with interest, but without incredulity. The Heavenly Twins never lied to each other.

"Yes," she answered impressively, "and I cut across the pine woods, and the big black shadows fluttered about me like butterfly bogies, and I wasn't afraid.   I threw my arms about, and ran, and jumped, and *breathed!*   Oh!" she exclaimed, "after holding your breath for twenty-four hours, in a house full of gaslight and groans, you learn what it is to be able to breathe freely out under the stars in the blessed dark.   And there was a little crescent moon above the trees," she added.

Diavolo had opened his great gray eyes, and looked out over her head through the wall opposite, watching her with enthusiasm as she "cut across the pine woods."   "And how did you get in?" he asked.

"At the back," she answered.   They looked into each other's intelligent faces, and grinned.   "Everybody is in bed," she added, "and I'm half inclined to return to the palace, and come back to-morrow in the carriage properly."

"I shouldn't do that," said Diavolo, feeling that such a proceeding would be an inartistic anticlimax.   "And it's to-morrow now, I should think."   He raised himself on his elbow, and peered at the clock on the mantelpiece.

Angelica held up the candle.   "It's two," she said.   "What do you do when you first wake up in the morning?"

"Turn round and go to sleep again," Diavolo grunted.

"*I* always look at the clock," said Angelica.   "But I want to tell you.   You know after you said I was a cyclone in petticoats?"

Diavolo nodded.   "So you are," he remarked.

"Well, I *am*, then," Angelica retorted.   "Have it so, only don't interrupt me.   I can't think why I cared," she added upon reflection ; "it seems so little now, and such a long way off."

"Is it as far from the point as you are?" Diavolo courteously inquired.

"Ah, I'm coming to that!" she resumed, and then she graphically recounted her late painful experiences, including the bishop's charge to Sir Mosley Menteith, and poor Edith's last piteous appeal to heaven and earth for the relief which she was not to receive.

"And did she die?" Diavolo asked in an awestruck whisper.

Being less sturdy and more sensitive than Angelica, he was quite shaken by the bare recital of such suffering.

"Not while I was there," Angelica answered.   "I heard her as I came out.   She was calling on God then."

They were both silent for some moments after this,   Angel-

ica fixed her eyes on the candle, and Diavolo looked up to
the unanswering heaven, full of the vague wonderment which
asks Why ? Why ? Why ?

"There is no law, you see," Angelica resumed, "either to
protect us or avenge us. That is because men made the law for
themselves, and that is why women are fighting for the right
to make laws too."

"I'll help them !" Diavolo exclaimed.

"Will you?" said Angelica. "That's right ! Shake
hands ! "

Having solemnly ratified the compact, Angelica boldly
asserted that all the manly men were helping women now,
including Uncle Dawne and Dr. Galbraith.

Then she thought she would go to bed. Of course she had
flung the door wide open when she entered, and left it so, and happening to glance toward it now, it seemed to her that there was
a horrible peculiar kind of pitchy black darkness streaming in.

"O Diavolo !" she exclaimed, "I'm frightened ! I daren't
go alone !"

" *You* frightened ! " he jeered, " after dancing home alone in
the dark, through the pine woods too ! "

"There were only birds, beasts, and bogies there—pleasant
creatures," she said. "But here, behind those rows and rows
of closed doors, there will be ghosts of tortured women, and I
shall hear them shriek !"

Her terror communicated itself to Diavolo's quick imagination, and he glanced toward the door apprehensively. Then
he deliberately arose, put on his dressing gown and slippers,
and lit a candle, by which time his face was steadily set.
"Come," he said. "I'll see you safely to your room."

"Diavolo, you're a real gentleman !" Angelica protested,
"for I know you're in as big a fright as I am."

Diavolo drew himself up and led the way.

Their rooms were far apart, it having been deemed advisable
to separate them when they first came to the castle, at which
time there had been a curious delusion that distance would do
this. The first part of their progress that night was nervous
work, but they had not gone far before the new aspect which
familiar things took on by the light of their candles arrested
their attention.

"The light makes great-grandpapa wink," said Angelica
looking up at a portrait. "And Venus has put on a cloak."

"She's *wrapt in shadow*," said Diavolo poetically.

They were talking quite unconcernedly by this time, and in their usual somewhat loud tone of voice, fear of discovery not being one of their characteristics. They were bound to have awakened any light sleeper, but it so happened that they passed no occupied rooms but their Uncle Dawne's. He, however, being up, heard them, and opened his door on them suddenly. They both jumped.

"What are you two doing?" he said; "and why are you here at all, Angelica?"

"I didn't think it delicate to stay at the palace any longer under the circumstances," she answered glibly.

Lord Dawne was struck by the extreme propriety of this reply. "And may I ask *when* you returned?" he said.

"Yesterday," she answered, "and I've had nothing to eat since."

"Oh!" he observed. "And you've not had time to remove your walking jacket either?" He looked hard at her. "I should like very much to know how you got in," he said, shaking his head.

The Heavenly Twins looked at him affably.

"Well," he concluded, knowing better than to question them—"I suppose you know where to find food, if that is your object!"

They both grinned.

"Come along, Uncle Dawne, and we'll show you!" Angelica burst out sociably.

"Yes, *do!*" Diavolo entreated. "Come and revel!"

The Heavenly Twins never worked on any regular plan; their ideas always came to them as they went on.

Lord Dawne felt that this was really claiming a kinship with him, and a picture which presented itself to his mind's eye, of himself foraging for food in his father's castle with the Heavenly Twins in the small hours of the night, appealed to him. It was an opportunity not to be lost.

"Very well," he said, putting his hands in the pockets of the short velvet jacket he was wearing, and preparing to follow. The twins led the way, holding their candles aloft, and descending the stairs in step. But exactly what the mysteries were into which they initiated their uncle that night nobody knows. Only they were all very late for breakfast next morning, and when Lord Dawne saw his sisters, he listened in silence to such explanations of Angelica's reappearance at the castle as they were able to offer.

Angelica herself forgot she was not at home, and came down to breakfast yawning unconcernedly. The exclamation of surprise with which she was greeted took her aback at first. She had intended to send a carriage, early in the morning, for her maid Elizabeth, and to walk in herself with her hat on when it returned, as if she had come in it ; but as she only remembered this intention when Lady Fulda exclaimed "Why, Angelica, how did you come ? " she was obliged to have recourse to the simple truth, and after answering blandly : " 1 walked, auntie," she left the matter there for others to elucidate at their leisure if they chose to make inquiries.

But the accustomed trouble with the Heavenly Twins seemed insignificant at this time compared with other perplexities which were pending at the castle. The old duke had been very queer lately. He had " been dreaming and seeing things," as Diavolo explained to Angelica.

" Storms and what dreams, ye holy gods, what dreams ! "

Father Ricardo said they were miraculous temptations of the devil, the implication being that the poor old duke's soul was more specially worth wrangling for than those of less exalted sinners. The one dear wish of Father Ricardo's life was to be mixed up in something miraculous. He was too humble to expect anything to be revealed to himself personally, but he had great hopes of the saintly Lady Fulda ; and certainly, if concessions are to be wrung from the Infinite to the Finite by perfect holiness of life and mind, she should have obtained some. She had become deeply read in that kind of lore under Father Ricardo's direction, and had meditated so much about occurrences of the kind that it would not have surprised her if she had met " Our Lady " anywhere, bright light, blue cloak, supernatural beauty, indefinite draperies, lilies, sacred heart, and all. She had, in fact, thought too much about it, and was becoming somewhat hysterical, which raised Father Ricardo's hopes, for he was not a scientific man, and knew nothing of the natural history of the human being and of hysteria ; and, besides, by dint of long watching, fasting, and otherwise outraging what he believed to have been created in the image of God, viz., his own poor body, and also by the feverish fervour with which he entreated Heaven to vouchsafe them a revelation at Morne for the benefit of Holy Church, he was worn to a shadow, and had become somewhat hysterical himself. The twins had discovered him on his knees before the altar in the chapel at night, and had been much interested in the " vain repetitions" and other audible ejaculations which he was offering up with many contortions of his attenuated form.

"Isn't he enjoying himself?" Diavolo whispered.

"He must be in training to wrestle with the devil when they meet," Angelica surmised.

But all this was having a bad effect upon the old duke. In private, he and Lady Fulda and the priest talked of nothing but apparitions and supernatural occurrences generally. Lord Dawne had obtained a hint of what was going on from some chance observations of the Heavenly Twins, but until the day after Angelica's return from the palace neither his father nor sister had spoken to him on the subject.

That morning, however, he happened to go into the chapel to see how the colours were lasting in some decorative work which he had done there himself years before, and there he found his father standing in the aisle to the right of the altar near the door of the sacristy, gazing up fixedly at a particular panel in the dark oakwork which covered that portion of the wall.

"Anything wrong, father?" he said, going up to him.

"Dawne," the old duke replied in an undertone, touching his son's arm with the point of the forefinger of his left hand, and pointing up to the panel with the stick he held in his right: "Dawne, if it were not for what that panel conceals—" he ended by folding his hands on the top of his stick, looking down at the pavement, and shaking his head. "I saw it in a dream first," he resumed, looking up at the panel. "But now it appears during every service. It comes out. It stretches its baby hands to me. It sobs, it sighs, it begs, it prays; and sometimes it smiles, and then there are dimples about its innocent mouth."

Some disturbance of the atmosphere caused Lord Dawne to look round at this moment, although he had heard nothing, and he was startled to find his sister Fulda standing behind him, looking as awestruck as the duke.

"We must tear down that panel!" the old man exclaimed, becoming excited. "We must exorcise, and purify, and cleanse the house. It is that—that "—shaking his stick at the panel—" which hinders the Event! Bury it deep! bury it deep! give it the holy rites, and *then!*" His voice dropped. He muttered something inaudible, and walked feebly down the aisle.

Lady Fulda followed him out of the chapel, but presently she returned. Her brother was still standing as she had left him,

looking now at the pavement and now at the panel, and deep
in thought. His grave face lighted with tenderness as he turned
to meet her. She was very pale.

"I am afraid all this is too much for you, Fulda," he said
seriously.

"No. This is nothing," she answered. "Nothing—no
human excitement ever disturbs me. But, Dawne, I have seen
it myself ! "

"It ! What, Fulda ? "

"The Child—just as he describes it. It appears there "—
looking up at the panel—" and stretches out its little hands to
me smiling, but when I move to take it, it is gone ! "

"My dear Fulda," Lord Dawne replied, with a shiver which
he attributed to the chill of the chapel, "people who live in
such an atmosphere as you do are liable to *see things !* "

"It would ease my mind," she said, clasping her hands on
his shoulder, and laying her cheek upon them : "it would ease
my mind if that panel were removed. There is something
behind it."

"It must be solid masonry then," he answered, smiling ;
and, stepping up to the panel, he tapped it hard with his
knuckles ; but, contrary to his expectations, the sound it
emitted was somewhat hollow. Then he examined it carefully,
and discovered that it was not fitted into grooves as the other
panels were, but was held in its place by four screws, the heads
of which had been carefully concealed by putty, stained and
varnished to the color of the oak. "I will see about this at
once," he said.

The message from the palace that morning, sent by Mrs.
Orton Beg, had been : "Edith still lingers," and Lord Dawne
had intended to go there to see the bishop (in times of sickness and sorrow he was everywhere welcome) ; but now he
went with the further intention of finding Dr. Galbraith. In
this he was successful, and they had a long talk about the state
of affairs at the castle, and it was finally arranged that Dr.
Galbraith should dine there that evening and remain for the
night.

"That panel must be removed," he said, "and it should be
done with great ceremony. The best time would be midnight.
But leave all that to Father Ricardo, and only insist upon one
thing, and that is the presence of the Heavenly Twins."

"Are you meditating a *coup de théâtre ?* "

"No, not at all, ' Dr. Galbraith replied. "Only I am quite

sure that if there is any exorcism to be done, the Heavenly Twins will accomplish it better than any priest."

Lord Dawne, however, remained somewhat uncertain about the wisdom of this recommendation, but as Dr. Galbraith had always managed his father's foibles and other difficult matters at the castle with admirable tact and delicacy he gave in.

The twins themselves soon perceived that there was something in the air. During the day several strange priests arrived, all looking more or less important ; but they did not dine with the duke. The demeanour of the latter was portentously solemn ; Diavolo tried to take him out of himself, but was reproved for his levity ; and Father Ricardo and Lady Fulda went about with exalted expressions of countenance, and looking greatly in need of food and rest. Even in the early part of the evening nobody talked much, and as the hours dragged on slowly toward midnight, the silence in the castle became oppressive. The servants stole about on tiptoe, and in pairs, being nervous about going into the big empty rooms, and down the long shadowy corridors alone. There was, besides, a general inclination to glance about furtively, as the hush of anxious expectancy settled upon everybody. The twins felt it themselves, but they were everywhere all the same, and if any particular preparations had been made, it would have been at the risk of their discovering them. The night was sultry and very dark. Dr. Galbraith and Lord Dawne stood together, stirring their coffee, at an open window in the great drawing room.

"It is curiously still," said Lord Dawne, looking out. "It reminds me of the legend of Nature waiting breathless for the happy release of an imprisoned soul. I wonder how that poor child Edith is ! "

"I would give—I would give anything that anybody could name," Dr. Galbraith said slowly, "to be quite sure that she would pass into peace to-night."

"Ah, poor girl ! poor innocent girl ! " Lord Dawne ejaculated ; and then he said, as if speaking to himself : "How long, O Lord, how long ? We are so powerless ; we accomplish so little ; the great sum of suffering never seems lessened, do what we will ! "

They were silent for some time after that, each occupied with painful thoughts, and then Dr. Galbraith spoke with an effort to change the direction of them.

"A storm to-night would be most opportune," he said.

"But things of that kind never do happen opportunely," Lord Dawne rejoined. Just as he spoke, however, a brilliant flash of lightning lit up vividly the precipitous side of the hill and the whole valley beneath them for a moment.

"Let us hope it is a happy omen," said Dr. Galbraith.

Toward midnight, the various members of the household who were privileged to be present at the coming ceremony began to assemble in the chapel; but the very first to arrive found that the Heavenly Twins were before them, and had secured the best seats for seeing and hearing. The chapel was dim and even dark at the corners and at the farther end, there being no light except from the candles which were burning upon the altar. Four priests were kneeling before it at the rails, and a fifth came out of the sacristy presently, and passed in. It was Father Ricardo, and as he made the genuflection, it was seen that his face was irradiated by profound emotion. He remained on his knees before the altar for some moments, then he arose, and at the same instant the chapel glowed in every colour of the prism. It was merely the play of the lightning through the stained glass windows, but the unexpected effect, combined with the electricity in the atmosphere and the tension of expectancy, wrought upon the nerves of all present.

The Heavenly Twins snuggled up close to each other. Lady Fulda's lips began to move rapidly in fervent prayer. Angelica noticed this, and as she watched her aunt, her own lips began to move in imitation, either involuntarily or in order to see if she could work them as fast.

But now the attention of all present became riveted upon the priests. Father Ricardo descended the altar steps, and two of the others followed him into the sacristy. They returned in the same order, but Father Ricardo was carrying a basin of holy water and an aspergillus, with which he proceeded to sprinkle all present, murmuring some inaudible adjuration the while. One of the strange priests held an open book, and the other carried some common carpenter's tools. During this interval the lightning flashed again, and was seen to play about the chapel in fantastic figures before the black darkness engulfed it. A long irregular roll of distant thunder succeeded, and then, after a perceptible pause, there was a sound as of hundreds of little feet pattering upon the roof. They were the advanced guard of rain drops heralding the approaching storm, and halted instantly, while the air in the chapel became perceptibly colder, and Dr. Galbraith himself began to experience sensations which made him fear it would have been wiser if a less appropriate time had been chosen to lay the ghost.

The priest now approached the panel, upon one corner of which a ray of light from the altar fell obliquely. Father Ricardo sprinkled it liberally from where he stood on the ground, repeating some formula as he did so, and then mounted a small pair of steps which had been placed there for the purpose, and began to search for the screws. As he found them, he cut out the hard putty that concealed them with a knife which one of the priests had handed up to him for the purpose, and when he had accomplished this he exchanged the knife for a screwdriver, and endeavoured to turn the screws ; but this required more strength than his ill-treatment of his poor body had left in it, and he was obliged to relinquish the task to one of the other priests. The two who had hitherto knelt at the altar now joined the group in front of the panel. All five looked unhealthy and frightened, but the one who next ascended the steps made a brave effort, and began to remove the screws. He was a muscular man, but it was hard work, requiring his full strength ; and those present held their breath, and anxiously watched him straining every sinew. And meanwhile the storm gathered overhead, the lightning and thunder flashed and crashed almost simultaneously, and the rain fell in torrents.

Having removed the screws, the priest descended the steps, which he pushed on one side, and inserting the screwdriver into a crevice, prised the panel outward. It resisted for some time, then, suddenly yielding, fell forward on his head, and crashed noisily to the ground. All present started and stared. The panel had concealed an aperture, a small niche rudely made by simply removing some of the masonry. It was long and low, and there lay in it what was unmistakably the body of a young child fully dressed. The priests fell back, Lady Fulda's parted lips became set in the act of uttering a word, the duke groaned aloud, while an expression of not being able to believe their own eyes settled upon the countenances of Lord Dawne, Dr. Galbraith, and the tutor, Mr. Ellis.

After the fall of the panel there was a pause, during which the very storm seemed to wait in suspense. Nobody knew what to do next. But before they had recovered themselves, Angelica broke the silence at the top of her voice.

"You pushed me !" she angrily exclaimed.

"I did *not* !" Diavolo retorted.

"You did !"

"I didn't!"

Smack! And Miss Hamilton-Wells stood trembling with rage in the aisle. Then she darted toward the aperture. The priests fell back. "I believe it's all a trick," she said, reaching up and seizing the child by its petticoats. Lady Fulda uttered an exclamation: the duke stood up, Angelica tugged the figure out of the niche, looked at it, and then held it to the light.

It was a huge wax baby-doll, considerably battered, which had once been a favourite of her own. Diavolo came out of his seat, hugging himself, and bursting in eloquent silence.

Father Ricardo wiped the perspiration from his face, Lord Dawne bit his under lip, Lady Fulda gathered herself up from her knees, and stood helpless. Everybody looked foolish, including the duke, whose eyebrows contracted nervously; then suddenly that treacherous memory of his landed him back in the old days. "By Jove!" he exclaimed aloud, "I'm more like Angelica, and less of a damned fool than I thought!"

"Come, Diavolo! this is no place for us!" Angelica cried. She seized his hand, and they both darted into the sacristy.

There was a bang, a scuffle, and then a dull thud; but the first to follow was only in time to see eight finger-tips clinging for a moment outside to the ledge of one of the narrow windows, which was open.

"They've jumped out!" "It's fourteen feet!" "Hush, listen!"

And then the congregation scattered hurriedly from the sacred precincts, leaving the candles burning on the altar, the doll lying on the pavement, the gaping niche and the fallen panel to bear witness to some of the incredible phases through which the human race passes on its way from incomprehensible nothingness to the illimitable unknown.

CHAPTER XI.

THE Heavenly Twins had disappeared for the night. Those who ran round to the outside wall of the sacristy to look for them found only a shred of Angelica's gown hanging on a shrub. Their footsteps could be followed cutting across the grass of a soppy lawn, but beyond that was a walk of hard asphalt, and there all trace of them was lost. But Lady Fulda said they must be found, and brought back; and sleepy servants were accordingly aroused and set to search the grounds, while grooms were sent off on horseback to scour the lanes. The storm was still muttering in the distance, but above Morne the sky had cleared, and the crescent moon shone out to facilitate the search. It was quite fruitless, however. From Morne to Morningquest the messengers went, passing backward and forward from the castle the whole night long. Lady Fulda never closed her eyes, and when the party assembled at breakfast next morning they were all suffering from want of sleep.

The duke, Lord Dawne, Dr. Galbraith, Mr. Ellis, Father Ricardo and the four strange priests were at table.

"What *can* have become of those children?" Lady Fulda was exclaiming for the hundredth time, when the door opened, and the twins themselves appeared hand in hand, smiling affably.

They looked as fresh as usual, and began to perform their morning salutations with their habitual self-possession.

"Where have you been?" the duke asked sternly.

"In bed, of course," Angelica answered—"till we got up, at least. Where else should we be?" She looked round in innocent inquiry.

"We just ran round to the garden door, you know," Diavolo explained, "and went to bed. You couldn't expect us to stay out on a dripping night like that!"

Lord Dawne afterward expressed the feeling of the whole household when he declared: "Well, it never did and it never would have occurred to me to look for them in their own rooms."

He remained behind with them in the breakfast room that morning when the others withdrew.

"I suppose we shall be sent for directly," said Angelica resignedly.

Diavolo grinned.

"I say, how did you feel last night when it was all going on?" she inquired.

"Awfully nice," he rejoined. "I had little warm shivers all over me."

"So had I," she said, "like small electric shocks; and I believed in the ghost and everything. I expect that is why that kind of supernatural business is kept up, because it makes people feel creepy and nice. You can't get the same sensation in any other way, and I dare say there are lots of people who wouldn't like to lose a whole set of sensations. I should think they're the kind of people who collect the remains of a language to save it when it begins to die out."

"I should say those were intelligent people," her uncle observed. Angelica looked at him doubtfully.

"Well, at any rate, *I* should like to believe in ghosts," said Diavolo.

"So should I," said Angelica, "in fun, you know; and I was thinking so last night; but then I could not help noticing what a fool Aunt Fulda was making of herself, and grandpapa looked such a precious old idiot too. They weren't enjoying it a bit. You were the only one of the family, Uncle Dawne, who believed and looked dignified."

"Who told you I believed?" he asked.

"Well, I'm not sure that you did," Angelica answered. "But at all events, your demeanour was respectful—hence the dignity, perhaps!"

"If yours were a little more respectful you would gain in dignity too, I imagine," Diavolo observed.

Angelica boxed his ears promptly, whereupon her uncle took her to task with unusual severity for him : "You are quite grown up now," he said. "You talk like a mature woman, and act like a badly brought up child of ten. You are always doing something ridiculous too. I should be ashamed to have you at my house."

Angelica looked amazed. "Well, it is your fault as much as anybody's," she burst out when she had recovered herself. "Why don't you make me something of a life? You can't expect me to go on like this forever—getting up in the morning, riding, driving, lessons, dressing, and bed. It's the life of a lapdog."

She got up, and going to one of the windows, which was open, leant out. Dawne and Diavolo followed her. As the former approached, she turned and looked him full in the face for an answer.

"You will marry eventually——" he began.

"Like poor Edith?" she suggested. Dawne compressed his lips. "That was her ideal," Angelica proceeded—"her own home and husband and family, someone to love and trust and look up to. She told me all about it at Fountain Towers under the influence of indignation and strong tea. And she was *an exquisite womanly creature!* No, thank you! It isn't safe to be an *an exquisite womanly creature* in this rotten world.

The most useful kind of heart for a woman is one hard enough to crack nuts with. Nobody could wring it then."

"You would lose all finer feeling——" Lord Dawne began.

"Including the heartache itself," she supplemented.

"But what *do* you want?" he asked.

"An object," she answered. "Something! something! something beyond the mere getting up in the morning and going to bed at night, with an interval of exercise between. I want to do something for somebody!"

Lord Dawne raised his eyebrows slightly. He had no idea that such a notion had ever entered her head.

At this point, a servant was sent by his Grace to request the twins to be so good as to go to him in the library at once.

"It is the inevitable inquiry," Angelica said resignedly. "Come with us, uncle, *do*," she coaxed. "It is sure to be fun!"

Lord Dawne consented.

On the way, Diavolo remarked ambiguously: "But I don't understand yet how there came to be a ghost as well!"

The inquiry led to nothing. The Heavenly Twins had determined not to incriminate themselves, and they refused to answer a question. They stood together, drawn up in line, with their hands behind their backs; changed from one leg to the other when they were tired, and looked exceedingly bored; but they would no. speak.

The duke stormed, Lady Fulda entreated, Father Ricardo prayed, even Lord Dawne begged them not to be obstinate; but it was all in vain, and their grandfather, losing all patience, ordered them out of the room at last.

As they retired, Diavolo asked Father Ricardo if he were thinking of thumbscrews.

"I feel quite sure that Angelica did not know the doll was there," Lord Dawne said when the twins had gone. "I fancy it was a trick Diavolo had played her."

Nobody mentioned the ghost again. It was felt to be a delicate subject. Lady Fulda was made to take rest and a tonic, the duke was rigidly dieted, and Father Ricardo was sent away for change of air. But the twins never ceased from troubling. As soon as the duke's temper was restored, they consulted the party collectively at afternoon tea in the oriel room on the subject of Angelica's dissatisfaction. Diavolo affected to share it, but that was only by way of being agreeable, as he inadvertently betrayed.

"I suppose I shall have to do something myself," he drawled in his lazy way.

"I should think marriage is the best profession for you!" said Angelica scornfully.

"Thank you. I will consider the question," Diavolo answered.

He was lying on the floor in his habitual attitude, with his head on the windowsill, beaming about him blandly.

"The army is the only possible profession for a gentleman in your position," the duke observed.

"Ah! that would not meet my views at present," Diavolo rejoined. "I am advised that the army is not a career for a man. It is a career for a machine—for a machine with a talent for converting other men into machines, and I haven't the talent. I suppose, if Uncle Dawne *won't* marry, I shall be obliged to go into the House of Lords eventually; but, in the meantime, I should like to be doing some good in the world."

"You might go into Parliament," his uncle suggested.

"Ah, no!" Diavolo answered seriously. "I should never dream of undertaking any of the actual work of the world while there are plenty of good women to do it for me. My modest idea was to be a musician, or philanthropic lecturer, or artist of some kind—something that gives pleasure, you know, and the proceeds to be devoted to the indigent."

"May I ask if you belong to the peace party?" said the duke.

"I am a peace party myself," Diavolo answered. "Anybody who has lived as long with Angelica as I have would be that— if he were not a party in pieces."

"I admire your wit!" said Angelica sarcastically.

Diavolo bestowed a grateful smile upon her.

"But everything is easy enough for a man of intellect," she went on, "whatever his position. It is *our* powers that are wasted."

"Vanity! vanity!" said Lady Fulda. "Why do you suppose that your abilities are superior?"

"I can prove that they are!" Angelica answered hotly. Then suddenly her spirits went up, and she began to be sociable.

For a few days after this the Heavenly Twins appeared to be very busy. They both wrote a great deal, and also practised regularly on their violins and the piano; and they made some mysterious expeditions, slipping away unattended into Morningquest. It was suspected that they had something serious on

hand, but Father Ricardo being away, the spy-system was suspended, so nobody knew. One morning, however, big placards,
which had been printed in London, appeared on every hoarding
in Morningquest, announcing in the largest type that Miss
Hamilton-Wells and Mr. Theodore Hamilton-Wells would
give an entertainment in the Theatre for the benefit of certain
of the city charities, which were specified. The programme
opened with music, which was to be followed by a speech from
Mr. Theodore Hamilton-Wells, and to conclude with a mono-
logue, entitled " The Condemned Cell," to be delivered by Miss
Hamilton-Wells, who had written it specially for the occasion.
This was the news which greeted Mr. Hamilton-Wells and
Lady Adeline upon their return from their voyage round the
world; and, like everybody else, when they first saw the placard,
which was as they drove from the station through Morningquest
to the castle, they exclaimed : " Who on earth is Mr. *Theodore
Hamilton-Wells ?* "

The old duke was rather taken with the idea of the entertainment. It was something quite in the manner of his youth,
and if it had not been for the inopportune arrival of his son-
in-law and daughter, the Heavenly Twins would probably have
carried out their programme under his distinguished patronage.
Dr. Galbraith was all in favour of letting them do it, Lord
Dawne was neutral; but Mr. Hamilton-Wells objected. He
caused the announcement to be cancelled, and handsomely
indemnified the various charities named to be recipients of the
possible proceeds.

Diavolo did not much mind. He was prepared to do all
that Angelica required of him, but when the necessity was
removed he acknowledged that it would have been rather a
bore, and afterward spoke disrespectfully of the whole project
as " The Condemned Sell."

Angelica raged.

But the energy which Mr. Hamilton-Wells had collected during his travels was not yet expended. He summoned a family
council at Morne to sit upon the twins, and having tried them
in their absence they were sent for to be sentenced without the
option of appeal. Angelica was to be presented at Court and
otherwise " brought out " in proper splendour immediately;
while, with a view to going into the Guards eventually, Diavolo
was to be sent to Sandhurst, as soon as he had passed the
necessary examinations, about which Mr. Ellis said there would
be no difficulty *if Diavolo chose.*

Diavolo shrugged his shoulders, and said that *he* didn't mind.

Angelica said nothing, but her brow contracted. Diavolo's indifference was putting an end to everything. It was not that she had any actual objection to going to Court and coming out, but only to the way in which the arrangement had been made—to the coercion in fact. She was too shrewd, however, not to perceive that, in consequence of Diavolo's attitude, rebellion on her part would be both undignified and ineffectual. So she held her peace, and went to walk off her irritation in the grounds alone; and there she encountered her fast friend of many years' standing, Mr. Kilroy of Ilverthorpe, who was just riding in to lunch at the castle. When he saw her he dismounted, and Angelica snatched the whip from his hand, and clenching her teeth gave the horse a vicious slash with it, which set him off at a gallop into the woods.

Mr. Kilroy let him go, but he was silent for some seconds, and then he asked her in his peculiarly kindly way: "What is the matter, Angelica?"

"Marry me!" said Angelica, stamping her foot at him— "Marry me, *and let me do as I like.*"

CHAPTER XII.

EVADNE spent eighteen months in Malta without going from the island for a change, but at the end of her second cold season she went to Switzerland with the Malcomsons and Sillingers, and Colonel Colquhoun went on leave at the same time alone to some place which he vaguely described as "The Continent."

When they met again, Evadne noticed a change in him, and she feared it was a change for the worse. He was out of health, out of temper, and depressed.

He had spent most of his leave at Monte Carlo, but he did not say so at first; he was waiting for her to question him. Had she done so he would have said something snappy about feminine curiosity; as she did not do so, he lost his temper, went off to the mess, and drank too much.

It is a terrible thing for a man to be brought into constant association with a woman who never does anything—in a small way—that he can carp at, or says a word he can contradict. She robs him of all his most cherished illusions; she shakes his confidence in his own infallible strength, discernment, knowledge, judgment, and superiority generally ; she outrages his prejudices on the subject of what a woman ought to be, and leaves him nothing with which to compare himself to his own advantage.   This is the miserable state to which Evadne was rapidly reducing poor Colonel Colquhoun—not, certainly, of malice-prepense, but with the best intentions. He did not like her opinions, therefore she ceased to express opinions in his presence.   He took exception to many of her observations, and so she let the words, " I think," fall out of her vocabulary, and confined her talk to a clear narrative of occurrences, un-- interrupted by comments.   It was an art which she had to acquire, for she had no natural aptitude for it, her faculty of observation having hitherto served as an instrument with which she could extract lessons from life ; a lens used for the pur- pose of collecting data on exact scientific principles as matter from which to draw conclusions ; but with practice she became an adept in the art of describing the one while at the same time withholding the other, so that her conversation interested Colonel Colquhoun without, however, giving him anything to cavil at.   It was like a dish exactly suited to his taste, but delicate to insipidity because his palate was hardened to pepper.   When she returned from Switzerland she gave him details of her own doings which were interesting enough to take him out of himself, until one day, when, unfortunately, it occurred to him that she was making an effort to entertain him, and he determined that he would *not* be entertained— like a child, indeed ! She might be a deuced clever woman and all that, but he wasn't going to have those feminine airs of superiority ; so he snubbed her into silence, and having suc- ceeded, he became exceedingly annoyed because she would not talk.   It was opposition he wanted, not acquiescence, but she was not clever enough with all her cleverness, this straight- forward nineteenth century young woman, to understand such subtleties. She had always heard that the contrariness of women was a cause of provocation, and she could never have been made to comprehend that the removal of the cause would be even more provoking than the contrariness.   The great endeavour of her life had been to cultivate or acquire the qualities in which she understood that women are wanting, and when she succeeded she expected to please ; but she found Colonel Colquhoun as "peculiar " on the subject as her father had been when she proved that, although of the imbecile sex, she could do arithmetic. Colonel Colquhoun waited a week to snap at her for asking him how he had spent his leave, but he was obliged at last to give up all hope of being questioned ; and then he felt himself aggrieved. She certainly took no interest in him whatever, he reflected ; she didn't care a rap if he went to the dogs altogether—in fact, she would probably be rather glad, because then she would be free. She would waste a world of attention and care upon any dirty little child she picked up in the street, but for him she had neither thought nor sympathy. Clearly she wanted to get rid of him ; and she should get rid of him. He felt he was going to the bad ; he *would* go to the bad ; it was all her fault, and she should know it. He had treated her with every possible consideration ; she had never had the slightest cause for complaint. He had even stuck up for her against his own interests with her old ass of a father—and, by Jove ! while she was treating him, Colonel Colquhoun, commanding a crack corps, and one of the smartest officers in her Majesty's service, with studied indifference, she was thinking affectionately of the same dear old pompous portly papa, to whom, in fact, she had never borne the slightest ill-will, Colonel Colquhoun was sure, although he had done her the injury of allowing her to marry herself to the kind of man whom it was against her principles even to countenance.

But at this point his irritation overflowed. He could contain himself no longer.

"Do you know where I spent most of my leave ?" he asked one morning at breakfast.

"No," Evadne answered innocently.

"At Monte Carlo," he said, with emphasis.

" I hope you enjoyed it. I have always heard it is a very beautiful place," she responded tranquilly.

"It's effect on my exchequer has not been beautiful," he observed grimly.

"Indeed," she answered. "Is it so expensive ?"

"Gambling is, when you lose," he declared.

"Ah, yes. I forgot the tables at Monte Carlo," she remarked quite cheerfully. "I suppose you can lose a great deal there."

"You can lose all you possess."

"Well, yes—of course you could if you liked ; but I am quite sure you would never do anything so stupid."

He looked at her curiously : "You don't disapprove of gambling, then ?" he asked.

"I? Oh—of course, I disapprove. But then you see I have no taste for it "—this was apologetically said to signify that she did not in the least mean to sit in judgment upon him.

"You have a fine taste for driving people to such extremities, then," he asserted.

She looked at him inquiringly.

"What I mean is this," he explained : "that if I could have been with you, I should not have gone to Monte Carlo."

Evadne kept her countenance—with some difficulty ; for just as Colonel Colquhoun spoke she recollected a conversation they had had at breakfast one morning under precisely similar circumstances, that is to say, each in their accustomed place and temper, she placidly content, he politely striving to bottle up the chronic form of irritation from which he suffered at that time of the day so as to keep it nice and hot for the benefit of his officers and men ; for Colonel Colquhoun in the presence of a lady was one person, but Colonel Colquhoun in his own orderly room or on parade was quite another. While in barracks he was in the habit of swearing with the same ease and as unaffectedly as he made the responses in church. He probably did it from a sense of duty, because he had been brought up in that school of colonel, and in the course of years would naturally come to consider that a volley of oaths on parade, although not laid down in the "Drill Book," was as much a part of his profession of arms as "Good Lord, deliver us!" is of the church service. At all events, he did both punctually at the right time and place, and never mixed his week-day oaths with his Sunday responses, which was creditable. In fact, he seemed to have the power of changing his frame of mind completely for the different occasions, and would be prepared in advance, as was evident from the fact that if a glove went wrong just as he was starting for church, he would send up for another pair amiably ; but if a similar accident happened when he was on his way to parade, he would swear at his man till he surprised him—the man not being a soldier servant.

But what very nearly made Evadne smile was the distinct recollection she had of having asked him earnestly to join her party in Switzerland when he went on leave, and of his answering "No," he should not care about that, and suggesting that she should meet him at Monaco instead. She fancied he must have a bad memory, but of course she said nothing ;

what is the use of saying anything ? She thought, however, that had she been under his orders, the invitation to go to Monaco would have been a command, and the present implied reproach a direct accusation.

She was most anxious that he should understand perfectly that she quite shrank from interfering with him in any way.

One night—not knowing if he were at home or not—she had occasion to go downstairs for a book she had forgotten. There was no noise in the house, and consequently when she opened the drawing room door she was startled to find that the room was brilliantly lighted, and that there was a party assembled there, consisting of three strange ladies, loud in appearance, one or two men she knew, and some she had not seen before. The majority were seated at a card-table playing, while the rest stood round looking on : and they must have reached a momentous point in the game, for Evadne had not heard a sound to warn her of their presence before she saw them.

Colonel Colquhoun was one of those looking on at the game, and one of the first to see her. He changed countenance, and came forward hastily, conscious of the strange contrast she presented to those women, flushed with wine and horrid excitement, gambling at the table, as she stood there, rooted to the spot with surprise, in her gold-embroidered, ivory-white draperies, with a half-inquiring, half-bewildered look on her sweet grave face. It was a vision of holiness breaking in upon a scene of sin, and his one thought was to get her away. There was always that saving grace of the fallen angel about him, he never depreciated what he had lost, but sometimes sighed for it sorrowfully.

"I beg your pardon for this intrusion," Evadne said, looking at him pointedly so as to ignore the rest of the party. " I did not even know that you were at home. I had forgotten a book and came for it. Will you kindly give it to me ? It is called "— she hesitated. " But it does not matter," she added quickly. " I will read something else. Good-night ! " and she turned, smiling, without seeming to have seen anyone but Colonel Colquhoun, and calmly swept from the room.

" St. Monica the Complacent, I should say," one of the men suggested.

"Or Vengeance smiling with murder in her mind," said another.

" No, a saint for certain," jeered one of the women.

" Why not say an angel at once ? " cried another.

" I shouldn't have thought Colquhoun could keep either upon the premises," laughed the third.

" The lady you are pleased to criticise is my wife, gentlemen," said Colonel Colquhoun, lashing out at them suddenly, his face blazing with rage.

The women tried not to be abashed ; the men apologised ; but the game was over for that night, and the party broke up abruptly.

When they had gone, Colonel Colquhoun looked about for Evadne's book, and found it—not a difficult matter, for she had a bad habit of leaving the book she was reading open and face downward on any piece of furniture not intended to hold books, by preference a chair where somebody might sit down upon it. This one happened to be upon the piano stool. Colonel Colquhoun glanced at the title as he picked it up, and reading " A Vision of Sin," understood why she had shrunk from naming it. He appreciated her delicacy, but he feared the discernment which had shown her the necessity for it, and he determined to disarm her resentment next day by making her a proper apology at once.

He went down late to breakfast, expecting black looks at least, and was surprised to find her calm and equable as usual, and busy, keeping his breakfast hot for him.

" I wish to apologise to you for the scene you witnessed last night," he began ceremoniously.

" I think I owe *you* an apology for taking you unawares like that," she interrupted cheerfully, giving her best attention to a very full cup of coffee she was carefully carrying round the table to him. " But I hope you understand it was an accident."

" I quite understood," he answered sullenly. " But I want to explain that those people were also here by accident—at least I was not altogether responsible for their presence. They were a party from one of the yachts in the harbour. I met them here at the door, just as I was coming in last night, and they forced themselves in uninvited. I hope you believe that I would not willingly bring anyone to the house whom I could not introduce to you."

" Oh, I quite believe it," she answered cordially. " You are always most kind, most considerate. But I fear," she added with concern, " that my being here must inconvenience you at times. Pray, pray, do not let that be the case. I should regret it infinitely if you did."

When Evadne left Colonel Colquhoun he threw himself into a chair, and sat, chin on chest, hands in pockets, legs stretched out before him, giving way to a fit of deep disgust. He had always had a poor opinion of women, but now he began to despair of them altogether. "And this comes of letting them have their own way, and educating them," he reflected. "The first thing they do when they begin to know anything is to turn round upon us, and say we aren't good enough. And, by Jove! if we aren't, isn't it their fault? Isn't it their business to keep us right? When a fellow's had too good a time in his youth and suffered for it, what is to become of him if he can't find some innocent girl to believe in him and marry him? But there soon won't be any innocent girls. Here am I now, a most utter bad lot, and Evadne knows it, and what does she do? apologizes for appearing at an inopportune time! Now, Beston's wife would have brought the house about his ears if she'd caught him with that precious party I had here last night; and that's what a woman ought to do. She ought to *care.* She ought to be jealous, and cry her eyes out. She ought to go down on her knees and take some trouble to save a fellow's soul,"—it may be mentioned, by the way, that if Evadne *had* done so, Colonel Colquhoun would certainly have sworn at her "for meddling with things she'd no business to know anything about"; it was, however, not what he *would* but what she *should* have done that he was considering just then. "That's the proper thing to do," he concluded; "and I don't see what's to be gained by this *cursed* cold-blooded indifference."

Articulation ceased here because the startling theory that a vicious dissipated man is not a fallen angel easily picked up, but a frightful source of crime and disease, recurred to him, with the charitable suggestion that a repentant woman of his own class would be the proper person to reform him; ideas which settled upon his soul and silenced him, being full-fraught for him with the cruel certainty that the end of "all *true* womanliness" is at hand.

CHAPTER XIII.

COLONEL COLQUHOUN'S first interest in Evadne lasted longer than might have been expected, but the pleasure of hanging about her palled on him at last, and then he fell off in his kind attentions. This did not happen, however, as soon as it would have done by many months, had their relations been other than they were. It began in the usual way. Little acts to which she had become accustomed were omitted, resumed again, and once more omitted, intermittently, then finally allowed to drop altogether. When the change had set in for certain, Evadne regretted it. The kindly feeling for each other which had come to exist between them was largely due to her appreciation of the numberless little attentions which it had pleased him to pay her at first; they had not palled upon her, and she missed them—not as a wife would have done, however, and that she knew; so that when the fact that there *was* to be a falling off became apparent, she found in it yet another cause for self-congratulation, and one that was great enough to remove all sting from the regret. What she was prepared to resent, however, was any renewal of the gush after it had once ceased; she required to be held in higher estimation than a toy which could be dropped and taken up again upon occasion—and Colonel Colquhoun gave her an opportunity, and, what was worse, provoked her into saying so, to her intense mortification when she came to reflect.

There was to be a ball at the palace one night, a grand affair, given in honour of that same fat foreign prince who had stayed with her people at Fraylingay, just before she came out, and had been struck by the promise of her appearance. In the early days of their acquaintance, Colonel Colquhoun had given her some very beautiful antique ornaments of Egyptian design, and she determined to wear them on this occasion for the first time, but when she came to try them with a modern ball-dress, she found that they made the latter look detestably vulgar. She therefore determined to design a costume, or to adapt one, which should be more in keeping with the artistic beauty of her jewels; and this idea, with the help of an excellent maid, she managed to carry out to perfection—which, by the way, was the accident that led her finally to adopt a distinctive style of dress, always a dangerous experiment, but in her case, fortunately, so admirably successful, that it was never remarked upon as strange by people of taste; only as appropriate.

Colonel Colquhoun dined at mess on the night of the ball, and did not trouble himself to come back to escort her. He said he would meet her at the palace, and if he missed her in the crowd there were sure to be plenty of other men only too glad to offer her an arm. He had been most particular never to allow her to go anywhere alone at first—rather inconveniently so sometimes, but that she had endured. She was reflecting upon the change as she sat at her solitary dinner that evening, and she concluded by cheerfully assuring herself that she really was beginning to feel quite as if she were married. But, afterward, when she found herself in the drawing room it seemed big and bare, and all the more so for being brilliantly lighted; and suddenly she felt herself a very little body all alone. There was no bitterness in the feeling, however, because there was no one neglecting her whose duty it was to keep her heart up; but it threatened to grow upon her all the same, and in order to distract herself she went downstairs to choose a bouquet. She had several sent her for every occasion, and they were always arranged on a table in the hall so that she might take the one that pleased her best as she went out. There were more than usual this evening. There was one from the Grand Duke, which she put aside. There was one from Colonel Colquhoun; he always ordered them by the dozen for the different ladies of his acquaintance. She picked it up and looked at it. It was beautiful in its way, but sent at the florist's discretion, not chosen to suit her gown, and it did not suit it, so that she could not have used it in any case; yet she put it down with a sigh. The next was of yellow roses, violets, and maidenhair fern, very sweet: "With Lord Groome's compliments," she read on the card that was tied to it. "He is back then, I suppose," she thought. "Funny old man! Very sorry, but you won't do." The next was from one of the survivals, a man she loathed. She thought it an impertinence for him to have sent her flowers at all, and she threw them under the table. The rest she took up one after the other, reading the cards attached, and admiring or disapproving of the different combinations without gratitude or sentiment; she knew that self-interest prompted all of the offerings that were not merely sent just because it was the right thing to do. There was one unconventional bunch, however, that caught her eye. It was a mere handful of scarlet flowers tied loosely together with ribbons of their own colour and the same tint of green as their leaves. It was from a young subaltern in the regiment, a boy whom she had noticed first because he was the same age and somewhat resembled her brother Bertram; and had grown to like afterward for himself. His flowers were the first to arouse her to any expression of pleasure. The arrangement was new at the time, but it has since become common enough.

"He has done that for me himself," she thought. "The

boy respects me ; I shall wear his flowers. They are beautiful too," she added, holding them off at arm's length to admire them—"the most beautiful of them all."

Almost immediately after she returned to the drawing room Mr. Price was shown in. He was the person of all others at that moment in Malta whom she would most have liked to see could she have chosen, and her face brightened at once when he entered.

" I have been dining with your husband's regiment to-night," he explained, "and I found that he could not come back for you to take you to the ball, and that therefore you would have to go alone ; and so I ventured to come myself and offer you my escort."

" Ah, how good you are," Evadne cried, feeling fully for the first time how much she had in heart been dreading the ordeal of having perhaps to enter the ball room alone.

The old gentleman surveyed her some seconds in silence.

" That's original," he said at last, with several nods, approvingly. " And that is a glorious piece of colour you have in your hand."

" Is it not ? " she said. " More beautiful, I think, than all my jewels."

" Yes," he agreed. " The flowers are the finishing touch."

The ball had begun when Evadne arrived, and the first person she encountered was the Grand Duke, who begged for a dance and took her to the ball room. A dance was just over, however, when they entered ; the great room was pretty clear, and the prince led her toward the further end where their hostess was sitting. There also was Colonel Colquhoun and and some other men, with Mrs. Guthrie Brimston. He had forgotten Evadne for the moment, and she was so transformed by the beautiful lines of her dress that he had looked at her hard and admiringly before he recognized her.

" Who's the lady with the Grand Duke ? " Major Livingston exclaimed.

" Someone with a figure, by Jove ! " said old Lord Groome.

" Loyal Egypt herself ! " said Mrs. Guthrie Brimston, always apt at analogy.

" Why—it's Evadne," said Colonel Colquhoun.

" Didn't know his own wife, by Jove ! " Lord Groome exclaimed.

" Well, I hope I may be pardoned at that distance," rejoined Colonel Colquhoun, confused.

" Royal Egypt is more audacious than ever," Mrs. Guthrie Brimston observed. " This is a new departure. The reign of ideas is over, I fancy, and a season of social success has begun."

Evadne danced till daylight, unconscious of the sensation she had made, and rose next morning fresh for the usual occupations of the day ; but her success of the night before had so enhanced her value in Colonel Colquhoun's estimation that he was inclined to be effusive. He returned to lunch, and hung about her the whole afternoon, much to her inconvenience, because he had not been included in her arrangements for some months now, and she could not easily alter them all at once just to humour a whim of his. But wherefore the whim? A very little reflection explained it. Looks and tones, and words of her partners of the previous night, not heeded at the time, recurred to her now, and made her thoughtful. But she could not feel flattered, for it was obviously not her whom Colonel Colquhoun was worshipping, it was success ; and the perception of this truth suggested a possible parallel which made her shudder. It was a terrible glimpse of what might have been, what certainly *would* have been, had not the dear Lord vouchsafed her the precious knowledge which had preserved her from the ultimate degradation and the insult which such an endeavour as that of a woman she had in her mind, to win back a wandering husband, would have resulted in. "*I* do not care," was her happy thought when she began to see less of Colonel Colquhoun ; " but a wife would feel differently, and it would have been just the same had I been his wife."

He was not surprised to find her submit to his extra attentions in silence that afternoon, because that was her way, but he found her looking at him once or twice with an expression of deep thought in her eyes which provoked him at last to ask what it was all about. " I was thinking," she answered, " of that painful incident in ' La Femme de Trente-ans ' where Julie so far forgot her self-respect as to try to re-awaken her husband's admiration for her by displaying her superior accomplishments at the house of that low woman Mme. de Sèricy. You remember she made quite a sensation by her singing : ' Et son mari, réveillé par le rôle qu'elle venait de jouer, voulut l'honorer d'une fantaisie, et la prit en goût, comme il eût fait d'une actrice.' I was thinking, when she became aware of what she had done, of the degradation of the position in which she had placed herself, how natural it was that she should depise herself, cursing marriage which had brought her to such a pass, and wishing herself dead."

Colonel Colquhoun became moody upon this : " My having stayed at home with you this afternoon suggests a parallel, I suppose, after your success of last night ?" he inquired. " And you have been congratulating yourself all day," he proceeded, summing up judicially, " upon having escaped the degradation of being the wife *de facto* of a man whose admiration for you could cool—under any circumstances ; and be revived again by a vulgar success in society ? "

She was silent, and he got up and walked out of the house. From where she sat she saw him go, twirling his blond moustache with one hand, and viciously flipping at the flowers as he passed with the stick he carried in the other ; a fine, soldier-like man in appearance certainly, and not wanting in intelligence since he could comprehend her so exactly ; but, oh, how oppressive when in an admiring mood ! This was her first feeling when she got rid of him ; but a better frame of mind supervened, and then she suffered some mortification for having weakly allowed herself to be betrayed into speaking so plainly. Yet it proved in the long run to have been the kindest thing she could have done, for Colonel Colquhoun was enlightened at last, and they were both the better for the understanding.

But the house seemed full of him still after he had gone that day, and she therefore put on her things, and, hurrying out into the fresh air, walked quickly to the house of a friend where she knew she would find a fresh moral atmosphere also. She was soul-sick and depressed. Life felt like the end of a ball, all confusion, and every carriage up but her own , torn gowns, worn countenances, spiteful remarks, ill-natures evident that were wont to be concealed, disillusion generally, and headache threatening. But, fortunately, she found a friend at home to whom she instinctively went for a moral tonic. This was a new friend, Lady Clan, the widow of a civil service official, who wintered all over the world as a rule, but had passed that year at Malta. She was a cheery old lady, masculine in appearance, but with a great, kind, womanly heart, full of sympathetic insight—and a good friend to Evadne, whom she watched with fear as well as with interest, doubting much what would come of all that was unaccustomed about the girl. The sweet grave face and half shut eyes appealed to her pathetically that afternoon in particular, as Evadne sat silently beside her, busy with a piece of work she had brought. Lady Clan thought her lips too firm ; as she grew older, she feared her mouth would harden in expression if she were not happy— and the old lady inwardly prayed Heaven that she might be saved from that ; prayed that little arms might come to clasp her neck, and warm little lips shower kisses upon *her* lips to keep them soft and smiling, lest they settled into stony cold-ness, and forgot the trick.

CHAPTER XIV.

MALTA was enlivened that winter by a joke which Mrs. Guthrie Brimston made without intending it.

Mrs. Malcomson had written a book. She was thirty years of age, and had been married to a military man for ten, and in that time she had seen some things which had made a painful impression upon her, and suggested ideas that were only to be got rid of by publishing them. Ideas cease to belong to an author as soon as they are made public ; if they are new at all somebody else appropriates them ; and if they are old, as alas ! most of them must be at this period of the world's progress, the mistaken reproducer is relieved of the horrid responsibility by kindly critics promptly. Blessed is the man who never flatters himself with the delusion that he can do anything original ; for, verily, he shall not be disappointed.

Mrs. Malcomson made no such vain pretension. She was quite clever enough to know her own limitations exactly. Out of everyday experiences everyday thoughts had come to her, and when she began to embody such thoughts in words she did not suppose that their everyday character would be altered by the process. She had not met any of those perfect beings who inhabit the realms of ideal prose fiction, and make no mistakes but such as are necessary to keep the story going ; nor any of the terrible demons, without a redeeming characteristic, who haunt the dim confines of the same territory for purposes invariably malign ; and it never occurred to her to pretend that she had. She was a simple artist, educated in the life-school of the world, and desiring above everything to be honest—a naturalist, in fact, with positive ideas of right and wrong, and incapable of the confusion of mind or laxity of conscience which denies, on the one hand, that wrong may be pleasant in the doing, or claims, on the other, with equal

untruth, that because it is pleasant it must be, if not exactly
right, at all events, excusable. So she endeavoured to represent things as she saw them, things real, not imaginary ; and
when her characters spoke they talked of the interests which
were daily discussed in her presence, and expressed themselves
as human beings do. She was too independent to be conventional, and it was therefore inevitable that she should bring
both yelp and bray upon herself, and be much misunderstood.
When asked why she had written the book, she answered candidly : ' For my own benefit, of course," which caused a perfect howl of disapprobation, for, if that were her object, there
could be no doubt that she would attain it, as the book had
been a success from the first ; but as people had hastily
concluded that she was setting up for a social reformer and
would fail, they were naturally disgusted. They had been
prepared to call the supposed attempt great presumption on
her part ; but when they found that she had merely her own
interests in view, and had not let their moral welfare cost her
a thought, they said she was not right-minded ; whereupon she
observed : "I don't mind having my morals attacked ; but I
should object to be pulled up for my grammar"—meaning
that she was sure of her morals, but was half afraid that her
grammar might be shaky. As is inevitable, however, under
such circumstances, this obvious interpretation was rejected,
and the most uncharitable construction put upon her words.
It was said, among other things, that she evidently could not
be moral at heart, whatever her conduct might be, because she
made mention of immorality in her book. Her manner of
mentioning the subject was not taken into consideration,
because such sheep cannot consider ; they can only criticise.
The next thing they did, therefore, was to take out the incident
in the book which was most likely to damage her reputation,
and declare that it was autobiographical. There was one man
who knew exactly when the thing had occurred, who the characters were, and all about it.

"Nunc dimittis !" said Mrs. Malcomson when she heard
the story ; "for the same thing has been said of the author of
any book of consequence that has ever appeared." And naturally she was somewhat puffed up. But it remained for Mrs.
Guthrie Brimston to cap the criticisms. Her smouldering
antagonism to Mrs. Malcomson was kept alight by a strong
suspicion she had that Mrs. Malcomson was wont to ridicule
her ; and as a matter of fact the best jokes of that winter *were*

made by Mrs. Malcomson at the expense of Mrs. Guthrie Brimston. It was not likely, therefore, that the latter would spare Mrs. Malcomson if she ever had an opportunity of crushing her, and she watched and waited long for a chance, until at last one night, at a dinner party, she thought the auspicious moment had arrived, and hastened to take advantage of it; but, unfortunately for her, she chose a weapon she was unaccustomed to handle, and in her awkwardness she injured herself.

Mr Price was giving the dinner, and Mrs. Malcomson was not there, but the Colquhouns and Sillengers were, and other friends of hers, kindly disposed, cultivated people, who spoke well of her, and were all agreed in their praise of her work.

Mrs. Guthrie Brimston stiffened as she listened to their remarks, but held her peace for a time, with thin lips compressed, and rising ire apparent.

"I cannot class the book," said Colonel Sillenger. "It does not claim to be fact exactly, and yet it is not fiction."

"Not a novel, but a novelty," Major Guthrie Brimston put in, clasping his hands on his breast, twiddling his thumbs, and setting his head on one side, the "business" with which he usually accompanied one of his facetious sallies.

"What I admire most about Mrs. Malcomson is her courage," said Mr. Price. "She ignores no fact of life which may be usefully noticed and commented upon, but gives each in its natural order without affectation. Do you not agree with me?" he asked, turning to Mrs. Guthrie Brimston who was standing beside him.

Her nostrils flapped. "If you mean to say that you *like* Mrs. Malcomson's book, I do *not* agree with you," she answered decidedly; "I consider it *improper*, simply!"

There was a momentary silence, such as sometimes precedes a burst of applause at a theatre; and then there was laughter! Such an objection from such a quarter was considered too funny, and when it became known, there was quite a run upon the book; for Mrs. Guthrie Brimston's stories were familiar to the members of all the messes, naval and military, in and about the island, not to mention the club men, and the curiosity to know what she did consider an objectionable form of impropriety in narrative made Mrs. Malcomson's fortune.

From that time forward, however, Mrs. Guthrie Brimston's influence was perceptibly upon the wane. Even Colonel Colquhoun wearied of her—to Evadne's great regret. For Mrs.

Guthrie Brimston's vulgarity and coarseness of mind were always balanced by her undoubted propriety of conduct, and her faults were altogether preferable to the exceeding polish and refinement which covered the absolutely corrupt life of a new acquaintance Colonel Colquhoun had made at this time, a Mrs. Drinkworthy, who would not have lingered alone with him anywhere in public, but dressed sumptuously at his expense the whole season. The different estimation in which he held the two ladies and his respect for Evadne herself was emphasised by the fact that he never brought Mrs. Drinkworthy to the Colquhoun House, nor encouraged Evadne to associate with her as he had always encouraged her to associate with Mrs. Guthrie Brimston. And there can be no doubt that the latter's influence was restraining, for, after his allegiance to her relaxed, Evadne noticed new changes for the worse in him, and regretted them all the more because she feared that a chance remark of her own had had something to do with weaning him from the Guthrie Brimstons. She had been having tea with him there one day, and on their way home Colonel Colquhoun said something to her about the Guthrie Brimstons having been unusually amusing.

"They only seemed unusually talkative to me," she answered; "but I always come away from their house depressed, and with a very low estimate of human nature generally. I feel that their mockery is essentially 'the fume of little minds'; and when they are particularly facetious at other people's expense, I leave them with the pleasing certainty that our own peculiarities will be put under the microscope as soon as we are out of earshot, a species of inquisition from which no human being can escape with dignity."

Colonel Colquhoun reflected upon this. His horror of being made to appear ridiculous may have hitherto blinded him to the possibility of such a thing—there is no knowing; but, at all events, it was from that time forward that he began to go less to the Guthrie Brimstons.

He was just at the age, however, when the manners of certain men begin to deteriorate, especially in domestic life. Their capacity for pleasure has been lessened by abuse, and they have to excite it with stimulants. They become less careful in their appearance, are not particular in their choice of words before the ladies of their own families, nor nice in their manners at table. If not already married, they look about for something young and docile on which to inflict their ill-humours, and expect to have their maladies of mind and body tenderly cared for in return for such ecstatic joy as young wives find in the sober certainties of board and lodging. Should they be married already, however, Heaven be good to their wives, for they will have no comfort upon earth !

But doubtless in the good time coming, all estimable wives will subscribe to keep up asylums to which their husbands can be quietly removed for treatment, so soon after the honeymoon as their manners show signs of deterioration. When they begin to be greedy, forget to say " please," "thank you," and "I beg your pardon ; " show no consideration for anyone's comfort but their own, no natural affection, and lose control of their tempers ; the best thing that can be done for them, and the kindest, is to place them under proper restraint at once. They cannot be treated at home. Opposition irritates them, and humouring such dreadful propensities submissively only con- firms them.

The deterioration of Colonel Colquhoun had certainly been delayed by the arrangement which in honour bound him to treat Evadne as a young lady, and not as a wife ; but that it should set in eventually, was inevitable. When it did begin, however, it was less in manner, for the same reason that had delayed it, than in pursuits, and therefore Evadne's position was not affected by it, and she continued to have a kindly, affectionate feeling for him, and to pity him still without bit- terness.

He began to stay out late at night, at this time, and she would hear him occasionally in the small hours of the early morning returning from a bachelor dinner party, or a big guest-night at mess, reeking, doubtless, of tobacco and stimu- lants. Verily, Ouida knows what she is writing about when she invariably adds " essences " to the toilet of her dissipated men. Evadne would wake with a start in the gray of the dawn some- times, and hearing Colonel Colquhoun pass her door with unsteady step on his way to his own room, would shudder to think what his wife must have suffered. And it was not as if the sacrifice of herself would have made any difference to him either. If she could have done any good in that way she might have tried ; but his habits were formed, and they were the outcome of his nature. Nothing would have changed him, and the longer she lived with him, the more reason she had to be convinced of this, and to be sure that her decision had been a right and wise one.

But Colonel Colquhoun did not agree with her. He cherished the vain delusion that, although her influence as a young lady whom he admired and respected had not availed to elevate him, her presence as a wife, whose feelings he certainly would not have felt bound to consider, and whose opinion he would not have cared a rap for, would have made all the difference.

They drifted into a discussion of this subject one hot afternoon when he happened to find Evadne idling for a wonder with a fan at an open window.

"You might have made anything you liked of me had you adopted a different course," he said. He had been carousing the night before, and was now mistaking nausea and depression for a naturally good disposition perverted by ill-treatment.

"No," she answered gently. "I do not flatter myself that I should have succeeded where Mrs. Beston and half a dozen other ladies I could name even here, in a little place like Malta, all more lovable, estimable, and stronger in womanly attributes generally than I am, have failed. Colonel Beston is always with your particular clique—and she is very unhappy."

"She makes herself miserable then," said Colonel Colquhoun, the natural man re-appearing as the *malaise* passed off or was forgotten. "What business is it of hers where he goes or what he does so long as he is nice to her when he *is* at home?"

"Just reverse the position, and consider what Colonel Beston's feelings would be if she took to amusing herself as he does, and maintained that he had no business to interfere with her private pursuits ; would he be satisfied so long as she was 'nice' to him at home?" Evadne asked.

Colonel Colquhoun's countenance lowered. "That is nonsense," he said. "Women are different. They must behave themselves."

Evadne smiled. "I am beginning to know that phrase," she said. "It puzzled me at first, because it is neither reason nor argument, but merely an assertion somewhat in the nature of a command, and equally applicable to either sex, if the other chose to use it. But I know that what you have just said with regard to Mrs. Beston having no occasion to make herself miserable is your true feeling on the subject, and therefore I am convinced that if I had 'adopted a different course,' it would not have been to your advantage in any way, and it would certainly have been very much to the reverse of mine. We are excellent friends as it is, because we are quite independent of each other, but had it been otherwise—I shudder to think of the hopeless misery of it."

Colquhoun was silent.

"There is no hope for me, then," he said at last, lamely. "I suppose the truth of the matter is you never cared for me at all; you just thought you would get married, and accepted me because I was the first person to propose, and your friends considered me eligible. I think you are cold-hearted, Evadne. I have watched you since you came out here, and I've never seen you fancy any man, even for a moment."

Evadne flushed angrily. It is one thing to consider ethical questions in relation to their bearing upon the future of the world at large, and another to have it suggested that you have been under observation yourself with a view to discovering if you found it possible to live up to your own ideas. It was a fact, however, that no man attracted Evadne during this period as Colonel Colquhoun himself had done. The shock of the discovery which had destroyed her passion for him had caused a revulsion of feeling great enough to subdue all further possibilities of passion for years to come, and even if she had been free to marry she would not have done so. All the energy of her nature had flashed from her heart to her brain in a moment, and every instinct of her womanhood was held in check by the superior power of intellect. Since the day of the marriage ceremony she had been a child in her pleasures, and only mature in the capacity for thought. Her senses had been stunned, and still slept heavily; but there remained to her a vivid recollection of the entrancing period which had followed their first awakening, and so she answered Colonel Colquhoun's last remark decidedly.

"You are mistaken," she said, "if you imagine that I did not care for you—that I was merely marrying you for the sake of marrying, and would have been quite as content with any-one else whom my friends might have considered eligible. My mother was very much disappointed because I did not accept an offer I had before I saw you from a man who was certainly 'eligible' in every way—I think you said my father had told you of it? I could not care for *him*; but I think my passion for *you* was blinder and more headlong, if anything, than is usually the case in very young girls. It possessed me from the moment I saw you in church that first time. You pleased my eyes as no other man has ever done, and I was only too glad to take it for granted that your career and your character were all that they ought to have been. But of course I did not love you, for passion, you know, is only the introduction to love. It is a flame that may be blown out at any time by a difference of opinion, and mine went out the moment I learnt that your past had been objectionable. I really care more for you now than I did in the days when I was 'in love' with you. For you have been very good to me—very kind in every possible way. So much so, indeed, that I have more than once felt the keenest regret—I have wished that there was no barrier between us."

"There is no hope for me, then?" he again suggested, but with hope in his heart as he spoke.

She shook her head sadly.

"It is what might have been that I regret," she answered; "but that does not change what has been—and is."

"I suppose you consider that I have spoilt your life?" he said.

"Oh, no!" she exclaimed. "Don't think that. Don't blame yourself. I have never blamed you since I was cool enough to reflect. It is the system that is at fault, the laxity which permits anyone, however unfit, to enter upon the most sacred of all human relations. Saints should find a reward for sanctity in marriage; but the Church, with that curious want of foresight for which it is peculiar, induced the saints to put themselves away in barren celibacy so that their saintliness could not spread, while it encouraged sinners satiated with vice to transmit their misery-making propensities from generation to generation. I believe firmly that marriage, when those who marry are of such character as to make the contract *holy* matrimony, is a perfect state, fulfilling every law of our human nature, and making earth with all its drawbacks a heaven of happiness; but such marriages as we see contracted every day are simply a degradation of all the higher attributes which distinguish men from beasts. For there is no contract more carelessly made, more ridiculed, more lightly broken; no sacred subject that is oftener blasphemed; and nothing else in life affecting the dignity and welfare of man which is oftener attacked with vulgar ribaldry in public, or outraged in private by the secret conduct of it. No. You are not to blame, nor am I. It is not our fault that we form the junction of the old abuses and the new modes of thought. Some two people must have met as we have for the benefit of others. But it has been much better with us than it might have been—thanks to your kindness. I have been quite happy here with you—much happier than I should have been at Fraylingay, I think, all this time. You have never interfered with my pursuits or endeavoured to restrict my liberty in any way, and consequently my occupations and interests have been more varied, and my content greater than it would have been at home after my father had discovered how very widely we differ in opinion. I am grateful to you, George, and I do hope that it has been as well with you as it has been with me since I came to Malta."

"Oh, yes. I have been all right," he answered—in a quite dissatisfied tone, however. But presently that passed, and then he slid into a better frame of mind, "You are a good woman, Evadne," he said. "You have played me a—ah—*very* nasty trick, and I don't agree with you—and I don't believe there are a dozen men in the world at the present moment who would agree with you. But, apart from your peculiar opinions, you are about one of the nicest girls I ever knew. Everything you do is well done. You're never out of temper. You don't speak ·much, as a rule, but you're always ready to respond cheerfully when you're spoken to—and you don't interfere. I wish from the bottom of my soul you had never been taught to read and write, and then you would have had no views to come between us. But since you think you cannot care for me, I shall not persecute you. I gave you my word of honour that I never would, and I hope I have kept it."

"Yes—*indeed.* You have been goodness itself," she answered.

"I wrote and told your father how very well we get on," he continued, "and tried to persuade him to make it up with you, but the old gentleman is obstinate. He has his own notion of a wife's duty, and he sticks to it. But I did my best, because I know you feel the separation from your own family, although you never complain. He can't get over your wanting a 'Christlike' man for a husband. He says he laughs every time he thinks of it. The first time he laughed at that idea of yours I was there, and a—eh—*very* unpleasant laugh it was. It got my back up somehow, and made me feel ready to take your part against him. It isn't a compliment, you know, to have your father-in-law laugh outright at the notion of your ever being able to come up to your wife's idea of what a man should be. And when he came down raging about your books, it was the recollection of that laugh, I believe, that made me

determine to get them for you.   I asked your mother to show
me your old rooms, and I just took all the books I could find;
and then I thought it would be a good idea to make your new
rooms look as much like the old ones as possible."

"It was a very kind thought," Evadne answered.

"I don't pretend to have been a saint; very much the contrary," Colonel Colquhoun proceeded with that assumption of
humility often apparent in the repentant sinner who expects to
derive both credit and importance from his past when he
frankly confesses it was wicked, "but I hope I have always
been a gentleman,"—with her "saint" and "gentleman" were
synonymous terms,—"and what I want to say is," he continued—"I don't quite see how to put it; but you have just
expressed yourself satisfied with the arrangements I have made
for you so far.   Well, if you really think that I have done all
I can to make your life endurable, will you do something for
me ?   I am a good deal older than you are.   In all human
probability you will outlive me.   Will you promise me that
during my lifetime you will not mix yourself up publicly—will
not join societies, make speeches, or publish books, which
people would know you had written, on the social subjects you
are so fond of."

"*Fond* of . " she ejaculated.

"Well, perhaps that is not the right expression," he conceded.

"No, very far from the right expression," she answered
gently.   "Social subjects seem to be forcing themselves on the
attention of every thoughtful and right-minded person just now,
and it would be culpable cowardice to shun them while there
is the shadow of a hope that some means may be devised to
put right what is so very wrong.   Ignoring an evil is tanta-
mount to giving it full licence to spread.   But I am thankful
to say I have never known anyone who found the knowledge
of evil anything but distressing—except Mrs. Guthrie Brimston,
and she only delights in it so long as it is made a jest of.   But
they are all alike in that set she belongs to.   Their ideas of
propriety are bounded by their sense of pleasure.   So long as
you talk flippantly, they will listen and laugh; but if you talk
seriously on the same subject, you make the matter disagreeable, and then they call it 'improper.' "

Colonel Colquhoun was standing with his arms folded on the
parapet of the veranda looking down a vista of yellow houses
at a glimpse there was of the sea, dotted with boats, hazy with

heat, intensely blue, and sparkling back reflections of the glaring sun. From where Evadne sat she saw the same scene
through the open balustrade over the tops of the oleanders
growing in the garden below, and gradually the heat, and
stillness, and beauty, stole over her, melting her mood to
tenderness, and filling her mind with sadly sweet memories of
the days of delight which preceded " all this." She thought
of the yellow gorse on the common, recalling its peculiar
fragrance; of the misty cobwebs stretched from bush to bush,
and decked with dazzling drops of dew; of the healthy happy
heath creatures peeping out at her shyly, here a rabbit and
there a hare; of a lark that sprang up singing and was lost to
sight in a moment, of a thrush that paused to reflect as she
passed. She thought of the little church on the high cliffs, the
bourne of her morning walks, of the long stretch of sand; and
of the sea; and she felt the fresh free air of those open spaces
rouse her again to a gladness in life not often known to ladies
idling on languid afternoons in the sickly heat essential to the
wellbeing of citron, orange, and myrtle; beloved of the mythi-
cal faun, but fatal to the best energies of the human race. And
by a very natural transition, her mind leaped on to that morning in church when the sense of loneliness which comes to all
young creatures that have no mate resolved itself into that
silent supplication, the petition which it is a part of the joy of
life in youth to present to a heaven which is willing enough to
hear; and she recalled the thrill of delight that trembled
through every nerve of her body when she looked up, and
found her answer, when she saw and recognized what she
sought in the glance which, flashing between them, was the
spark that first fired the train of her blind passion for Colonel
Colquhoun. She thought then that her prayer was answered
at that moment; and she believed still that it had been an ·
swered so; but for a special purpose which she had not then
perceived. Colonel Colquhoun was not the husband of her
heart, but the rod of chastisement for her rash presumption;
he had not been given to her for her own happiness, but that
she might act as she had done to set an example by which she
should have the double privilege of expiating a fault of her
own, and at the same time securing the peace in life of others.
It was in this way there hummed in her brain on that hot
afternoon results of the faith which had been held by her
ancestors; of the teaching which she had herself received
directly; with a curious glimmering of truths that were already

half apparent to her own acute faculties; an incongruous jumble all leavened by the natural instincts of a being rich in vitality, and wholesome physical force. With the recollection of the old days came back the shadow of the old sensation. The interval was forgotten for the moment. She saw before her the man whose every glance and word had thrilled her with pleasurable emotion, whom it had been a joy just to be with and see. It was the same man leaning there, fine of form and feature, with a dreamy look in his blue eyes softening the glitter which was apt to be hard and stony. If only—— At that moment Colonel Colquhoun looked round at her, hesitated, although his face flushed, and then exclaimed : " Evadne, you *do* love me ! "

" I *did* love you," she answered.

He sat down beside her, close to her : "Will you forget all this ? " he said. " Will you forget my past ; will you make me a different man ? Will you ? You can." He half stretched out his hand to take hers, but then drew back, a gentleman always in that he would not force her inclinations in any way. " If I do not change, we can be again as we are now, and there would be no harm done. Will you consent, Evadne, will you —my wife—will you ? "

He leant forward so close that her senses were troubled— too close, for she pushed her chair back to relieve herself of the oppression, and the act irritated him. Another moment, a little more persuasion and caressing of the voice, which he could use so well to that effect, and she might have given in to the kind of fascination which she had felt in his presence from the first ; but when she moved he drew back too, his coun- tenance clouded, and her own momentary yearning to be held close, close ; to be kissed till she could not think ; to live the intoxicating life of the senses only, and not care, was over.

" We could never be again as we are now," she answered. " There would be no return for me. A wife cannot feel as I do. And you—you would not change. Or at least you would only change your habits ; the consequences of them you will carry to your grave with you, and I doubt if you could ever change your habits once for all. You were a different man for a while when I first came out, but you soon relapsed. No. I can never regret my present attitude ; but I have seen several times already how much reason I should have to regret—a different arrangement."

"You make light of love," he said. "Many a girl has died of a disappointment."

"Many a girl is a fool," she answered placidly. "And what can love offer me in exchange for the calm content of my life just now? for my perfect health? for my freedom from care?"

"A reconciliation with your family," he suggested.

She sighed, and sat silent a little, lost in thought.

"I do not live with my family now," she answered at last. "They have all their own interests, their own loves, apart from mine; would a letter or two a year from them make up after all for the risk of misery I should be running—for the terrible, helpless, hopeless, incurable misery of an unhappily married woman, if I should become one?"

He rose and returned to his old position, leaning over the veranda, looking down to the sea.

"You are cold-blooded, I think, Evadne," he reiterated.

She said nothing, but rested her head on the back of her chair and smiled. She was not cold-blooded, and he knew it as well as she did. She was only a nineteenth century woman of the higher order with senses so refined that if her moral as well as her physical being were not satisfied in love, both would revolt. They were silent some time after that, and then he turned to her once more.

"Will you promise me that one thing, Evadne?" he asked. "Promise me that during my lifetime you will never mix yourself up—never take part publicly in any question of the day. It would be too deuced ridiculous for me, you know, to have my name appearing in the papers in connection with measures of reform, and all that sort of thing."

"I promise to spare you that kind of annoyance at all events," she answered without hesitation, making the promise, not because she was infirm of purpose, but because she was indefinite; she had no impulse at the time to do anything, and no notion that she would ever feel impelled to act in opposition to this wish of his.

"Thank you," he said, and there was another little pause, which he was again the first to break.

"You would have loved me, then, if I had lived a different life," he said.

"Yes," she answered simply, "I should have loved you. No other man has made me feel for a moment what I felt for you, while I believed that you were all that a man should be who proposes to marry ; and I don't think any other man ever will. You were born for me. Why, oh, why ! did you not live for me ?"

"I wish to God I had," he answered.

She rose impulsively, and stretched out her hands to him. Its was a movement of pain and pity, sorrow and sympathy, and he understood it.

"You meant to marry always," she said. "You treasured in your heart your ideal of a woman ; why could you not have lived so that you would have been *her* ideal too, when at last you met ?"

He took her two little outstretched hands and held them a moment in his, looking down at them. "I wish to God I had," he repeated.

"Did it never occur to you that a woman has her ideal as well as a man ?" she said : "that she loves purity and truth, and loathes degradation and vice more than a man does ?"

"Theoretically, yes," he answered ; "but you find practically that women will marry anyone. If they were more particular, we should be more particular too."

"Ah, that is our curse," said Evadne—"yours and mine. If women had been 'more particular' in the past, you would have been a good man, and I should have been a happy wife to-day."

He raised her hands, which he was still holding, placing them palm to palm, took them in one of his, and clasped them to his chest, bringing her very close to him ; and then he looked into her upturned face, considering it, with that curious set expression on his own, which always came at a crisis. Her lips were parted, her cheeks were pale, she still panted from the passion of her last utterance, and her eyes, as he looked down into them, were pained in expression and fixed. He let her hands drop, and once more returned to his old position, leaning upon the balustrade with his back to her, looking out over the sea. If it had been possible to have obtained the mastery he had dreamed of over her, mere animal mastery, the thought would have repelled him now. He might have dominated her senses, but her soul would only have been the more confirmed in its loathing of his life. He knew the strength of her convictions, knew that, so long as they were a few yards apart, she could always have ruled both herself and him ; and life is lived a few yards apart. It was the best side of his nature that was under Evadne's influence, and he had now some saving grace of manhood in him, which enabled him to appreciate the esteem with which she had begun to repay his consideration for her, and to admire the consistent self-respect which had brought her triumphantly out of all her difficulties, and won her a distinguished position in the place. He felt that he ought to be satisfied, and knew that he would have to be.

She remained standing as he had left her, and presently he turned to her again. "Forgive me," he said, "for provoking a discussion which has pained you needlessly. If repentance and remorse could wipe out the past, I should be worthy to claim you this minute. But I know you are right. There might have been hours of intoxication, but there would have been years of misery also—for you—as my wife. Your decision was best for both of us. It was our only chance of peace." He looked at her wistfully, and approached a step.

She met him more than halfway. She put her hands on his shoulders, and looked up at him. "But we are friends, George," she said with emotion. "I seem to have nobody now but you belonging to me, and I should be lonely indeed if——" She suddenly burst into tears.

"Yes, yes," he said huskily. "Of course we are friends; the best friends. We shall always be friends. I have never let anyone say a word against you, and I never will. I am proud to think that you are known by my name. I only wish that I could make it worthy of you—and, perhaps, some day—in the field——"

Poor fellow! The highest proof of moral worth he knew of was to be able to take a prominent part in some great butchery of his fellow-men, without exhibiting a symptom of fear.

Evadne had recovered herself, and now smiled up at him with wet eyelashes.

"Not there, I hope!" she answered. "Going to war and getting killed is not a proof of affection and respect which we modern women care about. I would rather keep you safe at home, and quarrel with you."

Colonel Colquhoun smiled. "Here is tea," he said, seeing a servant enter the room behind them. "Shall we have it out here? We shall be cooler."

"Yes, by all means," she answered.

And then they began to talk of things indifferent, but with a new and happy consciousness of an excellent understanding between them.

CHAPTER XV.

THE following day, as Colonel Colquhoun went out in the afternoon, he met Evadne coming in with Mrs. Malcomson and Mrs. Sillenger. Evadne was leaning on Mrs. Malcomson's arm. She looked haggard and pale, and the other two ladies were evidently also much distressed.

"Has anything happened?" Colquhoun asked with concern. "Are you ill, Evadne?"

"I am sick at heart," she answered bitterly.

"We have had bad news," Mrs. Malcomson said significantly.

Colonel Colquhoun stood aside, and let them pass in. Then he went on to the club, wondering very much what the news could be.

There he found Captain Belliot, Colonel Beston, and a few more of his particular friends, all discussing something in tones of righteous indignation. Mr. Price and Mr. St. John were there also. A mail had just arrived bringing the details of Edith's illness from Morningquest.

Mr. St. John turned from the group, and as he did so Colonel Colquhoun noticed that his gait was uncertain, and his face was white and distorted as if with physical pain. His impulse was to offer him a restorative and see him to his rooms, but Mr. Price anticipated the kind intention.

It was Mrs. Orton Beg who had written to Evadne, and she had brought Mrs. Sillenger and Mrs. Malcomson in to hear the letter read.

"Edith is quite, quite mad," she said, unconsciously choosing the poor girl's own expression; "and the most horrible part of it is, she knows it herself. She wants to do the most dreadful things, and all the time she feels as much horror of such deeds as we should. My aunt says her sufferings are too terrible to describe. But she was growing gradually weaker when the letter left."

"How *awful!*" Mrs. Sillenger ejaculated. "To think of her as we knew her, so beautiful, and so sweet and good and true in every way; and with her magnificent physique! and now not a soul that loves her, when they hear that she is 'growing gradually weaker,' would wish it otherwise."

"My aunt concludes her letter by saying: "I am telling you the state of the case exactly,'" Evadne continued, "'because I

did not agree with you when you were here. I had been so
shielded from evil myself that I could not believe in the danger
to which all women in their weakness are exposed. But I agree
with you now, perfectly. We must alter all this, and we can.
Put me into communication with your friends——'"

"And you will join us yourself, Evadne?" Mrs. Malcomson
exclaimed.

"Certainly I shall!" she answered emphatically. Then all
at once something flashed through her mind.

"Heaven!" she exclaimed. "I had forgotten! I cannot—
I cannot join you. I have given my word—to do nothing—so
long as Colonel Colquhoun is alive."

Up to this time, Evadne in her home life had been serene
and healthy minded. But now suddenly there came a change.
She began to ask: Why should she trouble herself? Nobody
who had a claim upon her wished her to do anything but dress
well and make herself agreeable, and that was what most of the
people about her were doing to the best of their ability. The
Church enjoined that she should do her duty. What was her
duty? Clearly to acquiesce as everybody else was doing, to
refuse to know of anything that might distress her, to be
pleased and to give pleasure. That was all that heaven itself
had to offer her, and if she could make heaven upon earth
now, with a fan and a book, and a few congenial friends, she
would.

This was the first consequence of her promise to Colonel
Colquhoun. It had cramped her into a narrow groove wherein
to struggle would only have been to injure herself ineffectually.
There comes a time when every intellectual being is forced to
choose some definite pursuits. Evadne had been formed for a
life of active usefulness; but now she found herself reduced to
an existence of objectless contemplation, and she suffered
acutely until she had recourse to St. Paul and the pulpit, from
which barren fields she succeeded at last in collecting samples
enough to make up a dose of the time-honoured anodyne sacred
to her sex. It is a delicious opiate which gives immediate
relief, but it soothes without healing and is in the long run
deleterious. And this was the influence under which Evadne
entered upon a new phase of life altogether. She gave up
reading; and by degrees there grew upon her a perfect horror
of disturbing emotions. She burnt any books she had with
repulsive incidents in them. She would not have them about
even, lest they should remind her. There were some pictures

also in her rooms which depicted scenes of human suffering—
a battle piece, a storm at sea, a caravan lost in the desert, and
a prison scene ; and those she had removed. She would have
ended all such horrors if she could, but as that was impossible,
she would not even think of them ; and accordingly, she had
those pictures replaced by soothing subjects—moonlit spaces,
sun-bright seas, clear brown rivulets, lakes that mirrored the
placid mountains, and flowers and birds and trees. She
would look at nothing that was other than restful ; she would
read nothing that harrowed her feelings ; she would listen to
nothing that might move her to indignation and reawaken the
futile impulse to resist ; and she banished all thought or reflection that was not absolutely tranquillizing in effect or otherwise
enjoyable.

But all this was extremely enervating. She had owed her
force of character to her incessant intellectual activity, which
had also kept her mind pure, and her body in excellent condition. Had she not found an outlet for her superfluous
vitality as a girl in the cultivation of her mind, she must have
become morbid and hysterical, as is the case with both sexes
when they remain in the unnatural state of celibacy with
mental energy unapplied. We are like running water, bright
and sparkling so long as the course is clear ; but divert us into
unprogressive shallows, where we lie motionless, and very soon
we stagnate, and every particle of life within us becomes
offence. This was the fate which threatened Evadne. As her
mind grew sluggish, her bodily health decreased, and the
climate began to tell upon her. Malta has a pet fever of its
own, of a dangerous kind, from which she had hitherto escaped,
but now, quite suddenly, she went down with a bad attack, and
hovered for weeks between life and death. Colonel Colquhoun
made arrangements to take her home as soon as she was
sufficiently strong to be moved ; but just at that time a small
war broke out, and his regiment was one of the first to be
ordered to the front. He was able to see her off, however,
with other ladies of the regiment, and he telegraphed to her
friends begging them to meet her at Southampton. The hope
of seeing them sustained Evadne during the voyage, but when
she arrived only Mrs. Orton Beg appeared. The latter was
shocked by the change in Evadne. Her hair had been cut
short, her eyes were sunken, her cheeks were hollow ; she was
skin and bone, and the colour of death.

Mrs. Orton Beg had gone on board the steamer, and Evadne

had been brought up on deck, supported by one of the ladies and her own maid.

She looked at her aunt, and then she looked beyond her. " Has my mother not come to meet me ? " she asked.

Mrs. Orton Beg looked at her compassionately.

" Is she ill ? " Evadne added.

" No, dear," her aunt replied.

Evadne burst into tears. It was a bitter disappointment, and she was very weak, and had suffered a great deal.

After her arrival her pompous papa continued "firm," as he called it, and as she was equally "firm" herself, he would not have her at Fraylingay. He repeated that if there were one human weakness which is more reprehensible than another, it is obstinacy, and he told Mrs. Frayling that she must choose between himself and Evadne. If she preferred the latter, she might go to see her, but she should not return to him. He meant to be master in his own house—and so on, at the top of his voice, with infinite bluster—to which it was that Mrs. Frayling submitted. She never could bear a noise.

Evadne, therefore, saw nothing of her mother or brothers or sisters, and must have been lonely, indeed, had it not been for Mrs. Orton Beg, who took charge of her and nursed her and brought her round, and remained with her until Colonel Colquhoun returned. They spent most of their time in the Western Highlands, but stayed also in London and Paris.

Colonel Colquhoun was absent a year, and made the most of every opportunity to distinguish himself. At the end of the war he was made C. B., and promoted to the rank of colonel ; and, his time with his regiment having expired, he was further honoured by being immediately appointed to the command of the depôt at Morningquest. Evadne was glad to see him again. She had missed him, and had waited anxiously for his return. She had no one to care for in his absence, no one, that is to say, who was specially her charge, to be attended to and made comfortable. He had narrowed her sphere of usefulness down to that by the promise he had exacted, and in his absence she had what to her was a useless, purposeless existence, wandering about from place to place. During this period she made few notes in the " Commonplace Book," but the few all bore witness to one thing, viz., her ever increasing horror of unpleasantness in any shape or form.

END OF BOOK III.

BOOK IV.

THE TENOR AND THE BOY.—AN INTERLUDE.

His words are bonds, his oaths are oracles ;
His love sincere, his thoughts immaculate ;
His tears pure messengers sent from his heart,
His heart as far from fraud as heaven from earth.
—Two Gentlemen of Verona.

CHAPTER I.

MORNINGQUEST, with the sunset glow upon it, might have made you think of Arthur's "dim rich city"; but Morningquest had already flourished a thousand years longer than Caerlyon, and was just as many times more wicked. And it was known to be so, although not a tithe of the crimes committed in it were ever brought to light; but even of those which were known and recorded, no man could have told you the half, so great was their number. Of course, as the place was wicked, the doctors were well to the fore, combating the wages of sin gallantly; and the lawyers also, needless to say, were busy; and so, too, were the clergy in their own way, ecclesiasticism being well-worked; Christianity, however, was much neglected, so that, for the most part, the devil went unmolested in Morningquest, and had a good time.

There were seventy-five churches besides the cathedral within the city boundary, and a large sprinkling of religious sects of all denominations, which caused ferment enough to prevent stagnation; and, of course, where so many churches were the clergy swarmed, and were made the subject of the usual well-worn pleasantries. If you asked what good they were doing, you would hear that nobody knew; but you would also be assured that at all events they were, as a rule, too busy about candles and vestments and what not of that kind of thing, discussing such questions with heat enough to convince anyone that the Lord in heaven cares greatly about the use of one gaud more or less in his service, to do much harm. But, upon the whole, the attitude of the citizens toward the clergy was friendly and unexacting. If nobody heeded them much, nobody opposed them much either, so that, as in any other profession, they enjoyed the liberty of earning their livelihood in their own way. The people considered them without reverence as a part of the population merely; their services were accepted as a necessity in the regular routine of life as bread-and-butter was, and doubtless they did good in some such way, although the one was as much forgotten as the other before it was well assimilated. If the citizens mentioned their teaching at all, it was merely to repeat what they said of the clergy themselves—that it did no harm.

This was a pleasantry of which they never wearied; but sometimes they would add to it another article of their faith. "The Lord is gracious," they would declare, "and when he sends dull preachers, he mercifully sends sleep also to comfort his afflicted people." So the preachers preached, and their congregations slumbered tranquilly, and everbody was satisfied. If the clergy squabbled amongst themselves, and with their churchwardens, their fellow-citizens were rather grateful to them than otherwise for varying the monotony, so that they were encouraged to wage their internecine combats to their hearts' content; and when these lapsed and they let each other alone, it was always interesting to see how they turned upon the bishop. But nobody was disturbed, for in such a sleepy old place—and the respectable part of it *was* sleepy!—men habitually view the vagaries of their friends with smiling tolerance, and if they comment upon them at all, it is without bitterness.

In general history there are always events, as there are people, that take prominent places and attract attention long after similar events are buried and forgotten. They owe their vitality less to their importance, perhaps, than to some gleam of poetry, pathos, or romance which distinguishes the actors in them; and most old places have a pet tragedy amongst their traditions, but Morningquest was an exception to this rule, for, although it had its particular tragedy, it was quite a new one. From the first, however, it was easy enough to foresee that this one event of all the sorrowful things which had happened in that bad old place, having as it were every desirable requirement of time, setting, and person to invest it with a proper, permanent and most pathetic interest, was the likeliest one to be remembered.

Morningquest was a city of singers, and the citizens were proud of their cathedral choir, which was chiefly recruited from amongst themselves, there being a succession of exquisite boy-voices constantly forthcoming to awaken the slumbering echoes in the ancient pile, and the sweet old sentiments in the people's hearts. Some of the lay clerks had been choristers themselves, and amongst them was one who had been especially noted as a boy for his birdlike treble. It seemed a thousand pities when it broke; but as he reached maturity, he found himself able to sing again, and eventually he developed a very true, if not very

powerful tenor voice, and rose in time to be the leading tenor
in the choir. People had flocked to hear him sing in his childhood, and as they still came, it was natural that he should continue to think himself the attraction, and also natural that he
should be somewhat puffed up in consequence. He wore a
moustache, he wore a ring, he put on airs, he scented his pocket-
handkerchiefs, he ogled the pretty ladies in the canon's pew
like an officer ; but he was an orphan, and had a poor old
kinswoman depending upon him, and kept her well ; he was
harmless, he never did anyone an ill-turn, nor said an evil thing,
and he could sing ; so that, taken all round, his good qualities
outweighed his weaknesses, and he was duly allowed the measure
of praise and respect which he earned.

But his rings, and his scents, and his affectations generally,
covered a secret ambition. He wanted to be more than a tenor
in the choir ; he wanted to be an opera singer, and he entered
into negotiations with a London *impressario.* He did so secretly,
being fearful of discouragement, and also because he wished to
surprise his friends, and when a personal interview became
necessary he did not ask for the means to make the journey ;
he had the management of the choir funds, and there being a
surplus in his hands at the moment, he made use of the money,
borrowing it in perfect good faith, and honestly sure that he
would be able to repay it before it was required of him. Had
he succeeded, the money would have been returned at once ;
but, alas, he did not succeed, the money was spent, his hopes
were shattered, and his honest career was at an end. " If only
he had come to me, the matter might have been put right,"
the dean said, and he publicly reproached himself for not knowing the hearts of his people better, so that he might have entered
with sympathy into their lives, and won their confidence.
The tenor ought to have trusted him, but he never thought of
such a thing. He was a poor crushed creature, and had
abandoned hope. But he went back to Morningquest nevertheless. Indeed, where else could he go ? He knew no other
place, and had never a friend elsewhere in the world. So he
went back mechanically, and he went to the cathedral, and
there he hid himself. And there three times a day for three
days he looked down from the clerestory, himself unseen,
looked into the faces he knew so well, faces which had been
friendly faces, eyes that had watched him kindly all his life ;
and, out there in the cold, he followed the services at which he
had been wont to assist, taking a leading part almost so long as

he could remember. And there in the grim solitude by day, and the added horror of ghostly darkness by night, he lived on thought, and suffered his agony of remorse, and the minor miseries of cold and hunger and thirst, till the need of endurance ceased to be felt. And then, amid the misty morning grayness of the fourth day he hanged himself from a ladder left by some workmen engaged in repairs, by whom his body was afterward found desecrating the sacred precincts.

These are the materials out of which Morningquest wove its pet tragedy. The event happened at the beginning of that important year which the Heavenly Twins spent with their grandfather at Morne, and doubtless they heard all about it, but, being very much occupied with a variety of absorbing interests at the time, it did not make any particular impression upon them. It was brought home to them eventually, however, when it might have been considered an old story ; but it had not become so then in anybody's estimation, nor has it since because of the pity of it which lent the pathetic interest that makes a story deathless and ageless ; the subtle something which influences to better moods, and from which the years as they pass do not detract, but rather pay it the tribute of an occasional addition thereto, by which its hope of immortality is greatly strengthened.

After the tenor's death, the difficulty had been who should succeed him. There was nobody immediately forthcoming, and this had put the dean and chapter in a fix, for it happened that there were services of particular importance going on in the cathedral at the time, to which strangers flocked from a distance, and it was felt that it would never do to disapppoint them of their music. So, on the morning of the great day of all, after the early service, the dean, the precentor, and the organist, having doffed their surplices, returned to the choir, and stood for some time beside the brazen lectern, discussing the subject.

While they were so engaged, a gentleman came up to the dean, and, after making a graceful apology for the intrusion, explained that he had heard of their difficulty, and begged to be allowed to sing the tenor part, and a solo, at the afternoon service.

The dean looked doubtful ; the precentor, judging by the stranger's appearance and tone that he might be somebody, was inclined to be obsequious ; the organist struck a neutral attitude, and stood by ready to agree to anything.

"I can sing," the applicant said modestly, answering the doubt he saw in the dean's demeanour ; "although I confess that I have not been doing so lately. I think I may venture to promise, however, that I shall not, at all events, spoil the service."

"Well, sir," the dean replied, "if you *can* help us, you will really be putting us under a great obligation, for we are in a most awkward dilemma. What do you say, Mr. Precentor ? "

"I should say, as the organist is here, if this gentleman would try his part this morning——"

"That is what I was about to suggest," the stranger interposed.

The precentor found the music, the organist retired to his instrument, the dean took a seat, and the stranger sang. When he paused, the dean arose.

"I thank you, sir," he said with effusion, "and I gratefully accept your offer."

The stranger bowed to his little audience, returned the music, and left the building.

He was a young man, tall and striking in appearance ; clean shaven, with delicate features, dark dreamy gray eyes, and a tumbled mop of golden hair, innocent of parting. He was well-dressed, but his clothes hung upon him loosely, as if he had grown thinner since they were made ; his face was pale too, and pinched in appearance, and his movements were languid, giving him altogether the air of a man just recovering from some serious illness. That he was a gentleman no one would have doubted for a moment, nor would they have been surprised to hear that he was a great man in the sense of being a peer or something of that kind, for there was that indefinable something in his look and bearing which people call aristocratic, and his manner was calm and assured like that of a well-bred man of the world accustomed to good society.

The people who flocked to the afternoon service that day regarded him with much curiosity, and he was certainly unlike anyone whom they had hitherto seen in the choir. A surplice had been found for him, and the dead white contrasted well with the brightness of his hair, and made the refined beauty of his face even more remarkable than it had been in his morning dress. Sitting with the lay clerks behind the choristers, he looked like the representative of another and a higher race, and even those of them whose personal attractions had hitherto been considered more than merely passable when they appeared beside him were suddenly seen to be hopelessly commonplace. But, although the interest he excited was evident enough, it was equally evident that he himself remained quite unaware of it. In his whole bearing there was not the slightest assumption. He entered with the choir, and might have been in the habit of doing so all his life, so perfectly unconscious did he seem of anything new or strange in the position. As soon as he was seated, without even glancing at the people, he had taken up his music, and continued lost in the study of it until the service opened ; and then he sang his part with ease and precision, which, however, attracted less attention at the moment than his appearance. The rest of the choir, animated by his presence, exerted themselves to the utmost, but were too delighted with their own performances to think much of his before the solo began.

Then, however, they awoke. The first note he uttered was a long *crescendo* of such rich volume and so sweet, that the people held their breath and looked up :

> This world recedes ; it disappears !
> Heaven opens my eyes ! my ears
> With sounds seraphic ring :
> Lend, lend your wings ! I mount ! I fly !
> O Grave ! where is thy victory?
> O Death ! where is thy sting ?

It was as if a delicious spell had been cast upon the congregation, which held them bound until the last note of the exquisite voice, even the last reverberation of the organ accompaniment, had trembled into silence, and then there was a movement, a flutter, a great sigh of relief heaved, so to speak, as if the pleasure had been too great, and nerves and senses were glad to be released from the tension of it.

The Tenor was slightly flushed when he resumed his seat, but otherwise his face was as serenely impassive as ever.

" It is some great singer from abroad," the people whispered to each other. " He is used to every kind of success, and does not even trouble himself to see if we are pleased. He has sung doubtless to gratify some whim of his own. Such artists are capricious folk." To which the answer was : " Long may such whims continue ! "

After the service, the dean hastened to thank the stranger. He shook his hand with emotion, and congratulated him upon his marvellous gift. " May I ask if you are a professional singer? " the old gentleman said.

"Not yet," was the answer ; " but I wish to offer myself for the vacant post of Tenor in the choir, if you are satisfied with my attainments."

The dean stared at him. "Oh—ah—" he stammered in his surprise ; and then he added something apologetically about references, and being obliged to ask a few questions.

"If you have the time to spare, I think I can satisfy you now," the stranger answered.

The dean, perceiving that he wished to speak to him alone, bowed courteously, and requested the applicant to accompany him to the deanery. The precentor, who had assisted at the interview up to this point, now watched them depart, and as he did so he pursed up his lips significantly. The stranger had sunk in his estimation from the possible rank of a Russian prince to that of a simple singer, a considerable drop ; but the precentor was a musician, and he asserted that the voice was of the finest quality, and trained to perfection. He wanted to know, however, what could bring a man with a fortune like that in his throat to bury himself alive in Morningquest, and he ventured to predict that it must be something " fishy."

The stranger had a long private interview with the dean, but what transpired thereat was never made public. It was known, however, that when he left the deanery the dean himself accompanied him to the door, and there shook hands with him cordially ; and it was immediately afterward announced that " Mr. Jones " was to be the new tenor.

"Mr. *Jones*, indeed ! " said Morningquest sarcastically. " As much *Jones* as the bishop ! " And the precentor was sure that the dean had been taken in by a clever impostor, which would not have been the case, he asserted, if the matter had been referred to him as it ought to have been. But Morningquest declared that there was no imposition about that voice, and as to antecedents, why, it was absurd to be too particular when everything else was so entirely satisfactory.

There happened to be a tiny tenement in the Close vacant when the new lay clerk began his duties as Tenor in the choir, and this he took. It was a detached house, one of a row which faced the apse on the south side of the cathedral. One step led down from the road into the little front garden, and another from that into the house, which was thus two steps below the road in front, but was level with the garden at the back. Tho passage ran right through the house, the garden door being opposite the front door ; the kitchen was behind a little sitting room on the right as you entered, and on the left were two other rooms when the Tenor took the house, the one looking into the back garden, the other into the front ; but these two rooms he immediately turned into one by having the dividing wall removed, and together they made a long, low, but comfortably proportioned apartment, with a French window at either end. The Tenor spent all his spare time when he first arrived in decorating this room, *"making* work for himself," as the people said ; and indeed that was just what he seemed to be doing, for he worked as a man does who feels that he ought to be occupied, but he takes no pleasure and finds no relief in any occupation. He frescoed the walls and ceiling of his room with admirable taste and skill, making it look twice the size by cunning divisions of the pattern on the walls, and by the well-devised proportions of dado and cornice.

The dean often went to watch him at his work, and sat on a packing case (the only article which the room contained at the time) by the hour together talking to him, a circumstance which, taken with the fact that other gentlemen in the neighbourhood also called upon him and lingered long on the premises, greatly exercised the inquisitive minds of the multitude, especially when it was perceived that the Tenor, instead of being elated by their condescension, accepted it as a matter of course, and continued always the same—sad, preoccupied, impassive, seldom smiling, never surprised, taking no healthy interest in anything.

When the painting was finished, furniture began to arrive, and this was another surprise for the Close, where houses were not adorned with the designs of any one period, but were filled with a heterogeneous collection of articles, generally aged and remarkably uncouth. Everything in the Tenor's long low room, on the contrary, even down to the shape of the brass coal scuttle and including the case of the grand piano, was in harmony with the colour and design of the frescoes on the walls and ceiling ; the floor, which was polished, being adorned here and there with rugs which suggested dim reflections of the tint and tone above. It was a luxurious apartment, but not effeminate. The luxury was masculine luxury, refined and significant ; there was no meaningless feminine fripperies about, nor was there any evidence of sensuous self-indulgence. It was the abode of a cultivated man, but of one who was essentially manly withal.

The fame of this apartment having been noised abroad, the precentor came one day to inspect it. There is no need to describe this precentor; one knows exactly what a man must be who calls things "fishy." He was an ordained clergyman, but not at all benevolent, neither was he a Christian, for he did not love his neighbour as himself, and his visit on this occasion was anything but friendly in intention. He was determined to know something more about the Tenor, he said, and he meant to question him. His theory was that the Tenor had been a public singer, but had disgraced himself, and was unable to appear again in consequence; and on this supposition he intended to proceed.

He found the Tenor with his hat in his hand on the point of leaving the house; but the precentor was not delicate about detaining him. He walked into the sitting room without waiting to be asked, pried impertinently into everything, and then sat down. The Tenor meantime had remained standing with his hat in his hand patiently waiting, and he still stood, but the precentor did not take the hint.

"You are an opera singer, I think you said," he remarked as soon as he was seated.

The Tenor looked at him inquiringly.

"Or was it concerts?" he suggested, a trifle disconcerted.

The Tenor looked gravely amused.

"It was not the music halls, of course?" the precentor persuasively insinuated.

"Well, hardly," said the Tenor, fixing his steady eyes upon the man in a way that made him wince. "I have some business to attend to in the town," he added. "Pray make yourself at home so long as it pleases you to remain;" with which he brushed his hand back over his glossy hair, put on his hat, and sauntered out, leaving his gentle guest to ruminate.

The interest which the Tenor had begun by exciting in the breasts of the quiet inhabitants of Morningquest did not diminish all at once, as might have been expected. He was only a lay clerk, to be sure, but then he was so utterly unlike any other lay clerk. He was always so carefully dressed, for one thing, and maintained so successfully that suggestion of good breeding which had been their first impression of him; was altogether so distinguished in appearance that it was a pleasure to hear strangers exclaim: "Who *is* that?" and to be able to surprise them with the off-hand rejoinder: "Oh, that is only our tenor."

Then he was a stranger from nobody knew where ; he went by the name of " Jones," which was not believed to be his ; he had a magnificent voice, and he remained in Morningquest in an obscure position, making nothing of it.   True, he must have means ; but what after all were the means which he appeared to possess compared with the means which he might be enjoying?   And further—and this was considered the most extraordinary circumstance of all—there was his attitude in the cathedral.   He followed the services devoutly ; and such a thing as attention, let alone devotion, on the part of a lay clerk had never been heard of in Morningquest.   There was not even a remote tradition in existence to prepare anybody's mind for such a contingency.

So that altogether the man was a mystery ; a mystery, however, toward which the kindly people were well-disposed. And no wonder.   For the Tenor's manners were as attractive as his appearance, and his ways were not at all mysterious when considered apart from the points already indicated, but, on the contrary, simple in the extreme : the ways of one who is kindly courteous and considerate on all occasions, paying proper respect to every man, and also rigorously exacting from each the respect that was due to himself.   He would always see people who called upon him, and though it was believed that he would rather not have been disturbed, he was too much of a gentleman to show it.   In fact, it was agreed that he was a gentleman before everything, and not at all like a " Jones " ; and therefore, acting on some instinctive perception of the fitness of things, the citizens dropped the offensive appellation altogether and called him " the Tenor " simply, as they might have called him " the Duke."

There was at first a good deal of wonder as to where the money came from with which he furnished his little house in the Close.   How did he manage to buy so many books and pictures? and how could he afford to give so much away in charity? For it was known beyond a doubt that he had on more than one occasion relieved the families of the other singers, and had relieved them, too, in a most substantial way.   It was evident that he had means ; but if he had means, why did he sing in the choir?   This question was the Alpha and Omega of all that concerned him.

It was asked everywhere and by everybody ; but no one could answer it save the dean, who was not to be approached upon the subject.   Finally, however, people grew tired of forming conjectures which were neither denied nor affirmed, and, becoming accustomed to the Tenor's presence amongst them, they ceased as a regular thing to discuss his affairs.

But this was not the case until a story had been circulated about him which was generally believed, although nobody knew from whence it emanated. He was, according to the story, the illegitimate son of an actress, and some great—in-the-sense-of-having-a-title—man, from whom he inherited his aristocratic appearance and a small income. His mother, it was said, had been an opera singer, which accounted for his voice ; and shame, they declared, on the discovery of his birth, had driven him into his present retirement, and caused him to renounce the world. As this story accounted in the most satisfactory manner for all that was strange about him, it was regarded in every respect as authentic ; and, after the wickedness of titled men and the frailty of acting women had been freely commented upon with much sage shaking of the head, as if only titled men were wicked and acting women frail, and Morningquest itself was a saintly city, innocent of any deed not strictly in accordance with its word, the matter was allowed to drop, and the Tenor was left to " gang his ain gait," which he would have done in any case, probably, but which he continued to do in a quiet, earnest, regular way that won him a friendly feeling from most men, and more than his share of sympathy and attention from the good women who had not self-love enough to be wounded by his indifference. Unsophisticated little maidens, just budding into womanhood, would peep after him shyly from the old-fashioned houses sometimes, and would feel in their tender little hearts a gentle pity for one who was so handsome and so unfortunate. Like the true hero of romance, he was believed by them to be supremely unhappy, and all they asked was to be allowed to comfort him ; but he noticed none of them. And so the little maidens blushed at first for having thought of him at all, and then forgot him for somebody else ; or, if the somebody else did not come quickly, they began to regard the Tenor with a totally different feeling—almost as if he had wronged them in some way. But the Tenor continued to "gang his ain gait," and was alike indifferent to their pity or their spite.

His little house, like most of those in the Close, had an old walled garden behind it, a large garden for the size of the house, and so sheltered that many things grew there which would not grow elsewhere in the open. The house itself was picturesque on that side, having a bright south aspect favourable to the growth of creepers, with which it was thickly covered, jasmine, clematis, honeysuckle, and roses succeeding each other in their regular order ; and the garden was always full of flowers. It was here that the Tenor spent much of his time, hard at work. He had evidently a passion for flowers, and was a most successful gardener, the conservatory and orchid house, which he had had built soon after his arrival, being always lovely even in the winter. The building of these two houses was considered an extravagance, and had caused the Close to point the finger at him for a while ; but when someone declared that the unfortunate Tenor had probably in-herited much of his mother's recklessness, and was not there-fore responsible as other people were, the suggestion was con-sidered reasonable enough, and from that time forward the Tenor's expensive tastes were held to be separate matter for commiseration ; the truth being that Morningquest could not bear to be on bad terms with the Tenor, and would have found an excuse for him had he outraged the best preserved pre-judices it ever held.

It was only necessary to glance at the Tenor's books to per-ceive that he was a student. Many valuable works in many languages were scattered about his house, and it was a well-known fact that he spent much of his leisure in poring over these. To what end his studies might be directed no one, of course, could tell, but it was assumed that he had acquired a respectable amount of knowledge from the fact that the dean, himself a learned man, delighted not a little in his conversa-tion. When this fact had been fully ascertained by careful observation, smouldering curiosity blazed up afresh, and sur-mise was once more busy with the Tenor's name. Did he write for the magazines, they wondered? It seemed likely enough, for it was notorious in Morningquest that people who did that kind of thing were not like the rest of the world ; and it soon came to pass that certain articles relating to various things, such as drainage, deep sea fishery, the coinage of Greece, competitive examinations in China, and essays on other subjects likely to interest an artistic man, were confi-dently assumed to be his. And the shy little girls in the old-fashioned houses, who never looked at anything in the maga-zines but the pictures and the poetry, were wont to credit him with certain passionate lays from which they got quite new ideas of eyes and dies and sighs, and other striking rhymes to musical metres which made their little hearts throb pleasurably.

But nothing more definite was known of the Tenor's labours than was known of anything else concerning him; and, fortunately for himself, there was that in his bearing which preserved him from being personally annoyed by impertinent curiosity, so that he was most probably pretty nearly the only person in the city who had no idea of the interest he himself excited.

Two years had glided by in great apparent tranquillity since the day the Tenor entered the choir; two years, during which he had trodden the path of life so uprightly, and so purely, that not even a suspicion of wrong-doing was ever breathed against him by gentle or simple, good or bad. It was a calm and passionless existence that he led, the life of an ascetic, but of a cultivated ascetic, devoted to the highest intellectual pursuits, and actuated by the belief that their value consisted, not in their market price, nor in the amount of attention called fame, which they might attract to himself, but in the pleasure they gave and in the good they did. Many a weary man whose life had been wasted in the toil of bringing himself before the world, when he had reached the summit of his ambition, might well have envied the Tenor his placid countenance and untroubled lot; some might even have perceived that there was more of poetry than of commonplace in the quiet life which glided on so evenly, soothed by the cathedral services, cheered by the chime, and guarded by the shadow of its gray protecting walls.

The Tenor's cheeks had been haggard and worn when he first settled in Morningquest, and dark circles round his eyes had betokened sleepless nights, and the ceaseless gnawing ache of a great grief. But all that had passed as the days wore on, giving place to a settled expression of peace—peace tinged with a certain sadness, but dignified by resignation. Gradually, too, although he remained slender, he ceased to be emaciated, and his cheeks assumed a healthy hue that very well became them.

CHAPTER II.

IT was thought at first that the dean's intimacy with the new Tenor arose from a sense of duty sharpened by the feeling of self-reproach with which he had regarded his fancied neglect of the old one; but, however that might have been, it was

continued from a genuine liking for the man himself.   No one
in Morningquest knew the Tenor half so well as the dean did,
no one could have had a truer regard for him, or watched the
passing of his trouble with more affectionate interest, or noted
the change for the better which had been wrought by the regular occupation of those peaceful days with greater satisfaction.
The dean knew the Tenor's story, so that their relations might
be called confidential ; but for two years no allusion had been
made by either of them to the past, neither had any plans been
formed for the future.

At the end of that time, however, the dean noticed signs of
awakening energy in his friend.   The Tenor performed his
duties less mechanically.   His apathy was broken by fits of
restlessness.   He had found the mornings long lately ; he had
thought the afternoons objectless ; and when evening came
and the lamps were lighted, he wearied of his books and music,
and chafed a little for something, not change exactly ; but he
was conscious of a desire—and this he only felt at times—a
desire for some trifling human interest which should make the
life he was leading fuller.   He had awakened, in fact, from his
long lethargy, and found himself alone.

The Dean of Morningquest was a remarkable man.   He had
the fine physique, the high-breeding, and the scholarly reputation common to that order of divines who keep up the dignity
of the Church without doing much for Christianity.   In person
he was tall, but stooped from the shoulders.   He had white
hair, a fine intellectual face ; fresh, and with that young look
in it which has been called saint-like, and is only seen on the
faces of those in whom passion has not died a natural death as
the vital powers decay, but has been brought into subjection,
and made to do good work instead of evil.   No man consorted
more habitually with his equals, or seldomer entertained the
notion that there were such people in the world as his inferiors.
He practised his religion to the last letter of church law,
and worshipped Christ the Son of God ; but there is no doubt
that he would have turned his exclusive back on Christ the carpenter's son, and had him prosecuted for an impostor had he
presented himself with no better pedigree.   He could tell the
story of the Saviour's sufferings with infinite pathos because he
knew who the Saviour was ; but he could not have told the
same story with the same power had the hero of it been merely
one common man sacrificing his life for others.   What affected
the dean was the enormous condescension.   It was the great-

ness of the Man, not the greatness of the deed, that appealed to him. A poor tradesman might sacrifice his life nobly also ; but, then, what is the life of a tradesman comparatively speaking ?

People called the dean proud and worldly wise, but this was not true of him. He may have believed that all the people of Palestine belonged to county families, and were therefore called the chosen people, but he never said so. A certain gentle humility of demeanour always distinguished him, no matter to whom he spoke ; and he was without doubt a thoroughly good nineteenth century churchman, living at his own level, of course, and true to his caste, toward the weaknesses of which he exercised much charity and forbearance, while he expressed his condemnation of its sins by rigorously excluding from his family circle any member of it who had been openly convicted of disgraceful conduct, just as he excluded professional men and other common citizens when they held no official position which he was obliged to recognize, and were not connected with the landed gentry. But these were the characteristics of his position, for as a dean he was required to be the slave of precedent ; as a man, however, he was known to be just and generous, and an excellent good friend to all who had any claim upon him, from the bishop who governed him down to the humblest chorister in the cathedral which he governed.

It was in the early spring when the dean first noticed what he took to be a change for the better in the Tenor's attitude toward life at large. The dean was susceptible himself to kindly changes in the season ; so much so, indeed, that, contrary to all precedent, he allowed himself to be tempted out after dark one night into the Close by the balmy mildness of the weather. His mind had been running all day upon the Tenor, and, noticing as he passed his little house that the blind was up, and the sitting room window wide open, showing the lamplit interior, and the object of his thoughts pacing restlessly to and fro, he determined to go in and have a chat. The Tenor received him cordially, but his manner was somewhat absent, and for a wonder the conversation flagged.

"Are you well ?" the dean asked at last. "You look somewhat fatigued, I think, and pale."

"Yes, I am well, thank you," the Tenor answered, brushing his hand back over his forehead and hair, a gesture which was habitual. "But I fancy," he added smiling, "that I am beginning to be a little "—he did not know what.

"Ah!" said the dean, looking at him with the grave, critical air of an anxious physician, and ruminating before he pronounced his diagnosis. "You have shown most extraordinary perseverance in the course of life you marked out for yourself," he finally observed; "and I trust your resolution is well recompensed by having obtained for you that peace of mind which you sought. But there is one thing I should like to be permitted to point out to you. I do not venture to advise, because, in the first place, it is always a difficult matter to decide on what would be best for another man's welfare; and, in the second"—the dean always spoke with great deliberation—"a man who has proved himself so capable of acting with prudence and determination, so competent to judge, and so firm in carrying out his convictions as you have been, might well consider advice from anyone presumptuous. And, therefore, I am merely going to observe that, lately, it has seemed to me to be a pity that your life should continue much longer to be a life of inaction. I hope, and indeed I think, that the years you have spent so well in this quiet way have been even more beneficial than you yourself imagine; that they have not only reconciled you to life, but have given you back the confidence and energy which should belong to your character and abilities, and the ambition to succeed in the world which should belong to your age. For some time past it has seemed to me that you are more restless than you used to be; and I have fancied, indeed I may say I have hoped, that you are at last beginning to long for change."

The Tenor sat silent and thoughtful for a while.

"No," he began at last, "I do not even yet long for change, as you would understand the longing. I have begun to feel a want, though I scarcely know of what—of companionship, perhaps, of some new interest; but I have no inclination for any change that would take me away from here. After the storm I passed through, this place has been for me a perfect haven of rest; and now that my peace of mind has returned to me, do you think it would be wise, by any voluntary act, to alter the present course of my life, seeing that it is so well with me as it is? When a man is content it does not seem to me that any change can be for the better; and, trifles apart, I really am content."

"God grant it may last," the dean responded earnestly. "Only I would warn you to be ready for change in case it comes to you in spite of yourself. I would warn you not to

feel too secure. For I have noticed this, that, for some mysterious reason which no mortal can fathom, it appears to be the
will of Heaven that when a man is able to say sincerely, ' I am
happy'; when he is most confident, believing his happiness to
be as firmly placed as earthly happiness can be, then is the
time for him to be most watchful, for then is change most
likely to be at hand. Indeed, it has seemed to me that this
feeling of security, or rather of content with things as they are,
is in itself an indication of coming change."

As he finished speaking the cathedral clock above them
began to strike the hour. Slowly the mellow notes followed
each other, filling the night with sound, and dying away in a
long reverberation when the twelfth had struck. Then came
silence, then the chime, voicelike, clear, and resonant :

He, watch-ing o-ver Is - ra - el, slumbers not, nor sleeps.

After which all was so still that the Tenor, looking up through
the open window at the moonlit cathedral, towering above him,
gray, shadowy, and mysterious, felt as if the world itself had
stopped, and all the life in it had been resolved into a moment
of intense self-consciousness, of illimitable passionate yearning
for something not to be expressed.

The next day was Saturday, and in the afternoon the Tenor
had to sing.

CHAPTER III.

THERE is human nature, both literally and figuratively
speaking, in Wagner's method of setting a character to a
tune of its own ; for, although our lives can hardly be said to
order themselves to one consistent measure, our days often do.

For months now, "When the orb of day departs," Schubert's
song, had accompanied the Tenor. It had soothed him, it had
irritated him ; it had expressed passionate longing, it had been
the utterance of despairing apathy ; it had marked the vainest
regret, and it had suggested hope ; it had wearied him, it had
comforted him ; but it had never left him. That Saturday
morning, however, when he awoke, his mind was set to another

measure. Schubert's song had gone as it had come, without conscious effort on his part ; but it had left a substitute, for the Tenor, as he lingered over his morning's work, found himself continually murmuring whole phrases of a chant which he had heard once upon a time when he was staying in an old town in France. It was the Litany of the Blessed Virgin sung at Benediction by some unseen singer with a wonderfully sympathetic mezzo-soprano voice. The Tenor had gone again and again to hear her in this chant, the music of which suited her as well as it did the theme. The words of adoration, "Sancta Maria, Sancta Dei Genetrix, Sancta Virgo virginum," were uttered evenly on notes that admitted of the tenderest expression, while the supplication, the "Ora pro nobis," rose to the full compass of the singer's voice, and was delivered in tones of passionate entreaty. At the end, in the "Agnus Dei," the music changed, dropping into the minor with impressive effect, the effect of earnestness wearied by effort but still unshaken ; and it was this final appeal in all its pathetic beauty that now recurred to the Tenor. He had not thought of the chant for years, nor had there been anything apparently to recall it now ; but all that day it possessed him, and at intervals he caught himself involuntarily singing it aloud :

> " Agnus Dei, qui tollis peccata mundi, parce nobis Domine,
> Agnus Dei, qui tollis peccata mundi, exaudi nos Domine,
> Agnus Dei, qui tollis peccata mundi, miserere nobis."

He sang it while he was dressing ; he whistled it with his hands in his pockets while he walked up and down the room waiting for his breakfast ; and at breakfast, with the newspaper before him, he hummed it to himself steadily. He began it again as he crossed the road to enter the cathedral for the early morning service ; he continued it while he was putting on his surplice ; he marched to it in the procession, and he rapped it out on his music book when he had taken his seat in the choir. He opened the book to study his solo for the afternoon service, but before he was halfway through his mind was busily rendering, not the music before him, but

> " Angus Dei, qui tollis peccata mundi, parce nobis Domine."

The haunting strain had become an intolerable nuisance by this time, and he made a vigorous effort to get rid of it by giving his mind to what was going on around him, and interesting himself in the people as they entered and took their places in stall and choir, and canon's pew, chancel and transept. Being Saturday, there was a good attendance even at this early service. Strangers from a distance came in to see the cathedral, and people in the place came in to see the strangers; so that there was plenty to observe, especially for one who (unlike the Tenor) was a little behind the scenes or had peeped beneath the surface and beheld the various incidents of the life-dramas which were constantly being enacted in the sacred edifice itself from service to service in the midst and with the help of psalms and hymns and spiritual songs, prayers and sermons, under the dean's very nose, and often in the presence of the bishop. The world at worship is a worldly sight, and there was a certain appropriateness in the Tenor's *miserere*; but he failed to apply it although it kept him company to the end, and was still faithful when he sallied forth from the gloom of the cathedral and went on his way with the rest in the sunshine and freshness of a glad new day.

As the time for the afternoon service approached, the people began again to flock to the cathedral, but in crowds now, for it had been rumoured that the Tenor was to sing.

The choir, from their lateral position on either side of the aisle, were able to look up and down the church, having on the one hand and opposite the distinguished visitors who were accommodated with seats in the stalls, the canon's and dean's pews; and on the other the officiating clergy and the congregation generally. It was an advantageous position for those who came to observe, but the Tenor had not hitherto been one of these. The music, when it was interesting, absorbed him; and when it was dull the monotony soothed him, so that he noticed nothing. It had done so this afternoon. During all the first part of the service he neither saw nor heard, but did his work mechanically like one in a dream; and in every pause of it the old chant recurred to him, filling his heart with a separate undercurrent of solemn supplication, now in French: "Agneau de Dieu, qui effacez les péchés du monde, ayez pitié de nous," and now in Latin: "Agnus Dei, qui tollis peccata mundi, miserere nobis."

The dean preached a *sermonette* on Saturday afternoon, which he took the precaution to deliver before the anthem, so that the people might still have something to look forward to and keep their seats. The *sermonette* over, the organ played the opening bars of the Tenor's solo, and the choir stood up.

While he waited for the note, the Tenor absently fixed his eyes on a lady in the canon's pew. The spell of the old chant was still upon him, and, instead of preparing his mind for his task, he let it murmur on : " Agnus Dei, qui tollis peccata mundi, parce nobis Domine "—while a rapt silence fell upon the congregation—not a ribbon rustled ; the expression of expectation was most intense. One would scarcely have expected the Tenor to take up the note at the right moment, his mind being preoccupied by another strain, but he did. The lady in the canon's pew held the music of the anthem before her, and had been following that ; but when the first clear notes of the Tenor's voice rang through the building she looked up as if in surprise, their eyes met, and with a shock the Tenor awoke from his lethargy, faltered for a moment, and then stopped. The organ played on, however, and he quickly recovered ; but the pause had been quite perceptible and the people were amazed. It was the first time that such a thing had happened with their Tenor, which made it a matter of moment ; and the wonder of it grew, parties being formed, the one to excuse the slip and call it nothing, the other to blame him for his carelessness, as people who never disappoint us are blamed, with bitterness, if for once by chance they err.

That night the Tenor's restlessness grew to a head. He was engaged upon a piece of work he wished to finish, but he could not settle to it ; and after making an ineffectual effort to concentrate his attention upon it, he took up his hat and strolled out.

It was a lovely moonlight night. The line of trees in the Close were in flower, and their sweetness was overpowering. He did not stay there, however, but wandered out into the city, with his hat pushed back from his forehead, and his hands in his pockets. The gas was not lighted in the streets as the moon was near the full ; and beneath her rays, all common objects, however obtrusively vulgar by daylight, were refined into beauty for the moment.

> " Pater de cœlis Deus, miserere nobis ;
> Fili Redemptor mundi Deus, miserere nobis,
> Spiritus sancte Deus, miserere nobis ;
> Sancte Trinitas unus Deus, miserere nobis "—

the Tenor sang softly to himself as he slowly pursued his way.

He had some sort of a vague idea that he would like to go and look at the quaint old market-place by moonlight ; and when he reached it, he stopped at the corner, interrupting his song to gaze in artistic appreciation at the silent scene before him, at the heavy masses of shade interspersed with intervals of mellow moonlight, and the angles of roof and spire and ornament cut clean as cameos against "the dark and radiant clarity of the beautiful night sky."

The market-place was an irregular square, picturesquely enclosed by tall houses of different heights and most original construction, among them the east end of a church and part of a public building of ancient date were crowded in ; without incongruous effect, however, the moonlight, crisp, cool, and clear, having melted hue and form of all alike into one harmonious whole, to the charm of which even the covered stalls, used in the day's dealings and now packed in the middle of the square, and the deserted footways added something.

A tall, slender lad of sixteen or seventeen was standing on the edge of the pathway, just in front of the Tenor. He was the only other person about, and on that account the Tenor had looked at him a second time. As he did so, a young woman came suddenly round the corner, and accosted the boy.

"Qu'il est beau !" she exclaimed, laying her hand on his arm, and smiling up into his face admiringly.

The Boy stepped back to avoid her, with an unmistakable gesture of disgust, and in doing so, he accidentally stumbled up against the Tenor.

He turned round, and apologised confusedly.

The Tenor raised his hat, and answered courteously. They were standing together side by side now, and remained so for some seconds, silently surveying the scene ; and then the Tenor all unconsciously began again to sing :

"Sancta Maria," he entreated, "Sancta Dei Genetrix, Sancta Virgo virginum, ora pro nobis."

The girl had been wandering off again, but at the first note of the supplication she stopped. A chord of memory stirred. She knew the words, she knew the tune. She had sung them both herself often and often at home in France. She was a Child of Mary then—and now ?

As the Tenor finished the last note of the phrase and paused, she clasped her hands convulsively, and gasped : "O mon Dieu ! mon Dieu ! ayez pitié de moi ! "

Her half-inarticulate cry did not reach the Tenor and the Boy, neither had they observed her distress, for just at that moment the city clock struck one, and both had raised their heads involuntarily in expectation of the chime. And presently out upon the night it rolled, a great wave of sound, swelling and spreading, muffled by distance somewhat, but still distinctly sweet and insistent :

He, watch-ing o - ver   Is - ra - el,   slumbers not, nor sleeps.

"Do you believe it?" said the Boy, glancing toward the girl, and repeating the gesture of disgust with which he had shrunk from her when she accosted him.

The Tenor lifted his hat, and brushed his hand back over his hair. "Do I believe it in spite of *that?* you would say," he answered, considering the girl with quiet eyes. "Yes, I believe it," he declared, "in spite of *that,* which has puzzled older heads than yours."

With which he turned to retrace his steps, taking up the Litany of the Blessed Virgin once more as he went, the supplication : "Agnus Dei, qui tollis peccata mundi, miserere nobis," being audible long after he was out of sight.

The Boy remained as he had left him for some time, apparently lost in thought ; and the girl still stood a little way off in a dejected attitude, her hands clasped before her, her eyes fixed on the ground. She looked ill and spiritless. The Boy, glancing at her carelessly, wondered at the intent expression of her face ; he did not perceive that she was praying, but she was.

The midnight stillness deepened about those two ; there was not another living creature to be seen. The irregular old buildings on every side looked ruinous in the shadowy moonlight, and the whole market-place presented to the Boy a picture of desolation which chilled him. He was about to turn away with a last cursory glance at the other solitary figure, when something suddenly occurred which arrested his attention. It seemed to startle him too, for he sprang back, with prompt agility, into a dark doorway behind him, from whence he watched what followed with the keenest interest, being careful, however, to conceal himself the while. He had not felt any movement of pity or kindly compassion for the girl ; perfect indifference had succeeded the first sensation of repugnance ; he would have left her there to any fate that might await her, and would have expected all right-minded people to do the same, It was therefore with unmitigated astonishment that he beheld the scene which was now being enacted before him. They were no longer alone. A tall and graceful lady of most dignified bearing, with a countenance of peculiar serenity and sweetness, had approached from the opposite direction, and was standing beside the girl, speaking to her evidently, but the Boy was too far off to hear what was said. He could see, however, that the girl's whole attitude had changed. She was no longer dejected, but eager : and she gazed in the lady's face as she listened to her words with an expression of admiration and wonder, one had almost said of adoration, upon her own, as though it were a heavenly visitant who had hailed her. The lady, as she spoke, pointed to a street opposite, and the girl cast a quick glance in that direction ; she seemed to be measuring a distance she was impatient to traverse, and moved a step forward at the same time, uttering some short sentence with rapid gesticulation. The pantomime was perfectly intelligible to the Boy, who understood that she was feverishly anxious to carry out some intention on the instant. The lady seemed to hesitate, then, laying her beautiful white ungloved hand on the girl's shoulder, and looking into her face, she spoke again earnestly. The girl answered with passionate protestations, and then the lady smiled, satisfied apparently, and led the way in the direction to which she had pointed, the girl following in haste. Her hat had fallen back, her hair was loosened, her countenance beamed with enthusiasm, as the Boy observed. He was stealing softly after them, skipping from shadow to shadow, in great enjoyment of the whole adventure.

The lady took the girl to a long low rambling house beside a church, at the door of which she knocked. It was opened immediately by a singularly venerable looking old man, evidently a priest, with a fine though rugged face, instinct with zeal and benevolence. He had his hat in his hand, and was just coming out ; but when he saw who had knocked, he stopped short, and bowed deferentially. The girl sank down upon the doorstep as if exhausted.

"I have brought Marie Cruchot home, father," the lady said.

"Ah, my daughter, is that you? We have been expecting you for many days," the old man exclaimed in French, taking the girl's hand and raising her gently as he spoke. "I have prayed for you day and night without ceasing, and only just now, as I passed the convent, I went to ask the night portress for tidings of our wandering sheep, and specially mentioned you. But enter. The good sisters are waiting for you, and will welcome you with joy."

One of two sisters of charity, who were standing behind the priest, now came forward and kissed the girl. The old man raised his hat, and, looking up into the clear depths of the quiet sky, murmured a blessing, and went his way. And then the door was closed.

"Humph!" said the Boy, who was lurking up an entry opposite. "So that is what they do at night, is it? and that is the young person who sold her sister Louise to Mosley Menteith. Now I am beginning to know the world; and what an extraordinary old world it is, to be sure! One half seems to be always kept busy mending the mischief the other half has made."

He peeped cautiously out of the entry, looking for the lady, but she had disappeared, and night and silence reigned supreme.

CHAPTER IV.

ALL that the Tenor had witnessed of the scene in the market-place made little or no impression on him, and he would probably never have thought of it again had he not encountered the Boy a few nights later, standing, idly observant as before, at the same time and almost in the same place.

The Tenor's first impulse was to pass on without speaking, but the Boy looked at him, and there was something in the look, half shy, half appealing, which caused him to stop, and having stopped, he was obliged to speak.

To his first commonplace remark the Boy answered nervously, and with quick glances instantly averted, as if he were afraid to meet the Tenor's eyes. The latter continued to talk, however, and after a little the Boy's timidity wore off, and his manner became assured.

"This is a curious old place, is it not?" he remarked; "and curiously named if you consider how very little *quest* there is for *morning* here, for the new day which would bring the light of truth after the darkness of error."

"It never struck me that the name could have any allegorical significance," the Tenor answered prosaically. "I believe it used to be Morn and Quest. It stands at the junction of the two rivers, you know, or rather just below it. They run their united race from hence to the sea."

"I know," said the Boy. "But it really is a romantic old place, especially by moonlight; and it teems with historical associations, as the guidebook has it, with its cathedral, cloisters, castle, and close—the closest in England, they say. Don't you feel remote from the world when you get in there, and the four old gates are shut upon you? The water-gate is the most interesting to me."

" Two of the others are architecturally beautiful where they haven't been spoilt by restoration," the Tenor rejoined.

"Ah!" the Boy ejaculated, and then continued boyishly: "You're not a native evidently, or you wouldn't speak so moderately. The inhabitants boast themselves black in the face about everything in the city. They made me believe that the whole earth began here originally, and that it was also the point of departure for the sea. It did wash their walls on the southern side once upon a time; but the sinfulness of the people compelled it to retire ages ago, and it has since enjoyed a purer moral atmosphere twenty miles away."

"Indeed," said the Tenor. "I did not know that the sea was so fastidious!"

"Oh, yes, it is, naturally," the Boy declared; "but it cannot choose its position for itself always any more than we can. But people are more entertaining than places," he pursued; "don't you think so? Now these people, how Godfearing and orthodox they are, and how admirably they make religion part of their daily life in the matter of stretching a point and using the right of Christian charity to be lenient when a too rigorous adhesion to principle would injure their interest. Their chief confectioner retired from business the other day, but they would not give their custom to his successor at first because of his religious opinions. They forsook him for his atheism, in fact; but in a very short time they returned to him for his ice-creams, which are excellent. If you ever feel any doubt about life being worth living, go and get one. It will reassure you."

They had been strolling on as they talked, and now the Tenor turned to look at his companion, being about to answer him, when something in the Boy's face struck him as familiar, and he paused, knitting his brows in a perplexed effort to think what it was. Measured beside himself the Boy was rather taller than he looked, but very slender, and his hands and feet were too small. He had dark eyebrows, peculiarly light luxuriant hair, and, as a natural accompaniment, a skin of extreme fairness and delicacy. In fact, he was too fair for his age, it made him look effeminate ; and had it not been for the dark eyebrows and eyelashes his colouring would have been insipid. As it was, however, there was no lack of character in his face ; and you would have called him "a pretty boy" while thinking it high time he had grown out of his prettiness. This was the Tenor's reflection, but his too earnest gaze apparently disconcerted the Boy, who returned it with one quick anxious glance, then seemed to take fright, and finally bolted, leaving the Tenor alone in the road. "That young rascal is out without leave, and is afraid of being recognized," he concluded.

It was some weeks before they met again, and during the interval the Tenor often thought of the Boy with curiosity and interest. There was something unusual in his manner and appearance which would have attracted attention even if his conversation had not been significant, and that it was significant the Tenor discovered by the continual recurrence to his mind of some one or other of the Boy's observations. He had not tried to find out who the Boy was, interest not having stirred his characteristic apathy in such matters to that extent, but he looked for him continually both by day and night, his thoughts being pretty equally divided between him and the lady whose brilliant glance had had such a magical effect upon him the first time he encountered it. She came to the cathedral regularly now, and always sat in the canon's pew ; and always when he sang she looked at him, and he knew that the look was an expression of appreciation and thanks. He knew, too, that the day she did not come would be a blank day for him.

CHAPTER V.

THE moon had grown old, but the nights were still scented by the lime-trees when the Tenor met the Boy again. He had begun to believe that the Boy did not live in Morningquest ; and, as often happens, he was thinking of him less than usual on this particular occasion, and hence he came upon him unawares.

The Boy was lolling against the iron railings that enclosed the grassy space round which the old lime-trees grew, in the middle of one arm of the Close. It was a bright, clear night, but chilly, and he was wrapped up in a greatcoat which lent a little substance to his slender figure. The Tenor would have passed him without recognizing him, but for his sandy hair, which shone out palely against the bark of one of the trees.

"I was waiting for you," the Boy said. "Why are you so late to-night?"

"How do you know I am later than usual to-night?" he asked.

"Because, generally, you come out about ten o'clock, and it is nearly twelve now."

"How do you happen to know I generally come out about ten o'clock?"

"Oh," the Boy answered coolly, "I watched you. I have been studying your habits in order to find out what manner of man you are; and I think you'll do," he added patronizingly, with a wise shake of the head. "I guess you were looking for me too, weren't you?"

The Tenor smiled again, and, lifting his hat, brushed his hand back over his hair. "What makes you think so?" he asked.

"I am accustomed to that sort of thing," the Boy replied, with a twinkle in his eyes. "People who meet me once try, as a rule, to cultivate my acquaintance," with which he raised himself from his lolling posture, and added : "I'll walk up and down with you, if you like, but you must give me your arm. I require support."

"Why? are you tired? What have you been doing to-day?" the Tenor asked as he acquiesced, smiling in his grave way, for the Boy pleased him.

"Oh, well"—considering—"I got up this morning."

"That was a serious business!"

"It was"—with emphasis—"for I had to settle a serious question before I arose. I had to make up my mind about free will and predestination. If I could believe in predestination I thought I might have breakfast in bed without self-reproach ; but if it were a matter of free will, I felt I should be obliged to get up."

"And how did you settle it?" The tenor asked.

"I didn't settle it," the Boy replied, "for just as I was coming to a conclusion the breakfast bell rang, and the force of habit compelled me to jump out of bed in a hurry. I don't call *that* free will ! And I think, on the whole, predestination had the best of it, perhaps, for my breakfast was sent up to me after all, without any action on my part, and I partook of it in the silence and solitude of my own chamber, with an easy conscience, and the luxuries of an open window and a book. I suppose you can do that every day if you like ? You have no one to interfere with you."

" I have no one to interfere with me," the Tenor repeated, thoughtfully. " Perhaps it would be better for me if I had."

" By better you mean happier," the Boy responded, clasping both hands round the Tenor's arm.

The latter looked down at him, wondering a little, but not displeased.

They were walking in the shadow of the houses just then, and could not see each other's faces, but the Tenor's heart warmed more and more to this curious Boy, and he pressed the hand that rested on his arm a little closer. It was a long time since the grave, large-hearted, earnest man had known anyone so young and spontaneous, or felt a touch of human sympathy, and in both he found refreshment—a something of that something which he knew he needed but could not name.

They took a turn up and down in silence, and then the Boy began again, boyishly : " I say, do you suffer from nerves ? You made rather a bungle of it the other day, didn't you ?"

" You mean when I broke down in that anthem ? Were you there ? Where did you sit ?"

" With the distinguished strangers, of course."

" I did not see you."

" Did you look behind you ? "

" No. But are you a stranger here ?"

" Well, not exactly," said the Boy, with a great affectation of candour.

They had passed out into the open now, and the Tenor could see the Boy's face. He had glanced at him as we do at the person we speak to, but something he saw arrested his glance, and caused him to look again keenly and closely—the something that had perplexed him before.

The Boy returned his gaze smiling and unabashed. " She put you out, didn't she ?" he asked with a grin. " Verily, she hath eyes—at least, I've been told so ; but I am no judge of such things myself."

The puzzled look passed from the Tenor's face. " I know what it is," he said. " You are exactly like her."

The Boy laughed. " I meant to keep it a secret. I was

going to make a mystery of myself," he said ; "but faculties like yours are not to be baffled, and since you have observed so much, I might as well confess that there are two of us, twins. They call us the Heavenly Twins."

"What, signs of the Zodiac ?" said the Tenor.

" No, signs of the times," said the Boy.

There was a little pause and then the Tenor observed : " I should hardly have thought you were twins, except for the like-ness. Your sister looks older than you do."

"Well, you see, she's so much more depraved," said the Boy. " And her lovely name is Angelica—excuse me. I must laugh." He slipped his hand from the Tenor's arm, leant his back against a railing, and exploded. "Excuse me," he re-peated, when he could contain himself. " I have suffered from this affliction all my life. I can't help laughing."

" So it seems," said the Tenor, " May I ask what provoked this last attack of your malady ?"

Before he could answer, they were accosted by a respectable looking man, a small farmer from a distance probably, who was making the most of a rare opportunity by trying to see as much as he could of the cathedral in the dark.

" I beg your pardon, sir," he said—the Boy was all gravity in a moment—"but could you tell me what flying buttresses are."

" A sign of rain," said the Boy, whereupon the Tenor seized him by the scruff of the neck and shook him incontinently. For a moment after he was released, the Boy seemed to be overcome by astonishment ; but this was rapidly succeeded by an attack of the malady he had declared to be congenital, apparently brought on by the shock of the chastisement, and the Tenor, who had walked on a little way with the countryman answer-ing his questions, left him laughing all over. He waited, lean-ing against the railing, until the Tenor returned.

" You little wretch——" the latter began.

" That's right, don't make a stranger of me," the Boy inter-rupted. " Treat me like a younger brother. You make me feel that I have succeeded in establishing confidential relations between us, which is what I want."

The Tenor was about to reply, but his voice was drowned by a sudden clangour of the bells above them. The clock struck, the chime rang, and while they waited listening, the Tenor raised his hat. They were standing at the corner of the cloisters, looking up to the clock tower and its tapering spire, which surmounted the Norman façade and entrance to the south transept.

"I must go," the Boy said, when he could hear himself speak.

"Will you not come in—to my house—I am afraid I am very wanting in hospitality," the Tenor exclaimed. " I should have asked you before. I live close by. I should be so glad——"

"Not to-night," the Boy interrupted hastily ; "another time. Good-bye ! "

CHAPTER VI.

WHEN next the Tenor saw Angelica after he had learnt that she was the Boy's sister, he felt that a new interest had been added to her attractions.

It was on a Saturday afternoon in the cathedral, as usual, and she came in late. But almost as soon as she had taken her seat she looked at the Tenor with an earnest, anxious glance that reminded him of her brother, and her colour deepened. The Boy had told her then, the Tenor thought, and he was glad she knew that they had met ; it was a bond of union which seemed to bring her nearer.

He noticed now how like in feature the brother and sister were. The girl looked taller as well as older, and was alto-gether on a larger scale, her figure being amply developed for her age, while the Boy's was fragile to a fault ; her hair was dark too, while his was light ; but with these slight differences there was likeness enough to show that they were twins. They both had the same shaped eyes, the same straight, well-defined, dark eyebrows and long lashes, the same features, the same clear skin and even teeth ; but the expression was differ-ent. There was never any devilment in the girl's face ; it was always pale and tranquil, almost to sadness, as the Tenor saw it, standing out in fair relief against the dark oak carving of the stalls. Her movements were all made, too, with a certain quiet dignity that seemed habitual. In the Boy, on the con-trary, there was no trace of that graceful attribute. He threw himself about, lolled, lollopped, and gesticulated, with as much delight in the free play of his muscles as if he were only let out to exercise them occasionally ; and it seemed as if he must always be at daggers drawn with dignity. But such a slender intellectual creature could not without absurdity acquire the ponderous movements and weight of manner of smaller wits and duller brains. In the girl, quiescence was the natural outcome of womanly reserve; in the Boy, it would have been mere affectation. His lightness and brightness were his great charm at present, a charm, however, which was much enhanced by moments of thoughtfulness, which gave glimpses of another nature beneath, with more substantial qualities. The Tenor had soon perceived that he was not all mischief, romp, and boyishness; all that was on the surface; but beneath there was a strong will at work with some purpose, or the Tenor was much mistaken; and there was daring, and there was originality. This was the Tenor's first impression, and further acquaintance only confirmed it.

Having formed his opinion of the Boy's abilities, the Tenor began to make plans for his future, and the selflessness of the man's nature showed itself in nothing more clearly, perhaps, than in the consideration he gave to the lad's career. His own had not cost him so much as a thought for years; but now he roused himself and became ambitious all at once for the Boy! He believed that there was the making of a distinguished man in him, and he allowed the hope of being able to influence him in some worthy direction to become as much a part of his daily life as another hope had become—a hope which was strongly felt but not yet acknowledged, except in so far as it took the form of a desire to see her, and made known its presence with force in the pang of disappointment which he suffered if by chance she failed to come as usual to the service on Saturday afternoon. He saw in the girl an ideal, and had found soul enough in the laughter-loving Boy to make him eager to befriend him.

And thus into the Tenor's life two new interests had found their way, and something which had hitherto been wanting to make the music of it perfect was heard at last in his wonderful voice when he sang.

CHAPTER VII.

ABOUT this time the weather changed; the nights were wet for a week, and when it cleared up the Tenor had begun to do some work for the dean which kept him at home in the evenings, so that he had no opportunity of seeing the Boy, who only seemed to come abroad at night, for some little time. He saw his sister, however, in the cathedral regularly once a week, and always she gave him a friendly glance, by which his days were rounded as by a blessing, and he felt content. His being so was entirely characteristic. Another man in his place would have lost the charm of the present in anxiety to reach some future which should be even more complete. But the Tenor took no thought for the morrow ; each day as it came was a joy to him, and his hopes, if he had any, were a part of his peace.

The work he was doing for the dean was interesting. He was making drawings to illustrate a history of Anglo-Norman times which the dean was writing. He drew well and with great facility ; but these drawings, many of which were architectural, required special care and accuracy, with the closest attention to detail, which made the work fatiguing, particularly as he had to do it at night, his only leisure time just then ; and more than once he had tired himself out, and been obliged to put it away and rest. On one of these occasions, instead of going to bed, he stretched himself in an easy-chair beside the open French window which looked out upon the cathedral, and prepared to indulge in the quiet luxury of a pipe while he rested his weary eyes. The great cathedral towered above him, and from where he sat the Tenor caught a beautiful glimpse of it anglewise, of the south transept and tower and spire ; the rich perpendicular windows of the clerestory, the bold span of the flying buttresses rising out of the plain but solid Norman base, every detail of which he knew and appreciated.

It was a fair, still, starry night without, and the light air that blew in upon him was sweet and refreshing. His mind wandered from subject to subject—a sleepy sign—as he smoked, and presently he put down his pipe and closed his eyes. He thought then that he had fallen asleep and was dreaming, and in his dream he fancied he heard himself sing. "This is a queer dream," he was conscious of saying. "That is my voice exactly. I have often wondered how it sounded to other people, and now I am listening to it myself, which is strange." But the strangest part of it was that the words to which the music shaped itself in his mind were not the words of any song he knew, but that expression of human nature which contains in itself some of the grandest harmony in the language :

" These our actors,
As I foretold you, were all spirits, and
Are melted into air, into thin air :
And, like the baseless fabric of this vision,
The cloud-capp'd towers, the gorgeous palaces,
The solemn temples, the great globe itself ;
Yea, all which it inherit, shall dissolve ;
And, like this insubstantial pageant faded,
Leave not a wreck behind.   We are such stuff
As dreams are made on, and our little life
Is rounded with a sleep."

The last words repeated themselves over and over again, on different notes and in another key each time, and with such powerful emphasis that at last it aroused the Tenor, upon whose sleepy brain the fact that it was not a voice but a violin to which he had been listening, dawned gradually, while his trained ear further recognized the tone of a rare instrument, and the touch of a master hand.   He got up and went to the window.   " Oh ! " he exclaimed, " is it you ? " and there was a world of pleasure in the exclamation.   "Come in."

The Boy, who was standing in the road, opened the little garden gate, and entered.   " I am glad you have relented," he said ; "for I meant to play until I had softened your heart, and had persuaded you to take me in ; and the hope deferred was making me sick."

"I was asleep," the Tenor answered.   "Why didn't you come in?   You must have known you would be welcome. Here is an easy-chair.   Sit down.   And, tell me, why do we only meet at night?   What do you do with yourself all day?"

"I am not a daylight beauty," the Boy declared.   "I look best at night."

"But seriously ?" the Tenor persisted.

"Oh, my tutor, you know—Sandhurst—exams—and that kind of thing."

"You are going into the army then ?"

But the Boy, smiling, put the question by.   The easy, pleasure-loving, sensuous side of his nature was evidently uppermost, and when that was the case it was so natural for him to shirk a disagreeable subject, that the Tenor had not the heart to pursue it further.

" Won't you take your hat off?" he said presently.

The Boy put up both hands to it.   "My head's a queer shape," he said, tapping it.   "You won't want to examine it phrenologically, will you ?"

"No," the Tenor answered, smiling. "Not if you object."

"I do object. I don't like to be touched."

The Tenor, still smiling, watched him as he carefully removed his hat. His head was rather a peculiar shape. It was too broad at the back, and too large altogether for his slight frame, though probably the thickness of his fluffy light hair, which stood up all over it, innocent of parting as the Tenor's own, added considerably to this last defect. There was nothing so very extraordinary about it, however, and the Tenor did not see why he should be sensitive on the subject, and rather suspected that the boy was gravely poking fun at him ; but as he could not be sure of this, and would not have hurt his feelings for the world, he forebore to make any remark.

The Boy glanced round the room. "What a wealthy luxurious fellow you are," he observed.

"These appearances of wealth, as you call it, are delusive," the Tenor answered. "I just happened to have money enough to furnish my house when I came here ; but I am a very poor man now. I have little or nothing, in fact, but my salary for singing in the choir."

"Oh," said the Boy. "And you might be so rich with your voice."

The Tenor brushed his hand back over his hair.

"Are you lazy ?" the Boy demanded.

"No," he answered, smiling again. The Boy kept him smiling perpetually.

"What is it, then ? Why don't you work ?"

"Well, I do work," the Tenor answered him.

"I mean, why don't you make money ?"

"Oh—because I have no one to make it for."

"If you had "—and the Boy leant forward eagerly—" would you ? Would you work for a lady who loved you if she gave herself to you ?"

"I would work for my wife," said the Tenor.

"Are you engaged ?" the Boy asked. There seemed no limit to his capacity for asking.

The Tenor shook his head, and shook the ashes out of his pipe at the same time.

"Are you in love ?" the Boy persisted.

The Tenor made no reply to this impertinence, but a glow spread over his face, forehead and chin and throat.

The Boy, whom nothing escaped, leant back satisfied. "I know what it is," he said. "She's married, and you don't like to ask her to run away with you. I expect she would, you know, if you did."

The Tenor threw himself back in his chair and laughed.

His mirth seemed to jar on the Boy, who got up and began to pace about the room, frowning and dissatisfied.

"You look pale," the Tenor said. "Have you been ill since I saw you?"

"No—yes," the Boy answered. "I had a bad cold. I was very sorry for myself."

The Tenor took up his violin, and examined it. "Where did you study?" he asked.

"Everywhere," was the ungraciously vague reply.

"I wish you would play again," the Tenor said, taking no notice of his ill-humour. "It would be a rare treat for a hermit like me."

"No," was the blunt rejoinder. "I don't want to make music. I want to explore."

"Well, make yourself at home," the Tenor said, humouring him good-naturedly.

"*Make* me at home," the Boy replied. "Confidential relations, you know. You may smoke if you like."

"Oh, thank you," the Tenor answered politely, sitting down in his easy-chair, from which he had risen to look at the violin, and taking up his pipe again.

The Boy was rummaging about now, and, finding much to interest him, he presently recovered his temper, and began to banter his host. But even this outlet was scarcely sufficient for his superfluous life and energy, so he emphasized his remarks by throwing a stray cushion or two at the Tenor ; he jumped over the chairs instead of walking round them, and performed an occasional *pas seul*, or pirouette, in various parts of the room. When these innocent amusements palled upon him, he took up his violin and played a plaintive air, to which he chanted :

> "There was a merry dromedary
> Waltzing on the plain ;
> Dromedary waltzing, dromedary prancing.
> And all the people said, it is a sign of rain,
> When they saw the good beast dancing ;"

executing grotesque steps himself at the same time in illustration.

"Oh, Boy, forbear ! " the Tenor exclaimed at last, " or you will be the death of me."

"That's it," the Boy responded cheerfully. "I mean to be life or death to you."

After this he sat down on a high-backed chair, with his hands in his pockets, his legs stretched out before him, and his chin on his chest, looking up from under his eyebrows at the Tenor thoughtfully. It was an interval of great gravity, and when he spoke again the Tenor looked for something serious.

"I say," he began at last.

The Tenor took his pipe from his mouth and waited, interrogatively.

"I say, I'm hungry."

The Tenor looked his dismay.

"Boys always are, you know," the youth added, encouragingly.

"And if there should be nothing in the house!" the poor Tenor ejaculated. "I'll go and see."

He returned quite crestfallen. "There *is* nothing," he said; "at least nothing but bread—no butter even."

"I don't believe you," said the Boy, rousing himself from his indolent attitude.

"Boy, you mustn't say you don't believe me."

"But I don't," said the Boy. "I don't believe you know where to look. Are the servants out?"

"Yes, my solitary attendant doesn't sleep here."

"Then I'll go and look myself."

"Oh, do, if you like," said the Tenor, much amused. And thinking the Boy would enjoy himself best if he were left to rummage at his own sweet will, he took up a book, brushed his hand back over his shining hair, and was soon absorbed. But presently he was startled by a wild cry of distress from the kitchen, and, jumping up hastily, he went to see what was the matter.

He found the Boy standing at one end of the kitchen, clutching a vegetable dish, and gazing with a set expression of absolute horror at some object quite at the other end. The Tenor strained his own eyes in the same direction, but could not at first make anything out. At last, however, he distinguished a shining black thing moving, which proved to be a small cockroach.

"Well, you *are* a baby!" he exclaimed.

"I'm not," the Boy snapped. "It's an idiosyncrasy. I can't bear creepy crawly things. They give me fits."

"I begin to perceive, Boy, that you have a reason for everything," the Tenor observed, as he disposed of the innocent object of the Boy's abhorrence.

"Put it out of sight," the latter entreated, looking nauseated.

But as soon as the Tenor had accomplished his mandate, his good humour returned, and he began to beam again. "What a duffer you are!" he said, taking the lid off the dish he held in his hand. "You have no imagination. You never lifted a dish cover. Why, I've found a dozen eggs—fresh, for I broke one into a cup to see; and here are a whole lot of cold potatoes."

"It doesn't sound appetizing; cold potatoes and raw eggs!"

"Sound! It isn't sound you judge by in matters of this kind. Just you wait, and you shall see, smell, and taste."

"Well, if it please you," the Tenor answered lazily. "I see something already. You have lighted a fire."

"Yes, and I've used all the dry sticks," said the Boy, with great glee. "Won't the old woman *swear* when she comes in the morning!"

The Tenor returned to his book, reflecting, as he prepared to resume it, on the wonderful provision of nature which endows the growing animal not only with such strong instincts of self-preservation, but with the power to gratify them, and to take itself off at the same time and be happy in so doing, thus saving those who have outgrown these natural proclivities from some of their less agreeable consequences.

Presently a hot red face appeared at the door. "Did you say you liked your eggs turned?" the Boy wanted to know.

"I didn't say; but I do, if you're frying them."

"And hard or soft?"

"Oh, soft."

"How many can you eat?"

"Half-a-dozen at least," the Tenor returned at random.

"And I can eat three"—with great gravity—"that will make nine, and leave three for your breakfast in the morning. I daresay you won't want more after such a late supper. I don't think I should myself."

"But do you mean me to understand that the voracity of the growing animal will be satisfied with less than I can eat?"

"Well, you see," the Boy explained apologetically, "the heat of the fire has taken a lot out of me."

"But the waste must be repaired."

"Yes, but the expenditure has been followed by a certain amount of exhaustion, and the power to repair the waste has yet to be generated ; it will come as a sort of reaction of the organs which can only set in after a proper period of repose—a sort of interregnum of their energies, you know."

The Tenor threw back his golden head. "Oh, Boy!" he expostulated, "don't make me laugh again to-night, don't, please !"

The Boy was very busy for the next ten minutes, arranging the table, and quite in his element ; cooing as he proceeded, and giving little muttered reasons to himself, in his soft contralto voice, for everything he did. That voice of his was wonderfully flexible ; he could make it harsh, grating, gruffly mannish, and caressing as a woman's, at will, but the tone that seemed natural to it was the deep, mellow contralto into which he always relapsed when not thinking of himself. The Tenor thought it hardly rough enough for a boy of his age, but it was in harmony with his fragile form, and delicate, effeminate features.

"Whom the gods love die young," flashed through his mind as he watched him now, coming and going ; and he sighed, it seemed so likely ; and felt already that he should miss the Boy ; and wondered, with retrospective self-pity, how he had managed to live at all with no such interest.

"A golden-headed, gray-eyed, white-toothed, fine-skinned son of the morning must be a sybarite," the Boy observed, entering the room at that moment ; "so I bring flowers, and also salad, just cut and crisp."

"May I ask how you knew there was salad in my garden ?"

"Well, you may *ask*," the Boy responded cheerfully ; "but—let me see, though—perhaps I had better tell you. I found that out the last time I was here. Perhaps you don't know that I came ? I wanted to discover the resources of the place, so I took advantage of your temporary absence on business one day, and inspected it."

"Where was I ?" the Tenor asked.

"You were busy at the fire insurance office opposite."

"Do you mean the cathedral ? Boy, I will not let you mock."

The Boy grinned. "It was the only time I could be at all sure of you," he pursued. "You were going to sing a solo. I saw it advertised in the paper, and laid my plans accordingly. But I *was* in a fright ! I thought you might just happen to feel bad and be obliged to come out, and catch me. I felt that strongly when I was picking your flowers in the greenhouse."

He left the room before the Tenor recovered, and returned with a tray on which was the result of his enterprise.

"If you don't like eggs and potatoes fried as I fry them, you'll never like anything again in this world," he asserted confidently, helping the Tenor as he spoke. "The thing is to have the dripping boiling to begin with, you know," he continued—("I'll only give you two eggs at a time)—then plunge them in, and as they brown take them off one by one and put them on a hot dish—I'm speaking of the potatoes now; but don't cover them up, it makes them flabby, and the great thing is to keep them crisp."

"They really are good," said the Tenor. But he had over-estimated his capacity, and could only dispose of three of the eggs.

The Boy was disgusted. However, he said it did not matter, since he was there to sacrifice himself in the interests of science, and preserve the balance of nature by eating the rest himself, a feat he accomplished easily.

"Now this is what I call good entertainment for man and beast," he observed.

"May I ask which is the beast?" the Tenor ventured.

"Why, I am, of course," said the Boy. "Did you ever know a boy who wasn't half a beast?"

"Yes. It is all a matter of early association and surroundings."

"Well, if you knew the kind of moral atmosphere I have to breathe at home, you would know also how little you ought to expect of me. But what shall we drink?"

"There is some beer, I believe," the Tenor said dubiously.

"Burgundy is more in my line."

"Burgundy! A boy like you shouldn't know the difference."

"A *boy* like me wouldn't, probably."

The Tenor smiled. "And what do you call yourself, pray? A man?" he asked.

"No; a bright particular spirit."

It was not inappropriate, the Tenor thought, and he got up. "It does not often happen so," he said; "but now I think of it I believe I have some Burgundy in the house. The dean sent me a dozen the last time I was out of sorts, and there is some left."

"I know," said the Boy. "It is in the cupboard under the stairs on the left hand side."

When the Tenor came back with the Burgundy the Boy settled himself in an easy-chair with a glass on the table beside him, and it was evident that his mood had changed. He was thoughtful for a little, sitting with solemn eyes, looking out at the cathedral opposite.

There was only one rose-shaded lamp left alight in the long low room, and the dimness within made it possible to see out into the clear night and distinguish objects easily.

"When I look out at that great pile and realize its antiquity, I suffer," the Boy said at last. "Do you know what it is, the awful oppression of the ages?"

The Tenor did not answer for a moment, then he said:

"I never see you at church.

"I should think not," the Boy replied, still speaking seriously. "You never see anyone but Angelica."

The Tenor flushed.

"Why do you never speak to that sweet young lady?" the Boy asked tentatively, after a little pause.

"I! How could I?"

"I fancy you ought to," the Boy went on, endeavouring to "draw" the Tenor. "You can't expect her to make up to you, you know."

"Oh, Boy! how can you be so young!" the Tenor exclaimed, with a gesture of impatience, but still amused.

The Boy sipped his wine, and gazed into the glass, delighting in the rich deep colour. "I should think she would be delighted to make the acquaintance of so great an artist," he said.

The Tenor bowed ironically. "May I ask if you are pursuing your investigations as to what manner of man I am?" he asked.

"Well, yes," was the candid rejoinder; "I was. I suppose you think that you ought not to speak without an introduction. Well, say I gave you one."

The Tenor laughed. He felt that he ought to let the subject drop, and at the same time yielded to temptation.

"What would your introduction be worth?" he asked.

"Everything," the Boy rejoined. "I am on excellent terms with Angelica. We have always been inseparable, and I get on with her capitally; and she's not so easy to get on with, I can tell you," he added, as if taking credit to himself.

" When she is good she is very good indeed,
But when she is naughty she is horrid.

And just now she's mostly naughty. She isn't very happy."

The interest expressed in the Tenor's attitude was intensified, and inquiry came into his eyes.

"She is not very happy," the Boy pursued with extreme deliberation, "because you come no nearer."

" Boy, you are romancing," the Tenor said, with a shade of weariness in his voice.

" I am not," the Boy replied. " I know all that Angelica thinks, and it is of you——"

"Hush !" the Tenor exclaimed. " You must not tell me."

" But she——"

" I will not allow it."

"Well, there then, don't bite," said the Boy; "and I won't tell you against your will that she thinks a great deal about you "—this *presto,* in order to get it out before the Tenor could stop him. " But I will tell you on my own account that I don't know the woman who wouldn't."

A vivid flush suffused the Tenor's face, and he turned away.

" I hope you never say things like that to your sister," he objected, after a time.

The Boy grinned. " Sometimes I do," he said, "only they're generally more so."

There was a long silence after this, during which the Tenor changed his attitude repeatedly. He was much disturbed, and he showed it. The Boy made a great pretence of sipping his wine, but he had not in reality taken much of it. He was watching the Tenor, and it was curious how much older he looked while so engaged. The Tenor must have noticed the change in him, which was quite remarkable, giving him an entirely different character, but for his own preoccupation. As it was, however, he noticed nothing.

" Boy," he began at last, in a low voice and hesitating. " I want you to promise me something." The Boy leant forward all attention. " I want you to promise that you will not say anything like that—anything at all about me to——"

"To Angelica ?" The Boy seemed to think. " I will promise," he slowly decided, "if you will promise me one thing in return."

" What is it ?"

"Will you promise to tell me everything you think about her."

The Tenor laughed.

"You might as well," the Boy expostulated. "I've got to look after you both and see that you don't make fools of your-selves. The youngness of people in love is a caution! And I should like to see Angelica safely settled with you. A man with a voice like yours is a match for anyone. There are obstacles, of course; but they can be got over—if you will trust me."

"Oh, you impossible child!" the Tenor exclaimed.

"It is you who are impossible," the Boy said, in dudgeon. "You are too ideal, too content to worship from afar off as Dante worshipped Beatrice. I believe that was what killed her. If Dante had come to the scratch, as he should have done, she would have been all right."

"Beatrice was a married woman," the Tenor observed.

The Boy shrugged his shoulders, but just then the cathedral clock struck three, and he hastily finished his wine.

"I'll disperse," he said, when the chime was over. "Take care of my fiddle. You'll find the case under the sofa. I left it the last time I was here. By-the-bye, you should make the old woman stay at home to look after the place when you're out. Unscrupulous people might walk in uninvited, you know. Ta, ta," and the Tenor found himself alone.

It was no use to go to bed, he could not rest. His heart burned within him. It was no use to tell himself that the Boy was only a boy. He knew what he was saying, and he spoke confidently. He was one of those who are wiser in their generation than the children of light. And he had said—what was it he had said? Not much in words, perhaps, but he had conveyed an impression. He had made the Tenor believe that she thought of him. He believed it, and he disbelieved it. If she thought of him—he threw himself down on the sofa, and buried his face in the cushions. The bare supposition made every little nerve in his body tingle with joy. He ought not to indulge in hope, perhaps; but, as the Boy himself might have observed, you can't expect much sense from a man in that state of mind.

A few days later the Tenor saw his lady again in the canon's pew, and he was sure, quite sure, she tried to suppress a smile.

"That little wretch has told her, and she is laughing at my presumption," was his distressed conclusion. "I'll wring his neck for him when he comes again."

But when the service was over, and he had taken his surplice off, she passed him in the nave, so close that he might have touched her, and looked at him with eyes just like the Boy when he was shy; gave him a quick half-frightened look, and blushed vividly; gave him time to speak, too, had he chosen. But the Tenor was not the man to take advantage of a girlish indiscretion.

When he went home, however, he was glad. And he opened his piano and sang like one inspired. "I am gaining more power in everything," he said to himself. "I could make a position for her yet."

CHAPTER VIII.

A FEW nights later the Tenor went out for a stroll, leaving the windows of his sitting room closed but not fastened, and the lamp turned down. On his return he was surprised to find the window wide open and the room lit up. The little garden gate was shut and bolted. He could easily have reached over and opened it from the outside, but knowing that it creaked, and not wanting to disturb his nocturnal visitor until he had ascertained his occupation, he jumped over it lightly, walked across the grass plot to the window, and looked in.

It was the Boy, of course. The Tenor recognized him at once, although all he could see of him at first were his legs as he knelt on the floor with his back to him and his head and shoulders under a sofa. "What, in the name of fortune, is he up to now?" the Tenor wondered.

Just then the boy got up, frowning, and flushed with stooping. He stamped his foot impatiently, and looked all round the room in search of something. Suddenly his face cleared. He had discovered his violin on the top of a bookshelf above him, and that was apparently what he wanted, for he made a dash at it, and took it down, and hugged it affectionately.

The Tenor smiled, and stepped down into the room. He did not wish to take his visitor unawares, but the carpet was soft and thick, and his quick step as he crossed to where the boy was standing with his back to him, absorbed in the contemplation of his beloved instrument, made no noise, so that when the Tenor laid his hand on the Boy's shoulder he did startle him considerably. The Boy did not drop his instrument, but he uttered an almost womanish shriek, and faced

round with such a scared white look that the Tenor thought he
was going to faint. He recovered immediately, however, and
then exclaimed angrily : "How dare you startle me so ?
Everybody knows I can't bear to be startled. If you are nothing but a blunderer you will spoil everything. And I bolted
the gate too. It would have made a noise if you had opened
it as you ought to have done, and then I should have known.
I've a good mind to go away now, and never come back
again."

"I am very sorry," said the Tenor. "But how was I to
know it was you ? It might have been a thief."

"Thieves don't come to steal grand pianos and armchairs
in lighted chambers with the windows open and the blinds up,"
the Boy retorted. "Don't you feel mean, spying around like
that ?"

"Are you an American ? " the Tenor interrupted blandly.

"Yes, I am "—with asperity—"and you must have known
quite well it was me. Who else could get into the Close after
the gates were shut ? "

"I never thought of that," said the Tenor. "And how *do*
you get in, pray ? By the postern ? "

"No," was the answer. "I come by the water-gate ; " and
his face cleared as he saw the Tenor's puzzled glance at his
garments.

"I'm not wet," he said. "I don't swim."

"But the ferry does not cross after six."

"No, but I do, you see. And now let us make music," he
added, his good humour restored by the Tenor's mystification.
"If you will be so good as to accompany me with your piano,
I will give you a treat. I brought my music the last time I
was here ; " and there it was, piled up, on a chair beside the
instrument.

The Tenor could have sworn that neither chair nor music
was there when he went out that evening, but what was the use
of swearing ? He felt sure that the Boy in his present mood
would have outsworn him without scruple had it pleased him
to maintain his assertion, so he opened his piano in silence,
and the music began. And it was a rare treat indeed which
the Tenor enjoyed that night. The Boy played with great
technical mastery of the instrument, but even that was not so
remarkable as the originality of his interpretations. He possessed that sympathetic comprehension of the masters' ideas
which is the first virtue of a musician ; but even when he was

most true to it, he managed to throw some of his strong individuality into the rendering, and hence the originality which
was the special charm of his playing. As an artist, he certainly
satisfied ; even the sensitive soul of the Tenor was refreshed
when he played ; but in other respects he was obviously deficient. So long as things were pleasant it was a question
whether he would ever stop to ask himself if they were right.
Acts which lead to no bodily evil, such as sickness or that lowering of the system which lessens the power of enjoyment, he
was not likely in his present phase to see much objection to ;
and for the truth, for verbal accuracy in his assertions that is,
he had no particular respect. All this, however, the Tenor was
more reluctant to acknowledge, perhaps, than slow to perceive.
He was one of those who expect a great soul to accompany
great gifts, and what he did know of the Boy's shortcomings he
condoned. He believed the young tone-poet's power was in
itself an indication of high aspirations, and those he thought
were only temporarily suppressed by a boyish affectation of
cynicism.

But the Boy did not give the Tenor much time to think.
His mind was quick-glancing, like his eyes when he was animated, and he carried the Tenor along with him from one
occupation to another with distracting glee. When he was
tired of making music, as he called it, he demanded food, and,
so long as he could cook it and serve it himself, he delighted
in bacon and eggs, as much as he did in Bach and Beethoven.

The Tenor tried to wean him of his nocturnal habits, but to
this the Boy would not listen. He said he liked to sit up all
night, and when he said he liked a thing, he seemed to think
he had adduced an unanswerable argument in its favour. The
Tenor complained of fatigue. The long nights affected his
voice, he said, and made him unfit for work ; but the Boy only
grinned at this, and told him he'd get used to it. Then he
threatened to shut up the house and go to bed if the Boy did
not come in proper time, and on one occasion he carried out
his threat ; but when the Boy arrived he made night hideous
with horrid howls until the Tenor could stand it no longer,
and was obliged to get up, and let him in, to preserve the peace
of the neighbourhood. After which the Tenor ceased to remonstrate, and it became one of the pleasures of his life to
prepare for this terrible hungry Boy. He worked in his garden early and late, cultivating the succulent roots which the
latter loved, the fruits and the vegetables, and, last, but not

least, the flowers, for he never could feed without flowers, he said, and the Tenor ministered to this exaction with the rest. "He is dainty because he is delicate," the Tenor thought, always excusing him. "When he is older and stronger he will grow out of all these epicurean niceties of taste. I must make him dig, too. and fence, and row. He'll soon develop more manliness."

That he was spoiling the Boy in the meantime never occurred to him, not even when he noticed that the latter took all these kindnesses as a matter of course, and only grumbled when some accustomed attention was omitted.

The Tenor was vexed sometimes, and obliged to find fault, but the Boy could always soothe him. "I am sure you love me," he would say. "Your life was not worth living until I came, and you could not live without me now. I am a horrid little brute I know, but I have my finer feelings too, my capacity for loving, and that raises me.

> "All love is sweet
> Given or returned."

When the Boy quoted or recited anything he really felt, he had a way of lingering over the words as if each syllable were a pleasure to him. The deep contralto of his voice was at its sweetest then, and he seldom failed to make his own mood felt as he intended.

The Tenor, justly incensed by some wicked piece of mischief, was often obliged to turn away that he might maintain his authority and not be seen to soften. But he never deceived the Boy, who could gauge the effect of his persuasion to a nicety, and would grin like a fiend behind the Tenor's back at the success of his own eloquence. No matter what he had done, by hook or by crook he always managed to bring about a reconciliation before they parted. He knew the Tenor's weak point—Angelica—and when everything else failed he would play upon that unmercifully. But he had a way of speaking of his sister which often made the Tenor seriously angry. He did not believe the Boy meant half the disrespect with which he mentioned her, but it galled him, nevertheless; and, on one occasion, when the Boy had repeated some scandalous gossip to which the Tenor objected, and afterward excused himself by saying that it was not his but his sister's story, the Tenor's indignation overflowed, and he lectured him severely.

"You should never forget that your sister is an innocent girl," he said, "and it is degrading to her even to have her name associated with such ideas."

But the Boy only grinned. "Bless you," he retorted, "don't make so much ado about nothing. She's quite as wise as we are."

The Tenor's eyes flashed. "I call that disloyal," he said. "Even if it were true—and it is not true—it would be disloyal ; and I am ashamed of you. If you ever dare to speak of your sister in that light way to me again, I'll thrash you."

For a moment the Boy was astonished by the threat. His jaw dropped, and he stared at the Tenor ; but, quickly recovering himself, he burst into an uncontrollable fit of laughter. "Oh, my !" he exclaimed. "What a brother-in-law you would be ! How do you know she is such a saint ?"

"You are a little brute," was all the answer the Tenor vouchsafed. But the question made him think. He could picture her to himself at any time as he saw her in the canon's pew, and the pale proud purity of her face, with the unvarying calm of her demeanour, were assurances enough for him. His dear lady. His delicate-minded girl. He would stop it. He would make this scapegrace brother of hers respect her, even as he had threatened, if necessary.

"Do you know what she calls you?" that youth asked presently, breaking in upon the Tenor's meditation in a confident way, as if he could not be mistaken about the subject of it.

But the Tenor was not to be beguiled all at once. "I have already requested you not to mention your sister to me," he said.

"I know," was the cool rejoinder. "But I promised on my word of honour to tell you what she calls you. She calls you Israfil—Is-ra-fil," he repeated, "the angel of song, you know."

But the Tenor made no sign. The Boy watched him a moment, and then continued unabashed, "I shall call you Israfil myself, I think, for the future. But I like your own name too !" he added. "I have only just found it out. Everybody here calls you the Tenor, you know."

"And how did you find it out, pray, if I may ask ?"

"I looked everywhere," said the Boy, glancing round him comprehensively ; "and at last I found it on the back of an old envelope that was in that Bible you keep in your bedroom.

Here it is," and he took it out of his pocket-book. " David
Julian Vanetemple, Esq., Haysthorpe Castle, Hays, N. B."

A painful spasm contracted the Tenor's face. "Oh, Boy,"
he said, in a deep stern voice that made the latter quail for
once ; "have you no sense of honour at all? You must give
that back to me immediately."

The Boy returned it without a word, and the Tenor went
upstairs. His step was listless, and when he came back he
looked pale and disheartened. He sat down in his accustomed
seat beside the fireplace farthest from the window that looked
out upon the cathedral, but facing it himself, and rested his
elbow on the arm of the chair and his head on his hand, taking
no notice of the Boy, however, who waited a while, casting
anxious glances at him, and then rose softly and stole away.

When the Tenor roused himself he found a slip of paper on
the table beside him, on which was written, "Dear Israfil, I
beg your pardon. I did it without thinking. I will never
hurt you like that again, only forgive me." And the Tenor
forgave him.

On another occasion, when there was peace between them,
and they were both in a merry mood, the Boy said he had a
grievance, and when the Tenor asked what it was, he complained that the Tenor had never taken interest enough in him
to ask him his name.

" No, now you mention it," the Tenor answered. "I never
thought of your having a name."

" Do you mean to say you think me such a nonentity ?"

" Just the opposite. Your individuality is so strongly
marked that you don't seem to require to be labelled like other
people. By-the-bye, what is your name ?"

" Claude."

The Tenor laughed ironically. "Oh, no," he said, "it is
Maude you mean ; delicate, dainty, white-fingered Maude."

But the Boy only roared. This kind of insinuation never
roused his resentment ; on the contrary, it delighted him.
" Imagine the feelings of the flowers," he said, with a burst of
laughter that convulsed him, "if my remarkable head, sunning
over with curls, were to shine out on them suddenly, and want
to be their sun !"

" I am afraid you are incorrigible," the Tenor answered.
" You seem to glory in being effeminate. If wholesome ridicule
has no effect, you'll die an old woman in the opprobrious sense
of the word."

"I'll make you respect these delicate fingers of mine, though," the Boy irritably interposed, and then he took up his violin. "I'll make you quiver."

He drew a long melodious wail from the instrument, then lightly ran up the chromatic scale and paused on an upper note for an instant before he began, with perfect certainty of idea and marvellous modulations and transitions in the expression of it, to make music that steeped the Tenor's whole being in bliss.

The latter had noticed before that it was to his senses absolutely, not at all to his intellect, that the Boy's playing always appealed; but he did not quarrel with it on that account, for music was the only form of sensuous indulgence he ever rioted in, and besides, once under the spell of the Boy's playing, he could not have resisted it even if he would, so completely was he carried away. The Boy's white fingers were certainly not out of place at such work. "Do I play like an old woman in the opprobrious sense of the word?" he demanded, mimicking the Tenor.

"Oh, Boy!" the latter exclaimed, with a deep drawn sigh of satisfaction. "You have genius. When you play you are like that creature in the 'Witch of Atlas':

" A sexless thing it was, and in its growth
It seemed to have developed no defect
Of either sex, yet all the grace of both."

But the Boy frowned for a moment at the definition, and then he said: "Is that what you call genius? Now I make it something like that, only different. I believe it is the attributes of both minds, masculine and feminine, perfectly united in one person of either sex."

The Tenor, lolling in his easy-chair, smiled at him lazily. There was no end to his indulgence of the Boy; but still he led him, by example principally, but also by suggestion, as on one occasion when the Boy had been sketching out a scheme of life in which self was all predominant, and the Tenor asked: "Do you never feel any impulse to do something for your suffering fellow-creatures?"

To which the Boy at first rejoined derisively: "Am I not one of the best of their benefactors? Would you say that a fellow who plays as I can does nothing for his fellow-creatures? To make music is my vocation, and I follow it like a man."

But after a moment's thought he confessed: "Once indeed I did try to do some good in the world, but I failed disastrously."

"What did you try?"

"I took a class in a Sunday school." He waited to enjoy the effect of this announcement on the Tenor. "I did, indeed," he protested; "but—eh—I cannot say that success attended the effort. In fact, both I and my class were forcibly ejected from the building before the school closed. You see, I had no vocation, and it was foolish to experiment."

The Tenor said no more on the subject, and did not mean to, but the Boy returned to it himself eventually, and it was evident that the wish to do something for somebody was taking possession of him seriously. This was the Tenor's tactful way with him; and from such slight indications of awakening thought he continued to augur well for the Boy.

CHAPTER IX.

SO time passed on, changing all things greatly, or with infinitesimal changes, according to their nature. The colours worn in crowded thoroughfares varied with the varying fashions; the tint of the summer foliage with sun and rain and dust. Doors, closed the whole long winter, were opened now and left so, and the young people passed to and fro, thronging to river banks, but lately deserted; to the cricket fields, garden, or wood, or lawn. The very faces of the streets were changing, enlivened by plaster and paint and polish: the face of the land with the certain advance of the season; the faces of friends with something not to be named, but visible, strange, and, for the most part, disheartening. It was the old story for ever and ever; all things changed always; but the chime was immutable.

As the days grew gradually to weeks, his one connecting link with the outer world became dearer and dearer to the lonely Tenor. The nights that brought the Boy were happy nights, looked forward to with eagerness, and prepared for with difficulty. For at this time the Tenor denied himself some of the bare necessaries of life, that he might buy him the Burgundy he loved to sip: he did no more than sip, and, therefore, the Tenor indulged him; drink was not to be one of his vices, evidently.

The Tenor, although he would not have acknowledged it, held that the Boy was a creature apart, and one, therefore, whom it was not fair to measure by the common standard. Doubtless the manner of their meeting had something to do with this idea. The Boy was associated in the Tenor's mind with many sweet associations; with the beautiful still night; with the Tenor's far off ideal of all that is gracious and womanly; with the music that was in him; and, further, with a sympathetic comprehension of those moments when gray glimpses of the old cathedral, or a warm breath of perfumed air from the garden, or some slight sound, such as the note of a night bird breaking the silence, fired a train of deep emotion, and set his whole poetic nature quivering, to the unspeakable joy of it; joy sanctified by reverence, and enlarged beyond comparison by love.

With such moods as these the Boy's own mood was always in harmony; so much so indeed that the Tenor thought it was then that he was himself, and that those wild ebullitions of spirits were only affected to disguise some deeper feeling of which, boy-like, he was ashamed. As their intimacy ripened there were times when, not only his whole demeanour, but his very nature seemed to change; when he craved for dimness and quiet; and when he would work upon the Tenor with little caressing ways that won his heart and drew from him, although he was habitually undemonstrative, expressions of tenderness which were almost paternal.

In his quieter moods the Boy would sit in the dim lamplight on a footstool beside the Tenor's chair, leaning his head against the arm of it, while the latter smoked, and the tap, tap, tap, of the clematis and honeysuckle on the window pane kept time to the thoughts of each. Long intervals of silence were natural to the Tenor, and it was generally the Boy who broke the charm. He would talk seriously then, and often about his sister, and was not to be silenced until he had had his say. He conquered the Tenor as usual by his persistence, but the latter was not much influenced by what he said at first. Gradually, however, and by dint of constant iteration, some of the Boy's assertions became impressed upon his mind. He began to believe that Angelica did wish to make his acquaintance, and to admit to himself that there might be a possibility of winning her regard eventually; but his high mindedness shrank from approaching a girl whose social position was so far above his own—in the matter of money that is. For of course the Tenor had a proper respect for art. He knew that to be a great artist, with the will and power to make his art elevating, is to be great in the greatest way ; and he also knew that his own gift was second to none. But would she link her lot with his? He yearned for some assurance. He had no ambition whatever for himself, but he would have toiled to succeed for her It was his weakness to require someone to work for as he was working for the Boy ; a purely personal ambition seemed to him a vexing, vain, and insufficient motive for action. All selfless people suffer from indolence when only their own interests are in question ; they require a strong incentive from without to arouse them. Such incentive as the Tenor had was in itself a pleasure to him, a refinement of pleasure which might be coarsened, which certainly would be impaired by any change. He had, however, begun to make plans. He was determined to go and take his place amongst the singers of the world ; but when, exactly, he had not decided. As the Boy declared, when it came to the point he found it difficult to tear himself away from Morningquest. Of course he would go, in fact he felt he must go, soon—say, when these drawings for his good friend the dean were finished.

"By the way, Boy," he asked one night, "what is your family name ? and who are your people ?"

"My family name is Wells," the boy answered demurely. "My father has a little place in the neighbourhood, and my grandfather lives here too."

"Wells," the Tenor repeated. "I seem to know the name."

"Oh, doubtless," the Boy observed. "This is a hotbed of Wellses. Israfil," he pleaded—he was nestling beside the Tenor in the dim half light, watching the latter smoke—"Israfil, tell me all about yourself ? Tell me about that old castle in the North to which your letter was addressed. Tell me who you are ? I want your sympathy"

"You have it all, dear Boy," the Tenor said.

"I shall not feel that I have until you ask for mine. You would not deny me this if you knew what a stranger I am to the luxury of loving. I want to cultivate the power to care for others. Just now I don't seem to be able to sympathise with anyone for more than a moment, and that is the cause of all you object to in me. But if you would confide in me, if you would make me feel that I am nearer to you than anybody else is, I believe I could be different."

The Tenor reflected for a little. "If I were to make you

my confidant, Boy, would you respect my confidence ? " he said at last.

"Assuredly," the Boy replied. "I promise on my honour. You shall tell her yourself."

The Tenor ignored this last impertinence, but the Boy was not abashed. "Israfil," he pursued, "they say you are the son of an actress and some great nobleman, and that when you found it out, your intolerable pride made you give up your profession, and come and bury yourself alive in Morningquest because you could not bear the stigma. Are you the son of such parents, Israfil ? "

The Tenor brushed his hand back over his hair. "Has your sister heard these reports ? " he asked.

"Yes."

"And what does she say ? "

"Oh, *she* doesn't mind ! She rather leans to the nobleman theory ; and when people of that kind—I mean the nobility and gentry," he exclaimed with a grin—"(the worst of being in society is that you are forced to know so many disreputable people) ; when they come to our house—and they do come in shoals, Angelica being the attraction, you know—then we speculate. Angelica feels quite sure that the Duke of Morning-quest himself is your father. He was a loose old fish, they say. And there is a sort of family likeness between you. Angelica thinks you came here that your presence might be a continual reproach to him."

"Not a very worthy thought," said the Tenor drily.

"Well," said the Boy with much candour. "I could not swear it was Angelica's. It has a strong family likeness to some of my own."

"It has," said the Tenor.

He was lolling in his deep easy-chair with his hands folded on his vest and his legs crossed, and now he laid his sunny head back wearily against the cushion, and looked up at the ceiling. It was his accustomed attitude in moments of abstraction, and the Boy let him alone for a little, watching him quietly. Then he grew impatient, and broke the silence : "*Is* it true, Israfil ? " he asked.

"Is what true ? " lowering his eyes to look at him without changing his position.

"Is it true that you are the son of an actress and a duke ? "

"Probably," the Tenor answered ; "anything is probable where the most absolute uncertainty prevails."

" Then you don't know who you are?" the Boy exclaimed, in a tone of deep disgust due to baffled curiosity.

"I haven't the most remote idea," said the Tenor.

" I don't believe you."

" Boy, I have already told you that I will not have my word doubted."

" I know," said the Boy. " You are always autocratic. But I can't believe you don't know who you are. It is incredible. You would never give yourself such airs if you hadn't something to go upon. And, besides, you command respect naturally, as well-bred people do. And you have all the manner and bearing of a man accustomed to good society. You have the accent, too, and all the rest of it The difficulty in your case is to believe in the actress. She was a very superior kind of actress, I suspect. And, at any rate, you must have been brought up and educated by somebody. Do tell me, Israfil. I am burning to know."

" Your curiosity is quite womanish, Boy."

" That is quite the right word," the Boy answered glibly. " Women are generous and elevated, and ' a generous and elevated mind is distinguished by nothing more certainly than an eminent curiosity.' "

The Tenor changed his position slightly, and, in doing so, absently laid his hand on the Boy's head : " What queer dry hair you have," he said.

The Boy drew back resentfully. " I wish you wouldn't touch my hair," he said. " I know it's nasty dry hair. It's a sore point with me. I think you should respect it."

" I beg your pardon," the Tenor answered. " I really didn't know you were so sensitive on the subject. But why on earth do you come so close ? You put that remarkable head of yours under my hand, and then growl at me for touching it. And really it is a temptation. If I were a man of science instead of a simple artist I should like to examine it inside and out."

The Boy put both hands up to his head and laughed, delighted as usual by any jest at his own expense. He had moved his footstool back a little now, and sat, stroking his upper lip thoughtfully, and looking at the Tenor. There was a mischievous twinkle in his eyes, and he seemed to have forgotten his desire to know the Tenor's secret history. " Why don't you wear a moustache ?" he said suddenly.

The Tenor looked at him lazily. " Well, I never did wear

one," he said. "But I could not in any case have worn one with a surplice."

The Boy nodded his head sagely. "I forgot," he said. "Of course that would have been bad form. A parson is always vulgarized in appearance by wearing a military moustache. The effect is as incongruous as a tail would be if added to a figure with wings. But, tell me, do you think my moustache will be the colour of my eyebrows when it comes?"

"Oh, Boy!" the Tenor exclaimed, "this is quite refreshing; especially from you. You will be quite young in time if you go on."

The Boy grinned in his peculiar way, and then got up and began to walk about the room. The Tenor thought from the expression of his face that he was meditating mischief; but before he had time to put it into effect the big bell boomed above them, striking the hour, and then came the chime.

The Boy hated the chime. He said it was flat; he said it was importunate, like an ill-bred person; he said it mingled inopportunely with everything; he declared it had a spite against him, and would do him an injury if it could; when he was good he said it made him bad, and when he was bad it made him worse. The Tenor had expected to hear him swear at it; but, oddly enough, considering some of his aberrations, the Boy never swore. His ideas were occasionally shocking, but, with the exception of certain *boyishnesses*, in the expression of them he was a purist.

He went off now, however, anathematizing the chime, and the Tenor was almost glad to get rid of him. The Boy's superabundant vitality alone was fatiguing, and when he added, as he often did, a certain something of manner to it which was perplexing and irritating in the extreme, he left the Tenor not only fatigued, but jarred all over. Yet he spent the interval which usually elapsed before the Boy returned in making excuses for him, and also in making preparations.

CHAPTER X.

THE Tenor was obliged to leave the window of his sitting room which looked out on the little grass plot in front of his house and the cathedral opposite, open always now, rain, blow, or snow, for the convenience of the Boy. The latter had changed his mind about forcing an entrance. If the

Tenor, he said, would not make it quite evident that he wanted him by leaving the window open so that he could come in his own way whenever he chose, he should not come at all. The window was his way; and on one occasion when he had found it shut he had gone home, intending, as he afterward declared, never to return; but he had changed his mind and reappeared after an unusually long interval, when the Tenor, to use the Boy's own phrase, "caught it" for his want of hospitality. Of course, he acknowledged, he might have come in by the door, or he might have knocked at the window; but then he did not choose to come in by the door or knock at the window, so that was all about it. If the Tenor wanted to see him he knew how to make him feel he was welcome, and so on until, for the sake of peace and quietness, the Tenor was again obliged to yield.

Oh, the moods of that terrible Boy! No two the same and none to be relied on! Sometimes he was like a wild creature, there was no holding him. no knowing what he would do next; and the Tenor used to tremble lest he should carry out one of his impossible threats, among which serenading the dean, upsetting the chime, climbing the cathedral spire on the outside, or throwing stones at the stained-glass saints in the great west window, were intentions so often expressed that there seemed some likelihood of one or other of them being eventually put into execution. Then again he would saunter in about midnight, and sit down in a dejected attitude, looking unutterably miserable; he would hardly answer when the Tenor spoke to him, and if he did not speak he resented it; neither would he eat, nor drink, nor make music, and if the Tenor sang he sometimes burst into tears.

On other occasions he was the most commonplace creature imaginable. He would talk about a book he had been reading, a new picture his "people" had bought. the society in the neighbourhood; anything, in fact, to which the Tenor would listen. and the latter was often astonished by the acuteness of his perceptions, and the worldly wisdom of his conclusions.

The Tenor made every allowance for these changes of mood, which, if they were trying at times—and certainly they were trying—were interesting also and amusing. He knew what an affliction the sensitive, nervous, artistic temperament is; what a power of suffering it hides beneath the more superficial power to be pleased; and he pitied the Boy, who was an artist in every sense. He also thought there had been mistakes made in his education.

"Did you ever go to a public school, Boy?" he asked one night.

"Well, no," the Boy rejoined. "I had the advantage of being educated with Angelica. They kindly allowed me to share her tutor. I was thrown in, you understand, just to fill up his time. And that is how it is I am so refined and cultivated."

"But seriously?" said the Tenor.

The Boy raised his eyebrows. "Seriously?" he repeated. "But do you think it delicate to question me so closely? Ah, I see, poor fellow! You don't know any better. But really your curiosity is quite womanish. I will tell you, however. I had the misfortune to sever my femoral artery when I was a brat, and, although it seems to have come quite right now, it was not thought advisable for me to rough it at a public school."

"But why on earth are they putting you in the army?" the Tenor asked.

"You mean I am much too pretty?" said the Boy, "not to mention my brains and manners. Well, there I must agree with you. It does seem a sad waste of valuable material. But it is only to fill up an interval. I shall be put into a permanent billet of another kind eventually, whether I like it or not."

"You mean you will be put into the earth to enrich it, I suppose?"

"Well, no. I was not so smart," said the Boy. "Now, that is rather a good one for you. Oh, I suspect, if I could plumb your depth, I should find myself but a simple, shallow child in comparison. No; what I meant was that eventually a certain amount of earth would come to me to enrich me."

"But what does your father think about this military manœuvre?"

"My father *think!*" roared the Boy. "O Lord! you don't know my father!" and he fairly curled himself up in convulsions of silent laughter, which the Tenor thought unseemly considering the subject of it, but he said no more. He knew that there was nothing to be done with such a boy but to wait and hope; and that was the attitude into which the Tenor found himself most prone to fall in these days with regard to things in general; being greatly cheered meanwhile by the sight of his lovely lady, who smiled at him now without doubt, and was seldom absent from her accustomed seat in the Canon's pew when he sang.

The Tenor looked better now, and more out of place than ever in the choir—better, that is to say, in the sense of being more attractive ; but he was not looking strong, and the common faces about him seemed commoner still when contrasted with the exceptional refinement of his own. The constant self-denial he had been obliged to exercise in order to indulge the fancies of that rapacious Boy, although a pleasure in itself, was beginning to tell upon him. His features had sharpened a little, his skin was transparent to a fault, and the brightness of his yellow hair, if it added to the quite peculiar beauty, added something also to the too great delicacy of his face. It was the brightness of his hair that suggested such names for him as "Balder the Beautiful " and " Son of the Morning " to the Boy, who invariably called him by some such fanciful appellation.

It was at this time, too, that a great painter came to Morning-quest and painted a picture called " *Music*," the interest of which centred in the Tenor himself singing, while Angelica gazed at him as if she were spell-bound.

The Boy used to describe this picture to the Tenor while it was in progress, but the latter. listening in his dreamy way, was under the impression for some time that the work was one of his young friend's own imagination only. By degrees, however, it dawned upon him that the picture was an actual fact, and then he was displeased. He thought that the artist had taken a liberty with regard to himself, and been guilty of an impertinence so far as his lovely lady was concerned.

" Well, so I told him," said the Boy. " But you know, dear Israfil, that in the interests of art as well as in the interests of science, men are carried away to such an extent that they sometimes forget to be scrupulous. It is curious," he broke off, gazing at the Tenor critically, "that Angelica should specially admire your chin. It is your mouth that appeals to me. You have a regular Rossetti-Burne-Jones-Dante's-Dream and-Blessed-Damosel kind of mouth, with full firm lips. I should think you're the sort of fellow that women would like to kiss. Don't try to look as if you wouldn't kiss a woman just once in a way, dear old chap ! Women hate men like priests, who mustn't kiss them if they would ; and they have no respect for other men who wouldn't kiss them if they could. I know Angelica hasn't ! "

The last words were delivered from outside in the garden after the Boy had made his escape through the window.

CHAPTER XI.

HOW long the Tenor's dream would have remained unbroken by action it is hard to say. His want of personal ambition, his perfect serenity of mind, and his thankfulness for a state of things so much more blissful than anything he had ever expected to fall to his lot again ; the languid summer weather, and his affectionate anxiety for the Boy, all combined to keep him in Morningquest, and to keep his indefinite plans for the future still in abeyance.

Other people, however, were not so apathetic. The dean's friendly remonstrances had been redoubled of late ; the Boy had become importunate ; and even the mild musicians of Morningquest, whose boast it was to have that bright particular star in their own little firmament, ventured to hint respectfully that he was not doing his duty by himself. All this kindly interest in his future career was not without its effect upon him, and if it did not actually rouse him to act, it put him in the mood to be aroused.

He was sitting alone one evening in his accustomed seat beside the fireplace, or rather beside the bank of ferns and flowering plants which he had arranged before the fireplace so as to hide it, at the instigation of the Boy. A shaded lamp stood on a table behind him, throwing its softened light from over his shoulder on to the big book which lay open on his knee. But he was not reading. He had placed his hands upon the book, and was resting his head on the back of the chair. His yellow hair seemed to shine out of the surrounding gloom with a light of its own ; but his face was in shadow.

The window at the further end of the room behind him was shut, and the creepers outside brushed gently against it, tapping now and then, and keeping up a continual soft rustle and murmur of leaves, like friendly voices, soothing insensibly.

The other window was open as usual, and as he sat now he could see the old cathedral opposite towering above him. It was a bright moonlight night ; the shadows were strong, and the details of the façade, flying buttress, gargoyle and cornice, with a glimpse of the apse and spire, were all distinct. But as the Tenor thoughtfully perused them, the whole fabric suddenly disappeared from view, blotted out by an opaque body round which the moonlight showed like a rim of silver, tracing in outline the slender figure of the Boy. The Tenor had forgotten him for once, and was startled from his reverie by the unexpected apparition ; but he did not alter his position or make any sign. The Boy preferred to come and go like that, ungreeted and unquestioned, and the Tenor of course humoured this harmless peculiarity with the rest.

The Boy sauntered in now in a casual way, arranged his hair at a mirror, threw himself into an armchair, leant back, crossed his legs, folded both hands on his hat, which he held on his knee, and looked at the Tenor lazily.

In the little pause that followed, the Tenor glanced at his book again, and then he closed it.

" Israfil," the Boy said suddenly, leaning forward to look at the book, as if to make sure, and speaking in an awestruck voice—" is that the *Bible* you were reading ? "

Any evidence of the Tenor's simple piety, which was neither concealed nor displayed, because it was in no way affected but quite natural to him, and he was, therefore, unconscious of it, had a peculiar effect upon the Boy. It seemed to shock him. But whether it made him feel ashamed or not, it is impossible to say. Sometimes, the first effect over, he would remain thoughtful, as if subdued by it ; but at others it appeared to have irritated him, and made him aggressively cynical.

To-night he was all subdued.

" You believe it, Israfil, don't you ? " he said. " ' He watch-ing ' is a fact for you ? "

The Tenor did not answer, except by folding his hands upon his book again, and looking at the Boy.

" Now *I* don't believe a word of it," the latter pursued, " but it makes me feel. I have my moments. The Bible is a wonderful book. I open it sometimes, and read it haphazard. I did last night, and came upon—oh, Israfil, the grand simpli-city of it all ! the wonderful solemn earnestness ! It brought me to my knees, and made me hold up my hands ; but I could not pray. I heard the chime, though, that night. It sounded insistent. It seemed to assert itself in a new way. It was as if it spoke to me alone, and I felt a strange sense of something pending—something for which I shall have to answer. ' He watching.' Yes. I feel all that. But "—dejectedly—" one feels so much more than one knows ; and when I want to know, I am never satisfied. Trying to find the little we know amongst the lot that we feel is a veritable search for mignonette seeds in sand."

The Tenor continued silent and thoughtful for a time. "But do you never pray, dear Boy ?" he said at last.

The Boy shook his head.

"*Did* you never ?"

"Oh, yes,"—more cheerfully. "I used to believe in all the bogies at one time."

"I am afraid you have been brought under some bad influence, then. Tell me, who was it ?"

"Angelica," said the boy.

"Oh, Boy ! your sister !"

"Ah, you don't know that young lady !" the Boy rejoined, with his cynical chuckle. "She is very fascinating, I allow ; but always, in her conversation, ' the serpent hisses where the sweet bird sings.'"

The Tenor toyed with the cover of his book, and was silent.

After a time the Boy spoke diffidently. "But do *you* pray, Israfil ?" he asked.

"Yes," the Tenor answered. "I try to make prayer the attitude of my mind always—I mean I try to be, and to do, and to think nothing that I could not make a subject of prayer at any time. But I do not think that a direct petition is the only or best way to pray. It seems to me that it is in a certain attitude of mind we find the highest form of prayer, a reverential attitude toward all things good and beautiful, by which we attain to an inexpressible tenderness, that enemy of evil emotions, and also to rest and peace and a great deep solemn joy which is permanent."

"I don't think I ever knew a man before who prayed regularly," the Boy observed thoughtfully, rising as he spoke, and standing with his hat on : "except the clergy, I suppose. But then that is their profession, and so one thinks nothing of it. But I wonder if many men of the world pray? I suppose they have to give up everything that makes life pleasant before they can conscientiously begin."

"Far from it," said the Tenor, smiling. "But you are going early ! Aren't you hungry ?"

The Boy grinned as if the insinuation were flattering. "No, I am not hungry," he answered. "I dined at home to-night for a wonder, and when I do that I don't generally want any

more for some time. By home I mean at my grandad's, where
they always have seven or eight courses, and I can't resist any
of them. I los͙ my self-respect, but satisfy my voracity, which
has the effect ҫ͏ improving the greediness out of my mind.
But I am in a hurry this evening, and I have already outstayed
my time. I only came in for a moment to ask you if you are
to sing to-morrow ? "

The Tenor nodded.

" In that case I am to beg you for ' Waft her, Angels.'
Angelica ventures to make the request. Good-night ! "

The words were scarcely spoken, and his flying footsteps
were still audible as he ran lightly up the Close, when the
cathedral clock began to strike. There was only one emphatic
throb of the iron tongue, followed by a long reverberation, and
then came the chime.

The Tenor, who had risen, stood listening, with upturned
face, until the end.

But the chime failed of its effect for once. There was something weary and enigmatical in the old worn strain. Hitherto,
it had always been a comfort and an assurance to him, but
to-night, for the first time, it was fraught with some portentous meaning. Was there any cause for alarm in what was
happening ? any reason for fear that should make it merciful to
prepare him with migivings ? It was no new thing for the
Tenor to be asked to sing something special, and he tried to
think such a request, although it came from Angelica—if
indeed it came from her, and was not a fabrication of the
Boy's—was a whim as trifling as the rest. But even if it were,
trifles, as all the world knows, are not to be despised. Someone has said already that they made up the sum of life, and it
may also be observed that the hand of death is weighted by
them.

CHAPTER XII.

THE Tenor happened to be entering the cathedral next
day for the afternoon service just as Angelica was being
handed from a carriage by a singular looking man who wore
pince-nez, was clean shaven, and had an immense head of hair.
Angelica very evidently called the attention of this gentleman
to the Tenor as he passed, and the latter heard the " Ach ! " of
satisfaction to which the stranger gave utterance when he had

adjusted his *pince-nez* with undisguised interest, and taken the Tenor in.

The latter felt that he had seen the man before, and while he was putting on his surplice he remembered who he was, an *impresario*, well-known by sight to regular opera goers and musicians generally. Having established his identity, the reason of his presence there that afternoon was at once apparent. The Tenor had been requested to sing a solo which was admirably calculated to display the range and flexibility of his voice to the best advantage, and the *impresario* had been brought to hear him. The mountain had come to Mahomet.

The Tenor never sang better than upon that occasion, and he had scarcely reached his cottage after the service was over, when the *impresario* burst in upon him, having, in his eagerness, omitted the ceremony of knocking. He seized the Tenor's hand, exclaiming in broken English :—"Oh, my tear froind, you are an ideal!" Then he flung his hat on the floor, and curvetted about the room, alternately rubbing his hands and running his fingers upward through his luxuriant hair till it stood on end all over his head. "And have I found you?" he cried sentimentally, apostrophising the ceiling. "Oh, have I found you? What a *Lohengrin!* Ach Gott! it is the prince himself. Boat "—and he stopped prancing in order to point his long forefinger at the Tenor's chest—"boat you are an actor born, my froind! You was the *Prince of Devotion* himself jus' now. You do that part as if you feel him too! Why "—jerking his head towards the cathedral with a gesture which signified that if he had not seen the thing himself he never could have believed it—"why, you loose yourself in there kompletely!" Then he asked the Tenor to sing again, which the Tenor did, being careful, however, not to give his excitable visitor too much lest the intoxicating draught should bring on a fit.

The music-mad-one had come to make the Tenor golden offers, and he did not leave him now until the Tenor had agreed to accept them.

The dean came in by chance in time to witness the conclusion of the bargain, adding by his congratulations and good wishes to the Tenor's own belief that such an opportunity was not to be lost. The drawings the Tenor had been doing for the dean were all but finished now, and it was arranged that the Tenor should enter upon his new engagement in one month's time.

When he found himself alone at last and could think the matter over, he was thoroughly content with what he had done, There could be no doubt now as to whose wish it was that he should go and make a name for himself, and he felt sure that the step he was about to take would not lead to the separation he dreaded, but rather to the union for which he might at last without presumption, after such encouragement, venture to hope.

CHAPTER XIII.

A FEW nights after the Tenor had signed the agreement the Boy burst in upon him, exclaiming in guttural accents : " Oh, my tear froind ! have I found you ? " Then he threw his hat on the floor and began to prance up and down, waving his hands ecstatically.

The Tenor picked up a cushion and threw it at him. "You wretched Boy ! " he said, laughing. "Who told you he did that ? "

"Oh, my *dear* Israfil ! " the Boy replied. "Why on earth do you ask who *told* me? You must know by this time, and if you don't you should, that genius does not require to be told. Given the man and the circumstances, and we'll tell you exactly what he'll do, don't you know," and the Boy showed his teeth.

But the Tenor was not convinced. " Knowing your patience and zeal when engaged in the pursuit of knowledge—I think that was the euphemism you employed the last time you had to apologize for the unscrupulous indulgence of your boundless curiosity," the Tenor, standing with his back to the Boy, observed with easy deliberation, as he filled and lighted a pipe, " I have little doubt that you assisted at the interview from some safe coigne of 'vantage—to borrow another of your pet expressions—perhaps from the closet under the stairs there——"

"Or from behind the sofa," the Boy suggested, with that enigmatical grin of his which the Tenor disliked, perhaps because it was enigmatical. " Like my new suit, Israfil ? " he demanded in exactly the same tone. He had on a spotless flannel boating suit, with a silk handkerchief of many colours, knotted picturesquely round his neck.

" It's too new," said the Tenor. "It looks as if you'd got it for private theatricals, and taken great care of it."

The Boy laughed, and then, assuming another character, he began to remonstrate with himself playfully in the Tenor's voice.

"Boy, will you never be more manly?" and "Don't mock, Boy!" and "Boy, you have no soul!" and "Oh, Boy, you're not high-minded." Then he did a love scene between the Tenor and Angelica. The Tenor tried to stop this last performance, but he only made matters worse, for the Boy argued the question out in Angelica's voice, taking the part of "dear Claude"—he still insisted that his name was Claude—and ending with: "Dear Israfil, we are so happy ourselves, I think Claude should have a little latitude to-night. He studies so hard, poor boy, he deserves some indulgence."

When this amusement ceased to divert him, he announced his intention of going on the stage, of not going home till morning, and of being rowed down the river in the meantime.

"But where will you get a boat at this time of night?" the Tenor objected.

"You're not a man of much imagination," said the Boy, "or you wouldn't have asked such a question. How do you suppose I come every night, after all the world is barred and bolted out of your sacred Close, and the alternative lies between the porter at the postern, whom you know I shun, and the water-gate?"

"Do you mean to say you row yourself down the river, every time you come?"

"I do," said the boy complacently.

"I didn't think you could!" was the Tenor's naïve ejaculation.

The Boy was delighted. "It never struck you, I suppose," he chuckled, "that my fragile appearance might be delusive? Haven't you noticed I never tire?"

"Yes," said the Tenor. "But I thought that you probably paid for these nights of dissipation by days of languor."

The boy laughed again. "Don't know the sensation," he declared. "Days of laziness would be nearer the mark. I have plenty of them."

It was a lovely night, all pervaded by the fragrance of the flowers in the gardens round about the Close.

They sauntered out, turning to the left from the Tenor's cottage, the cathedral being on their right, the cloisters in front. The Boy walked up to the latter and peeped in. "Come here, dear Israfil," he said obligingly, "and I will show

you the beauties of the place. These are the cloisters, and, as
you see, they form a hollow square, nearly two hundred feet
long, and twelve feet wide. Yon slowly rising moon shows the
bare quadrangle in the centre, and the tracery of the windows
opposite ; but the exquisite groining of the roof, and the
quaintly sculptured bosses, are still hidden in deep darkness.
The light, however, brightens in the northeast corner, and—if
you weren't in such a *hem* hurry, Israfil——" The Tenor
had walked on, but the Boy stayed where he was, and now
began to improve the occasion at the top of his voice.

The Tenor returned hurriedly. " For Heaven's sake hold
your tongue ! " he expostulated. " You'll wake the whole
Close."

" I was calling your attention to the details of the architec-
ture," the Boy rejoined politely ; and, as usual, for the sake of
peace and quietness, the unfortunate Tenor was obliged to hear
him out.

When he stopped, the Tenor exclaimed " Thank Heaven ! "
devoutly, then added, " No fear for your exams, Boy, if you
can cram like that. But I did not know you were a cultivated
archæologist."

" Nor am I," said the Boy with a shiver. " I hate architec-
ture, and I don't want to know about it, but I can't help picking it up. It is horrid to remember that that arch yonder was
built in the time of William the Conquerer. I never look at it
without feeling the oppression of the ages come upon me. And
when I get into this bigoted Close and think of the heathenish
way the people live in it, shutting themselves in from the rest
of the citizens with unchristian ideas of their own superiority,
I am confirmed in my unbelief. I feel if there were any truth
in that religion, those who profess it would have begun to
practice its precepts by this time ; they would not be content to
teach it for ever without trying it themselves. And oh ! "—
shaking his fist at the cathedral—" I loathe the deeds of darkness that are done there in the name of the Lord."

" What unhappy experience are you alluding to, Boy ? " said
the Tenor, concerned.

" I was thinking of Edith—poor Edith Beale," the Boy
replied. " But don't ask me to tell you that story if you
have not heard it. It makes my blood boil with indignation."

" I have heard it," the Tenor answered sadly. " But, Boy,
dear, every honest man **deplores** such circumstances as much
as you do."

"Then why do they occur?" the Boy asked hotly. "If the honest men were in earnest, such blackguardism would not go unpunished. But don't let us talk about it."

They went through the arm of the Close in the centre of which the lime trees grew round a grassy space enclosed from the road by a light iron railing. "This is grateful!" the Boy exclaimed, as they passed under the old trees, lingering a while to listen to the rustle and murmur of the leaves. Then they emerged once more into the moonlight, and took their way down the little lane that led to the water-gate. Here they found an elegant cockle-shell of a boat tied up, "a most lady-like craft," said the Tenor.

"I'll steer," said the Boy, fixing the rudder, and then arranging the cushions for himself, while the Tenor meekly took the oars.

With one strong stroke he brought the boat into mid-stream, then headed her down the river toward the sea, and settled to his oars with a long steady pull that roused the admiration of the Boy.

"You row like a 'Varsity man," he said.

"So I should," was the laconic rejoinder.

"*Are* you a 'Varsity man?"

"I am."

"Oxford, then, I'll bet. And did you take your degree?"

The Tenor nodded.

"Well, you *are* a queer chap!" said the Boy. "Were you expelled? The Tenor shook his head. "Did you do *anything* disgraceful?" The Tenor again made a sign of negation. "Then why on earth did you come and bury yourself alive in Morningquest?"

"That I might have the pleasure of rowing you down the river by moonlight, apparently," the Tenor answered, but without a smile.

"I'd give my ears to know!" the Boy ejaculated.

"I quite believe you would!" said the Tenor, pausing to speak; after which he bent to his oars with a will, and the banks became a moving panorama to their vision as they passed. Now they swept under a light iron bridge that crossed the river with one bold span, and connected a busy thorough-fare of the city with a pleasant shady suburb beyond. Then they wound round a curve, and on their left was a broad towing-path, and beautiful old trees, and a high paling made of sleepers shutting out the view; while on the right, those crowded dwellings of the poor which add so much to a picture, especially by moonlight, and so little to the loveliness of life, rose from the water's edge and straggled up the rising ground, tumbling over each other in every sort of picturesque irregularity. Ahead of them, the river was landlocked by a wooded hill ; and, also facing them, was an old round tower on the towing-path, above which the round moon shown in an empty indigo sky.

"Stop a minute, Israfil," said the Boy, "and turn your head. Who does it make you think of ?"

"Old Chrome," the Tenor answered, looking over his shoulder. "It is perfect."

The river was quite narrow here, and on either side were long lines of pleasure-boats moored to the bank, and an occasional flat tied up for the night, with its big brown sails, looking like webbed wings, hoisted to dry. Further on they met a barge coming up the river, and the Boy wished the man who was steering a polite good-night, and hoped he'd have a pleasant passage and no bad weather ; to which piece of facetiousness the bargee replied good-humouredly, having mistaken the boy's contralto for a woman's voice, an error of judgment at which the latter affected to rage, much to the amusement of the Tenor.

But they were out of the city by this time. On their right was a gentleman's park, well-wooded, and sloping up from the river to a gentle eminence crowned by a crest of trees; on their left, across some fields, the villas of that pleasant suburb before mentioned studded the rising ground, appearing also among old trees, beneath which they and their quiet gardens nestled peacefully. There were trees everywhere—beech and laburnum and larch, horsechestnut and lime and poplar, as far as the eye could reach, and the latter, standing straight up in the barer spots, were a notable feature in the landscape, as were also the alder-cars and occasional osier beds dotted about in marshy places.

The pleasant suburb straggled out to an ancient village, past which a reach of the river wound, but the Boy kept the boat to the main stream. They could see the village street, however, with the quaint church on the level ; and light warm airs brought them odours of roses and mignonette from the gardens. It had been a long pull for a hot night, and the Tenor shipped his oars here, and threw himself back in the bow to rest. He lay looking up at the sky while they drifted back

little by little with the tide. The balmy air, the lop-lop of the
water against the boat, the rock and sway and sense of dreamy
movement, and ever and anon the nightingales, made a time of
soft excitement, such as the Boy loved.

"O Israfil!" he burst out; "isn't it delicious just to be
alive?"

He was lolling in the stern with his hat off, his legs stretched
out before him, and a tiller rope in each hand, the image of
indolent ease. "Yes, this is perfect," he added; "it is paradise."

"Not for you, I should think," said the Tenor, "without an
Eve."

"Now, there you mistake me," the Boy replied. "If there
be one thing I deprecate more than another it is the impertinent intrusion of *sex* into everything."

"You surprise me," the Tenor answered idly. "When I
first had the pleasure of meeting you, love was a favourite topic
of yours."

"Ah! at that time, yes," said the Boy. "You see I was merely
pandering then to what I supposed to be your taste, in order to
ingratiate myself with you; but you may have noticed that
since I knew you better I have allowed the subject to drop—
except, of course, when I wanted to draw you."

"That is true," said the Tenor upon reflection. "And yet
you are the most sensuous little brute I know."

"Sensuous, yes; not sensual," said the Boy. "I take my
pleasures daintily, and this scene satisfies me heart and soul;
balmy air; moonlight with its myriad associations; a murmurous multitude of sounds like sighs, all soothing; the silent
drift and gentle rocking of the boat; and the calm human
fellowship, the brotherly love undisturbed by a single violent
emotion, which is the perfection of social intercourse to me. I
say the scene is hallowed, and I'll have no sex in my paradise."
The last words were uttered irritably, and he sat up as he
spoke, thrust his hands into his pockets, and frowned at the
silvery surface of the river. "Love!" he ejaculated. "Rot!
It is not love they mean. But don't let us desecrate a night
like this with any idea that lowers us to the level of a beastly
French novel reeking with sensuality."

"Amen, with all my heart," said the Tenor lazily. "But
don't introduce the disturbing element of violence either, dear
Boy. Your sentiments may be refined, but the same cannot be
said for the expressions in which you clothe them. In fact, to

describe the latter, I don't think *coarse* would be too strong a word."

"No, not coarse," said the Boy, with his uncanny grin. "Vigorous, you mean, dear. But now shut up. I want to think."

"You don't. You want to feel," said the Tenor.

The Boy threw his cap at him.

Then they resettled themselves, lolling luxuriously, the one in the bows, the other in the stern ; and the Tenor's soul was uplifted, as was the case with him in every pause of life, to the heaven of heavens which only could contain it ; while the Boy's roamed away to realms of poesy where it revelled amid blossoming rhymes, or rested satisfied on full blown verses, some of which he presently began to chant to himself monotonously.

"I like that," he broke off at last. "There is quite an idea in it—well worked out too ; don't you think so ?"

"What is the thing ?" the Tenor asked. "Who wrote it ?"

"I wrote it myself," said the Boy.

The Tenor roused himself, and got out the oars, but sat resting on them with a far-away look in his dreamy eyes. He was bareheaded, and the moon played on his yellow hair, making it shine ; a detail which did not escape the Boy, whose pleasure in the Tenor's beauty never tired.

"I didn't know you were a poet as well as a musician," the latter said at last.

"Ah ! you have much to learn," the Boy answered complacently, then added—"I am extremely versatile."

"Jack of all trades," said the Tenor.

"Now, don't be coarse," said the Boy.

"Well, I hope that is not the best specimen of your powers in that line," the Tenor drily pursued.

"By no means," was the candid rejoinder ; "but the most appropriate, seeing that I just made it for the occasion, which is not a great occasion, don't you know."

"I've heard something very like it before," said the Tenor.

"Yes," said the Boy, with a gratified smile, "that is the beauty of it. There is no new-fangled nonsense about me. My verses always tremble with agreeable reminiscences. They set the sensitive sympathetic chords of memory vibrating pleasurably. You can hardly read anything I write without being reminded of some one or other of your best friends in the language. I have written some verses which I can assure

you were a triumph of this art." He made an artistic pause
here, shook his head, and then ejaculated solemnly : "But,
Lord ! how I did rage when the fact was first pointed out to
me ! "

The Tenor got the boat round, and, with an occasional dip
of the oars to keep it in mid-stream, allowed it to drift slowly
back toward Morningquest.

"I am afraid you are precocious, Boy," he said at last.
"Don't be so if you can help it. The thing is detestable."

"I really think I shall be obliged to avoid you, Israfil," the
Boy rejoined. "If I let you be intimate, you will be giving
me good advice. Look there ! "

The Tenor turned hastily. But there was nothing wrong.
It was only that they had reached a point from which they
could obtain a view that pleased the Boy's excitable fancy ; a
bend of the river, a glimpse of upland meadows, woods with the
cathedral spire above them, and the square outline of the
castle overhanging the city from its dominant site on the hill,
and seeming to guard it as it slept.

The Tenor looked a little, then dipped his oars and rowed a
stroke or two. The Boy's mood had changed. He was keenly
susceptible to the refining influences of beautiful scenes. His
countenance cleared and softened as he gazed, and the Tenor
knew that he would jeer no more that night.

Presently they heard the city clocks striking the hour. Both
listened, waiting for the chime. The Tenor rested on his oars,
and after it had sounded, muffled by distance, but quite
distinct, he still sat so, gazing thoughtfully into the water.

"Boy, shall I tell you something ? " he said at last.

The Boy gravely responded with a nod.

"It was not far from where we are now," the Tenor continued, "that I first heard the chime—oh, ever so many years
ago ! " and he brushed his hand back over his hair.

"You were a boy then ?"

"Yes, a lad like you—perhaps younger. I had been working in a colliery. The work was too hard for me, and I was
coming up the Morne on a barge, to try and get something
lighter to do in one of the towns. We came up very slowly,
and it was a hot day, and I idled about for hours, looking at
the water over the side, and at the banks of the river as we
passed, but without thinking of anything. What I saw made
me feel. I was conscious of various sensations—pleasure,
wonder, amusement, and, above all, of a dreamful ease ; but I

could not translate sensations into words at that time ; they suggested no ideas.   There had been nothing in my life so far to rouse my mental faculties, and I was conscious without being intelligent, as I suppose the beasts of the field are.   I must have been happy then, but I did not know it.   As we approached Morningquest I heard the chime.   It was very faint at first, for we were still a long way off; but the next time it sounded we were nearer ; and the next it was quite distinct. And it seemed to me to mean something, so I asked the old bargee who was steering, and he told me.   I could neither read nor write at that time, and I had never heard of Christ, but I loved music, and the idea of a great beneficent being who slumbered not nor slept, but watched over us all forever, took possession of my imagination, and I caught up the notes and words and sang them with all my heart.   And when we got to the outskirts of the city, a gentleman who had been sitting on the towing-path, sketching the old houses on the opposite side of the river, heard me, and hailed the barge, and came on board.   'Which is your sweet singer?' he asked, and the old fellow who was steering nodded toward me, and answered : 'The lad there.'   And the gentleman said if I would go away with him he would have me taught music and make a great singer of me."

"And you went ?"

"Yes," said the Tenor, with his habitual gesture.

"The gentleman was a bachelor," he resumed, "with few near relations.   He was very rich, very liberal, and passion·ately fond of art in all its branches.   That was why he took me at first, but by and by he began to like me for myself.   He had me educated as his own son might have been, and I loved him as if he had been my father.   Oh, Boy, he was a good man !   You never would have scoffed at religion and truth had you been brought up by him.   I rested on his affection as securely as you rely on the obligation of your nearest of kin. I knew that, even if I had lost my voice or otherwise dis-appointed him, it would have made no difference.   Once my friend he would always have been my friend.   But I did not lose my voice, nor did I otherwise disappoint him, I trust." The Tenor paused a moment.   "He was always sure that I was gentle by birth," he resumed, "and all my tutors said I must have come of an educated race because I was so teach-able.   Everything in the new life came to me naturally.   I never had any trouble.   My friend tried hard to find my par·

ents, but all that was known of me in the place I came from
was that a collier, who lived alone in a little cottage, went home
late one night and found me asleep on his bed. They thought
I was only a few days old then, and had kept my clothes,
which were such as a gentleman's child would have worn, but
there was no mark on any of them, nor any clue by which I
could be identified, except the name, David Julian Vanetemple, scrawled on a scrap of paper in a woman's hand, an
educated hand. The collier brought me up somehow, though
Heaven alone knows how, considering my age and his own
occupation. Do you know, Boy, one of the most weary
things in life is the sense of an obligation you can never repay.
If I could only have done something to prove my gratitude to
my first foster father! But there! I must not think of it. It
is better to hope that all he did for me was a pleasure to himself at the time, though there must have been much more
trouble than pleasure at first. But he was very kind, and I
was very happy with him." Here the Tenor paused again for
a while, and then resumed. "When I was old enough he
took me down to the pit occasionally, but he would not let me
work until I was much past the age at which the other boys
began. He said I was not one of them ; my build was different, and I was quite unfit for such rough labour ; and so it
proved, but I persevered as long as he lived. It was not
very long, however, for he was killed one day by an explosion
of gas down in the mine while trying to rescue some other
poor fellows who had been blocked up in a gallery for days
by a fall. His dog was killed at the same time. He liked to
have his family with him, he said, and we were generally both
beside him when he was at work. But he sent me off on an
impossible errand to a neighbouring town that day. I did not
suspect it at the time, but I know now that it was to keep me
out of harm's way. And so I was left quite alone in the
world, and I thought the place where I had had a friend was
more desolate than strange places with which I had no such
tender associations would be ; and so I wandered away, and
wandered about until I was found by my next friend on the
barge, and the new life began for me."

"Then he never found out who you were ?" the Boy
exclaimed.

" No, never."

" And why did you leave him ? "

The Tenor shipped his oars. " He had a place in Scotland

to which we went every autumn for shooting," he began to answer indirectly, and then stopped.

The Boy was leaning forward, with his eyes riveted on the Tenor's face ; his delicate features were pale and drawn with excitement and interest; his lips were parted ; he scarcely seemed to breathe. There was a long pause. The moonlight still streamed down upon them. The water lapped against the sides of the boat, and sparkled and rippled all around them, its murmurs mingling with the rustle of leaves, the sighing of sleeping cattle, the manifold " inarticulate voices of the night," above which a nightingale in a copse hard by sang out at intervals divinely.

"My friend was not conventional in anything," the Tenor began again at last. " When he went out shooting, for instance, he liked to find his own game as he would have had to do in the wilds. All the sport of the thing lay in that, he said ; it was just the difference between nature and artifice. We were therefore in the habit of going out alone—that is to say, with a keeper or two and the dogs, but never with a party." Here again the Tenor paused, and all the minor murmurs of the water and from the land sounded aggressively, with that sort of sound which fills the ears but seems nevertheless to emphasize the silence and solitude at night.

The Boy moved restlessly once or twice, making the little boat rock, and the Tenor, yielding to the eager expectancy he saw in his eyes, resumed his story.

" Toward the end of the season of which I have been speaking," he said, "we had arranged an expedition for one particular morning ; but just as we were about to start my friend got a telegram from a man he knew, begging him as a favour to be at home that day to receive a yachting party who were anxious to come up and see the place, and had only a few hours to do it in. I wanted to stay and help him to entertain them, but he would not hear of it. My day's shooting was of more consequence to him than the entertainment of many guests, and he made me go alone. But I went reluctantly. I had been out alone often enough before, and had enjoyed it thoroughly, but that day, somehow, I hated to leave him, and only went to please him, he made such a point of it. Once fairly started, however, I began, as was natural, to enjoy the tramp over the moors. We intended to send back for any game we might shoot, so only one old gillie accompanied me. I carried out the plans we had made the night before, going the way we had intended to go. It was deer I was after, and as luck would have it I had some splendid sport, and had begun to enter into it thoroughly before we halted to refresh ourselves at noon. After a long rest we set off again up a wooded glen. The keeper had noticed a herd of deer only the day before feeding at the other side, and it seemed more than probable that we should get a shot when we reached the brow of the hill, or we might perhaps meet some of them coming down the glen to drink. The afternoon was waning then, and we had turned our faces homeward. When we got to the head of the glen the luck seemed still to be favouring us, for there, on our right, was a splendid fellow lording it alone on the very crest of the hill within range. I did not stop to consider, but raised my gun to my shoulder and fired instantly. But just as I pulled the trigger, someone sprang up from the heather between me and the stag—sprang up, uttered a cry, and reeled and fell "—the last words were spoken with a gasp, and the Tenor stopped for an instant, and then continued in a hoarse broken whisper to which his companion had to listen intently, leaning forward to do so, with his great eyes dilated, and his pale lips quivering. "'Lord, sir,' the gillie exclaimed, 'you've shot the master!'"

"And you had?"

"I had. Yes, I had shot him," the Tenor repeated.

"O Israfil!" cried the Boy, flinging himself down impetuously before him, and grasping his hands.

"When his guests had gone," the latter continued in a broken voice, "he strolled out to meet me. He had not said anything about coming, but he knew I meant to return by that glen. He did not, however, know on which side I should be, and he had therefore taken up his position on the brow of the hill from whence he could see every point at which I was likely to appear. Probably he never saw the stag—it was behind him ; and we—the gillie and I—neither of us saw anything else. And, indeed, had there been no game, we could hardly have distinguished him at that time of the day from the hillside till he moved, for the suit he wore was just the colour of the rocks and heather. We carried him home—but he was dead—dead—quite dead," and the Tenor moaned, covering his face with his hands.

"I remember now," the Boy said softly. "I heard all about it at the time, and read the case in the papers, but I never thought of associating it with you. Yet—how could I have been so dull ?   There was an inquest, and they tried——" he hesitated.

"They tried to make out that I had some motive—something to gain by his death," the Tenor went on ; "but everyone, and most of all his nearest of kin, his heir, came forward to exonerate me.   He had provided for me in his will by settling the allowance he always made me on me and my heirs forever. But he always said that my voice was my fortune, and he had no need to make enemies for me by giving me that which belonged by right to others.   He was a just man, singularly open in all his dealings, and it was not hard to clear me, but still—oh !"—he broke off—" it was awful ! awful ! "

"And afterward ? " the Boy ventured to ask.

"Afterward," the Tenor repeated slowly.   "Afterward— for some months—I wandered about.   They were all very kind. They wanted me to stay with them—they wanted to take me abroad—they would have done anything to help and comfort me.   But all I cared for was to be alone.   At first there was a blank—the faces about me had no meaning for me—the people when they spoke could scarcely make me understand.   I was mad in a way, but not mad enough to be insensible to sorrow. I felt the fearful calamity that had fallen upon me, but nothing else.   I told myself every hour of the day that he was dead— dead ; cruelly cut off in the midst of his happy life by me whom he loved—I could not have suffered more had I been guilty," the Tenor broke off.   "This lasted—I hardly know how long ; but eventually I began to fancy that he saw my agony of grief, and that it was a torment to him not to be able to come and comfort me.   Then one day—I was in Cornwall at the time—sitting on the sea shore—and all at once—it was the strangest thing in life—I heard the chime !   I had not been thinking of it.   I doubt if I had thought of it a dozen times since I heard it first.   But it sounded for me then :

He, watch-ing o - ver   Is - ra - el,   slumbers not, nor sleeps.

I heard it quite distinctly, and I got up and looked about me. It was the first thing outside myself that had arrested my attention since I had seen him drop on the moor.   I went back to the inn I was staying at, and asked about it ; but I could scarcely make them understand what I meant, and there was certainly no such chime in that neighbourhood. Then I felt it was a message sent specially to me, and I made my man pack up my things, and then I dismissed him, and started at once for Morningquest alone. It was a long journey, and although I travelled with all possible speed, I did not arrive until nearly forty-eight hours later. It was close on midnight then, and the first thing I heard, when I found myself alone in my room at the hotel, was the chime itself. Have you ever noticed—or is it only my fancy?—that it seems to strike louder at midnight, and with greater intensity of expression, as we ourselves strike final chords? It sounded so to me then, and suggested something—I can't tell what, I can't define it; but something that changed the current of my thoughts, and made me feel I had done right to come. And from that moment my grief was less self-centred, and the blessed power to feel for others began to return to me. Almost immediately after my arrival, I heard of the tragedy in the cathedral, the suicide of the tenor, and the trouble the dean and chapter were having to find a substitute; and when I had seen the quiet shady Close, and the beautiful old cathedral, and my little house with its high-walled garden at the back, standing, as it were, on holy ground, I longed to take up my abode there, where no one would know my story but those to whom the secret would be sacred, and no one would intrude upon my grief. So I applied for the tenor's place, and I knew as soon as I had taken the step that it was a wise one. I thought, if anything could restore the balance of my mind, it would be the regular employment, the quiet monotony, the something to do that I must do, the duty and obligation, which were just sufficient without being any tax on my powers to take me out of myself. And the being able to shut myself up from the world in the Close, as I said before, was another inducement, though by far the greatest were the daily services in the cathedral; while taking part in them I always feel that I am nearer him. When I applied for the place, and the dean heard who I was—of course, he knew the story; the whole world knew it at that time—and heard how I yearned for a life of devotion, he sympathized with me entirely, gladly acceded to my request, and agreed to keep my secret. He has told me since that he always hoped and believed the quiet regular life would restore me, and when it had he intended to urge me to go away, and make the most of my powers. Dear, kind old man! he has indeed been a good friend to me, and he is a good man himself, if ever there were one. But I seem to have known none but good men," the Tenor concluded thoughtfully.

"But your money, Israfil," the Boy said impatiently; "what did you do with that?"

The question provoked the ghost of a smile. "Oh. Boy! that is so like you!" the Tenor answered. "But since you wish to know I will tell you. My income has all been disposed of for some years to come. It was a great deal more than I should have required in any case, and a lay clerk with such means would have been an anomaly not to be tolerated. But he meant that I should enjoy it, and so I have. I have held it as a sacred trust left to me for the benefit of those who are worse off than myself. I keep the principal in my own hands, but I dispose of the interest. It does not go very far, alas! in my profession, where want is the rule, but it enables me to do something, and that, till I knew you, Boy, was my greatest pleasure in life. I have earned my own living almost ever since I came to Morningquest, and being obliged to do so has been a very good thing for me."

"And all these pensioners—or whatever you like to call them—of yours, do they know?"

"As a rule my lawyers manage the business delicately," the Tenor answered, smiling. He dipped his oars as he spoke, and began to row back with a will.

The Boy, shivering as if with cold, gathered up the tiller lines and steered mechanically. They were both subdued, and scarcely spoke till the boat touched the landing place at the water-gate, and then the Boy begged the Tenor to get out, saying that he must row himself home.

The Tenor jumped ashore, and then, with a long grip of each other's hands, and a long look into each other's eyes, they parted in silence.

The moon had set by this time, and the summer dawn was near.

CHAPTER XIV.

THE next night the Boy appeared again in his white boating suit, with his sandy hair tumbled more than usual. His restless eyes sparkled and glanced, and there was a glow beneath his clear skin which answered in his to a heightened colour in other complexions. He was evidently excited about something, and the Tenor thought he had never seen him look so well. What his mood was did not become immedi- ately apparent. The Tenor had learnt that the sparkle in his eyes either meant some mischievous design, or a strong de- sire to "make music." But this evening he was long in com- ing to the point. He began by pelting the Tenor with roses through the window, and then he entered and danced an im- promptu breakdown in the middle of the room; but these pre- liminaries might have been an introduction to anything, and it seemed as if his programme were not complete, for he next subsided into his accustomed seat on the sofa up against the wall opposite the fireplace, and remained there, with his hands in his pockets, looking at the Tenor thoughtfully for at least ten minutes.

The Tenor was also in his accustomed seat beside the hearth —or rather beside the stand of growing flowers and ferns that hid the hearth, with a book on his knee. He was sitting there when the first rose whizzed in out of the silence and solitude of night without warning upon him, announcing the arrival of the Boy. It startled him somewhat, but he did not wince from the shower that followed, nor did he move when the Boy chose to show himself, but merely smiled and closed his book and then sat watching the next part of the proceedings with the gravity of an eastern potentate. He sat so now, looking up at the great cathedral, seen dimly through the open window, towering above them, his profile turned to the Boy, and the roses all about him—on the floor, on the back of his chair, one on his shoulder, another on his book, and one he held in his hand. There were dozens of them of every hue, from that deep crimson damask which is almost black, to the purest white, fresh gathered from the trees apparently, with the dew still glistening on their perfumed petals and on the polished surface of the leaves. The Tenor, becoming conscious of the *Gloire de Dijon* he held in his hand, looked into its creamy depth with quiet eyes. The beauty of the flower was a pleas- ure to him—though, for the matter of that, everything was a pleasure to him now, He had no words to tell it, but his face was irradiated by the gladness of the hope which he cherished, from morning till night.

The Boy had been watching him admiringly. "You will be one of the beauties when you come out, dear Israfil," he said. "They will photograph you and put you into the shop windows, cabinet size two-and-sixpence Sounds rather vul-

gar, though, doesn't it? Savours of desecration, to my mind.
But, Israfil, you will certainly be the rage. One so seldom
sees a good-looking man ! Good-looking women are common
enough and they make themselves still commoner nowadays,"
—which remark coming from such a quarter amused the
Tenor, whereupon the Boy became irate. " Oh, jeer away ! "
he exclaimed ; " but when you know Angelica as well as I do
you will respect my knowledge of the subject."

But here the Tenor threw back his head, and groaned aloud.

" Boy, I protest ! " he exclaimed. " I can endure your gar-
rulousness, but I do bar your cynicism. If you can't be
agreeable, be still. You're in a horrid bad temper"—and so
saying the Tenor rose in his languid way, got a little table
which he placed beside his chair, spread out his pipes upon it,
and began to clean them with crows' quills, the Boy watching
the operation the while with cheerful intentness.

" Pipes and tobacco and roses ! " he said at last. " What a
mixture it sounds ! But it doesn't look bad, dear Israfil," he
added encouragingly.

The Tenor made no remark ; his pipes seemed to be all en-
grossing. He had just filled the bowl of one with a number
of fuseeheads, cut off short, and now he popped in a light and
corked them up. There was a tiny explosion on the instant,
followed by a rush of smoke through the shank of the pipe,
which swept it clean, and added musk and gunpowder to the
already heavy odour of roses that filled the room.

The Boy, still lolling on the sofa observing the Tenor's proceedings with interest, drew up one leg, clasping his hands
round it below the knee, and began to sing to himself in a
monotonous undertone as was his wont.

" By-the-bye," the Tenor said, like one who suddenly remembers, " I found some verses after you were here the other
night "—and he straightened himself to feel in his pockets—
" I suppose you dropped them. Here they are." And then
he leant back in his chair again and read aloud :

> " When the winter storms were howling o'er the ocean,
>   Leafless trees and sombre landscape cold and drear,
>   Bitter winds, and driving rains, or white commotion
>   Of the whirling snow that drifted far and near ;
>   Then my heart, which had been strong, was bowed and broken
>   I was crushed with sudden sense of loss and fear,
>   Dull as silence passed the days and brought no token
>   Of a light to make the darkness disappear.

Would the grief that wrecked my life forever hold me?
    Soon or later winter storms their ravage cease—
With the coming of the green leaves, something told me,
    With the coming of the green leaves there is peace.

When the bursting buds proclaim'd the spring time nearing,
    Song of birds and scent of flowers everywhere,
Drowsy drone of distant workers, and the cheering
    Hum of honey-seeking bees in all the air ;
Then my sorrow took swift wings and rose and left me ;
    And I knew no more the aching of despair ;
Came again to me the joy that seemed bereft me,
    And for hope I changed the dreary weight of care.
With the winter tempests pass'd the storms of feeling,
    Soon and surely did their power to pain me cease,
And the sunshine-lighted summer rose revealing
    With the coming of the green leaves there is peace."

The Tenor looked at the Boy when he had finished, shook
his head mournfully, struck a match, set fire to the paper upon
which the verses were written, and watched it burn with the
air of a disappointed man.

"Don't make any more rhymes, Boy," he said ; "don't
write any more, at least, until you get out of the sickly sentimental stage. I thought I was prepared for the worst, but I
really never imagined anything quite so bad as that."

·The Boy, although he had listened to the lines with a fine
affectation of enjoyment, was in no way discomposed by the
Tenor's adverse criticism ; he seemed, on the contrary, to
enjoy that too, for he chuckled and hugged himself ecstatically
before he replied.

"I should like to know," he said, with his uncanny grin,
"how you found out those lines were mine, for I certainly
never told you that I wrote them."

The Tenor's mind misgave him.

"Didn't you ? " he said, looking at the ashes.

The Boy threw himself back on the sofa.

"They were Angelica's ! " he said, with a shout of laughter.
"And now you look as if you would like to have them back
again. It will take you months to get over that ! "

The Tenor was certainly disconcerted, but he merely resumed his pipe, folded his hands, and looked up at the cathedral. He had been blessed all his life with the precious gift of
silence. Outside the night was very still. There was a fitful
little breeze which rustled the leaves, and made the creepers
tap on the window panes, but, beyond this, there was no sound,

no sign of life or movement, nothing to remind them of the
" whole cityful " so close at hand.

The Tenor lay back in his chair, looking somewhat dispirited.
The Boy got up and began to wander about the room ; a long
pause followed which was broken by the chime.

" I have been trying to say something all the evening, and
now that beastly chime has gone and made it impossible," the
Boy exclaimed, as soon as he could hear himself speak. " I,
hate it. I loathe it. It is cruel as eternal damnation. It is
condemnation without appeal. It is a judgment which acknowl-
edges none of the excuses we make for ourselves. I wish they
would change it. I wish they would make it say ' Lord, have
mercy ; Christ, have mercy upon us.' "

The Tenor put down his pipe, rose slowly, and went upstairs. In a few minutes he returned in flannels.

" You want exercise, Boy," he said. " You must come out.
It is a lovely night for the river, and I have been shut up in
the Close all day."

The Boy sprang to his feet. " Yes, yes," he exclaimed
with animation, " let us go, and I'll bring my violin. Where's
my hat ? "

" You came without one to-night—or perhaps you hung it
on the palings."

" No, I didn't," the Boy replied. " I must have forgotten
it altogether. But it doesn't matter. I'd rather be without
one. I always take it off when I can."

" So I have seen," said the Tenor, following him out.

As he walked through the Close, still a little behind the
Boy, he could not help noticing, by no means for the first
time, but more particularly than usual, what a graceful creature
the latter was. His slender figure showed to advantage in the
light flannels. They made him look broader and more manly
while leaving room for the free play of limb and muscle. He
had knotted a crimson silk scarf round his neck, sailor fashion,
and twisted a voluminous cummerbund of the same round his
waist, carelessly, so that one heavily fringed end of it came
loose, and now hung down to his knee, swaying with his body
as he moved. The Tenor remembered that his socks were
also of crimson silk, a detail which had caught his eye as the
Boy lolled on the sofa. It was evident that the costume had
cost him a thought, and, if somewhat theatrical, it was certainly
picturesque, and entirely characteristic. In one respect the
Boy's art was perfect : although he was quite conscious of his

good looks, he never had the air of being so ; every movement was natural and spontaneous, like the movements of a wild creature, and as agile. He seemed to rejoice in his own strength, to delight in his own suppleness ; and he walked on now with healthy elastic step, his violin held to his shoulder, his clear cut cheek leant down to it lovingly ; his luxuriant light hair all tumbled and tossed, while he kept time to an imaginary tune with the bow in his right hand, now flourishing it in the air, and now drawing it across the instrument, scarcely seeming to touch the strings, yet waking low Æolean harplike murmurs, or deep thrilling tones, or bright melodious cadences ; making it respond to his touch like a living creature, and glancing back over his shoulder at the Tenor as they proceeded, with a joyous face as if sure of his sympathy, but anxious to see if he had it all the same.

"I feel more amiable now," he said, between cadence and cadence. "Kindly consider that I have cancelled all my former misstatements. Cynicism can't exist in a healthy sensorium with sounds like these "—and he executed a magnificent *crescendo* passage on his violin. "When I want to play I feel that I must prepare myself. Making music is a religious rite to me, which can only be performed by one in perfect charity with all men."

They were seated in the boat by this time, the Tenor at the oars.

"Row, brothers, row !"

the Boy played—"and steer yourself," he said. "I can do nothing but accompany you."

And then he began in earnest, while the Tenor made the boat fly past river bank and towing-path, and house and wharf ; past bridge and tower and town—it seemed but a flash, and they were out in the open country ! flat meadows on the left, and on their right the green and swelling upland, dotted with slumbrous cattle and sheep, and shadowy with the heavy summer foliage of old trees. The Tenor stopped there, exhausted.

"There is madness in your music, Boy," he said. "It puts me beside myself."

The Boy laughed.

But in the pause that followed he shivered a little, and laid aside his instrument. It was not such a very fine night on the river as it had appeared to be in the Close. The moon would rise later, but at present there was no sign of her, and the sky, though cloudless, was not clear, the colour being that misty opaque gray which hangs low at the horizon on summer nights when the light never wholly departs, and is accompanied by a close and sultry atmosphere, surcharged with electricity, the harbinger of storms. It was so that night. There were no stars to relieve the murky heaviness, nor was it dark ; a sort of twilight reigned, as comfortless as tepid water, and there was no breeze now to rustle the leaves into life. All seemed ghostly still save for the muffled rush of the river, and the melancholy howling of a dog at some farm out of sight. And even the river was not its usual merry self, but a sullen heavy body that slipped by stealthily, making haste to the sea as if anxious to be away from the spot, without a ripple to break its level surface, and without the musical lop and gurgle and murmur with which it danced along at brighter times. In spite of the heat—or perhaps because of it—the air was full of moisture, and while the Tenor rested, a dead white mist began to appear above the low-lying meadows. It rose thinly, a mere film at first, which, coming suddenly, would have made a man brush his hand over his eyes, mistaking the haze for some defect of vision ; but gathering and gaining body rapidly, and rising a certain height clear from the ground, then seeming to hover, a thick cloud poised between earth and sky, not touching either, but drawn horizontally over the fields like a pall with ragged edges through which the trees showed in blurred outline, their leaves dripping miserably with an inter-mittent patter of uncertain drops as the moisture collected upon them and fell, and then collected again.

The fog was stationary for a time, and did not extend beyond the meadows, but it rose at intervals, though the clearance was only momentary, and had scarcely become perceptible before reinforcements of dull white vapour, tainted with miasma, rolled up from the marshy ground, bringing dank odours of standing water and weedy vegetation, half decayed, and gradually encroaching on the river, the smooth surface of which glowed with a greasy gleam beneath it, making it look like a river of oil.

"Let us go back," said the Boy. "My soul is sick with apprehension, and the damp will ruin my violin."

"I thought it was making you feel as if something were going to happen," the Tenor observed as he got the boat round.

The Boy ruffled his flaxen hair, and laughed uneasily. "Get away quick," he said. "If the elements do sympathize with man, there'll be a tragedy here before morning."

The Tenor pulled on steadily and in silence for some distance. But once out of sight of the mist and the meadows, the Boy's ever varying spirits rose again. He took up his violin, and drew soft sounds from it which seemed to float away far out into the night.

"Sing something," he said at last, playing the prelude to the most love-sweet song ever written.

"I arise from dreams of thee," the Tenor sang like one inspired.

The Boy uttered a deep sigh when he had finished ; he was speechless with pleasure.

But the Tenor went on. He sang of the sun and the sea, gliding from one strain to another, and unconsciously keeping time to the measure as he rowed, now making the little boat leap forward with a fine impulse, now almost resting on his oars till their progress through the water was scarcely perceptible, and now stopping altogether while he lingered on a closing cadence, looking up.

People who chanced to wake, as the windings of the river brought the singer past their homes that night, sat up in their beds and wondered. The music made them think of old tales of weird enchantment, in which strains, incomprehensibly sweet and thrilling like these, coming from nobody could tell where, had played a part. And one poor creature, who had long been dying in lingering pain, thought heaven had opened for her, and, smiling, passed happily away.

It would have been no great stretch of the imagination to have supposed that nature did sympathize with man in his moods just then, for gradually, as if to the music, the murky clouds had parted like a curtain at a given signal, and rolled away, leaving the vault of night high and bare and blue above them, with here and there a diamond star or two sparsely sprinkled from horizon to zenith, radiant at first, but presently paling before a slender shaft of light that shot up in the east, and then, opening fan-like was quickly followed by the great golden rim of the moon herself. She rose from behind a hill crested with fir trees, which appeared for a moment as if photographed on her disc, and then, mounting rapidly, hung suspended in a clear indigo sky above the quiet woods, the river and the little boat, which was motionless now—an ideal

moon in an ideal world with ideal music to greet her. But
the Boy dropped the violin on his knee and forgot to play as
he watched this beautiful transformation scene, and the
Tenor's song sank to a murmur while he also gazed and
waited, dipping his oars to keep the boat in mid-stream
mechanically. Joy and sadness are near akin in music ; they
are like pleasure and happiness, the one is the surface of feeling, the other its depth ; and there is solemnity in every
phase of absolute beauty which cannot fail to influence such
natures as the Tenor's and the Boy's. It was the Tenor,
though, that felt this moment most. His nature, if not deeper,
was more devout than the Boy's ; pleasure with him was a
veritable uplifting of the spirit in praise and thankfulness ;
and all the peace and quietness about them, the marvellous
light on hill and wood and vale, and even the nearness of the
unseen city, which he felt without perceiving it, and from
which there came to him that sense of fellowship and of the
sacredness of human life in which all the best qualities of man
are rooted ; these together sanctified the time. Although, for
the matter of that, to such a nature all times and seasons are
sanctified. For if ever a man's soul was purified on earth, his
was ; and if ever a man deserved to see heaven, he did.
Humanly speaking there was no stain on him ; in thought,
word, and deed he was immaculate and true as a little child.
This moment was therefore peculiarly his own, a moment of
deep happiness, which found expression, as all pleasurable
emotion did with him, in music. He lifted up his voice, that
wonderful voice which had no equal then upon earth, and
sang as he had sung once before on that very spot when the
first vague idea of the omnipresent majesty of a God possessed him, sang with all his heart, and it was the litany of the
Blessed Virgin, the one he had heard in France in days gone
by, the one he had been singing when first he met the Boy,
which recurred to him now—why or wherefore it would be
hard to say. He had not thought of it since. But perhaps
the moon, which was shining again as it had shone that night
on the old market-place, had helped to recall it, or perhaps it
satisfied him with a sense of appropriateness. For it was not
a dismal, monotonous product of mercenary dryness to which
the words were set, but the characteristic music of devotion
by which the spirit of prayer is made audible when words
fail, as they always do, to express it in all its force and fervour.

The Boy listened a while with parted lips. It was a new experience for him, and he was deeply moved. Then his musical instinct awoke, and presently he took up the strain, voice and violin, accompanying the Tenor, who rowed on once more, while the river banks resounded with, " Christe audi nos, Christe exaudi nos," and re-echoed " Miserere nobis."

At one point as they approached, a lady appeared suddenly, and stood with her hands clasped to her breast, looking and listening. She was a tall and graceful woman, wrapped in a long cloak and bareheaded, as if she had stepped out from somewhere just for the moment. She evidently recognized the singer ; and the Boy would have recognized the beautiful face, strong in its calm, sad serenity, and compassionate, had he looked that way ; but he did not look that way, and they swept on, the music growing fainter and fainter in the distance, till at last the boat was out of sight. Yet even then a few high notes continued to float back ; but these in turn quivered into silence, and all was still—only for a moment, though, for the clocks had struck unheeded, and now the chime rang out through the sultry air, voice-like, clear, and resonant :

He, watch-ing o - ver Is - ra - el, slumbers not, nor sleeps.

The lady listened, looking up as if the message were for her, but sighed.

" It will come right, I know," she said as she turned away. " But, Lord, how long ? "

CHAPTER XV.

AIR perfumed with flowers ; music, motion, warmth, and stillness ; moonlit meadows, shadowy woods, the river, and the boat ; it had been a time of delight too late begun and too soon ended. But exaltation cannot last beyond a certain time at that height, and then comes the inevitable reaction. It came upon the Tenor and the Boy quite suddenly, and for no apparent reason. It was the Boy who felt it first, and left off playing, then the song ceased, and the Tenor rowed on diligently. They were near the landing place by this time, but the Tenor did not know it.   He had not noticed the landmarks as they passed, and thought they had still some distance to go.

"Here, Boy," he said, breaking a long silence.   "Take the oars and row.   I am tired.   And it is your turn now."

"Oh!" the Boy exclaimed derisively.   "Just as if I would row and blister my lovely white hands when you are here to row me!"

"I cannot tolerate such laziness," the Tenor protested.   "It is sparing the rod and spoiling the child.   Here, take the oars or I'll throw you overboard," and he made a gesture toward him.

The Boy jumped up laughing, and flourishing his violin as if he would hit the Tenor on the head with it.   "Don't touch me," he cried, "or I'll——"

"Take care, for God's sake!" the Tenor exclaimed.

But too late.   His excitable companion, in the middle of cutting a fantastic caper, reeled, lost his balance, plunged head foremost into the water, and sank like a stone.

Without a moment's delay the Tenor dived in after him, the cockleshell of a boat, half capsizing as he went over, took in water enough to sink her to the gunwale, and the whole thing happened so quickly that a spectator on the bank who had seen the boat and its occupants one moment might have looked in vain the next for any trace of either.

The Tenor came to the surface alone.   His dive in the uncertain light had been unsuccessful, and now he had the strength of mind to wait—in what agony of suspense Heaven only knows!—till the Boy should rise.   It could only have been a few seconds, but it was long enough for the Tenor to lay another man's death at his own door, to realize the loss to himself the Boy would be, and his position when he would have to take the dreadful news to the family, only one member of which in all probability knew of their intimacy.   She knew —But, good Heaven! would she not blame him?   Oh, he had been to blame, to blame!—It was only a few seconds, yet it was time enough for the unfortunate Tenor to live over again the awful moment when he had seen his best friend drop dead, only there was a double pang, for time and space were confounded, and it was as if both father and brother—as they had been to him—had gone down at once, and both by his hand.

In that brief interval of suffering his face had become rigid and set, a stony mask with no visible sign of emotion upon it; and yet the man's strength and power of endurance were evident in this, that he had the courage to wait.

And presently the Boy rose to the surface within easy reach.

With an exclamation of relief the Tenor grasped him, and struck out for the shore—afraid at first that the Boy, who apparently could not swim, would cling about him in his fright and hamper his movements; and then afraid because the Boy did not cling about him, but suffered himself to be dragged through the water, inert, like a log, helpless, lifeless—no, not lifeless, the Tenor argued with himself. He could not be lifeless, you know. He had not been in the water long enough for that. The Tenor noticed that he had not let go of his violin, and thought : " The ruling passion strong in—no, not in death. How could a dead hand hold on like that? Boy, dear Boy !" But the Boy made no response. The Tenor had struck out for the nearest bank which, as luck would have it, brought him to the landing place at the watergate. His perception seemed singularly quickened ; every sense was actively alive to what was passing ; nothing escaped him ; and he rendered an account to himself of all that occurred, feeling it strange the while that he should be able to do so at such a time. He noticed some detail of the stonework in the arch as he swam toward it ; he noticed the poplars, some three or four of different heights, which stood up all stiff and vimi-neous as seen from below, beside it ; he remembered the Boy once saying they looked like hairy caterpillars standing on their heads, and smiled even now at the quaint conceit. When he reached the steps and clutched the handrail, it was with a sensation of joy that nearly paralyzed him. It was curious, though, what odd and trivial phrases rose to his lips, what irrelevant thoughts passed through his mind.

" Mustn't holloa till we're out of the wood," he warned himself, as he drew the Boy from the water with difficulty, and, getting him over his shoulder so that he could hold him with one hand and steady himself on the steep steps with the other began to stagger up. " I wonder what the Boy would say if he could see me now !" was his involuntary thought as he did so.

The Boy was heavier than his slender figure would have led one to suppose, or else the Tenor was not so strong as he thought himself ; at all events he swayed under his burden as he carried him through the silent Close, now putting out his hand flat against a wall to steady himself, and now staggering up to the gnarled trunk of one of the old lime trees, and pausing to take breath while he mentally calculated the distance between that and the next support at which he could stop to rest, noticing in the brief interval the blackness of the shadows ; noticing also a little shiver of leaves above him caused by a gust of air, the first forerunner of a breeze that was rapidly rising ; noticed this last fact particularly, partly because the wind chilled him in his thin wet flannels, and partly because it marked the change and contrast between the warm and happy time just over, the anxious present moment, and the dread of what might be yet to come. The next support was the corner of the wall which surrounded the dean's garden ; creeping on by that till it ended, he made an unsteady dash across the road for the wall of the cathedral, and then from that across again, zigzag, to his own little gate, where, gathering his strength for the last effort, he took the Boy, whom he apostrophised as a perfect Old Man of the Sea, in both arms, as a mother does her child, and a moment afterward laid him on the floor of the long low room where they had spent so many happy hours together, and from whence he had gone out a short time before all life and strength and youth and beauty : "Gone to his death !" The Tenor felt the phrase in his mind, but stifled it with a "Thank God !" as he laid him down.

He had been fatigued by the long row when the accident happened, and was now almost exhausted by excitement, terror for the Boy, and this last effort ; but still his mind went on with abnormal clearness noting every trifle, and continuing to force him, as it were, to render an account of each to himself. He noticed the perfume of roses, the roses the Boy had showered in upon him—so short a time before —and he found himself measuring the shortness of the interval again as if it would have been easier to bear the catastrophe had it not jostled a happier state of things so closely. He found himself wondering what the Boy would say if he knew he had brought him in by the front door instead of by the window ; he was sure he would have insisted on the mode of entrance he so much preferred had he been conscious, and felt as if he had taken a disloyal advantage of the Boy's helpless condition.

But while these trivial thoughts flashed through his brain he lost no time, not even in lighting a lamp, though the room was dark. What there was to be done must be done promptly, and with the same extraordinary lucidity of mind he remembered every simple remedy there was at his disposal. He ran upstairs, three steps at a time, for the blankets off his own bed. He had made up the kitchen fire, as was his wont, that evening, for the Boy to cook if it pleased him, and fortunately it was burning brightly still. He warmed the blankets there, and then returning, stripped the light flannel clothing from the Boy, loosened his fingers from the violin which he still clutched convulsively, rolled him up in them, and then, with an effort, lifted him on to the sofa, where he had sat and jested only a little while ago—and again the involuntary reckoning of time, to consider the contrast between the then and now, smote the Tenor to the heart with a cruel pang.

"Boy, dear Boy!" he called to him. He was kneeling beside him, but could only see a dim outline of his face in the obscurity of the room, and perhaps it was the darkness that made him look so rigid. "Boy, dear Boy!" he cried again, but the Boy made no sign. "O God, spare him!" the stricken man implored. And then he clasped the lad in his arms and pressed his cheek to his in a burst of grief and tenderness not to be controlled. He held him so for a few seconds, and it seemed as if in that close embrace, his whole being had expressed itself in love and prayer, as if he had wrestled with death itself and conquered, for all at once he felt the Boy's limbs quiver through their clumsy wrappings, and then he heard him sigh. Oh, the relief of it! The sudden reaction made him feel sick and faint. But the precious life was not yet safe. "There's many a slip"—so his mind began in spite of an effort to control it. "Restoratives—heat, stimulants, friction. He pulled the stand of ferns and flowering plants half round from the fireplace roughly, so that the pots fell up against each other, or rolled on the floor; then he fetched the burning coals from the kitchen, and heaped them on till the grate was full. The kettle had been boiling on the hob, so he brought it in now hissing, with brandy to make a drink. But he must have more light. Where are the matches? Nowhere, of course. They never are when they're wanted. However, it didn't matter, a piece of paper would do as well, and he twisted a piece up and stooped among the scattered roses to light it at the fire, and then he lit the lamp and turned to look at the Boy. All this had been done in a moment, as it seemed, and his face was still bright with hope, and prepared to smile encouragement. But—" God in heaven ! " he cried ; under his breath, as a man does who is too shocked to speak out.

Had some strange metamorphosis been brought about by that sudden immersion?

He pulled himself together with an effort, and walked to the other end of the room, where he stood with his back to the sofa, and his hands upraised to his head, trying to steady himself. Then he returned.

No, he had not been mistaken, he was not mad, he was not dreaming. It was the Boy who had plunged into the water headforemost, but this——

" God in heaven ! " he ejaculated again, under his breath, and then stood gazing like one transfixed.

For this, with the handsome, strong young face upturned, the smooth white throat, the dark brown braids pinned close to the head, all wet and shining ; this was not the Boy, but the Tenor's own lady, his ideal of purity, his goddess of truth, his angel of pity, as, in his foolishly fond way idealizing, he had been accustomed to consider her. It was Angelica herself ! Yet so complete had been the deception to his simple, unsuspicious mind, so impossible to believe was the revelation, and so used was he to associate some idea of the Boy with everything that occurred, that now, with his first conscious mental effort, he began to blame him as if her being there were due to some unpardonable piece of his mischief.

" The little wretch," he began, " how dare he "—he stopped there, realizing the absurdity of it, realizing that there was no Boy ; and no lady for the matter of that, at least none such as he had imagined. It had all been a cruel fraud from beginning to end.

It was a terrible blow, but the high-minded, self-contained dignity of the man was never more apparent than in the way he bore it. His face was unnaturally pale and set, but there was no other sign of what he suffered, and, the first shock over, he at once resumed his anxious efforts to restore—the girl—whose consciousness had scarcely yet returned, although she breathed and had moved. It was curious how the new knowledge already affected his attitude toward her. In preparing the hot drink he put half the quantity of brandy he would have used five minutes before for the Boy, and when he had to raise her head to make her swallow it, he did so reluctantly. It was only a change of idea really, the Boy was **a girl, that was all ; but what a difference it made, and would** have made even if there had been no question of love and marriage in the matter! At any other time the Tenor himself might have marvelled at the place apart we assign in our estimation to one of two people of like powers, passions, impulses, and purposes, simply because one of them is a woman.

The stimulant revived the girl, and presently she opened her eyes and met his as he bent over her.

"You are better now, I hope," he said coldly, moving away from her.

"I am better," she answered, and again their eyes met. But there was yet another moment of dazed semi-consciousness before she was able to attach any meaning to the change she saw in his face ; and then it flashed upon her. What she had hoped, feared, expected, and prevented every time they met had come to pass. He knew at last, and she could see at once what he thought of her. She would never again meet the tolerant loving glance he had had for the Boy, nor note the tender reverence of his face when her own name was mentioned. His idol was shattered, the dream and hope of his life was over, and from all that remained of them, herself as she really was, he shrank as from the dishonoured fragment of some once loved and holy thing—a thing which is doubly painful to contemplate in its ruin because of the importunate memories that cling about it.

Realizing something of this, she uttered a smothered ejaculation, and covered her face with a gesture of intolerable shame. There was always that saving grace of womanliness about Angelica, that when there was no excuse for her conduct, she had the honesty to be ashamed of herself ; in consequence of which she was one of those who never erred in the same way twice.

The Tenor turned to the fire, and then noticing her wet things scattered about he gathered them up : "I will take them and dry them," he said, and gladly made his escape. What he thought in the interval was : "I must marry her now, I suppose," and he could not help smiling ironically at this new way of putting it, nor wondering a little at the possibility of such a sudden change of feeling as that which had all at once transformed the dearest wish of his life into a distasteful, if not altogether repugnant, duty.

When the things were dry he took them to her.

"I will leave you to put them on," he said. "Will you

kindly call me when you are ready ?" And then he closed the window that looked out on the road, drew down the blind, and once more left her.

No reproach could have chilled and frightened her as this stiff and formal, yet cool acceptance of the position did. She feared it meant that all was over between them in a way she had never thought possible. But still she hoped to coax him round. She dreaded the next hour, the day of reckoning, as it were, but did not try to escape it. On the contrary, she hastened her dressing in order to get it over as quickly as possible.

" Israfil ! " she called to him boldly, as soon as she was ready.

The Tenor returned.

She was standing in the middle of the room when he entered, and she looked at him confidently, and just as the "Boy" would have done after a piece of mischief which he had determined to brazen out. The Boy had two moods, the defiant and the repentant ; it seemed that the girl—but here the Tenor checked his thoughts. It was very hard, though, to drop either of the two individualities which had hitherto been so distinct and different, and to realize that one of them at least had never existed.

She certainly brought more courage to the interview than he did, for he, the wronged one, found as he faced her now that he had not a word to say for himself. For the moment, she was master of the situation, and she began at once as if the whole thing were a matter of course.

Catching an involuntary glance of the Tenor's, she put both hands up to her head as the Boy would have done—so the Tenor, still confused between the two, expressed it to himself ; and the old familiar gesture sent another pang through his heart. The water had washed the flaxen wig away, but the thick braids of her hair were still pinned up tightly, accounting for the shape of the *remarkable head* about which the Boy had so often, and, as was now evident, so reck-lessly, jested.

Her hair was very wet, and she began deliberately to take it down and unplait it.

" I could not always make it—my head, you know—the same shape," she said, answering his thought ; " but you never noticed the difference, although you often looked. I **used** to wonder how **you** could look so intelligently and see

so little"—and she glanced down at herself, so unmistakably
a woman now that he knew. She had been like a conundrum,
the answer to which you would never have guessed for yourself, but you see it at once when you hear it, and then it seems
so simple. She was rather inclined to speak to the Tenor in
a half pitying, patronizing way, as to a weak creature easily
taken in ; but he had recovered himself by this time, and
something in his look and manner awed her, determined as
she was, and she could not keep it up.

He moved farther from her, and then spoke in a voice made
harsh by the effort it cost him to control it.

"Why have you done this thing?" he said sternly.

Her heart began to beat violently. The colour left her lips,
and she sank into a chair, covered once more with shame and
confusion. But, boy or girl, the charm of her peculiar personality was still the same, and it had its effect upon him even
at that moment, indignant as he was, as she sat there, her long
hair falling behind her, looking up at him with timid eyes and
with tremulous mouth.

It was pitiful to see her so, and it softened him.

"What was your object?" he asked, relenting.

"Excitement—restlessness—if I had any," she faltered.
" But I had no object. I am inventing one now because you
ask me ; it is an afterthought. I—I took the first step "—
with a dry sob—"and then I—I just drifted on—on, you
know—from one thing to another."

"But tell me all about it," he persisted, taking a seat as he
spoke. " Tell me exactly how it began."

There was no help for it now. He was sitting in judgment
upon her, and she felt that she must make an effort to satisfy
him.

"It began—oh, let me see ! how am I to tell you?" and
she twisted her hands, frowning in perplexity. " I don't want
to embellish the story so as to make it picturesque and myself
more interesting," and she looked at the Tenor with slightly
elevated eyebrows, as if pained already by her own inaccuracy.
There was something irresistibly comic in this candid avowal
of the force of habit, and all the more so because she was too
much in earnest for once to see the humour of it herself. The
Tenor saw it, however, but he made no sign.

" Well, begin," he said. " I ought to know your method
sufficiently well by this time to enable me to sift the wheat
from the chaff."

Angelica considered a little, and then she answered, hesitating as if she were choosing each word : " I see where the mistake has been all along. There was no latitude allowed for my individuality. I was a girl, and therefore I was not supposed to have any bent. I found a big groove ready waiting for me when I grew up, and in that I was expected to live whether it suited me or not. It did not suit me. It was deep and narrow, and gave me no room to move. You see, I loved to make music. Art ! That was it. There is in my own mind an imperative monitor which urges me on always into competition with other minds. I wanted to *do* as well as to *be*, and I knew I wanted to do ; but when the time came for me to begin, my friends armed themselves with the whole social system as it obtains in our state of life, and came out to oppose me. They used to lecture me and give me good advice, as if they were able to judge, and it made me rage. I had none of the domestic virtues, and yet they would insist upon domesticating me ; and the funny part of it was that, side by side with my natural aspirations was an innate tendency to conform to their ideas while carrying out my own. I believe I could have satisfied *them*—my friends—if only they had not thwarted me. But that was the mistake. I had the ability to be something more than a young lady, fiddling away her time on useless trifles, but I was not allowed to apply it systematically, and ability is like steam—a great power when properly applied, a great danger otherwise. Let it escape recklessly and the chances are someone will be scalded ; bottle it up and there will be an explosion. In my case both happened. The steam was allowed to escape at first instead of being applied to help me on in a definite career, and a good deal of scalding ensued ; and then, to remedy that mistake, the dangerous experiment of bottling it up was tried, and only too successfully. I helped a little in the bottling myself, I suppose, and then came the explosion. This is the explosion,"—glancing round the disordered room, and then looking down at her masculine attire. " I see it all now," she proceeded in a spiritless way, looking fixedly into the fire, as if she were trying to describe something she saw there. " I had the feeling, never actually formulated in words, but quite easy to interpret now, that if I broke down conventional obstacles—broke the hampering laws of society, I should have a chance——"

" It is a common mistake," the Tenor observed, filling up the pause.

"But I did not know how," she pursued, "or where to begin, or what particular law to break—until one evening. I was sitting alone at an open window in the dark, and I was tired of doing nothing and very sorry for myself, and I wanted an object in life more than ever, and then a great longing seized me. I thought it an aspiration. I wanted to go out there and then. I wanted to be free to go and come as I would. I felt a galling sense of restraint all at once, and I determined to break the law that imposed it; and that alone was a satisfaction—the finding of one law that I could break. I didn't suppose I could learn much—there wasn't much left to learn,"—this was said bitterly, as if she attached the blame of it to somebody else—"but I should be amused, and that was something; and I should see the world as men see it, which would be from a new point of view for me, and that would be interesting. It is curious, isn't it?" she reflected, that what men call 'life' they always go out at night to see; and what they mean by 'life' is generally something disgraceful?" It was to the fire that she made this observation, and then she resumed: "It is astonishing how importunate some ideas become—one now and then of all the numbers that occur to you; how it takes possession of you, and how it insists upon being carried into effect. This one gave me no peace. I knew from the first I should do it, although I didn't want to, and I didn't intend to, if you can understand such a thing. But my dress was an obstacle. As a woman, I could not expect to be treated by men with as much respect as they show to each other. I know the value of men's cant about protecting the 'weaker' sex! Because I was a woman I knew I should be insulted, or at all events hindered, however inoffensive my conduct; and so I prepared this disguise. And I began to be amused at once. It amused me to devise it. I saw a tailor's advertisement, with instructions how to measure yourself; and I measured myself and sent to London for the clothes—these thin ones are padded to make me look square like a boy. And then, with some difficulty, I got a wig of the right colour. It fitted exactly—covered all my own hair, you know, and was so beautifully made that it was impossible for any unsuspicious person to detect it without touching it; and the light shade of it, too, accounted for the fairness of my skin, which would have looked suspiciously clear and delicate with darker hair. The great difficulty was my hands and feet; but the different shape of a boy's shoes made my feet pass; and I crumpled my hands up and kept them out of sight as much as possible. But they are not of a degenerated smallness," she added, looking at them critically; "it is more their shape. However, when I dressed myself and put on that long ulster, I saw the disguise would pass and felt pretty safe. But isn't it surprising the difference dress makes? I should hardly have thought it possible to convert a substantial young woman into such a slender, delicate-looking boy as I make. But it just shows how important dress is."

The Tenor groaned. "Didn't you know the risk you were running?" he asked.

"Oh, yes!" she answered coolly. "I knew I was breaking a law of the land. I knew I should be taken before a police magistrate if I were caught masquerading, and that added excitement to the pleasure—the charm of danger. But then you see it was danger without danger for me, because I knew I should be mistaken for my brother. Our own parents do not know us apart when we are dressed alike."

"Oh, then there *are* two of you?" the Tenor said.

"Yes. I told you. They call us the Heavenly Twins," said Angelica.

"Yes, you told me," the Tenor repeated thoughtfully. "But then you told me so many things."

"Well, I told you nothing that was not absolutely true," Angelica answered—"from Diavolo's point of view. I assumed his manner and habits when I put these things on, imitated him in everything, tried to think his thoughts, and looked at myself from his point of view; in fact my difficulty was to remember that I was not him. I used to forget sometimes and think I was. But I confess that I never was such a gentleman as Diavolo is always under all circumstances. Poor dear Diavolo!" she added regretfully; "how he would have enjoyed those fried potatoes!"

The Tenor slightly changed his position. He only glanced at her now and then when he spoke to her, and for the rest he sat as she did, with his calm deep eyes fixed on the fire, and an expression of patient sadness upon his face that wrung her heart. Perhaps it was to stifle the pain of it that she began to talk garrulously. "Oh, I am sorry for the trick I have played you!" she exclaimed with real feeling. "I have been sorry all along since I knew your worth, and I came to-night to tell you, to confess and to apologize. When I first knew you all my *loving consciousness* was dormant, if you know what that is;

I mean the love in us for our fellow-creatures which makes it pain to ourselves to injure them. But you re-aroused that feeling, and strengthened and added to it until it had become predominant, so that, since I have known you as you are, I have hated to deceive you. This is the first uncomfortable feeling of that kind I have ever had. But for the rest I did not care. I was bored. I was always bored; and I resented the serene unconcern of my friends. Their indifference to my aspirations, and the way they took it for granted that I had everything I ought to want, and could therefore be happy if I chose, exasperated me. To be bored seems a slight thing, but a world of suffering is contained in the experience; and do you know, Israfil, I think it dangerous to leave an energetic woman without a single strong interest or object in life. Trouble is sure to come of it sooner or later—which sounds like a truism now that I have said it, and truisms are things which we habitually neglect to act upon. In my case nothing of this kind would have happened "—and again her glance round the room expressed a comprehensive view of her present situation—" if I had been allowed to support a charity hospital with my violin—or something; made to feel responsible, you know."

"But surely you must recognize the grave responsibility which attaches to all women——"

"In the abstract," Angelica interposed. "I know if things go wrong they are blamed for it; if they go right the Church takes the credit. The value attached to the influence of women is purely fictitious, as individuals usually find when they come to demand a recognition of their personal power. I should have been held to have done my duty if I had spent the rest of my life in dressing well, and saying the proper thing; no one would consider the waste of power which is involved in such an existence. You often hear it said of a girl that she should have been a boy, which being interpreted means that she has superior abilities; but because she is a woman it is not thought necessary to give her a chance of making a career for herself. I hope to live, however, to see it allowed that a woman has no more right to bury her talents than a man has; in which days the man without brains will be taught to cook and clean, while the clever woman will be doing the work of the world well which is now being so shame-fully scamped. But I was going to say that I am sure all my vagaries have arisen out of the dread of having nothing better

to do from now until the day of my death—as I once said to
an uncle of mine—but to get up and go to bed, after spending
the interval in the elegant and useless way ladies do—a ride,
a drive, a dinner, a dance, a little music—trifling all the time
to no purpose, not even amusing one's self, for when amusement begins to be a business, it ceases to be a pleasure. This
has not mended matters, I know," she acknowledged drearily ;
" but it has been a distraction, and that was something while
it lasted. Monotony, however luxurious, is not less irksome
because it is easy. A hardworking woman would have rest to
look forward to, but I hadn't even that, although I was always
wearied to death—as tired of my idleness or purposeless occupations as anybody could possibly be by work. I think if you
will put yourself in my place, you will not wonder at me, nor
at any woman under the circumstances who, secure of herself
and her position, varies the monotony of her life with an occasional escapade as one puts sauce into soup to relieve the
insipidity. Deplore it if you will, but don't wonder at it ; it
is the natural consequence of an unnatural state of things ,
and there will be more of it still, or I am much mistaken."

Again the Tenor changed his position. "I cannot, *cannot*
comprehend how you could have risked your reputation in
such a way," he said, shaking his head with grave concern.

" No risk to my reputation," she answered with the insolence
of rank. " Everybody knows who I am, and, if I remember
rightly, · That in the captain's but a choleric word which in the
soldier is rank blasphemy.' What would be an unpardonable
offence if committed by another woman less highly placed than
myself is merely an amusing eccentricity in me, so—for *my*
benefit—conveniently snobbish is society. Since I grew up,
however, I find that I am not one of those who can say flippantly, ' You can't have everything, and if people have talents
they are not to be expected to have characters as well.' Great
talent should be held to be a guarantee for good character ;
the loss of the one makes the possession of the other dangerous.
But what I do maintain is that I have done nothing by which
I ought in justice to be held to have jeopardised my character.
I have broken no commandment, nor should I under any circumstances. It is only the idea of the thing that shocks your
prejudices. You cannot bear to see me decently dressed as a
boy, but you would think nothing of it if you saw me half
undressed for a ball, as I often am ; yet if the one can be done

with a modest mind, and you must know that it can, so can the other, I suppose."

The Tenor was sitting sideways on his chair, his elbow resting on the back, his head on his hand, his legs crossed, half turned from her and listening without looking at her ; and there was something in the way she made this last remark that set a familiar chord vibrating not unpleasantly. Perhaps, after the revelation, he had expected her to turn into a totally different person ; at all events he was somewhat surprised, but not disagreeably, to perceive how like the Boy she was. This was the Boy again, exactly, in a bad mood, and the Tenor sought at once, as was his wont, to distract him rather than argue him out of it. This was the force of habit, and it was also due to the fact that his mind was rapidly adapting itself to a strange position and becoming easier in the new attitude. The woman he had been idolizing was lost irretrievably, but the charm which had been the Boy's remained to him, and he had already begun to reconcile himself to the idea of a wrong-headed girl who must be helped and worked for, instead of a wrong-headed boy.

"But why should you have chosen this impossible form of amusement in particular?" he said. "Why could you not interest yourself in the people about you—do something for them?"

"I did think of that, I did try," she answered petulantly. "But it is impossible for a woman to devote herself to people for whom there is nothing to be done, who don't want her devotion ; and, besides, devotion wasn't my vocation. But, after all," she broke off, defending herself, "I only arrived at this by slow degrees, and I never should have come so far at all if Diavolo had stuck to me ; but he got into a state of don't-care-and-can't-be-bothered, and separated his work from mine by going to Sandhurst. Then I found myself alone, and you cannot think how a woman must suffer from the awful loneliness of a life like mine when I had no one near me in the sense in which Diavolo has always been near, a life that is full of acquaintances as a cake is full of currants, no two of which ever touch each other."

The Tenor's habitual quiescence seemed to have deserted him. He changed his position incessantly, and did so now again ; it was the only sign he made of being disturbed at all; and as he moved he brushed his hand back over his hair, but did not speak.

"I kept my disguise a long time before I used it," she began again, another morsel of incident and motive recurring to her. "I don't think I had any very distinct notion of what I should do with it when I got it. The pleasure of getting it had been everything for the moment, and having succeeded in that and tried the dress, I hid it away carefully and scarcely ever thought of it—never dreamt of wearing it certainly until one night—it was quite an impulse at last. That night, you know, the first time we met—it was such a beautiful night! I was by myself and had nothing to do as usual, and it tempted me sorely. I thought I should like to see the market-place by moonlight, and then all at once I thought I *would* see it by moonlight. That was my first weighty reason for changing my dress. But having once assumed the character, I began to love it; it came naturally; and the freedom from restraint, I mean the restraint of our tight uncomfortable clothing, was delicious. I tell you I was a genuine boy. I moved like a boy, I felt like a boy; I was my own brother in very truth. Mentally and morally, I was exactly what you thought me, and there was little fear of your finding me out, although I used to like to play with the position and run the risk."

"It was marvellous," the Tenor said.

"Not at all," she answered, "not a bit more marvellous in real life than it would have been upon the stage—a mere exercise of the actor's faculty under the most favourable circumstances; and not a bit more marvellous than to create a character as an author does in a book; the process is analogous. But the same thing has been done before. George Sand, for instance; don't you remember how often she went about dressed as a man, went to the theatres and was introduced to people, and was never found out by strangers? And there was that woman who was a doctor in the army for so long—until she was quite old. James Barry, she called herself, and none of her brother officers, not even her own particular chum in the regiment she first belonged to, had any suspicion of her sex, and it was not discovered until after her death, when she had been an Inspector General of the Army Medical Department for many years. And there have been women in the ranks too, and at sea. It was really not extraordinary that an unobservant and unsuspicious creature like yourself should have been deceived."

This recalled the patronizing manner of the Boy at times, and the Tenor smiled.

" The meeting with you was an accident, of course," Angelica proceeded with her disjôinted narrative ; " but I thought I
would turn it to account.   I was, as you used to say, devoured
by curiosity, and my mind is always tentative.   I wanted to
hear how men talk to each other.   I didn't believe in goodness in a man, and I wanted to see badness from the man's
point of view.   I expected to find you corrupt in some particular, to see your hoofs and your horns sooner or later, and I
tried to make you show them : but that of course you never
did, and I soon realized my mistake.   I had a standing quarrel with your sex, however, and at first it pleased me to deceive
you simply because you were a man.   That was only at the
very first, for, as soon as I began to appreciate your worth, I
felt ashamed of myself.   Don't you see, Israfil, you have been
raising me all along,   It has been a very gradual process,
though, but still I *did* wish to undeceive you.   I would have
done so at once if you had not been so far above me.   If you
had spoken to me when I gave you that chance—in the cathedral after the service, don't you remember ?—it would have
been stepping down from your pedestal ; we should have been
on the same level then, and I need not have dreaded your
righteous indignation.   But as it was you maintained your
high position, and I was afraid—and I could not give you up.
It was delightful to look at myself—an ideal self—from afar
off with your eyes ; it made me feel as if I could be all you
thought me ; it made me wish to be so ; and it also made me
more sorry than anything to have you think so highly of me
when I did not deserve it.   All these were signs of awakening
which I recognized myself—and I did try over and over again
to undeceive you about my character, but you never would
listen to me.   I wish—I wish you had ! "

"Do you love me then ?" the Tenor asked her, and was
startled himself as soon as he had spoken by the immediate
effect of the question upon her.   It was evident that she had
received a terrible shock.   She changed colour and countenance, and swayed for a moment as if she were about to faint,
and he sprang up to catch her in his arms, but she recovered
herself sufficiently to check the impulse : " No, no," she
exclaimed hoarsely,—" stop ! stop ! you don't know—My God !
how could I have put myself in such a position ?—I mean—let
me tell you——" She shut her eyes and waited, the Tenor
looking at her in pained surprise.   He sank again on to the
seat from which he had risen, and waited also, wondering.

Presently she opened her eyes and looked at him : "The charm—the charm," she faltered, "has all been in the delight of associating with a man intimately who did not know I was a woman. I have enjoyed the benefit of free intercourse with your masculine mind undiluted by your masculine prejudices and proclivities with regard to my sex. Had you known that I was a woman—even you—the pleasure of your companionship would have been spoilt for me, so unwholesomely is the imagination of a man affected by ideas of sex. The fault is in your training ; you are all of you educated deliberately to think of women chiefly as the opposite sex. Your manner to me has been quite different from that of any other man I ever knew. Some have fawned on me, degrading me with the supposition that I exist for the benefit of man alone, and that it will gratify me above all else to know that I please him ; and some few, such as yourself, have embarrassed me by putting me on a pedestal, which is, I can assure you, an exceedingly cramped and uncomfortable position. There is no room to move on a pedestal. Now, with you alone of all men, not excepting Diavolo, I almost think I have been on an equal footing ; and it has been to me like the free use of his limbs to a prisoner after long confinement with chains." The expression which the Tenor's abrupt question had called into her countenance passed off as she spoke, and with it the impression it had made upon the Tenor. He mistook the remarks she had just been making for a natural girlish evasion of the subject, and he did not return to it, partly because he felt it to be an inopportune time, but also because he was pretty sure of her feeling for him, and thought that he would have ample leisure by and by, the leisure of a lifetime, to press the question. There were other explanations to be asked for too, which it seemed advisable to him to get over at once and have done with.

"But how have you managed to get out night after night," he asked, "without being missed ?"

"Not night after night," she answered. "If you remember, there were often long intervals. But I have told you, I was constantly alone. The house is large, none of the servants sleep near my room, and my husband——"

"Your—*what?*" the Tenor demanded, turning round on his chair to face her, every vestige of colour gone from his counterance, yet not convinced. "What did you say?" he repeated, aghast.

" My—husband," she faltered. " Mr. Kilroy of Ilver-thorpe."

Hitherto, he had uttered no reproach, but she knew that this reticence was due to self-respect rather than to any lin-gering remnant of deference, and now when she saw his face ablaze she was prepared for an outburst of wrath. All he said, however, was, speaking with quiet dignity : " You need not have allowed that part of the deception to go on. You should have told me that at once ; why did you not ? "

For the first time Angelica lost her presence of mind. "I— I forgot," she stammered.

The Tenor threw back his sunny head and laughed bitterly.

" It is a curious fact," Angelica remarked upon reflection, and as if speaking to herself, " but I really had forgotten.

The Tenor looked at the fire, and in the little pause that ensued Angelica suddenly lost her temper.

" If you are deceived in me you have deceived yourself," she burst out, " for I have tried my utmost to undeceive you. You go and fall in love with a girl you have never spoken to in your life, you endow her gratuitously with all the virtues you admire without asking if she cares to possess them ; and when you find she is not the peerless perfection you require her to be, you blame her ! oh ! isn't that like a man ? You all say the same thing : ' It wasn't me ! ' "

" What will your husband say ? " the Tenor ejaculated in an undertone.

" Well, you see the bargain was when I asked him to marry me——"

" When you *what ?* " said the Tenor.

" Asked him to marry me," Angelica calmly repeated. " The bargain was that he should let me do as I liked, there being a tacit understanding between us, of course, that I should do nothing morally wrong. I could not under any circumstances do anything morally wrong—not, I confess, because 1 am particularly high-minded, but because I cannot imagine where the charm and pleasure of the morally wrong comes in. The best pleasures in life are in art, not in animalism ; and all the benefit of your acquaintance, I repeat, has consisted in the fact that you were unaware of my sex. I knew that directly you became aware of it another element would be introduced into our friendship which would entirely spoil it so far as I am concerned."

It is a noteworthy fact, as showing how hopelessly involved

man's moral perceptions are with his prejudices and faith in custom even when reprehensible, that the Tenor was if anything more shocked by Angelica's outspoken objection to grossness than he would have been by a declaration of passion on her part.　The latter lapse is not unprecedented, and therefore might have been excused as natural ; but the unusual nature of the declaration she had made put it into the category to which all things out of order are relegated to be taken exception to, irrespective of their ethical value.　But he said nothing, only he turned from her once more, and gazed sorrowfully into the fire.

Angelica looked at him with a dissatisfied frown on her face. " I wish you would speak," she said to him under her breath ; and then she began again herself with her accustomed volubility : " Oh, yes, I married.　That was what was expected of me.　Now, my brother when he grew up was asked with the most earnest solicitude what he would like to be or to do ; everything was made easy for him to enter upon any career he might choose, but nobody thought of giving *me* a chance.　It was taken for granted that I should be content to marry, and only to marry, and when I expressed my objection to being so limited nobody believed I was in earnest.　So here I am.　And I won't deny," she confessed with her habitual candour, " that it did occur to me that I might have cared for you as a lover had I not been married.　But of course the thought did not disturb me.　It was merely a passing glimpse of a might-have-been.　When one has a husband one must be loyal to him, even in thought, whatever terms we are on."

The Tenor rose abruptly and walked to the farther end of the room, and stood there for a little leaning against the window-frame with his back to her, looking out at the cathedral.　He felt sick and faint, and found the fire and the smell of the roses overpowering.　But presently he recovered, and then he returned to her.　His face was set now, white and passionless, as it had been while he waited to rescue her from the river, and when he spoke there was no tone in his voice ; it was as if he were repeating some dry fact by rote.

" There is no excuse for you then," he said ; and she perceived with surprise that until he knew she was married he had tried to believe that there was.　" You were playing with me, cheating me, mocking me all the time."

Angelica looked at him in dismay.　" Israfil !　Israfil ?" she pleaded, springing to her feet and clasping his arm with both hands, her better nature thoroughly aroused, "O Israfil! forgive me!" She almost shook him in her vehemence, then flung him from her, and pressed her hands to her eyes for an instant. "Mocking you? Oh, no!" she protested. "Believe me—believe me if you can. I respected you almost from the first; I reverenced you at last. I used to tease you about myself to begin with, I repeat, because it did not occur to me that you could care seriously for a girl to whom you had never spoken. Then I began to perceive my mistake. Then I felt anxious to get you to go away and return, and be properly introduced to us."

"And so you schemed——"

"I arranged a future for you that is worthy of you. O Israfil, I have some conscience. I am not so bad as you think me. Even if I had not dared to tell you to-night, I should have sent you a full explanation as soon as you had gone. I thought when once you were engaged upon a new career, you would forget—all this."

"I am surprised to hear that you did not expect me to enjoy the joke at my own expense—the trick you have played me."

Angelica changed countenance·; it was exactly what she had expected.

"Don't speak bitterly to me," she exclaimed. "It is not natural for you to do so. Oh! I should know—I know only too well—all your good qualities. My heart has been wrung a hundred times—by the thought—of all—I have—lost—by my folly." She raised her hands with a despairing gesture. "Don't imagine that you suffer—alone—or more than I do. There is hope for you; there is none for me. But one thing has been a comfort. I knew you only cared for an ideal creature, not at all like me. I was not afraid you would break your heart for a phantom that had never existed. And for me as I am, I knew you could have no regard. I see"— she broke off—"I see all the contradictions that are involved in what I have said and am saying, and yet I mean it all. In separate sections of my consciousness each separate clause exists at this moment, however contradictory, and there is no reconciling them; but there they are. I can't understand it myself, and I don't want you to try. All I ask you is to believe me—to forgive me."

There was an interval of silence after this, and then the Tenor spoke again.

"It is nearly morning," he said. "I will see you safely home."

The Boy had been allowed to come and go as he liked, but with her it was different ; and the altered position made itself again apparent in this new-found need for an escort. It was evident, too, from the way the Tenor had allowed the subject to drop, tacitly agreeing to the assertion : " For me as I am I knew you could have no regard," that he considered there was nothing more to be said ; but Angelica retained her childish habit of talking everything out, and this did not satisfy her, it was such a lame conclusion.

She got up now, however, to accompany him. " My hair !" she exclaimed, recollecting. " What am I to do with my hair ? I suppose my wig is lost." Then she burst out passionately : " Oh, why did you save my life ! " and wrung her hands—"or why aren't you different now you know ? Can't you say something to restore my self-respect ? Won't you forgive me ? "

The Tenor's face contracted as with a spasm of pain. He had much to forgive, and he may be pardoned if he showed no eagerness; but he spoke at last. " I do forgive you," he said. Then all at once his great tender heart swelled with pity. " Poor misguided girl ! " he faltered with a broken voice; " may God in heaven forgive you, and help you, and keep you safe, and make you good and true and pure now and always."

She sank down at that, and clasped his feet and burst into a paroxysm of tears, which were as a fervent *Amen* to the Tenor's prayer.

" Come ! " he said, raising her. " Come, before it is too late. You must do something with your hair."

But she could not plait it, her hands trembled so, and he was obliged to help her. He got her a hat to roll it up under.

" The light is uncertain," he said, " and it is raining now. Even if we do meet anyone, I don't think they would notice— especially if I can find an umbrella for you."

He hunted one up from somewhere, and then he hurried her away, ferried her across the river, and left her at the lodge gate safely, his last words being:—" You will do some good in the world—you will be a good woman yet, I know—I know you will."

END OF BOOK IV.

BOOK V.

MRS. KILROY OF ILVERTHORPE.

Face to face in my chamber, my silent chamber, I saw her :
God and she and I only, there I sat down to draw her Soul through
The clefts of confession—" Speak, I am holding thee fast,
As the angel of recollection shall do it at last!"
                    " My cup is blood-red
                        With my sin," she said,
                " And I pour it out to the bitter lees.
As if the angel of judgment stood over me strong at last
                    Or as thou wert as these,"
                            —*Elizabeth Barrett Browning.*

            Howbeit all is not lost
            The warm noon ends in frost
            And worldly tongues of promise,
            Like sheep-bells die from us
            On the desert hills cloud-crossed:
            Yet through the silence shall
            Pierce the death-angel's call,
            And " Come up hither," recover all.
                Heart, wilt thou go ?
                        I go !
            Broken hearts triumph so."
                            —*Ibid.*

CHAPTER I.

HALF an hour after the Tenor parted from Angelica, she was sleeping soundly, not because she was dedolent but because she was exhausted; and when that is the case sleep is the blessed privilege of youth and strength, let what will have preceded it. She lay there in her luxurious bed, with one hand under her head, her thick dark hair—just as the Tenor had braided it—in contrast to the broad white pillow; her smooth face, on which no emotion of any kind had written a line as yet, placid as a little child's; to all appearance an ideal of innocence and beauty. And while she slept the rain stopped, the misty morning broke, the clouds had cleared away, and the sun shone forth, welcomed by a buzz of insects and chirrup of birds; the uprising of countless summer scents, and the opening of rainbow flowers. It was one of those radiant days, harmonizing best with tranquil or joyous moods, when, if we are disconsolate, nature seems to mock our misery, and callous earth rejoices forgetful of storms, making us wonder with a deeper discontent why we, too, cannot forget.

Angelica slept a heavy dreamless sleep, and when she did awake late in the morning, it was not gradually, with that pleasant dreamy languor which precedes mental activity in happy times, but with a sudden start that aroused her to full consciousness in a moment, and the recollection of all that had occurred the night before. Black circles round her eyes bore witness to the danger, fatigue, and emotion of her late experiences; she had a sharp pain in her head, too, and she was unaccustomed to physical pain; but she felt it less than the dull ache she had at her heart, and a general sense of things gone wrong that oppressed her, but which she strove with stubborn determination to stifle.

Her maid was busy in the dressing room, the door of which was open, and she called her.

"Elizabeth!"

"Yes, ma'am," and the maid appeared, smiling.

She was a good-looking woman of thirty or thereabouts. She had come to Angelica when the latter got out of her

nurse's hands, and remained with her ever since, Angelica
being one of those mistresses who win the hearts of their servants by recognizing the human nature in them, and appreciating the kindness there is in devotion rather than accepting
it as a necessary part of the obligation to earn wages.

"Bring me a cup of coffee, Elizabeth."

"Yes, ma'am," the maid rejoined. "It shall be ready for
you as soon as you have had your bath."

"But I want it now," said Angelica, springing out of bed
energetically, and holding first one slim foot and then the
other out to be shod.

There was a twinkle in the maid's eye as she answered:
"Please, ma'am, you made me promise never to give it to you,
however much you might wish it, until you had had your bath.
You said you'd be sure to ask for it, and I was to refuse,
because hot coffee was bad for you just before a cold bath, and
you really enjoyed it more afterward, only you hadn't the
strength of mind to wait."

"Quite so," said Angelica. "You're a treasure, Elizabeth,
really. But did I say you were to begin to-day?"

"No, ma'am; not to-day in particular. But the last time I
brought it to you early you scolded me after you had taken it,
and said if ever I let myself be persuaded again, you'd dismiss
me on the spot. And you warned me that you'd be artful and
get it out of me somehow if I didn't take care."

"So I did," said Angelica.

She had been brought up with a pretty smart shock the night
before, and was suffering from the physical effects of the same
that morning; the mental were still in abeyance. She felt a
strange lassitude for one thing, and was strongly inclined to
indulge it by being indolent. She breakfasted in her own
room, but could not eat, neither could she read. She turned
her letters over; then tried a book; then going back to her
letters again, she picked one out which she had overlooked
before. It was from her husband, and as she read it she
changed countenance somewhat, but it would be impossible to
say what the change betokened, whether pleasure or the reverse.

"Elizabeth," she said, speaking evenly as usual, "your
master is coming back to-day. He will be here for lunch."

The sickening sense of loss and pain which had assailed her
when she awoke that morning did not diminish as the day wore
on, nor did her thoughts grow less importunate; but she steadily refused to entertain any of them, or to let her mental dis-

comfort interfere with her occupations. After reading her
husband's letter she finished dressing, had a long interview
with her housekeeper, went round the premises as was her
daily habit, to see that all was in order, and then retired to her
morning room, and set to work methodically to write orders,
see to accounts, and answer letters. It was a busy day with
her, and she had only just finished when Mr. Kilroy arrived.
She went to meet him pleasantly, held up her cheek to be
kissed, and said she was glad he was in time for lunch. There
was no sign of the joy or effusion with which young wives
usually receive their husbands after an absence, but the greeting was eminently friendly. Angelica had always had a strong
liking for Mr. Kilroy, and, as she told him, marriage had not
affected this in any way. She had made a friend of him while
she was still in the schoolroom, and confided to him many
things which she would not have mentioned to anyone else, not
even excepting Diavolo; and she continued to do so still. She
was sure of his sympathy, sure of his devotion, and she
respected him as sincerely as she trusted him. In fact, had
there been any outlet for her superfluous mental energy, any
satisfactory purpose to which the motive power of it might
have been applied, she would have made Mr. Kilroy an excellent wife. She was not in love with him, but she probably
liked him all the better on that account, for she must have
been disappointed in him sooner or later had she ever discovered in him those marvellous fascinations which passion projects
from itself on to the personality of the most commonplace person. As it was, however, she had always left him out of her
day-dreams altogether. She quite believed that pleasure is the
end of life, but then her ideal of pleasure was nice in the
extreme. Nothing so vulgar and violent as passion entered
into it, and nothing so transient, so enervating, corroding, and
damaging both to the intellectual powers and the capacity for
permanent enjoyment; and nothing so repulsive either in its
details, its self-centred egotistical exaltation, and the self-
abasement which arrives with that final sense of satiety which
she perceived to be inevitable. That part of her nature had
never been roused into active life, partly because it was not
naturally strong, but also because the more refined and delicately
sensuous appreciation of beauty in life, which is so much a
characteristic of capable women nowadays, dominated such
animalism as she was equal to, and made all coarser pleasures
repugnant. It had been suggested to her that she might, with

her position and wealth, form a salon and lay herself out to attract, but she said: "No, thank you. One sees in the history of French salons the effect of irresponsible power on the women who formed them. I am bad enough naturally, without applying for a licence to become worse, by making myself so agreeable that everybody will excuse me if I do. And as to being a great beauty and nothing else, one might as well be a great cow; the comfort would be the same and the anxiety less, the amount of attention received not depending on a clear complexion or an increase of figure, and therefore necessitating no limit in the enjoyment of such good things as come with the varying seasons, the winter wurzel and summer state of being in clover."

It was to Mr. Kilroy that these remarks were made one day when she wanted a target to talk at, for her appreciation of her husband did not amount to any adequate comprehension of the extent to which he understood her. The truth was, however, that he understood her better than anybody else did, the complete latitude he gave to her to do as she liked being evidence of the fact, if only she could have interpreted it; but she had failed to do so, his quiet undemonstrative manner having sufficed to deceive her superficial observation of him as effectually as the treacherous smoothness of her own placid face when in repose, upon the unruffled surface of which there was neither mark nor sign to indicate the current of changeful moods, ambitious projects, and poetical fancies, which coursed impetuously within, might excusably have imposed upon him. He was twenty years older than Angelica and looked it, but more by reason of his grave demeanour than from any actual mark of age, for his life had been well ordered and as free from care as it had been from corruption. Mr. Kilroy was not a talkative man, and what he did say was neither original nor brilliant, yet he was generally trusted, and his advice oftener asked and followed than that of people whose reputations were at least as good, and whose abilities were infinitely better; the explanation of which was probably to be found in the good feeling which he brought to the consideration of all subjects. Some people whose brains would be at fault if they were asked to judge, are enabled by qualities of heart to feel their way to the most praiseworthy conclusions. Mr. Kilroy was one of those people, well-born and of ample means, whom society recognizes as its own, but without enthusiasm, the sterling qualities which make them such an addition to its ranks being

less appreciated than the wealth and position which they contribute to its resources; still, in his case it was customary for
women to describe him as "a thoroughly nice man," while "an
exceedingly good fellow" was the corresponding masculine
verdict.

He was in parliament now, and was consequently obliged to
be in London continually, but latterly Angelica had refused to
accompany him. She loved their place near Morningquest,
and she had begun to appreciate the ancient city with its
kindly, benighted, unchristian ways, its picturesqueness, and
all that was odd and old-world about it. There, too, she was
somebody, but in crowded London she lost all sense of her
own identity; though, to do her justice, she disliked it less for
that than for itself, for its hot rooms, society gossip, vapid men
and spiteful women. Mr. Kilroy could rarely persuade her to
accompany him, and never induce her to stay. Having her
with him was just the one thing that he was a little persistent
about, and her wilfulness in this respect had been a real
trouble to him. He had come now to see if she continued
obdurate, and he came meekly and with conciliation in his
whole attitude. She thought, however, that she knew how to
get rid of him, how to make him return alone in a week of his
own accord, so far as he himself knew anything about it, and
that, too, without thinking her horrid; and she laid her plans
accordingly. This was something to do; and so irksome did
she find the purposeless existence which the misfortune of having been born a woman compelled her to lead, that even such
an object was a relief, and her spirits rose. Something—anything for an occupation; that was the state to which she was
reduced. She began at once, and began by talking. All
through lunch she discoursed admirably, and at first Mr. Kilroy
listened fascinated, but by and by his attention became strained.
He found himself forced to listen; it was an effort, and yet he
could not help himself. He tried to check Angelica by assuming an absent look, but she recalled him with a sharp exclamation. He even took a letter out of his pocket and read the
superscription, but put it away again shamefacedly, upon her
gently apologizing for monopolizing so much of his attention.

"You see it is so long since I saw you," she said. "You
must forgive me if I have too much to say."

When lunch was over the carriage came round, and Angelica, all radiant smiles, took it for granted that Mr. Kilroy
would go with her for a drive. Now, if there were one thing

which he disliked more than another it was a stupid drive there and back without an object, but Angelica seemed so uncommonly glad to see him he did not like to refuse. He had many things to attend to, but he felt that it would be bad policy not to humour her mood, especially as it was such an extremely encouraging one, so he went to please her with per-fect good grace, although he could not help thinking regret-fully of the precious time he was losing, of the accumulation of things there were to be seen to about his own place, and of some important letters he ought to have written that afternoon. Angelica beguiled him successfully on the way out, however, so that he did not notice the distance, but on the way back her manner changed. So far she had been all brightness and animation; now she became lugubrious, and took a morbid view of things. She talked of all the men of middle age who had died lately, and of what they had died of, showing that most of them were taken off suddenly when in perfect health apparently, and usually without any premonitory symptoms of disease. It was all the result of some change of habits, she said, which was always dangerous in the case of men of middle age; and Mr. Kilroy began to feel uneasy in spite of himself, for he had been obliged to alter his own habits considerably when he married, and he was apt to be a little nervous about his health. Consequently he was much depressed when they returned, and finding that he had missed the post did not tend to raise his spirits. Angelica came down to dinner dressed in pale green, with something yellow on her head. Mr. Kilroy admired her immensely; she was the only subject upon which he ever became poetical, and somehow the combination of colours she wore on this occasion, with her lithe young figure and milk-white skin, made him think of an arum lily, and he told her so, and was very pleased with the pretty compliment when he had paid it, and with the dinner, and everything. The fatal age was forgotten, and he allowed himself to be cheered by hopes of success in his present mission. He had not yet mentioned it, but when they were left alone at dessert he began.

"Is my Châtelaine tired of seclusion, and willing to return with me to the great wicked city?" he ventured with an affec-tation of playfulness, which rather betrayed than concealed his very real anxiety. "A wife's place is by her husband."

"Your Châtelaine is not tired of seclusion," she answered in a cheerful matter of fact tone; "and it is a wife's duty to look after her husband's house and keep it well for him, especially in his absence. But how much will you give me to go? My private purse is empty."

Mr. Kilroy laughed. "It always is, so far as I can make out," he said. "But a mercenary arum lily! what an anomaly! I will give you a hundred pounds to buy dolls, if you will go back with me next week."

Angelica appeared to reflect. "I will take fifty, thank you, and stay where I am," she answered with decision.

Mr. Kilroy's countenance fell. "If you will not come back with me, you shall not have any," he said, with equal firmness.

"Then I shall be obliged to make it," she rejoined, with a schoolgirl grin of delight.

This threat to make money with her violin had kept her purse full ever since her marriage—not that it was ever really empty, for she had had a handsome settlement. Mr. Kilroy, however, was not the kind of man to inspect his wife's bank-book; and besides, whether she had money or not, if it amused her to obtain more, he never could be quite sure that she would not carry out that dreadful threat and try to make it. He knew she would be only too glad of an excuse, knew, too, that if ever she tried she would be certain to succeed, what with her talent, presence, family *prestige*, and the interest which the ill-used young wife of an elderly curmudgeon (that was the character she meant to assume, she said) was sure to excite.

She did not care for money. It was the pleasure of the chase that delighted her, the fun of extorting it. If Mr. Kilroy had given her all she asked for without any trouble, she would have soon left off asking; but he felt it his duty to refuse, by way of discipline. Seeing that she was so young, he did not think it right to indulge her extravagance, and he did his best to curb the inclination gently before it became a confirmed habit.

After dinner he went to the library to write those important letters, and Angelica retired to the drawing room. The night was close, doors and windows stood wide open, and she got a violin and began to tune it. She was too good a musician not to be able to make the instrument an instrument of torture if she chose, and now she did choose. She made it screak; she made it wail; she set her own teeth on edge with the horrid discords she drew from it. It crowed like a cock twenty-five times running, with an interval of half a minute between each crow. It brayed like two asses on a common, one answering the other from a considerable distance. And then it became ten cats quarreling *crescendo*, with a pause after every violent outburst, broken at well-judged intervals by an occasional howl.

Mr. Kilroy endured the nuisance up to that point heroically; but at last he felt compelled to send a servant to tell Angelica that he was writing.

"Oh," she observed, perversely choosing to misinterpret the purport of this tactful message, "then I need not wait for him any longer, I suppose. Bring me my coffee, please."

The man withdrew, and she proceeded with the torture. Mr. Kilroy good-naturedly shut his doors and windows, hoping to exclude the sound, when he found the hint had been lost upon her. In vain! The library was near the drawing room, and every note was audible.

Angelica was stumbling over an air now, a dismal minor thing which would have been quite bad enough had she played it properly, but as it was, being apparently too difficult for her, she made it distracting, working her way up painfully to one particular part where she always broke down, then going back and beginning all over again twenty times at least, till Mr. Kilroy got the thing on the brain and found himself forced to wait for the catastrophe each time she approached the place where she stumbled.

Presently he appeared at the drawing-room door with a pen in his hand, and a deprecating air. He suspected no malice, and only came to remonstrate mildly.

"Angelica, my dear," he began, "I am sorry to disturb you, but I really cannot write—I have been overworked lately—or I am tired with the journey down—or something. My head is a little confused, in fact, and a trifle distracts me. Would you mind——"

Angelica put down her violin with an injured air.

"Oh, I don't mind, of course," she protested in a tone which contradicted the assertion flatly. "But it is very hard." She took out her handkerchief. "You are so seldom at home; and when you *are* here you do nothing but write stupid letters, and never come near me. And this time you are horrid and cross about everything. It is such a disappointment when I have been looking forward to your return." Her voice broke. "I wish I had never asked you to marry me. You ought not to have done so—it was not right of you, if you only meant to neglect me and make me miserable. You won't do anything for me now—not even give yourself the trouble to write out a cheque for fifty pounds, though it would not take you a minute." Two great tears overflowed as she spoke, and she raised her handkerchief with ostentatious slowness to dry them.

Mr. Kilroy was much distressed. "My *dear* child!" he exclaimed, sitting down beside her. "There, there, Angelica, now don't, please"—for Angelica was shivering and crying in earnest, a natural consequence of her immersion on the previous night, and the state of mind which had ensued. "I am obliged to write these letters. I am indeed. I ought to have done them this afternoon, but I went out with you, you know. You really are unjust to me. I have often told you that I do not think it is right for you to be so much alone, but you will not listen to me. Come and sit with me now in the library. I would much rather have you with me. I would have asked you before, but I was afraid it might bore you. Come now, do!"

"No, I should only fidget and disturb you," she answered, but in a mollified tone.

"Well, then," he replied, "I will go and finish as fast as I can, and come back to you here. And don't fret, my dear child. You know there is nothing in reason I would not do for you." In proof of which he sent the butler a little later, by way of breaking the length of his absence agreeably, with what looked like a letter on a silver salver. Angelica opened it, and found a cheque for a hundred pounds. When she was alone again, she beamed round upon the silent company of chairs and tables, much pleased. Then her conscience smote her. "He is really very good," she said to herself—"far too good for me. I don't think I ever could have married anybody else.' But there was something dubious, that resembled a question, in this last phrase.

The next day was hopelessly miserable out of doors—raining, gusty, cold. Mr. Kilroy was not sorry. He had a good deal of business connected with his property to attend to, and did not want to go out. And Angelica was not sorry. She had some little plans of her own to carry out, which a wet day rather favoured than otherwise.

Having finished her accustomed morning's work, and being obliged to stay in, it was natural that she should try to amuse herself, also natural that she should try something in the way of exercise. So she collected some dozen curs she kept about the place, demonstrative mongrels for the most part, but all intelligent; and brought them into the hall, where she made them run races for biscuits, the *modus operandi* being to place a biscuit on the top step of a broad flight of stairs there was at one end of the hall, then to collect the dogs at the other, make them stand in a row—a difficult task to begin with, but easy enough when they understood, which was very soon, although not without much shrieking of orders from Angelica, and responsive barking on their part—and then start them with a whip. The first to arrive at the top of the stairs took the biscuit as a matter of course, and the others fought him for it. It was indescribably funny to see the whole pack tear up all eagerness, and then come down again, helter-skelter, tumbling over each other in the excitement of the scrimmage, some of them losing their tempers, but all of them enjoying the game; returning of their own accord to the starting point, waiting with yelps of excitement and eyes brightly intent, ears pricked, jaws open, tongues hanging, tails wagging, sides panting, till another biscuit was placed, then off once more—sometimes after a false start or two, caused by the impetuosity of a little yapping terrier, which *would* rush before the signal was given, and had to be brought back with the whip, the other dogs looking disgusted meanwhile, like honourable gentlemen at a cad who won't play fair. Angelica, shouting and laughing, made as much noise in her way as the dogs did in theirs, and the din was deafening; an exasperating kind of din too, not incessant, but intermittent, now swelling to a climax, now lulling, until there seemed some hope that it would cease altogether, then bursting out again. whip cracking, dogs howling and barking, feet scampering, Angelica shrieking worse than ever.

Presently, Mr. Kilroy appeared, with remonstrance written on every line of his countenance.

"My dear Angelica," he said, unable to conceal his quite justifiable annoyance. "I can do nothing if this racket continues. And"—deprecatingly—"is it—is it quite seemly for you——?"

"I used to do it at home," Angelica answered.

"But you are not at home now"—quick as light she turned and looked at him with her great grieved eyes. "I mean"— he grew confused in his haste to correct himself—"of course you are at home—very much so indeed, you know. But what I want to say is—as the mistress of a large establishment— dignity—setting an example, and all that sort of thing, don't you see?"

"None of the servants are about at this hour," Angelica

answered. "It is their dinner time. But I apologize for my thoughtlessness if I have disturbed you." She smiled up at him as she spoke, and poor Mr. Kilroy retired to the library quite disarmed by her gentleness, and blaming himself for a selfish brute to have interfered with her innocent amusement. In future, he determined, he would make more allowance for her youth.

Angelica, meanwhile, had collected her dogs and disappeared. But presently she returned, and followed Mr. Kilroy to the library. He was busy writing, and she went and stood in the window, looking idly out at the rain, and drumming— absently, as it seemed—on the panes with ten strong fingers, till he could bear it no longer.

"My dear child!" he exclaimed at last, "can't you get something to do?"

Angelica stopped instantly. If her thoughtlessness was exasperating, her docility was exemplary. But she seemed disheartened; then she seemed to consider; then she brightened a little; then she got some letters, sat down, and began to write—scratch, scratch, scratch, squeak, squeak, squeak, on rough paper with a quill pen, writing in furious haste at a table just behind her husband. Why did she choose the library, his own private *sanctum*, for the purpose, when there were half a dozen other rooms at least where she might have been quite as comfortable? Mr. Kilroy fidgeted uneasily, but he bore this new infliction silently, though with an ever-increasing sense of irritation, for some time. Finally, however, an exclamation of impatience slipped from him unawares.

"Do I worry you with my scribbling?" Angelica demanded with hypocritical concern. "I'm sorry. But I've just done," —and she went away with some half dozen notes for the post.

When they met again at lunch she told him triumphantly that she had refused all the invitations which had come for him since his arrival, on account of his health. She had told everybody that he had come home for perfect rest and quiet, which he much needed after the strain of his parliamentary duties; and as one of the notes at least would be read at a public meeting to explain his absence therefrom, and would afterward appear in the papers probably, she had made it impossible for him to go anywhere during his stay. Mr. Kilroy could not complain, however, for had he not himself said only last night that he was suffering from the effects of overwork, and so alarmed her? and he would not have complained in any case when he saw her so joyfully triumphant in the belief that she had cleverly eased him from an oppressing number of duties; but he determined to pick his excuses more carefully another time, for the prospect of a prolonged *tête-à-tête* with Angelica in her present humour somewhat appalled his peace-loving soul, and the thought of it did just stir him sufficiently for the moment to cause him to venture to suggest that in future it might be as well for her to consult him before she answered for him in any matter. Angelica replied with an intelligent nod and smile. She was altogether charming in these days in spite of her perverseness, and Mr. Kilroy, while groaning inwardly at her irritating tricks, was also touched and flattered by the anxiety she displayed for his comfort and welfare.

He hoped to enjoy a quiet cigar and a book after luncheon, but Angelica had another notion in her head. She went to the drawing room, opened doors and windows, sat down to the piano, and began to sing—shakes, scales, intervals, the whole exercise book through apparently from beginning to end, and with such good will that her voice resounded throughout the house. She had eaten nothing since breakfast so as to be able to produce it with the desired effect, and there was no escape from the sound. But poor Mr. Kilroy did not like to interfere with her industry as he had done with her idleness. He was afraid he had shown too much impatience already for one day, so he endured this further trial without exhibiting a sign of suffering; but after an hour or two of it, he found himself sighing for the undisturbed repose of his house in town, in a way that would have satisfied Angelica had she known it. At dinner she looked very nice, but she did not talk much. Conversation was not Mr. Kilroy's strong point, but he was good at anecdotes, and now he racked his brains for something new to tell her. She listened, however, without seeming to see the point of some, and others caused her to stare at him in wide-eyed astonishment as if shocked, which made him pause awkwardly to consider, half fearing to find some impropriety which his coarser masculine mind had hitherto failed to detect.

This caused the flow of reminiscences to languish, and presently to cease. Then Angelica began to make bread pills. She set them in a row, and flipped them off the table one by one deliberately when the servants left the room. This amusement ended, she pulled flowers to pieces between the courses, and hummed a little tune. Mr. Kilroy fidgeted. He felt as if he had been saying "Don't!" ever since he came home, and he would not now repeat it, but the self-repression disagreed with him, and so did his dinner, dyspepsia having waited on appetite in lieu of digestion.

After dinner Angelica induced him to go with her to the drawing room, and when she had got him comfortably seated, and had given him his coffee and a paper, and just peace enough to let him fall into a pleasurably drowsy state, accompanied by a strong disinclination to move, she began to pick out the "Dead March" in "Saul" and kindred melodies with one finger on the piano. Mr. Kilroy bore this infliction also; but when she brought a cookery book and insisted on reading the recipes aloud, he went to bed in self-defence.

CHAPTER II.

IF the first and second days at home were failures so far as Mr. Kilroy's comfort was concerned, the third was as bad, if not worse. It was a continual case of "Please don't!" from morning till night, and Angelica herself was touched at last by the kindly nature which could repeat the remonstrance so often and so patiently; but all the same she did not forbear. All that day, however, Mr. Kilroy made every allowance for her. Angelica was thoughtless, very thoughtless; but it was only natural that she should be so, considering her youth. On the next day, however, it did occur to him that she was far too exacting, for she would not let him leave her for a moment if she could help it; and on the next he was sufficiently depressed to acknowledge that Angelica was trying; and if he did not actually sigh for solitude, he felt, at all events, that it would cost him no effort to resign himself to it if she should again prove refractory and refuse to go back with him—and Angelica knew that he had arrived at this state just as well as if he had told her; but still she was far from content. She wanted him to go, and she wanted him to stay—she did not know what she wanted. She teased him with as much zeal as at first, but the amusement had ceased to distract her in the least degree. It had become quite a business now, and she only kept it up because she could think of nothing else to do. She was conscious of some change in herself, conscious of a racking spirit of discontent which tormented her, and of the fact that, in spite of her superabundant vitality, she had lost all zest for anything.   Outwardly, and also as a matter of habit, when she was with anybody who might have noticed a change, she maintained the dignity of demeanour which she had begun to cultivate in society upon her marriage; but inwardly she raged—raged at herself, at everybody, at everything; and this mood again was varied by two others, one of unnatural quiescence, the other of feverish restlessness.   In the one she would sit for hours at a time, doing nothing, not even pretending to occupy herself; in the other, she would wander aimlessly up and down, would walk about the room, and look at the pictures without seeing them, or go upstairs for nothing and come down again without perceiving the folly of it all.   And she was forever thinking.   Diavolo was at Sandhurst—if only he had been at Ilverthorpe!   She might have talked to him.   She tried the effect of a letter full of allusions which should have aroused his curiosity if not his sympathetic interest, but he made no remark about these in his reply, and only wrote about himself and his pranks, which seemed intolerably childish and stupid to Angelica in her present mood; and about his objection to early rising and regular hours, all of which she knew, so that the repetition only irritated her.   She considered Mr. Kilroy obtuse, and thought bitterly that anyone with a scrap of intelligent interest in her must have noticed that she had something on her mind, and won her confidence.

This reflection occurred to her in the drawing room one night after dinner, and immediately afterward she caught him looking at her with a grave intensity which should have puzzled her if it did not strike her as significant of some deeper feeling than that to which the carnal admiration for her person which she expected and despised, would have given rise; but she was too self-absorbed to be more observant than she gave him the credit of being.

The result of Mr. Kilroy's observation was an effort to take her out of herself.   He began by asking her to play to him. Not very graciously, she got out a violin, remarking that she was sorry it was not her best one.

"Where is your best one?" he asked.

"It is not at home," she answered.   "I left it with Israfil, my fair-haired friend, you know."   She spoke slowly, holding the end of the violin, and tightening the strings as she did so, the effort causing her to compress her lips so that the words were uttered disjointedly; and as she finished speaking, she raised the instrument to her shoulder and her eyes to Mr. Kilroy's face, into which she gazed intently as she drew her bow across the strings, testing them as to whether they were in tune or not, and seeming rather to listen than to look, as she did so. Mr. Kilroy, still quietly observing her, noticed that her equanimity had been suddenly restored; but whether it was the mellow tones of her violin or some happy thought that had released the tension he could not tell. It was as much relief, however, to him to see her brighten, as it was to her to feel when she answered him that a great weight had been lifted from her mind, and she would now be able "to talk it out," this trouble that oppressed her, unrestrainedly, as was natural to her.

When Mr. Kilroy accepted the terms upon which she proposed to marry him, namely, that he should let her do as she liked, she had voluntarily promised to tell him everything she did, and she had kept her word as was her wont, telling him the exact truth as on this occasion, but mixing it up with so many romances that he never knew which was which. He was in town when she first met the Tenor, but when he returned, she told him all that had happened, and continued the story from time to time as the various episodes occurred, making it extremely interesting, and also almost picturesque. Mr. Kilroy knew the Tenor by reputation, of course, and was much entertained by what he believed to be the romance which Angelica was weaving about his interesting personality. He suggested that she should write it just as she told it. "I have not seen anything like it anywhere," he said; "nothing half so lifelike."

"Oh, but then, you see, this is all *true*," she gravely insisted.

"Oh, of course," he answered, smiling. And now when she answered that she had left her best violin with the Tenor, it reminded him: "By the by, yes," he said. "How does the story progress? I was thinking about it in the train on my way home, but I forgot to ask you—other things have put it out of my head since I arrived."

"And out of mine, too," said Angelica thoughtfully—"at least I forgot to tell you—which is extraordinary, by the way, for matters are now so complicated between us that I can think of nothing else. It will be quite a relief to discuss the subject with you."

She drew up a little chair and sat down opposite to him, with her violin across her knee, and began immediately, and with great earnestness, looking up at him as she spoke. She described all that had happened on that last sad occasion minutely—the row down the river, the moonrise, the music, the accident, the rescue, the discovery, and its effect upon the Tenor; and all with her accustomed picturesqueness, speaking in the first person singular, and with such force and fluency that Mr. Kilroy was completely carried away, and declared, as on previous occasions, that she set the whole thing before him so vividly he found it impossible not to believe every word of it.

"And what are you going to do now?" he asked with his indulgent smile, when she had told him all that there was to tell at present. "You cannot end it there, you know, it would be such a lame conclusion."

"That was just what I thought," she answered, "and I wanted to ask you. As a man of the world, what would you advise me to do?"

"Well," he began—then he rose and held out his hand to help her up from her little chair. "Will you come out and sit on the terrace," he said, "and allow me to smoke? The night is warm."

Anelica nodded, and preceded him through one of the open windows.

"Well," Mr. Kilroy resumed, when he had lit his cigar, and settled himself in a cane chair comfortably, with Angelica in another opposite. "What a lovely night it is after the rain yesterday"—this by way of parenthesis. "Rather close, though," he observed, and then he returned to the subject. "I suppose you mean that you do not want it to be all over between you?"

"*Between the Tenor and the Boy,*" she corrected. "The whole charm of the acquaintance, don't you see, for me, consisted in that footing—I don't know how to express it, but perhaps you can grasp what I mean."

Mr. Kilroy reflected. "I am afraid," he said at last, "that footing cannot be resumed. The influences of sex, once the difference is recognized, are involuntary. But, if he has no objection, I do not see why you should not be friends, and intimate friends too; and with that sort of man you might make some advance, especially as you are entirely in the wrong. I am not saying, you know, that this would be the proper thing to do as a rule; but here are exceptional circumstances, and here is an exceptional man."

"Now, that is significant," said Angelica, jeering. "Society is so demoralized that if a man is caught conducting himself with decency and honour on all occasions when a woman is in question, you involuntarily exclaim that he is an exceptional man!''

Mr. Kilroy smoked on in silence for some time with his eyes fixed on the quiet stars. His attitude expressed nothing but extreme quiescence, yet Angelica felt reproved.

"Don't snub me, Daddy," she exclaimed at last. "I came to you in my difficulty, and you do not seem to care."

Mr. Kilroy looked at his cigar, and flicked the ash from the end of it.

"Tell me how to get out of this horrid dilemma," Angelica pursued. "I shall never know a moment's peace until we have resumed our acquaintance on a different footing, and I have been able to make him some reparation."

"Ah—reparation?" said Mr. Kilroy dubiously.

"Do you think it is impossible?" Angelica demanded.

"Not impossible, perhaps, but very difficult," he answered. "Really, Angelica," he broke off laughingly, "I quite forget every now and again that we are romancing. You must write this story for me."

"We are *not* romancing," she said impatiently, "and I couldn't write it, it is too painful. Besides, we don't seem to get any further."

"Let me see where we were?" Mr. Kilroy replied, humouring her good-naturedly. "It is a pity you cannot unmarry yourself. You see, being married complicates matters to a much greater extent than if you had been single. A girl might, under certain circumstances, be forgiven for an escapade of the kind, but when a married woman does such a thing it is very different. Still, if you can get well out of it, of course the difficulty will make the *dénouement* all the more interesting."

"But I don't see how I am to get well out of it—unless you will go to him yourself, and tell him you know the whole story, and do whatever your tact and goodness suggest to set the matter right." She bent forward with her arms folded on her lap, looking up at him eagerly as she spoke, and beating a "devil's tattoo," with her slender feet, on the ground impatiently the while.

"No," he answered deliberately, "that would not be natural. You see, either you must be objectionable or your husband must; and upon the whole I think you had better sacrifice the husband, otherwise you lose your readers' sympathy."

"Make *you* objectionable, Daddy!" Angelica exclaimed. "The thing is not to be done! I could never have asked you to marry me if you had been objectionable. And I don't see why I should be so either—entirely, you know. If I had been quite horrid, I should not have appreciated you, and the Tenor and Uncle Dawne and Dr. Galbraith—oh, dear! Why is it, when good men are so scarce, that I should know so many, and yet be tormented with the further knowledge that you are all exceptional, and crime and misery continue because it is so? What is the use of knowing when one can do nothing?''

Again Mr. Kilroy looked up at the quiet stars; but Angelica gave him no time to reflect.

''I don't see why I should be severely consistent,'' she said. ''Let me be a mixture—not a foul mixture, but one of those which eventually result in something agreeable, after going through a period of fermentation, during which they throw up an unpleasant scum that has to be removed.''

''That would do,'' Mr. Kilroy responded gravely.

''But just now,'' Angelica resumed, ''it seems as if I should be obliged to let matters take their course and do nothing, which is intolerable.''

''Oh, but you must do something,'' Mr. Kilroy decided; ''and the first thing will be to go to him.''

''Go to him!'' she ejaculated.

''Well, yes,'' he rejoined. ''Naturally you will feel it. Now that you are no longer *The Boy* made courageous by his unsuspicious confidence—I mean the Tenor's—it is quite proper for you to be shy and ashamed of yourself. As a woman, of course, you are not wanting in modesty. But there is no help for it; he would never come to you, so you must go to him. I quite think that you owe him any reparation you can make. And, knowing the sort of man he is—you have made his character well known in the place, have you not?''

Angelica nodded. ''Well, then, a visit from a lady of your rank will create no scandal, nor even cause any surprise, I should think, if you go quite openly; for you are known to be a musician, and might therefore reasonably be supposed to have business with one of the profession. I wish, by-the-bye, you had made him an ugly man, with kind eyes, you know; it would have been more original, I think. But you will find out who he is, of course?''

''No. I hardly think so!'' Angelica answered. ''But you would advise me to go to him?''—this by way of bringing him back to the subject.

"Yes"—with a vigorous attempt to draw his cigar to life again, it having gone all but out—"I should advise you to go to him boldly, by day, of course; and just make him forgive you. Insist on it; you will find he cannot resist you. Then you will start afresh on a new footing as you wish, and the whole thing will end happily."

"You forget though, he did forgive me."

"There are various kinds of forgiveness," Mr. Kilroy replied. "There is the forgiveness that washes its hands of the culprit and refuses to be further troubled on his behalf— the least estimable form of forgiveness; and there is that which proves itself sincere by the effort which is afterward made to help the penitent, that is the kind of forgiveness you should try to secure."

"But somehow it still seems unfinished," Angelica grumbled.

"If you had been single now," Mr. Kilroy suggested, "you would, in the natural course of events, have married the Tenor."

"Oh, no!" Angelica vigorously interposed. "I should never have wanted to marry him. Can't I make you understand? The side of my nature which I turned to him as *The Boy* is the only one he has touched, and I could never care for him in any other relation."

"Well, I don't know," Mr. Kilroy observed thoughtfully. "It may be so, of course, but it is unusual."

"And so am I unusual," Angelica answered quickly; "but there will be plenty more like me by and by. Now don't look 'Heaven forbid!' at me in that way."

"That was not in the least what I intended to express," he answered with his kindly smile-indulgent. "And I am inclined to think that your own idea of loving him without being in love with him is the best; it is so much less commonplace. But what do you think"—speaking as if struck by a bright idea—"what do you think of putting him under a great obligation which will bind him to you in gratitude, and secure his friendship? You might, with great courage and devotion, and all that sort of thing, you know, find out all about him, prove him to be a prince or something—the heir to great estates and hereditary privileges, with congenial duties attached. The idea is not exactly new, but your treatment of it would be sure to be original——"

Angelica interrupted him by a decisive shake of her head. "But about going to him?" she demanded—"you do not think, speaking as a man of the world yourself, and remembering that he knows the world too although he *is* such a saint; you do not think such a proceeding on my part will lower me still further in his estimation?"

"Well, no," Mr. Kilroy replied. "I feel quite sure it will have just the opposite effect. As a man of the world he will know what it has cost a young lady like you to humble herself to that extent: as a saint he will appreciate the act, looking at it in the light of a penance, which, in point of fact, it would be; and as a human being he will be touched by your confidence in him, and the value you set upon his esteem. So that, altogether, I am convinced it is the proper thing to do."

Angelica made no reply, but got up languidly after a moment's thought, carefully ruffled his hair with both hands as she passed, called him "Dear old Daddy!" and retired.

Mr. Kilroy did not like to have his hair ruffled in that way, particularly as he was apt to forget, and appear in public with it all standing up on end; but he bore the infliction as it was intended for a caress. Angelica's caresses always took some such form; she assured him he would like them in time, and he sincerely hoped he might, but the time had not yet arrived.

The following evening they were again in the drawing room together. Mr. Kilroy was reading the papers, Angelica was sitting with her hands before her doing nothing—not even listening, though she affected to do so. when he read aloud such news as he thought would interest her. The week was nearly over, and nothing more had been said about her return to town. She was just wondering now if Mr. Kilroy had found the week a long one. She had given him more than enough of her company and made him feel—at least so she hoped, slipping back to the mood in which he had found her upon his arrival—made him feel how pleasant a thing it is to dwell alone in your own house with no one to trouble you; and she quite expected to find, when it came to the point, that he would cheerfully take no for an answer.

Presently she rose, went to a mirror that was let into the wall, and looked at herself critically for some seconds.

"Should you think it possible for anybody to fall so hopelessly in love with my appearance that, when love was found to be out of the question, friendship would also be impossible?" she demanded in a tone of contempt for herself, turning half round from the mirror to look at Mr. Kilroy as she spoke.

Mr. Kilroy glanced at her over his *pince-nez*. That same

appearance which she disliked to be valued for was a never-failing source of pleasure to him, but he took good care to conceal the fact. On this occasion, however, he fell into the natural mistake of supposing that she was coquettishly trying to extricate a compliment from him for once, an amusing feminine device to which she seldom condescended.

"Well, I should think it extremely probable," he replied—"if he were not already in love with another woman."

"Or an idea?" Angelica suggested with a yawn; and Mr. Kilroy, perceiving that he had somehow missed the point, took up his paper, and finished the paragraph he had been reading. Then he said, looking up at her again with admiring eyes: "I do not think I quite like that red frock of yours. It seems to me that it is making you look alarmingly pale."

Angelica returned to the mirror, and once more looked at herself deliberately. "Perhaps it does," she answered; "but at any rate you shall not see it again." And having spoken she sauntered out on to the terrace with a listless step, and from thence she wandered off into the gardens, where the scent of roses set her thinking, thinking, thinking. She sought to change the direction of her thoughts, but vainly; they would go on in spite of her, and they were always busy with the same subject, always working at the one idea. Israfil! Israfil! There was nobody like him, and how badly she had treated him, and how good he had always been to her, and how could she go on day after day like this with no hope of ever seeing him again in the old delightful intimate way? and oh! if she had not done this! and oh! if she had not done that! It might all have been so different if only *she* had been different; but now how could it come right? A hopeless, hopeless, hopeless case. She had lost his respect forever. And not to be respected! A woman and not respected!

She went down to the lodge gate where they had parted, and remembered the chill misery of the moment, the gray morning light, the pelting rain. Ah—with a sudden pang—she only thought of it now. How wet he must have been! He had lent her his one umbrella, and she had kept it; she had it still; she had allowed him to walk back in the rain without wrap or protection of any kind.

And now she came to think of it, he had never changed his things after he had rescued her. He never did think of himself—the most selfless man alive; and she, alas! had never thought of him—never considered his comfort in anything.

Oh, remorse! If only she could have those times all over again, or even one of those times so recklessly misspent! He might have lost his life through that wetting. Or what if he lost his voice? Singers have notoriously delicate throats. But happily nothing so untoward had resulted; she was saved the blame of a crowning disaster—she knew, because she had heard of him going to the cathedral as usual; she had taken the trouble to inquire, not daring to go herself, and she had seen in that day's paper that he would sing the anthem to-morrow, so evidently he had not suffered, which was some comfort— and yet—how could he go to the cathedral every day and sing as usual, just as if nothing had happened? It might be forti- tude, but, considering the circumstances, it was far more likely to be indifference. And so she continued to torment herself; thinking, always thinking, without any power to stop.

The next day Mr. Kilroy returned to town alone. He had only once again alluded to his wish that she should accompany him, and that he did quite casually, for she had succeeded in making him content that she should refuse. She had con- vinced him that her exuberant spirits were altogether too much for him. He had not had an hour's peace since his arrival, though the place would have held a regiment comfortably; and what would it be if he shut her up in London, in a confined space comparatively speaking, and against her will too? He left by an early afternoon train, and she drove to the station with him to see him off. She had enjoyed his visit very much —so she said—especially the last part of it, when she had surpassed herself in ingenious devices to exact attention. All that, while it lasted, really had distracted her; but the occu- pation was not happiness—far from it! It was a sort of intoxicant rather, which made her oblivious for the moment of her discontent. At every pause, however, remorse possessed her, remorse for the past; yet it never occurred to her that her present misdemeanours would be past in time, and might also entail consequences which would in turn come to be causes of regret.

But, now, when she had succeeded in getting rid of Mr. Kil- roy, she was sorry. She stood on the platform watching the train until it was out of sight, and then she returned to her carriage with a distinct feeling of loss and pain. What should she do with the rest of the day? She even thought of the next, and the next, and the next; a long vista of weary days, through which she must live alone and to no purpose, a waste of life, a waste of life—a barren waste, a land of sand and thorns. She wished she was a child again playing pranks with Diavolo; and she also wished that she had never played pranks, since it was so hard to break herself of the habit; yet she enjoyed them still, and assured herself that she was only discontented now because she had absolutely nobody left to torment. Then she tried to imagine what it would be to have Diavolo with her in her present mood, and instantly a squall of conflicting emotions burst in her breast, angry emotions for the most part, because he was no longer with her in either sense of the word, because he was indifferent to all that concerned her inmost soul, and was content to live like a lady himself, a trivial idle life, the chief business of which was pleasure, unremunerative pleasure, upon which he would have had her expend her highest faculties in return for what? Admiring glances at herself—and her gowns *perhaps!*

"But what should she do with the rest of the day?" Her handsome horses were prancing through Morningquest as she asked herself the question; and there was a little milliner on the footway looking up with kindly envy at the lady no older than herself, sitting alone in her splendid carriage with her coachman and footman and *everything*—nothing to do included, very much included, being, in fact, the principal item.

"I should be helping her," thought Angelica. "She is ill-fed, overworked, and weakly, while I am pampered and strong; but there is no rational way for me to do it. If I took her home with me and kept her in luxurious idleness for the rest of her days, as I could very well afford to do, I should only have dragged her down from the dignity of her own honest exertions into the slough of self-indulgence in which I find myself, and made bad worse. *She* should have more and *I* should have less; but how to arrive at that? Isolated efforts seem to be abortive—yet——" she stopped the carriage, and looked back. The girl had disappeared. She desired the coachman to return, and kept him driving up and down some time in the hope of finding her, but the girl was nowhere to be seen, nor could they trace her upon inquiry. "Another opportunity lost," thought Angelica. "A few pounds in her pocket would have been a few weeks' rest for her, a few good meals, a few innocent pleasures—she would have been strengthened and refreshed; and I should have been the better too for the recollection of a good deed done."

The carriage had pulled up close to the curb, and the footman stood at the door waiting for orders.

"What is there to do?" thought Angelica. "Where shall I go? Not home. The house is empty. Calls? I might as well waste time in that way as any other." She gave the order, and passed the next two hours in making calls.

Toward the end of the afternoon, she found herself within about a mile of Hamilton House, and determined to go and see her mother. There was no real confidence between them, but Lady Adeline's presence was soothing, and Angelica thought she would just like to go and sit in the same room with her, have tea there, and not be worried to talk. These peaceful intentions were frustrated, however, by the presence of some visitors who were there when she arrived, and of others who came pouring in afterward in such numbers, that it seemed as if the whole neighbourhood meant to call that afternoon. Mr. Hamilton-Wells was making tea, and talking as usual with extreme precision. Angelica found him seated at a small but solid black ebony table, with a massive silver tea-service before him. He folded his hands when she entered, and, without rising, awaited the erratic kiss which it was her habit to deposit somewhere about his head when she met him; which ceremony concluded, he gravely poured her out a cup of tea, with sugar *and* milk, but *no* cream, as he observed; and then he peeped into the teapot, and proceeded to fill it up from the great urn which was bubbling and boiling in front of him. He always made tea in his own house; it was a fad of his, and the more people he had to make it for the better pleased he was. A servant was stationed at his elbow, whose duty it was to place the cups as his master filled them on a silver salver held by another servant, who took them to offer to the visitors who were seated about the room. Angelica knew the ceremony well, and slipped away into a corner, as soon as she could escape from her father's punctilious inquiries about her own health and her husband's; and there she became wedged by degrees, as the room grew gradually crowded. Beside her was a mirror, in which she could see all who arrived and all that happened, and involuntarily she became a silent spectator, the medium of the mirror imparting a curious unreality to the scene, which invested it with all the charm of a dream; and, as in a dream, she looked and listened, while clearly, beneath the main current of conversation, and unbroken by the restless change and motion of the people, her own thoughts flowed on consciously and continuously. Half turned from the rest of the room, she sat at a table, listlessly turning the leaves of an album, at which she glanced when she was not looking into the mirror.

She saw the party from Morne enter the room—Aunt Fulda and her eternal calm! She looked just the same in the market-place at Morningquest, that unlucky night when the Tenor met the Boy. She was always the same. Is it human to be always the same?

"Who is that lady?" Angelica heard a girl ask of a benevolent looking elderly clergyman who was standing with his back to her. "Oh, that is Lady Fulda Guthrie, the youngest daughter of the Duke of Morningquest," he replied. 'She is a Roman Catholic, a pervert as we say, but still a very noble woman. Religious, too, in spite of the errors of Rome, one must confess it. A pity she ever left us, a great pity—but of course *her* loss as well as ours. We require such women now, though; but somehow we do not keep them. And I cannot think why."

"Too cold," Angelica's thoughts ran on. "Hollow, shallow, inconsistent—loveless. Catholicism equals a modern refinement of pagan principles with all the old deities on their best behaviour thrown in; while Protestantism is an ecclesiastical system founded on fetish——"

"You are a stranger in the neighbourhood?" the benevolent old clergyman was saying. "Only on a visit? Ah! then of course you don't know. They are a remarkable family, somewhat eccentric. Ideala, as they call her, is no relation, only an intimate friend of Lady Claudia Beaumont's, and of the Marquis of Dawne. The three are usually together. The New Order is an outcome of their ideas, a sort of feminine *vehmgericht* so well as I can make out. But no good can come out of that kind of thing, and I trust as you are a very young lady——"

"Not so young—I am twenty-two."

"Indeed!" with a smile and a bow—"I should not have thought you more than nineteen. But twenty-two is not a great age either! and I do hope you will not be drawn into that set. They are sadly misguided The ladies scoff at the wisdom of men, look for inconsistencies, and *laugh* at them—actually! It is very bad taste, you know; and they call it an impertinence for us to presume to legislate exclusively in matters which specially concern their sex, and also object to the interference of the Church, as being a distinctly masculine organization, in the regulation of their lives. Men, they declare, have always said that they do not understand women, and it is of course the height of folly for them to presume to express opinions upon a subject they do not understand. Now, can anything be more absurd? And it is dangerous besides—absolutely dangerous."

"Yet I hear that they are very good women," the girl ventured, and Angelica thought that she detected a note of derision, levelled at the clerical exponent of these reprehensible ideas, beneath the demure remark.

"Oh, saintlike!" he answered cordially; "but still to blame. Misguided, you know, so I venture to warn you. How can they presume to reject proper direction? Their pride is excessive, but the Church will receive them, and extend her benefits to them still if only they will humble themselves——" Conversation over the room entered upon a *crescendo* passage at this moment, and Angelica lost the rest of the sentence in the general outburst.

A new voice presently claimed her attention. The speaker was a young man addressing another young man, and both had their backs turned to her, and were looking hard at a portrait of herself hung so low on the wall that they had to stoop to look into it.

"Painted by a good man," were the first words she heard.

"Rather fine face; who is it?"

"Daughter of the house, don't you know? Old duke's granddaughter. Married old Kilroy of Ilverthorpe."

"Ah! Then that was done some time ago, I expect."

"Oh, dear, no! Only last year. It was exhibited in the last Academy."

"Then she's still young?" He peered into the portrait once more with an evident increase of interest. "She looks as if she might be larky."

"Can't make her out, on my word, was the response, delivered in a tone of strong disapproval. "Married to an elderly chap—not old exactly, but a good twenty years older than herself; who gives her her head to an unlimited extent, yet she says she doesn't care to have a lot of men bothering about, and, by Jove! she acts as if she meant it. It's beastly unnatural, you know."

"Well, I must say I like a woman to be a woman," the other rejoined, surveying the portrait from this new point of view. "But that's the way with all that Guthrie lot—and you know Dawne himself is *pi!*"—so what can you expect of the rest? the tone implied.

Suddenly Angelica felt her face flush. One of her ungovernable fits of fury was upon her. She sprang to her feet, upsetting her chair with a crash, and turned upon the two young men, who, recognizing her, changed colour and countenance, and shrank back apologetically.

Her uncle, seeing something wrong, had hurried across the room to her with anxious eyes.

"Who are those people?" she asked him, indicating the two young men.

Lord Dawne, always all courtesy and consideration himself, was shocked by her tone.

"I think you have met Captain Leicester before," he gravely reminded her. "Let me introduce——"

"No, for Heaven's sake!" Angelica broke forth, glaring angrily at the offenders.

She walked away abruptly with the words on her lips, leaving Lord Dawne to settle with the delinquents as he thought fit. Her mother, who was seated at the farther end of the room talking to a charming-looking old lady Angelica did not know, stretched out a hand to her as she approached, and drew her to a seat beside her; and instantly Angelica felt herself in another moral atmosphere.

"This is my daughter, Mrs. Kilroy of Ilverthorpe," Lady Adeline said to the old lady, then added smiling: "There are so many Mrs. Kilroys in this neighbourhood, one is obliged to specify. Angelica, dear, Mrs. Power."

Angelica bowed, and then leaned back in her chair so that she might not have to join in the conversation, but she listened in an absent sort of way, feeling soothed the while by the tone of refinement, of earnestness and sincerity, in which every word was uttered: "No, I am sure," Lady Adeline was saying, "I am sure no one who can judge would mistake that lineless calm for a device to cover all emotion."

"I never have done so myself," Mrs. Power rejoined, "although I do not know her history. But I should say, judging merely from observation, that the fineness of her countenance, which consists more in the expression of it than in either form or feature, though both are good, is the result of long self-repression, self-denial, and stern discipline, the evidence of a true and beautiful soul, and of a noble mind at rest after some heavy sorrow, or some great temptation, which, being resisted, has proved a blessing and a source of strength.''

Angelica wondered of whom they were speaking, and, following the direction of their eyes, met those of Ideala fixed a little sadly, a little wistfully, upon herself. Young people, as they grow up, find their own life's history so absorbingly interesting that they think little of what may have happened, or may be happening, to those whom they have always known as "grown up"; and it had never occurred to Angelica that any one of the placid, gentle-mannered women among whom she had always lived, in contrast to them herself as a comet is to the fixed stars, had ever experienced any extremes of emotion. Now, however, she felt as if her eyes had been suddenly opened, and she looked with a new interest at her old familiar friends, and wondered, her mind busy for the moment with what she had just heard. She could not keep it there, however; involuntarily it slipped away—back—back to that first attempt of hers to see the hidden wheels of life go round —the market-place, the Tenor.

Suddenly she felt as if she must suffocate if she did not get out into the air, and rising quickly she stole from the room, and out of the house unobserved. But the babble of voices seemed to pursue her. She stood for a moment on the steps and felt as if the people were all preparing to stream out of the drawing room after her, to surround her, and keep up the distracting buzz in her ears by their idle inconsequent talk. Their horses were prancing about the drive; their empty carriages, with cushions awry and wraps flung untidily down on the seats, or even hanging over the doors and grazing the dusty wheels, gave her a sense of disorder and discomfort from which she felt she must fly.

"Where to, ma'am, please?" the footman asked, touching his hat when he had closed the door.

"Fountain Towers," Angelica answered. She would go and see Dr. Galbraith.

When the carriage drew up under the porch at Fountain Towers, she sat some time as if unaware of the fact; but the footman's patient face as he waited with his hand on the handle of the door, ready to help her to descend, recalled her.

She walked into the house as she had always been accustomed to do, and instantly thoughts of Diavolo came crowding. Why had Diavolo ceased to be all in all to her? She asked herself the question through a mist of tears which gathered in her eyes, but did not fall, and at the same moment her busy mind took note of the singular appearance of a statue on the staircase as she beheld it in blurred outline through her bedimmed vision.

She found Dr. Galbraith in the library sitting at his writing table. The door was half open, so she entered without knocking, and walked up to him.

He turned at the sound of her step, rose smiling, and held out his hand when he saw who it was.

"I have been thinking about you this afternoon," he remarked. "Sit down." But before she had settled herself his practised eyes had detected something wrong. "What is it?" he asked.

"Nerves," she answered. "Give me something."

He went to an inner room, and returned presently with a colourless draught in a medicine glass. She took it from him and drank it mechanically, and then he placed a cushion for her, and she leant back in the deep armchair, and closed her eyes. Dr. Galbraith looked at her for a few seconds seriously, and then returned to his writing. Presently Lord Dawne came in, and raised his eyebrows inquiringly when he saw Angelica, who seemed to be asleep.

"Overwrought," Dr. Galbraith replied to the silent inquiry.

"There was a *fracas* at Hamilton House just now," her uncle observed. "But how is all this going to end?"

"Well, of course; but you had better leave her to me."

Lord Dawne quietly withdrew.

"Oh, the blessed rest and peace of this place!" Angelica exclaimed shortly afterward.

Dr. Galbraith, who had resumed his writing, put down his pen again, and turned to her.

"Talk to me," she said. "I've lost my self-respect. I've lost heart. I'm a good-for-nothing worthless person. How am I to get out of this dreadful groove?"

"Live for others. Live openly," he answered slowly, looking up beyond her—into futurity—with a kindly light in his deep gray eyes, a something of hope, of confidence, of encouragement expressed in his strong plain face.

Angelica bowed her head. The familiar phrases had a new significance now, and diverted the stream of her reflections into another channel. She folded her hands on her lap and sat motionless once more, with her eyes fixed on the ground.

Dr. Galbraith was a specialist in mental maladies. He

knew exactly how much to say, and when to say it. If a text were as much as the patient required or could bear, he never made the mistake of preaching a sermon upon it in addition; and so for the third time he took up his pen and returned to his work, leaving Angelica engaged in sober thought, and happily quiescent.

CHAPTER III.

IT was late when at last she went home, but the drive of many miles in the fresh evening air helped to revive her. She had dreaded the return. The place seemed empty to her imagination, and strange and chill, as a south room in which we have sat and been glad with friends all the bright morning does, if by chance we return alone when the sun has departed.

And the place was dismal. There was no one to welcome her. Even her well-trained servants were out of the way for once, and she felt her heart sink as she crossed the deserted hall to go upstairs, and saw long lines of doors, shut for the most part, or, if open, showing big rooms beyond silent and tenantless. As she passed the library she had noticed her husband's chair half turned from his writing table, just as he had left it, probably, that very morning. It seemed a long time since then. He must have come to his journey's end—ages ago. She wondered if he had felt it as dreary on arriving as she did now, and an unaccustomed wish to be with him, in order to make things pleasanter for him, here obtruded itself. It was one of the least selfish thoughts she had had lately, and this was also one of the very few occasions on which his leaving her had not occasioned her a sense of liberty restored, which was the one unmixed delight she had hitherto experienced.

Her mind was racked by inconsistencies, but she did not perceive it herself, otherwise she must also have observed that she was running up the whole gamut of her past moods and experiences, only to find how unsatisfactory in its unstableness and futility was each. And she might still further have perceived how fatal the habit of living from day to day without any settled purpose, a mere cork of a creature on the waters of life at the mercy of every current of impulse, is to that permanent content to which a steady effort to do right at all events whatever else we may not do, and right only whatever happens, alone gives rise, making thereof a sure foundation of quiet happiness out of which countless pleasures, known only to those who possess it, spring perceptibly—or to which they come like butterflies to summer flowers, enriching them with their beauty and vitality while they stay, and leaving them none the poorer when they depart, but rather, it may be, gainers, by the fertilizing memories which remain.

Angelica had gone to her room to dress for the evening as usual. She had no idea of shirking the ordinary routine of daily life because her mind was perturbed. But that duty over, she descended to the drawing room to wait until dinner should be announced, and so found herself alone with her own thoughts once more. She went to one of the fireplaces, and stood with her hands folded on the edge of the mantelpiece, and her forehead resting on them, looking down at the flowers and foliage plants which concealed the grate.

"You cannot go on like this, you know," she mentally ejaculated, apostrophising herself.

Then she became conscious of a great sense of loneliness, the kind of loneliness of the heart from which there is no escape except in the presence of one who knows what the trouble is and can sympathize. She had been half inclined to confide in Dr. Galbraith, and now she regretted she had not, but presently, passing into a contrary mood, she was glad; what good could he have done? And as for her husband, an empty house was better than a bad tenant. This was before dinner was announced; but afterward, at dinner, sitting in solitary state with the servants behind her, and a book to keep her in countenance, she made a grievance of his absence, and then sighed for such company as the seven more who were entertained in that house which was swept and garnished for another purpose, she fancied, but she could not recollect what, and it was too much trouble to try—so her thoughts rambled on uncontrolled—only she believed they were merry, and that was what she was not; but she would be very soon in spite of everything—in pursuance of which resolve she wrote several notes after dinner, asking people she knew well enough to kindly dispense with the ceremony of a long invitation and come and lunch with her to-morrow; and she dispatched a groom on horseback with the notes that there might be no delay. She even thought of making up a house party, but here her interest and energy flagged, and she left the execution of that project till next day.

Then she relapsed into her regretful discontented mood. If only—if only that wretched accident had never occurred, how different would her feelings have been at this moment, was one of her reflections as she sat alone on the terrace outside the great deserted reception rooms. She would have been waiting now till the house was quiet, and then she would have dashed up to her room to dress, with that exquisite sense of freedom which made the whole delight of the thing, and in half an hour she might have been the *Boy* with Israfil.

"You cannot go on like this, you know," Angelica repeated to herself. "You must do something."

But what? Involuntarily her mind returned to the Tenor. If she could win his respect she felt she could start afresh with a clear conscience and a steadfast determination to—what was it Dr. Galbraith had suggested? "Live openly. Live for others."

But how to win the Tenor back to tolerate her? If she would make him her friend she knew that she must be entirely true—in thought, word, and deed; to every duty, to every principle of right; and how could she be that if there were any truth in the theory of hereditary predisposition, coming as she did of a race foredoomed apparently to the opposite course? It was folly to contend with fate when fate took the form of a long line of ancestors who had made a family commandment for themselves, which was: "Be decent to all seeming! but sin all the same to your heart's content," and had kept it courageously—at least the men had—but then the women had been worthy—in which thought she suddenly perceived that there was food for reflection; for was not this contradictious fact a proof that it was a good deal a matter of choice after all? And here the Tenor's parting words recurred to her, and with them came the recollection of the impression made at the moment by the deep yet diffident tone of earnest conviction in which he had uttered that last assurance: "You will do some good in the world—you will be a good woman yet, I know—I know you will."

Should she? was the question she now asked herself. Were the words prophetic? she wondered. And from that moment her thoughts took a new departure, and she was able, as it were, to stand aloof and look back at herself as she had been, and forward to herself as she might yet become. In this quiet hour of retrospect she was quite ready to confess her sins. She was sincerely sorry she had deceived the Tenor. But why was she sorry? Why, simply because he had found her out; simply because there was an end of a charming adventure— though less on that account than on others; for of course she knew that the end was near, that they must have parted soon in any case. It was the manner of the parting that caused her such regret. She had lost his affection, lost his confidence— lost the pleasure of his acquaintance, she supposed, which was more than she could bear. If he met her in the street he would probably look the other way. Would he? Oh! The very notion stung her. She sprang to her feet and threw up her hands; and then, as if goaded by a lash, but without any distinct idea, she ran down the steps headlong into the garden, and so on through the park till she came to the river. When she got there, she stopped at the landing place, not knowing why she had come, and as she stood there, trying to collect her thoughts, the absence of some familiar object forced itself upon her attention—her boat! It must have been lost the night of the accident. She did not know whether it had sunk or not, but there was no name on it, so that, even if it had been found, it could not have been restored to her unless she had claimed it. And while she thought this, she was conscious of another pang of regret. She knew that had the boat been there, her next impulse would have been to go to the Tenor just as she was, bareheaded, and in her thin evening dress. With what object, though? To beg for the honour of his acquaintance, she supposed! But, alas! she could not sneer in earnest, or laugh in earnest, at any absurdity she chose to think there was in the idea. For she acknowledged—in her heart of hearts she knew—that the acquaintance of such a man *was* an honour, especially to her, as she humbly insisted, although she had not broken any of the commandments, and never would, and never could.

Slowly she returned to the house. A servant met her on the terrace, and asked her if she should require anything more that night. Then she discovered the lateness of the hour, ordered the household to bed, and retired to her own room. There she extinguished the lights, threw the windows wider open, and sat looking out into the dim mysterious night.

Angelica loved the night. No matter what her mood might be she felt its charm, and something also of the pride-subduing, hallowed influence which is peculiarly its own; and now, as she leant, looking out, all the beauty of it, and its heavenly purity, began to steal into her heart and to soften it. Slowly, as the tide goes out when the sea is tempestuous, the waves returning again and again with angry burst and flow to cover the same spot, as if loath to leave it, but receding inevitably till in the further distance their harsh impetuous roar sinks to a babble when heard from the place where they lately raged, which itself seems the safer for the contrast between the now of quiet and firmness and the then of shifting sand and watery fury; so it was with Angelica s turmoil of mind, the foaming discontent, the battling projects—by slow degrees, they all subsided; and after the storm of uncertainty there came something like the calm of a settled purpose. To be good, to ascend to the higher life—if that meant to feel like this always she would be good—if in her lay such power. She could not be wholly without religion, because she found in herself a reverence for what was religion in others. And what after all is religion? An attitude of the mind which develops in us the power to love, reverence, and practise all that constitutes moral probity. But how to attain to this? By trying and trusting. Faith, that was it, faith in the power of goodness. Upon the recognition of this simple truth, her spirit wings unfurled, and slowly, as her senses ceased to be importunate, she became possessed by some idea of deathless love and longing which fired her soul with its heroism, and filled her heart with its pathos, until both mind and hands together unconsciously assumed the attitude of prayer.

She did not go to bed at all that night, but just sat there by the open window, patiently waiting for the dawn. Nor did she feel the time long. Her whole being thrilled to this new sensation and was subdued by it, so that she remained motionless and rapturously absorbed. It might only last till daybreak; but while it did last, it was certainly intense.

It lasted longer than that, however. It even survived the day and the luncheon party to which she had in a rash moment invited her friends. She had determined to go to the Tenor that very afternoon in the way her husband had suggested.

At first she thought she would drive, but it was a long way round by the road, much longer than by the river, and so she decided to walk, although the weather was inclined to be tempestuous. She crossed by the ferry, thinking she would, if possible, meet the Tenor as he came away from the afternoon service. In that hope, however, she was disappointed, for when she got to the cathedral she found the service over, the congregation dispersed, and the doors locked. There was nothing for it then but to go to his own house. With a fast beating heart she crossed the road, and paused at the little gate. She felt now that she had made a mistake. She should have taken her husband's advice and come in state; she would not have felt half so frightened and awkward if she could have sat in her carriage, and sent the footman to inquire if the Tenor would do her the favour to allow her to speak to him for a moment. And what would he say to her now? And what should she say? Suppose he refused to see her at all, should she ever survive it? Could she take him by storm as the Boy would have done, and demand his friendship and kind consideration as a right? Oh! for some of the unblushing assurance which had distinguished the Boy! It must have been part of the costume. But surely her confidence would return at the right moment, and then she would be able to face him boldly. Having to knock at the door and ask for him was like the first plunge into cold water. Just to think of it took her breath away. But the window was doubtless unfastened as usual; should she go in by that? No. It was absurd, though, how she hesitated, especially after all that had happened; but be deterred by this most novel and uncomfortable shyness she would not! She had come so far, and it should not be for nothing. She would not go back until——

But now, at last, with a smile at her qualms and nervous tremors, she knocked resolutely. There was a little interval before the knock was answered, and she filled it with hope. She knew just how radiant she would feel as she came away successful. She experienced something of the relief and pleasure which should follow upon this pain, and then the door was opened by the Tenor's elderly housekeeper. The woman had that worn and worried look upon her face which is common among women of her class.

"Is your master at home?" Angelica asked, not recollecting for the moment by what name he was known.

The woman looked at her curiously, as if to determine her social status before she committed herself. The question seemed to surprise her.

"He's gone," she answered dolefully. "Didn't you know?"

"Gone," Angelica echoed blankly. "Where?"

"Gone home," the woman answered.

"Gone home!' Angelica exclaimed, unable to conceal her dismay. "He has no home but this. Where is his home" '

The woman gave her another curious look, took a moment to choose her words, then blurted out: "He's dead, miss—didn't you know—and buried yesterday."

CHAPTER IV.

THE lonely man, after leaving Angelica that night, had returned to the Close, walking "like one that hath a weary dream." When he entered his little house, and the sitting room where the lamp was still burning, its yellow light in sickly contrast to the pale twilight of the summer dawn which was beginning to brighten by that time, the discomfort consequent on disorder struck a chill to his heart.

The roses still lay scattered about the floor, but they had been trampled under foot and their beauty had suffered, their freshness was marred, and their perfume, rising acrid from bruised petals, greeted him unwholesomely after the fresh morning air, and rendered the atmosphere faint and oppressive. The stand with the flower pots, much disarranged, stood as he had left it when he pulled it roughly aside to get at the grate, and the fire had burnt out, leaving blackened embers to add to the general air of dreariness and desertion. Angelica's violin lay under the grand piano where he had heedlessly flung it when he loosed it from her rigid grasp; and there were pipes and glasses and bottles about, chairs upset and displaced; books and papers, music and magazines, piled up in heaps untidily to be out of the way—all the usual signs, to sum up, which suggest that a room has been used over night for some unaccustomed purpose, convivial or the reverse, a condition known only to the early house-and-parlour maid as a rule, and therefore acting with peculiarly dismal effect upon the chance observer; but more dismal now to the weary Tenor than any room he had ever seen under similar circumstances by reason of the associations that clung about it.

He opened the window wide, extinguished the lamp, and began mechanically to put things away and arrange the chairs. The habit of doing much for himself prompted all this; anything that was not a matter of habit he never thought of doing. His things were drying on him, and he had forgotten that they had ever been wet. He had forgotten too that the night was past and over. He was heart sick and weary, yet did not feel that there was any need of rest. The extraordinary lucidity

of mind of which he had been conscious while his much
loved "Boy" was in danger had left him now, and only a
blurred recollection as of many incidents crowding thickly
upon each other without order or sequence recurred to him.
He suffered from a sense of loss, from an overpowering grief
—the kind of grief which is all the worse to bear because it
has not come in the course of nature but by the fault of man,
a something that might have been helped as when a friend is
killed by accident, or lost to us otherwise than by death the
consequence of disease.   But one persistent thought beset
him, the same thing over and over again, exhausting him by
dint of forced reiteration.   The girl he had been idolizing—
well, there was no such person, and there never had been;
that was all—yet what an *all!*   In the first moment of the
terrible calamity that had befallen him, it seemed now that
there could have been nothing like the misery of this home
returning—the barren, black despair of it.   It was the hopeless difference between pain and paralysis; then he had suffered, but at least he could feel; now he felt nothing except
that all feeling was over.

When he had finished the simple arrangement of his room,
he still paced restlessly up and down, shaking back his yellow
hair, and brushing his hand up over it as if the gesture eased
the trouble of his mind.

"If even the Boy had been left me!" he thought, and it
was the one distinct regret he formulated.

After a while his housekeeper arrived, a pleasant elderly
woman who had attended him ever since he came to Morningquest.

It was not in his nature to let any personal matter, whether
it were pain or pleasure, affect the temper of his intercourse
with those about him, and the force of habit helped him now
again to rouse himself and greet the woman in his usual kindly,
courteous way, so that, being unobservant, she noticed no
change in him except that he was up earlier than usual; but
then he was always an early riser.   She therefore set about her
work unsuspiciously, and presently drove him out of the sitting
room with her dust-pan and brush, and he went upstairs.
There, happening to catch a glimpse of his own haggard face
and discreditable flannels in the mirror, he began to change
mechanically, and dressed himself with all his habitual neatness and precision.   Then a little choir boy came to be
helped with his music.   It was the one who sang the soprano

solos in the cathedral, a boy with a lovely voice and much general as well as musical ability, both of which the Tenor laboured to help him to develop. He came every morning for lessons, and the Tenor gave him these, and such a breakfast also as a small boy loves; but the little fellow, to do him justice, cared more for the Tenor than the breakfast.

There were three services in the cathedral that day, and the Tenor went to each, but he did not sing. He seemed to have taken cold and was hoarse, with a slight cough, and a peculiar little stab in his chest and catching of the breath, which, however, did not trouble him much to begin with. But as the day advanced every bone in his body ached with a dull wearying pain, and he was glad to go to bed early. Once there, the sense of fatigue was overpowering, yet he could not sleep until long past midnight, when he dropped off quite suddenly; or rather, as it seemed to him, when all at once he plunged headlong into the river to rescue the Boy, and began to go down, down, down, to a never-ending depth, the weight of the water above him becoming greater and greater till the pressure was unbearable, and a horrid sense of suffocation, increasing every instant, impelled him to struggle to the surface, but vainly. He could not rise—and down, down, he continued to descend, reaching no bottom, yet dropping at last, before he could help himself, on a sharp stake, pointed like a dagger, that ran right through his chest. The pain aroused him with a great start, but the impression had been so vivid, that it was some time before he could shake off the sensation of descending with icy water about him; and even when he was wide awake, and although he was bathed in perspiration, the feeling of cold remained, and so did the pain.

It was during that night that the weather changed.

The next day it was blowing a gale. Heavy showers began to fall at intervals, chilling the atmosphere, and finally settled into a steady downpour, such as frequently occurs in the middle of summer, making everything indoors humid and unwholesome, and causing colds and sore throats and other unseasonable complaints.

The Tenor taught his little choir boy as usual in the morning, went to the three services, getting more or less wet each time, and then came home and tried to do some work, but was not equal to it—his head ached; then tried to smoke, but the pipe nauseated him; and finally resigned himself to idleness, and just sat still in his lonely room, lonely of heart himself, yet with his hands patiently folded, dreamily watching the rain as it beat upon the old cathedral opposite, and streamed from eave and gargoyle, and splashed from the narrow spouting under the roof, making spreading pathways of dark moisture for itself on the gray stone walls wherever it overflowed. It was all "His Will" to the Tenor, and for his sake there was nothing he would not have borne heroically.

He, watch-ing o-ver   Is - ra - el,   slumbers not, nor sleeps.

His cough was much worse that day, the pain in his chest was more acute, and his temperature rose higher and higher, yet he did not complain. He knew he was suffering from something serious now, but he derived from his perfect faith in the beneficence of the Power that orders all things an almost superhuman fortitude.

But as he sat there with his hands folded, his mind, busy with many things, returned inevitably to the old weary theme, just as, at the same time, Angelica's own was doing, but from the opposite point of view. Always, after a startling event, those who have been present as spectators, or taken some part in it, repeat their experiences, and make some remark upon them, again and again in exactly the same words, their minds working upon the subject like heat upon water that boils, forming it into bubbles which it bursts and re-forms incessantly. He began each time with that remark of Angelica's about the change which mere dress effects, and went on to wonder at the transformation of a strong young woman into a slender delicate-looking boy by it; and then went on to accept her conclusion that it was natural he should have been deceived seeing that, in the first place, he had not the slightest suspicion, and in the second he had never seen the "Boy" except in his own dimly lighted room, or out of doors at night— besides, it was not the first time that a boy had been successfully personated by a girl, a man by a woman; but here he found himself obliged to rehearse the instances which Angelica had quoted. Then he would reconsider the fact that the part had been well played; not only attitudes and gestures, but ideas and sentiments, and the proper expression of them had been done to perfection—which led up again to another assertion of hers. She had been a boy for the time being, there was no doubt about that. And yet if he had had the slightest suspicion! There had been the shyness at first, which had worn off as it became apparent that the disguise was complete; the horror of being touched or startled, of anything, as he now perceived, which might have caused a momentary forgetfulness, and so have led to self-betrayal; the boyishnesses which, alternating with older moods, might have suggested something, but had only charmed him; the womanishnesses of which, alas! there had been too few as seen by the light of this new revelation; the physical differences,—but they had been cleverly concealed, as she said, by the cut of her clothing, and pads; the "funny head," however, about which they had both jested so often—oh, dear! how sick he was of the whole subject! If only it would let him alone! But what pretty ways he had had—the "Boy"! What a dear, dear lad he had been with all his faults! Alas! alas! if only the Boy had been left him!

Then a pause. Then off again. He had been enchanted, like Reymond of Lusignan in olden times, by a creature that was half a monster. The Boy had been a reality to him, but the lady had never been more than a lovely dream, and the monster—well, the monster had not yet appeared, for that dark haired girl in the unwomanly clothes, with pride on her lips and pain in her eyes, was no monster after all, but an erring mortal like himself, a poor weak creature to be pitied and prayed for. And the Tenor bowed his sunny head and prayed for her earnestly through all the long hours of solitary suffering which closed that day.

Then came another sleepless night, and another gloomy morning which brought his little chorister boy, whom he tried to teach as usual; but even the child saw what the effort cost him, and looked at him with great tender eyes solemnly, and was very docile.

Before the early service one of his fellow lay clerks came in to see how he was. They had all noticed the feverish cold from which he had appeared to be suffering the whole week, and this one, not finding him better, begged him to stay in that day and take care of himself for the sake of his voice. The Tenor brushed his hand back over his hair. He had forgotten that he ever had a voice. But at all events he must go to the morning service; after that he would stay at home. He

longed for the Blessed Sacrament, which was always a "Holy
Communion" to him; but he did not say so.

That afternoon he fell asleep in his easy-chair facing the
window which looked out upon the cathedral—or into a
troubled doze rather, from which he awoke all at once with a
start, and, seeing the window shut, rose hurriedly to go and
open it for the "Boy." He had done so before at night often
when he chanced to forget it. But when he got to it now he
had to clutch the frame to support himself, and he looked out
stupidly for some seconds, wondering in a dazed way why the
sun was shining when it should be dark. Then suddenly full
consciousness returned, and he remembered. He should
never open the window again for the Boy, never again.

He returned to his chair after that, and sat down to think.

When he began to understand it thoroughly—the meaning
of the last incident—he was startled out of the apathy that
oppressed him.

It became evident now that he was not merely suffering, but
fast becoming disabled by illness, and it was time he let someone know, otherwise there might be confusion and annoyance
about—his work—finding a substitute; and there would be a
risk about—about—what was he trying to think of? Oh, her
name. He might mention it and be overheard by curious
people if he lost his head—Angelica—Mrs. Kilroy of Ilverthorpe—he wished he could forget; but he would provide
against the danger of repeating them aloud. He would telegraph to his own man—the fellow had written to him the other
day, being in want of a place: a capital servant and discreet—
glad he had thought of him. And then there were other matters—the sensible setting of his house in order which every
man threatened with illness would be wise to see to. There
were several letters he must write, one to the dean, amongst
others, to ask him to come and see him. Writing was a great
effort, but he managed with much difficulty to accomplish all
that he had set himself to do, and then his mind was at rest.

Presently his old housekeeper came in with some tea. She
was anxious about him.

"I've brought you this, sir," she said. "You've not tasted
a solid morsel since Tuesday morning, and this is Thursday
afternoon. Try and take something, sir, it will do you good.
You must be getting quite faint, and indeed you look it."

"Now, I call that good of you," the Tenor answered
hoarsely, as he took the cup from her hand. "I shall be glad

to have some tea. I've been quite longing for something hot to drink."

The woman was examining his face with critical kindness. She noticed the constant attempt to cough, and the painful catching of the breath which rendered the effort abortive.

"I am afraid you are not at all well, sir," she said, expecting him to deny it, but he did not.

"I am not at all well, to tell you the truth," he confessed. "I have just written to the dean to tell him, and——" a fit of coughing rendered the end of the sentence unintelligible. "I want you to post these letters," he was able to say at last distinctly; "send this telegram off at once to my servant, and leave this note at the deanery. That will do as you go home. The man should be here to-morrow, and anything else there may be can be attended to when he arrives."

"You'll let your friends know you're not very well, sir," the housekeeper suggested.

"Those letters"—indicating the ones she held in her hand—"are to tell them."

The woman seeing to whom the letters were addressed, and hearing the Tenor talk in an off-hand way about his manservant as if he had been accustomed to the luxury all his life, feared for a moment that his mind was affected; but then some of those wild surmises as to whom and what he might be, which were rife all over the ancient city when he first arrived, recurred to her, and there slipped from her unawares the remark: "Well, they always said you was *somebody*, and to look at you one might suppose you was a dook or a markis, sir, but I won't make so bold as to ask."

The Tenor smiled, "I am afraid I am only a Tenor with an abominable cold," he rejoined good-naturedly. "I really think I must nurse it a little. When I have seen the dean, I shall go to bed."

"You'll see the doctor first," she muttered decisively as she took up the tray and withdrew.

The Tenor overheard her, but was past making any objection. He had managed to take the tea, and, eased by the grateful warmth, he sank into another heavy doze from which the arrival of the doctor roused him. It was evening then.

He made an effort to rise in his courteous way to receive the doctor, was sorry to trouble him for anything so trifling as a cold, would not have troubled him in fact had not his officious old housekeeper taken the law into her hands; but now that he had come was very glad to see him; singers, as the doctor knew, being fidgety about their throats; and really —with a smile—even a cold was important when it threatened one's means of livelihood.

The doctor responded cheerfully to these cheerful platitudes, but he was listening and observing all the time. Then he took out a stethoscope in two pieces, and as he screwed them together he asked:

"Been wet lately?"

"Well, yes," the Tenor answered—"something of that kind."

"And you did not change immediately?"

"N-no, now I think of it, not for hours. In fact, I believe my things dried on me."

"Ah-h-h!" shaking his head. "And you'd been living rather low before that, perhaps? (Just let me take your temperature.) I should say that you had got a little down—below par, you know, eh?"

"Well, perhaps," the Tenor acknowledged.

"Humph." The doctor glanced at his clinical thermometer. "You have a temperature, young man. Now let me—" he applied the stethoscope. "I am afraid you are in for a bad dose," he said after a careful examination. "I wish you had sent for me twenty-four hours sooner. These things should be taken in time. And it is marvellous how you have kept about so long. But now go to bed at once. Keep yourself warm, and the temperature as even as possible. It is all a matter of nursing; but I'll save——" he had been going to say "your life" but changed the phrase—"your voice, never fear!"

The Tenor smiled: "Pneumonia, I suppose?" he said interrogatively.

"I am sorry to say it is," the doctor answered as he rose to depart; "and double pneumonia, to boot. I'll send you something to take at once"—and he hurried away before the housekeeper had time to speak to him.

When the medicine arrived, however, she had the satisfaction of administering a dose to her master, and she begged at the same time that she might be allowed to stay in the house that night in case he wanted anything, but this the Tenor would not hear of. He did not think he should want anything—(he could think of nothing unfortunately but the risk of mentioning Angelica's name). She might come a little earlier in the morning and get him some tea; probably he would be glad of some then. He was not going to get up in the morning, he really meant to take care of himself. The housekeeper coaxed, but in vain. There was no place for her to sleep in comfort, no bell to summon her, and as to sitting up all night that was out of the question; who would do her work in the morning? There would be plenty of people to look after him to-morrow. One night could make no difference.

Had she heard the doctor's orders she would have disobeyed her master, but as it was his manner imposed upon her, he spoke so confidently; and accordingly she left the house at the usual hour, to the Tenor's great relief.

When she had gone he was seized with an attack of hæmoptysis, and after he had recovered from that sufficiently he went to bed—or rather he found himself there, not knowing quite how it had come to pass, for the disease had made rapid progress in the last few hours, and he now suffered acutely, his temperature was higher, and the terrible sense of suffocation continued to increase.

It was at this time that the dean, in his comfortable easy-chair, looked up from the Tenor's note, and said to his wife deprecatingly: "He is ill, it seems, and wishes to see me. Do you think I need go to-night?"

"No, my dear, *certainly* not," was the emphatic reply. "There cannot be much the matter with him. I saw him out only yesterday or the day before. And at all events it will do in the morning. You must consider yourself."

So the dean stayed at home to lay up a lifelong regret for himself, but not with an easy conscience. He had a sort of feeling that it would be well to go, which his dislike to turning out on a raw night like that would not have outweighed without his wife's word in the scale.

Nothing was being done to relieve the Tenor. There were no medicines regularly administered, no soothing drinks for him, no equable temperature, no boiling water to keep the atmosphere moist with steam, the common necessaries of such a case; all these the Tenor, knowing his danger, had composedly foregone lest perchance in a moment of delirium he should mention a lady's name; and that he had had the foresight to do so was a cause of earnest thanksgiving to him when every breath of cold air began to stab like a knife through his lungs, and his senses wandered away for lengths of time which he could not compute, and he became conscious that he was uttering his thoughts aloud in spite of himself.

"It is not so very long till morning," he found himself saying once. "I will just lie still and bear it till then. I am drowsy enough—and in the morning——" but now all at once he asked himself, was there to be any more morning for him?

He was too healthy-minded to long for death, and too broken-hearted to shrink from it. His first feeling, however, when he realized the near prospect was nothing but a kind of mild surprise that it should be near, and even this was instantly dismissed. No more morning for him meant little leisure to think of her, and here he hastened to fold his hands and bow his golden head: "Lord, Lord," he entreated in the midst of his martyrdom, "make her a good woman yet."

The bells above him broke in upon his prayer. "Amen" and "amen," they seemed to say; and then the chime, full-fraught for him with promise, rang its constant message out, and as he listened his heart expanded with hope, his last earthly sorrow slipped away from him, and his soul relied upon the certainty that his final supplication was not in vain.

After this he was conscious of nothing but his own sufferings for a little. Then there came a blank; and next he thought he was singing.

He heard his own marvellous voice and wondered at it, and he remembered that once before he had had the same experiences, but when or where he could not recall. Now, he would fain have stopped; for every note was a dagger in his breast, yet he found himself forced to sing till at last the pain aroused him.

When full consciousness returned, a terrible thirst devoured him. What would he not have given for a drink!—something to drink, and someone to bring it to him.

What made him think of his mother just then? Where was his mother? It was just as well, perhaps, she should not be there to see him suffer.

He had never a bitter thought in his mind about any person or thing, nor did he dream of bemoaning the cruel fate which left him now at his death, as at his birth, deserted. What he did think of were the many kind people who would have been only too glad to come to his assistance had they but known his need.

But the torment of thirst increased upon him.

He thought of the dear Lord in *his* agony of thirst, and bore it for a time. Then he remembered that there must be water in the room. With great difficulty he got up to get it for himself. His face was haggard and drawn by this time, and there were great black circles round his sunken eyes, but the expression of strength and sweetness had been inten- sified if anything, and he never looked more beautiful than then.

It seemed like a day's journey to the washstand. He reached it at last, however, reached it and grasped the carafe ——with such a feeling of relief and thankfulness! Alas! it was empty. So also was the jug. The woman had forgotten for once to fill them, and there was not a drop of water to moisten his lips.

Tears came at this, and he sank into a chair. It was hard, and he was much exhausted, but still there was no reproach upon his lips. Presently he found himself in bed again with his pillows arranged so as to prop him up. The struggle for breath was awful, and he could not lie down. He had only to fight for a little longer, howev r, then suddenly the worst was over. And at the same moment, as it seemed to him, the chime rang out again triumphantly; and almost immediately afterward his first friend and foster father, the rough collier, grasped his hand. But he had scarcely greeted him when his second friend arrived, and bending over him called him as of old, "Julian, my dear, dear boy!" This reminded the Tenor. "Where *is* the Boy?" he said. "Is the window open? It is time he came."

"Israfil, I am here," was the soft response. The Tenor's face became radiant. All whom he had ever cared for were present with him, coming as he called them—even the dean, who was kneeling now beside his bed murmuring accustomed prayers. "What happiness!" The Tenor murmured. "I was so sorrowful this afternoon, and now! A happy death! a happy death! Ah, Boy, do you not see that he gives us our heart's desire? He slumbers not, nor sleeps," and the Tenor's face shone.

Then the chime was ringing again, and now it never ceased for him. He had sunk into the last dreamy lethargy from which only the clash of the bells above roused him hour by hour during the few that remained; but all sense of time was over; the hours were one; and so the beloved music accom- panied him till his spirit rose enraptured to the glory of the Beatific Vision itself.

It was just at the dawn, when the Boy was wont to leave him, that, according to his ancient faith, the dear-earned wings were given him, the angel guardian led him, and the true and beautiful pure spirit was welcomed by its kindred into everlasting joy.

CHAPTER V.

WHEN Angelica heard those dreadful words: "He's dead, miss, didn't you know? and buried yesterday"—her jaw dropped, and for a moment she felt the solid earth reel beneath her. The colour left her face and returned to it, red chasing white as one breath follows another, and she glared at the woman. For her first indignant thought was that she was being insulted with a falsehood. The thing was impossible; he could not be dead.

"And buried yesterday," the woman repeated.

"I don't believe you," Angelica exclaimed, stamping her foot imperiously.

The woman drew herself up, gave one indignant look, then turned her back, and walked into the house.

Angelica ran down the passage after her, and grasped her arm. "I beg your pardon," she said. "But, oh, do tell me —do make me understand, for I cannot believe it! I cannot believe it!"

The woman pushed open the sitting room door, and led her in.

"Was you a friend of his, miss—or ma'am?" she asked.

"I am Mrs. Kilroy of Ilverthorpe," Angelica answered. "Yes, I was a friend of his. I cared for him greatly. It is only a few days since I saw him alive and well. Oh! it isn't true! it isn't true!" she broke off, wringing her hands. "I cannot believe it!"

The woman sat down, threw her apron back over her face, and rocked herself to and fro.

Angelica, dazed and dry-eyed, stared at her stupidly. The shock had stunned her.

Presently the woman recovered herself, and seeing the lady's stony face, forgot her own trouble for the moment, and hastened to help her.

"I don't wonder you're took-to, my lady," she said. "It's bin a awful blow to a many, a awful blow. Oh! I never thought when they used to come and see him here in their fine carriages and with their servants and their horses and that, as it was anything but the music brought 'em—tho', mind you, he was as easy with them as they with him. Oh, dear! Oh, dear!''

Angelica's lips were so parched she could hardly articulate. "Tell me,'' she gasped, "tell me all. I cannot understand.''

The woman fetched her some water. "Lie back a bit in this chair, ma'am,'' she said, "and I'll just tell you. It'll come easier when you know. When one knows, it helps a body. You see, ma'am, it was this way''—and then she poured forth the narrative of those last sad days, omitting no detail, and Angelica listened, dry-eyed at first, but presently she was seized upon by the pitifulness of it all, and then, like scattered raindrops that precede a heavy shower, the great tears gathered in her eyes and slowly overflowed, forerunners of a storm which burst at last in deep convulsive sobs that rent her, so that her suffering body came to the relief of her mind.

"I wanted to stay with 'im that last night and see to 'im,'' the housekeeper proceeded, "for the doctor's very words to me was, when I went to fetch 'im, before ever 'e had come to see what was the matter, 'e ses, knowing me for a many years, 'e ses, 'You'll look after 'im well, I'm sure, Mrs. Jenkins,' 'e ses, and I answered, 'Yes, sir, please God. I will,' for I felt as something was 'anging over me then, I did, tho' little I knowed what it was. And I did my best to persuade 'im to let me stay that night and nurse 'im, but 'e wouldn't hear of it; 'e said there wasn't no need; and what with the way 'e 'ad as you didn't like to go agin 'im in nothing, and what with 'is bein' so cheerful like, 'e imposed upon me, so I went away. Oh, it's been a bad business''—shaking her head disconsolately—"a bad business! To think of 'im bein' alone that night without a soul near 'im, and it 'is last on earth. He'd not 'ave let a dog die so, 'e wouldn't.''

Angelica's sobs redoubled.

"But I couldn't rest, ma'am,'' the woman went on. "The whole night through I kep awaking up and thinking of 'im, and I 'eard every hour strike, till at last I couldn't stand it no longer, and I just got up and came to see 'ow 'e was. I'd 'a' bin less tired if I'd a sat up all night with 'im. And I came 'ere, and as soon as I opened the door, ma'am, there!'' she threw her hands before her—"I knew there was something! For the smell that met me in the passage, it was just for all the world like fresh turned clay. But still I didn't think. It wasn't till afterward that I knowed it was 'is grave. And I went upstairs, ma'am, not imaginin' nothin' neither, and tapped at 'is door, and 'e didn't answer, so I opens it softly, and ses: "Ow are you this mornin', sir?' I ses, quite softly like, in a whisper, for fear of wakin' 'im if 'e should be asleep. Oh, dear! Oh, dear! I needn't 'a' bin so careful! And I ses it agin: 'Ow are you, sir, this mornin'?' I ses: 'I 'ope you 'ad a good night,' I ses; but still 'e didn't answer, and some'ow it struck me, ma'am, that the 'ouse was very quiet—it seemed kind of unnatural still, if you understand. So, just without knowin' why like, I pushed the door open"—showing how she did it with her hands—"little by little, bit by bit, all for fear of disturbing 'im, till at last I steps in, makin' no noise—Oh, dear! Oh, dear!" She threw her apron up over her face again, and rocked herself as she stood. "And there 'e was, ma'am," she resumed huskily, "propped up by pillows in the bed so as to be almost sittin', and the top one was a great broad pillow, very white, for 'e was always most pertic'lar about such things, and 'ad 'em all of the very best. And 'is face was turned away from me as I came in, ma'am, so that I only saw it sidewise, and just at first I thought 'e was asleep—very sound." She wiped her eyes with her apron, and shook her head several times. "And there's a little window to 'is room what slides along instead of openin' up," she proceeded when she had recovered herself sufficiently, "with small panes, and outside there's roses and honeysucklers, what made shadows that flickered, for the mornin' was gusty though bright, and they deceived me. I thought 'e was breathin' natural. But while I stood there the sun shone in and just touched the edges of 'is 'air, ma'am, and it looked for all the world like a crown of gold against the white pillows, it did, indeed—eh! ma'am, I don't wonder you take on!" This emphatically upon a fresh outburst of uncontrollable grief from Angelica. "For I ses to myself, when the light fell on 'is face strong like that, 'It's the face of a angel,' I ses—"but there!" raising her hands palms outward, slowly, and bringing them down to her knees again—"I can't tell you! But 'is lips were just a little parted, ma'am, with a sort o' look on 'em, not a smile, you understand, but just a look that sweet as made you feel like smilin' yourself! and 'is skin that transapparent you'd 'ave expected to see through it; but that didn't make me think nothin', for it was always so—as clear as your own, ma'am, if you'll excuse the liberty; and some folks said it was because he was a great lord in disguise, for such do 'ave fine skins; and some said it was because 'e was so good, but I think it was both myself. But 'owever, ma'am, seein' 'e slept so sound, I made bold to creep in a little nearer, for 'e was a picter!'' shaking her head solemnly—''an' I was just thinkin' what a proud woman 'is mother would be if she was me to see 'im at that moment an' 'im so beautiful, when, ma'am''—but here her voice broke, and it was some seconds before she could add—''you might 'a' 'eard me scream at the cathedral. And after I 'ad screamed I'd 'a' given untold gold not to 'a' done it. For it seemed a sin to make a noise, and 'im so still. And, oh! ma'am, 'e'd bin dyin' the 'ole o' that last afternoon an' I never suspected 'e'd more nor a cold, though I knew it was bad. An' 'e'd bin alone the 'ole o' that blessed night a dyin', an' sensible they say to the last, an' not a soul to give 'im so much as a drink, an' the thirst awful, so I'm told. An' 'e'd been up to try an' get one for 'imself, for the bottle off the washstand was lyin' on the floor as if he'd dropped it out of 'is 'and—'e'd got up to get a drink for 'imself,'' she repeated impressively, ''an' 'im dyin', ma'am, *and there wasn't a drop o' water there.* I knowed it—I knowed it the moment I see that bottle on the floor. I'd forgot to bring up any before I left the day before, though I ses to myself when I did the room in the mornin'—'I must fetch that water at once,' and never thought of it again from that moment.''

''Oh, this is dreadful! dreadful!'' Angelica moaned.

''Eh!'' the woman ejaculated sympathetically. ''And the 'ardest part of it was the way they came when it was too late. Everybody. An' me, 'eaven forgive me, thinkin' 'im out o' 'is mind when 'e wrote to 'em an' said they was 'is friends. There was 'is lordship the Markis o' Dawne, and 'is two sisters, an' that other great lady what is with 'em so much. An' they didn't say much any of 'em except 'er, but she wept an' wrung 'er 'ands, and blamed 'erself and everybody for lettin' the master 'ave 'is own way an' leaving 'im, as it seems it was 'is wish to be left, alone with some trouble 'e 'ad. But they 'ad come to see 'im, too, Dr. Galbraith and the Markis 'ad, many times, for I let 'em in myself, an' never thought nothin' of it in the way of their bein' friends of 'is, I thought they came about the music. Eh!'' she repeated, ''they didn't say much, any of 'em, but you could see, you could see! An' the dean came, an' you should 'a' 'eard 'm! full o' remorse, 'e was, ma'am, for not 'avin' come the night before, though 'e was asked. An' they all went upstairs to see 'm, an' 'im lyin'

there so quiet and all indifferent to their grief, yet with such a
look of peace upon 'is face! It was sweet and it was sad
too; for all the world as if 'e'd bin 'urt cruel by somebody
in 'is feelin's but 'ad forgiven 'em, an' then bin glad to
go."

"Israfil! Israfil!" the wretched Angelica moaned aloud.
She could picture the scene. Her Aunt Fulda, prayerful but
tearless, only able to sorrow as saints and angels do; Ideala
with her great human heart torn, weeping and wailing and
wringing her hands; Aunt Claudia, hard of aspect and soft of
heart, stealthily wiping her tears as if ashamed of them; Uncle
Dawne sitting with his elbows on his knees and his face hidden
in his hands; and Dr. Galbraith standing beside the bed looking down on the marble calm of the dead with a face as still,
but pained in expression—Angelica knew them all so well, it
was easy for her imagination to set them before her in characteristic attitudes at such a time; and she was not surprised to
find that they had been friends of his although no hint of the
fact had ever reached her. They were a loyal set in that little
circle, and could keep counsel among themselves, as she knew;
an example which she herself would have followed as a matter
of course under similar circumstances, so surely does the force
of early associations impel us instinctively to act on the principles which we have been accustomed to see those about us
habitually pursue.

"An' they covered 'im with flowers, an' one or other of
those great ladies in the plainest black dresses with nothin'
except just white linen collar an' cuffs, stayed with 'im day an'
night till they took 'im to 'is long 'ome yesterday," the woman
concluded.

Then there was a long silence, broken only by Angelica's
heavy sobs.

"Can't I do nothin' for you, ma'am?" the housekeeper
asked at last.

"Yes," Angelica answered; "leave me alone awhile."

And the woman had tact enough to obey.

Then Angelica got up, and went and knelt by the Tenor's
empty chair, and laid her cheek against the cold cushion.

"It isn't true, it isn't true, it isn't true," she wailed again
and again, but it was long before she could think at all; and
her dry eyes ached, for she had no more tears to shed.

Presently she became aware of a withered rose in the hollow
between the seat of the chair and the back. She knew it must

be one of those she had thrown at him that night, perhaps the
one he had carelessly twirled in his hand while they talked,
now and then inhaling its perfume as he listened, watching her
with quiet eyes.

"Dead! dead!' she whispered, pressing the dry petals to
her lips.

Then she looked about her.

The light of day, falling on a scene which was familiar only
by the subdued light of a lamp, produced an effect as of chill
and bareness. She noticed worn places in the carpet, and a
certain shabbiness from constant use in everything, which
had not been visible at night, and now affected her in an inex-
pressibly dreary way. There was very little difference really,
and yet there was *some* change which, as she perceived it, began
gradually to bring the great change home to her. There was
the empty chair, first relic in importance and saddest in significance. There were his pipes neatly arranged on a little
fretwork rack which hung where bell handles are usually put
beside the fireplace. She remembered having seen him replace
one of them the last time she was there, and now she went
over and touched its cold stem, and her heart swelled. The
stand of ferns and flowers which he had arranged with such
infinite pains to please the "Boy" stood in its accustomed
place, but ferns and flowers alike were dead or drooping in
their pots, untended and uncared for, and some had been
taken away altogether, leaving gaps on the stand, behind
which the common grate, empty, and rusted from disuse,
appeared.

There was dust on her violin case, and dust on his grand
piano—her violin which he kept so carefully. She opened the
violin case expecting to find the instrument ruined by water.
But no! it lay there snugly on its velvet cushion without a
scratch on its polished surface or an injured string. She
understood. And perhaps it had been one of his last conscious acts to put it right for her. He was always doing
something for her, always. They said now that his income
had been insufficient, or that he gave too much away, and that
the malady had been rendered hopeless from the first by his
weakness for want of food. The woman who waited on him
had told her so. "He'd feed that chorister brat what come
every morning," she said, "in a way that was shameful, but
his own breakfast has been dry bread and coffee, without
neither sugar nor milk, for many and many a day—and his

dinner an ounce of meat at noon, with never a bite nor sup to speak of at tea, as often as not."

"O Israfil! Israfil!" she moaned when she thought of it. There had always been food, and wine too, for that other hungry "Boy," food and wine which the Tenor rarely touched —she remembered that now. To see the "Boy" eat and be happy was all he asked, and if hunger pinched him, he filled his pipe and smoked till the craving ceased. She saw it all now. But why had she never suspected it, she who was rolling in wealth? His face was wan enough at times, and worn to that expression of sadness which comes of privation, but the reason had never cost her a thought. And it was all for her —or for "him" whom he believed to be near and dear to her. No one else had ever sacrificed anything for her sake, no one else had ever cared for her as he had cared, no one else would ever again. Oh, hateful deception! She threw herself down on her knees once more.

"O Israfil! Israfil!" she cried, "only forgive me, and I will be true! only forgive me, and I will be true!"

It was trying to rain outside. The wind swept down the Close in little gusts, and dashed cold drops against the window pane, and in the intervals sprays of the honeysuckle and clematis tapped on the glass, and the leaves rustled. This roused her. She had heard them rustle like that on many a moonlight night—with what a different significance! And he also used to listen to them, and had told her that often when he was alone at night and tired, they had sounded like voices whispering, and had comforted him, for they had always said pleasant things. Oh, gentle loving heart, to which the very leaves spoke peace, so spiritually perfect was it! And these were the same creepers to which he had listened, these that tapped now disconsolately, and this was his empty chair—but where was he? he who was tender for the tiniest living thing —who had thought and cared for everyone but himself. What was the end of it all? How had he been rewarded? His hearth was cold, his little house deserted, and the wind and the rain swept over his lonely grave.

She went to the window and opened it. She would go to his grave—she would find him.

While she stood on the landing stage at the watergate waiting for the flat ferry boat, which happened to be on the farther side of the narrow river, to be poled across to her, the Tenor's little chorister boy came up and waited too. He had a rustic posy in his hand, but there was no holiday air in his manner; on the contrary, he seemed unnaturally subdued for a boy, and Angelica somehow knew who he was, and conjectured that his errand was the same as her own. If so he would show her the way.

The child seemed unconscious of her presence. He stepped into the boat before her, and they stood side by side during the crossing, but his eyes were fixed on the water and he took no notice of her. On the other side of the landing when they reached it was a narrow lane, a mere pathway, between a high wall on the one hand and a high hedge on the other, which led up a steep hill to a road, on the other side of which was a cemetery. The child followed this path, and then Angelica knew that she had been right in her conjecture, and had only to follow him. He led her quite across the cemetery to a quiet corner where was an open grassy space away from the other graves. Two sides of it were sheltered by great horse chestnuts, old and umbrageous, and from where she stood she caught a glimpse of the city below, of the cathedral spire appearing above the trees, of Morne in the same direction, a crest of masonry crowning the wooded steep, and, on the other side, the country stretching away into a dim blue hazy distance. It was a lovely spot, and she felt with a jealous pang that the care of others had found it for him. In life or death it was all the same; he owed her nothing.

The grass was trampled about the grave; there must have been quite a concourse of people there the day before. It was covered with floral tokens, wreaths and crosses, with anchors of hope and hearts of love, pathetic symbols at such a time.

But was he really there under all that? If she dug down deep should she find him?

The little chorister boy had gone straight to the grave and dropped on his knees beside it. He looked at the lovely hothouse flowers and then glanced ruefully at his own humble offering—sweetwilliam chiefly, snapdragon, stocks, and nasturtium. But he laid it there with the rest, and Angelica's heart was wrung anew as she thought of the tender pleasure this loving act of the child would have been to the Tenor. Yet her eyes were dry.

The boy pressed the flowers on the grave as if he would nestle them closer to his friend, and then all at once as he patted the cold clay his lip trembled, his chest heaved with sobs, his eyes overflowed with tears, and his face was puckered with grief.

Having accomplished his errand, he got up from the ground, slapped his knees to knock the clay off them, and, still sniffing and sobbing, walked back the way he had come in sturdy dejection.

All that was womanly in Angelica went out to the poor little fellow. She would like to have comforted him, but what could she say or do? Alas! alas! a woman who cannot comfort a child, what sort of a woman is she?

Presently she found herself standing beside the river looking up to the iron bridge that crossed it with one long span. There were trees on one side of the bridge, and old houses piled up on the other picturesquely. Israfil had noticed them the last time they rowed down the river. The evening was closing in. The sky was deepening from gray to indigo. There was one bright star above the bridge. But why had she come here? She had not come to see a bridge with one great star above it! nor to watch a sullen river slipping by—unless, indeed—— She bent over the water, peering into it. She remembered that after the first plunge there had been no great pain—and even if there had been, what was physical pain compared to this terrible heartache, this dreadful remorse, an incurable malady of the mind which would make life a burden to her forevermore, if she had the patience to live? Patience and Angelica! What an impossible association of ideas! Her face relaxed at the humour of it, and it was with a smile that she turned to gather her summer drapery about her, bending sideways to reach back to the train of her dress, as the insane fashion of tight skirts, which were then in vogue, necessitated. In the act, however, she became aware of someone hastening after her, and the next moment a soft white hand grasped her arm and drew her back.

"Angelica! how can you stand so near the edge in this uncertain light? I really thought you would lose your balance and fall in."

It was Lady Fulda who spoke, uttering the words in an irritated, almost angry tone, as mothers do when they relieve their own feelings by scolding and shaking a child that has escaped with a bruise from some danger to life and limb. But that was all she ever said on the subject, and consequently Angelica never knew if she had guessed her intention or only been startled by her seeming carelessness, as she professed to be.

The sudden impulse passed from Angelica, as is the way with morbid impulses, the moment she ceased to be alone. The first word was sufficient to take her out of herself, to recall her to her normal state, and to readjust her view of life, setting it back to the proper focus. But still she looked out at the world from a low level, if healthy; a dull, dead level, the mean temperature of which was chilly, while the atmosphere threatened to vary only from stagnant apathy to boisterous discontent, positive, hopeless, and unconcealed.

Moved by common consent, the two ladies turned from the river, and walked on slowly together and in silence. The feeling uppermost in Angelica's mind was one of resentment. Her aunt had appeared in the same unexpected manner at the outset of her acquaintance with the Tenor, and she objected to her reappearance now, at the conclusion. It was like an incident in a melodrama, the arrival of the good influence—it was absurd; if she had done it on purpose, it would have been impertinent.

The entrance to Ilverthorpe was only a few hundred yards from where they had met, and they had now reached a postern which led into the grounds. Angelica opened it with a latchkey and then stood to let her aunt pass through before her.

"I suppose you will come in," she said ungraciously.

But Lady Fulda forgave the discourtesy, and the two walked on together up to the house—passing, while their road lay through the park, under old forest trees that swayed continually in a rising gale: and somewhat buffeted by the wind till they came to a narrow path sheltered by rows of tall shrubs, on the thick foliage of which the rain, which had fallen at intervals during the day, had collected, and now splashed in their faces or fell in wetting drops upon their dresses as the bushes, struck by the heavy gusts, swayed to and fro.

Angelica, whose nervous system was peculiarly susceptible to discomfort of the kind, felt more wretched than ever. She thought of the desolate grave with mud-splashed, bedraggled flowers upon it and of the golden head and beautiful calm face beneath; thought of him as we are apt to think of our dead at first, imagining them still sentient, aware of the horror of their position, crushed into their narrow beds with a terrible weight of earth upon them, left out alone in the cold, uncomforted and uncared for, while those they loved and trusted most recline in easy chairs round blazing fires, talking forgetfully.

Something like this flashed through Angelica's mind, and a cry as of acute pain escaped from her unawares.

Her companion's features contracted for a moment, but otherwise she made no sign of having heard.

They had not exchanged a word since they had entered the grounds, but now the gentle Lady Fulda began again—with some trepidation, however, for Angelica's manner continued to be chilling, not to say repellent, and she could not tell how her advances would be received.

"I was looking for you," she said.

"For me?" raising her eyebrows.

"Yes. I went to his house this afternoon and heard from the housekeeper that a young lady had been there, and I felt sure from the description and—and likelihood—that it must be you. She said you had been wholly unprepared for the dreadful news, and it had been a great shock to you. And I thought you would probably go to see his grave. It is always one's first impulse. And I was going to look for you there when I saw you in the distance on the towing path."

Angelica preserved her ungracious silence, but her attention was attracted by the way in which her aunt spoke of the Tenor in regard to herself, apparently as if she had known of their intimacy. Lady Fulda resumed, however, before Angelica had asked herself how this could be.

"I am afraid you will think me a very meddling person," she said, speaking to her young niece with the respect and unassuming diffidence of high breeding and good feeling; "but perhaps you know—how one fancies that one can do something—or say something—or that one ought to try to. I believe it is a comfort to one's self to be allowed to try."

"Yes," Angelica assented, thinking of her desire to help the child, and thawing with interest at this expression of an experience similar to her own. "I felt something of that—a while ago."

They had reached the house by this time, and Angelica ushered her aunt in, then led her to the drawing room where she herself usually sat, the one that opened onto the terrace. This was the sheltered side of the house that day, and the windows stood wide open, making the room as fresh as the outer air. They sat themselves down at one of them from which they could see the tops of trees swaying immediately beneath, and further off the river, then the green upland terminating in a distance of wooded hills.

"I always think this is prettier than the view from Morne, although not so fine," Lady Fulda remarked tentatively. She was a little afraid of the way in which Angelica in her present mood might receive any observation of hers, however inoffensive. She had been looking out of the window when she spoke, but the silence which followed caused her to turn and look at Angelica. The latter had risen for some purpose—she could not remember what—and now stood staring before her in a dazed way.

"I am afraid you are not well, dear," Lady Fulda said, taking her hand affectionately.

"Oh, I am well enough," Angelica answered, almost snatching her hand away, and making a great effort to control another tempest of tears which threatened to overwhelm her. "But don't—don't expect me to be polite—or anything—to-day. You don't know——" She took a turn up and down the room, and then the trouble of her mind betrayed her. "O Aunt Fulda!" she exclaimed, clasping her hands, and wringing them, "I have done such a dreadful thing!"

"I know," was the unexpected rejoinder.

Angelica's hands dropped, and she stared at her aunt, her thoughts taking a new departure under the shock of this surprise. "Did he tell you?" she demanded.

"No," Lady Fulda stammered. "I saw you with him—several times. At first I thought it was Diavolo, and I did not wonder, he is so naughty—or rather he used to be. But when I asked with whom he was staying, everybody was amazed, and maintained that he had not been in the neighbourhood at all. So I wrote to him at Sandhurst, and his reply convinced me that I must have been mistaken. Then I began to suspect. In fact I was sure——"

Lady Fulda spoke nervously, and with her accustomed simplicity, but Angelica felt the fascination of the singular womanly power which her aunt exercised, and resented it.

"Is that all!" she said defiantly. "Why didn't you interfere?"

"For one thing, because I did not like to."

"Why?"

"On your account."

"Did you know I was deceiving him?"

"Yes—or you would not have been with him under such circumstances," Lady Fulda rejoined; "and then—I thought, upon the whole, it was better not to interfere"—she broke off, recurring once more to Angelica's question. "I was sure he would find you out sooner or later, and then I knew he would do what was right; and in the meantime the companionship of such a man under any circumstances was good for you."

"You seem to know him very well."

"Yes," Lady Fulda answered. "He was at the University with your Uncle Dawne and George Galbraith. They were great friends, and used to come to the castle a good deal at that time, but eventually Julian's visits had to be discontinued."

Lady Fulda coloured painfully as she made this last statement, and Angelica, always apt to put two and two together, instantly inserted this last fragment into an imperfect story she possessed of a love affair and disappointment of her aunt's, and made the tale complete.

She had heard that

> . . . never maiden glow'd,
> But that was in her earlier maidenhood,
> With such a fervent flame of human love,
> Which being rudely blunted glanced and shot
> Only to holy things ; to prayer and praise
> She gave herself, to fast and alms.

They must have been about the same age, Angelica reflected, as she examined the lineless perfection of Lady Fulda's face, and then there glanced through her mind a vision of what might have been—what ought to have been as it seemed to her: "But why should he have been banished from the castle because you cared for him?" she asked point blank.

Lady Fulda's confusion increased. "That was not the reason," she faltered, making a brave effort to confide in Angelica in the hope of winning the latter's confidence in return. "There was a dreadful mistake. Your grandfather thought he was paying attention to me, and spoke to him about it, telling him I should not be allowed to marry— beneath me; and Julian said, not meaning any affront to me,— never dreaming that I cared,—that he had not intended to ask me, which made my father angry and unreasonable, and he scolded me because he had made a mistake. Men do that, dear, you know; they have so little sense of justice and self-control. And I had little self-control in those days, either. And I retorted and told my father he had spoilt my life, for I thought it would have been different if he had not interfered. However, I don't know"; she sighed regretfully. "But when such absolute uncertainty prevailed it was impossible to say that Julian was beneath me by birth, and as to position—— But, there"—she broke off, "of course he never came amongst us any more."

"Otherwise I should have known him all my life," Angelica exclaimed, "and there would have been none of this misery."

They had returned to their seats, and she sat now frowning for some seconds, then asked her aunt: "Does Uncle Dawne know—did you tell him about my escapade?"

"No."

"You are a singularly reticent person."

"I am a singularly sore-hearted one," Lady Fulda answered, "and very full of remorse, for I think now—I might have done something—to prevent——" she stammered.

"The final catastrophe," Angelica concluded. "Then you are laying his death at my door?"

"Oh, no; Heaven forbid!" her aunt protested.

A long pause ensued, which was broken by Lady Fulda rising.

"It is time I returned," she said. "Come back with me to Morne. It will be less miserable for you than staying here alone to-night."

Angelica looked up at her for a second or two with a perfectly blank countenance, then rose slowly. "How do you propose to return?" she asked.

"I had not thought of that—I left the carriage in Morningquest," Lady Fulda answered.

"Really, Aunt Fulda," Angelica snapped, then rang the bell impatiently; "you can't walk back to Morningquest, and be in time for dinner at the castle also, I should think. The carriage immediately," this was to the man who had answered the bell.

"You will accompany me?" Lady Fulda meekly pleaded.

"I suppose so," was the ungracious rejoinder—"that is if you will decide for me. I am tired of action. I just want to drift."

"Come, then," said Lady Fulda kindly.

CHAPTER VI.

"I AM tired of action, I just want to drift. I am tired of action, I just want to drift," this was the new refrain which set itself as an accompaniment to Angelica's thoughts. She was tired of thinking too, but thought ran on, an inexhaustible stream; and the more passive she became to the will of others outwardly, the more active was her mind.

She leant back languidly in the carriage beside her aunt as they drove together through the city to Morne, and remained silent the whole time, and motionless, all but her eyes, which roved incessantly from object to object while she inwardly rendered an account to herself of each, and of her own state of mind; keeping up disjointed comments, quotations, and reflections consciously, but without power to check the flow.

There were a few blessed moments of oblivion caused by the bustle of their departure from the house, then Angelica looked up, and instantly her intellect awoke. They were driving down the avenue—"The green leaves rustle overhead," was the first impression that formulated itself into words. "The carriage wheels roll rhythmically. Every faculty is on the alert. There is something unaccustomed in the aspect of things—things familiar—this once familiar scene. A new point of view; the change is in me. We used to ride down that lane. Blackberries. The day I found a worm in one. Ugh! Diavolo, Diavolo—no longer in touch—a hundred thou· sand miles away—what does it matter? I am tired of action; I just want to drift. I am tired of action; I just want to drift, just want to drift—drifting now to Morne—a restful place; but I shall drift from thence again. Whither? Better be steered—no, though. I am not a wooden ship to be steered, but a human soul with a sacred individuality to be preserved, and the grand right of private judgment. What happens when such ennobling privileges are sacrificed? Demon worship—grandpapa.

"The old duke sat in his velvet cap in a carved oak chair in the oriel room—nonsense! And Aunt Fulda. As passive as a cow. Is she though? Is Angelica as passive as a cow for all that she's so still? Poor Daddy! Drudging at the House just now, not thinking of me. I hope not. Do I hope not? No, he belongs to me, and—I *do* care for him. The kind eyes, the kind caress, the kind thought. 'Angelica, dear'—

O Daddy! I'm sorry I tormented you—sorry, sorry—The lonely grave, the lonely grave—O Israfil! 'Dead, dead, long dead, and my heart is a handful of dust.' The horses' hoofs beat out the measure of my misery. The green leaves rustle overhead. The air is delicious after the rain. The dust is laid. Only this afternoon. I went to see him; what was I thinking of? Can I bring him back again? Never again! Never again! Only this afternoon, but time is not measured by minutes. Time is measured by the consciousness of it. 'He's dead, miss—haven't you heard? and buried yesterday.' ' Dead, dead, long dead—— '

> " The dearest friend to me, the kindest man,
> The best conditioned and unwearied spirit
> In doing courtesies.

"On through the dim rich city. A pretty girl and poor. Do you envy me, my dear? Stare at me hard. I am a rich lady, you see, asked everywhere:

> " The daughter of a hundred Earls,
> You are not one to be desired.

"The Palace—poor Edith! Here we are at the Castle Hill —and that idiot Aunt Fulda has forgotten her carriage. Shall I remind her? There is still time to turn back. No, don't trouble yourself. 'Let them alone and they'll come home.' I wish I had no memory. It is a perfect nuisance to have to think in inverted commas all the time. And Shakespeare is the greatest bore of all. The whole of life could be set to his expressions—that cannot be quite right; what I mean is the whole of life could be expressed in his words. Diavolo and I tried once to talk Shakespeare for a whole day. I made the game. But Diavolo could remember nothing but 'To be or not to be,' which went no way at all when he tried to live on it, so he said Shakespeare was rot and I pulled his hair—I wish I could stop thinking—suspend my thoughts—The pine woods:

> " From the top of the upright pine
> The snowlumps fall with a thud,
> Come from where the sunbeams shine
> To lie in the heart of the mud—

The heart of the mud, the heart of the mud—Oh, for oblivion! Nirvana—'The Dewdrop slips into the shining sea'—We're slipping into the courtyard of the castle. How many weary women, women waiting, happy women, despairing women, thoughtful women, thoughtless women, have those rows of winking windows eyed as they entered? Women are much more interesting than men—The lonely grave, the lonely grave——''

"Angelica!" Lady Fulda exclaimed as they drew up at the door, "I've left the carriage in Morningquest!"

"Yes, I know," said Angelica.

"My dear child, why didn't you remind me?"

Angelica shrugged her shoulders. "Let them alone and they'll come home," recurred to her, and then: "I must be more gracious. Aunt Fulda"—aloud—"who are here?"

"Your Uncle Dawne——"

"And Co., I suppose!" Angelica concluded derisively.

"Your Aunt Claudia and her friend are also here," Lady Fulda corrected her with dignity.

"Not exactly a successful attempt to be gracious," Angelica's thoughts ran on. "Ah, well! What does it matter? Live and let live, forget and forgive—forgetting *is* forgiving, and everyone forgets"—and then again *piano*—"The lonely grave, the lonely grave."

At dinner she sat beside her grandfather; her uncle being opposite, silent and serious as usual. But they were all subdued that night except the old duke, who, unaware of any cause for their painful preoccupation, and glad to see Angelica, who roused him as a rule with her wonderful spirits, chatted inconsequently. But Angelica's unnatural quietude could not escape the attention of the rest of the party, and inquiring glances were directed to Lady Fulda, in the calm of whose passionless demeanour, however, there was no consciousness of anything unusual to be read; and of course no questions were asked.

In the drawing room, after dinner, Angelica sat on a velvet cushion at her uncle's feet, and rested her head against his knee. Close beside her there was a long narrow mirror let into the wall of the room like a panel, and in this she could see herself and him reflected. At first she turned from the group impatiently; but presently she looked again, and began to study her uncle's appearance with conscious deliberation. It was as if she had never seen him before and was receiving a first impression.

Lord Dawne was one of those men who make one think of

another and more picturesque age. He would have looked natural in black velvet and point lace. He was about five and thirty at that time, to judge by his appearance—tall, well-made, and strong with the slim strength of a race horse, all superfluous flesh and bone bred out of him. His skin was dark, clear, and colourless; his hair black, wavy, and abundant; his eyes deep blue, a contrast inherited from an Irish mother. "A Spanish hidalgo in appearance," Angelica decided at this point.

It was a sad face, as high-bred faces often are. You would not have been surprised to hear that his life had been blighted at the outset by some great sorrow or disappointment. But it was a strong face too, the face of a manly man, you would have said, and of one with self-denial, courage, endurance, and devotion enough for a hero and a martyr.

"Angelica," her grandfather broke in upon her reflections with kindly concern. "You look pale. Do you not feel well, my dear child?"

"Not exactly, thank you," Angelica answered mendaciously, with formal politeness, hoping thereby to save herself the annoyance of further remarks; then inwardly added, "sick at heart, in very truth," to save her conscience, which was painfully sensitive just then. When anyone addressed her, thought was suspended by the effort to answer, after which the rush returned, but the current had usually set in a new direction, as was now the case. Her uncle, as seen in the mirror, gave place, when she had spoken, to the Tenor's long low room as she had seen it that afternoon; "The light shone in and showed the shabby places. Should the light be shut out to conceal what is wrong? Oh, no! Show up, expose, make evident. Let in knowledge, the light——"

But here her grandfather arose. The evening was to end with service in the chapel. "Will you come, Angelica?" he asked. "Do you feel equal to the exertion?"

"Oh, yes," Angelica answered indifferently, letting herself go again to drift with the stream.

The private chapel at Morne was lavishly decorated, an ideal shrine the beauty of which alone would have inclined your heart to prayer and praise by reason of the pleasure it gave you, and of the desire, which is always a part of this form of pleasure, to express your gratitude in some sort.

On this occasion the altar was brilliantly illuminated, and as she passed in before Lord Dawne, she was attracted like a child by the light, and stationed herself so as to see it fully, admiring it as a spectator, but only so. The scene, although familiar, was always impressive, being so beautiful; and as she settled herself on a chair apart her spirit revived under its influence enough to enable her to entertain the hope that, by force of habit and association, that sensation of well-being which is due to the refined and delicate flattery of the senses, a soothing without excitement, merging in content, and restful to the verge of oblivion, would steal over her and gradually possess her to the exclusion of all importunate and painful thought. And this was what happened.

It came at a pause in the service when the people bent their heads, and seemed to wait; or rather followed upon that impressive moment as did the organ prelude, and the first notes of a glorious voice—the voice of a woman who suddenly sang.

Angelica looked up amazed by the fervour of it, while a feeling, not new, but strange from its intensity, took possession of her, steeping her soul in bliss, a feeling that made her both tremble and be glad. She thought no more of the lonely grave, but of an angel in ecstasy, an angel in heaven. She looked around, she raised her eyes to the altar, she tried to seize upon some idea which should continue with her, and be a key with which she could unlock this fountain of joy here-after when she would. She almost felt for the moment as if it would be worthy to grovel for such opium at the knees of an oleosaccharine priest and contribute to his support forever. She tried to think of something to which to compare the feel-ing, but in vain. In the effort to fix it her mind and mem-ory became a blank, and for a blissful interval she could not think, she could only feel. Then came the inevitable moment of grateful acknowledgment when her senses brought of their best to pay for their indulgence—their best on this occasion being that vow to Israfil which presently she found herself renewing. She would indeed be true.

After this surfeit of sensuous distraction she retired to her room, the old room, as far away from Diavolo's as possible, which she had always occupied at the castle. She dismissed her maid, and sat down to think; but she was suffering from nervous irritability by this time, and could not rest. She drew up a blind and looked out of the open window. The night was calm, the air was freshly caressing, a crescent moon hung in the indigo sky, and there were stars, bright stars. Up from the pine woods which clothed the castle hill balsamic airs were wafted, and murmurs came as of voices inviting—friendly voices of nature claiming a kinship with her, which she herself had recognized from her earliest childhood. Out there in the open was the unpolluted altar at which she was bidden to worship, and in view of that, with the healthy breath of night expanding her lungs revivingly, she felt that her late experiences, in the midst of perfumes too sweet to be wholesome, and with the help of accessaries too luxurious to be anything but enervating, had been degrading to that better part of her to which the purity and peace of night appealed. She would go shrive herself in haunted solitudes, and listen to the voice which spoke to her heart alone. saying "Only be true," in the silence of those scenes incomparable which tend to reverence, promote endeavour, and prolong love.

She went to her door, opened it, looked out, and listened. The corridor was all in darkness: an excessive silence pervaded the place; the whole household had apparently retired.

With confident steps, although in the dark, Angelica went to Diavolo's room, and presently returned with a suit of his clothes. These she put on, and then, without haste, went downstairs, crossed the hall, opened a narrow door which led into a dark, damp, flagged passage, along which she groped for some distance, then descended a crooked stone staircase at the foot of which was a heavy door. This she opened with a key, careless of the noise she made, and found herself out in the open air, under the stars, on a gravel walk, with a broad lawn stretched before her. She stood a moment, breathing deeply in pure enjoyment of the air, then put up both hands to rearrange a little cloth cap she wore which was slipping from off her abundant hair. Then she threw up her arms and stretched every limb in the joy of perfect freedom from restraint; and then with strong bounds she cleared the grassy space, dashed down a rocky step, and found herself a substance amongst the shadows out in the murmuring woods.

When she returned she was making less vigorous demonstrations of superabundant strength and vitality, but still her step was swift, firm, and elastic; and she was running up the grand staircase from the hall when she saw that the door at the top, leading into the suite of rooms occupied by Lord Dawne when he was at the castle, was wide open, showing the room beyond, brilliantly lighted.

She would have to pass that open door or stay downstairs

till it was shut; but the latter she did not feel inclined to do,
so, with scarcely a pause to nerve herself for what might happen, she continued rapidly to ascend the stairs.

As she expected, when she reached the top, her uncle
appeared.

"Oh!" he exclaimed in surprise, seeing Diavolo as he supposed emerging from the darkness. "I thought it was Angelica's step. I fancied I heard her go down some time ago, and
I have been waiting for her. She complained of not feeling
well this evening, and I thought she might possibly want
something. Come in." He had turned to lead the way as he
spoke. "By-the-bye," he broke off, "what are you doing here,
you young rascal?"

Angelica, overcome by one of her mischievous impulses,
and grinning broadly, boldly followed her uncle into the
room.

"I had forgotten for a moment that you ought not to be
here, it is so natural to find you marauding about the place at
night," he pursued, bending down to adjust the wick of a
lamp that was flaring as he spoke. Angelica sat down, and
coolly waited for him to turn and look at her, which he did
when he had done with the lamp, meeting her dark eyes
unsuspectingly at first, then with fixed attention inquiringly.

"Angelica!" he exclaimed. "How can you!"

"I have been out in the woods," she rejoined with her
accustomed candour. "The suffocating fumes of incense and
orthodoxy overpowered me in the chapel, and I was miserable
besides—soul-sick. But the fresh air is a powerful tonic, and
it has exhilarated me, the stars have strengthened me, the
voices of the night spoke peace to me, and the pleasant creatures, visible and invisible, gave me welcome as one of themselves, and showed me how to attain to their joy in life."
She bent forward to brush some fresh earth from the leg of
her trousers. "But you would have me forego these innocent,
healthy-minded, invigorating exercises, I suppose, because I
am a woman," she pursued. "You would allow Diavolo to
disport himself so at will, and approve rather than object,
although he is not so strong as I am. And then these clothes,
which are decent and convenient for him, besides being a
greater protection than any you permit me to wear, you think
immodest for me—you mass of prejudice."

Lord Dawne made no reply. He had taken a seat, and
remained with his eyes fixed on the floor for some seconds

after she had spoken. There was neither agreement nor dissent in his attitude, however; he was simply reflecting.

"What is it, Angelica?" he said at last, looking her full in the face.

"What is what?" she asked defiantly.

"What is the matter?" he answered. "There is something wrong, I see, and if it is anything that you would like to talk about—I don't pretend to offer you advice, but sometimes when one speaks—you know, however, what a comfort it is to 'talk a thing out,' as you used to call it when you were a little girl." He looked at her and smiled. When she entered the room fresh from the open air a brilliant colour glowed in her cheeks, but now she was pale to her lips, which, perceiving, caused him to rise hastily, and add: "But I am afraid you have tired yourself, and"—glancing at the clock—"it is nearly breakfast time. I'll go and get you something."

After a considerable interval he returned with a tray upon which was a plentiful variety of refreshments, prawns in aspic jelly, cold chicken and tongue, a freshly opened tin of *paté de foie gras*, cake, bread, butter, and champagne.

"I think I've brought everything," he remarked, surveying the tray complacently when he had put it down upon a table beside her.

"You've forgotten the salt," snapped Angelica.

His complacency vanished, and he retired apologetically to remedy the omission.

"Do you remember the night you and Diavolo taught me where to find food in my father's house?" he asked when he returned.

"Yes," Angelica answered with a grin; and then she expanded into further reminiscences of that occasion, by which time she was in such a good humour that she began to feel hungry, and under the stimulating influences of food and champagne she told her uncle the whole story of her intimacy with the Tenor.

Lord Dawne listened with interest, but almost in silence. The occasion was not one, as it appeared to him, which it would be well to improve. He discussed the matter with her, however, as well as he could without offering her advice or expressing an opinion of her conduct; and, in consequence of this wise forbearance on his part, she found herself the better in every way for the interview.

CHAPTER VII.

ANGELICA awoke unrefreshed after a few hours of light and restless sleep, much broken by dreams. "Dead! dead!" was the first thought in her mind, but it came unaccompanied by any feeling. "Is Israfil really dead—buried—gone from us all forever?" she asked herself in a kind of wonder. It was not at the thought of his death that she was wondering, however, but because the recollection of it did not move her in any way. Reflections which had caused her the sharpest misery only yesterday recurred to her now without affecting her in the least degree—except in that they made her feel herself to be a kind of monster of callousness, coldness, and egotism. The lonely grave, looking deserted already, with the rain-bespattered, mud-bedraggled flowers fading upon it; the man himself as she had known him; his goodness, his kindness, the disinterested affection he had lavished upon her—she dwelt upon these things; she racked her brain to recall them in order to reawaken her grief and remorse, but in vain. Mind and memory responded to the effort, but her own heart she could not touch. The acute stage was over for the moment, and a most distressing numbness, attended by a sense of chilliness and general physical discomfort, had succeeded it. The rims of her eyes were red and the lids still swollen by the tears of the day before; but the state of weeping, with the nervous energy and mental excitement which had been the first consequence of the shock, was a happy one compared with the dry inhuman apathy of this, and she strove to recall it, but only succeeded in adding the old sensation of discontent with everything as it is and nothing is worth while to her already deep depression. She loved order and regularity in a household, but now the very thought of the old accustomed dull routine of life at the castle exasperated her. After her grandfather would come her uncle, and after him in all human probability Diavolo would succeed, and there would be a long succession of solemn servants, each attending to the same occupations which had been carried on by other servants in the same place for hundreds of years; horrible monotony, all tending to nothing! For she saw as in a vision the end of the race to which she belonged. They and their like were doomed, and, with them, the distinguished bearing, the high-bred reserve, the refined simplicity and

dignity of manner which had held them above the common
herd, a class apart, until she came, were also doomed. ''I am
of the day,'' she said to herself; ''the vulgar outcome of a
vulgar era, bred so, I suppose, that I may see through others,
which is to me the means of self-defence. I see that in this
dispute of 'womanly or unwomanly,' the question to be asked
is, not 'What is the pursuit?' but 'What are the proceeds?'
No social law-maker ever *said* 'Catch me letting a woman into
anything that pays!' It was left for me to translate the principle into the vernacular.''

She breakfasted upstairs so that she might not have to talk,
but went down immediately afterward in order to find somebody to speak to, so rapid were the alternations of her moods.
It was not in Angelica's nature to conceal anything she had
done from her friends for long, and before she had been
twenty-four hours at the castle she had taken her Aunt Claudia,
and the lady known to them all intimately as ''Ideala,'' into
her confidence; but neither of them attempted to improve the
occasion. They said even less than her uncle had done, and
this reticence perplexed Angelica. She would have liked them
to make much of her wickedness, to have reasoned with her,
lectured her, and incited her to argue. She did not perceive,
as they did, that she was one of those who must work out their
own salvation in fear and trembling, and she was angry with
them because they continued their ordinary avocations as if
nothing had happened when everything had gone so wrong
with her.

The weary day dragged its slow length along. A walk
about the grounds, luncheon, a long drive, calling at Ilverthorpe on the way back for letters; afternoon tea with her
grandfather in the oriel room, and afterward the accustomed
wait with bowed head for the chime, which floated up at last
from afar, distinct, solemn, slow, and weary like the voice of
one who vainly repeats a blessed truth to ears that will not
hear:

He, watch-ing o-ver   Is-ra-el,   slumbers not, nor sleeps.

Her grandfather raised his velvet cap, and held it above his
bald head while he repeated the words aloud, after which he

muttered a prayer for the restoration of "Holy Church," then rose, and, leaning heavily on his ebony stick, walked from the room with the springless step of age, accompanied by his daughter Claudia and his son, and followed by two deer hounds, old and faithful friends who seldom left him. When the door closed upon this little procession, Angelica found herself alone with her aunt Lady Fulda, to whom she had not spoken since the day before. They were sitting near to each other, Angelica being in the window, from whence she had looked down upon the tree-tops and the distant city while they waited for the chime, the melancholy cadence of which had added something to the chill misery of her mood.

"Do you still believe it?" she asked ironically, and then felt as if she were always asking that question in that tone.

Lady Fulda had also looked about as she listened, but now she left the window, and, taking a seat opposite to Angelica, answered bravely, her face lighting up as she spoke: "I do believe it."

"Then why did he let a man like that die?" Angelica asked defiantly. "Why did he create such a man at all merely to kill him? Wouldn't a commoner creature have done as well?"

"We are not told that any creature is common in his sight," Lady Fulda answered gently. "But suppose they were, would a common creature have produced the same effect upon you?"

"Do you mean to say you think he was created to please me——"

"Oh, no, not that," Lady Fulda hastily interposed, and Angelica, perceiving that she had at last found somebody who would kindly improve the occasion, turned round from the window, and settled herself for a fray. "And I don't mean," Lady Fulda pursued, "I dare not presume to question; but still—oh, I must say it! Your heart has been very hard. Would anything but death have touched you so? Had not every possible influence been vainly tried before that to soften you?"

Angelica smiled disagreeably. "You are insinuating that he died for me, to save my soul," she politely suggested.

Her aunt took no notice of the sneer. "Oh, not for you, alone," she answered earnestly; "but for all the hundreds upon whom you, in your position, and with your attractions, will bring the new power of your goodness to bear. You cannot think, with all your scepticism, that such a man has lived and died for nothing. You must have some knowledge or idea of the consequences of such a life in such a world, of the influence for good of a great talent employed as his was, the one as an example and the other as a power to inspire and control."

Angelica did not attempt to answer this, and there was a pause; then she began again; "I did grasp something of what you mean, I saw for a moment the beauty of holiness, and the joy of it continued with me for a little. Then I went to tell Israfil. I was determined to be true, and I should have been true had I not lost him; but now my heart is harder than ever, and I shall be worse than I was before."

"Oh, no!" her aunt exclaimed, "you are deceiving yourself. If you had found him there that day, your good resolutions would only have lasted until you had bound him to you —enslaved him; and then, although you would have carefully avoided breaking the letter of the law, you would have broken the spirit; you would have tried to fascinate him, and bring him down to your own level; you would have made him loathe himself, and then you would have mocked him."

"Like the evil-minded heroine of a railway novel!" Angelica began, then added doggedly: "You wrong me, Aunt Fulda. There is no one whose respect I valued more. There is nothing in right or reason I would not have done to win it—that is to say, if there had been anything I could have done. But I do not think now that there was." This last depressing thought brought about another of those rapid revulsions of feeling to which she had been subject during these latter days, and she broke off for a moment, then burst out afresh to just the opposite effect: "I do not know, though. I am not sure of anything. Probably you are right, and I deceived myself. I inherit bad principles from my ancestors, and it may be that I can no more get rid of them than I could get rid of the gout or any other hereditary malady, by simply resolving to cure myself. It is different with you. You were born good. I was born bad, and delight in my wickedness."

"Angelica!" her aunt remonstrated, "do not talk in that reckless way."

"Well, I exaggerate," Angelica allowed, veering again, as the wind does in squally weather before it sets steadily from a single quarter. "But what have I done after all that you should take me to task so seriously? Wrong, certainly; but still I have not broken a single commandment."

"Not one of the Decalogue, perhaps; but you have sinned against the whole spirit of uprightness. Has it never occurred to you that you may keep the ten commandments strictly, and yet be a most objectionable person? You might smoke, drink, listen at doors, repeat private conversations, open other people's letters, pry amongst their papers, be vulgar and offensive in conversation, and indecent in dress—altogether detestable, if your code of morality were confined to the ten commandments. But why will you talk like this, Angelica? Why will you be so defiant, when your heart is breaking, as I know it is?"

Angelica hid her face in her hands with one dry sob that made her whole frame quiver.

"Oh, do not be so hard!" the other woman implored. "Listen to your own heart, listen to all that is best in yourself; you have good impulses enough, I know you have; and you have been called to the Higher Life more than once, but you would not hear."

"Yes"—thoughtfully—"but it is no use—no help. I never profit by experiences because I don't object to things while they are happening. It is only afterward, when all the excitement is over and I have had time to reflect, that I become dissatisfied." And she threw herself back in her easy-chair, crossed one leg over the other so as to display a fair amount of slender foot and silk-clocked stocking, as it is the elegant fashion of the day to do; clasped her hands behind her head, and fixed her eyes on the ceiling, being evidently determined to let the subject drop.

Lady Fulda compressed her lips. She was baffled, and she was perplexed. A quarter rang from the city clocks. "Do you know," she began again, "I have a fancy—many people have—that a time comes to us all—an hour when we are called upon to choose between good and evil. It is a quarter since we heard the chime——"

"Only a quarter!" Angelica ejaculated. "It seems an age!"

"But suppose this is your hour," Lady Fulda patiently pursued. "One precious quarter of it has gone already, and still you harden your heart. You are asked to choose now, you are called to the Higher Life; you must know that you are being called—specially—this moment. And what if it should be for the last time? What if, after this, you are deprived of the power to choose, and forced by that which is evil in you to wander away from all that is good and pure and pleasant into the turmoil and trouble, the falseness, the illusion, and the maddening unrest of the other life? You know it all. You can imagine what it would be when that last loophole of escape, upon which we all rely—perhaps unconsciously—was closed, when you knew you never could return; when you came to be shut out from hope, a prey to remorse, a tired victim compelled to pursue excitement, and always to pursue it, descending all the time, and finding it escape you more and more till at last even that hateful resource was lost to you, and you found yourself at the end of the road to perdition, a worn out woman, face to face with despair!''

Angelica slowly unclasped her hands from behind her head, let her chin sink on her chest, and looked up from under her eyebrows at her aunt. Her eyes were bright, but otherwise her face was as still as a statue's, and what she thought or felt it was impossible to say. "It is idle to talk of choice," she answered coldly. "I *had* chosen—honestly. I told you; you see what has come of it!''

"Forgive me," said Lady Fulda, "but you had not chosen *honestly*. You had not chosen the better life—to lead it for its own sake, but for his. You wanted to bring yourself nearer to him, and you would have made goodness a means to that end if you could. But you see it was not the right way, and it has not succeeded.''

Angelica sat up, and the dull look left her face. She seemed interested. "You see through all my turpitude," she observed, affecting to smile, although in truth she was more moved than her pride would allow her to show.

Her aunt sighed, seeing no sign of softening. She feared it was labour lost, but still she felt impelled to try once more before she renounced the effort. She was nervous about it, however, being naturally diffident, and hesitated, trying to collect her thoughts; and in the interval the evening shadows deepened, the half hour chimed from the city clocks, and then she spoke. "Just think," she said sadly—"Just think what it will be when you have gone from here this evening—if you carry out your determination and return after dinner; just think what it will be when you find yourself alone again in that great house with the night before you; and your aching heart, and your bitter thoughts, and the remorse which gnaws without ceasing, for companions; and not one night of it only but all the years to come, and every phase of it; from the sharp pain of this moment to the dull discontent in which it ends, and from which nothing on earth will rouse you; think of yourself then without comfort and without hope." Angelica changed her position uneasily. "You still hesitate," Lady Fulda continued; "you are loath to commit yourself; you would rather not choose; you prefer to believe yourself a puppet at the mercy of a capricious demon who moves you this way and that as the idle fancy seizes him. But you are no puppet. You have the right of choice; you *must* choose; and, having chosen, if you look up, the Power Divine will be extended to you to support you, or—but either way your choice will at once become a force for good or evil."

She ended abruptly, and then there was another long pause.

Angelica's mind was alive to everything—to the rustle of summer foliage far below; to the beauty of the woman before her, to the power of her presence, to the absolute integrity which was so impressive in all she said, to her high-bred simplicity, to the grace of her attitude at that moment as she sat with an elbow on the arm of her chair, covering her eyes with one white hand; to the tearless turmoil in her own breast, the sense of suffering not to be relieved, the hopeless ache. Was there any way of escape from herself? Her conscience whispered one. But was there only one? The struggle of the last few days had recommenced; was it to go on like this forever and ever, over and over again? What a prospect! And, oh! to be able to end it! somehow! anyhow! Oh, for the courage to choose! but she must choose, she knew that; Aunt Fulda was right, her hour had come. The momentous question had been asked, and it must be answered once for all. If she should refuse to take the hand held out to help her now, where would she drift to eventually? Should she end by consorting with people like—and she thought of an odious woman; or come to be talked of at clubs, named lightly by low men—and she thought of some specimens of that class. But why should she arrive at any decision? Why should she feel compelled to adopt a settled plan of action? Why could she not go on as she had done hitherto? Was there really no standing still? Were people really rising or sinking always, doing good or evil? Why, no, for what harm had she done? Quick, answering to the question with a pang, the rush of recollection caught her, and again the vow, made, and forgotten for the moment, as soon as made, burned in her heart: "Israfil! Israfil! only forgive me, and I will be true."

She did not wait to think again. The mere repetition was a

renewal of her vow, and in the act she had unconsciously decided.

Slipping from her chair to the ground, she laid her head on Lady Fulda's lap.

"I wish I could be sure of myself," she said, sighing deeply. "You must help me, Aunt Fulda."

"Now the dear Lord help you," was the soft reply.

And almost at the same moment, the city clocks began to strike, and they both raised their heads involuntarily, waiting for the chime.

It rang at last with a new significance for Angelica. The hour was over which had been her hour; a chapter of her life had closed with it forever; and when she looked up then, she found herself in another world, wherein she would walk henceforth with other eyes to better purpose.

CHAPTER VIII.

ANGELICA drove back to Ilverthorpe alone directly after dinner, and went straight to bed. She slept from ten o'clock that night till the next morning, and awoke to the consciousness that the light of day was garish, that she herself was an insignificant trifle on the face of the earth, and that everything was unsatisfactory.

"Now, had I been the heroine of a story," she said to herself, "it would have been left to the reader's imagination to suppose that I remained forever in the state of blissful exaltation up to which Aunt Fulda wound me by her eloquence yesterday. Here I am already, however—with my intentions still set fair, I believe—but in spirit, oh, so flat! a siphon of soda-water from which the gas has escaped. Well, I suppose it must be recharged, that is all. Oh, dear! I *am* so tired. Just five minutes more, Angelica dear, take five minutes more!" She closed her eyes. "I'm glad I'm the mistress and not the maid—am I though? Poor Elizabeth! It spoils my comfort just to think of her always obliged to be up and dressed—with a racking headache, perhaps, hardly able to rise, but forced to drag herself up somehow nevertheless to wait upon worthless selfish me. Live for others"—Here, however, thought halted, grew confused, ceased altogether for an imperceptible interval, and was then succeeded by vivid dreams She fancied that she had wavered in her new resolutions, and gone back to her old idea.   If the conditions of life were different, *she* would be different, in spirit and in truth, instead of only in outward seeming as now appeared to be the case.   She was doing no good in the world; her days were steeped in idleness; her life was being wasted.   Surely it would be a creditable thing for her to take her violin, and make it what it was intended to be, a delight to thousands. Such genius as hers was never meant for the benefit of a little circle only, but for the world at large, and all she wanted was to fulfil the end and object of her being by going to work. She said so to Mr. Kilroy, and he made no objection, which surprised her, for always hitherto he had expressed himself strongly on the subject even to the extent of losing his temper on one occasion.   Now, however, he heard her in silence, with his eyes fixed on the floor, and when she had said her say he uttered not a word, but just rose from his seat with a deep sigh—almost a groan—and a look of weariness and perplexity in his eyes that smote her to the heart, and slowly left the room.   .

"I make his life a burden to him," she said to herself.   "I can do nothing right.   I wish 1 was dead.   I do."   And then she followed him to the library.

He was sitting at his writing table with his arms folded upon it, and his face bowed down and hidden on them, and he did not move when she entered.

The deep dejection of his attitude frightened her.   She hastened to him, knelt down beside him, and putting her arms round his neck drew him toward her; and then he looked at her, trying to smile, but a more miserable face she had never beheld.

"O Daddy, Daddy," she cried remorsefully, "I didn't mean to vex you.   I'll never play in public as long as I live—there! I promise you."

"I don't wish you to make rash promises," he answered hoarsely.   "But if you could care for me a little——"

"Daddy—*dear*—I do care for you.   I do, indeed," she protested.   "I like to know you are here.   I like to be able to come to you when—whenever I like.   1 cannot do without you.   If anything happened to you——"

The shock of such a dreadful possibility awoke her.   She was less refreshed than she had been when she first opened her eyes that morning, but she sprang out of bed in an instant.

The blinds were up and the windows open as usual; the sun had spun round to the south, and now streamed hotly in, making her feel belated.

"Elizabeth!" she called, then went to the bell and rang it, standing a moment when she had done so, and looking down as if to consider the blurred reflection of her bare white feet on the polished floor; but only for an instant, for the paramount feeling that possessed her was one of extreme haste. The painful impression of that dream was still vividly present with her, and she wanted to do *something*, but what precisely she did not wait to ask herself. As soon as she was dressed, one duty after another presented itself as usual, and, equally as usual with her in her own house, was carefully performed, so that she was fully occupied until lunch time, but after lunch she ordered the carriage, and drove into Morningquest to do some shopping for the household. This task accomplished, she intended to return, but as she passed the station the recollection of the dream, of her husband's bowed head, of the utter misery in his face when he looked up at her, of the pain in his voice when he spoke, and the effort he made in his kindly way to control it, so that he might not hurt her with an implied reproach when he said, "If you could care for me a little——" Dear Daddy! always so tender for her! always so kindly forbearing! What o'clock was it? The London express would go out in five minutes. It was the train he had gone by himself last time. How could she let him go alone? Stop at the station, write a line to Elizabeth—"Please pack up my things, and follow me to town immediately" Get me a ticket, quick! Here is the train. In. Off. Thank Heaven!

Angelica threw herself back in the centre seat of the compartment, and closed her eyes. The hurry and excitement of action suited her; her lips were smiling, and her cheeks were flushed. There was a young man seated opposite to her who stared so persistently that at last she became aware of his admiring gaze and immediately despised him, although why she should despise him for admiring her she could not have told. When he had left the carriage, a charming-looking old Quaker lady, who was then the only other passenger, addressed Angelica in the quaint grammar of her sect. "Art thee travelling alone, dear child?"

"Yes," Angelica answered, with the affable smile and intonation for which the Heavenly Twins were noted.

"Doubtless there are plenty of friends to meet thee at thy

journey's end,' the lady suggested, responding sympathetically to Angelica's pleasantness.

"Plenty," said Angelica—"not to mention my husband."
When she had said it she felt proud for the first time since her
marriage because she had a husband.

"Ah!" the lady ejaculated, somewhat sadly. "Well,"
she added, betraying her thought, "in these sad days the
sooner a young girl has the strong arm of a good man to protect her the better." Then she folded her hands and turned
her placid face to the window.

Angelica looked at her for a little, wondering at the delicate
pink and white of her withered cheek, and becoming aware of a
tune at the same time set to the words *A good man! A good
man!* by the thundering throbbing crank as they sped along.
Daddy was a good man—*suppose she lost him?* Nobody belonged
to her as he did—*suppose she lost him?* There was nobody else
in the world to whom she could go by right as she was going
to him, nobody else in whom she had such perfect confidence,
nobody on whose devotion to herself she could rely as she did
on his; she was all the world to him. *A good man! A good
man! Suppose—suppose she lost him?*

The sudden dread gripped her heart painfully. It was not
death she feared, but that worse loss, a change in his affection.
He was a simple, upright, honourable man—what would he say
if he knew? But need he ever know? The question was
answered as soon as asked, for Angelica felt in her heart that
she could bear to lose him and live alone better than be beside
·him with that invisible barrier of a deception always between
them to keep them apart. It was a need of her nature to be
known for what she was exactly to those with whom she lived.

The train drew up at the terminus, and the moment she
moved she was again conscious of that terrible feeling of haste
which had beset her more or less the whole day long.

"No one to meet thee?" the Quaker lady said.

"No, I am not expected," Angelica answered, with her
hand on the handle of the door. "I am a bad wife in a state
of repentance, going to give a good husband an unpleasant
surprise." She sprang from the carriage, hastened across the
platform, and got into a hansom, telling the man to drive
"quick! quick!"

On arriving at the house she entered unannounced, after
some little opposition from a new manservant who did not
know her by sight, and was evidently inclined to believe her to be

an impostor bent on pillage. This check on the threshold caused her to feel deeply humiliated.

Her husband happened to be crossing the hall at the time, but he went on without noticing the arrival at the door, and she followed him to his study. Unconscious of her presence, he passed into the room before her with a heavy step, and as she noted this it seemed to her that she saw him now for the first time as he really was—of good figure and quiet undemonstrative manners; faultlessly dressed; distinguished in appearance, upon the whole, if not actually handsome; a man of position and means, accustomed to social consideration as was evident by his bearing; and not old as she was wont to think him— what difference did twenty years'make at *their* respective ages? No, not old, but—unhappy, and lonely, for if she did not care to be with him who would? Her heart smote her, and she stepped forward impetuously, anxious above everything to make amends.

"Daddy!" she gasped, grasping his arm.

Startled, Mr. Kilroy turned round, and looked down into her face incredulously.

"Is it you—Angelica?" he faltered. "Is anything the matter, dear?" Then suddenly his whole being changed. A glad light came into his eyes, making him look years younger, and he was about to take her in his arms, but she coldly repulsed him, acting on one of two impulses, the other being to respond, to cling close to him, to say something loving.

"There is nothing the matter," she began. "I thought I should like to come back to you—at least"—recollecting herself—"that isn't true. But I do wish I had never separated myself from you in any way. I do wish I had been different." And she threw herself into a low, easy, leather-lined armchair, and leant back, looking up to him with appealing eyes.

Mr. Kilroy's pride and affection made him nicely observant of any change in Angelica, but still he was at a loss to understand this new freak, and her manner alarmed him.

"I am afraid you are not well," he said anxiously.

She sat up restlessly, then threw herself back in the chair once more, and lay there with her chin on her chest, in an utterly dejected attitude, not looking up even when she spoke. "Oh, I am well, thank you," she said, "quite well."

"Then something has annoyed you," he went on kindly. "Tell me what it is, dear child. I am the proper person to come to when things go wrong, you know. So tell me all about it. I –I——" he hesitated. She so often snubbed any demonstration of affection that he shrank from expressing what he felt, but another look at her convinced him that there was little chance of a rebuff to-day. He remained at a safe distance, however, taking a chair that stood beside an oval table near to which he happened to be standing.

Newspapers and magazines were piled up on the table, and these he pushed aside, making room for his right forearm to rest on the cool mahogany, on the polished surface of which he kept up a continual nervous telick-telick with the ends of his finger nails as he spoke. "If you do not come to me for everything you want, to whom will you go?" he inquired, lamely if pleasantly, being perturbed by the effort he was making to conceal his uneasiness and assume a cheerful demeanour both at once. "And there is nothing I would not do for you, as you know, I am sure." He tapped a few times on the table. "In fact, I should be only too glad if you would give me the opportunity"—tap, tap, tap—"a little oftener, you know"—tap, tap, tap. "What I want to say is, I should like you to consult me and, eh, to ask me, and all that sort of thing, if you want anything"—advice he had been going to add, but modestly changed the word—"money, for instance." And now his countenance cleared. He thought he had accidentally discovered the difficulty. "I expect you have been running into debt, eh?" He spoke quite playfully, so greatly was he relieved to think it was only that; "and you have been thinking of me as a sort of stern parent, eh? who would storm and all that sort of thing. But, my dear child, you mustn't do that. You should never forget 'with all my worldly goods I thee endow.' I assure you, ever since I uttered those words, I have felt that I held the property in trust for you and——" he had been going to add our children, but sighed instead. "I have, I know, remonstrated with you when I thought you unduly extravagant. I could not conscientiously countenance undue extravagance in so young a wife; but still I hope you have never had to complain of any want of liberality on my part in—in anything. In fact, what is the good of money to me if you do not care to spend it? Come, now, how much is it this time? Just tell me and have done with it, and then we will go somewhere, or make plans, and 'have a good time,' as the Americans call it. I have a better box than usual for you at the opera this year—I think I told you. And I never lend it to anybody. I like to keep it empty for you in case you care to go at any time. And I have season tickets, see"—he got up and rummaged in a drawer until he found them—"for everything, I almost think. I go sometimes myself just to see what is going on, you know, and if it is the sort of thing you would like, so as to know what to take you to when you come. And I accept all the nice invitations for you, conditionally, of course. I say if you are in town at the time, and I hope you may be (which is true enough always), you will be happy to go, or words to that effect. So you see there is plenty for you to do at any time in the way of amusement. I am always making arrangements, it is like getting ready to welcome you. When I am answering invitations or doing the theatres I feel quite as if I expected you. It is childish, perhaps, but it makes something to look forward to, and when I am busy preparing for you, somehow the days do not seem so blank."

Angelica felt something rise in her throat, but she neither spoke nor moved.

"Or we might go to Paris," he proceeded tentatively. "Shall we? I could pair with someone till the end of the session. We might go anywhere, in fact, and I should enjoy a holiday if—if you would accompany me." He looked at her with a smile, but the intermittent telick, telick, telick of his nervous drumming on the table told that he was far from feeling all the confidence he assumed. For in truth Angelica's attitude alarmed him more and more. On other occasions, when he had tried to be more than usually kind and indulgent, she had always called him a nice old thing or made some such affable if somewhat patronizing acknowledgment, even when she was out of temper; but now, finding that he was waiting for an answer, she just looked up at him once, then fixed her eyes on the ground again, and spoke at last in a voice so hopeless and toneless that he would not have recognized it.

"I think I have only just this moment learnt to appreciate you," she said. "I used to accept all your kind attentions as merely my due, but I know now how little I deserve them, and I wish I could be different. I wish I could repay you. I wish I could undo the past and begin all over again—begin by loving you as a wife should. You are ten thousand times too good for me. Yet I *have* cared for you in a way," she protested; "not a kind way, perhaps, but still I have relied upon you—upon your friendship. I have felt a sense of security in

the certainty of your affection for me—and presumed upon it.
O Daddy! why have you let me do as I like?"

Mr. Kilroy's face became rigid, and the fingers with which
he had kept up that intermittent tapping on the table turned
cold.

"What do you mean, Angelica?" he asked hoarsely. "Are
you in earnest? Have you done—anything—or are you only
tormenting me? If you are—it is hard, you know. I do care
for you; I always have done; and I have never ceased to look
forward to a time when you would love me too. God help me
if you have come to tell me that that time will never come."

Again that lump rose in Angelica's throat. A horrible form
of emotion had seized upon her: "I had better tell you and
get it over," she said, speaking in hurried gasps, and sitting
up, but not looking at him. "You will care less when you
know exactly. You will see then that I am not worth a
thought. I am suffering horribly. I want to *shriek.*" She
tore her jacket open, and threw her hat on the floor. "What
a relief. I was suffocating. I don't know where to begin."
She looked up at him, then stopped short, frightened by the
drawn and haggard look in his face, and tranquillised too,
forgetting herself in the effort to think of something to say to
relieve him. "But you do know all about it," she added,
speaking more naturally than she had done yet. "I told
you——"

"Told me *what?*"

"About—about—you thought I was inventing it—that story
—about the Tenor and the Boy."

Mr. Kilroy curved his fingers together and held them up
over the table for a moment as if he were about to tap upon it
again, and it was as if he had asked a question.

"It was all true," Angelica proceeded, "all that I told you.
But there was more."

Mr. Kilroy uttered a low exclamation, and hung his head as
if in shame. The colour had fled from his face, leaving it
ghastly gray for a moment like that of a dead man. Angelica
half rose to go to him, fearing he would faint, but he had
recovered before she could carry out her intention. She
looked at him compassionately. She would have given her
life to be able to spare him now, but it was too late, and there
was nothing for it but to go on and get it over.

"You remember the picture I had painted—'Music'?" Mr.
Kilroy made a gesture of assent. "That was his portrait."

"I always understood it was an ideal singer."

"An *idealized* singer was what I said; but it was not even that, as you would have seen for yourself if you had ever gone to the cathedral. It is a good likeness, nothing more."

"And you had yourself put into a picture with a common tenor, and exhibited to all the world!"

"Yes, and all the world thought it a great condescension. But he did not consent to it, or sit for it. He objected to the picture as strongly as you do. He was not a *common* tenor at all. He was an old and intimate friend of Uncle Dawne's and Dr. Galbraith's. They all—all our people—knew him. He was often at Morne before you came to Ilverthorpe; but I did not know it myself until afterward."

"Afterward?" he questioned.

"I had better go on from where I left off," she replied, her confidence returning. "I told you about the accident on the river, and his finding out who I was, and his contempt for me; and I told you I desired most sincerely to win his respect, and you advised me to go to him and endeavour to do so. Well, I went." She paused, and Mr. Kilroy looked hard at her; his face was flushed now. "And he was dead," she gasped.

Mr. Kilroy seemed bewildered. "I don't—understand," he exclaimed.

"I told you there was more, and that was it—that was all. He was dead," she repeated.

Mr. Kilroy drew a deep breath, and leant back in his chair. "I am ashamed to say I feel relieved," he began, as if speaking to himself; "yet I scarcely know what I expected." He looked down thoughtfully at his own hand as it lay upon the table. He wanted to say something more, but his mind moved slowly, and no words came at first. He was obliged to make a great effort to collect himself, and in the interval he resumed that irregular tapping upon the table. It maddened Angelica, who found herself forced to watch and wait for the recurrence of the sound.

"Let me tell you, though—let me finish the story," she exclaimed, at last unable to bear it any longer; and then she gave him every detail of her doings since last they parted.

Mr. Kilroy let his hand drop on the table, and listened without looking at her. "And that is all?" he said, when she had finished. "I mean—have you really told me all, Angelica?"

She met his eyes fearlessly, and there was something in her face, something innocent, an unsuspicious look of inquiry such as a child assumes when it waits to be questioned which would have made him ashamed of a degrading doubt had he entertained one.

"You were not—you did not care for him?"

"Oh, yes!" she exclaimed with most perfect and reassuring candour, "I cared for him. Of course I cared for him. Haven't I told you? No one could know such a man and not care for him."

"Thank God!" he said softly, with tremulous lips. "It would have broken my heart if he had not been such a man."

The words brought down upon him one of Angelica's tornado-tempests of unreasonable wrath. "Are you insinuating that my good conduct depended upon his good character?" she demanded. "Are you no better than those hateful French people who have no conception of anything unusual in a woman that does not end in gross impropriety of conduct; and fill their books with nothing else?"

Mr. Kilroy's face flushed. "Such an unworthy suspicion would never have occurred to me in connection with yourself," he said. "At the risk of appearing ungenerous, I must call your attention to the fact that it is you yourself who have been the first to allude to the bare possibility of such a thing. For my own part, if you chose to travel round the world alone with a man, at night or at any other time that suited your convenience, I should be content to know that you were doing so, especially if it amused you, such is my perfect confidence in your integrity, and in the discretion with which you choose your friends."

"I beg your pardon, forgive me!" Angelica humbly ejaculated. "You shame me by a delicacy which I can only respect and admire in you. I cannot imitate it; it is beyond me."

"I owe *you* an apology," he answered. "I should have spoken plainly. It was your feelings—your heart, not your conduct, that I suspected. You have never pretended to love me—to be in love with me, and your Tenor was a younger man, and more attractive."

"Not to me," Angelica hastily and sincerely asseverated.

She did not look up to see the effect of her words upon Mr. Kilroy. Her eyes had been fixed on his feet as she spoke, and now it struck her that they were exceedingly well-shaped feet, and well-booted in the quiet way characteristic of the man. Everything about him was unobtrusive as his own manner, but good as his own heart.

Angelica leant back in her chair, and a long silence ensued, during which she lapsed into her old attitude, lying back in her chair, her hands on the arms, her chin on her chest, her wandering glance upon the ground, so that she did not see that her husband was watching her with eyes that filled as he looked. What was to be the end of this? Should she lose his affection? Would she be turned out of the kind heart that had loved her with all her faults, and cherished her with a patient, enduring, self-denying fondness that was worth more, and had been a greater comfort to her, as she knew now, than all the things together, youth, beauty, rank, wealth, and talents, for which she was envied. If he said to her in his gentle way: "You had better return to Ilverthorpe, and live there," which would mean that he cared for her no longer, should she go? Yes, she would go without a word. She would go and drown herself.

But Mr. Kilroy was far from thinking harsh thoughts of her. On the contrary, he was blaming himself, little as he deserved it, for the circumstances which had brought Angelica to this bitter moment of self-abasement. He was not eloquent either in thought or speech, and with regard to his wife he had always felt more than he could express even to himself, though what he felt did find a certain form of expression, intelligible enough to a loving soul, in his constant care for her, and in the uncomplaining devotion which led him to sacrifice his own wishes to her whims, to absent himself when he perceived that she did not want him, and to suffer her neglect without bitterness, though certainly not without pain. And now he never thought of blaming her. What occurred to him was that this young half-educated girl had been committed to his care, and left by him pretty much to her own devices. He had not done his duty by her; he had not influenced her in any way; he had expected too much from her. It was the old story. Had he not himself seen fifty households wrecked because the husband, when he took a girl, little more than a child in years, and quite a child in mind and experience, from her own family, and the wholesome influences and companionship of father, mother, brothers, sisters, probably left her to go unguided, to form her character as best she could, putting that grave responsibility in her own weak hands as if the mere making a wife of her must make her a mature and sensible woman also? This was what he had done himself, and if Angelica had got into bad hands, and come to grief irreparable, there would have been nobody to blame but himself for it, especially as he knew she was headstrong, excitable, wild, original, fearless, and with an intellect large out of all proportion for the requirements of the life to which society condemned her; a force which was liable, if otherwise unemployed, to expend itself in outbursts of mischievous energy, although there was not a scrap of vice in her —no, not a scrap, he loyally insisted. For just look how she had come to him and told him! Would a girl who was not honest at heart have done that when she might so easily have deceived him? It was this confidence which touched him more than anything. She had come to him, as she should have done, the first thing, and she had come full of remorse and willing to atone. All this trouble was tending to unite them; it had brought her home; it would prove what is called a blessing in disguise after all, he hoped. His great love inspired him with insight and taught him tact in all his dealings with Angelica; and now it prompted him to do the one wise simple thing that would avail under the circumstances. He went to her, and bending over her, always delicately considerate of her inclinations even in the matter of the least caress, laid a kind hand on her shoulder, uttering at the same time brokenly the very words of her dream that morning: "If you could care for me a little, Angelica."

She looked up, amazed at first, then, understanding, she rose. The distressing tension relaxed in that moment, her heart expanded, her eyes filled with tears and overflowed; she could not command her voice to speak, but she threw herself impetuously into her husband's arms, and kissed him passionately, and clung to him, until she was able to sob out—"Don't let me go again, Daddy, keep me close. I am—I am grateful for the blessing of a good man's love."

END OF BOOK V.

BOOK VI.

THE IMPRESSIONS OF DR. GALBRAITH.

Nothing extenuate. nor set down aught in malice.
—*Othello*, Act V. Sc. II.

NOTE.—The fact that Dr. Galbraith had not the advantage of knowing Evadne's early history when they first became acquainted adds a certain piquancy to the flavour of his impressions, and the reader, better informed than himself with regard to the antecedents of his " subject," will find it interesting to note both the accuracy of his insight and the curious mistakes which it is possible even for a trained observer like himself to make by the half light of such imperfect knowledge as he was able to collect under the circumstances. His record, which is minute in all important particulars, is specially valuable for the way in which it makes apparent the changes of habit and opinion and the modifications of character that had been brought about in a very short time by the restriction Colonel Colquhoun had imposed upon her. In some respects it is hard to believe that she is the same person. But more interesting still, perhaps, are the glimpses we get of Dr. Galbraith himself in the narrative, throughout which it is easy to decipher the simple earnestness of the man, the cautious professionalism and integrity, the touches of tender sentiment held in check, the dash of egotism, the healthy-minded human nature, the capacity for enjoyment and sorrow, the love of life, and, above all, the perfect unconsciousness with which he shows himself to have been a man of fastidious refinement and exemplary moral strength and delicacy ; of the highest possible character ; and most lovable in spite of a somewhat irascible temper and manner which were apt to be abrupt at times.

CHAPTER I.

EVADNE puzzled me. As a rule, men of my profession, and more particularly specialists like myself, can class a woman's character and gauge her propensities for good or evil while he is diagnosing her disease if she consult him, or more easily still during half an hour's ordinary conversation if he happens to be alone with her. But even after I had seen Evadne many times, and felt broadly that I knew her salient points as well as such tricks of manner or habitual turns of expression as distinguished her from other ladies, I was puzzled.

We are not sufficiently interested in all the people we meet to care to understand their characters exactly, but a medical man who has not insight enough to do so at will has small chance of success in his profession, and when I found myself puzzled about Evadne it became a point of importance with me to understand her. She was certainly an interesting study, and all the more so because of that initial difficulty—a difficulty, by the way, which I found from the gossip of the place that everybody else was experiencing more or less. For it was evident from the first that whatever her real character might be, she was anything but a nonentity. Before she had been in the neighbourhood a fortnight she had made a distinct impression and was freely discussed, a fact which speaks for itself in two ways: first, her individuality was strongly marked enough to attract immediate attention, and secondly, there was that about her which provoked criticism. Not that the criticism of a community like ours is worth much, consisting as it does of carping mainly, and the kind of carping which reflects much more upon the low level of intelligence that obtains in such neighbourhoods than upon the character of the person criticised, for what the vulgar do not understand they are apt to condemn. Somebody has said that to praise moderately is a sign of mediocrity; and somebody might have added that to denounce decidedly shows deficiency in a multitude of estimable qualities, among which discernment must be specially mentioned—not, however, that there was any question of denouncing here, for Evadne was always more discussed for what she was not than for what she was. One lady of my acquaintance put part of my own feeling into words when she declared that Evadne *could* be nicer if *she would*, that part of it which first made me suspect that there was something artificial in her attitude towards the world at large, and more especially towards the world of thought and opinion, and that, had she been natural, she would have differed from herself as we knew her in many material respects. Naturainess, however, is a quality upon which too much stress is generally laid. If you are naturally nice it is all very well, but suppose you are naturally nasty? We should be very thankful indeed to think that some of our friends are not natural.

In looking back now, I am inclined to ask why we, Evadne's intimate friends, should always have expected more of her than we did of other people. That certainly was the case, and she disappointed us. We felt that she should have been a representative woman such as the world wants at this period of its progress, making a name for herself and an impression on the age; and it was probably her objection, expressed with quite passionate earnestness, to play a part in which we gathered from many chance indications that she was eminently qualified to have excelled, that constituted the puzzle. Her natural bent was certainly in that direction, but something had changed it; and here in particular the external tormenting difficulty with regard to her occurred with full force. At a very early period of our acquaintance, however, I discovered that her attitude in this respect was not inherent, but deliberately chosen.

"I avoid questions of the day as much as possible," she said on one occasion in answer to some remark of mine on a current topic of conversation. "I do not, as a rule, read anything on such subjects, and if people begin to discuss them in my presence I fly if I can."

"I should have thought that all such questions would have interested you deeply," I observed.

"They seem to possess a quite fatal fascination for people who allow themselves to be interested," she answered evasively, and in a tone which forbade further discussion of the subject.

But it was the evasion which enlightened me. She would not have been afraid of the "fatal fascination" if she had never felt it herself, and it was therefore evident that her objection was not the outcome of ignorant prejudice, but of knowledge and set purpose. It was the attitude of a burnt child.

The impression she made upon the neighbourhood was curious in one way—it was so very mixed. In the adverse part of the mixture, however, a good deal of personal pique was apparent, and one thing was always obvious: people liked her as much as she would let them. She even might have been popular had she chosen, but popularity comes of condescending to the level of the average, and Evadne was exclusive. She was *une vraie petite grande dame* at heart as well as in appearance, and would associate with none but her equals; and out of those again she was fastidious in the selection of her friends. To servants, people who knew their proper place, and retainers generally, with legitimate claims to her consideration, she was all kindly courtesy, and they were devoted to her; but she met the aspiring parvenu, seeking her acquaintance on false pretences of equality, with that disdainful civility which is more exasperating than positive rudeness because a lady is only rude to her equals.

And hence most of the animadversion.

But her manner was perfectly consistent. Her coldness cr cordiality to mere acquaintances only varied of necessity according to her position and responsibilities. In her own house, where the onus of entertaining fell upon her, she was charming to everybody to-day, neglecting none, and giving an equally flattering share of her attention to each; but if she met the same people at somebody else's place to-morrow, when she was off duty, as it were, she certainly showed no more interest than she felt in them. I do not believe, however, that she ever committed a breach of good manners in her life. When she spoke to you she did so with the most perfect manner, giving you her whole attention for the moment, and never letting her eyes wander, as underbred people so often do, especially in the act of shaking hands. Fairly considered, her attitude in society was distinguished by an equable politeness, in which, however, there was no heart, and that was what the world missed. She did not care for society, and society demands your heart, having none of its own. She certainly did her duty in that state of life, but without any affectation of delight in it. She went to all the local entertainments as custom required, and suffered from suspended animation under the influence of the deadly dulness which prevailed at most of them, but in that she was not peculiar, and she could conceal her boredom more successfully than almost anybody else I ever knew, and did so heroically.

In her religion too she was quite conventional. Like most people in these days, she was a good Churchwoman without being in any sense a Christian. She did not love her neighbour as herself, or profess to; but she went to church regularly and made all the responses, pleasing the clergy, and deriving some solace herself from the occupation—at least she always said the services were soothing. She was genuinely shocked by a sign of irreverence, and would sing the most jingling nonsense as a hymn with perfect gravity and without perceiving that there was any flaw in it. In these matters she showed no originality at all. She would repeat "my duty towards my neighbour is to love him as myself, and to do to all men as I would that they should do unto me" fervently, and come out and cut Mrs. Chrimes to the quick just afterward because she had the misfortune to be a tanner's wife and nobody's daughter in particular. It was what she had been taught. Any one of her set would have said "my duty to my neighbour" without a doubt of their own sincerity, and given Mrs. Chrimes the cold shoulder too; the inconsistency is customary, and in this particular Evadne was as much a creature of custom as the rest.

It was my fate to take Evadne in to dinner on the first occasion of our meeting. I did not hear her name when I was presented, and had no idea who she was, but I was struck by her appearance. Her figure was fragile to a fault, and she was evidently delicate at that time, not having fully recovered, as I was afterwards told, from a severe attack of Maltese fever; but her complexion was not unhealthy. Her features were refined and exquisitely feminine. She looked about twenty, and her face in repose would have been expressionless but for the slight changes about the mouth which showed that the mind was working within. Her long eyes seemed narrow from a trick she had of holding them half shut. They were slow-glancing and steadfast, and all her movements struck one at first as being languid, but that impression wore off after a time, and then it became apparent that they were merely rather more deliberate than is usual with a girl.

She answered my first remarks somewhat shortly; but certainly such observations as one finds to make to a strange lady while taking her from the drawing room to the dining room and arranging her chair at table are not usually calculated to inspire brilliant responses. She had the habit of society to perfection and was essentially self-possessed, but I fancied she was shy. Coldness is often a cover for extreme shyness in women of her station, and I did my best to thaw her; but the soup and fish had been removed and we had arrived at the last *entrée* before I made a remark that roused her in the least. I forget what I said exactly, but it was some stupid common-place about the difficulties of the political situation at the moment.

"I hate politics," she then observed. "Business is a dis-agreeable thing, whether it be the business of the nation or of the shop. I hear women say that they are obliged to interfere just now in all that concerns themselves because men have cheated and imposed upon them to a quite unbearable extent. But they will do no good by it. Their position is perfectly hopeless. And the mere trade of governing is a coarse pur-suit, and therefore most objectionable for us." She drew in her breath and tightened her lips. "But for myself," she added, "what I object to mainly is the thought. Why are they trying to make us think? The great difficulty is not to think. There are plenty of men to think for us, and while they are thinking we can be feeling. I, for one, have no joy in eventful living. Feeling is life, not thought. You need not be afraid to give us the suffrage," she broke off, with the first glimpse of a smile I had seen on her lips. "After the excitement of conquering your opposition to it was over we should all be content, and not one woman in a hundred would trouble herself to vote."

"I believe women are more public spirited than that," I answered. "They are toiling everywhere now for the further-ance of all good works, and they come forward courageously whenever necessity compels them to take such an extreme and uncongenial course. In times of war——"

She had been leaning back in her chair in a somewhat lan-guid attitude, but now suddenly she straightened herself, her face flushed crimson, and I stopped short. Something in the word "War" either hurt or excited her. Her long eyes opened on me wide and bright for the first time, and flashed a look into mine more stirring than the wine that bubbled in the glass between my fingers.

"She is beautiful!" I said to myself; but up to that moment I had not suspected it.

"War!" she exclaimed, speaking under her breath, but incisively. "Do not let us talk about it! War is the dirty work of a nation; it is one of the indecencies of life, and should never be mentioned!"

She looked straight into my face for a moment with eyes wide open and lips compressed when she had finished speaking, and then took her *menu* in her left hand, and began to study it with great apparent attention.

Having discovered that she thought politics a coarse, contaminating business, and war the dirty work of a nation, I felt curious to know her views on literature and art.

"I have just been reading a book that might interest you," I began; "it strikes me as being so true to life."

"I think I should be inclined to avoid it, then," she answered, "for I always find that 'true to life' in a book means something revolting."

"Unfortunately, yes, it often does," I agreed. "But still we ought to know. If we refused to study the bad side of life, no evil would ever be remedied."

"Do you think any good is ever done?" she asked.

"I am afraid you are a pessimist," I rejoined.

"But do you really like books that are true to life yourself?" she proceeded. "Don't you think we see enough of life without reading about it? For my own part I am grateful to anyone who has the power to take me out of this world and make me feel something—realise something—beyond. The dash of the supernatural, for instance, in 'John Inglesant,' 'Mr. Isaacs,' 'The Wizard's Son,' and 'The Little Pilgrim' has the effect of rest upon my mind, and gives me greater pleasure than the most perfect picture of real life ever presented. In fact, my ideal of perfect bliss in these days is to know nothing and believe in ghosts."

This also was a comprehensive opinion, and I felt no further inclination to name the book to which I had alluded. But now that she had begun to respond I should have been well content to continue the conversation. There was something so unusual in most of her opinions that I wanted to hear more. although I confess that what she said interested me less than she herself did. Before I could touch on another topic, however, the ladies left the table.

A big blond man, middle-aged, bald, bland, and with a heavy moustache, had been sitting opposite to us during dinner, and had attracted my attention by the way he looked at my partner from time to time. It was a difficult look to describe, because there was neither admiration nor interest in it, approval nor disapproval; he might have looked at a block of wood in exactly the same way, and it could hardly have been less responsive. Once, however, their eyes did meet, and then the glance became one of friendly recognition on both sides; but even after that he still continued to look in the same queer way, and it was this fact that struck me as peculiar.

When the ladies had gone I happened to find myself beside this gentleman, and asked him if he could tell me who it was I had taken in to dinner.

"Well, she is supposed to be my wife," he answered deliberately; "and I am Colonel Colquhoun."

He spoke with a decidedly Irish accent of the educated sort, and seemed to think that I should know all about him when he mentioned his name, but I had never heard of the fellow before. I rightly conjectured, however, that he was the new man who had come to command the Depôt at Morningquest while I had been abroad for my holiday.

CHAPTER II.

FIRST impressions are very precious for many reasons. They have a charm of their own to begin with, and it is interesting to recall them; and salutary, also, if not sedative. Collect a few, and you will soon see clearly the particular kind of ass you are by the mistakes you have made in consequence of having confided in them. When I first met Evadne I was still young enough, in the opprobrious sense of the word, to suppose that I should find her mentally, when I met her again, just where she was when she left me after our little chat at the dinner-table; and I went to pay my duty call upon her under that most erroneous impression. I intended to resume our interrupted conversation, and never doubted but that I should find her willing to gratify my interest in her peculiar views. It was a mistake, however, which anybody, whose delight in his own pursuits is continuous, might make, and one into which the cleverest man is prone to fall when the object is a woman.

I called on Evadne the day after the dinner. She was alone, and rising from a seat beside a small work-table as I entered, advanced a step, and held out a nerveless hand to me. She was not looking well. Her skin was white and opaque, her eyes dull, her lips pale, and her apparent age ten years more than I had given her on the previous evening. She was a lamplight beauty, I supposed. But her dress satisfied. It was a long indoor gown which indicated without indelicacy the natural lines of her slender figure, and she was innocent of the shocking vulgarity of the small waist, a common enough deformity at that time, although now, it is said, affected by third rate actresses and women of indifferent character only. The waist is an infallible index to the moral worth of a woman; very little of the latter survives the pressure of a tightened corset.

"Will you sit there?" Evadne said, indicating an easy chair and subsiding into her own again as she spoke. "Colonel Colquhoun is not at home," she added, "but I hope he will return in time to see you. He will be sorry if he does not."

It was quite the proper thing to say, and her manner was all that it ought to have been, yet somehow the effect was not encouraging. Had I been inclined to presume I should have felt myself put in my place, but, being void of reproach, my mind was free to take notes, and I decided off-hand that Evadne was a society woman of unexceptionable form, but ordinary, and my nascent interest was nowhere. My visit lasted about a quarter of an hour, during which time she gave me back commonplace for commonplace punctually, doing damage to her gown with a pin she held in her left hand the while, and only raising her eyes to mine for an instant at a time. Nothing could have been easier, colder, thinner, more uninspiring than the fluent periods with which she favoured me, and nothing more stultifying to my own brain. If it had not been for that pin my wits must have wandered. As it was, however, she inadvertently forced me to concentrate my attention upon the pin, with fears for her femoral artery, by apparently sticking it into herself in a reckless way whenever there was a pause, and each emphatic little dig startled my imagination into lively activity and kept me awake.

But, altogether, the visit was disappointing, and I left her under the impression that the glimpse of mind I had had the night before was delusive, a mere transient flash of intelligence caused by some swift current of emotion due to external influences of which I was unaware. Love, or an effervescent wine, will kindle some such spark in the dullest. But there was nothing in Evadne's manner indicative of the former influence; and as to the latter, the only use she ever made of a wineglass was to put her gloves in it.

As I gathered up the reins to drive my dogcart home that afternoon I was conscious of an impression on my mind as of a yawn. But I was relieved to have the visit over—and done with, as I at first believed it to be; but it was not done with, for during the drive a thought occurred to me with chastening rather than cheering effect, a thought which proves that my opinion of Evadne's capacity had begun to be mixed even at that early period of our acquaintance. I acknowledged to myself that one of us had been flat that day, and had infected the other; but which was the original flat one? Some minds are like caves of stalactite and stalagmite, rich in treasures of beauty, the existence of which you may never suspect because you bring no light yourself to dispel the darkness that conceals them.

CHAPTER III.

THE next time I saw Evadne it was at her own house also, and it was only a few days after my first visit. I was driving past, but encountered Colonel Colquhoun at the gate, and pulled up for politeness' sake, as I had not seen him when I called. He was returning from barracks in a jovial mood, and made such a point of my going in that I felt obliged to. We found Evadne alone in the drawing room, and I noticed to my surprise that she was extremely nervous. Her manner was self-possessed, but her hands betrayed her. She fidgeted with her rings or her buttons or her fingers incessantly, and certainly was relieved when I rose to go.

The little she said, however, impressed me, and I would gladly have stayed to hear more had she wished it. I fancied, however, that she did not wish it, and I accordingly took my leave as soon as I decently could.

As I drove home I found myself revising my revised opinion of her. I felt sure now that she was something more than an ordinary society woman. Still, like everybody else at that time, I could not have said whether I liked or disliked her. But I wanted to see her again. Before I had an opportunity of doing so, however, I received a request with regard to her which developed my latent curiosity into honest interest, and added a certain sense of duty to my half formed wish to know more of her.

The request arrived in the shape of a letter from Lady Adeline Hamilton-Wells, an intimate friend of mine, and one who has always had my most sincere respect and affection. She is a woman who lives altogether for others, devoting the greater part of her ample means, and all the influence of an excellent position, to their service; and she is a woman who stands alone on the strength of her own individuality, for Mr. Hamilton-Wells does not count. Her great charm is her perfect sincerity. She is essentially true.

When I saw her note on the breakfast table next day, I knew that somehow it would prove to be of more importance than the whole of my other letters put together, and I therefore hastened to open it first.

"Villa Mignonne, 15th March, 1880.

"Colonel Colquhoun, late of the Colquhoun Highlanders, has been appointed to command the depôt at Morningquest, I hear. Kindly make his wife's acquaintance at your earliest convenience to oblige me. She is one of the Fraylings of Fraylingay. Her mother is a sister of Mrs. Orton Beg's, and a very old friend of mine. I used to see a good deal of Mrs. Colquhoun up to the time that she met her husband, and she was then a charming girl, quiet, but clever. I lost sight of her after her marriage, however, for about two years, and only met her again last January in Paris, when I found her changed beyond all knowing of her, and I can't think why. She is not on good terms with her own people for some mysterious reason, but, apart from that, she seems to have everything in the world she can want, and makes quite a boast of her husband's kindness and consideration. I noticed that she did not get on well with men as a rule, and she may repel you at first, but persevere, for she *can* be fascinating, and to both sexes too, which is rare; but I am told that people who begin by disliking often end by adoring her—people with anything in them, I mean, for, as I have learnt to observe under your able tuition, the 'blockhead majority' *does* do despitefully by what it cannot comprehend. And that is why I am writing to you. I am afraid Evadne will come into collision with some of the prejudices of our enlightened neighbourhood. She is not perfect, and nothing but perfection is good enough for certain angelic women of our acquaintance. They will call her very character in question at the trial tribunals of their tea-tables if she be, as I think, of the kind who cause comment; and they will throw stones at her and make her suffer even if they do her no permanent injury. For I fear that she is nervously sensitive both to praise and blame, a woman to be hurt inevitably in this battle of life, and a complex character

which I own I do not perfectly comprehend myself yet, perhaps because parts of it are still nebulous. But doubtless
your keener insight will detect what is obscure to me, and I
rely upon you to befriend her until my return to England,
when I hope to be able to relieve you of all responsibility.

"Tell me, too, how you get on with Colonel Colquhoun.
I should like to know what you think of them both.

"ADELINE HAMILTON-WELLS."

My answer to this letter has lately come into my possession,
and I give it as being of more value probably than any subse-
quent record of these early impressions:

"FOUNTAIN TOWERS, 19th March, 1880.

"MY DEAR LADY ADELINE:

"I had made Mrs. Colquhoun's acquaintance before I
received your letter, and have seen her three times altogether.
And three times has not been enough to enable me to form a
decided opinion of her character, which seems to be out of the
common. Had you asked me what I thought of her after our
first meeting, I should have said she is peculiar; after the second
I am afraid I should have presumed to say not 'much'; but
now, after the third, I am prepared to maintain that she is
decidedly interesting. Her manner is just a trifle stiff to
begin with, but that is so evidently the outcome of shyness
that I cannot understand anybody being repelled by it. Her
voice is charming, every tone is exquisitely modulated, and
she expresses herself with ease, and with a certain grace of
diction peculiarly her own. It is a treat to hear English
spoken as she speaks it. She uses little or no slang and few
abbreviations; but she is perfectly fearless in her choice of
words, and invariably employs the one which expresses her
meaning best, however strong it may be, yet somehow the
effect is never coarse. Yesterday she wanted to know the
name of an officer now at the barracks, and made her husband
understand which she meant in this way: 'He is a little man,'
she said, 'who puts his hands deep down in his pockets,
hunches up his shoulders, and says *damn* emphatically.' How
she can use such words without offence is a mystery; but
she certainly does.

"All this, however, you must have observed for yourself,
and I know that it is merely skimming about your question,
not answering it. But I humbly confess, though it cost me

your confidence in my 'keen insight' forever, that I cannot answer it. So far, Mrs. Colquhoun has appealed to me merely as a text upon which to hang conclusions. I do not in the least know what she is, but I can see already what she will become—if her friends are not careful; and that is a phrase-maker.

"Colonel Colquhoun is likely to be a greater favourite here than his wife. Ladies say he is 'very nice!' 'so genial,' and 'a *thorough* Irishman!' whatever they mean by that. He does affect both brogue and blarney when he thinks proper. Per-haps, however, I ought to tell you at once that I do not like him, and am not at all inclined to cultivate his acquaintance. He strikes me as being a very commonplace kind of military man, tittle-tattling, idle, and unintellectual; and in the habit of filling up every interval of life with brandy and soda water. The creature is rapidly becoming extinct, but specimens still linger in certain districts. And I should judge him upon the whole to be the sort of man who pleases by his good manners those whom he does not repel by his pet vices—most people, that is to say. The world is constant and kind to its own.

"They are at As-You-Like-It, the gloomiest house in the neighbourhood. I fancy Colonel Colquhoun took it to suit his own convenience without consulting his wife's tastes or requirements, and he will be out too much to suffer himself, but I fear she will feel it. She is a fragile little creature, for whose health and well-being generally I should say that bright rooms and fresh air are essential. The air at As-You-Like-It is not bad, but the rooms are damp. That west window in the drawing room is the one bright spot in the house, and the sun only shines on it in the afternoon. I am sorry that I cannot answer your letter more satisfactorily, but you may rest assured that I shall be glad to do Mrs. Colquhoun any service in my power.

"Diavolo wrote and told me the other day that his colonel thinks him too good for the Guards, and has strongly advised him, if he wishes to continue in the service, to exchange into some other regiment! I have asked him to come and stay with me, and hope to discover what he has been up to. With your permission, I should urge him to apply for the Depôt at Morningquest. It would do the duke good to have him about again, and Angelica would be delighted; and, besides, Colo-nel Colquhoun would keep his eye on him and put up with more pranks probably than those who know not Joseph.

"Angelica is very well and happy. Her devotion to her husband continues to be exemplary, and he has been good-natured enough to oblige her by delivering some of her speeches in parliament lately, with excellent effect. She read the one now in preparation aloud to us the last time I was at Ilverthorpe. It struck me as being extremely able, and eminent for refinement as well as for force. Mr. Kilroy himself was delighted with it, as indeed he is with all that she does now. He only interrupted her once. 'I should say the country is going to the dogs, there,' he suggested. 'Then, I am afraid your originality would provoke criticism,' Angelica answered.

"When do you return? I avoid Hamilton House in your absence, it looks so dreary all shut up.

"Yours always, dear Lady Adeline,

"George Beton Galbraith."

CHAPTER IV.

HAVING despatched my letter, I began to consider how I might best follow up my acquaintance with Evadne with a view to such intimacy as should enable me at any time to have the right to be of service to her should occasion offer, and during the day I arranged a dinner party for her special benefit, not a very original idea, but by accident it answered the purpose.

The Colquhouns accepted my invitation, but when the evening arrived Evadne came alone, and quite half an hour before the time I had dressed, luckily, and was strolling about the grounds when I saw the carriage drive up the avenue, and hastened round the house to meet her at the door.

"The days are getting quite long," she said, as I helped her to alight. Then, glancing up at a clock in the hall, she happened to notice the time. "Is that clock right?" she asked.

"It is," I answered.

"Then my coachman must have mistaken the distance," she said. "He assured me that it would take an hour to drive here. But I shall not have occasion to regret the mistake if you will let me see the house," she added gracefully. "It seems to be a charming old place."

It would have been a little awkward for both of us but for

this happy suggestion; there were, however, points of interest enough about the house to fill up a longer interval even.

"But I am forgetting!" she exclaimed, as I led her to the library. "I received this note from Colonel Colquhoun at the last moment. He is detained in barracks to-day, most unfortunately, and will not be able to get away until late. He begs me to make you his apologies."

"I hope we shall see him during the evening," I said.

"Oh, yes," she answered, "he is sure to come for me."

There was a portrait of Lady Adeline in the library, and she noticed it at once.

"Do you know the Hamilton-Wellses?" she asked, brightening out of her former manner instantly.

"We are very old friends," I answered. "Their place is next to mine, you know."

"I did not know," she said. "I have never been there. Lady Adeline knows my people, and used to come to our house a good deal at one time; that is where I met her. I like her very much—and trust her."

"That everybody does."

"Do you know her widowed sister, Lady Claudia Beaumont?"

"Yes."

"And their brother, Lord Dawne?"

"Yes—well. He and I were 'chums' at Harrow and Oxford, and a common devotion to the same social subjects has kept us together since."

"He is a man of most charming manners," she said thoughtfully.

"He is," I answered cordially. "I know no one else so fastidiously refined, without being a prig."

She was sitting on the arm of a chair with Adeline's photograph in her hand, and was silent a moment, looking at it meditatively.

"You must know that eccentric 'Ideala,' as they call her, also?" she said at last, glancing up at me gravely.

"We do not consider her eccentric," I said.

"Well, you must confess that she moves in an orbit of her own," she rejoined.

"Not alone, then," I answered, "so many luminaries circle round her."

"Lady Adeline criticises her severely," she ventured, with a touch of asperity.

"*Les absents ont toujours torts,*" I answered. "But, at the
same time, when Lady Adeline criticises Ideala severely, 1 am
sure she deserves it. Her faults are patent enough, and most
provoking, because she could correct them if she would. You
don't know her well?"

"No."

"Ah! Then I understand why you do not like her. She
is not a person who shows to advantage on a slight acquaintance, and in that she is just the reverse of most people; her
faults are all on the surface and appear at once, her good
qualities only come out by degrees."

"1 feel reproved," Evadne answered, smiling. "But it is
really hard to believe that the main fabric of a character is
beautiful when one only sees the spoilt bits of it. You must
be quite one of that clique," she added, in a tone which
expressed "What a pity!" quite clearly.

"You are not interested in social questions?" I ventured.

"On the contrary," she answered decidedly, "I hate them all."
She put the photograph down, and looked round the room.

"Where does that door lead to?" she asked, indicating one
opposite.

"Into my study."

"Then you do not study in the library?"

"No. I read here for relaxation. When I want to work I
go in there.

"Let me see where you work?"

I hesitated, for I kept my tools there, and I did not know
what might be about.

"It is professional work I do there," I said.

She was quick to see my meaning: "Oh, in that case," she
began apologetically. "I am indiscreet, forgive me. I have
not realized your position yet, you see. It is so anomalous
being both a doctor and a country gentleman. But what a
dear old place this is! I cannot think how you can mix up
medical pursuits with the names of your ancestors. Were I
you I should belong to the Psychical Society only. The
material for that kind of research lingers long in these deep
recesses. It is built up in thick walls, and concealed behind
oak panels. Oh, how *can* you be a doctor here!"

"I am not a doctor here," I assured her, "at least only in
the morning when I make this my consulting room."

"I am glad," she said. "This is a place in which to be
human."

"Is a doctor not human, then?" I asked, a trifle piqued.

"No," she answered, laughing. "A doctor is not a man to his lady patients; but an abstraction—a kindly abstraction for whom one sends when a man's presence would be altogether inconvenient. If I am ever ill I will send for you in the abstract confidently."

"Well, I hope I may more than answer your expectations in that character," I replied, "should anything so unfortunate as sickness or sorrow induce you to do me the favour of accept-ing my services."

She gave me one quick grave glance. "I know you mean it," she said; "and I know you mean more. You will be-friend me if I ever want a friend."

"I will," I answered.

"Thank you," she said.

It was exactly what I had intended with regard to her since I had received Lady Adeline's letter, but a compact entered into on the occasion of our fourth meeting struck me as sud-den. I had no time to think of it, however, at the moment, for Evadne followed up her thanks with a question.

"How do you come to have an abode of this kind and be a doctor also?" she asked.

"The house came to me from an uncle, who died suddenly, just after I had become a fully qualified practitioner," I told her; "but there is not income enough attached to it to keep it up properly, and I wanted to live here; and I wanted besides to continue my professional career, so I thought I would try and make the one wish help the other."

"And the experiment has succeeded?"

"Yes."

"Are you very fond of your profession?"

"It is the finest profession in the world."

"All medical men say that," she remarked, smiling.

"Well, I can claim the merit—if it be a merit—of having arrived at that conclusion before I became——"

"Eminent?" she suggested.

"Before I had taken my degree," I corrected.

"So you came and established yourself as a doctor in this old place?"

She glanced round meditatively.

"That seems to surprise you?"

"It is the dual character that surprises me," she answered. "Your practice makes you a professional man, and you are a

county magnate also by right of your name and connec-
tions."

She evidently knew all about me already, and I was flattered
by the interest she showed, which I thought special until I
found that she was in the habit of knowing, and knowing
accurately too, all about everyone with whom she was brought
into close contact.

"I cannot imagine how you find time for it all," she continued; "you are not a general practitioner, I believe."

"Not exactly," I answered. "Of course I never refuse to
attend in any case of emergency, but my regular practice is all
consultation, and my speciality has somehow come to be
nervous disorders. Sometimes I have my house full of
patients—interesting cases which require close attention."

"I know," she said, "and poor people who cannot pay as
often as the rich who will give you anything to attend them."

"I should very much like you to believe the most exaggerated accounts of my generosity if any such are about," I hastened to assure her: "but honesty compels me to explain that
I benefit by every case which I treat successfully."

"Go to! you do not deceive me," she answered, laughing
up in my face.

Her manner had quite changed now. She recognized me as
one of her own caste, and knew that however friendly and
familiar she might be I should not presume.

When it was time to think of my other guests, she begged to
be allowed to remain in the library until they had all arrived.

"It would be such an exertion to have to explain to each
one separately how it is that I am here alone—and I do so
dislike strange people," she added plaintively. "It makes me
quite *ill* to have to meet them. And, besides," she broke out
laughing, "as it is a new place, perhaps I ought to try and
make myself interesting and of importance to the inhabitants
by coming in late! When you keep people waiting for dinner
you *do* become of consequence to them—to their comfort—
and then they think of you!"

"But not very charitably under such circumstances," I
suggested.

"That depends," she answered. "If you arrive in time to
save their appetites, they will associate a pleasant sense of
relief with your coming which will make them think well of
you for evermore. They mistake the sensation for an opinion,
and as they like it, they call it a good one!"

She looked pretty when she unbent like that and talked nonsense—or what was apt to strike you as nonsensical until you came to consider it. For there was often a depth of worldly wisdom and acuteness underlying her most apparently careless sallies that surprised you.

She lingered long in the library—so long that at first I felt impatiently that she might have remembered that I had an appetite as well as the strangers within my gates with whom it apparently pleased her to trifle, and I felt obliged, during an awkward pause, to account for the delay by explaining for whom we were waiting. If she were in earnest about wishing to make a sensation or attract special attention to herself, she had gained her end, for the moment I mentioned the name of Colquhoun, people began to speak of her, carefully, because nobody knew as yet who her friends might be, but with interest. I never supposed for a moment, however, that she was in earnest. There was something proudly self-respecting about her which forbade all idea of anything so paltry as manœuvring. I did at first think that she might have fallen asleep; but, afterward, on recollecting that she was a nervous subject, it occurred to me that her courage might have failed her, and that she would never present herelf to a whole room full of strangers alone. Excusing myself to my guests, therefore, as best I could, I went at last to the library, and found that this latter surmise was correct. She was standing in the middle of the room with her hands clasped, evidently in an agony of nervous trepidation. I went up to her, however, as if I had not noticed it, and offered her my arm.

"If you will come now, Mrs. Colquhoun," I said, "we will go to dinner."

She took my arm without a word, but I felt as soon as she touched me that her confidence was rapidly returning, and by the time we had reached the drawing room, and I had explained that Colonel Colquhoun had been detained by duty most unfortunately, but Mrs. Colquhoun had been kind enough to come nevertheless, she had quite recovered herself, and only a slight exaggeration of the habitual *noli me tangere* of her ordinary manner remained in evidence of her shyness.

When we were seated at table, and she was undoubtedly at her ease again, I expected to see her vivacity revive; but the nervous crisis had evidently gone deeper than her manner, and affected her mood. I had left her all life and animation, a mere girl bent upon pleasure, but with every evidence of considerable capacity for the pursuit; but now, at dinner, she sat beside me, cold, constrained, and listless, neither eating nor interested; pretending, however, courageously, and probably deceiving those about her with the even flow of polished periods which she kept up to conceal her indifference. I thought perhaps her husband's absence had something to do with it, and expected to see her brighten up when he arrived. He did not come at all, however, and only once at table did she show any sign of the genuine intellectual activity which I was now pretty sure was either concealed or slumbering in these moods. The sign she made was deceptive, and probably only a man of my profession, accustomed to observe, and often obliged to judge more by indications of emotion than by words, would have recognized its true significance. In the midst of her chatter she became suddenly silent, and one might have been excused for supposing that her mind was weary; but that, in truth, was the moment when she really roused herself, and began to follow the conversation with close attention. There was an old bore of a doctor at table that evening who would insist on talking professionally, a thing which does not often happen in my house, for I think, of all "shop," ours is the most unsuitable for general conversation because of the morbid fascination it has for most people. Ladies especially will listen with avidity to medical matters, perceiving nothing gruesome in the details at the moment ; but afterward developing nerves on the subject, and probably giving the young practitioner good reason to regret unwary confidences. I tried to stave off the topic, but the will-power of the majority was against me, and finally I found myself submitting, and following my friend's unwholesome lead.

"You must have some curious experiences, in your branch of the profession especially," the lady on my left remarked.

"We do," I said, answering her expectations against my better judgment, and partly, I think, because this was the moment when Evadne woke up. "I have had some myself. The extraordinary systems of fraud and deceit which are carried on by certain patients, for no apparent purpose, would astonish you. Their delight is essentially in the doing, and the one and only end of it all is invariably the same: a morbid desire to excite sympathy by making themselves interesting. I had one girl under my charge for six months, during which time she suffered daily from long fainting fits and other distressing symptoms which reduced her to the last degree of

emaciation, and puzzled me extremely because there was
nothing to account for them. Her heart was perfectly sound,
yet she would lie in a state of insensibility, livid and all but
pulseless, by the hour together. There was no disease of any
organ, but certain symptoms, which could not have been simu-
lated, pointed to extensive disorder of one at least. It was a
case of hysteria clearly, but no treatment had the slightest
effect upon her, and, fearing for her life, I took her at last to
Sir Shadwell Rock, the best specialist for nervous disorders
now alive. He confirmed my diagnosis, and ordered the girl
to be sent away from her friends with a perfect stranger, a
hard, cold, unsympathetic person who would irritate her, if
possible; and she was not to be allowed luxuries of any kind.
I had considered the advisability of such a course myself, but
the girl seemed too far gone for it, and I own I never expected
to see her alive again. After she went abroad I heard that
when she fainted she was left just where she fell to recover as
best she could, and when any particular food disagreed with
her, it was served to her incessantly until she professed to
have got over her dislike for it; but in spite of such heroic
treatment she was not at that time any better. Then I lost
sight of her, and had forgotten the case, when one day, without any warning whatever, she came into my consulting room,
looking the picture of health and happiness, and with a very
fine child in her arms. 'I suppose you are surprised to see me
alive,' she said. 'I am married now, and this is my boy—isn't
he a beauty? And I am very happy—or rather I should be
but for one thing—that illness of mine—when I gave you so
much trouble——' 'Oh, don't mention that,' I interrupted,
thinking she had come to overwhelm me with undeserved
thanks: 'My only trouble was that I could do nothing for you.
I hope you recovered soon after you went abroad?' 'As soon
as I thought fit,' she answered significantly, 'and that is what
I have come about. I want to confess. I want to relieve my
mind of a burden of deceit. Doctor—I was never insensible
in one of those fainting fits; I never had a symptom that I
could not have controlled. I was shamming from beginning
to end.' 'Well, you nearly shammed yourself out of the
world,' I said. 'Tell me how you did it?' 'I can't tell you
exactly,' she answered. 'When I wanted to appear to faint I
just set my mind somehow—I can't do it now that I am happy,
and have plenty of interests in life. At that time I had nothing to take me out of myself, and those daily doings were an

endless source of occupation and entertainment to me. But lately I have had qualms of conscience on the subject.' "

"And was she cured?" Evadne asked.

"Oh, yes," I answered. "There was no fear for her after she confessed. When the moral consciousness returns in such cases, and there is nothing but relief of mind to be gained by confession, the cure is generally complete."

"But what could have been the motive of such a fraud?" somebody asked.

"It is difficult to imagine," I answered. "Had it been more extensive the explanation would have been easier; but as myself and the young lady's parents were her only audience, I have never been able to account for it satisfactorily."

I noticed, while I was speaking, that Evadne was thinking the problem out for herself.

"She would not have given herself so much trouble without a very strong motive," she now suggested, "and human passions are the strongest motives for human actions, are they not?"

"Of course," I said, "but the question is, what passion prompted her. It could not have been either anger, ambition, revenge, or jealousy."

"No," she answered, in the matter-of-fact tone of one who merely arrives at a logical conclusion, "and it must therefore have been love. She was in love with you, and tried in that way to excite your sympathy and attract your attention."

"It is quite evident that view of the case never occurred to you, Galbraith," Dr. Lauder observed, laughing.

And I own that I *was* taken aback by it, considerably—not of course as it affected myself, but because it gave me a glimpse of an order of mind totally different from that with which I should have credited Evadne earlier in the evening.

"But how do you treat these cases?" she proceeded. "Is there any cure for such depravity?"

"Oh, yes," I answered confidently. "They are being cured every day. So long as there is no organic disease, I am quite sure that wholesome surroundings, patience and kind care, and steady moral influence will do all that is necessary. The great thing is to awaken the conscience. Patients who once feel sincerely that such courses are depraved may cure themselves—if they are not robbed of their self-respect. The most hopeless cases I have, come from that class of people who give each other bits of their mind—very objectionable bits, consisting of vulgar abuse for the most part, and the call-ing of names that rankle The operators seem to derive a solemn kind of self-satisfaction from the treatment themselves, but it does for the patient almost invariably.''

This led to a discussion on bad manners, during which Evadne relapsed. I saw the light go out of her eyes, and she showed no genuine interest in anything for the rest of the evening; and when I had wrapped her up, and seen her drive away, I somehow felt that the entertainment had been a failure so far as she was concerned, and I wondered why she should so soon be bored. At her age she should have had vitality enough in herself to carry her through an evening.

"Colonel Colquhoun will regret that he has not been able to come," she said as she wished me good-bye.

And I noticed afterward that she was always most punc-tilious about such little formalities. She never omitted any trifle of etiquette, and I doubt if she could have dined without "dressing" for dinner.

CHAPTER V.

COLONEL COLQUHOUN called next day himself to explain his absence on the previous evening. I forget what excuse he made, but it sufficed.

I saw Evadne, too, that same afternoon. She had been to make a call in the neighbourhood, and was waiting at a little country station to return by train. Something peculiar in her attitude attracted my attention before I recognized her. She was standing alone at the extreme end of the platform, her slender figure silhouetted with dark distinctness against the sloping evening sky. She might have been waiting anxiously for someone to come that way, or she might have been waiting for a train with tragic purpose. She wore a long dark green dress, the train of which she was holding up in her left hand. She showed no surprise when I spoke to her, although she had not heard me approach.

"What do the people here think of me?" she asked abruptly. "What do they say?"

"They have yet to discover your faults," I answered.

She compressed her lips, and looked down the line again.

"That is my train, I think," she said presently.

When I had put her into a carriage, she shook hands with

me, thanking me gravely, then threw herself back in her seat, and was borne away.

That was literally all that passed between us, yet she left me standing there, staring after her stupidly, and curiously impressed. There was always a suggestion of something unusual about her which piqued my interest and kept it alive.

During the summer and autumn I met her at various places, and saw her also in her own house, and she seemed, so far as an outsider could judge, as happily situated as most women of her station, and not at all likely to require any special service at the hands of a friend. Her husband was a good deal older than herself, but the disparity made no apparent difference to their comfort. When he was absent she never talked about him, but when he was present she treated him with unvarying consideration, and they appeared together everywhere. Mindful of my promise to Lady Adeline, I showed them both every attention in my power. I called regularly, and Colonel Colquhoun as regularly returned my calls, sometimes bringing Evadne with him.

The winter that year came upon us suddenly and sharply, and until it set in I had only seen her under the most ordinary circumstances; but at the beginning of the cold weather, she had an illness which was the means of my learning to know more of her true character and surroundings in a few days than I should probably have done in years of mere social intercourse. I stopped for a moment one morning as I drove past As-You-Like-It to leave her some flowers, and her own maid, who opened the door, showed me upstairs to a small sitting room, the ante-chamber to another room beyond, at the door of which she knocked.

I heard no answer, but the girl entered and announced me. I followed her in, and found myself face to face with Evadne. She was in bed. The maid withdrew, closing the door after her.

"What nonsense is this—I am exceedingly sorry, doctor!" Evadne exclaimed feebly. "That stupid girl must have thought that you were coming to see me professionally. But. oh! *do* let me look at the flowers!" and she stretched out her left hand for them, offering me her right at the same time to shake, and burying her face and her embarrassment together. Her hand was hot and dry.

"I don't require you in the least, doctor," she assured me,

looking up brightly from the flowers, "but I am very glad to see you."

"Why are you in bed?" I asked, responding cheerfully to this cheerful greeting.

"Oh, I have a little cold," she answered.

I drew a chair to the bedside, laid my hand on her wrist, and watched her closely as I questioned her—cough incessant; respiration rapid; temperature high, I judged; pulse 120.

"How long have you had this cold?" I asked.

"About a week," she said. "It makes me ache all over, you know, and that is why I am in bed to-day."

I saw at once that she was seriously ill, and I also saw that she was bearing up bravely, and making as little of it as possible.

"Why isn't your fire lit?" I asked.

"Oh, I never thought of having one," she answered.

"And what is that you are drinking?"

"Cold water."

"Well, you mustn't drink any more cold water, or anything else cold until I give you leave," I ordered. "And don't try to talk. I will come and see you again by and by."

I went downstairs to look for Colonel Colquhoun, and found him just about to start for barracks.

"I am sorry to say your wife is very ill," I said. "She has an attack of acute bronchitis, and it may mean pneumonia as well; I have not examined her chest. She must have fires in her room, and a bronchitis kettle at once. Don't let the temperature get below 70° till I see her again. Her maid can manage for a few hours, I suppose? But you had better telegraph for a nurse. One should be here before night."

"What a damned nuisance these women are," Colquhoun answered cheerfully. "There's always something the matter with them!"

I returned between five and six in the evening, walked in, and not seeing anybody about, went up to Evadne's sitting room. The door leading into the bedroom was open, and I entered. She was alone, and had propped herself up in bed with pillows. The difficulty of breathing had become greater, and she found relief in that attitude. She looked at me with eyes unnaturally large and solemn as I entered, and it was a full moment before she recognised me. The fires had not been lighted in either of the rooms, and she was evidently much worse.

"Why haven't these fires been lighted?" I demanded.

"This is only October," she answered, jesting, "and we don't begin fires till November."

I rang the bell emphatically.

"Do not trouble yourself, doctor," she remonstrated gently. "What does it matter?"

I went out into the sitting room to meet the maid as she entered.

"Why haven't these fires been lighted?" I asked again.

"I don't know, sir," she answered. "I received no orders about them."

"Where is Colonel Colquhoun?"

"He went out after breakfast, sir, and has not come back yet."

"Has the nurse arrived?"

"No, sir."

"Well, light these fires at once."

"I don't light fires, sir," she said, drawing herself up. "It isn't my work."

"Whose work is it?" I demanded.

"Either of the housemaids', sir, but they're both out," she answered, ogling me pertly.

I own that I was exasperated, and I showed it in such a way that she fled precipitately. I followed her downstairs to find the butler. I happened to know the man. His wife had been in my service, and I had attended her through a severe illness since her marriage.

"Do you know if there's such a thing as a sensible woman in this establishment, Williamson?" I demanded.

"Well, sir, the cook's sensible when she's sober," he answered, pinching his chin dubiously.

"Does she happen to be sober now?"

He glanced at the clock. "I'll just see, sir," he said.

When he returned he announced, with perfect gravity, that she was "passable sober, but busy with the dinner."

"Then look here," I exclaimed, out of all patience, "we must do it ourselves."

"Yes, sir," he said. "Anything I *can* do."

When I explained the difficulty, he suggested sending for his wife, who could manage, he thought, until the trained nurse arrived, and help her afterward. It was a good idea, and my man was despatched to bring her immediately.

"They're a bad lot o' servants, the women in this 'ouse at

present," Williamson informed me. "The missus didn't choose 'em 'erself"—and he shook his head significantly. ''But she knows what's what, and they're going. That's why they're takin' advantage."

I returned to Evadne. Her eyes were closed and her forehead contracted. Every breath of cold air was cutting her lungs like a knife, but she looked up at me when I took her hand, and smiled. I never knew anybody so patient and uncomplaining. She was lying on a little iron bedstead, hard and narrow as a camp bed. The room was bare-looking, the floor being polished and with only two small rugs, one at the fireplace and one beside the bed, upon it. It looked like a nun's cell, and there was a certain suggestion of purity in the sweetness and order of it quite consistent with the idea; but it was a north room and very cold. Evadne had unconsciously clasped my hand, and dozed off for a few minutes, holding it tight, but the cough re-aroused her. When she looked at me again her mind was wandering. She knew me, but she did not know what she was saying.

"I am so thankful!" she exclaimed. "The peace of mind —the peace of mind—I cannot tell you what a relief it is!"

Williamson came in on tiptoe and lit the fire, and Evadne's maid followed him in and stood looking on, half sheepishly and half in defiance. I noticed now that she was a hard-faced, bold-looking girl, not at all the sort of person to have about my delicate little lady, and when Mrs. Williamson arrived, I ordered her out of the room, and never allowed her to enter it again. During the week she left altogether, and I was fortunately able to procure a suitable woman to wait upon Mrs. Colquhoun. She has been with her ever since, by the way.

I felt pretty sure by this time that no nurse had been sent for, and I therefore despatched one of Colonel Colquhoun's men in a dogcart to Morningquest to telegraph for one. But she could not arrive before daylight even by special train, and it had now become a matter of life and death, and as Mrs. Williamson had no knowledge of nursing to help her good will, I determined to spend the night beside my patient.

When Colonel Colquhoun came in and found me making myself at home in his house he expressed himself greatly pleased.

"When I returned this afternoon to see how Mrs. Colquhoun

was progressing, I found that none of my orders had been carried out, and now she is dangerously ill," I said severely.

"Faith," he replied, changing countenance, "I'm very sorry to hear it, and I'm afraid I'm to blame, for I was in the deuce of a hurry when I saw you this morning, and never thought of a word you said from that moment to this. Now I'm genuinely sorry," he repeated. "Is there nothing I can do? Mrs. Orton Beg——"

"She's gone abroad for the winter."

"Ah, to be sure!"

"And everybody else is away who would be of any use," I added, "and I therefore propose, if you have no objection, to stay here to-night myself."

"You'd oblige me greatly by doing so," he answered earnestly. "I don't know what there is for dinner, but I shall enjoy it all the more myself for the pleasure of your company."

He made no special inquiries about his wife's condition, and never went near her; but as he was in a tolerably advanced state of intoxication before he retired for the night, it was quite as well, perhaps.

Mrs. Williamson had probably done her day's work before I sent for her, and, with all the will in the world to wake and watch, she fell fast asleep before midnight, and I let her sleep. There were only the fires to be attended to—at least that was all that I could have trusted her to do. Watching the case generally, and seizing opportune moments to administer remedies would not have been in her line at all.

Evadne knew me always, but she lost all count of time.

"You seem to come every day now, doctor," she said once during the night, "and I *am* glad to see you!"

For two hours toward dawn, when the temperature is sensibly lower, I gave my little lady up; but she was better by the time the trained nurse arrived, and eventually she pulled through—greatly owing, I am sure, to her own perfect patience. She was always the same all through her illness, gentle, uncomplaining, grateful for every trifle that was done for her, and tranquillity herself. My impression was that she enjoyed being ill. I never saw a symptom of depression the whole time; but when she had quite recovered, and although, as often happens after a severe illness, when so-called "trifles" are discovered and checked which would otherwise have been allowed to run on until they grew serious—although for this reason she was certainly stronger than she had ever been since

I became acquainted with her, no sooner did she resume her accustomed habits than that old unsatisfactory something in her, which it was so easy to perceive but so difficult to define, returned in full force.

I had ceased to be critical, however. Colonel Colquhoun's careless neglect of her had continued throughout her illness, and I thought I understood.

CHAPTER VI.

I HAD necessarily seen much of Evadne during her illness, and the intimacy never again lapsed.

Jealousy was not one of Colonel Colquhoun's vices. He always encouraged any man to come to the house for whom she showed the slightest preference, and I have heard him complain of her indifference to admiration.

"She'll dress herself up carefully in the evening to sit at home alone with me, and go out to a big dinner party in the dowdiest gown she's got," he told me once. "She doesn't care a hang whether she's admired or not—rather objects, if anything, perhaps"

Colonel Colquhoun rubbed his hands here with a certain enjoyment of such perversity. But I could see that Evadne did not relish the subject. It was one afternoon at As-You-Like-It. I was tired after a long day and had dropped in to ask for some tea. Colonel Colquhoun came up to entertain me, and Evadne went on with her work while we chatted familiarly.

"You were never so civil to any of your admirers, Evadne, as you were to that great boy in the regiment," Colonel Colquhoun continued, quite blind to her obvious and natural though silent objection to being made the subject of conversation—"a young subaltern of ours," he explained to me, "a big broad-shouldered lad, six feet high, who just worshipped Evadne!"

"Poor boy!" said Evadne, sighing. "He was cruelly butchered in a horribly fruitless skirmish with his fellow-creatures during that last small war. I was glad I was able to be kind to him. He was always very nice to me."

"Well, there's a reason for everything!" Colonel Colquhoun observed gallantly.

"Don't you like boys?" Evadne asked, looking up at me.

" The ones we have here at the depôt, when they first come, fresh from the public schools, are delightful, with their high spirits, and their love affairs ; their pranks, and the something beyond which will make men of them eventually. I can never see enough of *our* boys. But Colonel Colquhoun very kindly lets me have as many of them here as I like."

" Faith, I can't keep them out, for they're all in love with you," said Colonel Colquhoun.

" And I am in love with them all ! " she answered brightly, leaning back in her chair, and holding up her work to look at it. As she did so, the lower half of her face was concealed from me, and her eyes were cast down. I only glanced at her, but, in the act of doing so, I suddenly became aware, by one of those curious flashes of imperfect recollection which come to us all at times to torment us, that I had seen her somewhere. before I knew who she was, in that attitude exactly ; but where, or under what circumstance, I failed to recollect. The impression, however, was indelible, and haunted me ever afterward.

" Now, there's Diavolo," Colonel Colquhoun continued—the exchange I had suggested had been effected by this time, and Diavolo was quartered at the depôt—not exactly to Colonel Colquhoun's delight, perhaps, but he was very good about it. " Now, there's Diavolo. He tells me to my face that he was the first to propose to Mrs. Colquhoun, and always meant to marry her, and means it still. He said to me coaxingly, only last Friday, when I was coming out of barracks : ' Take me home with you to-day, sir.' And I answered, pretending to be severe, but pulling his sleeve, you know : ' Indeed I won't. You'll be making love to Mrs. Colquhoun.' And he got very red, and said quite huffily : ' Well, I think you might let a fellow look at her.' And of course I had to bring him back with me, and he sat down on the floor at her feet there, and got on with the most ridiculous nonsense. You couldn't help laughing ! ' I should like to kill you, and carry her off,' he said, for all the world as if he meant it. And no more harm in the boy, either, than there is in Evadne herself," Colonel Colquhoun added good-humouredly.

This is a specimen of the man at his best. Latterly I had seldom seen him in such a genial mood at home—abroad he brightened up. But in his own house *now*—for a process of deterioration had been going on ever since his arrival in Morningquest—his mind was apt to resemble a dark cave which is transformed diurnally by a single shaft of sunshine

which streams in for a brief space at a certain hour. The happy moment with him occurred about the time of the tenth brandy-and-soda, as nearly as I could calculate, and it lasted till the eleventh, when he usually relapsed into gloom again, and became overcast until the next recurrence of the phenomena. But whatever his mood was, Evadne humoured it. She responded always—or tried to—when he was genial; and when he was morose, she was dumb. I thought her a model wife.

CHAPTER VII.

AFTER her illness Evadne spent much of her time in the west window of the drawing room at As-You-Like-It with her little work-table beside her, embroidering. I never saw her reading, and there were no books about the room; but the work she did was beautiful. She used to have a stand before her with flowers arranged upon it, and copy them on to some material in coloured silks direct from nature. She could not draw either with pen or pencil, or paint with a brush, but she could copy with her needle quite accurately, and would do a spray of lilies to the life, or in the most approved conventional manner, if it pleased her. Her not being able to draw struck me as a curious limitation, and I asked her once if she could account for it in any way.

"I believe I am an example of how much we owe to early influences," she answered, laughing; "and probably I have the talent both for drawing and painting in me, but it remains latent for want of cultivation. My mother drew and painted beautifully as a girl, but she had given both up before I was old enough to imitate her, and only copied flowers as I do with her needle, and I used to watch her at her work until I felt impelled to do the same. If she had gone on with her drawing I am sure I should have drawn too; but as it was, I never thought of trying."

"Moral for mothers," I observed: "Keep up your own accomplishments if you would have your daughters shine."

Evadne was not enough in the fresh air at this time, and she was too much alone. I ventured once, in my professional capacity, to say that she should have friends to stay with her occasionally, but she passed the suggestion off without either accepting or declining it, and then I spoke to Colonel Colquhoun. He, however, pooh-poohed the idea altogether.

"She's all right," he said. "You don't know her. She always lives like that ; it's her way."

I also counselled regular exercise, and to that she replied : "I *do* go out. Why, you passed me yourself on the road only the other day."

I certainly had seen her more than once, alone, miles away from home, walking at the top of her speed, as if impelled by some strong emotion or inexorable necessity, and I did not like the sign. "One or two hours' walk regularly every day is what you should take," I told her. "The virtue of it is in the regularity. If you make a habit of taking a short walk daily you will have got more sunshine and fresh air, which is what you specially require, in one year than you will in two if you continue to go out in a jerky, irregular way. And you must give up covering impossible distances in feverish haste, as you do now. Walk gently, and make yourself feel that you have full leisure to walk as long as you like. You will find the effect tranquillizing. It is a common mistake to make a business of taking exercise. I am constantly lecturing my patients about it. If you want exercise to raise your spirits, brace your nerves, and do you good generally, it must be all pure pleasure without conscious exertion. Pleasurable moments prolong life."

"Thank you," Evadne answered gently. "I know, of course, that you are right, and I will do my best to profit by your advice, if it be only to show you how much I appreciate your kindness. But I must have a scamper occasionally, a regular *burst*, you know. Please don't stop that ! The indulgence, when I am in the mood, is my pet vice at present."

The great drawing room at As-You-Like-It, which I had mentioned in my letter to Lady Adeline as containing the one bright spot in that gloomy abode, was an addition tacked on to the end of the house, and evidently an afterthought. It was entered by a flight of shallow steps from the hall, and was above the level of the public road, which ran close past that end of the house, the grounds and approach being on the other side. It was lighted by three high narrow windows looking toward the north, and three more close together looking west, and forming a bay so deep as to be quite a small room in itself. It almost overhung the high-road, only a tall holly-hedge being between them, but so near that the topmost twigs of the holly grew up to the window-sill. It was a quiet road, however, too far from the town for much traffic, and Evadne could sit there with the windows open undisturbed, and enjoy the long level prospect of fertile land, field and fallow, wood and water, that lay before her.   She sat in the centre window, and I think it was from thence that she learnt to appreciate the charms of a level landscape as you look down upon it, about which I heard her discourse so eloquently in after days.   It was her chosen corner, and there she sat silent many and many an hour, with busy fingers and thoughts we could not follow, communing at times with nature, I doubt not, or with her own heart, and thankful to be still.

The road beneath her was one I had to traverse regularly, and it became a habit to look up as I drove past.   If she were in her accustomed seat she usually raised her eyes from her work for a moment to smile me a greeting.   Once she was standing up, leaning languidly against the window frame, twirling a rose in her fingers, but she straightened herself into momentary energy when she recognized me, and threw the rose at me with accurate aim.   It was the youngest and most familiar thing I had known her do—an impulse of pure mischief, I thought, for the rose was *La France*, and the sentiment, as I translated it, was : " You will value it more than I do ! "   For she hated the French.

There often occurs and recurs to the mind incessantly a verse or an apt quotation in connection with some act or event, a haunting definition of the impression it makes upon us, and Evadne in the wide west window, bending busily over her work, set my mind on one occasion to a borrowed measure of words which never failed me from that time forward when I saw her so engaged :

> There she weaves by night and day
> A magic web of colour gay.
> She has heard a whisper say,
> A curse is on her if she stay
>   To look down to Camelot.
> She knows not what the curse may be,
> And so she weaveth steadily,
> And little other care hath she,
>   The lady of Shalott.

But where was Camelot?   Fountain Towers, just appearing above the tree-tops to the north, was the only human habitation in sight.   I had a powerful telescope on the highest tower, and one day, in an idle mood, I happened to be looking through it with no definite purpose, just sweeping it slowly from point to point of the landscape, when all at once Evadne came into the field of vision with such startling distinctness that I stepped back from the glass. She was sitting in her accustomed place, with her work on her lap, her hands clasped before her, leaning forward looking up in my direction with an expression in her whole attitude that appealed to me like a cry for help. The impression was so strong that I ordered my dogcart out and drove over to As-You-Like-It at once. But I found her perfectly tranquil when I arrived, with no trace of recent emotion either in her manner or appearance.

When I went home I had the telescope removed. I had forgotten that we overlooked that corner of As-You-Like-It.

CHAPTER VIII.

THE idea that Evadne was naturally unsociable was pretty general, and Colonel Colquhoun believed it as much as anybody. I remember being at As-You-Like-It one afternoon when he rallied her on the subject. He had stopped me as I was driving past to ask me to look at a horse he was thinking of buying. The animal was being trotted up and down the approach by a groom for our inspection when Evadne returned from somewhere, driving herself.

She pulled up beside us and got out.

"I never see you driving any of your friends about," Colonel Colquhoun remarked. "You're very unsociable, Evadne."

"Oh, well, you see," she answered slowly, "I like to be alone and think when I am driving. It worries me to have to talk to people—as a rule."

"Well," he said, glancing at the reeking pony, "if your thoughts went as fast as Blue Mick seems to have done to-day, you must have got through a good deal of thinking in the time."

Evadne looked at the pony. "Take him round," she said to the groom ; and then she remarked that it must be tea-time, and asked us both to go in, and have some.

The air had brought a delicate tinge of colour to her usually pale cheeks, and she looked bright and bonny as she sat beside the tea-table, taking off her gloves and chatting, with her hat pushed slightly up from her forehead. It was an expansive moment with her, one of the rare ones when she unconsciously revealed something of herself in her conversation.

There were some flowers on the tea-table which I admired.

" Ah ! " she said, with a sigh of satisfaction in their beauty ; " I derive all my pleasure in life from things inanimate. An arrangement of deep-toned marigolds with brown centres in a glass like these, all aglow beneath the maiden-hair, gives me more pleasure than anything else I can think of at this moment."

" Not more pleasure than your friends do," I ventured.

" I don't know," she replied. " In the matter of love *surgit amari aliquid.* Friends disappoint us. But in the contemplation of flowers all our finer feelings are stimulated and blended, and yet there is no excess of feeling to end in regrets, or a painful reaction. When the flowers fade, we cheerfully gather fresh ones. But I hope I do not undervalue my friends," she broke off. " I only mean to say—when you think of all the uncertainties of life, of sickness and death, and other things more dreadful, which overtake our dearest, do what we will to protect them ; and then that worst thing whether it be in ourselves or others : I mean change—when you think of it all, surely it is well to turn to some delicate source of delight, like this, for relief—and to forget." and she curved her slender hand round the flowers caressingly, looking up at me at the same time as if she were pleading to be allowed to have her own way.

I did not remonstrate with her. I hardly knew the danger then myself of refusing to suffer.

It was some weeks before I saw her again after that. I had been busy. But one day, as I was driving into Morningquest, I overtook her on the road, walking in the same direction. I was in a close carriage, but I pulled the checkstring as soon as I recognized her, and got out. She turned when she heard the carriage stop, and seeing me alight came forward and shook hands. She looked wan and weary.

" Those are fine horses of yours," was her smileless greeting. " How are you ? "

" Have you been having a ' burst ' ? " I said—she was quite five miles from home. She looked up and down the road for answer, and affected to laugh, but I could see that she was not at all in a laughing mood, and also that she was already over-fatigued. I thought of begging to be allowed to drive her back, but then it occurred to me that, even if she consented, which was not likely, as she had a perfect horror of giving trouble, and would never have been persuaded that I was not going out of my way at the greatest personal inconvenience merely to pay her a polite attention ; but even if she had consented, she would probably have had to spend the rest of the day alone in that great west window, with nothing to take her out of herself, and nothing more enlivening to look at than dreary winter fields under a sombre sky, and that would not do at all. A better idea, however, occurred to me.

" I am going to see Mrs. Orton Beg," I said. " She is not very well.

Evadne had been staring blandly at the level landscape, but she turned to me when I spoke, and some interest came into her eyes.

" Have you seen her lately," I continued.

" N-no," she answered, as if she were considering ; " not for some time.

" Come now," I boldly suggested. " It will do her good. I won't talk if you want to think," I added.

Her face melted into a smile at this, and on seeing her stiffness relax, I wasted no more time in persuasion, but returned to the carriage and held the door open for her. She followed me slowly, although she looked as if she had not quite made up her mind, and got in ; but still as if she were hesitating. Once she was seated, however, I could see that she was not sorry she had yielded ; and presently she acknowledged as much herself.

" I believe I was tired," she said.

" Rest now, then," I answered, taking a paper out of my pocket. She settled herself more luxuriously in her corner, put her arm in the strap, and looked out through the open window. The day was mild though murky, the sky was leaden gray. We rolled through the wintry landscape rapidly— brown hedgerows, leafless trees, ploughed fields, a crow, two crows, a whole flock home-returning from their feeding ground ; scattered cottages, a woman at a door looking out with a child in her arms, three boys swinging on a gate, a man trudging along with a bundle, a labourer trimming a bank ; mist rising in the low-lying meadows ; grazing cattle, nibbling sheep ;—but she did not see these things at first, any of them ; she was thinking. Then she began to see, and forgot to think. Then her fatigue wore off, and a sense of relief, of ease, and of well-being generally, took gradual possession of her. I could see the change come into her countenance, and before we had arrived in Morningquest, she had begun to talk to me cheerfully of her own accord. We had to skirt the old gray walls which surrounded the palace gardens, and as we did so, she looked up at them—indifferently at first, but immediately afterward with a sudden flash of recognition. She said nothing, but I could see she drew herself together as if she had been hurt.

"Do you go there often?" I asked her.

"No—Edith died there; and then that child," she answered, looking at me as if she were surprised that I should have thought it likely.

"She shrinks from sorrowful associations and painful sights," I thought. But I did not know, when I asked the question, that our poor Edith had been a particular friend of hers.

We stopped the next moment at Mrs. Orton Beg's, and she leant forward to look at the windows, smiling and brightening again.

I helped her out and followed her to the door, which she opened as if she were at home there. She waited for me for a moment in the hall till I put my hat down, and then we went to the drawing room together, and walked in in the same familiar way.

Mrs. Orton Beg was there with another lady, a stout but very comely person, handsomely dressed, who seemed to have just risen to take her leave.

The moment Evadne saw this lady she sprang forward. "*Oh, Mother!*" she cried, throwing her arms round her neck.

"Evadne—my dear, dear child!" the lady exclaimed, clasping her close and kissing her, and then, holding her off to look at her. "Why, my child, how thin you are, and pale, and weak——"

"Oh, mother—I *am* so glad! I *am* so glad!" Evadne cried again, nestling close up to her, and kissing her neck; and then she laid her head on her bosom and burst into hysterical sobs.

I instantly left the room, and Mrs. Orton Beg followed me.

"They have not met since—just after Evadne's marriage," she explained to me. "Evadne offended her father, and there still seems to be no hope of a reconciliation."

"But surely it is cruel to separate mother and child," I exclaimed indignantly. "He has no right to do that."

" No, and he would not be able to do it with one of us," she answered bitterly; " but my sister is of a yielding disposition. She is like Mrs. Beale, one of the old-fashioned ' womanly women,' who thought it their duty to submit to everything, and make the best of everything, including injustice, and any other vice it pleased their lords to practise. But for this weakness of good women the world would be a brighter and better place by this time. We see the disastrous folly of sub-mitting our reason to the rule of self-indulgence and self-interest now, however ; and, please God, we shall change all that before I die. He will be a bold man soon who will dare to have the impertinence to dictate to us as to what we should or should not do, or think, or say. No one can pretend that the old system of husband and master has answered well, and it has had a fair trial. Let us hope that the new method of partnership will be more successful."

" Yes, indeed ! " I answered earnestly.

Mrs. Orton Beg looked up in my face, and her own counte-nance cleared.

" You and Evadne seem to be very good friends," she said. " I am so glad." Then she looked up at me again, with a curious little smile which I could not interpret. " Does she remind you of anybody—of anything, ever ? " she asked.

" Why—surely she is like you," I said, seeing a likeness for the first time.

" Yes," she answered, in a more indifferent tone. " There is a likeness, I am told."

I tried afterward to think that this explained the haunting half recollection I seemed to have of something about Evadne; but it did not. On the contrary, it re-awakened and con-firmed the feeling that I had seen Evadne before I knew who she was, under circumstances which I now failed to recall.

Thinking she would like to be alone after that interview with her mother, I left the carriage for her, and walked back to Fountain Towers ; and the state I was in after doing the ten miles warned me that I had been luxuriating too much in carriages lately, and must begin to practise what I preached again in the way of exercise, if I did not wish to lay up a fat and flabby old age for myself.

I made a point of not seeing Evadne for some little time after that event, so that she might not feel bound to refer to it in case she should shrink from doing so. But the next time we met, as it happened, I had another glimpse of her feeling

for her friends, which showed me how very much mistaken I
had been in my estimate of the depth of her affections.   It was
at As-You-Like-It.   I had walked over from Fountain Towers,
and dropped in casually to ask for some tea, and, Colonel Colquhoun arriving at the same moment from barracks, we went
up to the drawing room together, and found Evadne in her
accustomed place, busy with her embroidery as usual.   She
shook hands, but said nothing to show that she was aware of
the interval there had been since she saw me last.   When she
sat down again, however, she went on with her work, and there
was a certain satisfied look in her face, as if some little wish
had been gratified and she was content.   I knew when she
took up her work that she liked me to be there, and wanted
me to stay, for she always put it down when visitors she did
not care for called, and made a business of entertaining them.
But we had scarcely settled ourselves to talk when the butler
opened the door, and announced " Mr. Bertram Frayling," and
a tall, slender, remarkably handsome young fellow, with a
strong family likeness to Evadne herself, entered with boyish
diffidence, smiling nervously, but looking important, too.
Evadne jumped up impetuously.

" *Bertram !* " she exclaimed, holding out her arms to him.
" Why, what a big fellow you have grown ! " she cried, finding she could hardly reach to his neck to hug him. "And how
handsome you are ! "

" They say I am just like you," he answered, looking down
at her lovingly, with his arm around her waist. Neither of them
took any notice of us.

" This is your birthday, dear," Evadne said.   " I have been
thinking of you the whole day long.   I always keep all the
birthdays.   Did you remember mine ? "

" I—don't think I did," he answered honestly.   " But this
is my twenty-first birthday, Evadne, and that s how it is I
am here.   I am my own master from to-day."

" And the first thing you do with your liberty is to come and
see your sister," said Colonel Colquhoun.   " You're made of
the right stuff, my boy," and he shook hands with him heartily.

Evadne clung with one hand to his shoulder, and pressed
her handkerchief first to this eye and then to that alternately
with the other, looking so glad, however, at the same time,
that it was impossible to say whether she was going to laugh
or cry for joy.

" But aren't there rejoicings ? " she asked.

"Oh, yes!" he answered. "But I told my father if you were not asked I should not stay for them. I was determined to see you to-day." He flushed boyishly as he spoke, and smiled round upon us all again.

"But wasn't he very angry?" Evadne said.

"Yes," her brother answered, twinkling. "The girls got round him, and tried to persuade him, but they only made him worse, especially when they all declared that when they came of age they meant to do *something*, too! He said that he was afflicted with the most obstinate, ill-conditioned family in the county, and began to row mother as if it were her fault. But I wouldn't stand that!"

"You were right, Bertram," Evadne exclaimed, clenching her hands. "Now that you are a man, never let mother be made miserable. Did she know you were coming?"

"Yes, and was very glad," he answered, "and sent you messages."

But here Colonel Colquhoun and I managed to slip from the room. Evadne sent her brother back that day to grace the close of the festivities in his honour, but he returned the following week, and stayed at As-You-Like-It, and also with me, when he confirmed my first exceedingly good impression of him. Evadne quite wakened up under his influence, but, unfortunately for her, he went abroad in a few weeks for a two years' trip round the world, and, I think, losing him again so soon made it almost worse for her than if they had never been reunited, especially as another and irreparable loss came upon her immediately after his departure. This was the sudden death of her mother, the news of which arrived one day in a curt note written by her father to Colonel Colquhoun, no previous intimation of illness having been sent to break the shock of the announcement. I can never be thankful enough for the happy chance which brought about that last accidental meeting of Evadne with her mother. But for that, they would not have seen each other again; and I had the pleasure of learning eventually that the perfect understanding which they arrived at during the few hours they spent together on that occasion, afterward became one of the most comforting recollections of Evadne's life—"A hallowed memory," as she herself expressed it, "such as it is very good for us to cherish. Thank Heaven for the opportunity which renewed and intensified my appreciation of my mother's love and goodness, so as to make my last impression of her one which must stand out distinctly forever from the rest, and be always a joyful sorrow to recall. Do you know what a *joyful* sorrow is? Ah! something that makes one feel warm and forgiving in the midst of one's regrets, a delicious feeling ; when it takes possession of you, you cease to be hard and cold and fierce, and want to do good."

Mrs. Frayling died of a disease for which we have a remedy nowadays—or, to speak plainly, she died for want of proper treatment. Her husband gloried in what he called " a rooted objection to new-fangled notions," and would not send for a modern practitioner even when the case became serious, preferring to confide it entirely to a very worthy old gentleman of his own way of thinking, with one qualification, who had attended his household successfully for twenty-four years, during which time only one other member of his family had ever been seriously ill, and he also had died. But I hope and believe that my poor little lady never knew the truth about her mother's last illness. She was overwhelmed with grief as it was, and it cut one to the quick to see her, day after day, in her black dress, sitting alone, pale and still and uncomplaining, her invariable attitude when she was deeply distressed, and not to be able to say a word or do a thing to relieve her. As usual at that time of the year, everybody whom she cared to see at all was away except myself, so that during the dreariest of the winter months she was shut up with her grief in the most unwholesome isolation. As the spring returned, however, she began to revive, and then, suddenly, it appeared to me that she entered upon a new phase altogether.

CHAPTER IX.

DURING the first days of our acquaintance Evadne's attitude, whatever happened, surprised me. I could anticipate her action up to a certain point, but just the precise thing she would do was the last thing I had expected; I knew her feeling, in fact, but I was ignorant of the material it had to work upon, and by means of which it found expression. I had begun by believing her to be cold and self-sufficing, but even before her illness I had perceived in her a strange desire for sympathy, and foreseen that on occasion she would exact it in large measure from anyone she cared about. It was making much of a cut finger one day that she had led me to expect she would be exacting in illness, languishing as ladies do, to excite sympathy; and when the illness came I found I had been right in so far as I had believed that she would appreciate sympathy, but entirely wrong about the means she would employ to obtain it. Instead of languishing, when she found herself really suffering, she pulled herself together, and bore the trial with heroic calm. As I have said, she never uttered a complaint; and she had the strength of mind to ignore annoyances which few people in perfect health could have borne with fortitude. Certainly her attitude then had excited sympathy, and respect as well. It was as admirable as it was unexpected.

I had also perceived that she could not bear anything disagreeable. She seldom showed the least irritability herself, nor would she tolerate it for a moment in anyone else. Servants who were not always cheerful had to go, and the kind of people who snap at each other in the bosom of their families she carefully avoided, turning from them instinctively as she would have done from any perception revolting to the physical senses; and that she would fly disgusted from sickening sights or sounds or odours I never doubted. But here again I was wrong—or rather the evidence was utterly misleading. I found her one day sitting on the bridge of a little river that crossed a quiet lane near their house, and got down from my horse to talk to her, and as we stood looking over the parapet looking into the stream, the bloated carcase of a dead dog came floating by. She could only have caught a glimpse of it, for she drew back instantly, but she looked so pale and nauseated that I had to take her to the house, and insist upon her having some wine. And I once took her, at her own earnest request, to visit a children's hospital; but before we had seen a dozen of the little patients she cried so piteously I was obliged to take her away; and she could never bear to speak of the place afterward. And lastly, I had seen how she shrank from going to the palace because of the association with Edith's terrible death, and the chance of seeing her poor, repulsive looking little boy there.

Yet when it came to be a question of facing absolute horrors in the interests of the sufferers, she was the first to volunteer, and she did so with a quiet determination there was no resisting, and every trace of inward emotion so carefully obliterated that one might have been forgiven for supposing her to be altogether callous.

This happened after her mother's death, in the spring, when she had already begun to revive, and was the first startling symptom she showed of the new phase of interest and energy upon which I suspected she was entering. I hoped at the time that the great grief had carried off the minor ailments of the mind as the great illness did of the body, and that the change would prove to be for the better eventually, although the first outcome of it was not the kind of thing I liked at all—for her.

I had not seen her for a week or so when she was ushered one morning into my consulting room. She had not asked for an appointment, and had been waiting to take her turn with the other patients.

"Well, what can I do for *you?*" I said. I was somewhat surprised to see her. "You don't look very ill."

"No, thank goodness," she answered cheerfully; "and I don't mean to be ill. I have come to be vaccinated."

"Ah, that is wise," I said.

"You have heard, I suppose, that small-pox has broken out in the barracks?" she said when she was going. "There are fifteen cases, four of them women, and one a child, and they are going to put them under canvas on the common, and I shall be obliged to go and see that they are properly nursed. That is why I am in such a hurry. Military nursing is of the most primitive kind in times of peace. Our doctor is all that he should be, but what can he do but prescribe? It takes all his time just to go round and get through his ordinary duties."

"Did I understand you to say that you are going to look after the small-pox patients?" I asked politely.

"Yes," she answered defiantly. "I am going to be isolated with them out on the common. My tent is already pitched. I shall not take small-pox, I assure you."

"I don't see how you can be so sure," I said.

She gave me one of her most puzzling answers, one of those in which I felt there was an indication of the something about her which I did not understand.

"Oh, because it is such a relief!" she said.

"How a relief?" I questioned.

"Oh—I shall not take the disease," she repeated, "and I shall enjoy the occupation."

But this, I knew, was an evasion. However, I had no time to argue the point with her just then, so I waited until my consultations were over, and then went to see Colonel Colquhoun. I thought if he would not forbid he might at all events persuade her to abandon her rash design. I found him at his own place, walking about the garden with his hands in his pockets, and a cigar in his mouth. He was in a facetious mood, the one of his I most disliked.

" Now, you look quite concerned," he said, with an extra affectation of brogue, when I had told him my errand. " Sure, she humbugs you, Evadne does ! If you knew her as well as I do, you'd not be troubling yourself about her so much. I tell you, she'll come to no harm in the world. Now what do you think were her reasons for going to live in the small-pox camp ? "

" Then she *has* gone ! " I exclaimed.

" Oh, yes, she's gone," he answered. " The grass never has time to grow under that young woman's feet if she's an idea to carry out, I will say that for her. But what do you think she said when I asked her why she'd be going among the small-pox patients ? ' Oh,' she said, ' I want to see what they look like ! ' And she'd another reason, too. She'll make herself look like an interesting nurse, you know, and quite enjoy dressing up for the part."

I felt sure that all this was a horrid perversion of the truth, but I let it pass.

" You'll not interfere, then ? " I persisted.

" Not I, indeed ! " he answered. " She never comes commandering it over me, and I'm not going to meddle with her private affairs, so long as she doesn't come here bringing infection, that's all."

" But she may catch the disease herself and die of it, or be disfigured for life," I remonstrated.

" And she might catch her death of cold here in the garden, or be burnt beyond all recognition by a spark setting fire to her ball-dress the next time she wears one," he answered philosophically. " When you look at the chances, now, they're about equal.'

He smiled at me complacently when he had said this, and something he saw in my face inclined him to chuckle, but he suppressed the inclination, twirling his fair moustache instead, first on one side and then on the other, rapidly. In his youth he must have been one of those small boys who delighted to spear a bee with a pin and watch it buzz round. The boy is pretty sure the bee can't hurt him, but yet half the pleasure of the performance lies in the fact of its having a sting. It would not have been convenient for Colonel Colquhoun to

quarrel with me, because there had been certain money trans-
actions between us which left him greatly my debtor ; but he
thought me secured by my interest in Evadne, and indulged
himself on every possible occasion in the pleasure of opposing me. Not that he bore me any ill-will, either. I knew
that he would borrow more money from me at any time in
the friendliest way, if he happened to want it. I was his
honey bee, and he was fond of honey ; but it delighted him
also to see me buzz.

I was obliged to consider my own patients and keep away
from the small-pox camp during the epidemic, for fear of
carrying infection, and consequently I saw nothing of Evadne,
and only heard of her through the military doctor, for she
would not write. His report of her, however, was always the
same at first. She was the life of the camp, bright, cheerful,
and active, never tired apparently, and never disheartened.
This went on for some time, and then, one evening, there
came another report. She was just as cheerful as ever, but
looking most awfully done.

At daybreak next morning I drove out to the common, and,
leaving my dogcart outside the camp, went in to look for her.
I knew that she was generally up all night, and was therefore
prepared to find her about, and I met her making her way
toward her own tent. She was dressed like a French *bonne*,
in a short dark blue gown made of some washing material,
with a white apron and white cap, and a châtelaine with useful implements upon it hanging from her girdle, a very suitable costume for the work ; but she wore no wrap of any kind,
and the morning air was keen.

I noticed as she walked toward me that her gait was a little
uncertain. Once she put out her hand as if seeking something to grasp, and once she staggered and stopped. I
hastened to her assistance, and saw as I approached her that
she was colourless even to her lips; her eyes were bright and
sunken, with large black circles round them, and the lids were
heavy. I drew her hand through my arm without more formal
greeting, and she grasped it gratefully for a moment, then
dropped it and stepped back.

" I forgot," she said, " it seems so natural to see you anywhere. But don't touch me. I shall infect you."

" I shall have to go home and change in any case," I
answered briskly.

" I've been up all night with a poor woman," she said, " and

I'm just tired out. Don't look concerned, though. I shall not take small-pox. My own illness, you remember, was a blessing in disguise, and I am sure the absorbing distraction of helping to relieve others——" she stopped short, looked about her confusedly, and then exclaimed : " It is quite time I went to bed. I declare I don't know the Hospital Tent from the sandy common, nor a rabbit running about from a convalescent child, and the whin bushes are waltzing round me derisively." She swayed a little, recovered herself, tried to laugh, then threw up her hands, and fell forward into my arms.

I carried her to her tent, guided by one of the men. On the way Dr. James joined us. We laid her on her bed and looked anxiously for symptoms of the dreadful disease, but there were none.

" No, you see," Dr. James declared, " it's just what I expected—sheer exhaustion, and nothing else. But she'd better be got out of this atmosphere at once."

She was in a semi-unconscious, semi-somnolent state, half syncope, half sleep, and there was nothing to be gained by rousing her just then, so we wrapped her up warmly in shawls, sent for my dogcart, and lifted her on the back seat, where I supported her as best I could, while my man drove us to As-You-Like-It.

Colonel Colquhoun was not up when we arrived, but I waited to see her swallow some champagne after she had been put to bed, and in the meantime the bustle had aroused him. When he learnt the occasion of it, his wrath knew no bounds. He could not have abused me in choicer language if I had been one of his own subalterns. But I managed to keep my temper until I could get a word in, and then I mildly suggested that the best thing he could do, as he was so afraid of infection, was to give himself leave, and be off. " Nobody will expect *you* to stay and look after your wife," I said. " You'd better go to town."

It was what he would have done if I had not advised it, but the habit of opposing me was becoming so inveterate that he changed his mind, and, rather than act upon a suggestion of mine, ran the risk of living in barracks until all fear of infection was over.

Happily Evadne suffered from nothing worse than exhaustion, and soon recovered her strength ; but I never could agree with Dr. James about the merit of her conduct during the epidemic.

CHAPTER X.

IT was about this time, that is to say, immediately after the outbreak of small-pox was over, and in the height of the summer, that Mr. and Lady Adeline Hamilton-Wells returned from a prolonged absence abroad, and settled themselves for a few months at Hamilton House. I happened to be in London when they arrived, and saw them there as they passed through. Lady Adeline made particular inquiries about Evadne. "I don't think you, any of you, understand that girl," she said. "She is shy, and should be set going. She requires to be *induced* to come forward to do her share of the work of the world, but, instead of helping her, everybody lets her alone to mope in luxurious idleness at As-You-Like-It."

"She is never idle," I protested.

"I know what you mean," Lady Adeline answered. "She sits and sews; but that is idle trifling for a woman of her capacity. She was out of health and good-for-nothing when I saw her last with Mrs. Orton Beg in Paris, and therefore I held my peace; but now I mean to take her out of herself, and show her her mistake."

"I hope you will be able to do so," I said, and I was not speaking ironically; but all the same I scarcely expected that she would succeed. The day after my return home, however, which was only a week later, I called at Hamilton House, and it seemed to me then that she had already made a very good beginning. It was a brilliant afternoon, and I had walked through the fields from Fountain Towers, and found Lady Adeline alone for the moment, sitting out on the terrace under an awning, somewhat overcome by the heat.

"You have arrived at an acceptable time, as you always do," she said in her decided kindly way. "I am enjoying a brief period of repose before the racket begins again, and I invite you to share it."

"The racket?" I inquired.

"No, the repose," she replied. "Angelica is staying here, and Evadne——"

"Mrs. Colquhoun and racket!" I ejaculated.

"Well, it is difficult to associate the two ideas, I confess," she answered; "but you will see for yourself. Angelica makes the racket, of course, but Evadne enjoys it. I went to As-You-

Like-It as soon as I could, without waiting for her to call upon me, and I found her just as you had led me to expect, all staid propriety and precision, hiding deep dejection beneath an affectation of calm content—at least, that was my interpretation of her attitude—and inclined to be stiff with me; but I approached her as her mother's oldest and dearest friend, and she softened at once."

"And you brought her here?"

"That is quite the proper word for it," she rejoined. "I just brought her. I insisted upon her coming. I gave her no choice. And I also asked Colonel Colquhoun, but he declined. He said he thought Evadne would be all the better for getting away from home, and I agreed with him. He comes over, however, occasionally, and they seem to be very good friends. I don't dislike him at all."

This was said tentatively, but I did not care to discuss Colonel Colquhoun, and therefore, to change the subject, I asked Lady Adeline how she found Angelica.

"Very much improved in every way," she answered. "The happiest understanding has come to exist between herself and her husband since that dreadful occurrence. They are simply inseparable. She said to me the other day that her only chance of ever showing to any advantage at all would be against the quiet background of her husband's unobtrusive goodness. And I think myself that a great many people would never have believed in her if he had not. All her faults are so apparent, alas! while the very real and earnest purpose of her life is so seldom seen."

"She has been working very hard lately, I believe."

"Yes," Lady Adeline answered; "but I am thankful to say she has set up a private secretary, and who do you think it is? Our dear good Mr. Ellis!"

"I am heartily glad to hear of it," I said, "both for his sake and hers."

"Yes," she agreed. "It did not seem right that he should ever go away from amongst us, and you know how we all felt the severance after Diavolo went into the service, and there seemed no help for it, as his occupation was over. I am afraid, poor fellow, his experiences since he left us have been anything but happy. All that is over now, however, and it does seem so natural to have him about again!"

"He must make an admirable secretary," I said.

"Admirable!" she agreed—"in every way, for I don't

think Angelica would ever have got on quite so well with anybody else. He was always able to make her respect him, and now the habit is confirmed, so that he has more influence with her for good than almost anybody else—a restraining influence, you know. Her great fault still is impatience. She thinks everything should be put right the moment she perceives it to be wrong, and would raise revolutions if she were not restrained. It is always difficult to make her believe that evolution if slower is surer. But here they are."

As Lady Adeline spoke, Angelica, accompanied by Mr. Kilroy and Mr. Ellis, came out of the plantation to the left of the terrace upon which we were sitting, and walked across the lawn toward us, while at the same moment Diavolo and Evadne came round the corner of the house from the opposite direction and went to meet them. Evadne carried a parasol, but wore neither hat nor gloves. She looked very happy, listening to Diavolo's chatter.

Angelica carried a fishing rod, and I thought, as she approached, that I had never seen a more splendid specimen of hardy, healthy, vigorous young womanhood.

Evadne looked sickly beside her, and drooping, like a pale and fragile flower in want of water. The contrast must have struck Lady Adeline also, for presently she observed: " Evadne was as strong as Angelica once. Do you suppose her health has been permanently injured by that horrid Maltese fever ?"

" No," I said positively. "If she would give up sewing, and take a fishing rod, and go out with Angelica in a sensible dress like that, she would be as strong as ever in six months. But I fancy she would be shocked by the bare suggestion."

Angelica hugged Diavolo heartily when they met, and then, being the taller of the two, she put her arm round his neck, and all three strolled slowly on toward us, Mr. Ellis and Mr. Kilroy having already come up on to the terrace and sat down. While greeting the two latter I lost sight of the Heavenly Twins, and when I looked at them again something had evidently gone wrong. Angelica stood leaning on her rod berating Diavolo, who was answering with animation, while Evadne looked from one to the other in amazement, as the strange good child looks at the strange naughty ones. Whatever the difference was it was soon over, and then they came on again, talking and walking briskly, followed by four dogs.

" I *am* vulgar, decidedly, at times," Angelica acknowledged as she came up the steps. " I shouldn't be half so amusing if

I were not." She held out her hand to me, and then threw herself into the only unoccupied chair on the terrace, but instantly jumped up again. "I beg your pardon, Evadne," she said. "These are my society manners. When I am on the platform or otherwise engaged in *Unwomanly* pursuits outside the *Sphere*, I have to be more considerate."

Some more chairs were brought out, one of which Diavolo placed beside me. "This is for you," he said to Evadne; "I know you like to be near the Don." Evadne flushed crimson.

"Did you ever hear that story?" Angelica asked me.

Evadne's embarrassment visibly increased. "Angelica, don't tell it," she remonstrated; "It isn't fair."

Angelica laughed. "When Evadne first came here," she proceeded, "she sat next you at dinner one night, and didn't know who you were; but it seems you made such a profound and favourable impression upon her that afterward she had the curiosity to ask, when she learnt that you were a doctor. 'A doctor!' she exclaimed in surprise. 'He is more like a Don ¦than a doctor!' and you have been 'Don' to her intimates ever since."

"Well, I feel flattered," I said.

"I feel as if I ought to apologise," Evadne began—"only I meant no disrespect."

"My dear," Angelica interposed, "he is delighted to be distinguished by you in any way. But, by the pricking of my thumbs, something wicked"—and Colonel Colquhoun came out on to the terrace through the drawing room behind us. He shook hands with us all, his wife included, and then sat down.

"I say, Evadne——" Diavolo began.

"My dear boy," said Lady Adeline, "you mustn't call Mrs. Colquhoun by her Christian name."

"Christian!" jeered Diavolo. "Now, that *is* a good one! There's nothing Christian about Evadne. We looked her up in the dictionary ages ago, didn't we, Angelica? The name means Well-pleasing-one, as nearly as possible, and it suits her sometimes. Evadne—classical Evadne—was noted for her devotion to her husband, and distinguished herself finally on his funeral pyre—she ex-pyred there."

We all groaned aloud. "It was a somewhat theatrical exit, I confess," Diavolo pursued. "But, I say, Angelica, wouldn't it be fun to burn the colonel, and see Evadne do suttee on his body—only I doubt if she would!" He turned to Evadne.

"Mrs. Colquhoun," he began ceremoniously; "may I have the honour of calling you by your heathen name—as in the days beyond recalling?"

" When you are good," she answered.

"Ugh !" he exclaimed. "I should have had more respect for your honesty if you said 'no' at once. And it is very absurd of you, too, Evadne, because you know you are going to marry me when Colonel Colquhoun is promoted to regions of the blest. She would have married me first, only you stole a march on me, sir," he added, addressing Colonel Colquhoun. " However, I feel as if something were going to happen *now*, at last! There was a banshee wailing about my quarters in a minor key, very flat, last night. She had come all the way from Ireland to warn Colonel Colquhoun, and mistaken the house, I suppose."

" My dear——"

We all looked round. It was Mr. Hamilton-Wells addressing Lady Adeline in his most precise manner. He was standing in the open French window just behind us, tapping one hand with the *pince-nez* he held in the other.

" My dear, the cat has five kittens."

" My *dear !* " Lady Adeline exclaimed.

" They have only just arrived and——"

" Never mind them *now*," she cried hurriedly.

" But, my dear, you were anxious to know."

" I don't want to know in the least," she protested.

" But only this morning you said——"

" Oh, that was upstairs," she interrupted.

" What difference does that make ?" he wanted to know. " You don't mean to say you are anxious about the cat when you are upstairs, and not anxious when you come down ?"

Lady Adeline sank back in her chair, and resigned herself to a long altercation. Before it ended everybody else had disappeared, and I saw no more of Evadne on that occasion. But during the next few weeks I had many opportunities of observing the wonderful way she was waking up under the influence of the Heavenly Twins.

They gave her no time for reflection ; it was the life of action against the life of thought, and it suited her.

The ladies frequently made my house the object of an afternoon walk, and stayed for tea. Lady Adeline declared that the " girls " dragged her over because they wanted a new victim to torment with their superabundant animal spirits.

The superabundance was all Angelica's, I knew, but still Evadne was an accomplice, and they neither of them spared me in those days. They would rob my hot-houses of the best fruits and flowers, disarrange my books, turn pictures they did not like with their faces to the wall, drape my statues fantastically, criticise what they called my absurd bachelor habits, and give me good advice on the subject of marriage ; Lady Adeline sitting by meanwhile, aiding and abetting them with smiles, although protesting that she would not allow them to make me the butt of their idle raillery.

Evadne had a passion for the scent of gorse. She crammed pockets, sleeves, shoes, and the bosom of her dress with the yellow blossoms, and I often found these fragrant tokens of her presence scattered about my house after she had been there. Once, when we were all out walking together, she stopped to pick some from a bush, and as she was putting them into her bodice she made a remark which gave me pause to ponder.

"You will want to know why I do that, I suppose," she said. "You will be looking for a motive, for some secret spring of action. The simple fact that I love the gorse won't satisfy you. You would like to know why I love it, when I first began to love it, and anything else about it that might enable you to measure my feeling for it."

This was so exactly what I was in the habit of doing with regard to many matters that I could not say a word. But what struck me as significant about the observation was the obvious fact, gathered by inference, that, while I had been studying her, she also had been studying me, and I had never suspected it.

She walked on with Angelica after she had spoken, and I dropped behind with Lady Adeline.

" *Your* Evadne and Colonel Colquhoun's wife are two very different people," I said. "The one is a lively girl, the other a sad and bitter woman."

"Sad, not bitter," Lady Adeline corrected.

"I have heard her say bitter things !" I maintained.

"You may, perhaps, have heard her condemn wrong ones rather too emphatically," Lady Adeline suggested. "But all this is only a phase. She is in rather a deep groove at present, but we shall be able to get her out of it."

"I don't know," I answered dubiously. "I don't think it is that exactly. I believe there is some kind of warp in her mind I perceive it, but can neither define nor account for it yet. It is something morbid that makes her hold herself aloof. She has never allowed anybody in the neighbourhood to be intimate with her. Even I, who have seen her oftener than anybody, never feel that I know her really well—that I could reckon upon what she would do in an emergency. And I believe that there is something artificial in her attitude ; but why ? What is the explanation of all that is unusual about her ? "

Lady Adeline shook her head, and was silent for some seconds, then she said : " I once had a friend—but her moral nature quite halted. It was because she had lost her faith in men. A woman who thinks that only women can be worthy is like a bird with a broken wing. But I don't say that that is Evadne's case at all. Since she came to us she has seemed to be much more like one of those marvellous casks of sherry out of which a dozen different wines are taken. The flavour depends on the doctoring. Here, under Angelica's influence— why, she has filled your pocket with gorse blossoms ! "

It was true. In taking out my handkerchief, I had just scattered the flowers, and so discovered that they were there. " Then you give her credit for less individuality—you think her more at the mercy of her surroundings than I do," I said.

But before she could answer me, Evadne herself had joined us. I suppose I was looking grave, for she asked in a playful tone :

" Did he ever frolic, Lady Adeline, this solemn seeming— *Don* ? Was he always in earnest, even on his mother's lap, and occupied with weighty problems of life and death when other babes were wondering with wide open eyes at the irresponsible action of their own pink toes ? "

Which made me reflect. For if I were in the habit of being a dull bore myself it was no wonder that I seldom saw her looking lively.

The following week Evadne went home, and as soon as she was settled at As-You-Like-It, she seemed to relapse once more into her former state of apathy. I saw her day after day as I passed, sitting sewing in the wide west window above the holly hedge ; and so long as she was left alone she seemed to be content ; but I began to notice at this time that any interruption at her favourite occupation did not please her. The summer heat, the scent of flowers streaming through open windows, the song of birds, the level landscape, here vividly green with the upspringing aftermath, there crimson and gold where the poppies gleamed amongst the ripening corn—all such sweet sensuous influences she looked out upon lovingly, and enjoyed them—so long as she was left alone. On hot afternoons, Diavolo would go and lie at her feet sometimes, with a cushion under his head ; and him she tolerated ; but only, I am sure, because he always fell asleep.

I had to go to As-You-Like-It one day to transact some business with Colonel Colquhoun, and when we had done he asked me to go up into the drawing room with him. " Come, and I'll show you a pretty picture," he said.

It *was* a pretty picture. They had both fallen asleep on that occasion. It was a torrid day outside, but the deep bay where they were was cool and shady. The windows were wide open, the outside blinds were drawn down low enough to keep out the glare, but not so far as to hide the view. Behind Evadne was a stand of flowers and foliage plants. Diavolo was lying on the floor in his favourite attitude with a black satin cushion under his head, and was, with his slender figure, refined features, thick, curly, fair hair, and fine transparent skin, slightly flushed by the heat, a perfect specimen of adolescent grace and beauty. He looked like a young lover lying at the feet of his lady. Evadne was sitting in a low easy chair, with a high back, against which her head was resting. Half her face was concealed by a fan of white ostrich feathers which she held in her left hand, and the moment I looked at her the haunting certainty of having seen her in exactly that position once before recurred to me. She was looking well that afternoon. Her glossy dark brown hair showed bright as bronze against the satin background of the chair. She was dressed in a gown of silver gray cashmere lined with turquoise blue silk, which showed between the folds ; cool colours of the best shade to set off the ivory whiteness of her skin.

Colonel Colquhoun considered the group meditatively. " She keeps her looks," he observed in an undertone ; " and Diavolo's catching her up."

I looked at him inquiringly.

" She's six or eight years older than he is, you know," he explained ; " but you wouldn't think it now."

I wondered what he had in his mind.

" Times are changing," he proceeded. " Now, when I was a lad, if a lady had liked me as well as Evadne likes that boy, I'd have taken advantage of her preference."

"Not if the lady had been of her stamp," I said drily.

"Well, true for you," he acknowledged. "But it isn't the lady only in this case. It's that young sybarite himself. He's as particular as she is. He said the other day at mess—it was a guest night, and there was a big dinner on, and somebody proposed 'Wine and Women' for a toast, but he wouldn't drink it: 'Oh, spare me,' he said, in that slow way he has, something like his father's; 'Wine and women, as you take them, are things as coarse in the way of pleasure as pork and porter are for food.' We asked him then to give us his own ideas of pleasure; but he said he didn't think anybody there was educated up to them, even sufficiently to understand them!—and he wasn't joking altogether, either," Colonel Colquhoun concluded.

At that same moment Evadne opened her eyes wide, and looked at us a second before she spoke, but showed no other sign of surprise.

"I am afraid I have been asleep," she said, rising deliberately, and shaking hands with me across the prostrate Diavolo. "Do sit down."

She sank back into her own chair as she spoke, and fanned a fly from Diavolo's face. "I never knew anyone sleep so soundly," she said, looking down at him lovingly. "He rides out here nearly every day when he is not on duty, simply for his siesta. Angelica is jealous, I believe, because he will not go to her. He says there is no repose about Angelica, and that it is only here with me that he finds the dreamful ease he loves."

There was a sound of talking outside just then, and a few minutes later Angelica herself came in with her father.

"Oh, you *darling!* you *are* a pretty boy!" she exclaimed, when she saw Diavolo, and then she went down on her knees beside him, put her arms round his neck, pulled him up, and hugged him roughly, an attention which he immediately resented. "Ah, I thought it was you!" he said, opening his eyes. "Good-bye, sweet sleep, good-bye!" Then he sat up, and, turning his back to Evadne, coolly rested himself against her knee. "I suppose we can have tea now," he said. "There's always something to look forward to. Papa, dear, touch the bell, to save the Colonel the trouble."

Colonel Colquhoun laughed, and rang it himself good-naturedly.

"Diavolo!" Evadne exclaimed, pushing him away, "I am not going to nurse a great boy like you."

"Well, Angelica must, then," he said, changing his position so as to lean against his sister. Angelica laid her hand on his head, and her face softened. "Evadne *used* to like to nurse me," he complained. "She's not nearly so nice since she married. I say, Angelica, do you remember the wedding breakfast, when we agreed to drink as much champagne as the bridegroom? I swore I would never get drunk again, and I never have."

"Faith," said Colonel Colquhoun, "there are some who'd like to be able to say the same thing."

Some dogs had followed Angelica in, and had now to be turned out, because Evadne would not have dogs indoors. She said she liked a good dog's character, but could not bear the smell of him.

"And how are the children?" Mr. Hamilton-Wells asked affably, when this diversion was over.

"There are no children!" Evadne exclaimed in surprise.

"Are there not, indeed. Now, that is singular," he observed. Then he looked at me as if he were about to say something interesting, but I hastily interposed. I was afraid he was going to speculate about the natural history of the phenomenon which had just struck him as being singular. He knew perfectly well that Evadne had no children, but he was subject, or affected to be subject, to moments of obliviousness, in which he was wont to ask embarrassing questions.

"The weather is quite tropical," was the original observation I made. Mr. Hamilton-Wells felt if the parting of his smooth, straight hair was exactly in the middle, patted it on either side, then shook back imaginary ruffles from his long white hands, and interlaced his jewelled fingers on his lap.

"You were never in the tropics, I think you told me?" he said to Evadne, with exaggerated preciseness. "Ah! now, I have been, off and on, several times. The heat is very trying. I knew a lady, the wife of a Colonial Governor, who used to be so overcome by it that she was obliged to undo all her things, let them slip to the ground, and step out of them, leaving them looking like a great cheese. She told me so herself, I assure you, and she was an exceedingly stout person."

The Heavenly Twins went into convulsions suddenly.

"Is that tea at last?" Evadne asked.

Colonel Colquhoun and I both gladly moved to make room

for the servants who were bringing it in, and the conversation
was not resumed until they had withdrawn. Then Angelica
began : " I came to make a last appeal to you, Evadne. [
want to tell you about a poor girl——"

" Oh, don't break this lovely summer silence with tales of
woe ! " Evadne exclaimed, interrupting her. " I cannot do
anything. Don't ask me. You harrow my feelings to no purpose. I will not listen. It is not right that I should be forced
to know."

" Well, I think you are making a mistake, Evadne," Angelica
replied. " Don't you think so ? " looking at me. " She is
sacrificing herself to save herself. She imagines she can
secure her own peace of mind by refusing to know that there
is a weary world of suffering close at hand which she should
be helping to relieve. Suffering for others strengthens our
own powers of endurance ; we lose them if we don't exercise
them—and that is the way you are sacrificing yourself to save
yourself, Evadne. When some big trouble of your own, one.
of those which cannot be denied, comes upon you, it will
crush you. You will have lost the moral muscle you should
be exercising now to keep it in good working order and
develop it well for your own use when you require it. It
would not be worse for you to take a stimulant or a sedative
to wind yourself up to an artificially pleasurable state when at
any time you are not naturally cheerful—and that is what a
too great love of peace occasionally ends in."

Evadne waved her ostrich feather fan backward and forward slowly, and looked out of the window. She would not
even listen to this friendly counsel, and I felt sure she was
making a mistake.

I only saw her once again that summer under Lady Adeline's
salutary influence. It was a few days later, and Evadne was
in an expansive mood. She had been spending the day with
Lady Adeline, and the two had been for a drive together, and
had overtaken me on the road and picked me up on their way
back to Hamilton House. I had been for a solitary ramble,
and was then returning to work, but Evadne said I must go
back to tea with them : " For your own sake, because it is a
shame to waste a summer day in work—a glorious summer day
so evidently sent for our enjoyment."

" The greatest pleasure in life is to be in perfect condition
for the work one loves," I answered ; but I was settling myself
comfortably in the carriage as I spoke, such is the consistency

of man. But indeed it was not very difficult to persuade me to idle that afternoon. I had been inclining that way for weeks, under the influence of the intoxicating heat doubtless ; and presently, when I found myself comfortably seated on the wide stone terrace outside the great drawing room at Hamilton House, under a shady awning, looking down upon lawns vividly green and lovely gardens all aglow with colour and alive with perfume, which is the soul of the flowers, I yielded sensuous service to the hour, and gave myself up to the enjoyment of it unreservedly.

Mr. Hamilton-Wells was there, making tea in the precisest manner, and looking more puritanical than ever. How to reconcile his coldly formal exterior with the interior from which emanated his choice of subjects in conversation is a matter which I have not yet had time to study, 'although I am convinced that the solution of the problem would prove to be of great scientific value and importance. I was not in the habit of thinking of him as either a man or a woman myself, however, but as a specimen of humanity broadly, and domestically as a husband whom I always suspected of being a sharp sword of the law, although I had never obtained the slightest evidence of the fact.

Lady Adeline was lolling in a low cane chair, fatigued by her drive, and longing aloud for tea ; and Evadne was flitting about with her hat in her hand, laughing and talking more than any of us. She was wearing an art gown, very becoming to her, and suitable also for such sultry weather, as Mr. Hamilton-Wells remarked.

" I suppose you are a strong supporter of the æsthetic dress movement," he said, doubtless alluding to the graceful freedom of her delicate primrose draperies.

" Not at all," she answered, seating herself on the arm of a chair near Lady Adeline, and opening her fan gently as she spoke.

I was inspired to ask for more tea just then. Mr. Hamilton-Wells poured it out and handed it to me. "You take milk," he informed me, " but no sugar." Then he folded his hands and recommenced. " To return to the original point of departure," he began, " which was modern dress, if I remember rightly "—he smiled round upon us all, knowing quite well that he remembered rightly—"that brings us by an obvious route to another question of the day ; I mean the position of women. How do you regard their position at this latter end of the nineteenth century, Evadne ? "

" I do not regard it at all, if I can help it," she answered incisively.

Mr. Hamilton-Wells dropped his outspread hands upon his knees.

" If I remember rightly," he said, "you take no interest in politics either. That is quite a phenomenon at this latter end of the nineteenth century."

" I have my duties—the duties of my social position, you know," she answered, "and my own little pursuits as well, neither of which I can neglect for the affairs of the world."

" But are they enough for you ? " Lady Adeline ventured.

Evadne glanced up to see what she meant, and then smiled. " The wisdom of ages is brought to the training of each little girl," she said ; " and to fit her for our position, she is taught that a woman's one object in life is to be agreeable."

" You mean that a woman of decided opinions is not an agreeable person ? " Lady Adeline asked.

" Decided opinions must always be offensive to those who don't hold them," Evadne rejoined.

" A woman must know that the future welfare of her own sex, and the progress of the world at large, depends upon the action of women now, and the success attending it," Angelica observed comprehensively.

" Yes, but she knows also that her own comfort and convenience depend entirely on her neutrality," Evadne answered. " It is not high-minded to be neutral, I know, when it is put in that way ; but a woman who is so becomes exactly what the average man, taken at his word, would have her be, and he is, we are assured, the proper person to legislate."

She looked at us all defiantly as she spoke, and furled her fan ; and just at that moment Colonel Colquhoun joined us. He had come to fetch her, and his entrance gave a new turn to the conversation.

" It has been oppressively hot all day," he observed.

" Yes," Lady Adeline answered, " and I do so long for the mountains in weather like this."

" Oh, do you ? " said Evadne. " Are you subject to the magnet of the mountains ? I am not. I do not want to feel the nothingness of man ; I like to believe in his greatness, in his infinite possibilities. I like to think of life as a level plain over which we can gallop to some goal—I don't know what, but something desirable ; and the actual landscape pleases me best so. The great tumbled mountains make me melancholy, they are always foreboding something untoward, even at the best of times ; but the open spaces, windswept and evident—I love them. I am at home on them. I can breathe there—I am free."

This was the natural woman at last, in her aspirations unconsciously showing herself superior to the artificial creature she was trying to be.

" I hate the melancholy mountains," the ever-ready Angelica burst forth. " I loathe the inconstant sea. The breezy plain for a gallop ! It is there that one feels free !"

Colonel Colquhoun looked at Evadne meditatively, and slowly twisted each end of his heavy blond moustache. " I haven't seen you riding for some time now," he said, " and it's a pity, for you've a fine seat on a horse."

I was obliged to make up that night for the time lost in the afternoon, and the dawn had broken when at last I put my work away. I opened the study windows wider to salute it. A lark was singing somewhere out of sight—

> Die Lerche, die im augen nicht,
> Doch immer in den ohren ist—

and the ripples of undecipherable sound struck some equally inarticulate chord of sense, and fell full-fraught with association. The breeze, murmurous amongst the branches, set the leaves rustling like silk attire. Did I imagine it, or was there really a faint sweet perfume of yellow gorse in the air ? A thrush on a bough below began to flute softly, trying its tones before it burst forth, giving full voice to its enthusiasm in one clear call, eloquent of life and love and longing, and all expressed in just three notes—crotchet, quaver, crotchet and rest— which shortly shaped themselves to a word in my heart, a word of just three syllables, the accent being on the penultimate—" E-vad-ne ! E-vad-ne !"

Good Heavens !

I roused myself. Not a proper state of mind certainly for a man of my years and pursuits. Why, how old was I ? Thirty-five—not so old in one way, yet ten years older at least than—stop—sickly sentimentality. " Life is real, life is earnest," and there must be no dreams of scented gorse, of posing in daffodil draperies, for me. Must take a holiday and rest —take my " agreeable ugliness " off (I was amused when the Heavenly Twins told me their mother talked of my " agreeable ugliness " ; but, now, did I like it ? No. I was cynical when I said it) take my " agreeable ugliness " off to the mountains—" Turn thine eyes unto the mountains "—the magnet of the mountains. Yes, I felt it. I delighted to do so. I was not morbid. To the mountains ! to the cold which stays corruption, the snows which are pure, and the eternal silence ! By ten o'clock that night I was well on my way.

CHAPTER XI.

I WENT abroad that year for my holiday, but spent the last week of it in London on my way home. All the vapours of sentimentality had disappeared by that time. My nerves had been braced in the Alps, my mind had been calmed and refreshed by the warm blue Mediterranean, my sense of comparison emphasized in Egypt, where I perceived anew the law of mutability, the inevitable law, by the decree of which the human race is eternal, while we, its constituent atoms, have but a moment of intensity to blaze and burn out. Perishable life and permanent matter are we, with a limit that may be prolonged in idea by such circumstances as we can dwell on with delight, one love-lit day being longer in the record than whole monotonous years. It is good to live and love, but if we possess the burden of life unrelieved by the blessing of love, or the hope of it, well—why despair ? Man is matter animated by a series of emotions, the majority of which are pleasurable. Disappointment ends like success, and the futile dust of nations offers itself in evidence of the vanity of all attributes except wisdom, the wisdom that teaches us to accept the inevitable silently, and endure our moment with equally undemonstrative acquiescence, whether it comes full fraught with the luxury of living, or only brings us that which causes us to contemplate of necessity, and without shrinking, the crowning dignity of death.

I had come back ready for work, and could have cheerfully dispensed with that week's delay in London ; but I had promised it to an old friend, in failing health, whom I would not disappoint.

The people at Morne, the Kilroys, the Hamilton-Wellses, the Colquhouns, all my circle of intimate friends, had fallen into the background of my recollection during my tour abroad ; but, now again, when I found myself so near them,

the old habitual interests began to be dominant. I had sent
notes to apologize for not wishing them good-bye before my
sudden departure, but I had not written to any of them or
heard from them during my absence, and did not know where
they might all be at the moment ; and I was just wondering one
night as I walked toward Piccadilly from the direction of the
Strand—I was just wondering if they were all as I had left
them, if the civil war, as Angelica called it, was being waged
as actively as ever between herself and Evadne upon the all-
important point—and that made me think of Evadne herself.
I had banished her name from my mind for weeks, but now
some inexplicable trick of the brain suddenly set her before
me as I oftenest saw her, sitting at work in the wide west
window overlooking the road, and glancing up brightly at the
sound of my horse's hoofs or carriage wheels as I rode or
drove past, to salute me. A lady might wait and watch so at
accustomed hours for her lover ; but he would stop, and she
would open the window, and lean out with a flower in her
hand for him, and perhaps she would kiss it before she tossed
it to him, and he would catch it and go on his way rejoicing
—a pretty poetical dream and easy of fulfilment, if only one
could find the lady, suitably circumstanced.

I had arrived at Piccadilly Circus by this time, at the turn
into Regent Street where the omnibuses stop, and was delayed
for a moment or two by the casual crowd of loiterers and
people struggling for places, and by those who were alighting
from the various vehicles. Not being in any hurry myself, it
amused me to observe the turmoil, the play of human emotion
which appeared distinctly on the faces of those who approached me and were lost to sight again as soon as seen in
the eddy and whirl of the crowd. There was temper here,
and tenderness there ; this person was steadily bent on busi-
uess, that on pleasure, and one fussy little man escorting his
family somewhere was making the former of the latter.
There were two young lovers alone with their love so far as
any outward consciousness of the crowd was concerned ; and
there was a young wife silent and sad beside a neglectful
elderly husband. It was the 'buses from the west end I was
watching. One had just moved off toward the Strand, and
another pulled up in its place, and the people began to alight
—a fat man first in a frenzy of haste, a sallow priest whose
soul seemed to sicken at the sight of the seething mass of
humanity amongst which he found himself, for he hesitated per-

ceptibly on the step, like a child in a bathing machine who shrinks from the water, before he descended and was engulfed in the crowd. A musician with his instrument in a case, two fat women talking to each other, a little Cockney work-girl, and her young man, and then—a lady. There could be no mistake about her social status. The conductor, standing by the step, recognized it at once, and held out his arm to assist her. The gaslight flared full upon her face, the expression of which was somewhat set. She wore no veil, and if she did not court observation, she certainly did not shun it. She was quietly but richly dressed, and had one seen her there on foot in the morning, one would have surmised that she was out shopping, and looked for the carriage which would probably have been following her; but a lady, striking in appearance and of distinguished bearing, alighted composedly from an omnibus at Piccadilly Circus between nine and ten at night, and calmly taking her way alone up Regent Street was a sight which would have struck one as being anomalous even if she had been a stranger. But this lady was no stranger to me. I should have recognized her figure and carriage had her countenance been concealed. I had turned hot and cold at the first foreshadowing of her presence, and would fain have found myself mistaken, but there was no possibility of a doubt. She passed me without haste, and so close that I could have laid my hand upon her shoulder. But I let her go in sheer astonishment. What, in the name of all that is inexplicable, was Evadne doing there alone at that time of night? Such a proceeding was hardly decent, whatever her excuse, and it was certainly not safe. This last reflection aroused me, and I started instantly to follow her, intending to overtake her, and impose my escort upon her. She was out of sight, because she had turned the corner, but she could not have gone far, and I hurried headlong after her, nearly upsetting a man who met me face to face as I doubled into Regent Street. It was Colonel Colquhoun himself, in a joyful mood evidently, and for once I could have blessed his blinding potations. He recognized me, but had apparently passed Evadne.

"Ah, me boy, you here!" he exclaimed, with an assumption of facetious *bonhomie* particularly distasteful to me. "All the world lives in London, I think! It's where you'll always come across anyone you want. Sly dog! Following a lady, I'll be bound! By Jove! I wouldn't have thought it of you, Galbraith ! But you'll not find anything choice in Regent Street. Come with me, and I'll introduce you——"

" Excuse me," I interrupted, and hurried away from the brute. How had he missed Evadne ? Perhaps he was looking the other way. But what a position for her to be in. Supposing he had recognized her, my being so close would have made it none the better for her. And could I be sure that he had not seen her ? I did not think he was the kind of man, with all his faults, to lay a trap even for an enemy whom he suspected; but, still, one never knows.

Evadne was far ahead by this time, but the places of amusement were still open, and therefore there were few people in Regent Street. It is not particularly well lighted, but I was soon near enough to make her out by her graceful dignified carriage, which contrasted markedly with that of every other woman and girl I saw. In any other place her bearing would have struck me as that of a person accustomed to consideration, even if I had not known her; but here, judging by the confident way she held her head up, I should have been inclined to set her down either as a most abandoned person, or as one who was quite unconscious of anything peculiar in her present proceedings. In another respect, too, she was very unlike the women and girls who were loitering about the street, peering up anxiously into the face of every man they met. Evadne seemed to see no one, and passed on her way, superbly indifferent to any attention she might be attracting. The distance between us had lessened considerably, and I could now have overtaken her easily, but I hesitated. I could not decide whether it would be better to join her, or merely to keep her in sight for her own safety. I was inclined to blame her severely for her recklessness. She had already passed her husband, and might meet half the depôt, or be recognized by Heaven knows who, before she got to the top of the street; and, as it was, she was attracting considerable attention. Scarcely a man met her who did not turn when he had passed, and look after her; and anyone of these might be an acquaintance. My impulse had been to insist upon her getting into a hansom, and allowing me to see her safe home; but it had occurred to me, upon reflection, that I might compromise her more fatally by being seen with her under such circumstances than could happen if she went alone.

While I hesitated, a tall thin man with a gray beard, whom I thought I recognized from photographs seen in shop windows, met her, stared hard as he passed, stood a minute looking after her, and then turned and followed her. If he were the man I took him to be, he would probably know her, and my first impression was that he did so, and had recognised her, and been, like myself, too astonished to speak. If so, he quickly recovered himself, and, as he evidently intended to address her now, I was half inclined to resign my responsibility to him. Then I thought that if I joined her also nothing could be said. Two men of known repute may escort a lady anywhere and at any time. I quickened my steps, but purposely let him speak first.

Coming up with her from behind, he began in a tone which was more caressing than respectful. "It is a fine night," he said.

Evadne started visibly, looked at him, and shrank two steps away; but she answered, in a voice which I could hardly recognise as hers, it was so high and strident: "I should call it a chilly night," she said.

"Well, yes, perhaps," he answered, "for the time of the year. Are you going for a walk?"

"I—I don't know," she replied, looking doubtfully on ahead.

She was walking at a pretty rapid rate as it was, and her elderly interlocutor had some difficulty in keeping up with her.

"Perhaps if we turned down one of these side streets to the left, it would be quieter, and we could talk," he suggested.

"I don't think I want either to be quiet or to talk," she said, suddenly recovering her natural voice and tone.

"Well, what do you want, then?" he asked.

She looked up at him, and slackened her speed. "Perhaps, since you are so good as to trouble yourself about me at all," she said, "I may venture to ask if you will kindly tell me where in London I am?"

His manner instantly changed. "You are in Regent Street," he answered.

"And that lighted place behind us, where the crowd is—what is that?"

"You must mean Piccadilly Circus."

"And if I walk on what shall I come to?"

"Oxford Street. You don't seem to know London. Don't you live here?"

"I do not live in London"

"You have lost your way, perhaps; can I direct you anywhere?"

"No, thank you," she answered. "I can get into a hansom, you know, when I am tired of this."

"If I might venture to advise, I should say do so at once," he rejoined, slightly raising his hat as he spoke, and then he slipped behind her, and furtively hurried across the street, a considerably perplexed man, I fancied, and, judging by the way he peered to right and left as he went, one who was suffering from some sudden dislike to being recognised.

Evadne paid as little heed to his departure as she had done to his approach. A few steps farther brought her to a stand of hansom cabs. She hesitated a moment, and then got into one. I took the next, and directed the driver to follow her, being determined either to see her back to her friends, or to interfere if I found that she meant to continue her ramble. Her driver struck into Piccadilly at the next turn, and then drove steadily west for about half an hour. By that time we had come to a row of handsome houses, at one of which he stopped, and my man stoped also at an intelligent distance behind, but Evadne never looked back. She got out and ascended the steps with the leisurely air peculiar to her. The door was opened as soon as she rang, and she entered. A moment later a footman came out on to the pavement and paid the driver, with whom he exchanged a remark or two. As he returned, the light from the hall streamed out upon him, and I saw, with a sense of relief which made me realise what the previous tension had been, that he wore the Hamilton-Wells livery, and then I recognised the Hamilton-Wells' town house. The driver of the now empty hansom turned his horse, and walked him slowly back in the direction from which he had come. The incident was over; but what did it all mean? The whole thing seemed so purposeless. What had taken her out at all? Was it some jealous freak? Women have confessed to me that they watch their husbands habitually. One said she did it for love of excitement : there was always a risk of being caught, and nothing else ever amused her half so much. Another declared she did it because she could not afford to employ a private detective, and she wanted to have evidence always ready in case it should suit her to part from her husband at any time. Another said she loved her husband, and it hurt her less to know than to suspect. But I could not really believe that Evadne would do such a thing for any reason whatever. She was fearlessly upright and honest about her actions; and her self-respect would have restrained her if

ever an isolated impulse had impelled her to such a proceeding. But still——

"Will you wait until the lady returns, sir?" the driver
asked at last, peeping down upon me through the trap in the
roof. If he had not spoken I might have sat there half the
night, puzzling out the problem. Now, however, that he had
roused me, I determined to leave it for the present. I remembered my duty to the friend with whom I was staying, and
hurried back, resolving to go to Evadne herself next day, and
ask her point blank to explain. I believed she would do so,
for in all that concerned her own pursuits—the doings of the
day—I had always found her almost curiously frank. After
this wise determination, I ought to have been philosopher
enough to sleep upon the matter, but her ladyship's escapade
cost me my night's rest, and took me to her early next morning, in an angry and irritable mood.

I sent up my card, and Evadne received me at once in Lady
Adeline's boudoir.

"This is an unexpected pleasure," she said. "How did
you know I was in town?"

"I saw you in Regent Street last night," I answered bluntly.
"What were you doing there?"

"What were you doing there yourself?" she said.

The question took me aback completely, and the more so as
it was asked with an unmistakable flash of merriment.

"Answer me my question first," I said. "You could have
no business out alone in London at that time of night, laying
yourself open to insult."

"I don't recognise your right to question me at all," she
answered, unabashed.

"I have the right of any gentleman who does his duty when
he sees a lady making——"

"A fool of herself? Thanks," she said, laughing. "The
privilege of protecting a woman, of saving her even in spite
of herself from the effects of her own indiscretion, is one of
which a man seldom avails himself, and I did not understand
you at first. Excuse me. But how do you know I could have
no business out at that time of night? Do you imagine that
you know all my duties in life?"

I was bewildered by her confidence—by her levity, I may
say, but I persisted.

"I cannot believe that you had any business or duty which
necessitated your being in a disreputable part of London alone

late at night," I said. " But I hope you will allow me the
right of an intimate friend to warn you if you run risks—in
your ignorance."

" Or to reprove me if I do so with my eyes open ? " she
suggested.

" To ask for an explanation, at all events, if I do not understand what your motive could be."

" You are very kind," she said. " You want me to excuse
myself if I can, otherwise you will be forced to suspect something unjustifiable."

" That is the literal truth," I answered.

She laughed. " But you have not answered *my* question,"
she said. " What were you doing there yourself ? "

" I had been dining at the Charing Cross Hotel with a friend
who had just returned from India," I told her, " and I was
walking back to the house of the friend with whom I am
staying. He lives in a street off Piccadilly."

" But what were you doing in Regent Street ? "

" Following you."

She laughed again. " Did you see that old man speak to
me ? " she asked.

" Yes."

" Horrid old creature, is he not ? He gave me such a start !
Did you recognise him ? "

" Yes."

" I did not at first, but when I did, I thought I would make
him useful." She meditated for a little, then she said : " It
did me good."

" What ? " I asked.

" That start," she replied. " It quite roused me. But,
now, tell me. I should never have supposed that you had no
business anywhere at any time ; why are you not equally
charitable ? "

I was silent.

" Tell me what you think took me there ? "

" An unholy curiosity," I blurted out.

" That is an unholy inspiration which has only just
occurred to you, and you cannot entertain the suspicion for a
moment," she said.

This was true.

" But, after all," she pursued, " what business have you to
take me to task like this ? It is not a professional matter."

" I don't know that," I answered. This was another inspiration, and it disconcerted her, for she changed countenance.

" You have a nice opinion of me ! " she exclaimed.

" I have the highest opinion of you," I answered, " and nobody knows that better than yourself.   But what am I to think when I find you acting without any discretion whatever ? "

" Think that I am at the mercy of every wayward impulse."

" But I know that you are not," I replied ; " and I am unhappy about you.   Will you trust me ?   Will you explain ?   Will you let me help you if I can ?   I believe there is some trouble at the bottom of this business.   Do tell me all about it ? "

" Well, I *will* explain," she said, still laughing.   " I was driving past, and seeing you there, I thought I would horrify you, so I stopped the carriage——"

" You got out of an omnibus ! " I exclaimed.

" Well, that was my carriage for the time being," she answered, in no way disconcerted.   " You do not expect me to own that I was in an omnibus, do you ? "

" I wish you would be serious for a moment," I remonstrated.   " I wish you would tell me the truth."

" As I always do tell the truth if I tell anything, I think we had better let the subject drop," she said, with a sigh, as if she were tired of it.

" You mean you cannot tell me ? "

" That is what I mean."

I reflected for a moment.   " Does Lady Adeline know that you were out last night ? " I asked.

" No," she replied.   " She was out herself and I returned before she did.

" Then you have not told her either ? "

She shook her head.

" I would really rather you confided in her than in me, if you can."

" Thank you," she answered drily.

" Can you ? " I persisted.

" No, I cannot," was the positive rejoinder.

I rose to go.   " Forgive my officiousness," I said.   " I ventured to hope you would make use of me, but I am afraid I have been forcing my services upon you too persistently."

She rose impulsively, and held out both hands to me.   " I wish I could thank you," she said, looking up at me frankly and affectionately.   " I wish I could tell you how much I

appreciate your goodness to me, and all your disinterestedness. I wish I deserved it !" She clasped my hands warmly
as she spoke, then dropped them ; and instantly I became
conscious of an indescribable sense of relief ; and prepared to
depart at once ; but she stopped me again with a word as I
opened the door.

" Dr. Galbraith," she began, with another flash of merriment, "tell me, you *were* horrified, now, were you not?"

I jammed my hat on my head and left her. I did not mean
to slam the door, but her levity had annoyed me. I fancied
her laughing as I descended the stairs, and wondered at her
mood, and yet I was re-assured by it. She would not have
been so merry if there had been anything really wrong, and it
was just possible that the half explanation she had given me
and withdrawn was the true one. She might have been in an
omnibus for once for some quite legitimate reason, and while
it waited at Piccadilly Circus she might have seen me as she
had described, and got out in a moment of mischief to astonish me. If that were her object, she had certainly succeeded, and it seemed to me more likely than that she should
just have gone and returned for the sake of doing an unusual
thing, which was the only other explanation that occurred to
me.

I saw Lady Adeline before I left the house, and found that
Colonel Colquhoun was not staying with them, nor did she
seem to know that he had been in town.

CHAPTER XII.

A CRUEL misfortune robbed me of a near relation at this
time, and added the rank of baronet, with a considerable
increase of fortune, to my other responsibilities. The increase
of fortune was welcome in one way, as it enabled me to
enlarge a small private hospital which I had established on my
Fountain Towers estate, for the benefit of poor patients.
Attending to these, and to the buildings which were at once
put in progress, was the one absorbing interest of my life at
that time.

During the next three months 1 only called once on Evadne,
and that was a mere formal visit which I felt in duty bound
to pay her. I did not drive past the house, either, oftener
than I could help, but when I was obliged to go that way I

saw her, sitting sewing in her accustomed place, and she would smile and bow to me—brightly at first, but after a time with a wistful, weary expression, or I fancied so. It was of necessity a hurried glimpse that I had, although my horse would slacken his speed of his own accord as we approached the holly hedge that bounded her bower ; but I began to be uneasily aware of a change in her appearance. I might be mistaken, but I certainly thought her eyes looked unnaturally large, as if her cheeks had fallen away, and the little patient face was paler. In the early summer, when she was well, she had been wont to flush upon the least occasion, but now her colour did not vary, and I suspected that she was again shutting herself up too much. Mrs. Orton Beg was at Fraylingay, Diavolo was keeping his grandfather company at Morne, the Kilroys were in town, the Hamilton-Wellses had gone to Egypt, and Colonel Colquhoun had taken two months' leave and gone abroad also, so that she had no one near her for whom she had any special regard. Colonel Colquhoun had called on me before he left, and told me he was sure Evadne would hope to see a good deal of me during his absence, and he wished I would look after her—professionally, I inferred, and of course I was always prepared to do so. But, so far, she had not required my services, happily, and for the rest— well, my time was fully occupied, and I found it did not suit me to go to As-You-Like-It. When I noticed the change in her appearance, however, I began to think I would look in some day, just to see how she really was, but before I could carry out the half formed intention she came to me. It was during my consulting hours, and I was sitting at my writing table, seeing my patients in rotation, when her name was announced. She sauntered in in her usual leisurely way, shook hands with me, and then subsided into the easy-chair on my right, which was placed facing the window for my patients to occupy.

" I have a cold," she said, " and a pain under my right clavicle, and the posterior lobe of my brain—oh, dear, I have forgotten it all ! " she broke off, laughing. " How *shall* I make you understand ? "

" You are in excellent spirits," I observed, " if you are not in very good health."

" No, believe me," she answered. " The pleasure of seeing you again enlivened me for a moment ; but I am really rather down."

I had been considering her attentively from a professional point of view while she was speaking, and saw that this was true. The brightness which animated her when she entered faded immediately, and then I saw that her face was thin and pale and anxious in expression. Her eyes wandered somewhat restlessly ; her attitude betokened weakness. She had a little worrying cough, and her pulse was unequal.

"What have you been doing with yourself lately?" I asked, turning to my writing table and taking up a pen, when I had ascertained this last fact.

"Dreaming," she said.

The answer struck me. "Dreaming," I repeated to myself, and then aloud to her, while I affected to write. "Dreaming?" I said. "What about, for example?"

"Oh! the Arabian Nights, the whole thousand and one of them, would not be long enough to tell you," she replied. "I think my dreams have lasted longer already."

"Are you speaking of day-dreams?" I asked.

"Yes."

"You imagine things as you sit at work, perhaps!"

"Yes." She spoke languidly, and evidently attached no special significance either to my questions or her own answers, which was what I wished. "Yes, that is my best time. While I work, I live in a world of my own creating ; in a beautiful happy dream—at least it was so once," she added, with a sigh.

"I have heard you say you did not care to read fiction. You prefer to make your own stories, is that the reason?"

"I suppose so," she said; "but I never thought of it before."

"And you never write these imaginings?"

"Oh, no! That would be impossible. It is in the tones of voices as I hear them ; in the expression of faces as I see them; in the subtle, indescribable perception of the significance of events, and their intimate relation to each other and influence on the lives of my dream friends that the whole charm lies. Such impressions are too delicate for reproduction, even if I had the mind to try. Describing them would be as coarse a proceeding as eating a flower after inhaling its perfume."

"Did I understand you to say that this is the habit of years? Has your inner life been composed of dreams ever since you were a child?"

"No," she replied. "I don't think as a child I was at all imaginative. I liked to learn, and when I was not learning I lived an active, outdoor life."

"Ah! Then you have acquired the habit since you grew up?"

"Yes. It came on by degrees. I used to think of how things might be different; that was the way it began. I tried to work out schemes of life in my head, as I would do a game of chess; not schemes of life for myself, you know, but such as should save other people from being very miserable. I wanted to do some good in the world,"—she paused here to choose her words—"and that kind of thought naturally resolves itself into action, but before the impulse to act came upon me I had made it impossible for myself to do anything, so that when it came I was obliged to resist it, and then, instead of reading and reflecting, I took to sewing for a sedative, and turned the trick of thinking how things might be different into another channel."

She was unconsciously telling me the history of her married life, showing me a lonely woman gradually losing her mental health for want of active occupation and a wholesome share of the work of the world to take her out of herself. To a certain extent, then, I had been right in my judgment of her character. Her disposition was practical, not contemplative; but she had been forced into the latter attitude, and the consequence was, perhaps—well, it might be a diseased state of the mind; but that I had yet to ascertain.

"And are you happy in your dreams?" I inquired.

"I was," she said; "but my dreams are not what they used to be."

"How?" I asked.

"At first they were pleasant," she answered. "When I sat alone at work, it was my happiest time. I was master of my dreams then, and let none but pleasant shapes present themselves. But by degrees—I don't know how—I began to be intoxicated. My imagination ran away with me. Instead of indulging in a daydream now and then, when I liked, all my life became absorbed in delicious imaginings, whether I would or not. Working, walking, driving; in church; anywhere and at any time, when I could be alone a moment, I lived in my world apart. If people spoke to me, I awoke and answered them; but real life was a dull thing to offer, and the daylight very dim, compared with the movement and brightness of the land I lived in—while I was master of my dreams."

"Then you did not remain master of them always ? "

"No. By degrees they mastered me ; and now I am their puppet, and they are demons that torment me. When I awake in the morning, I wonder what the haunting thought for the day will be ; and before I have finished dressing it is upon me as a rule. At first it was not incessant, but now the trouble in my head is awful."

I thought so ! But she had said enough for the present. The confession was ingenuously made, and evidently without intention. I merely asked a few more questions about her general health, and then sent her home to nurse her cold, promising to call and see how it was the next day.

When I opened my case book to make a note of her visit and a brief summary of the symptoms she had described and betrayed, I hesitated a moment about the diagnosis, and finally decided to write provisionally for my guidance, or rather by way of prognosis, the one word, " Hysteria ! "

CHAPTER XIII.

NEXT day I found that Evadne's cold was decidedly worse, and as the weather was severe I ordered her to stay in her own rooms.

" Am I going to be ill ? " she asked.

" No," I answered, pooh-poohing the notion.

" Doctor, you dash my hopes ! " she said. " I am always happy when I am ill. It *is* such a relief."

I had heard her use the phrase twice before, but it was only now that I saw her meaning. Physical suffering was evidently a relief from the mental misery, and this proved that the trouble was of longer standing than I had at first suspected. She had used the same expression, I remembered, when I first attended her, during that severe attack of pneumonia.

Colonel Colquhoun had returned, she told me, but I did not see him that day, as he was out. Next morning, however, I came earlier on purpose, and encountered him in the hall. He was not in uniform, I was thankful to see, for he was very apt to assume his orderly room manners therewith, and they were decidedly objectionable to the average civilian, whatever military men might think of them.

"Ah, how do you do?" he said. "So you've been having honours thrust upon you? Well, I congratulate you. I'm sure, sincerely, in so far as they are a pleasure to you; but I condole with you from the bottom of my heart for your loss. I'm afraid Mrs. Colquhoun is giving you more trouble. Now, don't say the trouble's a pleasure, for I'll not believe a word of it, with all you have to occupy you."

"It is no pleasure to see her ill," I answered. "How is she to-day?"

"On my word I can't tell you, because I haven't seen her. I haven't the *entrée* to her private apartments. But come and see my new horse," he broke off—he was in an exceedingly good humour—"I got him in Ireland, and I'm inclined to think him a beauty, but I'd like to have your opinion. It's worth having."

The horse was like Colonel Colquhoun himself, showy; one of those high steppers that put their feet down where they lift them up almost, and get over no ground at all to speak of. Having occupied, without compunction, in inspecting this animal, half an hour of the time he considered too precious to be wasted on his wife, Colonel Colquhoun summoned Evadne's maid to show me upstairs, and cheerfully went his way.

But that remark of his about the *entrée* to his wife's apartments had made an impression. I was in duty bound to follow up any clue to the cause of her present state of mind, and here was perhaps a morbid symptom.

"Why have you quarrelled with your husband?" I asked in my most matter-of-course tone, as soon as I was seated, and had heard about her cold.

"I have not quarrelled with my husband," she answered, evidently surprised.

"Then what does he mean by saying that he hasn't the *entrée* to your private apartments?"

"I am sure he made no complaint about that," she answered tranquilly.

This was true. He had merely mentioned the fact casually, and not as a thing that affected his comfort or happiness in any way.

"Colonel Colquhoun and I are better friends now, if anything, than we have ever been," she added of her own accord, with inquiry in her eyes, as if she wanted to know what could have made me think otherwise.

I should have said myself that they were excellent friends,

but what precisely did " friends " mean ? I scented something anomalous here. However, it was not a point that I considered it advisable to pursue. I had ascertained that there was no morbid feeling in the matter, and that was all that I required to know. I only paid her a short visit that morning, and did not return for two days ; but I had been thinking seriously about her case in the interval, and carefully prepared to inquire into it particularly ; and an evident increase of languor and depression gave me a good opening.

"Tell me how you are to-day," I began. "Any trouble ? "

" The worry in my head is awful ! " she exclaimed. " Let me go downstairs. I am better there."

She was essentially a child of light and air and movement, requiring sunshine indoors as well as out to keep her in health. An Italian proverb says where the sun does not come, the doctor does, and this had been only too true in her case. It was pure animal instinct which had made the west window of the drawing room her favourite place. Nature, animal and vegetable, is under an imperative law to seek the sun, and she had unconsciously obeyed it for her own good. But she required more than that transient gleam in the western window ; a sun bath daily, when it could be had, is what I should have prescribed for her ; and from her next remark I judged that she had discovered for herself the harm which the deprivation of light was doing her.

" I can see the sun all day long beyond the shadow of the house," she continued, " but I want to feel it, too. I would like it to shine on me in the early morning, and wake me up and warm me. There is no heat so grateful ; and I only feel half alive in these dark, damp rooms. I never had bronchitis or was delicate at all in any way until we came here. Let me go down, won't you ? "

"Well, as your cold is so much better, you may go downstairs if you like. But you mustn't go out," I answered. " How are you going to amuse yourself ? "

" Oh ! "—she looked around the room as if in search of something—" I don't know exactly. Work, I suppose."

" You don't read much ? "

" No, not now." she answered, leaning forward with her hands clasped on her lap, and looking dreamily into the fire.

" Does that mean that you used to read once ?" I pursued. " You have plenty of books here."

She looked toward the well-filled cases.   "Yes," she said,
"old friends.   I seldom open any of them now."

"Do you never feel that they reproach you for losing interest in them?"

She smiled.   "I think perhaps they are relieved because I
have ceased from troubling them—from requiring more of
them than they could give me," she answered, smothering a
sigh.

"May I look at them?" I asked, anticipating her permission by rising and going toward them.

"Yes; certainly," she answered, rising herself, and following me languidly.   The books were arranged in groups—
science, history, biography, travels, poetry, fiction; with
bound volumes of such periodicals as the *Contemporary Re-
view, The Nineteenth Century,* and the *Westminster*.   I read
the titles of the volumes in the science divisions with surprise,
for she had never betrayed, nor had I ever suspected, that she
had added the incident of learning to the accident of brains.
But if she knew the contents of but half of these books well
she must be a highly educated woman.   I took out several to
see how they had been read, and found them all carefully
annotated, with marginal notes very clearly written, and containing apposite quotations from and references to the best
authorities on the various subjects.   This was especially the
case with books on the natural sciences; the physical ones
having apparently interested her less.

"These are not very elegant books for a lady's boudoir,"
she said, referring to the plain dark bindings.   "I dislike
gorgeously bound books, and could never make a pet of one.
They are like over-dressed people; all one's care is concentrated upon their appearance, and their real worth of character, if they have any, escapes one."

"Were you ever an omnivorous reader?" I asked.

"No, I am thankful to say," she answered, her natural
aptitude for intellectual pursuits overcoming her artificial
objection to them, as she looked at her books and became
interested in them in spite of herself; "for I notice that the
average reader who reads much remembers little, and is
absurdly inaccurate.   It is as bad to read everything as to eat
everything; the mind, when it is gorged with a surfeit of
subjects, retains none of them."

She had a fairly representative collection of French, Italian,
and German books, all equally well-read and annotated, each

in its own language, the French and Italian being excellent, but the German imperfect, although, as she told me, she liked both the language and the literature very much the best of the three. "German suggested ideas to me," she said, "and that is why I paid less attention to the construction of the language, I think. But I am afraid you will find no elegancies in any tongue I use, for language has always been to me a vehicle of thought, and not a part of art to be employed with striking effect. Now, here is Carlyle, the arch phrasemaker. I always admired him more than I loved him; but his books are excellent for intellectual exercise. He forced those phrases from his brain with infinite pains, and, when you take them collectively, you find yourself obliged to force them into yours in like manner."

She had become all interest and animation by this time, and I had never known her so delightful as she was that morning while showing me her books. She had no objection to lending me any that I chose, although I told her that I only wanted them to read her notes. I took a variety, but found no morbid tendency in any remark she had made upon them.

I paid my visit late in the afternoon next day, and found Evadne in the drawing room. She was standing in the window when I entered, but came down the room to greet me.

"I have been watching for you," she said. "I hoped you would come early. And I have also been watching that party of jubilant ducks waddling down the road. Come and see them. I believe they belong to us. They must have escaped from the yard. But aren't they enjoying the ramble! That old drake is quite puffed up with excitement and importance! He goes along nodding his head, and saying again and again to the ducks: 'Now, didn't I tell you so! and aren't you glad you took my advice and came?' And all the ducks are smiling and complimenting him upon his wisdom and courage. They ought to be driven back, but I haven't the heart to spoil their pleasure just yet by informing against them."

I was standing beside her in the window now, and she looked up at me, smiling as she spoke. She was brighter under the immediate influence even of the watery winter sun, now a red ball, glowing behind the brown branches of the leafless trees, than she had been in her gloomy north room; and I took this lively interest in the adventurous ducks to be a glimpse of the joyous, healthy mind, seeing character in all things animate, and gifted with sympathy as well as insight, which must naturally have been hers.

"When am I to go out?" she asked. "I begin to long for a sight of my fellow-creatures. I don't want to speak to them. I only want to see them. But I am sociable to that extent—when I am in my right mind."

"Tell me about this mental malady," I begged.

"Ah," she began, laughing up at me, but with a touch of bitterness. "I interest you now! I am a case! You do not flatter me. But I mean to give you every help in my power. If only you could cure me!" She clasped her hands and held them out to me, the gesture of an instant, but full of earnest entreaty.

"Come from the window," I said. "It is chilly here."

"Yes, come to the fire," she rejoined, leading the way; "and sit down, and let us have tea, and talk, and be cosey. You want me to talk about myself, and I will if I can. I was happy just now, but you see I am depressed in a moment. It is misery to me to be so variable And I constantly feel as if I wanted something—to be somewhere, or to have something; I don't know where or what; it is a sort of general dissatisfaction, but it is all the worse for not being positive. If I knew what I wanted, I should be cured by the effort to obtain it."

She rang the bell, and began to make up the fire; and I sat down and watched her because she liked to do those things in her own house. "Strangers wait upon me," she said; "but my friends allow me to wait upon them."

When the servant had brought tea and retired, she began again.

"Now question me," she said, "and make me tell you the truth."

"I am sure you will tell me the truth," I asserted.

"I am sure I shall try," she replied; "but I am not so sure that I shall succeed. If you provoke me, I shall fence with you; if you confuse me, I shall unwittingly say 'yes' when I mean 'no.' In fact, I am surprised to find myself confiding this trouble to you at all! It has come about by accident, but I am very glad; it is such a relief to speak. But how *has* it come about?" she broke off. "Did **you** suspect?"

"Suspect what?"

"That I am insane."

"You are not insane," I answered harshly.

She looked at me as if my words or manner amused her. "I remember now." she said. "I complained of the worry in my head, and then you questioned me."

"It is not an uncommon complaint," I rejoined.

"Is it not?" she answered. "Well, I don't know whether to be sorry for the other sufferers, or relieved to think that I am not the only one, which is what you intend, I believe. But, doctor, the misery is terrible, especially now that it has become almost incessant. It drives me—fills my mind with such dreadful ideas. I have actually meditated murder lately."

"Murder in the abstract, I suppose?"

"No, murder actually, murder for my own benefit, or what I fancy in that mood would be for my benefit ; the murder of one poor miserable creature whom I pity with all my heart and really care for—when I am in my right mind."

My heart sank. It was not necessary for me to know, and I had no inclination to ask, who the "one poor miserable creature" was.

"And when the impulse is on you, what do you do?" I said.

"It is not an impulse exactly," she answered ; "at least, it is nothing which I have ever had the slightest inclination to act upon. I am just possessed by the idea—whatever it may be—and then I cannot sit still. I have to rush out."

"Into Regent Street, for example?" I suggested, her last remark having thrown a sudden side-light upon that occurrence.

"Yes," she said. "But I didn't know I was going to Regent Street. I had read of Dickens prowling about the streets of London late at night when he was suffering from the effects of overwork, and recovering his tranquillity and power in that way, and I thought I would try the experiment ; so I went out and just walked on until I was tired, and then I got into an omnibus, so as to be with the people, and when it stopped and they all got out, I got out too, and walked on again, and then that horrid old man spoke to me. It was a great shock, but it had the happiest effect. I woke up, as it were, the moment I got rid of him, and felt quite myself again ; and then I hurried back, as you know. You still disapprove? Well, in one way, perhaps you are right ; but still it did me good." She stopped, and looked into the fire thoughtfully; and then she smiled. "Forgive me, do!" she said. "I know I behaved badly next day; I could not help it. The sudden relief to my mind had sent my spirits up inordinately for one thing; and then your face! Your consternation was really comical! If I had injured you irreparably in your estimation of the value of your own opinion of people, you could not have cared more. But I am sorry, very, very sorry," she added, with feeling, "that you should have lost your respect for me."

"What could make you think that I had lost my respect for you?" I asked in surprise.

"Because, you know, you have never come to see me since, as you used to do." · She looked at me a moment wistfully, and I knew she half expected me to explain or make some excuse; but I could not, unfortunately, do either without making bad worse. I could assure her, however, honestly, that I had not lost my respect for her.

"And I came to see you when you required me," I added.

But she was not satisfied. "I know your philanthropy," she said. "But I would rather have you come as of old because you believed in me, and like and respect me. I value your friendship, and it pains me to find that you can only treat me now like any other suffering sinner. Is it going to be so always?"

("Will the child kill me with her innocent talk?")

She had not alluded to the discontinuance of my visits before. I thought she had not missed me, and, being in a double mood, had been somewhat hurt by the seeming indifference, although I would not have had her want me when I could not come. Now, however, I was greatly distressed to find the construction she had put upon my absence, and all the more so because I could not explain.

"Do not say that!" I exclaimed. "You have always had, you always will have, my most sincere respect. It is part of an unhealthy state of mind which makes you doubt the attachment of your friends."

She was glad to accept this assertion. "Ah, yes!" she said. "I know the symptoms, but I had forgotten for the moment. Thank you. I *am* so glad to see you again!" She sighed, leaned back in her chair, folded her hands on her lap, and looked at me—"if only as a doctor," she added slowly. "You have some mysterious power over my mind. All great doctors have the power I mean ; I wonder what it is. Your very presence restores me in an extraordinary way. You dispel the worry in my head without a word, by just being here, however bad it is. I used to long for you so on those days when you never came, and I used to watch for you and be disappointed when you drove past ; but then I always said, 'He will come to-morrow,' and that was something to look forward to. I used to think at first you would get over my escapade, or learn to take another view of it ; but then, when you never came, I gradually lost heart and hope, and that is how it was I broke down, I think."

This guileless confidence affected me painfully.

"But I want to discover the secret of a great doctor's success," she pursued. "What is your charm? There is something mesmeric about you, I think, something inimical to disease at all events. There is healing in your touch, and your very manners make an impression which cures."

"Knowledge, I suppose, has nothing to do with it ?" I suggested, smiling.

"No, nothing," she answered emphatically. "I have carried out directions of yours successfully which had been previously given to me by another doctor and tried by me without effect. You alter the attitude of one's mind somehow—that is how you do it, I believe."

"Well, I hope to alter the present attitude of your mind completely," I answered. "And to resume. I want you to tell me how you feel when one of those tormenting thoughts has passed. Do you suffer remorse for having entertained it ?"

"Only an occasional pang," she said. "I do not allow myself to sorrow or suffer for thoughts which I cannot control. I am suffering from a morbid state of mind, and it is my duty to fight against the impulses which it engenders. But my responsibility begins and ends with the struggle. And I am quite sure that it is wiser to try and forget that such ideas ever were than to encourage them to haunt me by recollecting them even for purposes of penitential remorse."

"And when it is not a criminal impulse that affects you——"

"*Criminal!*" she ejaculated, aghast at the word.

I had used it on purpose to see its effect upon her, and was satisfied. The moral consciousness was still intact.

"Yes," I persisted. "But when it is not an impulse of that kind, what is it that disturbs your mind?"

"Thoughts of the suffering, the awful, needless suffering that there is in the world. The perception of it is a spur which goads me at times so that I feel as if I could do almost anything to lessen the sum of it. But then, you see, my hands are tied, so that all I can do is think, think, think."

"We must change that to work, work, work," I said.

"It is too late," she answered despondently. "Body and mind have suffered—mind and body. All that is not wrong in me is weak. I would have it otherwise, yes. But give me some anodyne to relieve the pain; that is all you can do for me now."

"I will give you no anodyne, either actual or figurative," I answered, rising to go. "If you had no recuperative force left in you there would be less energy in your despair. It rests with yourself now entirely to be as healthy-minded as ever again if you like."

I never could remember whether I said good-bye to her that day, or just walked out of the room, like the forgetful boor I sometimes am, with the words on my lips.

CHAPTER XIV.

A MEDICAL man who does not keep his moral responsibility before him in the consideration of a case must be a very indifferent practitioner, and, with regard to Evadne, I felt mine to such an extent that, before the interview was over, I had decided that I was not the proper person to treat her. I doubted my judgment for one thing, which showed that for once my nerve was at fault; and I had other reasons which it is not necessary to give. I therefore determined to run up to town to consult Sir Shadwell Rock about her. He was a distinguished colleague and personal friend of mine, a man of vast experience, and many years my senior; and I knew that if he would treat her, she could not be in better hands.

When I left As-You-Like-It I found that I had just time to drive to Morningquest and catch the last train to town. It was a four hours' journey, but fortunately there was a train in the early morning which would bring me back in time for my own work.

I knew Sir Shadwell was in town, and telegraphed to him to beg him to see me that night at half-past eleven if he possibly could, and, on arriving, I found him at home—very much at home, indeed, in a smoking jacket and slippers over a big fire in his own private sanctum, enjoying his bachelor ease with a cigarette and the last shilling shocker.

I apologised for my untimely visit, but he put me at my ease at once by cordially assuring me that I had done him a favour. "I was going to a boring big dinner this evening when your telegram arrived, and your coming in this way suggested something sufficiently important to detain me, so I sent an excuse, and have had a wholesome chop, and—eh—*a real good time*," he added confidentially, tapping the novelette. "Extraordinary production this, really. Most entertaining. I can't guess who did it, you know, I can't indeed—but, my dear boy, to what do I owe the pleasure? What can I do for you?

" First of all give me a wholesome chop if you have another in the house, for I'm famishing."

"Oh, a thousand pardons for my remissness!" he exclaimed, ringing the bell vehemently. "Of course you haven't dined. I ought to have thought of that. Something very important, I suppose?"

" A most interesting case."

" Mental ?"

" Yes. A lady."

" Well, not another word until you've had something to eat. Suitable surroundings play an important part in the discussion of such cases, and suitable times and seasons also. Just before dinner one isn't sanguine, and just after one is too much so. When you have eaten, take time to reflect—and a cigarette if you are a smoker." He had been holding his book in his hand all the time, but now he pottered to a side-table with an old man's stiffness, peeped at the paragraph he had been reading, marked his place with a paper cutter, and muttered—" Very strange, for if she didn't steal the jewels, who did? Mustn't dip though ; spoils it." He put the book down, and returned to me, taking off his spectacles as he came, and smoothing his thick white hair. "Now don't say a word if you've read it," he cautioned me. " I always owe everybody a grudge who tells me the plot of a story I'm interested in. But, let me see, what was I saying? Oh! Take time, that was it ! There is nothing like letting yourself settle if you are at all perplexed. When the memory is

crowded with details the mind becomes muddy, and you mus
let it clear itself. That is the secret of my own success. It
any difficulty I have always waited. Don't try to think.
Much better dismiss the matter from your mind altogether,
make yourself comfortable in the easiest chair in the room,
get a rousing book—the subject is of no importance, so long
as it interests you—and in half an hour, if the physical well-
being is satisfactory, you will find the mental tension gradually relax. Your ideas begin to flow, your judgment becomes
clear, and you suddenly see for yourself in a way that
astonishes you."

"Then pray oblige me by resuming your seat and cigarette," I answered, "and let me transfer my difficulty to you
while the moment lasts—*your* moment!"

"When you have dined," he said good-humouredly.
" I won't hear a word while you are famishing. Tell me how
you are yourself, and what you are doing. My dear boy, it is
really a pleasure to see you! Why aren't you married?"

" Now, really, do you expect me to answer such an important question as that with my mind in its present muddy condition!" I retorted upon him. "My many reasons are all
rioting in my recollection, and I can't see one clearly."

The old gentleman smiled, and sat patting the arms of his
chair for a little. "You're looking fagged," he remarked
presently. "Work won't hurt you, but beware of worry!"

My dinner was brought to me on a tray at this instant, and
the dear old man got up to see that it was properly served.
He tried the champagne himself, to be sure it was right, and
gave careful directions about the coffee. His interest in
everything was as fresh as a boy's, and nothing he could do
in the way of kindness was ever a trouble to him.

" You have been coming out strong in defence of morality
lately," I remarked, when I had dined. "You have somewhat startled the proprieties."

" Startled the pruderies, you mean," he answered, bridling.
" The proprieties face any necessity for discussion with
modest discretion, however painful it may be."

"Well, you've done some good, at all events," I answered.
I did not tell him, but only that very day I had heard it said
that his was a name which all women should reverence for
what he had done for some of them.

" Well," he said, "the clergy have had a long innings.
They have been hard at it for the last eighteen hundred years,

and society is still rotten at the core. It is our turn now. But come, draw up your chair to the fire and be comfortable. Well, yes," he went on, rubbing his hands, " I suppose eventually morality will be taught by medical men, and when it is much misery will be saved to the suffering sex. My own idea is that a woman is a human being ; but the clerical theory is that she is a dangerous beast, to be kept in subjection, and used for domestic purposes only. Married life is made up to a great extent of the most heartless abuse of a woman's love and unselfishness. Submission, you know——!"

When I had given him the details of Evadne's case, so far as I had gone into it, he asked me what my own theory was.

" I feel sure it is the old story of these cases in women," I answered. " The natural bent has been thwarted to begin with."

" Yes," he commented, " that is a fruitful source of mischief even in these days, when women so often listen to the voice of the Lord himself speaking in their own hearts, and do what he directs in spite of the Church. The restrictions imposed upon women of ability warp their minds, and the rising generation suffers. But how has the natural bent been thwarted in this case ?"

" I have not ascertained," I said. "She is a woman of remarkable general intelligence, but she makes no use of it, and she does not seem to have any one decided talent that she cares to cultivate, and consequently she has no absorbing interest to occupy her mind, no purpose for which to live and make the most of her abilities. She attends punctually to her social duties, but they do not suffice, and she has of necessity many spare hours of every day on her hands, during which she sits and sews alone. I suppose a woman's embroidery answers much the same purpose as a man's cigarette. It quiets her nerves, and helps her to think. If she is satisfied and happy in her surroundings her reflections will probably be tranquil and healthy, but if her outward circumstances are not congenial, she will banish all thoughts of them in her hours of ease, and her mind will gradually become a prey to vain imaginings—pleasant enough to begin with, doubtless, but likely to take a morbid tone at any time if her health suffers. This has been the case with Evadne——"

" With *whom* ? " Sir Shadwell interrupted.

"With my patient," I stammered. "I have been accustomed to hear her spoken of by her Christian name."

"Humph!" the old gentleman grunted, enigmatically.

"She has one of those minds which should be occupied by a succession of lively events, all helping on some desirable object," I proceeded—"the mind of a naturally active woman."

"Well," he answered, "it seems to be another instance of the iniquitous folly of allowing the one sex to impose galling limitations upon the other. It is not an uncommon case so far as the mental symptoms go. How does she get on with her husband? does she contradict him?"

"No, never," I answered. "She is always courteous and considerate."

"Ah, now, I thought so," he chuckled. "A happily married woman contradicts her husband flatly whenever she thinks proper. She knows she is safe from wrangling and bitterness. I think you will find that the domestic position is the difficulty here. You don't seem to have inquired into that very carefully."

I made no answer, and he looked at me sharply for a moment, then asked me how old my patient was.

"Twenty-five," I told him.

"Twenty-five," he repeated; "and you are intimate with both her and her husband. Now, have you ever had any reason to doubt her honesty—her verbal honesty of course I mean?"

"Quite the contrary," I answered. "I have always found her almost peculiarly frank."

"A woman may be accurate, you know, in all she says of other people," he observed; "but that is no proof that she will be so concerning herself."

"I know," was my reply; "but I feel quite sure of this lady's word."

"And during the time that you have known her she now confesses that she has suffered more or less?"

"Yes. She mentioned one interval during which she said a new interest in life took her completely out of herself."

"What was the interest?"

"I did not ask her."

"She fell in love, I suppose, and you happened to know the fact."

"I neither know, nor suspected such a thing,"

"That was it, you may be sure," Sir Shadwell decided. "When a young and attractive woman, who speaks to her husband with marked courtesy and consideration, instead of treating him familiarly, talks of having an interest in life which takes her completely out of herself, you may take it for granted almost always that the new interest is love."

"It is more likely to have been the small-pox epidemic," I rejoined, and then I gave him an account of that episode.

"Ah, well, perhaps," he said. "We are evidently dealing with a nature full of surprises." He pursed up his mouth and eyed me attentively. "My dear boy," he said at last, "I think I see your difficulty. You had better turn this case over to me altogether."

"Thank you," I answered. "That is what I should like to have suggested."

"Then send the lady up to town, and I will do my best for her."

CHAPTER XV.

SIR SHADWELL ROCK was exactly the kind of man Evadne had had in her mind, I felt sure, when she spoke of the peculiar influence which distinguished men of my profession exercise upon their patients. He was a man of taking manners to begin with, sympathetic, cultivated, humane; and, I need hardly add, scrupulously conscientious and exact. I could confide her to his care with the most perfect reliance upon his kindness, as well as upon his discretion and skill—if she would consent to consult him at all; but that was a little difficulty which had still to be got over. I anticipated some opposition, because I felt sure she had not realized that there was any-thing threatening to be serious in her case, and would there-fore see no necessity for further advice. This made the arrangement difficult. It would not do to arouse any appre-hension about her own state of mind; but how to induce her to go to London to consult an eminent specialist without doing so was the question. Had Lady Adeline been at home the suggestion would have come best from her, but in her absence there was nobody to make it except that impossible Colonel Colquhoun. If he chose to order Evadne to consult Sir Shadwell Rock, I knew she would do so at once, for she never opposed him, and he was so apt to be unreasonable and capri-cious that she would probably not think that the order signified much. But the further question was, would he give it? After I had finished my morning's work, I drove to the depôt to see. The men were on parade when I entered the barrack square. They were drawn up in line, and the first thing I saw was Colonel Colquhoun himself prancing about on his charger, and not in the most amiable mood possible, I imagined, from the way he was blackguarding the men. He sat his horse well, and was a fine soldierlike man in uniform, and a handsome man too, of the martial order, when his bald head was hidden by his cocked hat, and his blond moustache had a chance; the sort of man to take a woman's fancy if not the kind of character to keep her regard.

An unhappy old mounted major had got into trouble just as I came up. His palfrey was an easy ambler, but he was the sort of old gentleman who would not have been safe in a rocking chair with his sword drawn and his chief complimenting him.

"You ride like a damned tailor, sir," Colonel Colquhoun was thundering at him just as I drove up.

An officer in undress uniform, Captain Bartlet, and Brigade Surgeon James, who was in mufti, were standing at an open window in the ante-room, and I joined them there, and looked out at the parade.

"I don't know how you fellows stand that kind of thing, and before the men, too," I remarked, à *propos* of a fresh volley of abuse from Colonel Colquhoun.

"Oh! by Jove! we've got to stand it, many of us, for weighty considerations quite apart from our personal dignity," Captain Bartlet rejoined. "A man with a wife and five children depending upon him will swallow a lot for their sake. It would be easy enough to answer him, but self-interest keeps us quiet—a deuced sight oftener than discipline, by the way. However," he added cheerfully, "all C. O.'s are not so bad as that brute out there, nor the half of them for the matter of that."

"But, still, it's a wonder what you stand, you combatants," Dr. James observed.

"Shut up, doctor," Captain Bartlet rejoined good-naturedly, "Don't presume upon your superior position. *Your* promotion doesn't depend upon the colonel's confidential report, nor your peace in life upon his fancy for you. You can disagree with him in your own line, but we can't in ours."

"Is Colonel Colquhoun often so?" I asked. He had just been assuring that unfortunate major that a billet in the Commissariat department, with a pound of beef on one spur and a loaf of bread on the other to prevent accidents, was the thing for him.

"More or less," was the answer. "He's notorious all through the service. He brought his own regiment up to a high state of efficiency, I must say that for him, and led it into action like a man ; but, between ourselves, I expect there's never been a time since he got his company when there wasn't a bullet ready for him. You remember, James, in India ? of course it was an accident ! "

The doctor nodded. "The men call him Bully Colquhoun," he supplemented.

"But surely his character is known at the Horse Guards ? " I said.

"Ah, you see he's a smart officer," Captain Bartlet re-joined ; "and what are officers for ? To knock about and to be knocked about. Just look at him now ! See how he's buck-eting those men about ! He was a militiaman, and that's a militiaman all over ! A man who's been through Sandhurst has carried a rifle for a year himself, and he knows what it is, and gives his men their stand easy ; but a militiaman has no more feeling for them than a block."

"Well, I can't see why you seniors don't remonstrate," I rejoined. "The War Office is bound to support you if you show good cause."

"Yes, and cashier you too for very little, if you make your-self obnoxious by giving them trouble," Bartlet replied. "Roy-lance was the only fellow that ever really stood up to Col-quhoun. He was a young subaltern that had just joined, but an awful devil when he was roused, and he swore in the ante-room that if the colonel ever blackguarded him before the men, or anywhere else, or presumed upon his position to address him in terms which one gentleman is not permitted to use to another, he'd give him as much as he got. Well, the very next day, on parade, Roylance got the men into a muddle. Colquhoun's a good soldier, you know, and nothing riles him like inefficiency ; and, by Jove ! he was down on the lad like shot ! He poured his whole vocabulary on him, and then, for want of a worse word, he called him ' a damned dissipated subaltern.' Well, Roylance just stepped back so as to make himself heard, and shouted coolly : ' Dissipated ! that comes well from you, sir, considering the reason for the singular ar-rangement of your own *ménage !* ' with which he handed his sword to the adjutant, and walked off to his quarters ! You should have seen Colquhoun's face! He went on leave im‹ mediately afterward, and of course the matter was hushed up. Roylance exchanged. He'd lots of money. It's the men without means that have to stand that kind of thing."

My voice was husky and I could scarcely control it, but I managed to ask: "What was the insinuation?"

"What, about Roylance? Just a lie! The lad's life was as clean as a lady's."

"I meant about the marriage?"

"Oh, don't you know? Colquhoun himself told us all about it in his cups one night. Just as they were starting on their wedding trip she got a letter containing certain allegations against him, and she gave him the slip at the station, and went off by herself to make inquiries, and in consequence of what she learnt, she declined to live with him at all at first. But he has a great horror of being made the subject of gossip, you know, and her people were also anxious to save scandal, and so, between them, they managed to persuade her just to consent to live in the house, he having given his word of honour as a gentleman not to molest her; and that has been the arrangement ever since. Funny, isn't it? ' Truth stranger than fiction,' you know, and that kind of thing, Yet it seems to answer. They're excellent friends."

The parade had been dismissed by this time, but I had changed my mind, and did not wait to see Colonel Colquhoun. I had to hurry back to make arrangements with regard to my patients in the hospital, and then I returned to town, and midnight saw me closeted once more with Sir Shadwell Rock.

CHAPTER XVI.

THE revolting story I had heard in the barracks haunted me. I had thought incessantly of my poor little lady taken out of the school room to face a position which would be horrifying, even in idea, to a right minded woman of the world. What the girl's mental sufferings must have been only a girl can tell. And ever since—the incubus of that elderly man of unclean antecedents! All that had been incomprehensible about Evadne was obvious now, and also the mistake she had made.

During the most important part of the time when a woman

is ripe for her best experiences, when she should be laying in a store of happy memories to fall back upon, when memory becomes her principal pleasure in life, Evadne had lived alone, shut up in herself, her large intelligence idle or misapplied, and her hungry heart seeking such satisfaction as it could find in pleasant imaginings. As she went about, punctually performing her ineffectual duties, or sat silently sewing, she had been to all outward seeming an example to be revered of graceful wifehood and womanliness ; but when one came to know what her inner life had become in consequence of the fatal repression of the best powers of her mind, it was evident that she was in reality a miserable type of a woman wasted. The natural bent of the average woman is devotion to home and husband and children ; but there are many women to whom domestic duties are distasteful, and these are now making life tolerable for themselves by finding more congenial spheres of action. There are many women, however, above the average, who are quite capable of acquitting themselves creditably both in domestic and public life, and Evadne was one of these. Had she been happily married she would undoubtedly have been one of the first to distinguish herself, one of the foremost in the battle which women are waging against iniquity of every kind. Her keen insight would have kept her sympathies actively alive, and her disinterestedness would have made her careless of criticism. That was her nature. But nature thwarted ceases to be beneficent. She places us here fully equipped for the part she has designed us to play in the world, and if we, men or women, neglect to exercise the powers she has bestowed upon us, the consequences are serious. I did not understand at the time what Evadne meant when she said that she had made it impossible for herself to act. I thought she had deliberately shirked her duty under the mistaken idea that she would make life pleasanter for herself by doing so ; but I learnt eventually how the impulse to act had been curbed before it quickened, by her promise to Colonel Colquhoun, which had, in effect, forced her into the disastrous attitude which we had all such good reason to deplore. It seemed cruel that all the most beautiful instincts of her being, her affection, her unselfishness, even her modest reserve and womanly self-restraint, should have been used to injure her ; but that is exactly what had happened. And now the difficulty was : how to help her ? How to rouse her from the unwholesome form of self-repression which had brought about her present morbid state of mind.

I was sitting up late the night after my second visit to Sir Shadwell Rock, considering the matter. Sir Shadwell's advice was still the same : " Send her to me." But the initial difficulty, how to get her to go, remained. How to draw her from the dreary seclusion of her *Home in the Woman's Sphere,* and persuade her that hours of ease are only to be earned in action. I thought again of Lady Adeline, and sat down to write to her.

The household had retired, and the night was oppressively silent. I felt overcome with fatigue, but was painfully wide awake, as happens very often when I am anxious about a bad case. But this was the third night since I had been in bed, and I thought now I would go when I had finished my letter to Lady Adeline, and do my best to sleep. As I crossed the hall, which was in darkness save for the candle I carried in my hand, I fancied I heard an unaccountable sound, a dull thud, thud, coming from I could not tell whence for the moment. The senses are singularly acute in certain stages of fatigue, and mine were all alive that night to any impression, my hearing especially so ; and there was no mistake. I had stopped short to listen, and, impossible as I knew it would have been at any other time, I was sure that I could distinctly hear a horse galloping on the turf of the common more than a mile away, a mounted horse with a rider who was urging him to his utmost speed ; and in some inexplicable manner I also became conscious of the fact that the horseman was a messenger sent in all haste for me.

Mechanically I put my candle down and opened the hall door. It was a bright night. The fresh invigorating frosty air seemed to clear my mental vision still more strongly as it blew in upon me. Diavolo in mess dress, his cap gone, his fair hair blown back by the wind ; breathless with excitement and speed ; with thought suspended, but dry lips uttering incessantly a cry for help—" Galbraith ! Galbraith ! Galbraith ! " My pulses kept time to the thud of the horse's hoofs on the common. I waited. I had not the shadow of a doubt that I was wanted. But I did not ask myself by whom.

The sound only ceased for a perceptible second or so at the lodge gates. Were they open ? Had he cleared them ? What a jump ! Thud ! He must be well-mounted ! On the drive now ! The gravel is flying ! Across the lawn—Diavolo. Good speed indeed !

Scarcely five minutes since I heard him first till he stopped at the steps in the starlight, hoarsely panting " Galbraith ! Galbraith ! "

" I am here, my boy ! What is it ? "

" Come ! Come to her at once ! Colonel Colquhoun is dead."

The mind, quickened by the shock of a startling piece of intelligence, suddenly sums up our suspicions for us sometimes in one crisp homely phrase. This is what mine did. " The murder is out ! " I thought, the moment Diavolo spoke. Evadne—was this the end of it ! Such a state of mind as hers had been lately, might continue for the rest of her life, to her torment, without influencing her actions ; but, on the other hand, an active phase might supervene at any moment.

Diavolo had dismounted and sat down on one of the steps, utterly exhausted. " Here, take the reins," he said, " and mount. I'm done. I'll look after myself. Don't waste a moment."

I needed no urging.

" I have actually meditated murder lately. Murder—murder for my own benefit."

The horrible phrases, in regular succession, kept time to the rhythmical ring of the iron shoes on the frozen ground as the horse returned with me, still at a steady gallop, to As-You-Like-It.

I had recognized the animal. It was the same fine charger which Colonel Colquhoun himself had been riding so admirably on parade the last time I saw him. Only yesterday morning ! " Murder actually, murder for my own benefit." No ! no !—stumble. Hold up ! only a stone. Shall we ever be there ? Suspense—" Murder actually "—no, it shall not be that ! Hope is the word I want. Beat it out of the hardened earth ! Hope, hope, hope, hope, nothing, nothing but hope !

We had arrived at last. No one about. Doors open, lights flaring, and a strange silence.

Leaving the horse to do as he liked, I walked straight up-stairs, and on the first landing I met Evadne's maid.

" I hoped it was you, sir. Come this way," she whispered, and pushed open a door which stood already ajar, gently, as if afraid of disturbing some sleeper.

It was Colonel Colquhoun's bedroom, large and luxurious, like the man himself. He was stretched upon the bed, in evening dress, his gray face upward. One glance at *that* sufficed. But almost before I had crossed the threshold I was conscious of an indescribable sense of relief. There were four persons in the room, that poor old "begad" major, who could not ride, and Captain Bartlet, both hastily summoned from the depôt evidently, and still in mess dress; Dr. James in ordinary morning costume, with a covert coat on; and Evadne herself in a black evening dress, open at the throat. It was her attitude that relieved my mind the moment I saw her. She was seated beside the bed, crying heartily and healthily. The three gentlemen stood just behind her, gravely concerned; silent, sympathetic, helpless, waiting for me. No one spoke.

For the dead, reverence. I stood by the bed looking down on the splendid frame, prone now and inert, and again I thought of the last time I had seen him, a fine figure of a man, finely mounted, and exercising his authority arrogantly. I looked into the blank countenance. No other man on earth had ever called forth curses from my inmost soul such as I had uttered, to my shame, in one great burst of rage that had surprised me and shaken my fortitude the night before as I journeyed back alone, without the slightest prospect, that I could see, of saving her. The blank face, decently composed. His right hand, palm upward, was stretched out toward me as if he were offering it to me; and thankful I was to feel that I could clasp it honestly. I had not a word or look on my conscience for which I deserved a reproach from the dead man lying there. I took his hand: a doctor doing a perfunctory duty? No, a last natural rite, an act of reconciliation. In that solemn moment, still holding his hand and gazing down into his face, I rejoiced to feel that the trouble had passed from my soul, that the rage and bitterness were no more, and that only the touching thought of his kindly hospitality and perfect confidence in my own integrity—a confidence impossible in a man who has not himself the saving grace of a better nature—would remain with me from that time forth forever.

I laid my hand on Evadne's shoulder, and she looked up.

"Ah! have you come?" she cried, her voice broken with sobs that shook her. "Is it really true? Can nothing be done? Oh, poor, poor man! What a life! What a death!

A miserable, miserable, misspent life, and such an end—in a moment—without a word of warning—and all these years when I have been beside him, silent and helpless. If only I could have done something to help him—said something. Surely, surely there was *something* I might have done ? " She held her clasped hands out toward me, the familiar gesture, appealing to me to blame her.

" Thank Heaven ! " I inwardly ejaculated. " This is as it should be."

In the presence of eternal death, her own transient sufferings were forgotten, and healthy human pity destroyed any sense of personal injury she might have cherished.

We four men stood awkwardly, patiently by for several minutes, listening to her innocent self-upbraidings, knowing her story, and touched beyond expression by the utter absence of all selfish sentiment in any word she said.

When she was quite exhausted, I drew her hand through my arm, and took her to her own room.

Cardiac syncope was the cause of death. Colonel Colquhoun had been out that evening, and had, through some mistake of the coachman's, missed his carriage, and walked home in a towering rage. The exertion and excitement, acting together on a heart already affected, had brought on the attack. He was storming violently in the hall, with his face flushed crimson—so the servants told us—when all at once he stopped, and called " Evadne ! " twice, as if in alarm; and Mrs. Colquhoun ran down from the drawing room ; but before she could reach him he fell on the floor, and never spoke again.

CHAPTER XVII.

MUCH of my time during the next few months was devoted to the consideration of Evadne's affairs. Her father made no sign, and she had no other relation in a position to come forward and share the responsibility ; but, happily, she had very good friends. I had noticed that Diavolo was singularly agitated when he brought the terrible news that night to Fountain Towers, but thought little of it, as I knew the boy to be emotional. The shock to his own feelings did not, however, prevent him thinking of others, and the next thing I heard of him was that he had been to Morningquest and waited till the telegraph office opened, in order to send the news to his own people, and beg them to return at once, if they could, on Evadne's account ; and this they did, in the kindest manner, with as little delay as possible.

"I have only come to fetch Evadne," Lady Adeline said when she arrived. "I am going to take her away at once from this dreadful house and this dreary English winter to a land of sunshine and flowers and soft airs, and I hope to bring her back in the spring herself again—as *you* have never known her!"

Mr. Hamilton-Wells stayed behind, at considerable personal inconvenience, to consult with me about business. Colonel Colquhoun had died intestate and also in debt. What he had done with his money we could not make out, except that a large sum had been sunk in an annuity, which of course died with him. But one thing was quite evident, which was that Evadne would have little or nothing besides her pension from the service, and that would be the merest pittance for one always accustomed to the command of money as she had been. Mr. Hamilton-Wells wished to impose a handsome sum on her yearly by fraud and deceit, out of his own ample income.

"Really, ladies are so peculiar about money matters," he said. "I feel quite sure she would not accept sixpence from me if I were to offer it to her. But she need not know where the money comes from. It can be paid into her account at the bank, you see, regularly, and she will take it for granted that she is entitled to it."

"I am not so sure of that," I answered with some heat, "but at any rate the plan is not possible."

"Now, my dear Galbraith," Mr. Hamilton-Wells remonstrated, "do not put your foot down in that way. I am the older man, and I may also say, without offence, the older friend, and I am married ; and Lady Adeline will strongly approve of what I propose."

"I do not doubt it," I maintained ; "but it cannot be done."

"She is not the kind of person to marry for money," Mr. Hamilton-Wells observed, looking up at the ceiling.

"Who? Mrs. Colquhoun?" I asked. "I don't understand you."

"Oh," he answered. "it occurred to me that you might be thinking such a consideration would weigh with her in the choice of a second husband."

I stared at the man. He was sitting at a writing table in

my library, with the papers we had been going through spread
out before him, and I was standing opposite ; and, as he spoke,
he leant back in his chair, with his elbows on the arms of it,
brought the tips of his long white fingers together, and smiled
up at me, bland as a child, innocent of all offence. I am inclined to think he did secretly enjoy the effect of unexpected
remarks without in the least appreciating the permanent
impression he might be making. But I don't know. Some of
these apparently haphazard observations of his were pregnant
with reflection, and I believe, if his voice had been strong and
determined instead of precise and insinuating ; if he had
brushed his hair up, instead of parting it in the middle and
plastering it down smoothly on either side of his head ; if his
hands had been hardened by exposure and use instead of
whitened by excessive care ; if he had worn tweed instead of
velvet, Mr. Hamilton-Wells would have been called acute, and
dreaded for his cynicism. But looking as he did, inoffensive
as a lady's luggage, he was allowed to pass unsuspected ; and
if his mind were an infernal machine, concealed by a quilted
cover, the world would have to have seen it to credit the fact.

I put my hands in my pockets after that last remark, and
walked to the window glumly; but as I stood with my back to
him, I could not help wondering if he was making faces at
me, or up to any other undignified antics by way of relaxation.
Did he ever wriggle with merriment when he was alone ? I
turned suddenly at the thought. He was calmly perusing
a paper through his pince-nez, with an expression of countenance at once so benign, silly, and self-satisfied, that I felt I
should like to have apologised for the suspicion.

"There is nothing for it, Galbraith," she said, "that I can
see. She must either be poverty-stricken or have an income
provided for her."

"She has enough to go on with for the present," I answered.

"You can provide the money yourself if you would rather,"
he suggested, in the tone of one who gives in good-naturedly
to oblige you. "I don't care, you know, where the money
comes from, so long as the source is disinterested and respectable."

I had returned to the table, but now again I walked to the
window.

"But, I think," he continued, while I stood with my back to
him, "as you say, for the present nothing need be done. Give
her time for a rope—eh? What I do deprecate is leaving her

to be driven by poverty to marry for money. **My dear Galbraith,**" he broke off, protesting, "you have been on the prance for the last half-hour. For a medical man, you have less repose of manner than is essential, I should say. In fact, you quite give me the notion that you are impatient. But perhaps I am detaining you?"

"Oh, not at all," I assured him.

"Well, as I was saying," he pursued, "give her time to marry again. That would be the most satisfactory settlement of her difficulties. She is, I quite agree with you, a very attractive person. Now, there is the Duke of Panama already, Lady Adeline says—but she seems to have an objection to princes, especially if they are at all obese. I do not like obese people myself. Now, do *you* ever feel nervous on that score?"

"What score?"

"The score of obesity. You are just nicely proportioned at present for a man of your age and height. *I*, of course, am far too slender. But if you were to get any stouter by and by, it would be such a dreadful thing! I hope flesh is not in your family on both sides. On one I know it is. Now, my people are all slender. There is a great deal in that, I notice."

He was doing up the documents now with much neatness and dexterity.

"These had better go to my lawyer," he remarked.

"Why not to mine?" I suggested.

"Oh, allow me," he said, with great suavity—"as the older man. Of course, as a question of right, we neither of us have any claim to the privilege of being allowed to help this lady. Eventually, however, one of us may secure the right; but there is many a slip, you know, and perhaps it would be less awkward afterward if a person whose disinterestedness is quite above suspicion had had the direction of affairs from the first."

There could be no doubt of what he meant by this time, and the argument was unanswerable.

"Do you feel inclined to return with me to Mentone?" he asked.

"I am afraid I cannot get away just now."

"Ah! I suppose it *is* too soon. Well, she is quite safe with us, and we will bring her back to Hamilton House in the spring." Mr. Hamilton-Wells smiled complacently as he took his seat in his carriage. I almost expected him to thank me for the sport I had been giving him, he looked so like a man who had been enjoying himself thoroughly. I thought about that last remark of his after he had gone, and pitied Lady Adeline. It must be trying to be liable at any moment to have words, which one deliberately chooses to hide one's thoughts, set aside as of no consequence, and the thoughts themselves answered naïvely. However, there was no real reason for hiding my thoughts any longer on that subject. I had done my best manfully, I hope, while the necessity lasted, to mask my feeling for her, even from myself; but there was now no further need for self-restraint. I might live for her and love her honestly and openly at last; and, accordingly, when Sir Shadwell Rock came to me for a few days at Christmas, I did not attempt to conceal my intention from him.

"It is a great risk," he said gravely, "a very great risk. Of course, now that the first cause of all the trouble is removed, the mental health may be thoroughly restored. So long as there is no organic brain lesion there is hope in all such cases. But I tell you frankly that the first call upon her physical strength may set up a recurrence of the moral malady, and you cannot foresee the consequences. However, you know as much about that as I do, and I can see it's no use warning you. You have made up your mind."

"Yes," I answered. "I shall be able to take good care of her if only I am fortunate enough to win her."

"Well, well, she seems to be a loyal little body," the old gentleman replied; "and I wish you success with all my heart. She will have much in her favour as your wife, and since you are determined to run the risk, let us hope for the best."

And that was just what I did while I waited for the spring, and to such good purpose that I became light-hearted as a schoolboy. I watched the birds building; I noticed the first faint green shadow on the hedges, and the yellowing of the gorse; I listened in the freshness of the dawn to the thrush that sang "Evadne." And when at last Mr. Hamilton-Wells walked in one day unexpectedly, and explained, somewhat superfluously, that he had come, I could have thrown up my hat and cheered!

"But without the ladies," he added.

"Have you left them behind you?" I demanded, trying not to look blank.

"Yes," he answered very slowly, then added: "At Hamilton House." I suppose nobody ever thought of kicking anything so "slender" as Mr. Hamilton-Wells, or associated such a vulgar idea as would have been involved in the suspicion of a deliberate intention to "sell" you with a person of such courteous and distinguished manners. But one did occasionally wonder what he was like at school, and if blessings and abuse were often showered on him then at one and the same time, as had come to be the case in later life.

He had come to ask me to dinner that evening, and when I arrived he was standing on the hearthrug, gracefully, with a palm-leaf fan in his hand. Evadne greeted me quietly, Lady Adeline with affectionate cordiality, and Diavolo, who was the only other member of the party, with a grave yet bright demeanour which made him more like his Uncle Dawne in miniature than ever.

"'In the spring,'" Mr. Hamilton-Wells observed precisely, waving his fan to emphasise each word, and addressing a remote angle of the cornice, "'In the spring a young man's fancy lightly turns to thoughts of love.'"

Diavolo flushed crimson, Lady Adeline looked annoyed, but Evadne sat pale and still, as if she had not heard.

I was right about her not being likely to leave her affairs in anybody's hands. Very soon after her arrival she insisted upon having an accurate statement of accounts, and begged me to go over to Hamilton House one morning to render it, as she found Mr. Hamilton-Wells quite unapproachable on the subject.

She received me in the morning room alone, and began at once in the most business-like way. "Mr. Hamilton-Wells' reticence convinces me that I am a beggar," she said cheerfully. "Tell me the exact sum I have to depend upon?"

I named it.

"Oh, then," she proceeded, "the question is, What shall I do? I cannot possibly live in the world, you know, on such a sum as that."

"What do you propose to do?" I asked, her tone having suggested some definite plan already formed.

"Go into a sisterhood, I think," she answered.

"Nonsense!" I exclaimed.

She raised her eyebrows.

"I beg your pardon," I said. "But you are not fit for such a life. Why, in a month you would be seeing visions and dreaming dreams."

"But I am afraid I shall do that now in any case, wherever I am," she sighed; and then she added, smiling at her own cynicism ; " and I think I had better go where such things can be turned to good account. I have had no horrid thoughts, by the way, since I left As-You-Like-It, but of course I shall relapse."

" No, you will not," I blurted out, " if you marry happily." Her face flushed all over at the word.

" Will you, Evadne," I proceeded—" or rather could you— be happy with me ? " She rose, and made me a deep courtesy. " Thank you," she answered scornfully, " for your kind consideration, Sir George Galbraith ! I always thought you the most disinterested person I ever knew, but I had no idea that even you could go so far as that ! "

And then she left me alone with my consternation.

How in the name of all that is perplexing had I offended her ?

Lady Adeline came in at that moment, and I put the question to her, telling her exactly what I had said. She burst out laughing.

" My dear George ! " she exclaimed, " forgive me ! I can't help it ! But don't you think yourself you were a little bit abrupt ? You do not seem to have mentioned the fact that you feel any special affection for Evadne. It did not occur to you to protest that you loved her, for instance ? "

" No, it did not," I answered ; " I should think that the fact is patent enough without protestations."

" She may have overlooked it, all the same," Lady Adeline suggested, still laughing at me. " I would advise you to find out the next time you have a chance."

" Where is she ? " I demanded, going toward the door.

" Oh, you won't see her again to-day, you may be sure," she rejoined ; " and it is just as well, you bear, if you mean to make love to her with that kind of countenance ! "

But I would not be advised.

I strode straight up to her room, which I happened to know, and knocked at the door.

She answered " Come in ! " evidently not expecting me, and when she saw who it was she was furious.

" I cannot understand what you mean by such conduct ! " she exclaimed.

" Well, then, I'll make you understand ! " I retorted.

Mr. Hamilton-Wells insinuated afterward that Evadne only accepted me to save her life. But I protested against the libel. I have never, to my certain knowledge, uttered a rough word either to or before my little lady in the whole course of our acquaintance. But why, when she loved me, she should have gone off in that ridiculous tantrum simply because I did not begin by expressing my love for her, I shall never be able to understand. She might have been sure that I should have enough to say on that subject as soon as I was accepted.

The day after the engagement was announced Diavolo called upon me. Needless to say he found me in the seventh heaven. I had been walking about the house, unable to settle to anything, and when I heard he had come I thought it was to congratulate me, and I hurried down; but the first glimpse of his face caused my heart to contract ominously.

" Well, you have played me a nice trick," he said, with concentrated bitterness, " both of you. You knew what *my* intentions were and you gave me no hint of your own. You preferred to steal a march on me. I could not have imagined such a thing possible from you. I should have supposed that you would have thought such underhand conduct low."

" Diavolo ! " I gasped, " are you in earnest ? "

" Am I in earnest ! " he ejaculated. " Look at me ! I suppose you think I am incapable of deep feeling."

" If only I had known ! " I exclaimed. " Yet—how could I guess? The difference of age—and, Diavolo, my dear boy, believe me, I do sympathise with you most sincerely. This is a bitter drop in the cup for me. But—but—even if I had known—will it make it worse for you if I say it ?—it is me she loves. She would not have accepted anyone but me. Even if I *had* withdrawn in your favour——"

He waved his hand to stop me. " Don't distress yourself," he said. " It is fate. We are to be punished with extinction as a family for the sins of our forefathers. My case will be the same as Uncle Dawne's—only," he added suddenly, and clenched his fists, " only, if you treat her badly, I'll blow your brains out."

" I hope you will," I answered.

He looked hard at me with a pained expression in his eyes. " Ah, I'm a fool," he said ; " forgive me ! I don't know what I'm saying. I'm mad with disappointment, and grief, and rage. Of course, if she loves you, I never had a chance. Yet the possibility of giving me one, had you known, occurred to you. Well, I will show you that I can be as generous as you are." He held out his hand. " I—I congratulate you," he faltered. " Only, make her happy. But I know you will."

He felt about for his hat, and, having found it, walked with an uncertain step toward the door, blinded with tears.

I stood long as he had left me.

> Ah, brother ! have you not full oft
> Found, even as the Roman did,
> That in life's most delicious draught
> *Surgit amari aliquid?*

Lady Adeline met me sadly the next time I went to Hamilton House.

" Do you blame me ? " I faltered.

" No, oh, no ! " she generously responded. " None of us— not one of us—not even Angelica, suspected for a moment that he was in earnest. It had been his wolf-cry, you know, all his life. Evadne herself has no inkling of the truth."

" I hope she never will," I said.

" If it rests with Diavolo, she will not," his mother answered, proud of him, and with good cause.

It is a salient feature of the Morningquest family history that not one of them ever had a great grief which they did not make in the long run a source of joy to other people. Diavolo's first impulse was to go and see service abroad; but he soon abandoned that idea, although it would have afforded him the distraction he so sorely needed, and resigned his commission instead; and then took up his abode at Morne, in order to devote himself to his grandfather entirely, and it was in Diavolo's companionship that the latter found the one great pleasure and solace of his declining years. The old duke had been wont to say of Diavolo at his worst : " That lad is a gentleman at heart, and, mark my words, he will prove himself so yet ! "

And so he has.

His was the first and loveliest present Evadne received. He did not come to her second wedding, but, then, nobody else did except his father and mother, for it pleased us all to keep the ceremony as quiet and private as possible; so that his absence was not significant ; and, afterward, he rather made a point, if anything, of not avoiding us in any way. In fact, the only change I noticed in him was that he never again made any of those laughing protestations of love and devotion to Evadne with which he used to amuse us all in the dark days of her captivity.

CHAPTER XVIII.

WE were married in London, and when the final arrangements were being discussed, I asked her where she
would like to go after the ceremony.

"Oh, let us go home, Don," she said—she insisted on calling me "Don." I told her the name conveyed no idea to me,
but she answered that I was obtuse, and she was sure I should
grow to love it in time, even if I did not understand it, if it
were only because it was *fetish,* and nobody could use it but
herself; to which extent, by the way, I was very soon able to
endorse her opinion. "Don't let us go to nasty foreign hotels.
I hate travelling, and I hate sight-seeing—the kind of sight-
seeing one does for the sake of seeing. We will go home and
be happy. No place could be half so beautiful to me as yours
is now."

That she should call it "home" at once, and long to be
settled there, was a good omen, I thought. But she was
happy, beyond all possibility of a doubt, in the anticipation of
her life with me.

Soon after our return I took her into Morningquest, and left
her to lunch with her aunt, Mrs. Orton Beg. I had business
on the other side of the city which detained me for some hours,
and when at last I could get away, I hurried back, being
naturally impatient to rejoin her. Mrs. Orton Beg was alone
in the drawing room, and I suppose something in the expression of my face amused her, for she laughed, and answered a
question I had not asked.

"Out there," she said, meaning in the garden.

I turned and looked through the open French window, and
instantly that haunting ghost of an indefinite recollection was
laid. Evadne was sleeping in a high-backed chair, with the
creeper-curtained old brick wall for a background, and half
her face concealed by a large summer hat which she held in
her hand.

"I thought you would remember when you saw her so,"
said Mrs. Orton Beg. "It was just after that unhappy marriage fiasco. She had run away, and sought an asylum here,
and when you were so struck by her appearance, I could not
help thinking it was a thousand pities that you had not met
before it was too late."

"And then you asked me to use the Scottish gift of second

sight—I was thinking at the moment that she was the kind of girlie I should choose for a wife, and so I said she should marry a man called George——"

" Which made it doubly a Delphic oracle for vagueness to me," said Mrs. Orton Beg, " because Colonel Colquhoun's name was also George."

" Now, this is a singular coincidence ! " I exclaimed.

" Ah ! " she ejaculated. " But I do not talk of ' coincidences '—there is a special providence, you know."

" Which deserts Edith and protects Evadne ? "

" You are incorrigible ! "

" You are a demon worshipper ! The Infinite Good gives us the knowledge and power if we will use it. Evadne *was* a Seventh Wave ! "

" ' The Seventh Waves of humanity must suffer,' you said." We looked at each other. " The oracle was ominous. But surely she has suffered enough ? Heaven grant her happiness at last ! "

" Amen," I answered fervently.

As soon as we were settled, I tried to order her life so as to take her mind completely out of the old groove. I kept her constantly out of doors, and never let her sit and sew alone, for one thing, or lounge in easy chairs, or do anything else that is enervating.

I made her ride, too, and rise regularly in the morning; not too early, for that is as injurious in one way as too late is in another ; the latter enervates, but the former exhausts. Regularity is the best discipline. I taught her also to shoot at a mark, and took her into the coverts in the autumn ; but she could not bear the sight of suffering creatures, and unfortunately she wounded a bird the first time we were out, and I was never able to persuade her to shoot at another. However, there was active exercise enough for her without that, so long as she was able to take it, and when it became necessary to curtail the amount, she drove both morning and afternoon, and took short walks and pottered about the grounds in between times.

I had bought As-You-Like-It while she was abroad with the Hamilton-Wellses, and had had the whole place pulled down, and the site converted into a plantation, so that no trace was left of that episode to vex her. In fact, I had done all that I could think of as likely in any way to help to re-establish her health, and certainly she was very happy. Everything

1 wished her to do seemed to be a pleasure to her; and mind and body grew rapidly so vigorous that I lost all fear for her. She said she was a new creature, and she looked it.

When we had been married about a year, Sir Shadwell Rock came to pay us a visit. Evadne was quite at her best then, and I introduced her to him triumphantly.

He asked about her progress with kindly interest when we were alone together, and declared heartily that she was certainly to all appearance thoroughly restored, that he was quite in love with her himself, and hoped to see her in the van of the new movement yet.

She took to the dear old man, and told him his great reputation did not frighten her one bit; and she would lean on his arm familiarly out in the grounds, pelt him with gorse blossom, fill his pockets with rose leaves surreptitiously, till they bulged out like bags behind, and keep him smiling perpetually at her pretty ways. He had been going abroad for a holiday, but we persuaded him to stay with us instead, and when we parted with him at last reluctantly, he declared that Evadne had made him young again, and the wrinkles were all smoothed out.

His last words to me were: "So far so good, Galbraith," and I knew he meant to warn as well as to congratulate. "Don't keep her in cotton wool too much. Make her face sickness and suffering while she is well herself. Take warning by the small-pox epidemic. She has no morbid horror of that subject, because she knows practically how much can be done for the sufferers. If she devote herself to good works, she will be sanguine because so much is being accomplished, instead of dwelling despondently on the hopeless amount there is still to do."

Soon after this, however, I began to hope that a new interest in life was coming to cure her of all morbid moods for ever. I was anxious at first, but she was so quietly happy in the prospect herself, and she continued so well in spite of the drain upon her strength, that I soon took heart again.

"You have got to be very young, Don, since I was so good as to marry you," she said to me one day.

She had come in with some flowers for me, and had caught me whistling instead of working.

Sir Shadwell had consented, in his usual kind and generous way, to share the responsibility of this time with me. He came down to us for an occasional "week-end," just to see how she progressed, and his observations, like my own, continued to be satisfactory. It was a crucial test, we knew. If we could carry her safely through this trying time, she would be able to take her proper place with the best of her sex in the battle of life, to fight with them and for them, which was what we both ardently desired to see her do.

There had been never a word of the mental malady since Colquhoun's death. I had judged it well to let her forget she had ever suffered so if she could, and I had no reason to suspect that she ever thought of it. She had had hours, and even days, of depression since our marriage, but had always been able to account for them satisfactorily; and now, although of course she got down at times, she was less often so than is usually the case under the circumstances, and was always easily consoled.

She paid me a visit in my study one day. She had a habit of coming occasionally when I was at work, a habit that happily emphasized the difference between my solitary bachelor days and these. She was shy of her caresses as a rule, but would occasionally make my knee her seat, if it happened to suit her convenience, while she filled the flower vases on my table; or she would stand behind me with her hands clasped round my neck, and lean her cheek against my hair. She did so now.

"You love your work, Don, don't you?" she said.

"Yes, sweetheart," I answered; "next to you, it is the great delight of my life."

"But, Don, you find it all-absorbing; don't you?"

"No, not *all*-absorbing, *now*."

"But sufficiently so to be a comfort to you if you ever had any great grief? After the first shock, you would return to your old pursuits, would you not? And, by and by, you would find solace in them?"

I unclasped her hands from my neck, and drew her round to me. There was a new note in her voice that sounded ominous.

"What is the trouble, little woman!" I whispered, when I had her safe in my arms.

"I don't think I could die and leave you, Don, if I thought you would be miserable."

"Well, then, don't allow yourself to entertain any doubt on the subject," I answered; "for I should be more than 'miserable.' I should never care for anything in the world again."

" But if I should have to die——"

"There is no need to distress either yourself or me by such an idle supposition, Evadne," I answered. "There is not the slightest occasion for alarm."

" I am not *alarmed*," she said, and then she was silent.

A few days later, I found her sitting on the floor in the library, reading a book she had taken from one of the lower shelves. It was a book of Sir Shadwell Rock's on the heredity of vice. I took it from her gently, remarking as I did so : "I would rather you did not read these things just now, Evadne."

" I suppose you agree with Sir Shadwell Rock," she said.

"Let me help you up," I answered.

" Do you ?" she persisted.

"Of course. He is our chief authority," I answered. " But promise me, Evadne, not to look at any of those books again without consulting me. I shall be having you like the medical students who imagine they have symptoms of every disease they study."

" It would mark a strange change in my mind," she answered; " for I used to be able to study any subject of the kind without being affected in that way."

That her mind had changed, alas ! or rather, that it had been injured by friction and pressure of the restrictions imposed upon it, was the suspicion which necessitated my present precaution, but I could not say so.

She held out her hands for me to help her to rise. "Why are women kept in the dark about these things?" she said, pointing to the books on heredity. " Why are we never taught as you are? We are the people to be informed."

" You are quite right," I said. " It is criminal to withhold knowledge from any woman who has the capacity to acquire it. But there is a time for everything, you know, my sweetheart."

" Now, that poor Colonel Colquhoun," she went on as if I had not spoken. " He for one should never have been born. With his ancestry, he must have come into the world foredoomed to a life of dissipation and disease. It is awful to think we may any of us become the parents of people who can't be moral without upsetting the whole natural order of the universe. O Don ! it is dreadful to know it, but it is sinful to be ignorant of the fact."

" But there is no fear for our children, Evadne," I said.

" Ah ! that is what I want to know !" she exclaimed, clasping her hands round my arm.

" Come out into the grounds then, sweetheart," I answered, affecting a cheerfulness I was far from feeling ; " and I will tell you the whole family history."

I had to go out that evening to see a serious case in consultation with a brother practitioner. I had ordered the dogcart for ten o'clock, and Evadne came out into the hall with me from the drawing room, where I had been reading to her since dinner, when it was brought round.

" *Must* you go ?" she said listlessly.

" I am afraid I must," I answered ; " it is a matter of life and death. But why shouldn't you come too ! It will be much better than staying here alone. I ought to have thought of it sooner. Do come ! I will send the dogcart back, and have the brougham."

" It would delay you," she said, hesitating.

" Oh, no ! Two horses in the brougham will get over the ground faster than one in the dogcart. Come ! Let me get you some wraps."

" But when we arrive, my presence will be an inconvenience," she objected.

" In no way," I answered. " It will not be a long business, and you can wait very well in the carriage with a book and a lamp."

She came out and looked at the night, still undecided. The weather was damp and uninviting.

" I don't think I'll go, Don," she said, shivering. " Goodbye and safe home to you ! "

As I drove along, I cast about in my own mind for a suitable companion for Evadne, someone who would vary the monotony for her when I had to be out. She had no ladyloves, as so many women have. Mrs. Orton Beg was at Fraylingay again, and Lady Adeline was the only other friend I knew of who would be congenial just then ; but she had multifarious duties of her own to attend to, and it would not have been fair to ask her, especially as she was sure to come if she knew she was wanted, however great the inconvenience to herself. I knew nothing at that time of two other friends of Evadne's, Mrs. Sillinger and Mrs. Malcomson, to whom I afterward learnt that she was much attached. Owing, I think, to the unnatural habit of reticence which had been forced upon her, she had not mentioned them to me, although she continued to correspond with them. It took her some time to realize that every interest of hers was matter of moment to me. A certain colonel and Mrs. Guthrie Brimston had recently settled in the neighbourhood, in order, as they gave out, to be near the Morningquest family, with whom they claimed relationship, on the ground, I believe, that they also were Guthries. Colonel Guthrie Brimston led people to suppose that he had left the service entirely on the duke's account, his disinterested intention being to vary the monotony for the poor old gentleman during his declining years. They had claimed Evadne's acquaintance with effusion, but she had not responded very cordially.

"Let them have a carriage and horses whenever they like, Don," she said, "and give them plenty to eat; but don't otherwise encourage them to come here."

Recollecting which, I now inferred that Mrs. Guthrie Brimston would not answer my present purpose at all.

This was the first time Evadne had shown any objection to being left alone. She used to insist upon my going away sometimes, because, she said, I should be so very glad to come back to her! But she was never exacting in any way, and never out of temper. And she had such pretty ways as a wife! little endearing womanly ways which one felt to be the spontaneous outcome of tenderness untold, and inexpressible. It was strange how her presence pervaded the house; strange to me that one little body could make such a difference.

Foolishly fond if you like. But if every man could care as much for a woman, hallowed would be her name, and the strife-begetting uncertainties of heaven and hell would be allowed to lapse in order to make room for healthy human happiness. Our hearts have been starved upon fables long enough; we demand some certainty; and as knowledge increases, waging its inexorable war of extermination against evil, our beautiful old earth will be allowed to be lovable, and life a blessing, and death itself only a last sweet sleep, neither to be sought nor shunned—"The soothing sinking down on hard-earned holy rest," from which, if we arise again, it shall not be to suffer. No life could be fuller of promise than mine at this moment. Nothing was wanting but the patter of little feet about the house, and they were coming. Doubts and fears were latent for once. My hopes were limitless, my content was extreme.

"May you have quiet rest to-night, my darling; may your heart grow strong, and your faith in man revive at last."

About halfway to my destination, I met the gentleman who had asked me out in consultation, returning. He was on his way to my house to tell me that the patient was dead. My presence could therefore be of no avail, and I turned back also. I had not been absent more than an hour, but I found, on entering the house, that Evadne had already retired. It was a good sign, I thought, as she had been rather fidgety the whole day. I had some letters to write, and went at once to my study for the purpose, taking a candle with me from the hall. The servants, not expecting me back until late, had turned out most of the lights downstairs. The lamp in my study, however, was still burning. It stood on the writing table, and the first thing I saw, on entering the room, was a letter lying conspicuously on the blotting pad. It was from Evadne to me.

She had evidently intended me to get it in the morning, for a tray was always left for me in the dining room in case I should be hungry when I came in late, and my chances were all against my going to the study again that night. I put my candle down, and tore the note open with trembling hands. The first few lines were enough. " I am haunted by a terrible fear," she wrote. " I have tried again and again to tell you, but I never could. You would not see that it is prophetic, as I do—in case of our death—nothing to save my daughter from Edith's fate—better both die at once." So I gathered the contents. No time to read. I crumpled the note into my pocket. My labouring breath impeded my progress a moment, but, thank Heaven ! I was not paralyzed. Involuntarily I glanced at my laboratory. It was an inner room, kept locked as a rule, but the door was open now—as I knew I had expected it to be. I seized the candle and went to the shelf where I kept the bottles with the ominous red labels. One was missing.

" Evadne ! " I shouted, running back through the study and library into the hall, and calling her again and again as I went. If it were not already too late, and she had heard my voice, I knew she would hesitate. I tore up the stairs, and I must have flown, although it seemed a century before I reached her room. I flung open the door.

She *had* heard me.

She was standing beside a dressing table in a listening attitude, with a glass half raised to her lips, and her eyes met mine as I entered

My first cry of distress had reached her, and the shock of it had been sufficient. Had that note fallen into my hands but one moment later—but I cannot bear to think of it. Even at this distance of time the recollection utterly unmans me. The moment I saw her, however, I could command myself. I took the glass from her hand, and threw it into the fireplace with as little show of haste as possible.

"To bed now, my sweetheart," I said ; "and no more nonsense of this kind, you know."

She looked at the fragments of the broken glass, and then at me, in a half wondering, half regretful, half inquiring way that was pitiful to see. Shaken as I was, I could not bear it. While the danger lasted, it was no effort to be calm; but now I broke down, and, throwing myself into a chair, covered my face with my hands, thoroughly overcome.

In a moment she was kneeling beside me.

"O Don !" she exclaimed, " what is it ? Why are you so terribly upset ? "

Poor little innocent sinner ! The one idea had possessed her to the exclusion of every other consideration. I said nothing to her, of course, in the way of blame. It would have been useless. She was bitterly sorry to see me grieved ; but her moral consciousness was suspended, and she felt no remorse whatever for her intention, except in so far as it had given me pain. The impulse had passed for the moment, however, and I was so sure of it that I did not even take the fatal phial away with me when I went to my dressing-room ; but for forty-six days and nights I never left her an hour alone. The one great hope, however, that the cruel obliquity would be cured by the mother's love when it awoke amply sustained me.

She was well and cheerful for the rest of the time, greatly owing, I am sure, to the influence of Sir Shadwell Rock, who came at once, like the kind and generous friend he was, without waiting to be asked, when he heard what had happened ; and announced himself prepared to stay until the danger was over. I heard Evadne laugh very soon after his arrival, and could see that " the worry in her head," as she described it, had gone again, and was forgotten. The impulse, which would have robbed me of all my happiness and hopes had she succeeded in carrying it out, never cost her a thought. The saving suffering of an agony of remorse was what we should like to have seen, for in that there would have been good assurance of healthy moral consciousness restored.

It seemed to be only the power to endure mental misery which had been injured by those weary days of enforced se-clusion and unnatural inactivity, for I never knew anyone braver about physical pain. It was the strength to contem-plate the sufferings of others, which grows in action and is best developed by turning the knowledge to account for their benefit, that had been sapped by ineffectual brooding, until at last, before the moral shock of indignation which the view of preventable human evils gave her, her right mind simply went out, and a disordered faculty filled the void with projects which only a perverted imagination could contemplate as be-ing of any avail.

Whatever doubts we may have had about her feeling for the child when it came were instantly set at rest. Nothing could have been healthier or more natural than her pride and delight in him. When she saw him for the first time, after he was dressed, I brought him to her myself with his little cheek against my face.

" O Don !" she exclaimed, her eyes opening wide with joy. " I love to see you like that ! But what is she like, Don ? Give her to me ! "

" *She*, indeed !" I answered. "Don't insult my son. He would reproach you himself, but he is speechless with indig-nation."

" O Don, don't be ridiculous ! " she cried, stretching up her arms for him. " Is it really a boy ? Do give him to me ! I want to see him so !" When I had put him in her arms, she gathered him up jealously, and covered him with kisses, then held him off a little way to look at him, and then kissed him again and again.

" Did you ever see a baby before ? " I asked her.

" No, never ! never ! " she answered emphatically ; " never such a darling as this, at all events ! His little cheek is just like velvet ; and, see ! he can curl up his hands ! Isn't it wonderful, Don ? He's like you, too. I'm sure he is. He's quite dark."

" He's just the colour of that last sunset you were raving about. I told you to be careful."

" O Don, how can you ! " she exclaimed. It was beautiful to see her raptures. She was like a child herself, so unaf-fectedly glad in her precious little treasure, and so surprised ! The fact that he would move independently and have ideas of his own seemed never to have occurred to her.

So far so good, as Sir Shadwell said ; and we soon had her about again ; but the first time she sat up, after her cushions had been arranged for her, and her baby laid on her lap, when I stooped to give them both a kiss of hearty congratulation, she burst into tears.

"It is nothing, Don, don't be concerned," she said, trying bravely to smile again.   " I was thinking of my mother.   This would have been such a happy day for her."

This made me think of the breach with her father.   I had forgotten that she had a father, but it occurred to me now that a reconciliation might add to her happiness, and I wrote to him accordingly to that effect, making the little grandson my excuse.   Mr. Frayling replied that he had heard indirectly of his daughter's second marriage, but was not surprised to receive no communication from herself on the subject, because her whole conduct for many years past had really been most extraordinary.   If, however, she had become a dutiful wife at last, as I had intimated, he was willing to forgive her, and let bygones be bygones ; whereupon I asked him to Fountain Towers, and he came.

He was extremely cordial.   I had a long talk with him before he saw Evadne, during which I discovered from whence she took her trick of phrase-making.   He expressed himself as satisfied with me, and my position, my reputation, and my place.   He also shook his watch chain at my son, which denoted great approval, I inferred ; and made many improving remarks, interspersed with much good advice on the subject of babies and the management of estates.

Evadne had been very nervous about meeting him again, but the baby broke the ice, and she was unfeignedly glad to make friends.   Upon the whole, however, the reconciliation was not the success that I had anticipated.   Father and daughter had lost touch, and, after the first few hours, there was neither pleasure nor pain in their intercourse ; nothing, in fact, but politeness.   The flow of affection had been too long interrupted.   It was diverted to other channels now, and was too deeply imbedded in them to be coaxed back in the old direction.   Love is a sacred stream which withdraws itself from the sacrilegious who have offered it outrage.

It was an unmitigated happiness, however, to Evadne to have her brothers and sisters with her again, and from that time forward we had generally some of them at Fountain Towers.

Mrs. Kilroy of Ilverthorpe, otherwise known to her friends as Angelica, was one of the first people privileged to see the baby.

"Oh, you queer little thing!" she exclaimed, pointing her finger at it by way of caress. "I've been thinking all this time that babies were always Speckled Toads. And you are all rosy, and dimpled, and plump, you pretty thing! I wish I had just a dozen like you!"

Poor erratic Angelica, with all her waywardness, "but yet a woman!" There was only the one man that I have ever known who could have developed the best that was in Angelica, and him she had just missed, as so often happens in this world of contraries. I am thinking of our poor Julian, known to her as the Tenor, whom she had met when it was too late, and in an evil hour for us and for herself apparently, the consequences having been his death and her own desolation. Yet I don't know. Those were the first consequences certainly, but others followed and are following. The memory of one good man is a light which sheds the brightest rays that fall on the lives of thousands—as Mr. Kilroy has reason to know; with whom, after the Tenor, Angelica is happier than she could have been with any other man. And then, again, she has Diavolo. The close friendship between them, which had been interrupted for some years, was renewed again in some inexplicable way by the effect of my marriage on Diavolo, and since then they have been as inseparable as their respective duties to husband and grandfather allow. And so the web of life is woven, the puzzling strands resolving themselves out of what has seemed to be a hopeless tangle into the most beautiful designs.

Some of Evadne's ideas of life were considerably enlarged in view of the boy's future.

"I am so glad you are a rich man," she said to me one day, "and have a title and all that. It doesn't matter for you, you know, Don, because you *are* you. But it will give the baby such a start in life."

She summoned me at a very early period of his existence to choose a name for him, and having decided upon George Shadwell Beton, she had him christened with all orthodox ceremony by the Bishop of Morningquest as soon as possible. That duty once accomplished must have relieved her mind satisfactorily with regard to a *Christian* name for him, for she has insisted on calling him by the heathen appellation of Donino ever since, for the flattering reason that his temper when thwarted is exactly like mine.

"I am sure when you were his age you used to kick and scream just as he does when his wishes are not carried out on the instant," she said. "You don't kick and scream now when you are vexed; you look like thunder, and walk out of the room."

"Baby seems to afford you infinite satisfaction when he kicks and screams. You laugh and hug him more, if anything, in his tantrums than when he is good," I remarked.

"I take his tantrums for a sign of strength," she answered. "He is merely standing on his dignity, and demanding his rights as a rule. It was the same thing with his father when he frowned and walked out of the room. He wouldn't be sat upon either, and I used to see in that a sign of self-respect also. It is a long time now since I saw you frown and walk out of the room, Don."

"It is a long time since you attempted to sit upon me," I said.

"I am afraid I neglect you," she answered apologetically; "you see, Donino requires so much of my time."

She continued to be cheerful for months after the birth of the boy, and we waited patiently for some sign which should be an assurance of her complete restoration to mental health; or, so far as I was concerned, for an opportunity of testing her present feeling about the subject that distressed her. I had given up expecting a miraculous cure in a moment, and now only hoped for a gradual change for the better.

The opportunity I was waiting for came one winter's afternoon when she was playing with the baby. It was a moment of leisure with me, the afternoon tea-time, which I always arranged to spend with her if possible, and especially if she would otherwise have been alone, as was the case on this occasion.

I had been responding for half an hour, as well as I could, to incessant appeals for sympathy and admiration—not that I found it difficult to admire the boy, who was certainly a splendid specimen of the human race, although perhaps I ought not to say so; but my command of language never answered his mother's expectations, somehow, when it came to expressing my feelings.

"Do you think you care as much for him as I do, Don?" she burst out at last.

"More," I answered seriously.

" Why ? How ? " she demanded, surprised by my tone.

" Because I never could have hurt him."

" Hurt him ! " she exclaimed, gathering him up in her arms.
" Do you mean that I could hurt him ! hurt my baby ! Oh ! "
She got up and stood looking at me indignantly for a few
seconds with the child's face hidden against her neck ; and
then she rang the bell sharply, and sent him away.

" What do you mean, Don ? " she said, when we were alone
together again. " Tell me ? You would not say a cruel thing
like that for nothing."

" I am referring to that night before he was born," I said,
taking the little bottle from my pocket. This seems to me
to have been the cruellest operation that I have ever had to
perform.

" O Don ! " she cried, greatly distressed. " I understand.
I should have killed him. But why, why do you remind me
of that now ? "

" I want to be quite sure that you have learnt what a mistaken notion that was, and that you regret the impulse."

She sat down on a low chair before the fire, with her elbows
on her knees and her face buried in her hands, and remained
so for some time. She wanted to think it out, and tell me
exactly.

" I do not feel any regret," she said at last. " I would not
do the same thing now, but it is only because I am not now
occupied with the same thoughts. They have fallen into the
background of my consciousness, and I no longer perceive
the utility of self-sacrifice."

" But do you not perceive the sin of suicide ? "

" Not of that kind of suicide," she answered. " You see, we
have the divine example. Christ committed suicide to all
intents and purposes by deliberately putting himself into the
hands of his executioners ; but his motive makes *them* responsible for the crime ; and my motive would place society in a
similar position."

" Your view of the great sacrifice would startle theologians,
I imagine," was my answer. " But, even allowing that Christ
was morally responsible for his own death, and thereby set
the example you would have followed to save others from
suffering ; tell me, do you really see any comparison between
an act which had the redemption of the world for its object.
and the only result that could follow from the sacrifice of one
little mother and child ? "

"What result, Don?"

"Breaking your husband's heart, spoiling his life, and leaving him lonely forever."

She started up and threw herself on her knees beside me, clasping her hands about my neck.

"O Don, don't say that again!" she cried. "Don't say anything like that again—ever—will you?"

"You know I should never think of it again if I could be sure——"

She hid her head upon my shoulder, but did not answer immediately.

"I am seeking for some assurance in myself to give you," she said at last; "but I feel none. The same train of thought would provoke me again—no, not to the same act, but to something desperate; I can't tell what. But I suffer so, Don, when such thoughts come, from grief, and rage, and horror, I would do almost anything for relief."

"But just think——" I began.

"No, don't ask me to think!" she interrupted. "All my endeavour is not to think. Let me live on the surface of life, as most women do. I will do nothing but attend to my household duties and the social duties of my position. I will read nothing that is not first weeded by you of every painful thought that might remind me. I will play with my baby by day, and curl up comfortably beside you at night, infinitely grateful and content to be so happily circumstanced myself— Don, help me to that kind of life, will you? And burn the books. Let me deserve my name and be 'well pleasing one' to you first of all the world, and then to any with whom I may come in contact. Let me live while you live, and die when you die. But do not ask me to think. I can be the most docile, the most obedient, the most loving of women as long as I forget my knowledge of life; but the moment I remember I become a raging fury; I have no patience with slow processes; 'Revolution' would be my cry, and I could preside with an awful joy at the execution of those who are making the misery now for succeeding generations."

"But, my dear child, it would surely be happier for you to try to alleviate——"

"No, no," she again interrupted. "I know all you can say on that score; but I cannot bear to be brought into contact with certain forms of suffering. I cannot bear the contradictions of life; they make me rage."

"What I want to say is that you should act, and not think," I ventured.

"How can I act without thinking?" she asked.

"You see, if you don't act you must think," I pursued; "and if you do think without acting, you become morbid. The conditions of an educated woman's life now force her to know the world. She is too intelligent not to reason about what she knows. She sees what is wrong ; and if she is high-minded she feels forced to use her influence to combat it. If she resists the impulse her conscience cannot acquit her, and she suffers herself for her cowardice."

"I know," she answered. "But don't let us discuss the subject any more."

We were silent for some time after that, and then I made a move as if to speak, but checked myself.

"What is it?" she asked.

"I was going to ask you to do something to oblige me ; but now I do not like to."

"Oh !" she exclaimed, much hurt; "do you really think there is anything I would not do for you, if I could?"

"Well, this is mere trifle," I answered. "I want you to take that sturdy much be-ribboned darling of yours to see my poor sick souls in the hospital. A sight of his small face would cheer them. Will you?"

"Why, *surely*," she said. "How *could* you doubt it? I shall be delighted."

"And there was another thing——"

"Oh, don't hesitate like that," she exclaimed. "You can't think how you hurt me."

"I very much wish you would take charge of the flowers in the hospital for me, that was what I was going to say. I should be so pleased if you should make them your special care. If you would cut them yourself, and take them and arrange them whenever fresh ones are wanted, you would be giving me as much pleasure as the patients. And you might say something kind to them as you pass through the wards. Even a word makes all the difference in their day."

"Why didn't you ask me to do this before?" she said, reproachfully.

"I was a little afraid of asking you now," I answered.

"I shall begin to-morrow," she said. "Tell me the best time for me to go?"

There is a great deal in the way a thing is put, was my trite reflection afterward. If I had given Evadne my reason for particularly wishing her to visit the hospital, she would have turned it inside out to show me that it was lined with objections; but, now, because I had asked her to oblige me simply, she was ready to go ; and would have gone if it had cost her half her comfort in life. This was a great step in advance. As in the small-pox epidemic, so now at the hospital, she had no horror of anything she *saw.* It was always what she imagined that made her morbid.

CHAPTER XIX.

FOLLOWING these days there came a time of perfect peace for both of us. Evadne's health was satisfactory; she led the life she had planned for herself; and so long as she shut out all thought of the wicked world and nothing occurred to remind her of the "awful needless suffering" with which she had become acquainted in the past, she was tranquilly happy.

Donino rapidly grew out of arms. He was an independent young rascal from the first, and would never be carried if he could walk, or driven from the moment he could sit a pony— grip is the word, I know, but his legs were not long enough to grip when he began, and his rides were therefore conducted all over the pony's back at first. His object was to keep on, and in order to do so without the assistance he scorned, he rode like a monkey.

Evadne was proud of the boy, but she missed the baby, and complained that her arms were empty. It was not long, however, happily,—and *à propos* of the number of my responsibilities, I was taken to task severely one day, and discovered that I had in my son a staunch supporter and a counsellor whose astuteness was not to be despised.

I was finishing my letters one afternoon in the library when Evadne came in with her daughter in her arms, and Donino clinging to her skirt. I expected the usual "Don, I am sure you have done enough. Come and have some tea," and turned to meet it with the accustomed protest: "Just five minutes more, my sweetheart." But Evadne began in quite another tone.

"I have just heard such a *disgraceful* thing about you," she said.

" A disgraceful thing about me ! " I exclaimed.

" Yes. I hear you were asked the other day how many children you had, and you answered ' *Two or three !* ' Now, will you kindly count your children, and when you are quite sure you know the number off by heart, repeat it aloud to me, so that I may have some hope that you will not commit yourself in that way again."

" Oh," I answered, " I know how many *babies* there are ; my difficulty is about you. I am never quite sure whether to count you as a child or not."

" Now, I call that a mean little score," she said, carrying her baby off with an affectation of indignation which deceived Donino.

He had been standing with his back to the writing table and his feet firmly planted before him, gravely watching us, and now when his mother left the room he came to my knee and looked up at me confidentially.

" Ou bin naughty, dad ? " he asked.

" It looks like it," I answered.

" Ou say ou sorry," he advised.

" What will happen then ? " I wanted to know.

" Den de missus 'ill kiss ou," he explained. " Den *dat* all right."

" Truly ' a wise son maketh a glad father,' " I observed.

Donino knitted his brows, and grumbled a puzzled but polite assent. I saw signs of reflection afterward, however, which warned me not to be too sure that I knew exactly where the limits of the little understanding were. But one thing was evident. The boy was being educated on the principle of repent and have done with it. Old accounts are not cast up in this establishment.

Donino watched me putting my writing things away ; he was waiting to see me through my trouble. When I was ready, he took as much of my hand as he could hold in his, protectingly, and led me to the drawing room with a dignified air of importance. Sir Shadwell Rock was staying with us at the time, and my daughter was creeping from her mother to him as we entered the room, and receiving a large share of his attention. Donino glanced at him, fearing, perhaps, that his presence as audience would make matters more unpleasant for me.

" Mumme," he said, " dad's tum."

Evadne looked up inquiringly.

"I've come to say I am sorry," I exclaimed.

"Oh," said Evadne, a little puzzled, "that's right."

Donino looked from one to the other expectantly ; but as his mother made no move, he edged up to her side, and repeated with emphasis : "Dad's sorry."

"That's right," his mother answered, putting her arm round him, and caressing him fondly.

He drew away from her dissatisfied, and walked to the window, where he stood, with his thumbs in his belt, and his chin on his chest.

"O Don," Evadne whispered, "do look at yourself in miniature ! But what is the matter ? What have I done to disturb him ? or left undone ?"

"I said I was sorry, and you haven't kissed me," I replied.

Evadne grasped the situation at last, and got up.

"I suppose I must kiss you," she said. "I hope you won't be naughty again."

The boy made no sign at the moment, but presently he sauntered back to the tea-table as if he were satisfied.

When the children were gone Sir Shadwell asked for an explanation.

"It is beautiful to watch the mind of a young child unfold," he observed ; "to notice its wonderful grasp, on the one hand, of ideas one would have thought quite beyond its comprehension, and, on the other, its curious limitations. Now, that boy of yours reasons already from what he observes."

"Clearly," I answered. "He observes that my position in this house is quite secondary, and therefore, although he sees his mother 'naughty' every day, he never thinks for a moment of suggesting that she should 'own up' to me."

"Don, you are horrid !" Evadne exclaimed.

The next day she went out early in the afternoon to pay calls.

Sir Shadwell and I accompanied her to the door to see her into her carriage, and she drove off smiling, and kissing her hand to us.

"Now," I said, as we lingered on the doorstep, watching the carriage glint between the trees : "what do you think about the wisdom of my marriage ?"

"Oh," he answered, his eyes twinkling. "You didn't explain, you know, so I naturally concluded that you were merely marrying for your own gratification, in which case you would have been disappointed when you found what I foresaw, that, under the circumstances, the pleasure would not be unmixed. You should have explained that your sole purpose was to make a very charming young lady healthy-minded again and happy, if you wanted to know what I thought of your chances of success."

"You're a confounded old cynic," I said, turning into the house.

Sir Shadwell went out into the grounds, and there I found him later, patiently instructing Donino in the difficult art of stringing a bow, his white head bowed beside the boy's dark one, and his benign face wrought into wrinkles of intentness.

I was busy during the afternoon, but I fancied I heard the carriage return. Evadne did not come to report herself to me, however, as was her wont after an expedition, and I therefore thought that I must have been mistaken, and more especially so when she did not appear at tea-time. After tea, Sir Shadwell settled himself with a book, and I left him. In the hall I met the footman who had gone out with Evadne.

"When did you return?" I asked.

"I can't say rightly, Sir George," the man replied. "We only paid one call this afternoon, and then came straight back. Her ladyship seemed to be poorly."

I ran upstairs to my wife's sitting room. She was lying on a couch asleep, her face gray, her eyelids swollen and purple with weeping, her hair disordered. As I stood looking down at her, she opened her eyes and held up her arms to me. She looked ten years older, a mere wreck of the healthy, happy, smiling woman who had driven off kissing her hand to us only a few hours before.

"Tell me the trouble, my sweetheart," I said, kneeling down beside her. "Where did you go to-day?"

"Only to Mrs. Guthrie Brimston," she answered. "But Mrs. Beale was there with Edith's boy, and we talked—O Don!" she broke off. "I wish my children had never been born! The suffering! the awful needless suffering! How do I know that they will escape?"

Alas! alas! that terrible cry again, and just after we had allowed ourselves to be sure that it had been silenced at last forever.

I did not reason with her this time. I could only pet her, and talk for the purpose of distracting her attention, as one does with a child. So far, I had never for a moment lost heart and hope. I could not believe that the balance of her

fine intelligence had been too rudely shaken ever to be perfectly restored ; but now at last it seemed as if her confidence
in her fellow-creatures, the source of all mental health, had
been destroyed forever, and with that confidence her sense of
the value of life and of her own obligations had been also injured or distorted to a degree which could not fail to be dangerous on occasion.   There are injuries which set up carci-
noma of the mind, we know, cancer spots confined to a small
area at first, but gradually extending with infinite pain until
all the surrounding healthy tissue is more or less involved,
and the whole beautiful fabric is absorbed in the morbid
growth, for which there is no certain palliative in time, and
no possible prospect of cure except in eternity.   Was this to
be Evadne's case?   Alas! alas!   But, still, doctors sometimes mistake the symptoms, and find happily that they have
erred when they arrived at an unfavourable diagnosis.   So
I said to myself, but the assurance in no way affected the
despair which had settled upon my heart, and was crushing it.

Late that night I was sitting alone in my study.   I had
been reading Solomon's prayer at the dedication of the
temple, and the book still lay open before me.   It was a habit
of mine to read the Bible when I was much perturbed.   The
solemn majestic march of the measured words seldom failed
to restore my tranquillity in a wonderful way, and it had done
so now.   I felt resigned.   " Hearken therefore unto the supplication of Thy servant "—I was repeating to myself, in
fragments, as the lines occurred to me—" that Thine eyes may
be upon this house day and night . . . hear Thou from Thy
dwelling place, even from heaven ; and when Thou hearest
forgive."

I must have dozed a moment, I think, when I had pronounced the words, for I had heard no rustle of trailing garments in the library beyond, yet the next thing I was
conscious of was Evadne kneeling beside me.   She put her
arms round my neck, and drew my face down to her.

" Don," she said, with a great dry sob, " I am sorry.   I have
annoyed you somehow———"

" Not annoyed me, my wife."

" Hurt you then, which is worse.   I have taken all the heart
out of you—somehow—I can see that.   But I cannot—cannot
tell what it is I have done."   She looked into my face piteously, and then hid her own on my shoulder, and burst into
a paroxysm of sobs and tears.